D1492268

Death's Jest-Book

The jest is, the dead won't lie still in the grave . . .

Three times DCI Pascoe has wrongly accused dead-pan joker Franny Roote. This time he's determined to leave no gravestone unturned as he tries to prove that the ex-con and aspiring academic is mad, bad and dangerous to know.

Meanwhile, Edgar Wield rides to the rescue of a child in danger, only to find he's got a rent-boy under his wing. In return, the boy tips him off about the heist of a priceless treasure, and soon Wieldy is torn between protecting the boy and doing his duty.

His superiors might have worries, but DC Bowler is looking forward to a blissful New Year with the girl of his dreams. Unfortunately, her dreams are filled with a horror too terrible to tell . . .

And over all this activity broods the huge form of Mid-Yorkshire CID's First Mover, DS Andy Dalziel. As trouble builds, the Fat Man discovers (as many deities before him) that omniscience can be more trouble than it's worth, and that sometimes all om-nipotence means is that you can have any colour you like, as long as it's black.

Death's Jest-Book

REGINALD HILL

LONDON NEW YORK SYDNEY TORONTO

This edition published 2002
by BCA
by arrangement with Collins Crime
an imprint of HarperCollins*Publishers*

CN 104371

First reprint 2002

Extracts from 'This Be the Verse' from *Collected Poems* by
Philip Larkin
(published by Faber and Faber Ltd) and
'The Child Dying' from *Collected Poems* by Edwin Muir
(published by Faber and Faber) reproduced by permission of
Faber and Faber Ltd.

'Total Eclipse of the Heart' words and music by
Jim Steinman © 1983,
EMI Music Publishing Ltd.

Set in PostScript Linotype Janson by
Rowland Phototypesetting Limited, Bury St Edmunds, Suffolk

Printed and bound in Germany by
GGP Media, Pössneck

For Julia
who never hassles
thanks

The woodcut illustrations which prefigure each
of the novel's thirteen sections are taken from
Hans Holbein the Younger's *Dance of Death*
and the decorated letters at the start of each chapter
derive from the same artist's *Alphabet of Death*.

For death is more 'a jest' than Life, you see
Contempt grows quick from familiarity.
I owe this wisdom to Anatomy.

T. L. BEDDOES *Lines to B.W. Proctor*

...fat men can't write sonnets
T. L. BEDDOES *The Bride's Tragedy* i.ii.

The Physician

Imagined Scenes

from

AMONG OTHER THINGS:
The Quest for Thomas Lovell Beddoes

by Sam Johnson MA, PhD (first draft)

Clifton, Glos. June 1808

'That's it, man. Hold her head, hold her head. For God's
sake, you behind, get your shoulder into it. Come, girl.
Come, girl.'

The shouter of these instructions, a burly man of about
fifty years with a close-cropped head and a face made to
command, stands halfway up a broad sweeping staircase. A
few stairs below him a rustic, his naturally ruddy complexion
even more deeply incarnadined by exertion, is leaning backwards like the anchor in a tug-o'-war, pulling with all his
strength on a rope whose lower end is tied round the neck
of a large brown cow.

Behind the beast a nervous-looking footman is making
encouraging fluttering gestures with his hands. From the
marble-floored hallway below a housekeeper and butler
watch with massive disapproval, while over the balustrade of
the landing lean a pair of housemaids, arms full of sheets, all
discipline forgotten, their faces bright with delight at this
rare entertainment, and especially at the discomfiture of the
footman.

Between them kneels a solemn-faced little boy, his hands
gripping the gilded wrought iron rails, who observes the
scene with keen but unsurprised gaze.

3

'Push, man, push, it can't bite you!' roars the burly man.

The footman, used to obey and perhaps aware of the watching maids, takes a step forward and leans with one hand on each of the cow's haunches.

As if stimulated by the pressure, the beast raises its tail and evacuates its bowels. Caught full in the chest by the noxious jet, the footman tumbles backwards, the maids squeal, the little boy smiles to see such fun, and the cow as if propelled by the exuberance of its own extravasation bounds up the remaining stairs at such a pace that both the rustic and the burly man are hard put to retreat safely to the landing.

Below, the butler and the housekeeper check that the bemired footman is unhurt. Then the woman hastens up the stairs, her face dark with indignation, which the maids observing, they beat a hasty retreat.

'Dr Beddoes!' she cries. 'This is beyond toleration!'

'Come now, Mrs Jones,' says the burly man. 'Is not your mistress's health worth a little labour with brush and pan? Lead her on, George.'

The rustic begins to lead the now completely cowed cow along the landing towards a half-open bedroom door. The man follows, with the small boy a step behind.

Mrs Jones, the housekeeper, finding no answer to the doctor's reproof, changes her line of attack.

'A sick room is certainly no place for a child,' she proclaims. 'What would his mother say?'

'His mother, ma'am, being a woman of good sense and aware of her duty, would say that his father knows best,' observes the doctor sardonically. 'A child's eye sees the simple facts of things. It is old wives' fancies that give them the tincture of horror. My boy has already looked unmoved on sights which have sent many a strapping medical student tumbling into the runnel. 'Twill stand him in good stead if he chooses to follow his father's example. Come, Tom.'

So saying, he takes the boy by the hand and, passing in front of the cow and its keeper, he pushes open the bedroom door.

This is a large room in the modern airy style, but rendered

dark by heavily draped windows and illumined only by a single taper whose glim picks out the features of a figure lying in a huge square bed. It is a woman, old, sunken cheeked, eyes closed, pale as candle wax, and showing no sign of life. By the bedside kneels a thin black-clothed man who looks up as the door opens and slowly rises.

'You're too late, Beddoes,' he says. 'She is gone to her maker.'

'That's your professional opinion, is it, Padre?' says the doctor. 'Well, let's see.'

He goes to the window and pulls aside the drapes, letting in the full beam of a summer sun. In its light he stands looking down at the old woman, with his hand resting lightly on her neck.

Then he turns and calls, 'George, don't hang back, man. Lead her in.'

The rustic advances with the cow.

The parson cries, 'Nay, Beddoes, this is unseemly. This is not well done! She is at peace, she is with the angels.'

The doctor ignores him. Helped by the rustic and observed with wide unblinking eyes by his son, he manoeuvres the cow's head over the still figure in the bed. Then he punches the beast lightly in the stomach so that it opens its jaws and exhales a great gust of grassy breath directly into the woman's face. Once, twice, three times he does this, and on the third occasion the cow's long wet tongue licks lightly over the pallid features.

The woman opens her eyes.

Perhaps she expects to see angels, or Jesus, or even the ineffable glory of the Godhead itself.

Instead what her dim vision discovers is a gaping maw beneath broad flaring nostrils, all topped by a pair of sharp pointed horns.

She shrieks and sits bolt upright.

The cow retreats, the doctor puts a supporting arm round the woman's shoulders.

'Welcome back, my lady. Will you take a little nourishment?'

5

Her gaze clearing and the agitation fading from her features, she nods feebly and the doctor eases her back on to her pillows.

'Take Betsy out, George,' says Beddoes. 'Her work is done.'

And to his son he says, 'You see how it is, young Tom. The parson here preaches miracles. We lesser men have to practise them. Mrs Jones, a little nourishing broth for your mistress, if you please.'

Clifton, Glos, December 1808

Another bedroom, another bed, with another still figure stretched on it, arms crossed on breast, eyes staring sightlessly at the ceiling. But this is no old woman paled into a simulacrum of death by illness and debility. She, by the mercy of God and the ministrations of her doctor, still lives, but now Thomas Beddoes Sr, aged only forty-eight and looking as strong and wilful as ever he did in life, has leapfrogged his ancient patient into the grave.

Two women stand by the bed, one with her face so scored by grief she looks more fit to be laid on a bier than her husband, the other, some years older, with her arm round the wife's waist, offering comfort.

'Do not give yourself over so utterly to grief, Anne,' she urges. 'Remember the children. You must be their strength now, and they will be yours.'

'The children . . . yes, the children,' says Anne Beddoes distractedly. 'They must be told . . . they must be shown and take their farewells . . .'

'Not all of them,' says the other gently. 'Let Tom do for all. He is a thoughtful child for his age and will know how best to tell the others. Shall I fetch him now, Sister?'

'Please, yes, if you think it best . . .'

'But first his eyes . . . should we not close his eyes?'

They look down at the strong staring face.

7

'The parson tried but could not draw the lids down,' says Anne. 'He was in his prime, so full of energy ... I do not think he was ready to leave the world he could see for one which is invisible ...'

'It is a great loss, to you, to us all, to the poor of Bristol, to the world of science. Compose yourself a little, Sister, and I will fetch young Tom.'

She leaves the room, but does not have far to go.

Little Thomas Lovell Beddoes is sitting on the top stair, reading a book.

'Tom, my sweet, you must come with me,' she says.

The boy looks up and smiles. He likes his Aunt Maria. To the world she is Miss Edgeworth, the famous novelist, and when he told her that one day he too would like to write books, she didn't mock him but said seriously, 'And so you shall, Tom, else you would not be your father's son.'

Also she tells him stories. They are good stories, well structured, but lacking a little of the colour and excitement he already prefers in a narrative. But this is no matter as when he retells the tales to his brother and sisters, he is quite capable of adding enough of these elements to give them nightmares.

He stands up and takes his aunt's hand.

'Is Father well again?' he asks.

'No, Tom, though he is in a place where all are well,' she says. 'He has left us, Tom, he has gone to Heaven. You must be a comfort to your dear mama.'

The little boy frowns but does not speak as Aunt Maria leads him into the bedroom.

'Oh, Tom, Tom,' sobs his mother, embracing him so tightly he can hardly breathe. But all the time as she presses his head against her breast, his eyes are fixed upon the still figure on the bed.

His aunt prises him loose from the sobbing woman and says, 'Now say goodbye to your papa, Tom. Next time you see him will be in a better world than this.'

The boy goes to the bedside. He stands a little while, looking down into those staring eyes with a gaze equally unblinking. Then he leans forward as if to plant a kiss on the dead man's lips.

But instead of a kiss, he blows. Once, twice, thrice, each time harder, aiming the jet of warm breath at the pale mouth and flared nostrils.

'Tom!' cries his aunt. 'What are you doing?'

'I'm bringing him back,' says the boy without looking up.

He blows again. Now the assurance which had marked his mien till this moment is beginning to fade. He is gripping his father's right hand, and squeezing the fingers in search of a respondent pressure. And all the time he is puffing and blowing, his face red with effort, like an athlete straining for the tape at the end of a long race.

His aunt moves swiftly forward.

'Tom, stop that. You are upsetting your mama. Tom!'

She seizes him, he resists, not blowing now but shouting, and she has to pull him away from the corpse by main force. His mother stands there, clenched fist to her mouth, shocked to silence by this unexpected turn.

And as he is dragged out of the bedroom by his aunt, and across the landing, and down the stairs, his cries fade away like the calls of a screech owl across a darkling moor which still echo disturbingly in the mind long after they have died from the ear.

'Fetch the cow ... Fetch the cow ... Fetch the cow ...'

The Robber

St Godric's College

Cambridge

Fri Dec 14th   The Quaestor's Lodging

Dear Mr Pascoe,

Cambridge! St Godric's College! The Quaestor's Lodging!

Ain't I the swell then? Ain't I a Home Office commercial for the rehabilitating powers of the British penal system?

But who am I? you must be wondering. Or has that sensitive intuition for which you are justly famous told you already?

Whatever, let me end speculation and save you the bother of looking to the end of what could be a long letter.

I was born in a village called Hope, and it used to be my little joke that if I happened to die by drowning in Lake Disappointment in Australia, my cruciform headstone could read

Here lies
Francis Xavier Roote
Born in
HOPE
Died in
DISAPPOINTMENT

Yes, it's me, Mr Pascoe, and guessing what could be your natural reaction to getting mail from a man you banged up for what some might call the best years of his life, let me hasten to reassure you:

13

THIS ISN'T A THREATENING LETTER!

On the contrary, it's a REASSURING letter.

And not one I would have dreamt of writing if events over the past year hadn't made it clear how much you need reassurance. Me too, especially since my life has taken such an unexpected turn for the better. Instead of grubbing away in my squalid little flat, here I am relaxing in the luxury of the Quaestor's Lodging. And in case you think I must have broken in, I enclose the annual conference programme of the Romantic and Gothic Studies Association (RAGS for short!). There's my name among the list of delegates. And if you look at nine o'clock on Saturday morning, there you will see it again. Suddenly I have a future; I have friends; out of Despair I have found my way back to Hope and it's starting to look as if after all I may not be heading for the cold waters of Disappointment!

Incidentally, I shared my macabre little jest with one of my new friends, Linda Lupin MEP, when she took me to meet another, Frère Jacques, the founder of the Third Thought Movement.

What brought it to mind was we were standing in the grounds of the Abbaye du Saint Graal, the Cornelian monastery of which Jacques is such a distinguished member. The grounds opened with no barrier other than a meandering stream choked with cresses on to a World War One military cemetery whose rows of white crosses ran away from us up a shallow rise, getting smaller and smaller till the most distant looked no larger than the half-inch ones Linda and I carried on silver chains round our necks.

Linda laughed loudly. Appearances can deceive (who knows that better than you?) and finding Linda possessed of a great sense of humour has been a large step in our relationship. Jacques grinned too. Only Frère Dierick, who has attached himself to Jacques as a sort of amanuensis with pretensions to Boswellian status, pursed his lips in disapproval of such out-of-place levity. His slight and fleshless figure makes him look like Death in a cowl, but in fact he's stuffed to the chops with Flemish phlegm. Jacques happily, despite being tall, blonde and in the gorgeous ski-instructor mould, has much more of Gallic air and fire in him, plus he is unrepentantly Anglophile.

Linda said, 'Let's see if we can't dispose of you a bit further south in Australia, Fran. There's a Lake Grace, I believe. Died in Grace, that's what Third Thought's all about, right, Brother?'

This reduction of the movement to a jest really got up Dierick's bony nose but before he could speak, Jacques smiled and said, 'This I love so much about the English. You make a joke of everything. The more serious it is, the more you make the jokes. It is deliciously childish. No, that is not the word. Childlike. You are the most childlike of all the nations of Europe. That is your strength and can be your salvation. Your great poet Wordsworth knew that childhood is a state of grace. Shades of the prison house begin to close about the growing boy. It is the child alone who understands the holiness of the heart's affections.'

Getting your Romantics mixed there, Jacques, old frère, I thought, at the same time trying to work out if the bit about shades of the prison house was a crack. But I don't think so. By all accounts Jacques' own background is too colourful for him to be judgmental about others, and anyway he's not that kind of guy.

But it's funny how sensitive you can get about things like a prison record. These days I know that some ex-cons make a very profitable profession out of being ex-cons. That must really piss you and your colleagues off. But I'm not like that. All I want to do is forget about my time inside and get on with my life, cultivate my garden, so to speak.

Which is what I was doing quite successfully, and ultimately literally, till you came bursting through the hedge I'd built for protection and privacy.

Not once, not twice, but three times.

First with suspicion that I was harassing your dear wife!

Next with allegation that I was stalking your good self!!

And finally with accusation that I was involved in a series of brutal murders!!!

Which is the main reason I'm writing to you. The time has come, I think, for some straight talking between us, not in any spirit of recrimination but just so that when we're done, we can both continue our lives, you in the certainty that neither you nor those you love need fear any harm from me, and myself with the assurance that, now my life has taken such a strong turn for the better, I needn't concern myself with the possibility that once again the tender seedlings in my garden shall feel the weight of your trampling feet.

All we need, it seems to me, is total openness, a return to that childlike honesty we all possess before the shades of the prison house begin to close, and perhaps then I can persuade you that during my time in Yorkshire's answer to the Bastille, Chapel Syke Prison, I never once fantasized about taking revenge on my dear old friends, Mr Dalziel and Mr Pascoe. Revenge I have studied, certainly, but only in literature under the tutelage of my wise mentor and beloved friend, Sam Johnson.

As you know, he's dead now, Sam, and so, God damn his soul, is the man who killed him. Unless of course you pay any heed to Charley Penn. Doubting Charley! Who trusts nobody and believes nothing.

But even Charley can't deny that Sam's dead. He's dead.

When thou know'st this, thou know'st how dry a cinder this world is.

I miss him every day, and all the more because his death has contributed so much to the dramatic upturn in my life. Strange, isn't it, how tragedy can be the progenitor of triumph? In this case, two tragedies. If that poor student of Sam's hadn't overdosed in Sheffield last summer, Sam would never have moved to Mid-Yorkshire. And if Sam hadn't moved to Mid-Yorkshire, then he wouldn't have become one of the monstrous Wordman's victims. And if that hadn't happened, I would not be basking in the glow of present luxury and promised success here in God's (which, I gather, is how the illuminati refer to St Godric's!)

But back to you and your fat friend.

I'm not saying that I felt any deep affection for the pair of you or gratitude for what you'd done to me. If I thought of you at all it was in conventional terms, good cop, bad cop; the knee in the balls, the shoulder to cry on, both of you monsters, of course, but the kind that no stable society can do without, for you are the beasts that guard our gates and let us sleep safe in our beds.

Except when we're in prison. Then you cannot protect us.

Mr Dalziel, the ball-crushing knee, would probably say that we have foregone your protection.

But not you, dear Mr Pascoe, the damp shoulder. What I've heard and seen of you over the years since our first encounter makes me think you are more than just a role-player.

I'd guess you've got doubts about the penal system as it stands. In fact I suspect you've got doubts about many aspects of this creaky old society of ours, but of course being a career policeman makes it difficult for you to speak out. Doesn't stop your good lady, though, dear Mrs Pascoe, Ms Soper as she was in those long lost days when I was a young and fancy-free student at Holm Coultram College. How delighted I was to hear that you'd got married! News like that brings a little warmth and colour seeping through even the damp grey walls of Chapel Syke. Some unions seem to be made in heaven, don't they? Like Marilyn and Arthur; Woody and Mia; Chas and Di . . .

All right, can't win 'em all, can we? But at the time each of those marriages had that things-are-looking-up feel-good quality and, in terms of survival, yours looks like it could be the exception that proves the rule. Well done!

But, as I was saying, within those walls not even the

nice worrying cops like you can do much to protect the rights of young and vulnerable cons like me.

So even if I'd wanted to plan revenge, I wouldn't have had time to do it.

I was too busy looking for a route to survival.

I needed help, of course, for one thing I quickly worked out.

You can't survive alone in prison.

As you well know, I'm not defenceless. My tongue is my chief weapon, and given room to wield it in, I reckon I can nimble my way out of most predicaments.

But if one nasty con is twisting your arms up your back while another's sticking his cock in your mouth, wagging your tongue tends to be counter-productive.

This was the likely fate a guy I got banged up with on remand took some pleasure in mapping out for me if I got sent down to the Syke. Good-looking, blond, blue-eyed boy with a nice slim figure would be made very welcome there, he assured me, adding with a bitter laugh that he used to be a good-looking blond blue-eyed boy himself.

Looking at his scarred, hollow-cheeked, broken-nosed, ochre-toothed face, I found it hard to believe, but something in his voice carried conviction. Something in his judge's too, and next time we met was when we arrived at Chapel Syke together.

He was an old hand at this and though I soon sussed out that he was far too far down the pecking order to have any value as a protector, I squeezed every last detail I could get out of him about how the place worked as we went about our new-boy task of cleaning the bogs.

The main man was a ten-year con called Polchard, first name Matthew, known to his intimates as Mate, though not because of any innate amiability. He wasn't much to look at, being scrawny, bald, and so white faced it was like seeing the skull beneath the skin. But his standing was confirmed by the fact that during 'association' he always had a table to himself in the crowded 'parlour' which is what they called the association room. There he sat, scowling down at a chessboard (Mate: gerrit?) and studying a little book in which he occasionally made notes before moving a piece. From time to time someone would bring him a mug of tea. If anyone wanted to talk to him, they stood patiently by, a couple of feet from the table, till he deigned to notice them. And on rare occasions if what they said was of particular interest, they'd be invited to pull up a chair and sit down.

Polchard himself didn't do sex, my 'friend' informed me, but his lieutenants were always on the lookout for new talent and if he gave them the go-ahead, I might as well touch my toes and think of England.

But in the short term, he went on to say, I was most at risk from a freelancer like Brillo Bright. You may have encountered him and his twin brother, Dendo. God knows where their names came from, though I have heard it suggested that Brillo got his after spending some time in a padded cell (Brillo Pad, OK?) At some point Brillo had decided that having a spread eagle tattooed across his bald pate and beetling brow with its talons wrapped around his eye sockets was a good way of improving his facial beauty. He might have been right. What it certainly must have improved was the odds on his being recognized whenever he pursued his chosen profession of armed robbery, which possibly explained why he'd spent half of his thirty-odd years in jail. Brother Dendo was by comparison an intellectual, but only by comparison, being an unpredictably vicious thug. The Brights were the only cons to have an existence independent of Polchard. On the surface they were all chums together, but in fact they were far too unstable for Polchard to risk the hassle of a confrontation. So they existed like the Isle of Man, offshore, closely related to the mainland, but in many ways a law unto themselves.

And helping themselves to a tasty newcomer would be a way for Brillo and Dendo to affirm their independence without risking any real provocation of the main man.

To survive I had to find a way of getting myself under Polchard's protection which didn't involve getting under one of his boys. Not that I've got any serious objection to a close same sex relationship, but I knew from anecdote and observation that letting yourself become a centre-fold spread in prison means you're pinned down at the bottom of the heap just as surely as if you'd got a staple through your belly button.

First off, I had to show I wasn't to be messed with. So I laid my plans.

A couple of days later I waited till I saw Dendo and Brillo go into the shower room, and I followed them.

Brillo looked at me like a fox who's just seen a chicken come strolling into his earth.

I hung my towel up and stepped under the shower, plastic shampoo bottle in hand.

Brillo said something to his brother who laughed, then he moved towards me. He wasn't all that well hung for such a big man, but what there was certainly had a strong sense of anticipation.

'Hello, girlie,' he said. 'Like someone to do your back?'

I unscrewed the top of my shampoo bottle and said, 'Have you got that chicken sitting on your head so everyone will know you've got scrambled egg for brains?'

It took him a moment to work this out, then his eyes bulged in fury, which was fine as it doubled my target area.

As he lunged towards me, I raised the bottle and squeezed and sent a jet of the lavatory cleaning bleach I'd filled it with straight into his eyes.

He screamed and started to knuckle at his eyes and I gave the skinned end of his rampant dick another quick burst. Now he didn't know what to do with his hands. I stooped, hooked his left ankle from under him, then stood back as he tumbled over, hitting his head against the wall with such force that he cracked a tile.

All this in the space of a few seconds. Dendo

meanwhile had been standing there in sheer disbelief but now he began to advance. I waved the shampoo bottle towards him and he halted.

I said, 'Either get bird-brain here to a medic or buy him a white stick.'

Then I picked up my towel and retreated.

You see how I'm putting myself in your hands, my dear Mr Pascoe. A confession to assault and grievous bodily harm occasioning death. For it turned out that Brillo had a surprisingly thin skull for so thick a man, and there was damage which led to a tardily diagnosed meningeal problem which led to his demise. You could probably get an investigation going even after all this time. Not that I think the authorities at the Syke would applaud you. They went through the motions at the time, but brother Dendo who couldn't bring himself to co-operate with the Law even in circumstances like these, lost it when one of the screws dissed his dead brother and broke his jaw.

That got him out of the way for which I was mightily relieved. Of course all the cons knew what had happened, but in the Syke no one grassed without Polchard's say-so, and as there was a touch of negligence in Brillo's death, the screws were glad to bury him and the affair, very few questions were asked.

That was stage one. Polchard too probably wasn't sorry to see the back of the Brights, but there were plenty of people around who would be happy to do Dendo a favour, so I still needed the top man's protection.

So to stage two.

At the next period in the parlour, I approached his table and stood at what I'd worked out was the appropriate petitioning distance.

He ignored me completely, not even glancing up under his bushy eyebrows.. Conversation and activity went on elsewhere in the room but it had that hushed unreal quality you get when people are simply going through the motions.

21

I studied the chessboard as he worked out his next move. He'd obviously started with an orthodox Queen's Pawn opening and countered it with a variation on the Slav defence. Playing yourself is a form of exercise by which the top-flight chess-player can keep his basic skills honed, but the only real test, of course, lies in pitting them against the unpredictability of an equal or superior player.

Finally after what must have been twenty minutes and with only another five of the association period left, he made his move.

Then, still without looking up, he said, 'What?'

I stepped forward, picked up the black bishop and took his knight.

The room went completely silent.

Leaving the knight open to the bishop was a trap, of course. One which he'd laid for himself and would therefore not have fallen into. But I had. What he needed to know now was, had I done it out of sheer incompetence, or did I have an agenda of my own?

At least that's what I hoped he needed to know.

After a long minute, still without looking up, he said, 'Chair.'

A chair was thrust against the back of my legs and I sat down.

He spent the remaining period of association studying the board.

When the bell went to summon us back to our cells he looked me in the face for the first time and said, 'Tomorrow.'

And thus I moved out of the first, which is the most dangerous, stage of my prison career, Mr Pascoe. If I'd just sat around rehearsing revenge on yourself, I would by this point probably have been raped, possibly mutilated, certainly established as everyone's yellow dog, to be kicked and humiliated at will. No, I had to be pragmatic, deal with the existing situation as best I could. Which is what I'm doing now. I make no bones about it. I no longer want to be constantly glancing back over my shoulder, fearful that you are out there, driven to pursue me by your own fears.

Perhaps one day we may both come to recognize that flying from a thing we dread is not so very different from pursuing a thing we love. If and when that day comes, then I hope, dear Mr Pascoe, that I may see your face and take your outstretched hand and hear you say, ' esus bloody Christ!' said Peter Pascoe.

'Yes, I know it's that time of year,' said Ellie Pascoe who was sitting at the other side of the breakfast table looking without enthusiasm at a scatter of envelopes clearly containing Christmas cards. 'But is it fair to blame a radical Jewish agitator for the way western capitalism has chosen to make a fast buck from his alleged birthday?'

'The cheeky sod!' exclaimed Pascoe.

'Ah, it's a guessing game,' said Ellie. 'OK. It's from the palace saying the Queen is minded to make you a duchess in the New Year's Honours list. No? OK, I give up.'

'It's from bloody Roote. He's in Cambridge, for God's sake!'

'Bloody Roote? You mean Franny Roote? The student? The short story writer?'

'No, I mean Roote the ex-con. The psycho criminal.'

'Oh, that Roote. So what's he say?'

'I'm not sure. I think the bastard's forgiving me.'

'Well that's nice,' yawned Ellie. 'At least it's more interesting than these sodding cards. What's he doing in Cambridge?'

'He's at a conference on *Romantic Studies in the early nineteenth century*,' said Pascoe looking at the programme enclosed with the letter.

'Good for him,' said Ellie. 'He must be doing well.'

'He's only there because of Sam Johnson,' said Pascoe dismissively. 'Here we are. Nine o'clock this morning. Mr Francis Roote MA will read the late Dr Sam Johnson's paper entitled *Looking for the laughs in Death's Jest-Book*. That sounds a bundle of fun. What the hell does it mean?'

'*Death's Jest-Book*? You remember Samuel Lovell Beddoes, whose life Sam was working on when he died? Well, *Death's Jest-Book* is this play that Beddoes worked at all his life. I've not read it but I gather it's pretty Gothic. And it's a revenge tragedy.'

'Revenge. Aha.'

'Don't make connections which aren't there, Peter. Let's have a look at the letter.'

'I'm not finished yet. There's reams of the bloody thing.'

'Well, give us the bit you've read. And don't take too long reading the rest. Time and our daughter wait for no man.'

There had been a time when an off-duty Saturday meant a long lie in with the possibility of breakfast or, if he was very lucky, even tastier goodies in bed. But this was before his daughter Rosie had discovered she was musical.

Whether any competent authority was going to confirm this discovery, Pascoe didn't know. While not having a tin ear, his musical judgment wasn't sufficiently refined to work out whether the faltering and scrannel notes he could even now hear issuing from her clarinet were much the same as those produced by a pre-pubescent Benny Goodman, or whether this was as good as it got.

But while he was waiting to find out, Rosie had to have lessons from the best available teacher, viz. Ms Alicia Wintershine of the Mid-Yorkshire Sinfonietta, whose excellence was evidenced by the fact that the only session she had available (and that only because another budding virtuosa had discovered ponies) was nine o'clock on Saturday morning.

So goodbye to breakfast in bed, and all that.

But a man is still master in his own head if not his own house, and Pascoe buttered himself another piece of toast and settled down to the rest of Roote's letter.

Sorry about the hiatus!

I was interrupted by the entrance of a train of porters carrying enough luggage to keep the Queen of Sheba going for a long state visit. Behind them was a small lean athletic man with a shock of blond hair which looked almost white against his deeply tanned skin, whom I recognized instantly from his dust-jacket photos as Professor Dwight S. Duerden of Santa Apollonia University, California (or St Poll Uni, CA, as he expressed it). He seemed a little put out to find himself sharing the Quaestor's Lodging with me, even though I had modestly chosen the smaller bedroom.

(You will already, I'm sure, have worked out that I'm not the Quaestor – whatever that is – of God's, but merely a temporary occupant of his rooms during the conference. The Quaestor himself is, I gather, conducting a party of Hellenophiles around the Aegean on a luxury cruise liner. This is a line of work that interests me strangely!)

Professor Duerden and most of his luggage have now finally disappeared into his bedroom. If he intends a complete unpacking, he may be some time, so I shall continue.

Where was I? Oh yes, in the midst of what looks dangerously like becoming a rather tedious philosophical digression, so let me get back to straight narrative.

The following day, I played Polchard to a draw. I think I could have beaten him, but I wouldn't like to swear to it. Anyway, a draw seemed best for starters.

After that we played every day. At first he always had white but after our third draw he turned the board round and thereafter we alternated. The sixth game I won. There was a moment of cenotaph silence in the room, only more in anticipation of sacrifice than remembrance of it, and as I made my way back to my cell, men who'd become quite friendly over the past couple of weeks drew away from me.

I paid no heed. They were thinking of Polchard as King Rat, I was thinking of him as Grand Master. There's no fun playing someone not good enough to beat you, and less in playing someone who's good enough but too scared. My long-term survival plan depended on establishing equality.

That was my thinking, but I knew I could be wrong. I dreamt that night I was in that scene in Bergman's *Seventh Seal* where the Knight plays Death at chess. I woke up in a muck sweat, thinking I'd made a terrible mistake.

But next day he was sitting with the board set up and I knew I had been right.

Now all I had to do was find a way of letting him beat me without him spotting it.

But not straight off, I thought. That would be too obvious, and for him to catch me losing would be worse than constantly winning. So I played my normal game and planned ahead. Then Polchard made a move three times quicker than usual, and when I studied the board I realized I didn't need to worry. All that solitary exercise had turned him into a fine defensive player. Well, it's bound to when you're resisting attacking gambits you've devised yourself. But the bastard had been soaking up the details of the way I played and suddenly he'd gone into full attacking mode and I was in trouble.

It would have been easy to fold up before his onslaught, but I didn't. I twisted and turned and weaved and ducked, and when I finally knocked over my king, we both knew he'd beaten me fair and square.

He smiled as he re-set the pieces. Like a ripple on a dark pool.

'Chess, war, job,' he said. 'All the same. Get them thinking one way, go the other.'

Not a bad game plan I suppose if you're a career criminal.

After that I stopped worrying about results.

Now everyone was my friend again but I played it cool. I wanted to be accepted as an equal not envied as a favourite. I knew as long as I played my cards, and my pieces, right, I'd got a fully paid-up ticket to ride my stretch as comfortably as I could hope.

But make yourself as comfortable as you like in a noisy stinking overcrowded iron-barred nineteenth-century prison and it's still a fucking jail.

Time to turn my energies to my next project, which was to get myself an exeat.

You can see why I didn't have any time for the luxury of plotting revenge! I had a delicate balancing act to perform, staying Polchard's friend and at the same time getting myself a sufficient reputation as a reformed character to get a transfer to a nice open prison. Despite all evidence to the contrary, the Powers That Be still have a touching belief in a correlation between education and virtue, so I did an Open University degree, opting for a strong sociological element on the grounds that this would give me the best opportunity to impress the PTB with my revitalized sense of civic responsibility. Also it's the easiest stuff imaginable. Anyone with half a mind can suss out in ten minutes flat which buttons to press to get your tutors cooing over your essays. Whisk up a froth of soft left sentiments with a stiffening of social deprivation statistics and you're home and dry, or home and wet as the old unreconstructed Thatcherites would see it. With that out of the way, I started on an MA course on the same lines. My dissertation was on the theme of Crime and Punishment, which gave me the chance to really strut my born-again-citizen stuff. But it was so deadly dull!

It would have been all right if I could have told them the truth about my fellow cons, which was that to most of them crime was a job like any other, except there was no unemployment problem. Treating prison as a retraining opportunity is pointless when you're dealing with people who think of themselves as out of circulation rather than out of work. Better to spend all that public money sending them on holidays abroad in the hope they'd get food poisoning or Legionnaire's. But I knew that advancing such a theory wasn't going to get me letters after my name, so I dripped out the usual gunge about socialization and rehabilitation and in the fullness of time became Francis Roote, MA.

But I was still in the Syke, though by now I'd hoped to have smoothed my way out to Butlin's, which is what my ingenious fellow felons called Butler's Low, Yorkshire's newest and most luxuriously appointed open prison on the fringe of the Peak District.

I couldn't understand why I didn't seem to be making any progress in that direction. OK, I played chess with Polchard, but I wasn't one of his mob in the heavy sense. I put this to one of the screws I'd sweet-talked into semi-confidential mode.

'You lot can't keep giving me black marks for playing chess,' I protested.

He hesitated then said, 'Maybe it's not us who're giving you the black marks.'

And that was it. But it was enough.

It was Polchard who was making sure I didn't get a transfer.

He didn't want to lose the only guy on the wing, probably in the whole of the Syke, who could give him a run for his money on the chessboard and all he had to do to keep me was let the screws know that losing me would make him, and therefore everyone else, very unhappy.

I could see no way of changing this, so I had to find a way of countering it.

I needed some big hitters in my corner. But where to look?

The Governor was too busy watching his back against political do-gooders to have any time for individual cases, while the Chaplain was an old-fashioned whisky priest whose alcoholic amiability was so inclusive he even spoke up for Dendo Bright, who, thank God, had been transferred to some distant high-security unit.

As for my obvious choice, the Prison Psychiatrist, this was a jolly little man with the unreassuring nickname of

Bonkers, whom it was generally agreed you'd have to be mad to consult. But then came a Home Office inspection, which led to a temporary improvement in menu and the permanent removal, under some kind of cloud, of a still-smiling Bonkers.

A short time later all over the jail ears and other things pricked when it was announced that a new trick cyclist had been appointed, and that it was a woman!

Professor Duerden has interrupted me again.

I see now that I misinterpreted his reaction when he first saw me. He wasn't dismayed to find he was sharing the Quaestor's Lodging but puzzled to find he was sharing it with someone he'd never met and never heard of.

An Englishman would have slid around the subject, and some Americans can be pretty devious too, but he was of the straight-from-the-shoulder school.

'So where're you working, son?' he asked me.

'Mid-Yorkshire University,' I replied.

'That so? Now remind me, who's running your department these days?'

'Mr Dunstan,' I said.

'Dunstan?' He looked puzzled. 'Would that be Tony Dunstan the medievalist?'

'No, it would be Jack Dunstan, the head gardener,' I said.

Once he got over his surprise, that really tickled him, and I saw no reason not to be completely open with him. I explained about being Sam Johnson's pupil and how Sam had got me a job in the gardens, and how, as well as being Sam's student, I'd also been a close friend and was, through the good offices of his sister, his literary executor.

'Sam was scheduled to present a paper at the conference,' I concluded, 'and when the Programme Committee contacted me to ask if I would be willing to read his paper, I felt I owed it to him to accept. I presume my name's been substituted for his all down the line, which is how I come to be in the Quaestor's Lodging.'

He said, 'Yeah, that must be it,' but I suspect he didn't really reckon that even Sam rated high enough to be his roomy.

In fact, I've been wondering about this myself and I think I've got it sussed. The programme says that special thanks are due to Sir Justinian Albacore, the Dean of St Godric's, under whose auspices we are the guests of the college. That name rings a bell. Could this be the same J. C. Albacore whose study of the Gothic psyche, *The Search for Nepenthe*, you probably know? I've never read it myself, but I often saw it propping up the broken leg of a sofa in Sam Johnson's study. For this man was the great hate of Sam's life. According to Sam, he'd given a lot of help to Albacore when he was writing *Nepenthe*, and the man had shown his gratitude by ripping off his Beddoes project! Sam got suspicious on finding someone had been ahead of him when he delved into a couple of rare and apparently unrelated archives. Finally it emerged that Albacore was also working on a Beddoes critical biog. to appear in 2003, the bicentenary of TLB's birth. And not long before his death, Sam was spitting fire at the news heard on the grapevine that Albacore's publishers intended to pre-empt the field by publishing at the end of 2002.

I described myself to Dwight as Sam's literary executor, which wasn't precisely true. What in fact occurred, as you probably heard, was that Linda Lupin, MEP, Sam's half-sister and sole heir, decided out of the generosity of her spirit to place the reins of Sam's researches into my hands. It probably won't surprise you to learn that the publisher with whom Sam's biography was contracted wasn't best pleased.

I can see his point of view. Who am I, after all? In literary terms, nobody, though my 'colourful' background was something their sales department felt they might have been able to use if the field had remained clear. But with Albacore's book already being hyped around as the 'definitive' biography, their judgment now was that setting

31

me up to carry on where Sam had left off was throwing good money after bad.

So, sorry, mate, but no deal for the big book that Sam was aiming at.

They did however make an alternative proposal.

Because Beddoes' life is so thinly documented, Sam had been interlarding his script with what he clearly labelled 'Imagined Scenes'. These, as he explains in a draft preface, made no claim to be detailed accounts of actual incidents. Though some were based on known facts, others were simply imaginative projections, devised in order to give the reader a sense of the living reality of Beddoes' existence. Many would, I believe, have been much modified in or totally expunged from the finished book.

How would I feel, I was asked, about cutting out most of the hard-core lit. crit. stuff, working up a few more of these 'Imagined Scenes', well spiced with a sprinkling of sex and violence, and producing one of those pop-biogs which had done so well in recent years?

I didn't need the time offered to think about it.

I told them to get stuffed. I owe Sam a lot more than that.

But while I was still reeling from the injustice of it all came this invitation for me to take up Sam's place at the conference.

I'd taken it on face value as the programmers paying a posthumous tribute to a valued colleague and at the same time saving themselves the bother of rejigging their programme. But this was no explanation of why, instead of being stuck in a student's pad like the commonalty of lecturers, I was queening it in the Q's lodging alongside Dwight Duerden. There had to be another motive and, since seeing Albacore's name, I've been suspecting he might have hopes of sweet-talking Sam's Beddoes research database out of me.

Maybe I'm being paranoid. But the groves of academe are crowded with raptors, so Sam always assured me.

Anyway, I'll be in a better position to judge once I've actually met the conference organizers, which will be at the Welcome Reception and Introductory Session in fifteen minutes' time.

Now where was I? Oh yes, the new female psych. Her name, believe it or not, was Amaryllis Haseen!

Sporting with Amaryllis in the shade was, you will recall, one of the alternatives to writing poetry which Milton's most un-Puritanical imagination suggested to him. My only acquaintance with the flower is the garishly fleshy specimens that sometimes turn up at Christmas. Well, by those standards, Ms Haseen lived up to her name and was generally regarded by most of the sex-starved cons as an early Christmas prezzie. As one of Polchard's top lads said dreamily, 'Tart like that you can tell all your sexual fancies to, it's better than pulling your plonker over *Women on Top*.'

Everyone developed psychological problems. Ms Haseen was no fool, however. Her purpose in taking on the Chapel Syke consultancy was to garner material for a book on the psychology of incarceration, which she hoped would put more letters after her name and more money in her bank. (It came out last year, called *Dark Cells*, lots of nice reviews. I'm Prisoner XR pp.193–207, by the way.) She quickly sorted out the wankers from the bankers. When Polchard's lieutenant complained that he'd been dumped while I'd got a twice-weekly session, I smiled and said, 'You've got to make 'em feel they can help you, and that doesn't mean flashing your bone and asking her to give it the once over like you did!' That made even Polchard smile and thereafter whenever I came back from a session I had to face a barrage of obscene questions as to the progress I was making towards getting into her underwear.

To tell the truth, I think I might have managed it, but I didn't even try. Even if successful, what would I have got out of it?

A few top-C's of mindless delight (no chance in the

circumstances for more than a quick knee-trembler) and a coda of post-coital sadness that might stretch for years!

For I had to be a realist. Even if Amaryllis could be seduced into enjoying a bit of sport in the shade, when she walked out into the bright sunshine beyond the Syke's main gates and thought of her promising career and her happy marriage, she was going to shudder with shame and fear and pre-empt any future accusations I might make by marking me down as a dangerous fantasist. (You think I'm being too cynical? Read on!)

So I set my mind to finding out what it was that she wanted from me professionally and making sure that she got it.

There was another danger here. You see, what she really wanted was to get a clear picture of what made me tick. And the trouble was that this subject fascinated me also.

I've always known I'm not quite the same as other people, but the precise nature of this otherness eludes me. Is it based on an absence or a presence? Do I have something others lack, or am I lacking in something that others possess?

Am I, in other words, a god among mortals or merely a wolf among sheep?

The temptation to let it all hang out before her and see what her professional skills made of the fascinating tangle was great. But the risks were greater. Suppose her conclusion was that I was an incurable sociopath?

So, regrettably, I felt I had to postpone the pleasures of complete analytical honesty till such time as I could pay for it out of my pocket rather than out of my freedom.

Instead I devoted my energies to letting Amaryllis find what suited us both best – that is, a slightly fractured personality which would make an interesting paragraph in her book.

It was good fun. The checkable facts about my background I was careful to leave intact. But after that, it was creativity hour as, like Dorothy after the twister, I stepped out of the black and white world of Kansas into the bright bold colours of Oz. Like most of these trick cyclists, she was fixated on my childhood and I had a great time inventing absurd stories about my dear old dad, who actually vanished from my life so early that I have no recollection of him whatsoever. You'll find most of them in her book. I knew I had a talent for fiction long before I won that short-story competition.

Yet at the same time I was very aware that Amaryllis was no one's fool. I had to assume she knew that my agenda was to help myself by apparently helping her. So, as with my chess games, I needed to play on many levels.

It didn't take many sessions before I began to think I was truly in control.

Then she took me by surprise. Her opening was to ask me, 'How do you feel about the people you hold responsible for putting you in the Syke?'

'Apart from myself?' I said.

This seemed like a good answer, but she just grinned at me as if to say, 'Come off it!'

So I smiled back and said, 'You mean the policemen who arrested me and built the case against me?'

'If that's who you think responsible,' she said.

'I don't feel anything,' I said. 'In fact I've hardly thought about them since the trial.'

'So revenge never enters your mind? No little fantasies to while your nights away?'

It was funny, I'd been feeding her lies and half-truths for weeks, and now when I was telling her it like it is, no prevarication whatsoever, I was getting that disbelieving grin.

'Read my lips,' I said distinctly. 'Thoughts of revenge haven't broken my sleep nor troubled my waking hours. Cross my heart. Kiss the Book. Swear on my father's grave.'

I meant it, every word. Still do.

35

'Then how do you explain the topic you propose for your PhD thesis?' she asked.

This took my breath away for two reasons.

First, how the hell did she know what my proposed thesis topic was?

And second, how did I explain it?

The Revenge Theme in the English Drama.

Could it be that all the time I thought I was coolly, calmly and collectedly planning my future like a rational man, deep down inside me some bitter scheming fury was obsessed with thought of vengeance against you and Mr Dalziel?

Well, since then I've had a lot of time to think about it, and I can put my hand on my heart and declare with complete honesty that not one thought of you or Mr Dalziel crossed my mind as I chose my thesis topic.

Like I said earlier, I was bored to tears by all the sociological crap I'd had to shovel out for my degrees. I wanted something different. I wanted something to do with real people feeling real passion and I knew I had to turn from sociology to literature for that, and to the theatre in particular. I remembered an old English teacher who used to say there are three springs of action in the drama – love, ambition and revenge – and the greatest of these is revenge. So I started reading the Elizabethans and Jacobeans and very soon realized he was right. In terms of dramatic energy, nothing was more productive than revenge. Love moved, ambition drove, but revenge exploded! I knew I had found my theme, but it was an artistic, an academic, an autotelic choice, having nothing to do with extraneous matters like my own situation.

But I could see how it must look to Amaryllis with her Freudian squint.

I opened my mouth to argue, decided this was the wrong tactic, and said instead, 'I'd really never thought of that. Good God. And here's me thinking . . . well, I never!'

Let her see me gobsmacked, I thought. Let her feel completely in charge.

And all the time my brain was racing to work out how she knew about my proposal. I'd never mentioned it to her. Indeed I'd only put it together myself last week and sent it off to the extra-mural department of the University of Sheffield who had still to reply . . .

That was it! Her husband. I knew from the grapevine he was a university teacher. Her presence at the Syke meant it was likely it was one of the Yorkshire universities. I'd assumed his discipline would be the same as hers, but why should it be?

If I was right . . . but first check it out.

I could see no easier way than the most direct.

I said, 'This would be your husband telling you about my application, I presume? And you filling him in about me. Funny that. Don't the usual rules of patient confidentiality and pastoral responsibility apply in the case of convicted felons then?'

A fishing expedition she might have wriggled away from, but this was a grenade lobbed into the water.

She did her best but she was floundering belly-up from the start.

'No, really, nothing sinister,' she said, flashing me an all-sophisticates-together smile from those tubulous lips. 'Just one of life's little coincidences. Jay, that's my husband, happens to be in the English Department there, you see, and he happens to chair the committee which looks at these things, and he happened to mention that there'd been an application from someone in Chapel Syke . . .'

An expert interrogator like yourself would have easily spotted the symptoms of evasion, too many *happenses*, trying to cover the fact that when she leaves here, she heads home and chats away quite happily with her poncy husband about the funny things her banged-up clients have been telling her, fuck professional confidentiality, probably livens up the chat round the dinner table with

37

little anecdotes plucked from our soul-baring confessions. For a moment I felt genuinely indignant till I recalled that most of what I personally had told her was crap, more arsehole-baring than soul-baring.

I said, 'Well, that's handy. Maybe you could give me a hint how my application's going, seeing as they're taking forever to respond to me direct. I was thinking of having a word with the Visitor about it. He's always banging on about prisoners' rights.'

That gave her something to think about. Lord Threlkeld, our Chief Visitor, must be familiar to you. I bet he's one of old Rumbletummy's pet hates, being a notorious bleeding heart who likes nothing better than a good case of professional misconduct either from the police or the prison service to wave at his peers in the House.

She gathered her wits and answered, 'It's not for me to say, of course, but I think they're really impressed by the quality of your proposal. I know that Jay in particular is keen to see that you get approval . . . all things being equal, of course . . .'

Oh my Amaryllis, is chess one of the sports you play in the shade? I wondered, hiding a smile as I interpreted her words. Good old Jay would love to be your advocate, but that might be difficult if you're making some silly complaint about his wife . . .

'Now that would be kind,' I said. 'Is there any chance your husband would be interested in supervising me himself?'

'Oh no,' she said hurriedly. 'He's taking up a new post next term in his old college, so he won't be around, you see. But there is a colleague of his, Dr Johnson, who's showing a very positive interest . . .'

And that was the first time I heard dear Sam's name, but I hardly felt it as an epiphanic moment, I was more concerned with pressing home my advantage.

'So now you've happened to find out about my PhD proposal, what do you reckon it shows about me?' I asked.

'Do you really think I'm secretly harbouring thoughts of revenge against the people I blame for putting me here?'

'That's putting it too strongly, perhaps,' she said. 'I don't see you as a strongly vengeful personality. While it would be surprising if you didn't feel some resentment, I see your choice of thesis subject as a sublimation of these feelings. In other words, it's part of the healing process rather than part of the trauma.'

This was *Reader's Digest* stuff, I thought gleefully. This was the kind of simple diet I wanted the boneheads who decided my future to be fed on.

'So in fact, Doctor, you think the topic of my PhD proposal, and its acceptance at Sheffield, will be a help in getting me transferred to Butler's Low? I mean, I wouldn't want to be too far away from my supervisor, would I?'

'I can see that,' she said, nodding and making a note. 'That makes a lot of sense.'

I took that as a yes, and a yes is what it proved to be, though in fact I got transferred to Butlin's before I had my PhD proposal accepted. So it was there I met Sam for the first time. I was glad later that he never had to come to the Syke and see me in that context, and smell me too, probably, for one of the first things they told me when I reached Butlin's was that I'd brought the prison stink with me. You don't notice it yourself, but the others notice it, and I noticed it myself later when a new transferee arrived.

Curious, the creative power of a smell! It took me straight back to slamming doors and crowded cells and slopping out and constant fear – oh yes, even when you were Polchard's chess playmate, you still lived in fear – a sadistic screw, some nutter running amuck, dodgy smack, a new king rat knocking Polchard off his perch – you never knew what deadly changes the day might bring. So that smell was a potent incentive to behave myself in Butlin's. Here we were in the Land of Beulah. Every day we could look across the river to the Promised Land.

Only a fool would ever let himself be sent back to that other place.

I wasn't a fool then and I'm not a fool now.

I can see you might find it hard to believe my prison experience has rehabilitated me, but you can surely understand it's left me resolved never ever to risk going back inside.

So, no threats of revenge, nor even any thoughts of revenge, not even under provocation – and you must admit you have been somewhat provocative, dear Mr Pascoe.

What I want from life I can get by simple honest means, or at least what passes for such in the groves of academe! I look around me – at the old oak panelling of the room I'm writing in, its honeyed depths returning the glow of the open fire which fends off the chill of the crisp winter day whose pale sunlight fills the quiet quad outside my window.

I only arrived a couple of hours ago and, as I've told you, I'm only here for the weekend, but I knew the moment I set foot in the place that this or something very like it is what I want. That's why I'm writing to you, Mr Pascoe. I'd been thinking for some time it would be nice to clear the air between us, but now I know it's essential, as much I admit for my own selfish reasons as to ensure your peace of mind.

Have I said enough? Perhaps, perhaps not. I'll check later. But now I've got to go. It's the opening session of the conference in five minutes. Dwight has already left, pointing to his watch then making a drinking motion with his hand.

It wouldn't do for a new boy to be late. There's a post box by the porter's lodge so I'll drop this in when I go down. I don't expect I'll be writing to you again, dear Mr Pascoe. I hope that I've cleared the air between us. The past is Hades, the past is the cities of the plain; look back and disaster strikes. My eyes are set firmly on the future.

I must admit to feeling somewhat nervous, but also very excited.

This could be the beginning of the rest of my life. Wish me luck!

And a Very Merry Christmas to you and yours!

Franny Roote

llie Pascoe was a fast reader and soon she was picking up his discarded sheets and she snatched the last one from his fingers before he could let it fall.

Pascoe watched her finish it then said, 'So what do you think?'

'Well, it's always nice to have one's judgment confirmed.'

'Your judgment being like the court's, that Roote is a devious amoral psychopath?'

'Is that what the judge said? I must have missed it. I thought he was found guilty of being an accessory to murder. In any case, the judgment I refer to is the one by which Charley Penn and me awarded him first prize in the *Gazette* short-story competition. He writes very entertainingly, doesn't he?'

'Does he? I'd rather read a gas meter.'

'Each to his own taste. But you've got to give it to him. He's really making the most of his opportunities.'

'That's a good working definition of most crimes.'

'I didn't see any reference to crimes.'

'Killing Brillo wasn't a crime?'

'The fault, dear Peter, lies not in our Fran but in the system that put him there.'

'How about blackmailing Haseen to get him into Butlin's? And what about conning Linda Lupin into taking him under her wing? The poor cow had better keep her eyes skinned else she'll find she's got a permanent stowaway on the European gravy train.'

'Haseen seems to have behaved unprofessionally, so she had it coming. As for Loopy Linda, she deserves everything she gets.

And besides, I suspect she can look after herself. She certainly doesn't waste much energy looking after anyone else.'

Pascoe smiled, knowing he wasn't going to get anywhere inviting sympathy for Linda Lupin, who was a Tory MEP and a particular *betesse noire* of the left-wing feminist tendency. The fact that she was also the late lamented Sam Johnson's half-sister and sole heir had come as a shock to Ellie, but to Franny Roote it had clearly come as an opportunity which he'd grasped with both hands.

'And aren't you being a touch paranoid?' continued Ellie. 'All he's doing is telling you he's doing well for himself, so why should he be nursing grudges?'

'Doing well for a criminal involves criminality,' muttered Pascoe.

'Maybe. But what better area for the legitimate use of criminal talent than the life academic?' said Ellie, who since being officially confirmed as a creator by acceptance of her first novel tended to look back rather patronizingly at her old existence as a college lecturer. 'Anyway, he's paid his debt and all that, and he'd probably never have come to your notice again if you hadn't gone after him in a not very subtle way.'

This was so unjust it might have taken Pascoe's breath away if life with Ellie hadn't left him pretty well permanently breathless.

He said mildly, 'I only turned him up in the first place because someone was threatening you and he looked a possible candidate.'

'Yeah, and the other times? Pete, admit it, you've always gone in hard with Franny Roote. Why is that? There must be something about him that bugs you specially.'

'Not really. Except he's weird, you've got to admit that. No? OK, let's look at it another way. Don't you think it's just a little bit screwy to be writing to me like this?'

'You're acting like this is a threatening letter,' said Ellie. 'Despite the fact that he goes out of his way to say this isn't a threatening letter! What more does he have to say?'

'A man comes towards you in a dark street,' said Pascoe. 'He stops in front of you and says reassuringly, "It's OK, I'm not going to rape you." How reassured do you feel?'

'A lot more reassured than if he's stark naked and waving a knife, like Dick Dee when young Bowler rode to the rescue. How is he, by the way?'

'He looked fine when I saw him on Thursday. Should be back with us by the middle of next week, if he doesn't overtax his strength this weekend.'

'Doing what?'

'Seems Rye Pomona, his light of love, is showing her gratitude by taking him away for a long weekend at some nice romantic hotel in the Peaks. He was full of it on Thursday. Well, it should either make him or break him.'

'How nice it must be to have a part of you that's eternally adolescent,' said Ellie. 'But I'm glad he's come through it all OK. How about the girl?'

'Oddly enough, she looked a lot worse than him last time I saw her.'

'Why oddly?'

'He was the one who got his skull fractured and ended up in hospital, remember?'

'And she was the one who nearly got raped and murdered,' retorted Ellie.

They sat in silence for a while, each recollecting the dramatic climax of what came to be known as the Wordman case. The prime suspect, Dick Dee, head of the public library reference section, had lured his assistant, Rye Pomona, out to a remote country cottage. When DC Hat Bowler, who was madly in love with her, had discovered this, he'd gone rushing off to the rescue, with Pascoe and Dalziel in hot pursuit. Bowler had arrived to discover Rye and Dee, both naked and covered with blood, locked in a deadly struggle. In the fight that followed, Hat had managed to get hold of the knife Dee was wielding and stab the man fatally, but not before receiving severe head injuries himself. Pascoe, who'd been next on the scene, had feared the young man might die from his wounds, a fear compounded by his own sense of guilt that he had allowed too much of his own attention to be diverted by the presence among the list of suspects of the man who had come once more to disturb the even tenor of his ways – Franny Roote.

He'd been wrong then. Perhaps he was over-reacting now. Ellie certainly thought so.

She returned to the attack.

'Getting back to our Fran,' she said. 'We are entering the season of comfort and joy, or so the telly ads keep telling us, the season for making contact with people far away in space and time, hence all these sodding cards, which incidentally you might care to help me open. It's the time to put records and relationships straight. What's so odd about Roote wanting to do that, especially now things are looking up for him?'

'OK, I give in,' said Pascoe. 'I accept Roote's forgiveness. But I'm not going to send him a Christmas card. Jesus, look at the size of this one.'

He'd opened an envelope to reveal a reproduction of some alleged Old Master showing what looked like a bunch of sheep rustlers gazing up in understandable alarm at what could have been a police helicopter spotlight surrounded by an all-girl jazz band.

'And who the hell's Zipper with three kisses?' he asked, opening the card. 'We don't send cards to anyone called Zipper, do we? I certainly hope we don't.'

'Zipper. Rings a bell. Let me see . . .'

Ellie turned the envelope over and said, 'Shit. It's addressed to Rosie. Zipper was that little boy Rosie took up with on holiday. Parents were hang-'em-high Tories. We'd better reseal it else she'll report us to the Court of Human Rights.'

'Why not just bin it? Can't have our daughter mixing with the wrong set, can we?'

Ellie ignored his satirical intent and said, 'It's her first billy-doo. Girls treasure such things. I'll take it up to her and tell her to get her coat on. If you can drag yourself away from your own fan mail, shouldn't you be getting the car started? You know what it's like these cold mornings. You really ought to take more care of it.'

This was unjust enough to provoke rebellion. The reason Pascoe's car froze outside most nights was that Ellie's ancient vehicle usually occupied the garage on the basis of first come, first protected.

He said, 'Seeing your wreck is so highly tuned, why don't you take Rosie?'

'No chance. I'm meeting Daphne for coffee in Estotiland at ten, then we're going to break the back of Christmas shopping or die in the attempt. Unless you want to swap?'

'You for Daphne, you mean? Might be OK ... Sorry! But Rosie might be happy to trade in Miss Wintershine for Estotiland.'

Estotiland was a huge R&R complex (R&R standing for Recreation and Retail, and also for Rory and Randy, the Canadian Estoti brothers who'd developed the concept) built on a mainly brownfield site across the boundary between South and Mid-Yorkshire. The Estotis boasted that Estotiland provided everything a man, woman or child could reasonably want. It was as user friendly as such a place could be, with clubs and sports facilities as well as retail floors, and its Junior Jumbo Burger Bar and associated play areas had become the site of choice for kids' parties.

'The girl wants to be an infant prodigy, prodigious is what she's going to be,' said Ellie, who saw enough of herself in Rosie to be up to all her wiles. 'I'll get her moving.'

She went out. Pascoe shoved the rest of his toast into his mouth, emptied his coffee cup, thrust Roote's letter into his pocket and headed out to his car.

As forecast, it showed a reluctance to start to match his own and its morning cough was a lot worse. Some time during its third or fourth bout, Rosie climbed into the passenger seat. She sat there in silence for a while then said in her nobly suffering martyr's voice, 'When I go with Mum, I'm never late.'

'Funny that,' said Pascoe. 'My experience has been precisely the opposite. Gotcha!'

The cough turned into a splutter then a rhythmic rattle and finally into something like the sound of an internal combustion engine ready to go about its proper business.

'Now let's see who's late,' said Pascoe.

Ms Wintershine lived in St Margaret Street, which unfortunately meant taking the main road into the city centre. At first they made reasonable progress then the traffic began to thicken.

'Jesus,' said Pascoe. 'There's not a football match on or something, is there?'

'It's Christmas shopping,' said Rosie. 'Mum said we should have set off a lot earlier.'

'You weren't ready a lot earlier,' returned Pascoe. Which might have been worth a point if he'd been sitting in the drive with the engine revving when Rosie got into the car.

Gradually the traffic declined from a meander to a crawl and finally to a stop.

Rosie said nothing, but she had inherited from her mother the ability to communicate I-told-you-so by an almost indiscernible flexing of her nose muscles.

'OK,' said Pascoe. 'Here's something your mother can't do.'

He reached into the back seat, picked up his magnetic noddy light, opened the window, slammed it on to the roof, and pulled into the empty bus lane to his left.

Siren howling, light flashing, he raced past the stationary traffic.

Rosie expressed her delight at this turn of events by beaming from cheek to cheek and waving madly at the people in the stalled cars.

'Do me a favour, love,' said Pascoe. 'Cut the Royal Progress act. Either look like a dying infant being rushed to hospital or a deadly criminal on her way to jail.'

With some complacency he saw from the clock on St Margaret's Church as they turned into St Margaret Street that they had almost five minutes to spare. All the parking spaces in front of the house were filled so he pulled into the Hearses Only spot in front of the church, switched off the siren, and said to Rosie, 'There we are. Early.'

She gave him a quick kiss and said, 'Thanks, Dad. That was great.'

'Yeah. But do me another favour. Don't tell your mum. See you in an hour.'

He watched her run along the pavement. She paused at the top of the steps leading up to the terraced house, waved at him, then disappeared inside.

He relaxed in his seat. Now what? With the shopping traffic

the way it was, there was little point in heading home as he'd have to turn round and come back almost straight away. Too early for weddings or funerals, so he might as well wait here. Something to read would have been nice. He should have brought a newspaper. Or a book.

All he had was Franny Roote's letter.

He took it out of his pocket and started at the beginning again.

What's the bastard up to? he thought as he read.

In his mind's eye he could see that pale oval face with its dark unblinking eyes, which somehow managed to be at the same time compassionate and mocking, whether their owner was beating him over the head, lying in a bath with his wrists slit, or merely observing what a lovely day it was.

Had he got anything to reproach himself with in his relationship with Roote? Did his legitimate questioning of the man in pursuit of his investigative duties have any smack of persecution about it?

No! he told himself angrily. If there was any persecution going on here, it was quite the other way round. The obsessiveness was all Roote's. And why the hell was he worrying about him anyway? At this very moment the bastard would be standing up to deliver the late Sam Johnson's paper on *Death's Jest-Book*.

'Hope he gets hiccoughs!' declared Pascoe, glaring towards the church as if challenging it to condemn his lack of charity.

He found himself looking straight into Roote's dark unblinking eyes.

He was standing on the path which ran down the side of the church, partially obscured by a large memorial cross in weathered white marble. The distance was thirty or forty feet, but the expression of compassionate mockery was as clear as a close-up.

The church clock started striking the hour.

For two strikes of the bell they looked at each other.

Then Pascoe started to open the car door but found he'd parked too close to a wizened yew tree, so he slid over to the passenger side and scrambled out.

As he stood upright and looked towards the church, the clock's ninth strike sounded.

The churchyard was empty.

48

He went through the gate and hurried down the path past the white cross to the rear of the church.

Nothing. Nobody.

He returned to the cross and checked the ground. The grass was still laced with morning frost and showed no sign of any footprint.

He raised his eyes to look at the inscription carved on the cross.

It was dedicated to the memory of one Arthur Treebie who quit this vale of tears aged ninety-two, grievously deplored by his huge family and armies of friends. Possibly Treebie himself, anticipating the gap he was going to leave, had chosen the consoling text:

'Lo, I am with you alway, even unto the end of the world.'

Pascoe read it, shivered, glanced once more around the empty churchyard, and hurried back to the comfort of his car.

arlier that same Saturday morning, Detective Constable Hat Bowler had awoken from a dream.

Ever since the incident in which he sustained the serious head injury he was officially still recuperating from, his sleep had been broken by lurid nightmares in which he struggled once more with the naked blood-slippery figure of the Wordman. The difference from the reality was that in his dreams he always lost and lay there helpless while his towering assailant clubbed him again and again with a heavy crystal dish till he slipped into unconsciousness with the despairing screams of Rye Pomona echoing through his broken head. And when he awoke into a tangle of sweat-soaked sheets, it was the memory of those screams as much as his own pain and fear that he brought with him out of the dark.

This morning he woke once more into a tangle of sheets and a memory of Rye calling out, but this time there was nothing of fear or pain in his memory, only love and joy.

In his dream he'd been lying in his hotel bed, his body a burning brand in a cold, cold waste of circumspection, wondering whether he was a wise man or an idiot not to have pressed his suit with Rye to either a conclusion or a rejection, when he had heard his door open and next moment a soft naked body had fused its warmth with his and a voice had murmured in his ear, 'Thank God for equal opportunities, eh?' And after that she had spoken no more till those final wordless but oh so eloquent cries which had climaxed their passionate coupling.

He groaned softly at the sweet memory of the dream, tried to relax once more into that happy slumber, rolled over in the broad bed, and sat up wide-awake.

She was there. Either he was still dreaming, or . . .

Her arms went round him and drew him down.

'How's your head?' she whispered.

'I don't know. I think I'm having delusions.'

'So why don't we delude ourselves again?'

If this was dreaming, he was happy to sleep forever.

Afterwards they lay intricately twined together, listening to the hotel coming to life around them and the birds, later than the humans on these dark mornings, beginning to waken outside.

'What's that?' she said.

'Goldfinch.'

'And that?'

'Mistle thrush.'

'I like a man who knows more than I do,' she said. 'Hungry?'

'What had you in mind?'

'Sausage, bacon and egg, for starters.'

She rolled away from him, picked up the bedside phone and dialled.

He listened as she ordered the full English for two in his room.

'Have you no shame?' he asked.

'Just as well I haven't,' she said. 'Or were you planning to surprise me last night?'

He shook his head and said, 'No. I'm sorry. I wanted to, Jesus, how I've been wanting to! But I just lost my bottle . . .'

'Why?' she said curiously. 'You've never struck me as the retiring virgin type, Hat.'

'No? Well, usually . . . not that there's been a lot . . . but in most cases it didn't matter, being turned down, I mean. Some you lose, some you win, that sort of thing. But with you I was terrified I'd lose everything by pressing too hard. I had to be sure you really fancied me.'

'Girl fixes up a three-night break in a romantic country hotel and you're not sure?' she said incredulously.

'Yeah, well, I thought . . . then we got here and you'd booked separate rooms.'

'Fail-safe in case . . . anyway, you had the cue to look disappointed and say, "Hey, do we really need two rooms?"'

'Oh, I was disappointed,' he said with a grin. 'If I'd been on duty, I'd have gone out and arrested the first ten people I saw smiling and charged them with being happy. So, disappointed yes, but maybe not altogether surprised.'

'Meaning?'

'Meaning that during these past few weeks you've been concerned and caring and great fun to be with, all those things, but I always felt there was some kind of limit, you know: this far is fine but one more step and it's on your bike, buster! Am I making sense?'

She was listening to him with a frowning intensity.

She said, 'You think I was playing hard to get?'

'Crossed my mind,' he admitted. 'But it didn't seem your style. Though a couple of weeks back when things seemed to be going really well . . . do you remember? And I was thinking, this is the night! Then you got a headache! Jesus! I thought. A headache! How unoriginal can you get?'

'You've been mixing with too many dishonest people, Hat,' she said. 'If I say I've got a headache, I mean I've got a headache. So you thought because I didn't jump into bed with you the first time you got horny, I must be . . . what? What have you been thinking these past few weeks, Hat?'

He looked away then looked back straight into her eyes and said, 'I sometimes thought, maybe you're just grateful because of what happened. Maybe that's the limit, whatever gratitude can give but no more. Well, I couldn't have put up with that forever, but I wasn't ready yet to take the risk of making you say it. So that's the kind of wimpish wanker you've got yourself mixed up with.'

'Wimp you may be, but you can give up the wanking, eh, Constable?' she said, drawing him close to her. 'I love you, Hat. From now on in, you're safe with me.'

Which seemed to Hat even in these days of equal opportunity a slightly odd way of putting it, but he wasn't about to complain, and indeed in her arms he felt so utterly invulnerable to anything fate could hurl against him, even if it took the form of Fat Andy Dalziel in berserker mode, that perhaps she had the right of it.

blizzard rages across a desolate landscape, thunder rolls, wolves howl. Away in the distance there is movement. Gradually as the swirling snow parts the viewer sees that it's a horse, no, three horses, pulling a sleigh. And as it gets nearer the passengers became visible, a man and a woman and two children, and they are all smiling, and as the din of the raging storm dies to be replaced by the swelling strains of Prokofiev's "Troika" music, the viewpoint swings round to show over the horses' tossing heads the turrets and towers of what looks like a small city emerging from the white plain, above which arcs with a brilliance like the Northern Lights the word ESTOTILAND.

'Christmas starts in Estotiland,' intones a voice like the voice of a transatlantic God. 'Here in Estotiland you'll get so much fun out of shopping you'll never think of dropping. And don't forget, Estotiland is open from eight a.m. to ten p.m., and all day Sunday. So all you kids, git your mom and pop to hitch up the pony to the sleigh and head out here first thing tomorrow. But be careful. You may never want to go home again!'

Music climaxes as the sleigh, which is now seen to be the point of a broad arrow of many other sleighs, leads them all into the shining city.

'What a load of crap,' observed Andy Dalziel from his sitting-room door.

'Andy. Didn't hear you come in.'

'Not surprised, with that din on. Do I get a kiss or will that make you miss your favourite commercial?'

He leaned over the sofa and pressed what a less welcoming

53

and resilient recipient than Cap Marvell might have felt as a blow rather than a buss on her lips.

The advertising break was ending and the presenter of Ebor TV's early evening show was revealed half-engulfed in a deeply yielding armchair.

'Welcome back,' he said. 'Just to remind you, my guest tonight is that man of many hats, lawyer, campaigner, charity worker and historian, Marcus Belchamber.'

The picture changed to a shot of a man of early middle age, wearing a dinner jacket of immaculate cut, who was sitting in a sister chair to the presenter's, but with no threat to his steadiness of posture or alertness of mien. Steady grey eyes looked out of the head of an idealized Roman senator topped by lightly greying locks so immaculately groomed that they might indeed have been set there by a maestro's chisel rather than a barber's craft. This was a gentleman in whom you could place an absolute trust.

Dalziel made a farting noise with his lips.

'Mind if I watch this item, love?' said Cap.

'I'll get us a drink,' said the Fat Man, heading for the kitchen.

He and Cap Marvell didn't cohabit, but as their relationship matured, they'd exchanged keys, and now one of the delights of returning home for Dalziel was the possibility of finding a light on, a fire burning and Cap sitting on his sofa, or sleeping in his bed. She assured him that she felt the same, though he'd exercised his privilege of entry to her flat with great care after the occasion on which he'd been woken, stark naked on her hearth rug, by the scream of a campaigning nun who was her house guest.

From the sitting room he could hear the presenter's voice.

'Before we talk more about the Round Table Disadvantaged Children's Christmas Party which you're in charge of this year, Marcus, I'd like to have a word with you about another treat for both adults and kids which you've helped make available for us over the next few weeks. This is the chance, possibly for most of us the last chance, to see the Elsecar Hoard. For anyone out there that doesn't know it, I should say that under one of his many hats, Marcus is President of the Mid-Yorkshire Archaeological Society and is acknowledged nationally, indeed I might say internationally, as one of the country's foremost experts on Yorkshire during the Roman occupation.'

'You're too kind,' said Belchamber in that rich timbred voice which some had compared not unfavourably with that of the late Richard Burton.

'Perhaps you'd give us a bit of background just in case there's anyone left in the county who hasn't been following the saga?'

'Certainly. The Elsecar Hoard is perhaps Yorkshire's most precious historical treasure, though strictly – and herein lies the nub of the problem which emerged about a year ago – it doesn't belong to Yorkshire but to the Elsecar family. The first Baron Elsecar emerged as a power in the county at the end of the Wars of the Roses and the family flourished for the next three centuries, but a natural conservatism, with a small c, left them ill-prepared for the industrial revolution and by midway through Victoria's reign they had fallen on hard times. The greater part of their land, much of which later proved to be rich in minerals and coal, was sold at depressed agricultural prices to pay off their debts.

'In 1872, the eighth baron was draining a boggy section of one of the few remaining estates, in what any competent geologist could have told him was a vain hope of finding coal, when his workers hauled up a bronze chest.

'When opened, it proved to contain a large quantity of Roman coinage mainly of the fourth century, plus, more importantly, numerous ornaments of widely varied provenance, ranging from native Celtic designs to Mediterranean and Oriental. Particularly striking was a golden coronet formed of two intertwining snakes –'

'Ah yes,' interrupted the presenter, who had the TV personality's terror that if left out of shot long enough he would cease to exist. 'This is what's known as the serpent crown, right? Isn't it supposed to have belonged to some brigand queen?'

'A queen of the Brigantes, which is not quite the same thing,' murmured Belchamber courteously. 'This was Cartimandua, who handed over Caractacus to the Romans, but her connection with the crown is tenuous and owes more, I believe, to Victorian sentimental horror at the betrayal than any historical research. Snakes in our Christian society have come to be linked with treachery and falsehood. But, as you know, in the symbolism of Celtic art they have quite a different significance . . .'

'Yes, of course,' said the presenter. 'Quite different. Right. But this Hoard, where did it actually come from? And was it simply a question of finders keepers?'

'In law, there is no such thing as a simple question,' said Belchamber, smiling.

'You can say that again, you bastard,' muttered Dalziel in the kitchen.

'Scholars theorized that the Hoard was probably the collection of an important and well-travelled Roman official who found himself, either through choice or accident, isolated in Britain when the Roman rule broke down early in the fifth century. The big legal question was whether the chest had been deliberately hidden by its owner, thinking it prudent to conceal his treasure till quieter times came, in which case it would have been treasure trove and the property of the Crown; or whether it had been simply been lost or abandoned, in which case it was the property of the land-owner. Fortunately for the Elsecars, the matter was settled in their favour when further drainage revealed the remains of a wheeled vehicle, suggesting the chest was being transported somewhere when accident or ambush had caused the carriage to overturn and sink in the swamp.'

'So it was theirs, no question? Why didn't they sell it straight away if they were so hard up?' asked the presenter.

'Because good things like bad often come in bundles, and at just about the same time the heir apparent to the baronetcy caught himself a rich American heiress, so they stowed the Hoard in the bank vault against a rainy day . . .'

'Which has now arrived,' interrupted the presenter, seeing his producer making for-God's-sake-hurry this-along signals from the control room.

Dalziel clearly felt much the same. He'd returned with drinks and was sitting next to Cap on the sofa, glowering at the screen with an intensity of hatred which he usually only saved for winning Welsh rugby teams.

'So Lord Elsecar has put the Hoard on the market,' continued the presenter at a gallop. 'The best offer to date has been from America, the British Museum has been given the chance to match it, but so far, even with lottery money and a public appeal, they're still well short of the mark. So as a last gasp, and following a suggestion made, one might even say a pressure exerted, by the Yorkshire Archaeological Society led by yourself, the Elsecars have agreed for the Hoard to go on tour, with all profits from admission charges to go to the Save Our Hoard Fund. Will they do it?'

Belchamber made hopeful noises. Cap Marvell laughed derisively.

'Not a hope,' she said. 'They're so far short they'd need everyone in Yorkshire to go five times to get anywhere near! First time I've seen a lawyer who can't add up!'

'That's great,' said the presenter. 'So there you are, all you culture vultures, take the family along to see the money your ancestors spent and what they spent it on back in the Dark Ages. The Hoard will be on exhibition in Bradford till the New Year, then in Sheffield till Friday, January twenty-fifth, after which it moves to Mid-Yorkshire. Don't miss it! And now the Christmas Party. How many kids are you hoping to get this year, Marcus?'

Dalziel stood up and said, 'Like another drink?'

'I've hardly touched this one,' said Cap as she picked up the remote control and zapped the sound off. 'But I can take a hint. Is there some all-in wrestling on another channel you want to watch?'

'No. It's just I hear quite enough of yon turd, Belcher, without letting him into my own parlour,' said Dalziel.

'I take it this means he represents criminals and does a rather good job of it?'

'He does better than a good job,' said Dalziel grimly. 'He bends the law till it nigh on breaks. Every top villain in the county's on his books. I'm late tonight 'cos there was a scare with our one witness in the Linford case, and guess who's representing Linford.'

'You're not suggesting that Marcus Belchamber, solicitor,

gentleman, scholar and philanthropist, goes around intimidating witnesses?'

'Of course not. But I don't doubt it's him as told Linford's dad, Wally, that the case was hopeless unless they got shut of our witness. Any road, it turned out a false alarm and I left Wieldy soothing the lad.'

'Oh yes. Is the sergeant a good soother?'

'Oh aye. He tells 'em if they don't calm down, he'll have to stay the night. That usually does the trick.'

Cap, who sometimes had a problem working out when Dalziel's political incorrectness was post-modern ironical and when it was prehistoric offensive, turned the sound back on.

'You look awfully smart, Marcus,' the presenter was saying. 'Off clubbing tonight?'

Belchamber gave the weary little smile with which in court he frequently underlined some prosecution witness's inconsistency or inanity, and said, 'I'm driving to Leeds for the Northern Law Society's dinner.'

'Well, don't drink too much or you could end up defending yourself.'

'In which case I would have a fool for a client,' said Belchamber. 'But rest easy. I shall be spending the night there.'

'Only joking! Have a good night. It's been a privilege having you on the show. Ladies and gentlemen, Marcus Belchamber!'

Belchamber rose easily from the depths of his chair, the presenter struggled to get upright, the two men shook hands, and the lawyer walked off to enthusiastic applause.

'He's a fine-looking man,' said Cap provocatively.

'He'd look better strapped on the end of a ducking stool,' said Dalziel.

'And did you notice that DJ? Lovely cut. Conceals the embonpoint perfectly with no suggestion of tightness. Next time you see him, you really must ask who his tailor is.'

This was a provocation too far.

'Right, lass, if you just came round here to be rude, you can bugger off back to that fancy flat of thine. What did you come round for anyway?'

She grinned at him and ran her tongue round the rim of her glass.

'Actually I just thought I'd pop round to see what you wanted for Christmas,' she said languorously.

'I'll need at least thirty seconds to have a think,' said Dalziel. 'But it's not a tangerine in a sock, I can tell you that for starters.'

etective Sergeant Edgar Wield was in a good mood as he mounted his ancient but beautifully maintained Triumph Thunderbird and said farewell to Mid-Yorkshire's Central Police Station with a quite unnecessary crescendo of revs. A couple of uniformed constables coming into the yard stood aside respectfully as he rode past them. He was still a man of mystery to most of his junior colleagues, but whether you thought of him as an ageing rocker who ate live chickens as he did the ton along the central reservation of the M1 or believed the rumours that he was matron-in-chief of a transvestite community living in darkest Eendale, you didn't let any trace of speculation and/or amusement show. Dalziel was more obviously terrifying, Pascoe had a finger of iron inside his velvet glove, but Wield's was the face to haunt your dreams.

It had been a long day but in the end quite productive. With time running out, a suspect had finally cracked under the pressure of Wield's relentless questioning and unreadable features. Then, just as he was leaving, Dalziel had tossed into his lap the job of reassuring Oz Carnwath, the Linford case witness, that the burly man on his doorstep talking about death really had been an undertaker who'd mixed up addresses. He'd left the young man happy and arranged for a patrol car to stop by from time to time during the night. Then he'd returned to the station to put on his leathers and pick up his bike, and finally he was on his way home with all the pleasures of a crime-free Sunday in the company of Edwin Digweed, his beloved partner, stretching ahead. Nothing special, he doubted if they'd get further than the Morris, their local, or perhaps take a stroll along the Een whose valley had the bone structure to remain lovely even in midwinter, or go up to Enscombe Old Hall to check how Monte, the tiny marmoset he'd 'rescued' from a pharmaceutical research laboratory, was coping with the cold weather.

Things must be beautiful which, daily seen, please daily, or something like that. One of Pascoe's little gags which usually drifted across his hearing with small trace of their passage, but that one had stuck. As he recalled it now, he tried superstitiously not to let the thought *I am a very lucky man* join it in his head.

He came to a halt at traffic lights. Straight ahead the road which tracked the western boundary of Charter Park stretched out temptingly. Parks are the lungs of the city, and the fact that Mid-Yorkshire possessed an abundance of beautiful countryside, easy of access and to suit all tastes, did not mean the founding fathers had stinted when it came to pulmonary provision in the towns. Over the years many unsentimental eyes had looked greedily at these priceless green sites, but that lust for 'brass' which is proper to a Yorkshireman comes a poor second in his defining characteristics to the determination that 'what's mine's me own, and no bugger's going to take it from me'. Try as they might, not an acre of ground, not a spadeful of earth, not a blade of grass, had the developers ever managed to wrest from the grip of Charter Park's owners in perpetuity – the taxable citizenry. So the road alongside the park stretched straight and wide for a mile or more and a man on a powerful machine might hit the ton, though it's doubtful if he'd have much time to digest a live chicken.

Wield let himself be tempted. It was a safe indulgence. Over the years he had grown sufficiently strong in resisting temptation to be able to drink the heady potion more deeply than most men.

The lights turned green, the engine roared, but it was the roar of an old lion saying he could run down that wildebeest if he wanted but on the whole he thought he'd probably stretch under a bush and have a nap.

The sergeant moved forward sedately and legally.

It was his slowness that permitted him to see the attempted abduction taking place in the car park which ran much of the length of the park.

Separated from the main road by a long colonnade of lime

trees, it was in fact more like a parallel thoroughfare. During the day, visitors to the park left the cars there in a single line. On a summer night it might be quite crowded, but in the middle of winter, apart from the odd vehicle whose steamed-up windows advertised the presence of young love or old lust, there was rarely much activity. But as he went by, Wield saw a man trying to drag a young boy into his slow-moving car.

He braked sharply, went into a speedway racer's skid, straightened up to negotiate the gap between two lime trees, found it was already occupied by a bench, realigned his machine at the next gap, went through, lost a bit of traction on the loose shaley surface as he straightened up, and lost some time wrestling the Thunderbird back under control. All the while he was blasting out warnings of his approach on the horn. Prevention was better than cure and the last thing he wanted was a high-speed chase through city streets in pursuit of a car carrying a kidnapped child.

It worked. Ahead he saw the boy sprawling on the ground with the abductor's vehicle roaring off in a cloud of dust which, aided by the fact that the car's lights weren't switched on, made it impossible to get the number plate.

He pulled up alongside the boy, who had pushed himself into a sitting position. He looked about ten, maybe a bit older, twelve, say. He had big dark eyes, curly black hair and a thin pale face. He had grazed his hand on falling and he was holding it to his mouth to wash it and ease the pain. He looked angry rather than terrified.

'You OK, son?' said Wield, dismounting.

'Yeah, I think so.'

His accent was local urban. He began to rise and Wield said, 'Hold on. Got any pain anywhere?'

'Nah. Just this fucking hand.'

'You sure? OK. Easy does it.'

Wield took his arm and helped him up.

He winced as he rose then moved all his limbs in turn as if to show they worked.

'Great,' said Wield. He reached inside his leathers and pulled out his mobile.

'What you doing?' demanded the boy.

'Just getting someone to look out for that guy who grabbed you. Did you notice the make of car? Looked like a Montego to me.'

'No. I mean, I didn't notice. Look, why bother? Forget it. He's gone.'

A very self-possessed youngster.

'You might forget it, son. But that doesn't mean he's not going to try again.'

'Try what?'

'Abducting someone.'

'Yeah . . . well . . .'

The boy thrust his hands deep into the pockets of his thin windcheater, hunched his shoulders and began to move away. He looked waif and forlorn.

'Hey, where are you going?' said Wield.

'What's it to you?'

'I'm worried, that's all,' said Wield. 'Look, you've had a shock. You shouldn't be wandering round here at this time of night. Hop up behind me and I'll give you a lift.'

The boy regarded him speculatively.

'Lift where?' he said.

Wield considered. Offering to take the boy home might not be a good move. Maybe it was what awaited him at home that sent him wandering the streets so late. Best way to find out could be a low-key, friendly chat, unencumbered by the revelation that he was a cop. He put the phone away. The car would be long gone by now and what did he have anyway? A dark blue Montego, maybe.

'Fancy a coffee or a Coke or something?' he said.

'OK,' said the boy. 'Why not? You know Turk's?'

'Know of it,' said Wield. 'Hop on. You got a name?'

'Lee,' said the boy as he swung his leg over the pillion. 'You?'

'You can call me Mac. Hold on.'

The boy ignored the advice and sat there loosely as if not anticipating any need for anchorage. Wield said nothing but accelerated along the car park till the lime trees began to blur, then braked to swing between them and rejoin the main road.

63

He smiled as he felt the boy's arms swing round his midriff and lock on tight.

Turk's caff was situated in the lee of the Central Station. It was basic just this side of squalid, but had the advantage of staying open late, the theory being it would catch hungry travellers after the station snack-bars pulled down their shutters early in the evening. In fact the regular – indeed one might say the permanent – clientele seemed to consist of solitary men in shabby parkas hunched over empty coffee mugs, who gave few signs that they ever contemplated travelling anywhere. The only person who showed any sign of life, and that only enough to offer a customer slow and resentful service, was the morose and taciturn owner, the eponymous Turk, whose coffee was reason enough to keep a country out of the EU, never mind Human Rights, thought Wield, as he watched the boy drink Coke and tuck into a chunk of glutinous cheesecake.

'So, Lee,' he said. 'What happened back there?'

The boy looked at him. He'd shown either natural courtesy or natural indifference when Wield had removed his helmet to reveal the full ugliness of his face, but now his gaze was sharp.

'Nowt. Just a bit of hassle, that's all.'

'Did you know the guy in the car?'

'What difference does it make?'

'Could make the difference between some nutter driving around trying to kidnap kids and a domestic.'

The boy shrugged, chewed another mouthful of cake, washed it down with Coke, then said, 'What're you after?'

'What do you mean?'

'Getting mixed up with this.'

'You mean I should've ridden on by?'

'Mebbe. Most would.'

'I didn't.'

'OK, but the chat and this –' he waved the last forkful of cheesecake in the air then devoured it – 'what's all that for? You some sort of do-gooder?'

'Sure,' said Wield. 'Let me buy you another piece then I'll save your soul.'

This amused the boy. When he laughed, his age dropped back to the original low estimate. On the other hand, being smart put as many years on him.

'OK,' he said. ' 'Nother Coke too.'

Wield went up to the counter. The cheesecake looked like it contravened every dietary regulation ever written, but the boy needed fattening up. Watch it, Edgar, he told himself mockingly. You're thinking like your mother! Which thought provoked him into buying a ham sandwich. Edwin was going to be miffed that he was even later than forecast, and it wouldn't help things if Wield disturbed the even tenor of their pristine kitchen with his 'disgusting canteen habits'.

As he resumed his seat, the boy pulled a face at the sandwich and said, 'You gonna eat that? He makes them out of illegals who didn't survive the trip.'

'I'll take my chances,' said Wield. 'OK. Now, about your soul.'

'Sold up and gone, long since. What's your line?'

'Sorry?'

'What you do for dosh? Let's have a look . . .'

He took Wield's left hand and ran his index finger gently over the palm.

'Not a navvy then, Mac,' he said. 'Not a brain surgeon neither.'

Wield pulled his hand away more abruptly than he intended and the boy grinned.

He's sussed me out, thought Wield. A couple of minutes and he's got to the heart of me. How come someone this age is so sharp? And what the hell signals am I sending out? I told him to call me Mac! Why? Because Wield sounds odd? Because only Edwin calls me Edgar? Good reasons. Except nobody's called me Mac since . . .

It was short for Macumazahn, the native name for Allan Quartermain, the hero of some of Wield's beloved H. Rider Haggard novels. It meant he-who-sleeps-with-his-eyes-open and had been given to him by a long-lost lover. No one else had ever used it until a few years ago a young man had briefly entered his life . . .

He put the memory of the tragic end of that relationship out of his mind. This wasn't a young man, this was a kid, and, thank

God, he'd never fancied kids. It was time to wrap things up here and get himself back to the domestic peace and safety of Enscombe.

He finished his drink, pushed his chair back and said, 'OK, let's forget saving your soul and get your body delivered safely home.'

'Home? Nah. It's early doors yet.'

'Not for kids who're roaming the streets getting into fights with strange men.'

'Aye, you're right, it's been my night for strange men, hasn't it? Anyway, not sure if I want to get back on that ancient time machine of yours. No telling where you'd take me.'

Again the knowing grin. It was time to stop messing around. Wield took out his wallet and produced his police ID.

'I can either take you home or down the nick till we find out where home is,' he said.

The boy studied the ID without looking too bothered.

He said, 'You arresting me, or wha'?'

'Of course I'm not arresting you. I just want to make sure you get home safe. And as a minor if you don't co-operate by giving me your address, then it's my job to find it out.'

'As a minor?'

The boy reached into his back pocket, pulled out a billfold thick with banknotes and from it took a ragged piece of paper. He handed it over. It was a photocopy of a birth certificate which told Wield he was in the company of Lee Lubanski, native of this city in which he'd been born nineteen years ago.

'You're nineteen?' said Wield, feeling foolish. He should have spotted it from his demeanour straight off . . . but kids nowadays all acted grown up . . . or maybe he hadn't been looking at the youth like a copper should . . .

'Yeah. Always getting hassled in pubs is why I carry that around. So no need to see me home, Mac. Or should I call you sergeant now? I should have sussed when you went on about domestics. But you seemed . . . OK, know what I mean?'

He smiled insinuatingly.

Wield now saw things very clearly. He said, 'That car . . . he wasn't trying to pull you in, he was pushing you out.'

Lee said, 'That's right. Don't do the park any more, upmarket, that's me. But I were at a loose end, went for a stroll and this guy . . . well, he seemed all right, said the money was fine but he only gave me half upfront and, when we'd done the business, he tossed the rest out the window. Didn't surprise me, lot of 'em are like that, gagging for it till they've had it then they can't get away quick enough. But when I picked it up I saw it were twenty light. I got the door open as he tried to drive away and . . . well, you saw the rest.'

'Yes, I saw the rest. Why are you telling me this, Lee?'

'Just wanted to save you the bother of putting out a call on that Montego. Unless you fancy getting my money back? But you wouldn't want your mates to know how wrong you got things, would you? Can't imagine what you were thinking of,' he said, grinning.

'Me neither,' said Wield. 'Thought you were in trouble. Well, you are in trouble, Lee. But I reckon you know that. OK, no use talking to you now, but one day maybe you'll need someone to talk to . . .'

He handed the youth a card bearing his name and official phone number.

'Yeah, thanks,' said Lee. He looked surprised, as if this wasn't the reaction he was expecting. 'Bit of a do-gooder after all, are you, Mac?'

'Sergeant.'

'Sorry. Sergeant Mac. Look, don't rush off, my treat now. Have a bit of cheesecake, it's not bad. Could be an antidote to that immigrant ham.'

'No thanks, Lee. Got a home to go to.'

'Lucky old you.'

He said it so wistfully that for a second Wield was tempted to sit down again. Then he caught the gleam of watchful eyes beneath those long, lowered lashes.

'See you, Lee,' he said. 'Take care.'

'Yeah.'

Outside, Wield mounted the Thunderbird with a sense of relief, of danger avoided.

Through the grubby window of Turk's he could see the boy

still sitting at the table. No audience to impress now, but somehow he looked more waif and forlorn than ever.

Making as little noise as possible, Wield rode away into the night.

The Knight

St Godric's College

Cambridge

Sat Dec 15th   The Quaestor's Lodging

My dear Mr Pascoe,

Honestly, I really didn't mean to bother you again, but things have been happening that I need to share and, I don't know why, you seemed the obvious person.

Let me tell you about it.

I got down to the Welcome Reception in the Senior Common Room, which I found to be already packed with conference delegates, sipping sherry. Supplies of free booze are, I gather, finite at these events and the old hands make sure they're first at the fountain.

The delegates fall roughly into two groups. One consists of more senior figures, scholars like Dwight who have already established their reputations and are in attendance mainly to protect their turf while attempting to knock others off their hobby-horses.

The second group comprises youngsters on the make, each desperate to clock up the credits you get for attendance at such do's, some with papers to present, others hoping to make their mark by engaging in post-paper polemic.

I suppose that to the casual eye I fitted into this latter group, with one large difference – they all had their feet on the academic ladder, even if the rung was a low one.

Of course I didn't take all this in at a glance as you might have done. No, but I related what I saw and heard to what Sam Johnson had told me in the past and also to the more recent and even more satirical picture painted by dear old Charley Penn when he learned I was about to attend what he called my first 'junket'.

'Remember this,' he said. 'However domesticated your academic may look, he is by instinct and training anthropophagous. Whatever else is on the menu, you certainly are!'

Anthropophagous. Charley loves such words. We still play Paronomania, you know, despite the painful memories it must bring him.

But where was I?

Oh yes, with such forewarning – and with the experience behind me of having been thrown with even less preparation into Chapel Syke – I felt quite able to survive in these new waters. But in fact I didn't even have to work at it. Unlike at the Syke where I had to seek King Rat out and make myself useful to him, here at God's he came looking for me.

As I stood uncertainly just within the doorway, the only person I could see in that crowded room that I knew was Dwight Duerden. He was talking to a long skinny Plantagenet-featured man with a mane of blond hair so bouncy he could have made a fortune doing shampoo ads. Duerden spotted me, said something to the man, who immediately broke off his conversation, turned, smiled like a time-share salesman spotting an almost hooked client, and swept towards me with the American in close pursuit.

'Mr Roote!' he said. 'Be welcome, be welcome. So delighted you could join us. We are honoured, honoured.'

Now the temptation is to class anyone who talks like this, especially if his accent makes the Queen sound Cockney and his manner is by Irving out of Kemble and he's wearing a waistcoat by Rennie Mackintosh with matching bow tie, as a prancing plonker. But Charley's warning still sounded in my mind so I didn't fall about laughing, which was just as well as Duerden said, 'Franny, meet our conference host, Sir Justinian Albacore.'

I said, 'Glad to meet you, Sir Justinian.'

The plonker flapped a languid hand and said, 'No titles, please. I'm J. C. Albacore to my readers, Justinian to my acquaintance, plain Justin to my friends. I hope you will feel able to call me Justin. May I call you Franny?'

'Wish I had a title I could ignore,' said Duerden sardonically.

'Really, Dwight? That must be the one thing Cambridge and America have in common, a love of the antique. When I worked in the sticks, they'd have thrown stones at me if I'd tried to use my title. But here at God's, antiquity both in fact and in tradition is prized above rubies. Our dearest possession is one of the earliest copies of the *Vita de Sancti Godrici*, you really must see it while you're here, Franny. Gentlemen –' this to a group of distinguished looking old farts – 'let me introduce Mr Roote, a new star in our firmament and one which we have hopes will burn very brightly.'

Like Joan of Arc, I thought. Or Guy Fawkes.

During all this prattle, I was trying to work out Albacore's game. Did he really think I was such an innocent abroad that simply by giving me a nice room and bulling me up in front of the nobs he could sweet talk Sam's unique research notes out of me in time to incorporate them in his own book?

Perhaps looking down on the world from the mountain deanery of a Cambridge college gives a man a hearty contempt for the little figures scuttling around below. If so, I assured myself grandiloquently, he would soon find that he'd underestimated me.

Instead, I quickly came to realize that I'd underestimated him.

After the reception we all adjourned to a lecture room where the official business of the conference began with a formal opening followed by a keynote address from Professor Duerden on the theme 'Imagining What We Know: Romanticism and Science'.

It was interesting enough, he had a dry Yankee wit

(he comes from Connecticut; fate and a tendency to bronchitis took him to California) and was a master in the art of being provocative without going out on a limb. I listened with interest from my reserved seat on the front row, but part of my mind remained concentrated on the puzzle of Albacore, whose duties as chair of the meeting kept him from his other task of stroking my ego.

But when the lecture and subsequent discussions were over and we were all dispersing to our rooms, my new friend Justin was at my side again, his hand on my elbow as he guided me out into the quad and away from the general drift of delegates.

'And what did you think of our transatlantic friend?' he said.

'It was a real honour to hear him,' I gushed. 'I thought he put things so well, though I've got to admit, a lot of it was well over my head.'

I'd decided to have a bit of fun with this idiot by playing the eager and enthusiastic but not too bright student and seeing where that led. I didn't expect my performance to provoke cynical laughter.

'Oh, I don't think so, young Franny,' he said, still chuckling. 'I think an idea would have to be very deep indeed to be over your head.'

This didn't sound like simple flannel any more.

'Sorry?' I said. 'Don't quite follow.'

'No? I'm simply letting you know what a great respect I've got for your mental capacities, dear boy.'

I said, 'That's very flattering, but you hardly know me.'

'On the contrary. You and I are long acquainted and I know all your ways.'

He looked down at me from his height, eyes twinkling like distant stars.

And suddenly I was there.

J.C. to his readers. Justinian to his acquaintance. Justin to his friends.

And to his wife, Jay.

I said, 'You're Amaryllis Haseen's husband.'

It seems so obvious now. Probably you with your fine detective mind got there long before me. But you can see how the revelation bowled me over, especially as I'd spent so much time earlier today raking up that bit of my past for your benefit. Nothing is for nothing in this life, so Frère Jacques preaches. The past isn't another country. It's just a different part of the maze we travel through, and we shouldn't be surprised to find ourselves re-entering the same stretch from a different angle.

Albacore was spelling things out.

'My wife developed a very high opinion of your potential, Franny. She says that in terms of simple academic cleverness you are bright enough to hold your own in most company. But she also detected in you another kind of cleverness. How did she put it? A mind fit for stratagems, an eye for the main chance, nimble of thought, sharp in judgment, ruthless in execution. Oh yes, you made a big impression on her.'

I said, 'And on you too, from the sound of it.'

'Hardly,' he said, smiling. 'I was amused when she told me how you neatly got her in a neck lock. But at the time I was on my way from the ghastly wasteland of South Yorkshire back to God's own college, and apart from a little chortle at the idea of dear Sam Johnson being landed with a cunning convict as a PhD student, I never gave you another thought. Not of course till I heard about poor Sam's sad demise. Couldn't make the obsequies myself, but a friend described the dramatic part you played in them, and I thought, hello, could that be that chappie whatsisname? Then I heard that Loopy Linda had appointed you as Sam's literary heir or executor or some such thing, which was when I asked Amaryllis to dig out all her old case notes.'

'I'm surprised you didn't just read her book,' I said.

He shuddered and said, 'Can't stand the way she writes, dear boy. Subject matter is generally tedious and her style is what I call psycho-barbarous. In any case, it's

75

the marginalia of her case notes that make the most interesting reading. Unless she is wrong, which she rarely is, you are someone I can do business with.'

'The business being the redistribution of Sam Johnson's Beddoes research,' I said.

'There. I knew I was right. No need to soft soap a supple mind.'

'No? Then why do I feel so well oiled?' I wondered. 'The Q's Lodging, all these flattering introductions.'

'Samples,' he said. 'Simply samples. When you're getting down to a trade-off, you have to give the man you're trading with a taste of your wares. You see, I'm very aware that while I know what you have to offer, you may have doubts about what's in my poke. It's little enough unless it's what you want, and then it's the world. It is this –'

He made a ring master's gesture which comprehended the quad, and all the buildings around it, and much much more.

'If it is something you're not interested in, then we must look for other incentives,' he went on. 'But if, as from my brief observation of you in person I begin to hope, this cloistered life of ours, in which the intellect and the senses are so deliciously catered for, and the inhibiting morals kept firmly in their place, has some strong attraction, then we can get down to business straight off. I have influence, I have contacts, I know where many bodies are buried, I can put you on a fast-track academic career, get you on the cultural chat shows, if that is your desire, I can put you in the way of editors and publishers. In short, I can be thy protector and thy guide, in thy most need to go by thy side. So, do I judge right? Can we do business?'

This was straight talking with a vengeance. This was complete no-holds-barred honesty, which is always a cause for grave suspicion.

Time to test him out with some of the same.

'If I want these things you offer,' I said, 'what is to stop me getting them for myself? I am, as you

76

acknowledge, bright. I may be, as your wife alleges, ruthlessly manipulative. Your book, I presume, is mainly a reworking of the few known facts of Beddoes' Continental life, embellished, no doubt, by whatever you were able to lift from Sam before he became aware of your perfidy.'

That hit home, just a flicker of reaction, but I got used to reading flickers in the Syke when not to read them could mean losing a game of chess. Or an eye.

I pressed on.

'Sam, however, as your interest confirms you know, had tracked down a substantial body of new material in various forms. Wherever your book stood in relation to his, coming before or after, it was always going to stand in the shade.'

I paused again.

He said, 'And your point is . . . ?'

I said, 'And my point is, why should I bargain for what is already within my grasp?'

He smiled and said, 'You mean, complete Sam's book yourself, bathe in what would be mainly a reflected glory, then make your own way onward and upward? Perhaps you could do it. But it's a hard road, and other men's flowers quickly wilt. I naturally cannot be expected to agree with what you say about my book being in the shade, though what I am certain of is that it will be in the way. But if you can find someone willing to take a punt on a total unknown, then perhaps you should go ahead, dear Franny.'

He knew, the bastard knew, that Sam's pusillanimous publishers had developed feet so cold they were walking on chilblains.

He saw my reaction and pressed his advantage.

'How's your thesis going, by the way? Have you found a new supervisor? Now there's a thought. Perhaps I could offer my own services? It would mean moving to Cambridge, but if you're heading high, no harm starting on the upper slopes, is there?'

Perhaps I should have said, get thee behind me,

77

Satan! But any belief I might have had in my own divine indestructibility vanished back at Holm Coultram College when, despite my very best efforts, you managed to finger my collar.

So, please don't despise me, I said I'd think about it.

I thought about it all evening, paying little attention to the conference sessions I attended and barely picking at the buffet supper that was laid on for us. (There's a big formal dinner in the college hall tomorrow night, but meanwhile, sherry apart, it's the appetites of the intellect that are being catered for.)

And I'm still thinking about it now even as I write. Please forgive me if I seem to be going on at unconscionable length, but in all the world there is no one I can talk to so fully and frankly as I can to you.

Time for bed. Will I sleep? I thought I had learned in prison how to sleep anywhere in any conditions, but tonight I think I may find it hard to close my eyes. Thoughts wriggle round my head like little snakes nesting in a skull. What do I owe to dear Sam? What do I owe to myself? And whose patronage was the more precious, Linda Lupin's or Justin Albacore's? Which would a wise man put his trust in?

Goodnight, dear Mr Pascoe. At least I hope it will be for you. For me I see long white hours lying awake pondering these matters, and above all the problem of how I'm going to reply to Albacore's offer.

I was wrong!

I slept like a log and woke to a glorious morning, bright winter sunshine, no wind, a nip in the air but only such as turned each breath I took into a glass of champagne. I was up early, had a hearty breakfast, and then went out for a walk to clear my head and still my nerves before I read Sam's paper at the nine o'clock session. I left the college by its rear gate and strolled along beside the Cam, admiring what they call the Backs. The

Backs! Only utter certainty of beauty allows one to be so throwaway about it. Oh, it's a glorious spot this Cambridge, Mr Pascoe. I'm sure you know it well, though I can't recall whether you're light or dark blue. This is a place for youth to expand its soul in, and despite everything, I still feel young.

I didn't see Albacore until I arrived in the lecture theatre a few minutes before nine and saw his cunicular nose twitch with relief. He must have been worrying that his 'straight talk' last evening had been too much for my weak stomach and I'd done a runner!

He'd arranged for me to have a plenary session and every chair was taken. He didn't hang about – perhaps recognizing more than I did at that moment just how nervous I was – but introduced me briefly with, mercifully, only a short formal reference to Sam's tragic death, while I sat there staring down at the opening page of my lost friend's paper.

Its title was, 'Looking for the Laughs in *Death's Jest-Book*'.

I read the first sentence – *In his letters Beddoes refers to his play* Death's Jest-Book *as a satire: but on what?* – and tried to turn the printed words into sounds coming from my mouth, and couldn't.

There was a loud cough. It came from Albacore, who had taken his place in the front row. And next to him, looking up at me with those big violet eyes I recalled from our sessions in the Syke, was his wife, Amaryllis Haseen.

Perhaps the sight of her was the last straw that broke what remained of my nerve.

Rising from my chair was the hardest thing I'd ever done in my life. I must have looked like a drunk as I walked the few steps to the lectern. Fortunately it was a solid old-fashioned piece of furniture, otherwise it would have shaken with me as I hung on to it with both hands to control my trembling. As for my audience, it was as if they were all sitting at the bottom of a swimming pool and I was trying to see them through a surface broken by ripples and sparkling with sun-starts. The effort made me quite nauseous and I raised my eyes to the back of the lecture theatre and stared at the big clock hanging on the wall there. Slowly its hands swam into focus. Nine o'clock precisely. The distant sound of bells drifted into the room. I lowered my eyes. The swimming-pool effect was still evident, except in the case of one figure sitting in the middle of the back row. Him I could see pretty clearly with no more distortion than might have come if I'd been looking through glass. And yet I knew that this must be completely delusional.

For it was you, Mr Pascoe. There you were, looking straight at me. For a few seconds our gazes locked. Then you smiled encouragingly and nodded. And in that moment everyone else came into perfect focus, I stopped trembling, and you vanished.

Wasn't that weird? This letter I'm writing must have created such a strong subconscious image of you that my mind, desperately seeking stability, externalized it in my time of need.

Whatever the truth of it, all nerves vanished and I was able to put on a decent show.

I even managed to say a few words about Sam, nothing too heavy. Then I read his paper on *Death's Jest-Book*. Do you know the play? Beddoes conceived it at Oxford when he was still only twenty-one. 'I am thinking of a very Gothic-styled tragedy for which I have a jewel of a name – DEATH'S JESTBOOK – of course no one will ever read it.' He was almost right, but as he worked on it for the rest of his short life, it has to be pretty central to any attempt to analyse his genius.

Briefly, it's about two brothers, Isbrand and Wolfram, whose birthright has been stolen, sister wronged, and father slain by Duke Melveric of Munsterberg. Passionate for revenge, they take up residence at the ducal court, Isbrand in the role of Fool, Wolfram as a knight. But Wolfram finds himself so attracted to the Duke that, much to Isbrand's horror and disgust, they become best buddies.

80

Sam's theory is that the whole eccentric course of Beddoes' odd life was dictated by his sense of being left adrift when his own dearly beloved father died at a tragically early age. One aspect of the poet's search for ways to fill the gap left by this very powerful personality is symbolized, according to Sam, by Wolfram finding solace not in killing his father's killer but rather in turning him into a substitute father. Unfortunately, for the integrity of the play that is, this search had many other often conflicting aspects, all of which dominate from time to time, leading to considerable confusion of plot and tone. As for Death, he is by turns a jester and a jest, a bitter enemy and a seductive friend. Keats, you will recall, claimed sometimes to be *half in love with easeful death*. No such pussy-footing about for our Tom. His was a totally committed all-consuming passion!

Back to my conference debut. I finished the paper without too much stuttering, managed to add a few comments of my own, and finally took questions. Albacore was in there first, his question perfectly weighted to give me every chance to shine. Thereafter he managed the session like an expert ringmaster, guiding, encouraging, gentling, and always keeping me at the centre of things. Afterwards I was congratulated by everyone whose congratulation I would have prayed for. But not Albacore. He didn't come near me, though I caught his eye occasionally through the crowd and received a friendly smile.

I knew what he was doing, he was showing me what he could do.

And I discovered by listening and asking questions some interesting things about the set-up here. At God's the Master is top dog, the present one being a somewhat remote and ineffectual figure, leaving the real power in the hands of his 2i/c, the Dean. (The Quaestor, incidentally, is what they call their bursar.) Albacore in fact is presently deputizing for the Master, who's on a three-month sabbatical at the University of Sydney. (Sydney, for godsake! During an English winter! These guys know how to arrange things!) On his return he will be entering the last year of his office. Albacore naturally enough is in the van of contenders for his job, but, this being Cambridge, the succession is by no means cut and dried. A big successful book, appearing just as the hustings reached their height, would be a very useful reminder to the electorate (which is to say, God's dons – sounds like the Vatican branch of the Mafia, doesn't it?) that Albacore could still cut the mustard academically, and its hoped-for popular success would give him a chance to demonstrate that he had Open Sesames to the inner chambers of that media world where so many of your modern dons long to strut their stuff.

Oh, the more I got the rich sweet smell of it, the more I thought, *this is the life for me!* Reading and writing, wheeling and dealing, life in the cloisters and life in the fast lane running in parallel, with winters in the sun for those who made the grade.

But I wasn't going to rush into a decision as important as this. I slipped away back here to the Lodging to think it all through and there seemed no better way of doing this than pouring out all my thoughts and hopes to you. Like that vision I had of you this morning, it's almost like having you here in the room with me. I can sense your approval at the now final decision I have reached.

This quiet, cloistered but not inactive nor unexciting life in these most ancient and fructuous groves of academe is what I want. And if giving up Sam's research is the only way for me to get it, I'm sure that's what he'd have wanted me to do.

So the die is cast. I'll stroll out now and post this letter, then perhaps catch one of the afternoon sessions. If I bump into Albacore, I won't give him any hint of the way I'm thinking. Let him sweat till tonight at least!

Thanks for your help.

Yours in gratitude,

Franny Roote

n Monday morning, the mail had arrived just as Pascoe was about to leave.

He took it into the kitchen and carefully divided it into three piles – his own, Ellie's and mutual (mainly Christmas cards).

In his pile there were two envelopes bearing the St Godric's coat of arms.

Ellie was on the school run, which gave him a free choice of reaction and action.

He tore open the first letter. Not that he knew it was the first as it had exactly the same postmark on it as the second. But a quick glance down the opening page confirmed this one started where the previous letter had left off.

When he came to the bit about Roote's vision of himself at the back of the lecture theatre, he stopped reading for a minute while he debated whether it should make him feel more or less worried about himself. Less, he decided. Or maybe more. He read on. He had no ocular delusion of the man's presence as he read but he could feel Roote's influence reaching out of the words and trying to tie him into his life. To what end? It wasn't clear. But to no good end, of that he was absolutely certain.

Perhaps the second letter would make things clearer.

He felt curiously reluctant to open it, but sat for some while with it in his hand, growing (his suddenly Gothic imagination told him) heavier by the minute.

A noise brought him out of his reverie. It was the front door opening. Ellie's voice called, 'Peter? You still here?'

Now he could get what he'd been wishing for not very long ago, Ellie's sane and sensible reaction.

Instead he found himself stuffing both letters, the read and the unread, into his pocket.

'Here you are,' she said, coming into the kitchen. 'I thought you'd have been gone by now. It's the Linford case today, isn't it? I hope they lock the bastard up and throw away the key.'

Ellie's usually tender heart stopped bleeding and became engorged with indignation at mention of Liam Linford.

'Don't fret,' he said to Ellie now. 'We've got the little shitbag tied up. Rosie OK?'

'You bet. It's all Nativity Play rehearsals. She's taken young Zipper's card, allegedly to prove to Miss Martingale that angels really did play the clarinet. But I reckon she wants to boast about her sexual conquests to her mates.'

'Oh God. The Nativity Play. When is it? Friday? I suppose we have to go?'

'You bet your sweet life,' she said. 'What's happened to the great traditionalist who nearly blew a gasket when there was that petition to ban it on the grounds it was ethnically divisive? What was it you said? "Give in on this and it's roast turkey and poppa-doms next." Now you don't want to go! You're a very confused person, DCI Pascoe.'

'Of course I want to go. I've even asked Uncle Andy to guarantee I've got God's own imprimatur. I'm just worried a non-speaking angel's part isn't going to satisfy Rosie.'

'At least Miss Martingale has persuaded her that having Tig in the manger would not be such a good idea, and I don't doubt she'll talk her out of the clarinet solo too.'

'Maybe. But she told me last night that it seems odd to her that when the innkeeper told Mary there was no room, the angels didn't come down and give him a good kicking.'

'It's a fair point,' said Ellie. 'Having all that power and not using it never made much sense to me either.'

He kissed her and went out. She was right, as usual, he thought. He was a very confused person, not at all like the cool, rational, thoughtful mature being Franny Roote pretended to believe in.

The unread letter bulked large in his pocket. Maybe it should stay unread. Whatever game Roote was playing clearly required two players.

On the other hand, why should he fear a contest? What was it Ellie had just said? 'Having all that power and not using it never made much sense to me.'

He turned out of the morning traffic stream into a quiet side street and parked.

It was a long, long letter. Two-thirds of the way through it he reached for his morning paper which he hadn't had time to read yet, and found what he was looking for on an inside page.

'Oh, you bastard,' he said out loud, finished the letter, started the car, did a U-turn and reinserted himself aggressively into the traffic flow.

St Godric's College

Cambridge

Sun Dec 16th (very early!)

My dear Mr Pascoe,

Again so soon! But measured by swings of emotion, how very much time has passed!

Still buoyed up by my sense of having made a wise decision, and been approved in it by you, I went down to dinner tonight, posting my last letter en route, and found Albacore waiting to offer me a choice of dry or very dry sherry. I displayed my independence by refusing both and demanding gin. Then, because I wanted to relax and enjoy myself, I relented and told him that, subject to detail and safeguards, he had a deal.

'Excellent,' he said. 'My dear Franny, I couldn't be more pleased. Amaryllis, my love, come and renew old acquaintance.'

She hadn't hung around after my paper, but here she was in a sheer silk gown cut low enough to make a man forget the spur of fame. She greeted me like an old friend, kissing me on the lips and chatting away about other inmates of the Syke as though we were talking of old acquaintance from the tennis club.

It really was an excellent night. Everything about it – the setting, the food, the wine, the atmosphere, the conversation – confirmed the wisdom of my decision. I was seated between Amaryllis and Dwight Duerden, there being too few female delegates to allow the usual gender

86

hopping (academia is equal opportunity land, but not that equal!) and the pressure, too frequent to be coincidental, from Amaryllis's thigh, made me wonder if this happy night might not be brought in every sense to a fitting climax.

Perhaps fortunately, the opportunity didn't arise. After the dinner Albacore invited some few of us (the most distinguished plus myself) back to the Dean's Lodging, all men save for Amaryllis, and she soon retired as the cigars came out and the atmosphere thickened with aromatic fumes. It was deliciously old fashioned, and I loved it.

Albacore was by now treating me like a younger brother, and when Dwight requested a tour of the Lodging, he put his arm round my shoulder and the two of us led the way.

The D's Lodging was a sort of early eighteenth-century annexe to the original college building and must have stuck out like a new nose on an old star's face for a time. But Cambridge of all places has the magic gift of taking unto itself all things new and wearing their newness off them with loving care till in the end they too are part of the timeless whole. It was a fine old building with that feel I so much love of a lived-in church, infinitely more splendid than the Q's suite of rooms (what must the Master's Habitation, a small mansion situated on a grassy knoll in the college grounds overlooking the river, be like?) and full of what should have been a stylistic hodge-podge of furniture, statuary and paintings had they not also succumbed to the unifying aura of that magical world.

I lusted for it all, and I think Justin sensed my yearning, and felt how much closer it bound me to his desires, and grappled me to him ever more tightly as the tour proceeded.

The study was for me the sanctus sanctorum, lit with a dim religious light, its book-lined walls emanating that glorious odour of old leather and paper which I think of as the incense of scholarship. At its centre stood a fine old desk, ornately carved and with a tooled leather top large enough for a pair of pygmies to play tennis on.

Dwight, miffed perhaps to find himself behind me in the Dean's pecking order, said, 'How the hell do you work in this gloom? And where do you hide your computer?'

'My what?' cried Alabacore indignantly. 'Compute me no computers! When my publisher suggested that in the interest of speed it would be useful if he could have my Beddoes book on disk, I replied, "Certainly, if you can provide me with a large enough disc of Carrara marble and a monumental mason capable of transcribing my words!" Press keys and produce letters on a screen and what have you got? Nothing! An electronic tremor which an interruption of the electrical supply can destroy. Show me one great work which has been produced by word-processing. When I write with my pen, I am writing on my heart and what is inscribed there will take the rubber of God to erase.'

I sensed that Dwight, who probably had a computerized khazi, was drunk enough to tell his host he was talking crap, so, not wanting this atmosphere I was so much enjoying to be soured by dissent, I essayed a light-hearted diversion.

'God uses rubbers, does he?' I said. 'Must have burst when he was into Mary.'

Such blasphemous vulgarity is evidently much enjoyed at High Tables. Like kids saying bum, says Charley Penn, they're excited by their own outrageousness. Certainly it worked here, everyone responding with their own kind of amusement, the well-born Brits with that head-nodding chortle which passes for laughter in their class, the plebs with loud guffaws, and Dwight and couple of fellow Americans with a kind of whooping bray.

After that Dwight asked in a conciliatory tone how then did Justin work, and Albacore, apologizing now for being a silly old Luddite, showed him his complex but clearly highly efficient card-index system and opened drawers to reveals reams of foolscap (no vulgar A4 for our Justinian!) closely covered with his elegant scrawl.

'And this is your new book?' said Dwight. 'The only copy? Jesus, how do you sleep sound at a night?'

'A lot easier than you do, I suspect,' responded Albacore. 'My handwritten pages hold no attraction for a burglar. A computer on the other hand is something worth stealing, as are discs. Also no one can hack into manuscript and see what I'm up to, or copy chunks in a couple of seconds to pre-empt my ideas. Your electronic words, dear Dwight, are by comparison the common currency of the air. Someone coughs a continent away and you can catch a killing virus.'

I headed off what might have been a provoking defence of the computer by asking Albacore to what extent he felt his book might bring Beddoes in out of the cold at the perimeter of British romantic literature and into its warm centre.

'I don't even try,' he retorted. 'It's my thesis that to understand him we must treat him not as a minor English but as a significant European writer. He was – most appositely at this present period in our history – a very good European. Byron's the only other who comes close to him. They both loved Europe, not merely because they found it warmer and cheaper than back home, but for its history and culture and peoples.'

He expanded on this for a little while, almost addressing me directly. It was as if now that he'd won our little contest he wanted to put the memory of the arm-twisting and near-bribery behind us and demonstrate that he was a serious Beddoes scholar.

The others listened happily too, sitting on the deep leather armchairs and sofa which the spacious room afforded, drinking from their brandy balloons and puffing on their genuine Havanas till the aromatic smoke almost hid the decorated ceiling. I sometimes think that it will not be the least of the twentieth century's philistinisms that it has destroyed the art of enjoying tobacco. Like the poet said, a fuck is only a fuck, but a good cigar is a smoke.

Long before he bored his audience (the great talkers are also masters of timing) Albacore stopped talking about Beddoes and invited us all to admire the copy of the *Vita S. Godrici* which he mentioned to me earlier and which he'd brought from the secure room of the college library for our delectation. Merely to handle something of such beauty and antiquity was enough for most of us, but Dwight with that lack of embarrassment about money which is the mark of a civilized American, cut to the chase and said, 'How much would it fetch on the open market?'

Albacore smiled and said, 'Why, this is a pearl worth more than all your tribe, Dwight. Think what you have here. A contemporary copy of the contemporary life written by a man who actually visited Godric in his hut at Finchale, Reginald of Durham, a man himself of such piety and erudition that these qualities are said by tradition to be accorded to all subsequent clerks who bear that name and title. In other words you are touching the book that touched the hand of a man who touched the hand of the saint himself. Who could put a price on something like this?'

'Well,' said Dwight, unputdown, 'I know a dealer called Trick Fachmann in St Poll who'd take a shot at it.'

Even Albacore laughed, and now the conversation became general, running like quicksilver from tongue to tongue, good thing following good thing, wisdom and wit doled out in a prodigality of plenty, and I felt tears prick my eyes at the sense of privilege and pleasure in being part of this company in this place at this time.

If it were now to die, 'twere now to be most happy . . .

I could have stayed there forever, but all things have their natural foreordained ends, and finally we dispersed, some to their student staircases, Dwight and I making our unsteady way back to the Q's Lodging, arm in arm for mutual support.

I undressed and climbed into bed, but I could not go to sleep. At first it was because of my excitement at the world of profit and delight which seemed to be opening up before me. But then a sudden and complete reversal took place ... *from the might / Of joy in minds that can no further go, / As high as we have mounted in delight / In our dejection do we sink as low.* Which is why, dear Mr Pascoe, my old leech-gatherer, I am sitting here propped up against my pillow, penning these words to you. Have I done the right thing in giving in to Albacore? In my last letter I was sure I had your approval. Now I am equally certain that you with your strong principles and unmoveable moral convictions will despise me for my venality. It's so very important for me to get you to see my side of things. I am an innocent abroad here, a pygmy jousting with giants. It is not always given to us to choose the instruments of our elevation. You must have felt this sometimes in your relationship with the egregious Dalziel. You may well have wished on occasion that the glittering prizes of your career were not in the gift of such a one. And by indignities men come to dignities. And it is sometimes base.

So if I seem to be asking for your blessing, it is beca

Another interruption!

What soaps my letters are turning out to be, every instalment ending in a cliffhanger!

And this time what a climactic interruption, fit to rank with those end-of-series episodes of shows like *Casualty* and *ER* designed to whet your what-happens-next appetite to such an edge that you will return as hungry as ever after the summer break.

But I mustn't be frivolous. What we have here isn't soap, it's reality. And it's tragic.

It was the fearful clamour of a bell which distracted me.

I leapt out of bed and rushed to the open window.

Since my time in the Syke, I always sleep with my window open whatever the season. Looking out into the quad I could see nothing, but I could hear away to the right a growing hubbub of noise and, when I thrust my head out into the night air and looked towards it, it seemed to me that the dark outline of the building forming that side of the quad was already being etched against the sky by the rosy wash of dawn.

Except it was far too early for dawn and anyway I was looking north.

Pausing only to thrust my feet into my shoes and drag a raincoat round my shoulders, I rushed out into the night.

Oh God, the sight I saw when I passed from the Q's quad to the D's quad!

It was the Dean's Lodging, no longer a thing of beauty but now crouched there, squat and ugly as a marauding monster, with a great tongue of flame coiling out of a downstairs window and greedily licking its facade.

I hurried forward, eager to help but not knowing how I could. Firemen bearing hoses from the engine, which seemed to have got wedged under a Gothic arch that gave the only vehicular approach to this part of the college, some wearing breathing apparatus, moved around me with that instancy of purpose which marks the assured professional.

'What's happening for God's sake?' I cried to one who paused beside me to cast an assessing eye over the scene.

'Old building,' he said laconically. 'Lots of wood. Three centuries to dry out. These places are bonfires waiting to be lit. Who're you?'

'I'm a . . .' What was I? Suddenly I didn't know. 'I'm at a conference here.'

'Oh,' he said losing interest. 'Need someone who knows who's likely to be in there.'

'I do know,' I said quickly.

He turned out to be the Assistant Chief Fire Officer,

a good-looking young man in a clean-cut kind of way.

I told him that, as far as I knew, Sir Justinian and Lady Albacore were the only inmates of the Lodging and tried to indicate from my memory of our tour where they were likely to be found. All of this he repeated into his walkie-talkie. Behind him as we talked, I could see that the fire had reached the upper storeys. My heart began to misgive me that we were witnessing a truly terrible tragedy. Then his radio crackled with the good news that Amaryllis was safe and well. But my joy at hearing this was immediately diluted by the lack of any news about Justin.

It began to rain quite heavily at this point, which was good news for the firefighters. I could see no point in catching my death of cold watching a fire, so I returned to my room and letter. Might as well go on writing as I doubt if I shall be able to fall asleep.

Wrong again!

I was woken in my chair by Dwight shaking my shoulder.

As I struggled out of sleep I could see from his face the news was not good.

Indeed it was the worst.

They'd found Justinian Albacore's body on the ground floor where the fire had been at its fiercest.

I was devastated. I had little cause to love the man but perhaps something in his mockingly subtle character appealed to me and I'd found last night that I had no problem with the prospect of spending much time in his company.

Dwight wanted to talk but all I wanted was to be left to myself.

I got dressed and went outside. The shell of the Dean's Lodging, gently steaming in a Fennish drizzle, stood as a dreadful illustration of the power of flames. As I stood and contemplated it I was joined by my handsome young Fire Officer who gave me the fullest picture they could piece together of last night's events.

It seems that Amaryllis had been woken by Justin getting out of bed in the early hours. Drowsily she asked him what was up, to which he replied he thought he'd heard something downstairs but it was probably nothing so why didn't she go back to sleep, which she did. She woke again some time later to find the room full of smoke. On the landing outside her bedroom she found things even worse with flames plainly visible at the foot of the stairs. She retreated into her room and rang the fire brigade. Then, pausing only to put on slacks, T-shirt, several warm pullovers and a little make-up, she opened the bedroom window which overlooked the roof of an architecturally incongruous conservatory, built by an orchidomaniac Victorian dean before there were such things as conservation orders, on to which she descended with the help of a drainpipe and from which she slid into the arms of the first fireman on the scene.

As for Justin, all that is possible at the moment is speculation.

It seems likely that when he descended the stairs he found his study already well ablaze. His awareness that lying within was the college's greatest treasure, Reginald of Durham's *Vita S. Godrici*, which he had personally and recklessly removed from the college library, must have blinded his judgment. Instead of raising the alarm, he probably rushed inside to rescue the precious manuscript but found himself driven back by the heat to the threshold where, overcome by fumes, he collapsed and died.

From what I can see for myself and from what my new friend told me, it's pretty clear that not only has the *Vita* been reduced to ashes, but not a page of Albacore's Beddoes manuscript or a single card from his card-index system can have survived the inferno.

It is still early days to reach conclusions about causes, but when I told the Fire Officer that we had all been sitting around the study last night drinking brandy and smoking cigars, his large blue eyes sparkled and he made a note in his note-pad.

The conference has naturally been cancelled and, after a morning spent answering questions and making statements, I am sitting here once more writing to you, dear Mr Pascoe, in the hope of clearing my thoughts.

I know you will think me selfish, but deep down beneath all my real sorrow over Justinian's death is a tiny nugget of self-pity. All my hopes have died too, all the glorious dreams of a Cambridge future I was having only last night.

Poor old me, eh?

One more interruption, this one, I hope, definitely the last!

As I wrote my last self-pitying sentence, Dwight came into the room and said with that American directness, 'So what are your plans now, Franny, boy?'

'Plans?' I said bitterly. 'Plans need a future and I don't seem to have one.'

He laughed and said, 'Jesus, Fran, don't go soft on me. It's an ill wind . . . Seems to me you've got a great future. From what I've picked up over the last couple of days, you've inherited a half-written book about Beddoes which looks like it's got the field clear after what happened last night. Tell me, you got any deal going with a Brit publisher?'

'Well, no,' I said and explained the situation.

'And there's no way these guys can come back at you now and say they've got a claim to anything that Dr Johnson did while he was taking their money?'

'No. In fact I've got a written disclaimer. It seemed a good thing to ask for . . .'

'I'll say!' he said approvingly. 'So now you can go ahead and finish the book any which way you want and make your name, right?'

I thought about it. This was an aspect of the tragedy

that hadn't occurred to me before. Truly, God works in a mysterious way!

He said, 'Ever think about getting it published in the States? Lot of interest in Beddoes over there, you know. Lot of money available too, if you know where to look.'

I said, 'Really? I wish I knew where to look then!'

'I do,' he said. 'My own university publishers have been stirring themselves recently. They're just waking to the truth I've been telling them for years, either you grow or you die. Tell you what, I'm going to pack now, then I'm being driven up to London . . .'

'Down,' I said.

'Sorry?'

'I think from Cambridge you always go down to London. Or anywhere.'

He came close to me and said, 'Listen Fran, that's the kind of thinking you want to get out of your head. OK, Cambridge was once the place to be, but that was costume drama time. Nothing stays still. Either you go away from it or it goes away from you. Hell, I was in Uzbekistan recently and being an old Romantic I wanted to take a look at the Aral Sea. Well, I got to where my battered Baedeker said it ought to be and you know what I found? Nothing. Desert. The Russkis have been siphoning off so much water for so long that it's shrunk to half its size. I talked to this old guy still living in the house he was born in and he pointed to the cracked stony ground outside his front door and said that when he was a kid he used to run out of the house naked on a summer morning and dive straight into the waves. Now he'd have to run two hundred fucking miles! Same thing with Cambridge. It's all dried up. Look real close at it and what do you see? It's an old movie set where they once did a few good things, but now the cameras and the lights and the action have moved on. Nothing as sad as an old movie set that's been left to rot in the rain. Think about it, Fran. I'll be moving out in an hour. Hope you'll be with me.'

Well, after that I needed a walk to clear my head.

Once more I strolled along the Backs. Only this time I looked at all those ancient buildings with a very different eye.

And you know what I saw this time? Not temples to beauty and learning, not a peaceful haven where a man could drop anchor and enjoy shore leave for ever more.

No, I saw it with eyes from which Dwight had removed the scales, and what I saw was an old movie set, looking sad as hell in the rain!

Why on earth would I want to spend my days gossiping and bitching and boozing my life away in a dump like this?

So now I'm packed – my few things only take a minute to throw together – and waiting for Dwight. He should be ready soon, so at last I'll bring this letter to a conclusion rather than an interruption.

I hope I've cleared the air between us. Perhaps some time in the future I may be moved to write to you again. Who knows? In the meantime, as the year draws to its close, may I once again wish yourself and your lovely family a very Merry Christmas?

Yours on the move *per ardua ad astra!*

Franny Roote

ore arse and rusty bum,' said Andy Dalziel.

'What?'

'The Aral Sea. Christ, I've not thought of that for years. You never know what's going to stick, do you? Is it really drying up?'

'I don't know, sir,' said Peter Pascoe. 'But does it matter? I mean . . .'

'Matters if you dive in and it's not there,' said Dalziel reprovingly. 'Sore arse and rusty bum! Old Beenie would be chuffed.'

Pascoe looked at Edgar Wield and saw only an incomprehension to match his own.

His decision to bring up Roote's letters at the CID meeting was mainly pragmatic. He'd spent much of the morning so far following up various lines of enquiry relating to Roote and did not doubt that the eagle eye of Andy Dalziel above and the cat eye of Edgar Wield below would have noticed this, so it was best to make it official. But that triumphant feeling that his enemy had delivered himself into his hands had gradually faded. Indeed recollecting it now made him feel faintly ashamed. The investigation of crime should be a ratiocinative process, not a crusade. So he had introduced the letters in calm measured tones and passed them to his colleagues without (he hoped) letting it show how desperate he was for their confirmation that here was cause for concern.

Instead he was getting the Fat Man, like some portly prophet, speaking in tongues!

The rambling continued.

'He once said to me, old Beenie, "Dalziel," he said, "if ever I want to torture a man of letters, I'll make you read blank verse to him." Right sharp tongue on him, knew how to draw blood. But, God, it were a long boring poem! Mebbe that's why I recall the end, because I were so pleased it had got there!'

'What poem?' said Pascoe, abandoning his efforts to swim against this muddy tide.

'I told you. Sore arse and rusty bum, did you learn nowt at that poncy kindergarten of thine?' said Dalziel. Then relenting he added, '"Sohrab and Rustum" were its Sunday name, but we all called it sore arse and rusty bum. Do you not know it?'

Pascoe shook his head.

'No? Oh well, I expect by the time you got to school, it 'ud be all this modern stuff, full of four letter words and no rhymes.'

'Blank verse doesn't rhyme,' said Pascoe unwisely.

'I know it bloody doesn't. But it doesn't need to 'cos it sounds like poetry, right? And it's a bit miserable. This poem's right miserable. Sore Arse kills Rusty Bum and then finds out the bugger's only his own son. So he sits there all night next to the body in the middle of this sort of desert, the Chorasmian waste he calls it, while all around these armies are busy doing what armies do, one of the saddest scenes in Eng. Lit., Beenie said, and this river, the Oxus, keeps on rolling by. Bit like "Ol' Man River" really.'

'So where's the Aral Sea come in?' asked Pascoe.

'I'm telling you,' said Dalziel.

He struck a pose and started to declaim in a sing-song school-boy kind of way, end-stopping each line with no regard for internal punctuation or overall sense.

.... *till at last.*
The long'd-for dash of waves is heard and wide.
His luminous home of waters opens bright.
And tranquil from whose floor the new-bathed stars.
Emerge and shine upon the Aral Sea.

'Now that's fucking poetry, no mistake,' he concluded.

'And that's the end of this sore and rusty poem?' said Pascoe. 'And old Beenie . . . ?'

'Mr Beanland, MA Oxon. He could have thrown chalk for England. Put your eye out at twenty feet. He went on and on about this Aral Sea, how remote and beautiful and mysterious it were. And now this Yank says it's drying up, and tourists go to see it, and it's not there. Like life, eh? Like fucking life.'

'It isn't a correspondence that leaps up and hits me in the eye,' said Pascoe sourly.

'Which is what I'd do if I had a stick of chalk,' growled the Fat Man. 'Any road, talking of correspondence, why'm I wasting precious police time reading your mail?'

'Because it's from Franny Roote, because it contains implied threats, because in it he admits complicity in several crimes. And,' Pascoe concluded, like an English comic at the Glasgow Empire seeing his best gags sink in a sea of indifference and desperately reaching for any point of contact, 'because he refers to you as Rumbleguts.'

But even this provocation to complicity failed.

'Oh aye. When you've been insulted by experts that sounds like a term of endearment,' said the Fat Man indifferently.

'Glad to find you so philosophical,' said Pascoe. 'But the threats . . .'

'What threats? I can't see no threats. How about you, Wieldy? You see any threats?'

The sergeant glanced apologetically at Pascoe and said, 'Not as such.'

'Not as such,' mimicked Dalziel. 'Meaning not at fucking all! The bugger goes out of his way to say that he's not writing a threatening letter. In fact he seems to rate you so highly, it wouldn't surprise me if he ended up sending you a Valentine card!'

'That's all part of it, don't you see? Like this play he goes on about, *Death's Jest-Book*, it's all some kind of grisly joke. That stuff about the ambiguities of revenge, one brother becoming dead friendly with the Duke, the other bursting with hate, that's Roote telling me how he feels.'

'No it's not. In fact I recall he says quite clear he feels like the friendly brother. And all these crimes you're going on about, what would they be?'

Pascoe opened the file he was carrying and produced several sheets of paper.

'You've not been playing with your computer again?' said Dalziel. 'You'll go blind.'

'Harold Bright, known as Brillo,' said Pascoe. 'Banged up in the Syke the same time as Roote. Had an accident in the shower. Cracked his head. Traces of ammonia-based cleansing fluid found in eyes but never explained. Complications during treatment. Died.'

'And good riddance,' said Dalziel. 'I remember the Brights. Hospitalized two of ours when they got arrested, one of 'em had to take early retirement. Dendo still inside?'

'No. Finished in Durham, but he got out last month.'

'Problem solved then. Send him Roote's address. He sorts out your lad, we bang Dendo up again for the duration. Two for the price of one.'

Over the years Pascoe had come to a pretty good understanding of when the Fat Man was joking, but there were still some grey areas where he felt it better not to enquire.

He said, 'My point is, we know a man died, and now we have Roote's confession.'

'Bollocks,' said Dalziel. 'His admission might as well have been written by Hans Anderson. And, like he says himself, where are you going to get witnesses? Any road, if he did do it, he deserves a medal. Owt else?'

'I checked that Polchard was there the same time as Roote, and the Syke's Chief Officer remembers they played chess together,' said Pascoe sulkily.

'You going to do Roote for cheating then? I remember Mate Polchard. Right tricky sod. He out yet?'

Wield whose job it was to know everything said, 'Yes, sir. Came out in the summer. Went off to his place in Wales to recuperate.'

Polchard was out of the normal run of thugs in more than just his penchant for chess. Not for him the comforts of a Spanish villa with a plethora of Costa fleshpots on his doorstep. His preferred hideaway was a remote Welsh farmhouse in Snowdonia. But when it came to protecting his interests, he ran true to type. Shortly after he bought the farm, a barn belonging to it was burnt down and a message sprayed on a wall in Welsh with under it a helpful translation. *Go home Englishman or next time it's the house.* A few days later the local leader of the main Welsh activist group awoke in the early hours to find three men in his room. They were unarmed and unmasked, which he found more worrying than reassuring. They spoke to him politely, showing him a list of the addresses of perhaps a dozen members of his group, his own at the head, and assured him that in the event of any further interference with Mr Polchard's property, every one of these houses would be reduced to rubble within a fortnight. Then they left. Fifteen minutes later his garden shed blew up and burned with such ferocity it was a pile of cinders long before the fire brigade got near. No complaint was made, but Police Intelligence soon picked up the story, which Dalziel retailed now, at length, to signal his interest in Roote was over.

But Pascoe listened with barely concealed impatience to the oft-told tale and used it as a cue to wrest the subject back.

'Polchard's not the only one who's good at fires,' he said. 'This fire Roote writes about at St Godric's, I've got several newspaper reports here and I've been on to the Cambridge Fire Service Investigation Department and they're getting back to me . . .'

'Hold on, lad. Stop right there,' said Dalziel. 'I've not had this letter X-rayed and tested for poisoned ink like you, but I have read it, and I don't recall owt in it coming in hosepipe distance of an admission of arson! Did I miss summat? Wieldy, how about you?'

The sergeant shook his head.

'No, definitely no admission, not as such . . .'

'There you go again. Not as such! As what then if not such?' Pascoe had had enough.

He interrupted angrily, 'For Christ's sake, what's up with you two? It's as plain as the nose on your face, he's mocking us, that's the whole point of the letter. Even without the letter, I'd have known something was wrong. Look at the facts. Franny Roote is a nobody, an ex-con, working as a gardener. Then his tutor, Sam Johnson, gets killed and Roote manages to sweet-talk Johnson's sister into dropping his almost completed book on Beddoes into Roote's lap. Suddenly from being an academic nobody, he's set for the big league. One obstacle – there's competition in the shape of this guy Albacore, who looks set to get his oeuvre in the shops several months earlier. Roote and Albacore meet. Albacore thinks he's cut a deal. Take Roote on board, squeeze the juice of Johnson's researches out of him, and then, of course, he'd be able to drop Roote like the nasty little turd he is. Only he doesn't know yet that this turd's got teeth.'

Dalziel who'd been listening with his great maw open in maximum gobstopped mode burst out, 'A turd with teeth! I told thee, this is what comes of reading modern poetry!'

Pascoe who was a trifle vain about his style looked embarrassed but pressed on, 'But what happens? There's a fire and Albacore ends up dead and his work goes up in smoke. Coincidence? I don't think so. Like I say, I'd have been suspicious if I'd read about it in the paper. But that's not enough for the scrote! He has to write to me and gloat about it!'

'Gloat? I got no gloat. How about you, Wieldy? You step in any gloat? And if you say not as such, I'll pull your tongue out and ram it up your neb!'

Wield touched his lips with his tongue as if rehearsing the manoeuvre and said, 'Not . . . that I could say definitely was gloating. But like I say, if Pete's got a feeling . . . and I agree that Roote's a tricky bastard . . .'

'Not so tricky we didn't bang him up,' said Dalziel complacently.

'He's had the benefit of a prison education since then,' said Wield.

He was speaking figuratively but the Fat Man pretended to take him literally.

'Fair do's but,' he said. 'He didn't come out a sociologist like most of the buggers as get educated inside. I really hate it when I hear one of them bastards on the chat shows.'

The DCI closed his eyes and Wield said quickly, 'Mebbe we should wait and see what the Cambridge fire people say.'

The phone rang so aptly that he wasn't in the least surprised when Pascoe, who'd snatched it, up mouthed *Cambridge* at them.

Eyes less keen than Dalziel's and Wield's could have worked out it wasn't good news.

Pascoe said, 'Thanks a lot. If anything else comes up . . . yes, thank you. Goodbye.'

He put the receiver down.

'So?' said Dalziel.

'Nothing suspicious,' said Pascoe. 'As far as they can make out, the fire started in a leather armchair, probably caused by a lighted cigar butt which had slipped down behind the cushion. Only sign of any accelerant was an exploded brandy decanter.'

'Aye, well, bunch of drunken dons smoking big cigars in a building that's probably failed every fire regulation laid down over five hundred years, that's asking for trouble,' said Dalziel. 'Well, I'm glad we've got that out of the way.'

'For God's sake,' said Pascoe, 'you don't think that someone like Roote was going to get to work with a can of paraffin, do you? No, he was there, he tells us he was there, puffing away on a cigar with the best of them. That's what probably gave him the idea.'

'Oh aye? You got second sight now, Peter?' said the Fat Man. 'Pity they don't take account of that in the Criminal Evidence Act. I think that's enough about Roote for one day. I don't mind my officers having a hobby so long as they do it in their own time.'

Angrily Pascoe retorted, 'And how do you feel about your officers ignoring prima-facie evidence of crime? Sir?'

'Prima facie? That 'ud be an Italian waiter with his throat cut and Roote standing over him with a knife in his hand? Wieldy, them statistics I'm doing for the Chief, how'm I getting along with them?'

'You've finished them, sir.'

'Have I? Jesus, I must've sat up half the night. It's no fun being a superintendent. You'd best come along to my office in five minutes and tell me what I think of them afore I pass them on to Desperate Dan. How's young Ivor settling back in, by the way?'

Ivor was Dalziel's sobriquet for DC Shirley Novello, who had taken a bullet in the shoulder during the summer and only recently returned to work full time.

'Looking fine, sir,' said Wield. 'Very sharp and eager to make up for lost time.'

'Grand. Now we just need Bowler back and we'll only be slightly under fucking strength instead of seriously under fucking strength. When's he due to start?'

'This week, Wednesday I think, sir.'

'Not till Wednesday?' said Dalziel incredulously. 'You'd think the bugger had had major surgery. Here, pass us that phone and I'll give him a wake-up call.'

Up till now Dalziel had made little effort to hurry Bowler from his sickbed, knowing how easy it was for a convalescent hero to be turned into a gung-ho cop who'd killed a suspect through use of excessive force. But now the Board of Enquiry had finally cleared Bowler of all culpability, the case was altered.

'Shouldn't bother,' said Pascoe. 'I gather Ms Pomona's taken him away for a weekend of rest and recuperation. They won't be back till later today.'

'What? Off with his light o' love, is he? If a man's fit enough to shag, he's fit enough to work, says so in the Bible. Wait till I see him. Wieldy, them figures, five minutes right? By the way, Pete. Chief's taking me out to lunch. His treat for all my hard work. With luck I won't be back till tea-time, so if anyone wants me, you'll have to do.'

'Yes, sir. Except I'll be in court myself this afternoon,' said Pascoe.

'Oh aye, the Linford committal. Nowt to worry about there, we've got the scrote sewn up tighter than a nun's knickers, right?'

'Right,' said Pascoe. 'Though Belchamber will be looking to do a bit of snipping . . .'

'Sod the Belcher,' growled Dalziel. 'Nowt he can do long as your witness, the Carnwath lad, stays strong. No second thoughts after that scare on Saturday?'

'Oz is rock solid,' said Pascoe. 'And they can't get at him directly. Not married, no current girl, parents dead. Only close family is a sister in the States. She is coming over for Christmas, but not till Wednesday, by which time it'll be sorted, God willing.'

'Then what are you moaning about? Wieldy, five minutes.'

The Fat Man left.

Pascoe watched the great haunches swing out of sight and

said, 'You've made yourself indispensable to Rustybum, Wieldy. Could be a fatal mistake.'

'No, way I look at it is, if the station goes up in flames and Andy can only get one person out, it'll be me over his shoulder and down the drainpipe. Talking of flames . . .'

He looked significantly at the letters lying on the desk in front of Pascoe.

'You think I'm overreacting too?'

'I think something about Franny Roote's got to you in a big way. And I think that he knows it and he's enjoying jerking you around.'

'So you agree that he's setting out to provoke me with these confessions . . . all right, half-confessions?' said Pascoe hopefully.

'Mebbe. But that's all they are, provocations. One thing I'm certain of about our Franny is, he's not going to put himself at risk.'

'So your advice is . . . ?'

'Forget it, Pete. He'll soon get tired and concentrate on manipulating his new friends.'

'You're probably right,' said Pascoe gloomily.

Wield observed his friend closely, then said, 'There's something else, isn't there?'

'No. Well, yes. It's silly but . . . look, Wieldy, if I tell you this, not a word to Andy, eh?'

'Guide's honour,' said Wield girlishly.

Pascoe smiled. Even though he was now living openly with his partner, Edwin Digweed, at work Wield rarely let slip the mask with which he'd concealed his gayness for so many years. This brief flash of campness was a reassurance stronger than a dozen notarized oaths sworn on Bibles and mothers' graves.

He said, 'In the letter, you remember the bit where Roote stands up to give Sam Johnson's paper? He looks at the clock and it's nine o'clock on Saturday morning, and then he looks down and he sees . . . here it is . . . *it was you, Mr Pascoe. There you were, looking straight at me.*'

He raised his eyes from the paper and looked at Wield with such appeal that the sergeant touched his arm and said urgently, 'Pete, it's just a try-on. It's that German *doppelgänger* stuff he's picked up from Charley Penn. It's for frightening kids with . . .'

'Yes, I know that, Wieldy. Thing is, last Saturday I took Rosie to her music lesson in St Margaret Street, and I parked outside the church to wait for her. And I saw him.'

'The teacher?'

'No, dickhead! Roote. In the churchyard, standing there looking straight at me. St Margaret's clock began striking nine. I saw him for two chimes of the bell. Then I started getting out of the car and, by the time I'd got out, he'd vanished. But I saw him, Wieldy. At nine o'clock like he says. I saw Franny Roote!'

It came out more dramatically than intended. Not *thought I saw* or *imagined I saw*, the plain assertion *I saw!* He waited impatient for Wield's reaction.

The phone rang.

Wield picked it up, said, 'Yes?' listened, said, 'OK. Turk's. But not for an hour,' and replaced the receiver. He stood in thought for a long moment till Pascoe said, 'Well?'

'What? Oh, just someone, owt or nowt.'

Normally such imprecision would have aroused Pascoe's curiosity but now it merely aggravated his impatience.

'I mean about Roote,' he said.

'Roote? Oh yes. You thought you saw him but he's in Cambridge. Had your eyes tested lately, Pete? Look, I'd best get along to make sure Andy understands what he's going to be telling Dan. Good luck with Belchamber. See you later.'

'Thanks a bunch,' said Pascoe to the empty air. 'It's bad enough seeing things but it gets worse if you turn invisible at the same time.'

And was relieved to find he could still laugh.

The Newly-Wed

I t had been the best weekend of Hat Bowler's life, no competition, not even from the winter weekend a couple of years ago when he'd trudged back from a long unproductive stint in a hide looking for a reported Rock Thrush and there it had been, perched on the bonnet of his MG where it stayed long enough to get three good shots with his camera.

It hadn't just been the sex but the sense of utter togetherness they shared in everything they did. Saturday had been a perfect day till dinner when she'd pushed away her plate and said, 'Shit, I'm getting one of my headaches.' At first he'd laughed, taking it as a joke, then had felt a huge pang of selfish disappointment as he realized it wasn't. But this had quickly been blanked by anxiety as her face drained of colour. She'd assured him it was nothing, taken a tablet, and when, instead of retiring to her own room, she lay willingly and trustingly in his arms the whole night through, this had seemed an affirmation of love more powerful than sex. Gradually the next morning the colour had returned to her cheeks and by lunchtime she was as active and joyous as ever, and that night . . . if ever joy was unconfined, it was in the boundless universe which was their bed that night.

They didn't leave the room till halfway through Monday morning, and only then because they were due to check out. Slowly they drove back into Mid-Yorkshire. They were in Rye's Fiesta – Hat's MG was taking even longer than its owner to recover from the injuries sustained during the rescue mission – but it was lack of volition rather than lack of power which dictated their speed. Both knew from experience that joy is a delicate fabric and life's shoddy sleeve has a thousand tricks up it which can be played to bankrupt poor deluded humans even as they rake their winnings in. This journey was a time-out. In the car with them they carried all the joyous certainties of that hotel room, but what lay ahead could never be certain. Out of some part of Hat's subconscious, the existence of which he had hitherto not even suspected, the Gothic fancy leapt that if they had been driving along a narrow mountain road with a rock face on one side and a precipice on the other, it might have been well to seize the wheel and send them plunging to their deaths. Happily a hawthorn hedge and a turnip field didn't offer quite the same incentive, so it was a fancy easy to resist and one he decided to keep to himself. What after all was he feeling so pessimistic about? Had not Rye promised he would be safe with her, and he certainly intended exerting all his strength to ensure she stayed safe with him.

Impulsively he leaned over and kissed her, nearly bringing the turnip field into play.

'Hey,' she said, 'don't they do road safety in the police any more?'

'Yeah, but some of us get special exemption.'

She reached over and touched him intimately.

'And that's a special exemption, is it? Hang on.'

The turnip field came to an end to be followed by a meadow full of sheep with a rutted overgrown lane in between. Rye swung the wheel over and they bumped up the lane for twenty yards or so before jolting to a halt.

'Right,' she said, undoing her seat belt. 'Let's have a road safety lesson.'

For the rest of the journey his heart was like a nest of singing birds which permitted no discordant future possibilities to be heard. The world was perfect and all that lay ahead was an eternity exploring its perfections.

But, for all his certainties, he was sorry when the journey came to an end and they turned into Peg Lane where Rye lived. Somehow, cocooned in the car, they had seemed as solitary as Adam and Eve at the world's dawn. Still, God was obviously smiling upon them as there was a parking space right in front of Church View, the big converted townhouse which contained Rye's flat.

He followed her up the stairs, wondered as she inserted the key in the lock whether it would be naff to offer to carry her over the threshold, decided it wouldn't and who the hell cared anyway? put the cases down and stepped forward as the door swung open.

And saw over her suddenly rigid shoulder that the flat had been burgled.

The flat was a mess. It looked as if stuff had been removed from cupboards and drawers and hurled about recklessly in a desperate search, but as far as he could see the only thing that had been broken was a Chinese vase in the bedroom. It lay beneath the shelf it had fallen from. It struck Hat as he stood there looking down at it that this was the first time he'd been in Rye's bedroom. But not the last, he told himself complacently.

Then he saw her face and all such smug self-congratulation vanished.

She was staring at the shards of the broken vase, her face as pale as the fine white dust which surrounded them.

'Oh shit,' said Hat.

He could guess what the vase had held. Aged fifteen, her twin brother Sergius had been killed in the car accident which left his sister with the head injury whose healing was marked by a distinctive silver blaze in her rich brown hair. The twins had been close in life, he knew that, but just how close Sergius had stayed in death he hadn't known till now.

How he would have felt about bedding down with Rye in the presence of her brother's ashes, he didn't know. Not that there looked any likelihood of being put to the test in the near future. He tried to put a comforting arm round her shoulders but she turned out of his grasp without a word and went back into the living room.

Personal contact not getting through, he tried professional, urging her not to touch any more than was necessary, but she didn't seem to hear him as she moved around the living room and the kitchen, checking drawers, boxes, private hiding places.

'What's been taken?' he asked.

'Nothing,' she said. 'So far as I can see. Nothing.'

Didn't seem to make her happy. Come to think of it, it didn't make him happy either.

He looked around himself, hoping to find a gap. She didn't own a TV set or hi-fi equipment, the obvious targets. Lot of books, wouldn't be able to check those till they were back on the shelves, but they didn't seem a likely target. He went back into the bedroom. What the hell was she going to do about those ashes? Her clothes, which had been tipped out of drawers, were scattered over them. Not the kind of thing you wanted to find in your undies, he thought with that coarseness policemen learn to use as a barrier between themselves and the paralysing effect of so much of what they see.

There was a lap-top open on a table by the bed. Funny that hadn't gone. Expensive model, easily portable. He noticed it was in sleep mode.

'You always leave your computer on?' he called.

'No. Yes. Sometimes,' she said from the living room.

'And this time?'

'I can't remember.'

He ran his fingers at random over the keyboard and waited. After a while it got the message and began to wake up.

Now the screen came into focus. There were words on it.

BYE BYE LORELEI

Then they vanished.

He turned to see Rye had come into the room. She was holding the power cable which she had just yanked out of the wall socket.

'Why did you do that?' he asked.

'Because,' she said, 'if I want a detective, I'll dial 999.'

'And are you going to dial 999?'

She rubbed the side of her head where the silver blaze shone in the rich brown hair.

'What's the point?' she said. 'You lot will only make more mess. Best just to tidy up, get some better locks.'

'Your choice,' he said, not wanting to force the issue. 'But maybe you ought to make absolutely sure nothing's missing before you make up your mind. You won't be able to claim unless your insurance company sees a police report.'

'I told you, nothing's missing!' she snapped.

'OK, OK. Right then, let's do a bit of tidying up, or would you like a drink first?'

'No,' she said. 'No. Look, I'll do the tidying up myself. I'd prefer it.'

'Fine. Then I'll make us a coffee . . .'

'Christ, Hat!' she exclaimed, her hand at her head again. 'What happened to that guy who was so oversensitive he couldn't make a pass? I'll spell it out. I don't want a fuss, Hat. I've got a headache, Hat. I would rather be alone, Hat.'

Of course she would. He forced himself not to glance towards the shattered vase.

He nodded and said brightly, 'I think I've got that. OK. I'll ring you later.'

'Fine,' she said.

He went to the door, stood looking down at the lock, and said, 'Thanks for a great weekend. I had the best time of my life.'

She said, 'Me too. Really. It was great.'

He looked back at her now. She managed a smile but her face was pale, her eyes deep shadowed.

He almost went back to her but had the wit and the will not to.

'Later,' he said. 'We'll talk later.'

And left.

s Sergeant Wield approached Turk's his clear and well-ordered mind, long used to separating the various areas of his life into water-tight compartments, had no problem with setting out what he was doing.

He was an officer of Mid-Yorkshire CID, on duty, going to meet a nineteen-year-old rent boy who might possibly have information which would be of interest to the police.

He was alone because said rent boy was not a registered informant (which would have required the presence of two officers at any meeting) but a member of the public who had indicated he wanted to speak to Wield only.

So far, so normal. The only abnormality was that he was having to remind himself!

Then through the grubby glass of the cafe window, he saw Lee sitting at the same table they'd occupied on Saturday night, looking like a kid who'd bunked off school, and he broke his stride to remind himself again.

Turk returned his greeting with his usual glottal grunt and poured him a cup of coffee. Lee's face, which had lit up with pleasure or relief on Wield's entrance, had resumed its usual watchful suspicious expression by the time the sergeant sat down.

'How do?' said Wield.

'I'm fine. Survived your sarney then?'

'Looks like it.'

There was silence. Sometimes in such circumstances, Wield let the combination of the silence and his unreadably menacing face work for him. Today he judged that whatever point was going to be reached would require a path of small talk. Or maybe he just wanted to talk.

He said, 'Lubanski. Where's that come from?'

'My mam's name. She were Polish.'

'Were?'

'She's dead. When I were six.'

'I'm sorry.'

'Yeah? Why?' His tone was sceptically aggressive.

Wield said gently, 'Because no age is good to lose your mam, and six is worse than most. Old enough to know what it means, too young to know how to cope. What happened then?'

He didn't need to ask. Like Pascoe in pursuit of Franny Roote, he'd done some research that morning. Lee Lubanski had a juvenile record, nothing heavy: shop-lifting, glue-sniffing, absconding from a children's home. Nothing there about rent-boy activities. He'd been lucky, or clever, or protected. A con-scientious social worker had pieced together a brief family history when the boy first went into care. Grandfather was a Polish shipworker active in the Solidarity movement. A widower with dodgy lungs and a fifteen-year-old daughter, when General Jaru-zelski cracked down on Walesa and his supporters in 1981, Lub-anski, fearful that he wouldn't survive a spell in jail and fearful too of what might become of his daughter if left to run loose, had somehow got out of the country on a ship which docked at Hull. Seeing no reason why the UK authorities should be very much different from those back home, he'd slipped through the immigration net into the murky waters of metropolitan York-shire, only to find that what he'd fled from in Poland awaited him here. After a few months of precarious existence, he died of untreated TB, leaving a pregnant daughter with a basic know-ledge of English and no obvious way of making a living other than prostitution, which was her profession when Lee slithered into this unwelcoming world.

The new mother touched surface just long enough for her son to be registered officially and for her to get the minimum benefits offered by a caring state, but then her father's fear of authority took over and she slipped out of sight again until Lee came of school age. Now the Law got a line on her, but by the time it was ready to pronounce on her status as an illegal alien, she was too far gone with her father's illness for there to be argument over anything but who was going to pay for the coffin.

Her son too was, as might be expected, tubercular, but happily at an early enough stage for treatment. The assumption of the social worker's report was that he'd been the product of an unprotected encounter with a client, but in this alone did Lee's fragmented account differ from what Wield had read.

'My mam were going to get married, but she couldn't 'cos she were only fifteen, so she had to wait till she were sixteen, and something must have happened with my dad . . .'

Had some bastard lied to the girl in order to get her into bed for nothing? Or had she lied to her son so that he wouldn't have to grow up thinking he was the product of a five-quid shag up against a garage wall?

Whatever, it was clearly important to the boy. To the young man. To the nineteen-year-old male prostitute who'd got him here on the promise of useful information.

Wield sat up straight and looked at his watch to break the thread of confidentiality.

'OK, Lee,' he said. 'I've got things to do. So what did you want to see me about?'

For a moment Lee looked hurt, then his features became watchful and knowing.

'Thought you might like to hear about a heist that's coming off,' he said with an effort at being casual.

'A heist?' said Wield, hiding his smile at the use of this Hollywood word.

'That's right. You interested or wha'?'

'Won't know till you tell me a bit more,' said Wield. 'Like, what? Where? When?'

'Friday. Security van.'

'Good. Any particular security van?'

'You wha'?'

'You may not have noticed, lad, but the streets of our city are pretty well jammed with security vans at the busy times of day.'

'Yeah, well, it's one of Praesidium's.'

This was better. Praesidium was a newish Mid-Yorkshire

118

security company which by aggressive marketing was making its presence felt in a growth industry.

Wield close-questioned Lee about the cargo, time and location, but the boy just shrugged, and his only response to enquiries about the source of his information was it was guaranteed good, this with a double dose of that knowing look.

'OK, Lee,' said Wield. 'It's not much to go on, but I'll mention it to my boss. He's a payment-by-results man, by the way.'

'Payment? What payment?' said the youth angrily.

'You'll be wanting something for your trouble, won't you?'

'It was no trouble, just a favour, for what you did for me last night. Or should I have offered you money for that? Or summat else maybe?'

The implication was clear, but the indignation seemed genuine.

Wield said, 'Sorry, lad. Picked you up wrong. My line of work, you think . . . well, you know, you don't often get owt for nowt. Sorry.'

'Yeah, well, that's all right,' said Lee.

'Good. OK. Listen, how can I get hold of you?'

'Why should you want to get hold of me?'

'Just in case anything comes up. About the . . . heist.'

Lee thought a moment then said, 'I'll be in touch if there's owt, don't worry.'

Wield said, 'Sure, that's fine,' not doubting he could get a line on the young man whenever he wanted. 'Got to go now. Cheers. You take care of yourself.'

This time he didn't look into the cafe as he walked by the window, not wanting to risk another glimpse of vulnerability. For the moment all that mattered was this tip. It was too vague to be of much use as it stood. He could imagine what Dalziel would tell him to do, so he might as well do the do-able part before he got told.

Back on his bike, he headed for the estate that housed Praesidium Security.

Praesidium's boss, Morris Berry, a fleshy man with sweaty palms, was unimpressed. He called up the job sheets for Friday on his computer and after a quick examination opined that, if

the tip were true, they must be dealing with a singularly unambitious gang of heisters as the only job worth the risk of a hit was
the rural wages round. This delivered wage packets to various
small businesses across the county. OK, with Christmas bonuses
included, the initial amount carried was larger than usual, but it
still only amounted to thousands rather than hundreds of thousands, and of course with each delivery, it got less.

Wield checked for himself and had to agree with the conclusion. At least it narrowed down the likely time of the hit as
the gang must know that the longer they waited, the less they
were going to get. Berry laughed and asked what made him
think crooks were that clever. This lot must be really thick to
contemplate attacking one of his state-of-the-art vans with the
latest tracker devices installed so he knew their exact location
all the time.

He demonstrated this with a computerized map of Yorkshire
which showed van-shaped icons flashing away at various loca-
tions. Then he zoomed in on one of them.

'There we are, Van 3 on the A1079 approaching The Fox and
Hen. If the bastard stops there, he's fired!'

The bastard, happily for him, kept going. Wield, impressed
enough to have even more doubts about Lee's tip, glanced at
his watch. Jesus, it was two o'clock. Time for a pint and pie in
what should by now be the CID-free zone of the Black Bull.

eter Pascoe felt nervous. Despite all his assurances first to Ellie then to the Fat Man that the Linford case was well under control, he still had misgivings. At the heart of them stood Marcus Belchamber, advocate solicitor, of what was generally regarded as Yorkshire's premier law firm, Chichevache, Bycorne and Belchamber.

It was universally acknowledged that if you wanted to sue your loving gran for feeding you toffees at five to the detriment of your pancreas at thirty, or if you wanted rid of your spouse but not your spouse's assets, you retained Zoë Chichevache. If you wanted to draw up a commercial contract which would leave you keeping your fortune when all about you were losing theirs and blaming it on you, you retained Billy Bycorne. But if you simply wanted to stay out of jail, you sent for Marcus Belchamber.

He was of course an ornament of Yorkshire society, exuding reliability and respectability. His standing as a minor man of learning, particularly in the field of Roman Britain, was unassailable. Even his one approach to flashness was an unobtrusive learned jest in that he drove a Lexus bearing the numberplate JUS 10, which, if you took the digit 1 as letter I could be translated as *Behold the Law!*

Dalziel had a dream. 'One day the bastard 'ull overreach himself and I'll have his bollocks for breakfast.'

But, in the private opinion of the Fat Man's colleague, such a culinary treat was unlikely ever to be on the menu. Why should one who could so easily gather the golden apples free ever risk lending his clients his arm to shake the tree?

And today Belchamber was appearing for the accused, Liam Linford.

Pascoe had been in on this case almost from the start, which was late one November night when John Longstreet, twenty-six, taxi driver, had arrived home from his honeymoon with his wife, Tracey Longstreet, nineteen. Home was a flat in Scaur Crescent on the Deepdale Estate. Because the street in front of the flats was lined with cars, Longstreet had parked opposite. As he unloaded the cases, his young wife, eager to enter her new home, had set out across the road, pausing in the middle of it to turn and ask him if their honeymoon had left him so weak he needed a hand.

As he started to reply to the effect that he'd soon show her how weak he was, a car came round the corner at such speed it threw his wife ten feet into the air and thirty feet forward so that she crashed down on the windscreen of the braking vehicle, slid along the bonnet and rolled off under the wheels. The low-slung machine trapped her beneath the chassis, dragging her along the road for two hundred yards before finally scraping itself free of what remained, and accelerating away into the night.

Pascoe first saw John Longstreet forty-five minutes later at the City Hospital. He was advised by the attendant doctor that he was in such deep shock it was pointless talking to him. Indeed, when Pascoe, ignoring the advice, took a seat next to the man the only coherent phrase he managed to get out of him was 'black skull' repeated over and over.

But for Pascoe it was enough. He put it together with another phrase elicited from the one extremely distant independent witness to the effect that it was a 'yellow sporty job going a hell of a lick', and he set off towards the substantial residence of Walter Linford.

Wally Linford was an entrepreneur who'd ostensibly made his fortune out of a travel company in the loadsamoney eighties, but in CID it was known this side of proof that his true metier was the financing of crime. Not directly, of course. Projects would be vetted, proposals assessed, terms agreed, at some distance from the man himself. And his approval would never be written, indeed often not spoken, but just made manifest in the form of a nod. If things went wrong, Wally stayed right, able to enjoy the fruits of his investments and bask in the respect and approval of his fellow citizens, to whom he appeared as a fair employer, a generous supporter of good causes, and a loving father.

This last at least was true. He had one son and heir. It was perhaps all he wanted because, contrary to the common run of things in which the new mother under pressure of all her new responsibilities shows a disinclination for sex, it was Wally who vacated the marriage bed after Liam's birth. His wife, a quiet, rather introverted young woman, neither complained about nor commented on this state of affairs for some five years until, rather belatedly catching a whiff of the rampant feminism strutting the streets of Mid-Yorkshire in the eighties, she appeared one night in her husband's room to petition for her rights only to find the situation already filled. By a muscular young man.

In divorces generally, judges are inclined to favour the mother in matters of custody. In cases like this, it is more than an inclination, it is almost an inevitability.

But Wally had turned to Chichevache, Bycorne and Belchamber who specialized in avoiding the inevitable. And Liam had grown up under the sole tutelage of his father.

And yet he had by no means turned out as his father might have wished him.

Loud, louche, and loutish, he made no effort to win the respect of the common citizenry, or indeed of anyone. He seemed to see it as his bounden duty to dispose of as much of his father's wealth as he could in the pursuit of personal pleasure with no regard whatsoever for the rights and comforts of others. And his father, apparently blind to his defects, did nothing to disabuse him of this belief. His eighteenth birthday present six months earlier had been a canary yellow Lamborghini Diablo and he'd already run up nine penalty points on his licence for speeding. In fact it was suggested by some that had it not been for Wally's standing in the community and close friendship with several members of the Bench, Liam would have been disqualified long since.

Well, that was between them and their conscience, thought

Pascoe as he headed straight round to the Linford mansion. What was more interesting to him was the fact that Liam had thought to enhance the beauty of his machine by having a grinning black skull stencilled on the bonnet.

There was a car in the driveway of Linford's house, but it was a Porsche, not a Lamborghini. Wally Linford himself answered the door, courteously invited him in. Liam was in the lounge, enjoying a drink with his friend, Duncan Robinson, known as Robbo, another young man whose parents had more money than anything else. Pascoe enquired after the Lamborghini. Oh yes, Liam replied, he had been driving it that night. He'd gone to the Trampus Club, met some friends, had a dance and a few drinks, just a few but he realized when he got up to leave that he might be over the limit, so like a good citizen he had accepted a lift home with his old mate, Robbo. Check it out, the Diablo should still be in Trampus's car park.

Pascoe made a call. They sat and waited. The reply came. The car wasn't there.

Shock! Horror! It must have been stolen, declared Liam.

And I'm to be Queen of the May, said Pascoe and arrested him. He tested positive both for booze and coke. Put him in the car and he was going down for a long, long time.

But this didn't prove easy. Robbo vigorously confirmed Liam's story, and several other people at the club recalled hearing the lift being offered and accepted before the two of them left together. The Diablo was found nearly eighty miles away, burned out, despite which Forensic managed to find enough traces of blood to make a match with the dead girl's. So it was definitely the accident vehicle, but the distance involved gave further support to Liam's story. No way would he have had time to drive that far, torch the car and get back home before Pascoe arrived to arrest him. CPS were shaking their heads very firmly.

Then a witness came forward, Oz Carnwath, a student at the local Poly earning some money by working at Trampus's as an occasional barman. He'd been dumping rubbish in the big wheelie bin at the rear door when he saw Liam and his friend cross the car park, each get in his own car, then drive away separately. He'd kept his mouth shut at first, not wanting to get involved, and believing that Liam would get his come-uppance without any help from himself. But when the youth reappeared in the club, boasting that he was home and free, this stuck in Carnwath's throat and he went to the police.

So far Robbo had stuck to his story, though not without uneasiness in face of Pascoe's assurance that, if Liam was found guilty, the police wouldn't rest till he joined him in jail for attempting to pervert the course of justice. But clearly he was even more scared of what Wally Linford would do if he came clean. In addition he must have been mightily reassured to see the firm of Chichevache, Bycorne and Belchamber retained for the defence.

But Pascoe suspected Wally wouldn't put all his trust in legalities, and ordered a close watch to be kept on Carnwath till they got his evidence into the record at the committal proceedings. So far the business with the lost undertaker had been the only scare. And yet . . .

He saw Marcus Belchamber coming through the main entrance of the court complex and felt relieved that soon the action would commence. Then it dawned on him that Belchamber was alone. No Liam. No Wally.

No sodding trial!

'Mr Pascoe, I'm so sorry, but it seems we are wasting our time today. Young Mr Linford is too ill to attend. Possibly the advance guard of this new flu virus which is rife in London. Kung Flu, they call it, a play I assume on Kung Fu, because it knocks you down and leaves you helpless. I have the necessary medical certificate, of course. Forgive me. I must go and apprise the Bench.'

The man smiled apologetically. One civilized cultured guardian of the law exchanging courtesies with another, both of them engaged in the great pursuit of justice.

And yet as Pascoe left the court he felt more stitched up than the Bayeux Tapestry.

ith Fat Andy being lunched by the Chief Constable and Pascoe locked in mortal combat with Marcus Belchamber, Wield anticipated having the Black Bull pretty much to himself. And if there were any junior colleagues taking advantage of their superiors' absence to linger late, one glower from the most frightening features in the Force would send them scurrying back to their desks.

But the two DCs he saw as he entered the bar showed no signs of scurrying.

They were Hat Bowler and Shirley Novello, deep in conversation. Slightly surprising, as he got the impression that Bowler regarded Novello as his most potent rival. Perhaps, both having been wounded in the line of duty, they were swapping scars.

They stopped talking as he approached.

'Nice to see you, lad,' he said. 'When are you due back? Wednesday, isn't it? Breaking yourself in gradual, is that the idea?'

'Actually, I was hoping to see you, Sarge,' said Hat.

'Is that right?' said Wield. 'I'll just get myself a pie and a pint first.'

'My shout,' said Novello.

As she waited at the bar, she saw Bowler talking earnestly to Wield. She guessed he was telling him the story of returning to his girlfriend's flat and finding it burgled. He'd come in, looking for Wield, but when she told him that the sergeant had gone out at the end of the morning and not reappeared yet, he had started talking to her, not because he regarded her as a confidante, she guessed, but merely as a rehearsal for what he was going to say to Wield. She suspected there was more to his tale than he'd told her, but now that his true audience was here, she'd probably get to hear the lot.

When she returned to the table Bowler was just reaching a rhetorical climax.

'So, you see, it's got to be Charley Penn!' he pronounced with all the fervour of Galileo reaching the end of his detailed proof that the earth went round the sun.

Wield was regarding him with all the enthusiasm of an over-worked Inquisition officer who didn't fancy having to attend yet another bonfire at the height of an Italian summer.

'Why so?' he said.

'Because Lorelei's that German stuff he messes with, and because he hates me and Rye, and because I've got a description . . . oh hell!'

'Well well well! What's this? A wounded heroes' conference? It's purple hearts all round! And mine's a pint!'

Andy Dalziel had burst through the bar-room door, radiating more geniality then a Harrods Santa Claus, but Hat Bowler flinched away from the glow like a scientist in the presence of a reactor gone critical.

How could this be? he asked himself aghast. Hadn't he in his cleverness rung the station and established that Pascoe was in court and the Fat Man wasn't expected back from lunch with the Chief before dusk, leaving the way clear for him to button-hole Wield in the Bull?

What Bowler hadn't made allowances for was that chief con-stables earned their extra thousands by being even cleverer than detective constables. Dan Trimble, knowing from experience that lunch with Dalziel could blend imperceptibly into high tea then supper, had arranged to be bleeped by his secretary. The bleep had come with their puddings, the meal already having begun to stretch, but the loss of a crème brulée seemed a small price to pay for an early escape. He made a brief phone call, put on a concerned look, then explained with much apology that urgent business required his instant return to his office. 'No need for you to rush, Andy,' he said as he rose. 'Enjoy your pudding. Have a drink with your coffee. I'll leave the bill open.'

Trimble was a decent man and it was guilt that made him utter these words, but the guilt even of a decent man is a delicate flower and his had faded before he reached his car, leaving him asking himself, aghast, 'Did I really say that?'

Behind him Dalziel finished his bread and butter pudding, sampled the Chief's crème brulée, ordered two more with the comment, 'Tell the chef this is nice nosh, only he don't give a man enough to put in his eye!' then, washing down his Stilton with a large port, he applied himself to the serious business of choosing what malt to drink while his coffee went cold.

Despite this he was on his way back to the station at half past two, which was a lot earlier than he'd anticipated. He was in a taxi, having gone to the restaurant in the Chief's official car, and thinking it a shameful thing for a man to have no better place to go to on an afternoon he'd regarded as taken care of than his place of work, he commanded the driver to divert to the Black Bull.

He paid off the cab with a generous tip which went down on the receipt he collected to send to Trimble's office for reimbursement. The thought of the Chief's face when he saw it (hopefully at the same time as he registered the extra crème brulées and the malts) had filled him with a delight which had bubbled over into his somewhat over-effusive reaction at the sight of Hat Bowler.

'What did I say, Wieldy?' he went on. 'Out of his hospital bed and into his lass's, he'll be so full of vim, he'll not be able to wait to get back to work! Isn't that what I said?'

'Not as such,' said Wield, observing that young Bowler, once Dalziel's *bete noir*, did not seem delighted at his apparent upgrading to palace favourite, even though it was in the presence of Novello, his main rival for the spot. She had returned from the bar with Dalziel's drink. To get Wield's, she'd had to wait her turn, but at the sight of Dalziel, Jolly Jack, the lugubrious landlord, had pulled a pint in a reaction worth a Pavlovian paper.

'There's that not as such again, Wieldy,' reproved the Fat Man, sinking into a chair and taking his glass from Novello.

He drank half of it like a traveller in an antique land who hadn't seen liquid for many a hot day, and said, 'Thanks, Ivor. Now what's the crack?'

Wield hesitated. He'd already begun to suss there was something not quite right about this burglary report. The youngster had escorted his girlfriend home after what had been (if Wield read the signs right) a sexually and emotionally successful holiday and had found her flat had been burgled. Naturally, being a DC, the boy would have promised to kick-start a thorough CID investigation. Which a phone call would have done. Instead of which Bowler had turned up at the Bull and, what was even odder, a couple of hours must have lapsed since the burglary.

There were other things too, and Wield would have been happy to let the full story emerge at the DC's own pace. But now the case was altered.

He said, 'DC Bowler was just reporting a burglary to me, sir.'

'Ee, that's champion. On the job, off the job, back on the job, all in the twinkle of an eye. That's the stuff a good detective's made of. So, fill me in, lad.'

With all the enthusiasm of a politician admitting a bribe, Hat began his story again.

Dalziel soon interrupted, picking up points Wield had not yet commented upon.

'So nowt taken. She says. You believe her?'

'Of course.' Indignantly. 'Why should she lie?'

'Summat she was embarrassed by. Sex aids. Pictures of her six illegitimate kids. Summat she didn't care to tell a cop about. Bag of shit. Bundles of used notes she'd got on the black and wasn't going to let on to the Revenue about. Summat she didn't want her employers to hear about. Expensive books she'd liberated from the reference library. Why should a woman lie about anything, lad? Mebbe just because they've got a talent for it! Am I right or am I right, Ivor?'

Shirley Novello said, 'You know I think you're always right about everything, sir.'

Dalziel looked at her suspiciously, then his face lit up and he exploded into laughter.

'There, young Bowler, see what I mean! Fortunately us fellows have got a talent for sussing out lies, or ought to have. So, I'll ask you again. You believe your lass?'

'Yes,' said Hat sullenly.

'That your head or your hormones speaking?'

'My head.'

'Grand. No sign of forced entry, you say?'

'Couple of little scratches round the lock, but nothing positive.'

'Never mind, we'll know for sure when we take the lock to pieces.'

Hat looked even more unhappy, but the Fat Man was in full spate.

'So, just this message on her computer then. OK, what's it say?'

'Bye bye Lorelei.'

'Lorelei? What's that? Hang about. Weren't Lorelei the name of someone in a film . . .'

'*Gentlemen Prefer Blondes*. Marilyn Monroe,' said Wield.

'You been checking on the opposition, Wieldy? Lovely girl. Shame about yon fellow.'

Whether Dalziel's objection was to baseball players, playwrights or Kennedys wasn't clear, nor about to be made so as he pressed on. 'So what's its significance here? Come on, lad. Don't tell me you've not got a theory. When I were your age I had as many theories as I had erections, and I couldn't go upstairs on a bus without getting an erection.'

Hat took a deep breath and said, 'Well, sir, Lorelei's a sort of water nymph in this German fairy tale. There's this big rock or cliff on the Rhine, that's called the Lorelei too, and she sits there singing, and it's so beautiful that fishermen sailing by get distracted listening to her and run their boats on the rock and drown.'

'Used to feel like that about Doris Day,' said Dalziel. 'Sounds like one of them sirens.'

'They're Greek I think, sir,' said Wield.

'All in the bloody European Union, aren't they?' said the Fat Man, his geniality beginning to fade like morning dew. Airy-fairyness he could put up with from his DCI when more down to earth approaches were looking unproductive, but it wasn't something he encouraged in DCs making preliminary reports about burglaries. 'So we're into a German fairy tale now. Hope it's got a happy ending, lad.'

Bowler, who was beginning to learn that life with Dalziel meant having to put up with four injustices before breakfast, pressed on manfully.

'I looked it up. Seems this German poet, Heine, wrote a poem about this Lorelei . . .'

'Hold on. This yon Heinz that Charley Penn's always going on about?' said Dalziel suspiciously.

'Heine, yes,' said Hat.

'I thought I heard you mention Charley when I came into the room,' said Dalziel. 'I hope this isn't leading where I think it's leading?'

It was time to get this out in the open, thought Wield.

He said, 'Yes, sir, DC Bowler was just telling me of three links he made putting Penn in the frame. The message was one, the second was . . . remind me, Hat.'

'Because he hates Rye, and me,' said Bowler.

'Charley Penn hates every bugger,' said Dalziel. 'What makes you two so special?'

'Because we were both involved in the death of his best friend, Dick Dee,' said Hat defiantly. 'I'm sure he doesn't believe Dee was the Wordman. And he reckons that I killed Dee because I was jealous that he was getting it off with Rye, and that the pair of us covered it up by fitting Dee up with responsibility for the Wordman killings. And you all went along with it because it meant you could tell the media you'd got the bastard.'

Now Dalziel was right out of Santa Claus mode.

'You reckon that's what Charley thinks?' he said. 'He's not said it to me, but you'll know that, seeing he's not walking round with his head shoved up his arse. Wieldy?'

'He said some pretty way-out things to start with,' admitted the sergeant. 'But since then I've not heard him sounding off.'

'That could be because he thinks it's pointless making a fuss and he's planning to do something,' said Hat.

'Like breaking into your girlfriend's flat?' said Dalziel. 'Why?'

'Looking for something to support his story, I suppose. Or maybe he thought he'd find her there and . . .' Hat tailed off, not wanting to encourage them to follow him down the alleys of his more lurid imaginings.

Then, seeing the scepticism on their faces, he burst out, 'And he was round there a couple of days ago, I'm ninety-nine per cent sure of it. I went and knocked at some doors in Church View. And I got two witnesses, Mrs Gilpin who lives on one side of Rye and Mrs Rogers on the other. They both saw a strange man outside Rye's flat last Saturday morning, and the description they gave fits Charley Penn to a T.'

This was stretching things a bit. True, Mrs Gilpin, a voluble lady who had lived in the block long enough to regard it as her personal fiefdom, had described a skulking villainous creature who with only a little prompting had been shaped into Penn. But Mrs Rogers, a younger but much more retiring woman, had at first said that, having only just moved in, she didn't really know which people she saw were residents, which visitors. At this point Mrs Gilpin, who unbeknown to Hat had followed him to Mrs Rogers' door, came in with a graphic description which the other woman, perhaps in self-defence, admitted put her in mind of someone she thought she might have seen perhaps on Saturday morning. Upon which Hat, fearful that the sound of Mrs Gilpin's voice, which a town-crier would not have been ashamed to own, might bring Rye to her door, had swiftly brought the interviews to a conclusion.

Wield's face didn't show much, but his words made it clear he was starting to feel annoyed.

'You're admitting that you discovered a crime and, instead of ringing it in and getting a proper investigation under way, you wasted time poking around, disturbing the ground and probably making sure anything you did find will get tagged as inadmissible in court?'

'No, Sarge. Well, yes, in a way. But not really.'

'We'll be into not-as-such land just now,' said Dalziel. 'I'm a fair man, young Bowler, and I'll not see someone hanged without giving him a chance for an explanation, so why don't you have a stab at one while I tie this knot?'

'The thing is, there isn't a crime, sir. I mean, there's a crime, but there isn't a complaint. Rye, Miss Pomona, says she doesn't want to pursue it.'

Now all was clear to Wield. The love-sick lad's investigation had to be unofficial because officially there was nothing to investigate. He'd come to the Bull in search of a sympathetic ear, and while the sergeant felt faintly flattered that he'd been the sympathetic ear that Hat had come in search of, he wondered what it was the boy had expected him to do. Nothing, possibly. Maybe the sympathy would have been enough.

Dalziel said, 'Well, God's jocks, now I've heard it all. Wasting police time on a load of nowt . . .'

'I'm still on sick leave, sir, so it's my own time I'm wasting,' snapped Hat unwisely.

'I'm not talking about your sodding time, which I agree isn't worth much,' grated Dalziel. 'I'm talking about my time, which is worth millions, and the sergeant's time, which is worth quite a lot. Tell me this, lad. You're quick enough to spout accusations against Penn. You find something bad about your girl, you going to be as quick letting us know?'

Hat did not answer.

'Right. Then sod off out of here and next time I see you, bedtime 'ull be over and I'll not make allowances.'

Hat, blank faced, only a certain rigidity around the shoulders indicating any feeling, left, not closing the door behind him because he didn't trust himself not to slam it.

The Fat Man glowered after him then redirected the glower at Shirley Novello.

'Let that be a lesson to you, lass.'

'Yes, sir. What about, sir?'

'About the price of tea, what d'you think? And while you're at it, what *do* you think?'

'I think being in love doesn't necessarily make a man stupid, sir.'

'Aye, but it helps mebbe. You not got any work to do, lass?'

'Yes. What about you?' was the answer that orbited Novello's mind without getting anywhere near escape velocity. She was also wondering, being the kind of cop who could think of several things at the same time, whether she should mention the broken vase containing the ashes of Pomona's twin brother. Hat had mentioned this as he poured out the story to her, and maybe her raised eyebrow reaction had kept it out of the version he gave both Wield and Dalziel. Probably wise. She shuddered to think what the Fat Man would have made of it. As for herself, the questions to answer were, was it relevant? And was there any professional advantage in revealing it?

Answer to both at the moment was, not so far as she could see.

'Just going, sir,' she said. And went.

'So, Wieldy, what do you make of it?'

The sergeant shrugged, 'Owt or nowt, sir.'

'Aye. Owt or nowt,' said Dalziel thoughtfully. 'I'll have a word with Penn. You watch Bowler, OK? I think the bugger's given me indigestion. I'd best have another pint.'

Wield took the hint and stood up. When he returned, the Fat Man was eating his pie.

'Glad to see that lunch with the Chief hasn't spoilt your appetite, sir,' he said.

'Watch it! Sarcasm I'll take from buggers with letters after their name, they can't help it. But sergeants ought to talk as plain as they look.'

This looked like a cue, so Wield told him about the Praesidium heist tip.

'Bit vague. No names? Times? Details?'

'No, sir.'

'Source reliable?'

'Can't say, sir. This is a first.'

'Aye, but in your judgment?'

Wield considered then said, 'Don't think they'd deliberately jerk me around, but that doesn't mean they're not just trying to impress.'

'And how much did this excuse for a tip-off cost us?' said Dalziel.

'Nothing. Down to civic duty.'

'Oh, aye? Don't see much of that these days. Not getting yourself a fan club, are you, Wieldy?' said Dalziel, shooting him that keen glance which was one of the few missiles Wield did not feel his inscrutable features a complete defence against.

'Just came up in casual conversation,' he said.

'Bit too bloody casual for me. Not till Friday, but? That gives

134

you time to see if you can get a bit of flesh on your new chum's bones then. By God, this pie's good. Jack must've changed his barber. You not eating, Wieldy?'

'No, sir. Things to do. See you back at the station.'

He rose, intending to make a dash for the door, when it opened and Pascoe came in.

'My God,' said Dalziel. 'What's up wi' thee? You look like a hen that got shagged by an ostrich and feels an egg coming on. And why aren't you in court?'

'Postponed till tomorrow. Belchamber says his client's too ill to attend. Reckons he's got this Kung Flu.'

'Kung arseholes! And the beak bought it?'

'Belchamber produced a doctor's certificate. But give the beak his due, he said, "All right, same time Wednesday, but take notice, Mr Belchamber. If your client is still too ill to attend, we shall proceed in his absence." Which got an unctuous reassurance and a little apologetic glance in my direction. There's something about that bastard . . . I need a drink.'

'I'll have one with you. Man shouldn't drink alone.'

The Fat Man watched Pascoe go to the bar, then said, 'Don't often see Pete letting someone rattle his cage, not unless he's called Roote. What do you think, Wieldy? Yon greaseball Belchamber up to summat?'

'Wouldn't know, sir.'

'Why not? He's one of yours, isn't he?'

'Meaning gay?' said Wield unfazed. 'Wouldn't surprise me, but it doesn't mean we meet in the Turkish baths and exchange confidences. How about you in the Gents, sir?'

This was a good riposte, but not a counter accusation. 'The Gents' was short for the Mid-Yorkshire Gentlemen's Club, of which Dalziel was a member mainly because so many people had wanted to blackball him.

'Most on 'em think the sun shines out of his arse,' said Dalziel. 'Wankers. Couldn't separate steak from kidney in a pudding.'

Wield looked sadly at the few crumbs of his pie remaining on the plate, then took his leave once more and made for the door. Pascoe returned from the bar with two pints. Normally he wasn't much of a beer drinker at lunchtime, but the Belcher left a nasty taste.

As he sat down he said, 'Sir. I've been thinking . . .'

'Sod thinking. Try drinking. All things come to him who sups.'

Pascoe raied his glass.

'For once, sir,' he said, 'you may be right. Kill all the lawyers!'

'I'll drink to that,' said Dalziel.

The Cemetery

usk comes early even on the brightest December day and when the clouds sag low like dusty drapes over an abandoned bier, there's never much more light than you'll catch in the gloaming of a dead man's eyes.

So though it was not yet four o'clock, the streetlamps of Peg Lane were already kindling as Rye Pomona slipped out of Church View.

Under her arm she carried a Hoover bag.

At first she had tried with brush and pan to retrieve the fine ash which, if the undertaker were to be believed, comprised the selfsame molecules that had once danced around each other to form the limbs and organs of her beloved twin, Sergius.

But, do what she might, shards of china, household dust, carpet fluff, and all the cosmetic debris of her bedroom had been inseparably commingled in the pan while traces of ash remained beyond the reach of bristle in cracks and crannies from which it could only be summoned by Gabriel's trumpet on Judgment Day.

Or a Hoover if you couldn't wait that long.

This was the gallows humour with which she diverted herself as she went about the task of vacuuming her room. What else could she do? Sing a hymn? Speak a prayer? No, Serge would have found the absurdity of the situation hilarious and she would not let him down by relapsing into maudlin solemnity.

In fact, come to think of it, Serge would have found the whole business of keeping his ashes in a jar on her bedroom shelf ridiculous. 'Abso-fucking-lutely typical!' she could hear him cry. 'I always said you were made for the stage. You're a true-born drama queen!' Well, the accident had ended her career plans. Not much future even in this age of teleprompts for an actress whose mind went blank not just of her lines but of language itself whenever she walked onstage. But, oh! how small a price this seemed to be to pay for causing the death of her closest kin, her dearest friend, the better half of herself. And the Furies had thought so too, pursuing her to the frontiers of madness – no, beyond – in their quest for retribution. She should have been warned. The records of history and of literature are unanimous. Only the detail varies of the horrors that invariably attend all man's attempts to raise the dead. That period of her life seemed to her now like a journey through a Gothic landscape by night whose veil of dark was torn aside from time to time by brief jags of lightning to show sights that made the returning blackness welcome. That journey was over, thank God, but the past was not another country which you could simply leave behind. Travel as far and as fast as you could, there were parts of it you dragged with you. Only Hat offered her any hope of freedom. With him she found complete if temporary oblivion. In him she regained all she had lost and more. The half of herself that died with Sergius had been the irreplaceable closeness of kin, but in Hat's embrace she found a new completeness of kith which promised to make her whole again.

But the Kindly Ones know their stuff. Guilt, horror, self-loathing, these are coals of the selfsame fire. Heap them high and they can get no hotter. There is a deep which has no lower; a worst where pangs wring no wilder. So what's a frustrated Fury to do?

Aeons past they had learned their answer.

You don't pour water on a drowning man, you show him dry land.

Waking in Hat's arms, for a moment she could look ahead to a green and pleasant landscape whose rolling hills were bathed in golden sunshine. And then a band of white-hot metal snapped around her skull and her head was twisted round till she saw once more what it was she trailed behind her.

She was a murderer; worse, a serial killer, one of those monsters they paraded before you on tele-documentaries, inviting you to marvel how ordinary they seemed, to speculate what warped gene, what ruined childhood had brought them to this monstrosity.

She had killed nine people – no, not that many – the first two, the AA man and the boy with the bazouki, she had only assisted at their deaths, which she had taken as signs that she was on the right track – a track which had led her beyond all mathematical equivocation to seven indisputable murders, by knife, by poison, by gunshot, by electrocution . . .

Deluded (it was a delusion. Wasn't it? She knew that now. Didn't she?) into believing that through an alphabetically sign-posted trail of blood she could come once more to her dead brother, and talk with him, and give him back something of that lost life her wilful selfish stupidity had stolen from him, she had done these dreadful things. And not unwillingly, not under constraint, but eventually with eagerness, with glee even, revel-ling in her sense of power, of invulnerability, until the trail led her to her last victim, her boss at the library, Dick Dee, a man she liked and admired.

That was torment enough to give her pause. And when she saw the imagined signs pointing clearly towards the man she was coming to love, to Hat Bowler, she began to wake as it were from a dream, only to find herself pinned by black memory in a nightmare.

Was atonement possible? Or – God forbid – relapse?

She did not know. Nothing, she knew nothing . . . sometimes even the horrors seemed so far beyond her comprehension that she almost believed they had indeed been a dream . . . she needed help, she knew that . . . but who was there to talk to? Only Hat, and that was unthinkable.

So forget the future, she had no future, she had exchanged it for the past. Hardly a fair swap, screamed the Furies. We want change! But it would have to do. We creep under what comfort we can find in a whirlwind.

Getting rid of Sergius's ashes wasn't a step forward, but it was a step in that marking of time which kept her in the present.

Ashes to ashes . . . dust to the dustbin. That was the obvious way to dispose of them. But she found herself unable to do it.

Instead, holding the bag tight against her breast, she crossed the narrow road and pushed open the squeaky gate into the churchyard. Ahead loomed the tower, black on dark grey against the wintry sky. This was an old burial place. Here a marbled angel folded her grieving wings, there a granite obelisk pointed an accusing finger at the sky, but for the most part the memorials were modest headstones, many so flaky and lichened their messages to the living were almost impossible to trace with finger or with eye. Few were of such recent vintage that family members still kept them tidy or laid anniversary flowers. A cold wind whispered through the long grass and a hunting cat miaowed an almost silent protest at her for interrupting his patient vigil, then sinewed away.

Distantly she could perceive the glow of the populous city and hear the chitter of its traffic, but these lights and sounds had nothing to do with her. She stood like a ghost in a ghostly world whose insubstantiality was her proper medium now. Some memory might remain in this other place of that other place, but the laws of physics by which mortals walk and drive and fly over the earth and by which the earth itself and all the planets and all the stars swing round each other in their crazy reel, were the dreams of an amoeba. She felt as if she could float up through the looming tower and with one small step be on the invisible moon.

You stupid bitch! she said to herself in an attempt at a rescuing anger. Getting rid of Serge's ashes is meant to be a move away from all this crazy crap!

And with a series of movements like an orgasmic spasm, she shook the dust out of the Hoover bag.

The wind caught it and for a moment she could see the fine powder twisting and coiling in the air as if trying to hold together and reconstitute itself in some living form.

Then it was gone.

She turned away, eager to be out of this place.

And shrieked as she saw a figure standing beside an ancient headstone which leaned to one side as if something had just pushed it over to open a passage from the grave.

'I'm sorry,' said a voice. 'I didn't mean to startle you, but I was worried . . . are you all right?'

Not Serge! A woman. She was relieved. And disappointed? God, would it never stop?

'Yes, I'm fine. Why shouldn't I be? And who the hell are you?'

Speaking abruptly was the easiest way to control her voice.

'Mrs Rogers . . . I think we're neighbours . . . it is Ms Pomona, isn't it?'

'Yes. My neighbour, you say?'

Her eyes, accustomed now to the dark, could make out the woman's features. Mid to late thirties perhaps, a round face, not unattractive without being remarkable, her expression a mixture of embarrassment and concern.

'Yes. Just since last week though. We haven't met but I saw you going into your flat a couple of times. I was just walking down the lane now and I saw you . . . I'm sorry . . . none of my business . . . sorry if I startled you.'

She gave a nervous smile and began to turn away. Not once had her gaze gone to the Hoover bag – which must have been quite an effort, thought Rye. You spot someone emptying their vacuum cleaner in a churchyard, you're entitled to wonder if there's anything wrong!

'No, hold on,' she said. 'You're going back to Church View? I'll walk with you.'

She fell into step beside Mrs Rogers and said, 'My name's Rye. Like the whisky. Sorry I was so brusque, but you gave me a shock.'

'I'm Myra. I'm sorry but I thought that anything in a place like this . . . even a polite cough's going to sound a bit creepy!'

'Especially a polite cough,' said Rye, laughing. 'Which flat are you then?'

'The other side of you from Mrs Gilpin.'

'Ah, you've met Mrs Gilpin. No surprise there. Not meeting Mrs Gilpin is the hard thing.'

'Yes,' smiled the other woman. 'She did seem quite . . . interested.'

'Oh, she's certainly that.'

They had reached the gate. Across the road they saw a figure standing at the front door of Church View. It was Hat.

Rye came to a halt. She wanted to see him but she didn't want him to see her, not coming from the churchyard with a Hoover bag in her hand.

Mrs Rogers said, 'Isn't that the detective?'

'Detective?'

'Yes, the one who was round earlier asking if we'd seen anyone suspicious hanging around the building over the weekend.'

'Ah. That detective,' said Rye coldly.

She watched Hat out of sight along the street, then opened the gate.

'And did you see anyone?' she asked.

'Well, there was a man last Saturday morning. I hardly noticed him, but Mrs Gilpin seems to have got a closer look.'

'I'm amazed. Look, do you fancy coming in for a coffee? Unless your husband's expecting you . . .'

'Not any more,' said Myra Rogers. 'That's why I needed to find a new flat. Yes, a coffee would be lovely. Are you planning to use that bag again?'

They were at the front door and Mrs Rogers looked significantly down the basement steps to where the building's rubbish bins stood.

'My domestic economy hasn't sunk that low,' said Rye, smiling.

She went down the steps, took the lid off a bin and dumped the empty bag inside.

'Now let's get that coffee,' she said.

Sunday Dec 16th

Night,
somewhere in England,
heading north

Dear Mr Pascoe

It was only a few hours since I posted my last letter to
you, and yet it seems light years away! Train travel does
that to you, doesn't it? Stop time, I mean.

You will recall I was on the point of leaving
Cambridge in the company of Professor Dwight Duerden
of Santa Apollonia University, CA. During the drive to
London we talked naturally enough about the recent
unhappy events at God's, and Dwight returned once more
to his theme of good from evil, urging me to at least
explore the possibility of completing Sam's book myself
and finding a new publisher. He would be returning to
St Poll for the holidays, and he promised me again that he
would make enquiry of his university press. When we
arrived at the Ritz we exchanged addresses and farewells
and he instructed his driver to take me anywhere I wanted.

I had travelled to Cambridge via London, spending
the night at Linda's flat in Westminster, and, rather than
risk the purgatory of a Sunday train journey, I decided to
take advantage of her kindness again, so that's where I told
the driver to go. The flat is a hangover from the days
when Linda was an MP before she spread her wings and
flew to Europe. It's quite small – a tiny bedroom and a
tinier sitting room plus a shower – but comfortable
enough and conveniently placed. So, having a longish
lease, she decided to keep it on as a pied-à-terre. A crone
who lives a troglodyte existence in the basement has
charge of the spare key and, if you're on the list of

favoured friends, it provides a nice central location to lay your head on a visit to town.

On my first visit, the scowling crone had required three proofs of identity before she would hand over the key. This time I got a friendlier welcome, but I soon realized this was down to the pleasure of telling me I was too late, the flat was already occupied.

That's the trouble with generous people, they can be so indiscriminate.

I was turning away when she tried to rub salt in my wounds by making it clear it was no use me dossing down on a park bench and coming back in the morning.

'It's Miss Lupin's foreign clerical friend,' she said. 'He'll be staying several days.'

'Not Frère Jacques?' I said. 'Is he in? I must say hello.'

And I ran up the stairs before she could reply.

I had to knock twice before Jacques opened the door. He was clad in slacks and a string vest and looked a bit ruffled. But he smiled broadly to see me and I stepped inside without waiting for an invitation. And stopped dead when I saw he wasn't alone.

There was a young woman sitting on the solitary armchair.

Now Jacques is a man of indisputable holiness but also a man, if I am any judge, in whom the testosterone runs free, and it wouldn't have surprised me to find that his love of things English included our gorgeous girls.

But the easy way he introduced me was so guilt-free that I reproved myself for my suspicions, and even more so when I realized what he was saying.

This lovely young woman regarding me with an indifference worse than hostility was Emerald Lupin, Linda's daughter. Even if innate holiness and religious vows weren't enough to keep the old Adam at bay, surely, being a man of considerable good sense, Jacques wasn't going to take the slightest risk of getting up the nose of one of his movement's most influential patrons!

146

It occurs to me that I am assuming in you an at least passing familiarity with the Third Thought Movement, but in case I'm wrong, let me give you the briefest of outlines.

To begin at the beginning, which in this case is the movement's founder, Frère Jacques. He is a brother of the Cornelians, an Order little known outside the region of Belgium which contains its sole monastery, L'Abbaye du Saint Graal. From various sources I gather that Jacques led an active life as a soldier till he was invalided out of the army seriously wounded during service in a UN peace-keeping unit. Happily for him, and for all of us, his birthplace was close by the Cornelian Abbaye and a relapse necessitated a move to their Infirmary, followed by a long convalescence in their Stranger House. During this time he experienced that sense of peace and acceptance of whatever must come which later he was to formulate into the Third Thought philosophy, and eventually he presented himself to the monks as a candidate for admission to their order.

Their vote was unanimous. I say vote because the Cornelians are peculiar in that all major decisions are taken by the full brotherhood, one monk, one vote. Indeed they are a very liberal and democratic Order, which perhaps explains why Rome not too secretly hopes they will wither on the vine. Their founder, Pope Cornelius, you will recall, was banished and beheaded after a bitter doctrinal dispute in which he argued the Church's capacity to forgive apostates and other mortal sinners. Not much sign that he'd win the argument today, is there?

Jacques, not unnaturally, had found himself much preoccupied by death, particularly death unexpected, which it is, he assures me, even in battle. You always think it will be the next guy! He himself had grown up in the heart of the great Flanders killing grounds where it's still not possible to spend an hour digging in your garden without turning up a button or a bullet or a piece of bone, and none of this had put him off joining the army.

But his own close encounter had been something of an epiphany, and as he worked in the hospice section of the abbey infirmary, it occurred to him that while the patients there all knew that the end was in sight and were preconditioned to try and come to terms with it, for the vast majority of people, it was a bolt from the blue.

Something happens, we turn out to be the next guy, and which of us is ready?

What was needed, he decided, was a kind of hospice of the mind, a state of life like his own during his stay in the Infirmary and Stranger House, which admitted rather than ignored death, a condition of mind like Prospero's when he returned to Milan where, he says, *every third thought shall be my grave.*

Thus was born Third Thought Therapy, whose aim, simply stated, is to give Death his proper standing in our lives, even when youth, health, happiness and prosperity seem to make him an irrelevance. Then whenever he comes, he will not find us unprepared.

But even Jacques would find it hard to spare a thought for death in the presence of Emerald Lupin!

I knew Linda had a couple of daughters, but I suppose I'd pictured them as young clones of Linda herself. Don't misunderstand me. Though far from conventionally beautiful, Linda is not unattractive in a formidable way, like one of those pele towers in the Border country which age and weathering have given a Romantic cast. In her youth, however, I would guess that Linda, like a tower newly built, was just plain daunting!

But Emerald . . . ! How shall I convey her to you? Think summer, think sunshine, think golden roses filling the bowers with rich perfume, think soft white doves tumbling through clear blue air – oh, think whatever you judge loveliest and liveliest and most desirable in the worlds of flesh and spirit, and you may get a glimpse of this fair jewel.

Do I sound as if I'm in love? Perhaps I am. There's a first for everything!

It was explained to me (in too much detail?) that Emerald too had turned up unexpectedly and found Jacques in occupation. Being family she did not require the intermediacy of the crone but had her own key. She had burst in upon him in mid-toilette, but her natural spontaneity and his Continental sang-froid had lifted them high above embarrassment and they'd settled to a debate as to who should vacate the field.

I doubt if Emerald would have had any qualms about dispossessing me if I'd got there first. But she was bent on assuring Jacques that London was full of friends gagging to offer her hospitality. I believed it. Who in their right mind would turn her away?

Another factor in giving Jacques possession now appeared in the form of his personal ghost, Frère Dierick, who was going to bed down in the sitting-room chair. He'd been out viewing the sights and seemed as unimpressed by them as he clearly was by sight of me. But the notebook came out of his robe straightaway to record even the most monosyllabic utterance of his great guru.

Jacques had come to London to help promote the English version of his new book propounding the Third Thought philosophy. He presented me with a copy complete with a flattering inscription, which I let Emerald see in the hope that she'd dilute her bad opinion, but she didn't seem impressed. Can't say I blame her. Authors give away their books like drug barons give free snorts, hoping to start an expensive addiction.

So it was settled. Jacques would remain *in situ* while Emerald went off to a friend's.

'But what about you, Franny?' said Jacques. 'Perhaps we can squeeze you in here?'

The thought of a night spent in close proximity to Dierick didn't appeal, so I said that if I hurried I could execute Plan B, which was catching the last train back to Mid-Yorkshire from King's Cross.

'I'm heading up to Islington,' said Emerald. 'I can give you a lift.'

She's warming to me! I thought. Or she just wants to make sure I catch my train!

I accepted, Jacques said he'd come along for the ride, Dierick was told firmly by Emerald there wouldn't be room for him in her small car, and the three of us set off. On the stairs, I excused myself, saying I'd meant to use the loo and now it was urgent.

The tiny loo was off the bedroom. I really did want to use it, believe me, but I couldn't help noticing as I passed the bed that the coverlet was pretty crumpled. OK, so Jacques had had a lie-down. I did what I had to do and came out. Perhaps there is a bit of the detective in me too, Mr Pascoe, which is why I feel such an affinity with you, but I found myself crouching to look under the bed. And there I found — I know this sounds squalid — a used condom! I felt no shock or surprise, only a little envy.

'What are you doing?' asked a cold voice.

I looked up to see Frère Dierick standing over me.

I have no excuse for what I did then. I should have told a lie about dropping some money or something. Instead I stood up with the condom between finger and thumb, pulled open the pocket in his robe where he kept his notebook, and dropped it in, saying, 'There you go, Dierick. Make sure you put that in your notes.'

Then I trotted off to join the others.

At King's Cross, Jacques said he would see me on to my train. Emerald, illegally parked, had to stay with the car. Not that she'd have wanted to come anyway, I thought disconsolately. But to my surprise, as I stooped to say my thanks, she gave me a peck on the cheek and wished me safe journey.

And as we walked to my platform, Jacques took the chance to fill me in on Emerald.

I knew no more of Linda's family background than that she'd once been married to Harry Lupin, the cut-price airline entrepreneur. After the divorce, Linda got custody of the two children, Emerald, then aged eight, and her sister Musetta, seven. (The latter, it seems, takes after her mother. All the gorgeous genes in the family came Emerald's way.)

Emerald after a couple of years got fed up of coming second to politics and decided she wanted to live with Daddy. Six months later, realizing she was now coming third to business and bimbos, she returned to her mother, and thereafter shuttled between both parents and the country's top boarding schools, each of which in turn declared her uncontrollable and ineducable. Now at twenty she is in her final year at Oxford.

Meanwhile Musetta, known to her intimates as Mouse, lived down to her sobriquet by keeping very quiet and only emerging from her nest for food. She's some kind of teacher in Strasbourg, and, as Jacques put it, working on the principle that we love most the apple that falls closest to the tree, she is the pippin of her mother's eye.

Emerald on the other hand seems to have bounced and rolled a long long way.

Without saying anything which would have stood up in a court of law, Jacques conveyed a strong warning that if I wanted to maintain my good relationship with Linda, I should adopt a rigorous hands-off approach to either or both of her daughters.

You old hypocrite! I thought, recalling the condom.

But then I looked into those bright blue eyes in that most open and attractive of faces, and I felt ashamed. How could I condemn him for doing what I longed to do?

We embraced with real feeling. It's been a long time since someone hugged me in that affectionate familial way. I don't recall my father, and my mother was never a hugger. But my thoughts as I sat on the train were all of Emerald. I clung desperately to that final peck on the cheek she'd given me. Wasn't there something of affection in that too? Perhaps she's screwing Jacques merely as an act of defiance against her mother?

I needed help, I needed reassurance. For want of anything else, I dug Jacques' book out of my bag to see if his words could bring me any peace of mind and body.

I let fate open the pages, and lo! the first paragraph my gaze fell upon was this.

> *To say that man must die alone is a trite and fallacious cynicism. Find if you can a man or woman – friend, guru, mentor, father-figure, mother-figure, use what term you will – but someone you can view as the still centre of all your turbulent thoughts – someone before whom you can pour out unstintingly and without reserve all your hopes and fears and passions and desires – and you will have taken a large step towards that peace of mind which is the end of all our endeavours.*

And it hit me, this is what I have found in you, dear Mr Pascoe! This is what I am doing now, writing another letter to you on this oh so slow train journey north. Out there night presses on the grimy window. Lights move by – traffic, street lamps, urban houses, isolated cottages – all indicative of human presence, I know, but not of human community; no, they might as well be will-o'-the-wisps flitting across some dreary bog for all the comfort they bring. And my fellow passengers, each cocooned in that private time capsule we enter on a long train journey, might as well be alien beings from a distant galaxy.

But I have you, and it hardly matters if I think of you as guru or friend or even, despite your youth, the father-figure I never knew. What does matter is my awareness now that whatever my initial motivation in writing, I am using you as a Third Thought Therapy! I hope you don't mind. Perhaps you might find it in you to reply to me, or even (dare I ask it), call round to see me now I'm back in Mid-Yorkshire? Which is where, incredibly, the Dalek in control of the train intercom system has just announced that shortly we will be arriving.

Oh dream of joy! is this indeed The light-house top I

see? Is this the hill? Is this the kirk? Is this mine own countree?

I do believe it is. I'll finish this tomorrow.

Hello again! How quickly things change. Just in case you did think of dropping in on me over the next few days, don't bother, I'm not here. Or rather, not there!

Here's what happened. I awoke this morning quite early – Syke conditioning! I'm not due back at work till tomorrow and my renewed hopes that I might once more be able to find a publisher for Sam's Beddoes biography made me keen to get back to work on it. I headed straight out to the university library, planning to spend the day there, probably without a break, which is the way I like to work once I've got my teeth into something.

But I'd hardly started work before I was interrupted by the arrival of Charley Penn.

Charley has many excellent qualities and he has been most helpful in encouraging my literary ambitions, giving me many tips both creative and practical. In all of us there is both light and shade; in some one predominates, in others, the other. But in Charley there is a darkness which sometimes blots out the brightness altogether. Where does it spring from? Perhaps it's part of the German psyche. Though he has taken on much colouring from his Yorkshire upbringing, he is in many ways a true scion of his Teutonic ancestry.

It was Charley who drew my attention to a poem of Arnold's called 'Heine's Grave'. Fine poem, a moving tribute to the dead poet and a sharp assessment of what made him tick. In it Arnold speculates that it was Heine that Goethe had in mind when he wrote that some unnamed bard had 'every other gift but wanted love'.

So it seems to me with Charley. The one person who drew love out of him and returned it to him was Dick Dee. Dee's death and the revelation that he was probably the killer of so many people, including, God damn his soul, my beloved Sam, has quite overthrown Charley. Oh, for much of the time he seems the same, saturnine, savagely humorous, unblinkingly perceptive, but that darkness which always exists in the depths of a pine forest has in his case now spread out to envelope even the crowns of the trees.

Evidence of this came when I asked him what brought him here away from his usual perch in the town reference library.

'She's away on holiday, so I thought I'd take a break too,' he said laconically.

I didn't need an explanation. *She* is Ms Pomona who came so close to being the Wordman's final victim. Charley is so convinced of his friend Dee's innocence that he has persuaded himself there must have been a conspiracy to conceal the truth. But I'm sure that you know all about this already, Mr Pascoe, as you and Rumbleguts, who were first on the scene after Dee's death, are marked down as the head conspirators! Charley, I think, has the Gothic fancy that his accusing presence in the Reference when Ms Pomona is on duty will eventually wear her down and bring a confession.

I can't say that I was too pleased to see him as my head was full of ideas, but I owe him a lot for recent kindnesses and could not decently refuse his invitation to pop out for a coffee and a chat.

As we drank our coffee, I told him about my excitements in Cambridge, which he found mildly entertaining, but I could tell his mind was elsewhere.

Finally I said, 'Charley, you seem a bit down. Book going badly?'

'No, that's going fine, except I sometimes wonder, what's the point? Heine, Beddoes, we work our knackers off to produce "the definitive work", except of course it never is. At best it replaces the last definitive work and with a bit of luck we may pop our clogs before it gets replaced by the next one. Why do we do it, Fran?'

'You know why,' I said rather pompously. 'We pursue the Holy Grail of Truth.'

'Oh yeah? Well there's only one truth I want to pursue and I've been getting nowhere.'

Oh God, I thought. Here we go. Dick Dee is innocent, OK!

I said, 'Charley, if you're getting nowhere, maybe it's 'cos there's nowhere to get.'

He shook his head and said, 'Not true. But they're clever, I'll give 'em that. This is a fucking X-file. The truth is out there, under Andy Dalziel's fat buttocks or up yon Pascoe's tight arse. I wanted to do this by myself, but I'm not too proud to admit I need help. If the authorities won't listen to me, I've got friends that will!'

I wasn't sure what this meant. I don't think he's wrong about needing help, but I suspect that's not the kind of help he's got in mind. I could speculate, but I'm not going to. Frankly, if Charley's obsession leads him into illegalities, I don't want to know. A man in my situation needs to keep his relationship with the Law plain and unambiguous.

Which is why I feel I need to pass on my fears that Charley is so obsessed with proving his friend's innocence that he's capable of almost anything.

I do this not in any spirit of delation – my time at the Syke has conditioned me irredeemably to regard a grass as the lowest form of life – but in the sincere hope that by alerting you to Charley's state of mind, you might be able to head him off from any indiscretion or, worse, illegality of behaviour.

Enough of that. On my return to the library, I found I was uncomfortably aware of Charley's presence at the next table. It was like having Poe's raven or Beddoes' old crow of Cairo (which Sam amusingly points out is homophonous with the Christian monogram *chi-rho*, a pretty fancy which he plays with entertainingly for a page and a half before discarding it) brooding at my shoulder. So, though as I said before, I normally hate to be interrupted at my work, it was quite a relief when my mobile began to vibrate.

To my surprise it was Linda ringing from Strasbourg. Instantly I started to fantasize that Emerald had been on the phone to her, telling her she'd met me and later realized that I was the only man on earth for her! What idiots sex makes of us, eh?

Naturally it was nothing like this, though she knew of my meeting with Emerald as she'd been talking to Jacques on the phone. What concerned her more was the account she'd read in her paper of the events at God's.

She questioned me closely, asked if I was all right, then with that savage ability to cut to the chase which is her political hallmark went on to say, 'At least this means that you have a clear field for Sam's book. You'll want to get down to some serious work. When we met in Belgium, you mentioned that there were still a few things Sam had been working on about Beddoes' time in Basel and Zurich. Worth following up, you reckon?'

'Well, yes, I suppose so,' I said. 'I mean, even if they turn out dead ends, the only way to be sure is to follow them as far as possible . . .'

'Quite right. Like in politics, always cover your back so that you don't find some pushy little squirt second-guessing you. Right, here's what we do. Some chums have got a place in Switzerland. They're heading for warmer climes for a month or two so they've given me use of their bunkhouse while they're away and I'll be spending Christmas there with a few people. It's called Fichtenburg-am-Blutensee in Canton Aargau. The chalet there's the perfect place for you to work, lovely and quiet – my party won't be turning up till the twenty-fourth – and there's easy access to both Zurich and Basel. How's that sound?'

'It sounds very nice,' I said. 'But maybe . . .'

'Good,' she said. 'You'll join us for the festivities, but otherwise you'll be your own master. I've spoken to the housekeeper, Frau Buff, and she'll expect you this evening . . .'

'This evening!' I exclaimed. It dawned on me that Linda wasn't discussing possibilities but dictating arrangements! It had been the same when she'd contacted me last month to say that she was in Brussels for a meeting and had decided to spend the weekend in the Stranger House at Frère Jacques' monastery and wouldn't it be a good idea for me to actually meet the founder of Third Thought face to face? While I was still wondering how to refuse politely, she was telling me about my travel arrangements!

The same thing was happening now. I was booked on a tea-time flight from Manchester and my ticket would be waiting for me at the airport. A taxi driver would meet me at the arrivals gate at Zurich.

She rattled on in that peremptory manner of hers for a little while, but after the initial shock, I found that all I could think of was, will Emerald be there at Christmas?

I said, 'That sounds marvellous, Linda. Both for the work, and for Christmas. It was beginning to look like being a bit lonely. But I don't want to intrude on your family . . .'

'You won't,' she said brusquely. 'It will be a couple of political chums. And Frère Jacques will be with us, God willing. So, all fixed, right?'

And now disappointment made me dig my heels in a bit.

'Getting to Manchester might be a problem. My car's knackered . . . and there's my work . . .'

'Take a cab, bill it to me. As for work, that's why you're going,' she snapped.

'I meant, my job in the university gardens . . .'

I heard that snort of disbelief so familiar to millions of British viewers and listeners from her appearance on various chat shows. It had also been a distinctive punctuation of Labour speeches in parliamentary broadcasts before she fell out with her own leadership and flounced off to give the Europeans the benefit of her incredulity.

'You're a full-time scholar now, Fran, so it's no longer necessary to cultivate your garden. The book's the thing.'

Strange, I thought, that after so many years of estrangement from her stepbrother while he was alive she should be such an enthusiast of his work now that he was dead.

In the end, I did what most people do when Linda comes at them with their lives mapped out. I gave in.

And indeed the more I thought about her plan, the more attractive it seemed.

I really did want to do some serious work and what better place to do it in than a luxurious house (the wooden shack image of chalet I'd immediately discounted as the kind of pseudo-modest understatement by which the rich emphasize their wealth) in beautiful countryside with a nice motherly housekeeper to take care of my comfort?

I didn't really need the uni library for anything other than a chair, as Linda had told me to extract from Sam's personal library all those books I felt relevant to his researches. And I would be completely free from the oppressive presence of poor old Charley.

I went back in to collect my things and tell him of my change of plan.

He said indifferently, 'Switzerland? Don't stand in front of any cuckoo clocks.'

Finally I scribbled a note to Jack Dunstan, the Head Gardener, offering him my thanks and my notice.

So where am I now? On another train, that's where! This time heading for Manchester. Some innate parsimony made me unable to take up Linda's kind suggestion of travelling there by taxi. It would cost a fortune, and this train gets me there with plenty of time to spare.

So there we are. I hope you and dear Mrs Pascoe and your lovely little girl have a merry Christmas, and now that I know why I'm writing to you, I hope you won't

think it an imposition if I drop you another line in what
looks like it might be a very Happy New Year indeed!

Fondly yours

Franny

'I don't believe it!' said Pascoe. 'Here's another one.'

'Another what?'

'Letter from Roote.'

'Oh good. Anything's better than these round robins so many people send with their cards. It's the modern disease. The media's full of it. The obsession with trivia.'

'So how come you find Roote's trivia so interesting?'

'How come you find it so significant? Come on, let's have a look.'

'Hang on. There's reams of it again.'

As he read, Ellie picked up the discarded pages and read in tandem.

Finishing just behind him she regarded his long pensive face across the breakfast table and said, 'Well, friend, guru, father-figure, what's bugging you this time?'

'I feel . . . stalked.'

'Stalked? That's a bit strong, isn't it? A couple of letters . . .'

'Four. I think four letters constitutes a nuisance if not a stalking, especially when each of them separately is long enough to make several normal letters!'

'In this e-mad age, perhaps. But there's something rather touching about someone taking the time to write a good old-fashioned long narrative letter. And I don't see how your detective neuroses can find anything even vaguely threatening in this one. In fact he goes out of his way to warn you to watch out for Charley Penn who, I must admit, has been rather odd since Dee's death. Not that he ever says anything to me about it, being as I'm compromised by shagging one of the chief conspirators, but I can tell there's something simmering down there somewhere.'

Ellie knew Penn much better than Pascoe. She'd been a member of a literary group he ran, and with the publication of her first novel scheduled for the spring, he had admitted her to the adytum of real writerhood and their acquaintance had taken a step towards friendship till Dee's death had brought the barriers down.

'You don't think Charley's going to come after me with a poisoned ballpoint, do you?' said Pascoe.

'There you go, paranoid every time. If he does have a go, he's more likely to start sniping at you in print. That would be his way of attack. He's a word man, after all.'

She realized what she'd said even as she said it. The last Wordman who'd touched their lives had used more than words to dispose of his many victims.

'Well, there's a comfort,' said Pascoe. 'So you think I should write to Roote and thank him fulsomely for his kind concern? Maybe invite him over for supper so that we can have a heart to heart about his love life?'

'Could be interesting,' said Ellie as if she took him seriously. 'I think I could help him. There was a piece in one of the supplements not so long back about famous mothers and disaffected daughters, you know, the kind of thing hacks dredge up when they don't have an original idea in their heads, which is ninety per cent of the time.'

'And you treated it with the contempt it deserved, of course.'

'No, I devoured every word avidly on the grounds that a few years hence, when I'm a rich and famous author, it could be my revolting child they're writing about. Loopy Linda and her Emerald got a couple of paras. That girl sounds like she's made it her life's mission to disoblige her parents. So it could be Fran's right and she's just using the fornicating *frère* for her own ends.'

He said, 'She'd better watch out if she tries that on Roote. She'll need to get up very early in the morning to use that clever sod.'

'From what he says, all she'll need to do is go to bed very early in the evening,' said Ellie. 'But no need for you to lose any sleep, love. Even if he is planning to destroy you, Franny Roote is safely stowed in faraway Switzerland for the rest of the month, so we can concentrate all our attention on trying to survive the more conventional perils of Christmas, to wit, bankruptcy, mental breakdown and chronic dyspepsia.'

'To wit?' said Pascoe. 'I hope getting published isn't going to turn you precious.'

'Piss off, noddy,' said Ellie, grinning. 'That basic enough for you?'

'I hear and obey,' said Pascoe, finishing his coffee. He rose, stooped over Ellie to give her a lingering kiss which she much appreciated. But her appreciation didn't prevent her from noticing that during its execution, he slipped Franny Roote's letter into his pocket.

In his office he read it again. Was he over-reacting? There was nothing in this letter which a just and rational man could interpret as a threat. And he could see how his attempt to turn the account of the fire at St Godric's into a mockingly oblique confession of arson might appear to have more to do with neurotic prejudice than rational thought. He hadn't got anything from the Cambridge Fire Department to back up his suspicions of criminality. The call he'd made to the Cambridge police had been more diplomatic than detective, just to put it on record that he'd been talking to the fire people. He'd spoken briefly to what sounded like an overworked sergeant, referred vaguely to a couple of cases of suspected arson in Mid-Yorkshire educational establishments and the usefulness of correlating statistics nationally, and asked to be kept informed of any developments. No mention of Roote. Why risk feelers being put out along that intricate net of unofficial police contacts which is just as important to the Force as the National Computer, resulting in the firm establishment of Franny Roote as dotty DCI Pascoe's King Charles's head?

He unlocked a drawer in his desk and took out an unlabelled file. When during the course of a couple of recent cases Roote had drifted back into his ken – or, as some might say, been dragged back – Pascoe had quite legitimately collated all existing material on the man. That remained in the official records. But this file, for private consumption only, contained copies and digests of that official material plus much unofficial stuff including all the recent letters, carefully marked with date of receipt.

It occurred to Pascoe that if it hadn't been for the very first case of all, his path and Ellie's, so divergent since their student days, might never have crossed again.

So Roote could claim to be their Cupid. Or Pandarus.

Not that he'd ever made such a claim, Pascoe rebuked himself. Stick with the facts.

And the facts were that this man had served his time, been a model prisoner earning maximum remission, co-operated fully with the services administrating his release programme, and settled down to a couple of worthy jobs (hospital portering and gardening) while pursuing a course of studies which would settle him eventually in the academic world, a shining example of the regenerative powers of the British penal system.

Hooray. Wild applause all round.

So why am I the only person sitting on his hands? wondered Pascoe.

In his eyes, Roote was neither reformed nor deterred, he was just a lot more careful.

But no defences are impregnable, else the country wouldn't be full of ruined castles.

The phone rang.

'DCI Pascoe.'

'Hello. DCI Blaylock, Cambridge here. You were talking to one of my sergeants yesterday about the fire at St Godric's and I gather you've been asking the local fire people about the way the fire started too. Something about possible parallel cases involving educational establishments on your patch? Would that be at one of the Yorkshire universities then? I don't recall reading anything recently.'

It was little wonder. The allegedly possibly related cases with which Pascoe had salved his conscience had been two junior school fires, one of which had been set by disaffected pupils while the other had been started by an errant rocket on Bonfire Night.

Pascoe felt it was time to come at least partially clean.

163

He explained in measured rational tones that, happening to know that one of the delegates at the St Godric's conference was an ex-con to whom the destruction of Professor Albacore's research papers might afford some small advantage, he had thought it worth enquiring if there were any suspicious circumstances.

'My sergeant picked you up wrong then?' said Blaylock.

'Let us rather say that I could see no reason to add to your CID workload by suggesting otherwise without any supporting evidence. Therefore my call, which was in the nature of a courtesy marker rather than a passing on of information, perhaps erred on the side of underplaying my slight and distant interest. The fault if any is mine.'

Such circumlocution might bamboozle a plain-speaking Yorkshireman, but those working in the shadow of our older universities are more practised in threading their way through verbal mazes.

'So you had a hunch but didn't want to put it upfront because Fat Andy thinks it's a bladder full of wind,' said Blaylock.

'You know Superintendent Dalziel?'

'Only like a curate knows Beelzebub. Heard a lot about him, but hope I'll never have the pleasure of meeting him personally.'

Something defensive almost formed on Pascoe's lips, but he let it fade unspoken. As Dalziel himself once said, when offered the sympathy vote, sigh deeply and limp a bit.

'Anyway, sorry I stuck my nose in without talking to the main man. Incidentally, are you so overstaffed down there, they put DCIs in charge of non-suspicious fire cases?'

'No, just something one of the smart young chaps who wants my job mentioned, so I stuck my nose in and found to my surprise that it rubbed against yours. Thought it worth giving you a bell just in case you knew anything I ought to.'

'So what was it your smart young chap mentioned?' said Pascoe, trying to keep the hopeful excitement out of his voice.

'It's probably nothing. You know how keen these youngsters are to make mountains out of molehills so they can climb up 'em.'

Blaylock had a deep reassuringly mellow voice reminding

Pascoe of the kind of actor cast in the role of Scotland Yard inspector in black-and-white thrillers made before the war. Perhaps he wore a tweed jacket and smoked a pipe. Cambridge, city of dreaming squires, gleaming in the wide flat fens like a jewel on the brow of a submerged toad. How nice to work there. What beauty in your daily life, what sense of history, what opportunity for cultural contact and intellectual stimulus . . .

Jesus, I'm even sharing dreams with Roote now!

'I quite like mountains myself,' said Pascoe.

'It was just that the PM on Albacore showed death from smoke inhalation, but it also mentioned some possible damage to the back of his head. Hard to be sure though as the body was badly burnt. In any case, as he was overcome by smoke, he'd probably go down pretty hard and might well have cracked his head.'

'What about the way he was found?' said Pascoe. 'What I'm getting at . . .'

'I know what you're getting at,' said Blaylock in a kindly voice. 'We read all the training manuals down here too. My bright boy checked. Albacore was found lying face-down across the threshold of his study, facing in. But the experts assure me it means nothing. Unable to see and choking, victims often end up so disorientated they head back towards the source of a fire, and once they go down they may roll over several times in their efforts to escape.'

Pascoe was now very excited indeed, but he put a lid on it and asked negligently, 'So you found yourself wondering if someone could have whacked Albacore on the head and left him to die in the burning study.'

'That's what my bright boy wanted me to wonder. But he couldn't get anything out of the arson experts to suggest the fire had been started deliberately. So I made a note in the file and was getting on with more pressing matters, till I heard about your interest, Mr Pascoe. But if in fact all you've got is the vague notion you just outlined to me, then it's not much help, is it? Nothing plus nothing equals nothing, right?'

Not if, deep down inside, you know you're right, thought Pascoe. But what was the point of trying to explain to a man he didn't know a hundred plus miles away what his nearest and dearest face to face had listened to with unconcealed scepticism?

'You're right,' he said.

'I've been glancing through the file as we talked,' said Blaylock. 'I see this man Roote made a statement, just like all the rest of them. Any point in reeling him back in and putting a bit of pressure on him, do you think?'

Pascoe thought of Franny Roote, of that pale still face, of those eyes whose surface candour concealed what lay beneath, of that quietly courteous manner. Pressure applied here was like pressure applied to quicksand. It either sucked you in and destroyed you, or, if you managed to withdraw, it showed no sign that you'd touched it.

'No point whatsoever,' he said. 'Listen, it was just a passing notion. If I did find anything positive, I'd get straight in touch. And perhaps you could keep me posted if . . .'

'Don't worry, you'd hear from me,' said Blaylock, his mellow voice taking on a slight edge of menace.

So that was that, thought Pascoe as he replaced the phone. The unofficial network would be alerted. The news would soon be out. Hieronimo is mad againe.

'So what?' he said aloud.

'Does my heart good to see a man too deep in his work to hear a knock at his door.'

Dalziel stood on the threshold, had been standing there God knows how long.

The unofficial Roote file was open on the desk. Pascoe closed it, not, he prayed, over-casually, and said, 'Must be going deaf. Come in, do.'

'Owt interesting going off?' said Dalziel, his eyes fixed on the unlabelled file.

Taking the bull by the horns was better than waiting to be gored.

'Got another letter from Roote this morning. Would probably have binned it, but I've just had an interesting call from a DCI Blaylock at Cambridge.'

'Never heard of him.'

'He's heard of you,' said Pascoe.

He gave the gist of his conversation, convinced Dalziel had heard his half of it anyway.

As he spoke, the Fat Man ran his eyes over the letter, and Pascoe took advantage of the distraction to slide the file into a drawer. When he'd finished reading, he dropped the letter on to the desk, farted gently and asked, 'So what's this Bollock decided to do next?'

'Blaylock. Nothing. No evidence of crime. Leave it alone.'

'But you reckon Albacore caught Roote with a flame-thrower in his hand, and then the lad whacked him on the head and left him to barbecue, right? What do you think he's confessing to in his latest, then? Plans to scupper the Swiss Navy?'

'No,' said Pascoe, aiming at reasonableness. 'Nothing concrete to bother us here.'

'You reckon?' said Dalziel. 'This stuff about Charley Penn, doesn't that bother you?'

'No, not really,' said Pascoe, surprised. 'Nothing new there, is there? We all know how hard it's been for Penn to accept that his best mate was a killer.'

'How about what young Bowler said yesterday?'

Pascoe looked blank and the Fat Man said accusingly, 'I told you all about it in the Bull, but I could tell it weren't going in.'

'Yes it did,' protested Pascoe. 'Something about a break-in at his girl's flat. You can't think Penn had anything to do with that? He may be a bit stretched out at the moment, but I can't see him breaking and entering, can you? Anyway, didn't Bowler say there was no sign of forced entry? I don't see Charley as a dab hand with a picklock!'

'Always got a trick or two up his lederhosen, your Hun. Frogs thought the Maginot Line 'ud keep 'em out in 1940, look what happened there. Any road, he's a writer. Learn all kinds of dirty tricks, them writers. It's the research as does it. Look at yon Christie. All them books, all them murders. Can't touch pitch and not get defiled, lad.'

An idiot might have been tempted to suggest that maybe he was confusing his Christies, but Pascoe knew that Dalziel in frolicsome mood was like an elephant dancing, the wise man did not complain it was badly done, he just steered well clear.

But he couldn't resist a dig.

He said, 'I see what you mean. But it's a bit like this Roote thing, isn't it? No complaint, no evidence, so no case. How do you see yourself proceeding, sir?'

Dalziel laughed, ran a massive finger round the space on the desk where the file had been, and said, 'Like the Huns in 1940. Blitzkrieg! Seen owt of Wieldy?'

'Got another mysterious call and went out.'

'God, I hope he's not going to come back with another half-baked tip.'

'You reckon there's nothing in this Praesidium business then?' said Pascoe, determined to show how closely he had been listening in the Bull.

'I'm not holding my breath,' said the Fat Man.

'He's usually a pretty good judge,' said Pascoe loyally.

'True. But hormones can jangle a man's judgment worse than a knock on the head. Look at Bowler. Love's a terrible enemy of logic. I think I read that in a cracker.'

'Love . . . I don't see how Edwin Digweed can have anything to do –'

'Who mentioned Digweed? What if our Wieldy's playing away? Nay, don't stand there like a hen with the gapes. It happens. Is it coffee time yet? I could sup a cup.'

Pascoe, uncertain how serious Dalziel was about Wield, but knowing from experience that the Fat Man's basic instincts sometimes got to places that a cruise missile couldn't reach, recovered his composure and said brightly, 'Going down to the canteen, sir?'

'No way. Buggers stop talking when I show my face there. I like a bit of *Klatsch* with my *Kaffee*. Pardon my Kraut, must've picked it up off Charley Penn. If anyone wants me, tell 'em I've gone down the Centre in search of a bit of cultural enlightenment. Ta-rah!'

The Ship

alziel was right. If you wanted your coffee with *Klatsch*, not to mention *Schlag*, *latte*, or other even more exotic additives. then you headed for Hal's café-bar on the mezzanine floor of the Heritage, Arts and Library Centre.

If on the other hand you wanted it with a cloaking background of distant train noises and all too close punk rock, then Turk's was the only place to be.

At least, thought Wield sourly, Ellie Pascoe wouldn't need to agonize over the working conditions of those who had picked the beans to produce this social experience. Anyone with a hand in the process which led to this muck deserved everything they got.

His sourness was caused by the fact that Lee Lubanski hadn't turned up. Twenty minutes of sitting alone in this atmosphere listening to this racket under Turk's indifferent gaze made you wonder if the life you enjoyed outside this place wasn't just a dim memory of people and places long lost. You began to fear that if you stayed too long you might lose all power of decision and end up a permanent fixture like the silent, solitary men hunched over empty cups who surrounded him.

Time to go. He should feel relieved. But he didn't.

He pushed the cup away and began to rise. The door opened and Lee came in.

His young face was twisted with anxiety. He looked like a child who's lost contact with his mam in a supermarket and is experiencing a fear teetering on the edge of panic.

Then he saw Wield and his face lit up. He came straight to the table and apologies began to tumble out of him at such a rate the detail was lost in the torrent.

'Shut up and sit down afore you do yourself an injury,' said Wield.

'Yeah ... sure ... sorry ...'

He sat down and stopped talking but his face still glowed with pleasure at finding Wield waiting. Time to switch off the light.

'Passed on that so-called tip of yours to my boss,' growled Wield. 'He wasn't much impressed. Like I said to you, we don't have the men or the time to follow every bleeding Praesidium van for a whole day. You got any more details?'

The youth shook his head.

'Sorry, nowt about that, but I got something else.'

'Oh yes? What's it this time? A sub-post-office job somewhere in the North of England? Or is it not as definite as that?'

Lee's light was now definitely flickering.

'Not very definite, no,' he said defensively. 'But I can only tell you what I heard. You don't want me making things up, do you?'

There was something touchingly ingenuous about this, but Wield did not let his reaction show.

'Too bloody true,' he said. 'All right, let's have it.'

'It's that Liam Linford case. They're fixing it so the wanker gets off.'

Now it was his intense interest that Wield was concealing.

'Fixing it? Who is? How?'

'His dad, Wally, who fucking else?' said Lee with a show of aggression reminding Wield that under the facade of innocent kid lurked a streetwise rent boy. 'And all I know is they're fixing for that Carnwath to change his evidence so it never gets to Crown Court, and it's no use going on at me for more 'cos that's all I fucking know.'

'Yeah yeah, keep your voice down,' said Wield. The music was loud and no one was paying any attention, but too much animation in a place like Turk's was like laughter at a funeral. 'What you do know is where this info comes from.'

A sullen, stubborn expression settled like a pall across the boy's pale features.

A client, guessed Wield. He's not going to risk giving up a regular source of income. And maybe it's someone he's a bit scared of.

What he should be trying to do was sign Lee up as an official snout to compensate for any possible loss of earnings, but he didn't think it was worth the effort. Or maybe he simply didn't want to. Once on the books, his identity would be known at least to Dalziel and Pascoe, neither of whom would hesitate to use him any which way they could, and he would only remain useful as long he remained a rent boy.

'OK, forget that. How about an educated guess at what they're going to try to do to Carnwath? Anything at all, Lee. You're right, I don't want you to make things up, but I don't want you not to say anything either just 'cos you think it doesn't sound important.'

His softer tone had an immediate effect. The sullenness vanished to be replaced by a childish concentration.

'Nothing . . . except he did say something about someone arriving Wednesday . . . no use asking who or where or when . . . I don't know . . . just they're due in Wednesday . . .'

Wield didn't press. If there was anything else to come, which he doubted, pressure wasn't going to induce it. He said, 'That's good, Lee. Thanks a lot.'

And his heart ached again at the pleasure his praise clearly caused the boy.

He took some coins out of his pocket and said, 'Here, get yourself a Coke.'

'Nah, that's all right, my treat. 'Nother coffee?'

Without waiting for an answer, Lee went to the counter where the inscrutable Turk offered no response to his chirpy greeting but supplied the requested drinks with the indifference of an Athenian executioner pouring hemlock.

'So, Lee,' said Wield. 'Tell me a bit more about yourself. You got a trade at all?'

'Trade? Oh, I get plenty of trade,' he replied with a knowing laugh.

'Not what I meant,' said Wield. 'I meant a trade to get a proper living at. What you're talking about will likely kill you in the end, you know that.'

'So what if it does? Anyway, if men've got to pay 'cos that's the only way they can get what they want, where's the harm? Thought you'd have understood that.'

The bold stare reminded Wield that he'd been sussed.

He didn't look away.

'I don't pay for sex, Lee,' he said. 'Anything not available because someone doesn't want to give it to me, I do without.'

'Yeah, well, you're one of the lucky ones then,' said the boy, dropping his gaze. 'How about lasses, you ever try it with a girl?'

The question came out of nowhere and Wield let his surprise show.

'Sorry, I didn't mean . . . I were just wondering . . .'

'It's OK,' said Wield. 'Yes, I tried it with girls. When I were your age . . . younger . . . Before you understand the truth about yourself, wanting to be like everyone else makes you think there's something wrong, doesn't it?'

As he spoke, he realized he was making a stupid assumption. Being a rent boy didn't mean you had to be gay. But Lee's response confirmed what he'd assumed.

'Yeah, know what you mean,' he said moodily. 'It's like everyone's going to the match and you just want to be heading the other way.'

He took a pull at his Coke, then said, 'You're not drinking your coffee. It's OK, is it?'

Wield put the cup to his lips and let a tide of turgid muddy foam break over his teeth.

'Yeah,' he said. 'It's fine.'

Meanwhile back in *latte* land, Hal's café-bar, popular at any time of year, by eleven o'clock on a December morning well into the pre-Christmas shopping season was crowded with bag-laden Yorkshire maids and matrons, eager to rest their weary feet and refresh themselves with a sophisticated coffee or a traditional strong tea.

All the tables were taken and nearly every chair occupied. The only hint of vacancy was at a table for four at which a lone man sat, but the scatter of books and papers which covered the surface of table and chairs suggested that he was not eager for company. Mid-Yorkshire women in search of rest and recuperation are not so easily put off, however, and from time to time a party would boldly advance to essay an assault on this pathetic creature. Alas for their hopes! Alerted to their approach, the man would let them get within a couple of paces, then turn on them a scowl of such ferocity, in which misanthropy vied with lycanthropy for control of his hollow-cheeked, sunken-eyed, raggedy-bearded features, that even the Red Cross Knight might have quaked in his armour. Most fled in search of easier prey, but one, a youngish not unfetchingly dumpy woman with a round amiable face advanced as if she simply didn't recognize antagonism and seemed about to take a seat when suddenly a still more fearful shape loomed behind the monster and bellowed in its ear, 'What's up, lad? Pubs not open?'

The woman retreated, visibly shocked, and Charley Penn, for it was he, jumped about three inches out of his seat before twisting round and responding weakly, 'I could ask you the same, you fat bastard.'

'Nay,' said Andy Dalziel. 'I'm a common working man, got to go where the job takes me. You're a scholar and an artist. It's mostly going on in your noddle. You can take your work any-where, long as you don't lose your head. You've not lost your head recently, have you, Charley?'

The Fat Man brushed the papers off one of the chairs and sank heavily on to it, splaying its spindly metal legs across the tiled floor with a protesting squeal.

'Best get another for the other half of your arse, Andy,' said Penn, recovering.

'Nay, it'll hold, and if it don't, I can sue them. You've not answered my question.'

'Remind me.'

'Short-term memory going? They say that's a bad sign.'

'What of?'

'I've forgotten.'

Penn laughed. It didn't make him look less wolfish.

'Have I lost my head recently? Figuratively, I assume you mean? Rather than physically? Or perhaps metaphysically? Or even metempsychotically?'

'I love it when you talk down to me, Charley. Makes me really humble to be the friend of someone so famous.'

Penn's limited fame and fortune rested on his authorship of a sequence of historical romances which had been turned into a popular romping claret-and-cleavage TV series. His hopes of a lasting reputation rested on the critical biography of Heinrich Heine he'd been researching for many years, researches which had provided him with much of the material he used in his fictions. This was an irony which confirmed his cynical outlook on the way things were arranged. As if, he declared, the Venerable Bede had found the only way he could keep body and soul together was by selling plastic crucifixes that lit up in the dark and played 'Swing Low Sweet Chariot'.

'Andy, let's both cut the blunt down-to-earth Yorkshire crap. Just tell me what it is you think I've done that brings you out here looking for me.'

A waitress approached and enquired timidly if she could help them.

'Aye,' said Dalziel. 'Coffee. One of them frothy ones with bits of chocolate. And a hot doughnut. Charley? My treat.'

'By God, it must be serious. Another double espresso, luv. Right, Andy, spit it out.'

Dalziel settled more comfortably in his chair, spreading its legs a little wider.

'First off,' he said, 'I've not come here looking for you, I was on my way to the Reference when I clocked you. Though happen I did think I might find you sitting in your usual spot in the library. I've just bought one of your books, thought I'd get you to sign it for me, make it more valuable when I send it up to Sotheby's.'

He tossed on to the table the paperback he'd picked up at the Centre bookstall when he'd spotted Penn in Hal's. It was entitled *Harry Hacker and the Ship of Fools*. Its cover showed a ship crowded with agitated men in a turbulent sea being driven on to rocks on which basked several well-endowed women in a state of deshabille.

Penn frowned at it and said, 'So what made you pick this one?'

'Liked the cover. Ship driven on the rocks. Seemed to say something about you, Charley.'

'Like what?'

'Like out of control, mebbe.'

This seemed to reassure the writer. He pushed the book aside and said, 'If it's not me you're after in the Reference, then what is it?'

'Well, it's related to you in a way,' said Dalziel. 'Just tell me straight, Charley. You know where Ms Pomona, the librarian, lives?'

For a moment Penn went still, like a wolf freezing when the wind brings it some trace of its prey.

'Got a flat in Peg Lane, hasn't she?' he said.

'That's right. Church View House. You been round there recently?'

'Why should I? We're not exactly on social visiting terms.'

'Question answered with a question is a question answered, that's what they taught us at police college,' said the Fat Man. 'Thanks, luv.'

He raised the cappuccino the waitress had set in front of him to his mouth and licked the chocolate-flecked foam with an apparently prehensile tongue.

'And a suspect beaten with a table is a criminally damaged table,' said Penn. 'Bet they taught you that as well.'

'Hope it won't come to that,' said the Fat Man, studying his doughnut with the keen eye of a man expert at finding where the sac of jam is hidden. 'So?'

Penn let out a long sigh and said, 'OK, you've got me bang to rights. I did call round there for a chat, last weekend it was. No harm in that, is there?'

'When at the weekend?'

'Oh, Saturday I think,' said Penn vaguely. 'No one home, so I came away.'

Dalziel chose his point of incision, raised the doughnut to his mouth and bit.

Through red-stained teeth he said, 'Precision is important, Charley, else you miss the full pleasure. Saturday. When on Saturday?'

'Morning, was it? Yes, morning. Does it matter?'

'Morning starts at twelve midnight. Between twelve and one, was it?'

'Don't be daft!'

'One and two then? No? Two and three? No? Give us a clue at least, Charley!'

'And spoil your game? Play's important to kids, isn't that what the psychs say?'

'How about between eight and half past?' said Dalziel, pushing the rest of the doughnut into his maw.

'That would be about right, I dare say,' said Penn.

'Thought it might, as a man matching your description were seeing lurking in Church View around eight twenty-five.'

'Can't have been me,' said Penn indifferently. 'I gave up lurking years back. Case of mistaken identity then.'

'We got a description,' said Dalziel, taking out a notebook and looking at a blank sheet. 'Bearded, furtive, mad-looking. Like a nineteenth-century Russian anarchist who'd just planted a bomb.'

'Yeah, that does sound like me,' said Penn. 'So I called at about eight fifteen and she wasn't in so I left. So what?'

'Bit early for a social call, weren't it?'

'You know what they say about early birds, Andy.'

'Catch colds, don't they? Still sounds a bit odd to me. Can't remember the last time I called on a lass so early. Not unless I had a warrant and wanted to catch 'em afore they got their clothes on.'

'No such ambition. I just wanted to catch her before she went to work.'

'Works Saturdays, does she?'

'Aye. In the mornings. Mostly.'

'Yes, you'd know that 'cos you'd be in the library yourself most days, right, Charley? So why not have your little chat with her there?'

'Because it's hard to be private there.'

'Private? So there was something private you wanted to discuss with her, Charley?'

'Not particularly.'

'Not particularly? But particularly enough to call on her at sparrow-fart! Come on, Charley! There's only one thing you're interested in discussing with Ms Pomona and it's not something

178

that Ms Pomona would want to discuss with you any time, seeing as it was a nasty traumatic experience which she'll have been doing her very best to forget! So what do you think she was going to say if she opened her door at eight a.m. and saw Cheerful Charley Penn standing there? Sod off! That's what she was going to say.'

Penn drank his coffee, then asked quietly, 'Andy, what's going off here? She made some kind of complaint about me?'

'Not yet.'

'Meaning, but she will? Doesn't surprise me. She has to be dancing to your tune in this, no other way I can see it working.'

'I won't ask you what that means 'cos I don't like hitting a man I've just invested a coffee in. So what you're saying, Charley, is, you've never been in Ms Pomona's flat?'

'You're slow, Andy, but you get there in the end.'

'That's what all the girls tell me. So if we happened to find one of your fingerprints in Ms P's flat, you'd be hard put to explain how it got there?'

Penn raised his coffee cup, looked at it speculatively and said, 'If you took this cup and left it in the Vatican, you'd find my print there, but that doesn't mean I'm the Pope. Andy, don't you think it's time you told me what you're really after here?'

'Just having a coffee with an old friend.'

Penn made a play of looking round then said, 'Must have missed him.'

Dalziel emptied his cup and said, 'No rest for the wicked, eh? Oh, just one thing more. Lorelei. What's one of them when it's at home?'

'Why do you ask, Andy? Owt to do with little Miss P's intruder?'

Dalziel didn't answer but just stared at the writer till he raised his hands in mock surrender and said, 'She's a German nymph who lives on the Rhine. Her beautiful song lures fishermen to steer their boats on the rocks and drown. Heine wrote a poem about her. "*Ich weiß nicht was soll es bedeuten Daß ich so traurig bin. Ein Märchen aus alten Zeiten, Das kommt mir nicht aus dem Sinn.*"'

'You're hard enough to follow in English, Charley.'

'"I don't know of any good reason For me to feel so sad. A legend from some old season Keeps running around in my head."'

'Sounds like you, Charley.'

'How so?'

'Well, you've got everything most men want, a bit of fame, a bit of fortune, but you still droop around like you got the world on your back. And this Lorelei, beautiful young woman luring ships to destruction. Seems to run around in your head all right. Like in this book of yours, if the cover's owt to go on.'

'It's an imaginative interpretation.'

'That's all right then. What happened to Lorelei in the end? Some questing knight stick his lance into her?'

'Not that I know of,' said Penn. 'Not many fishermen on the Rhine nowadays, but I don't suppose she's averse to going for bigger prey, the odd pleasure boat full of trippers. No, I'd say that Lorelei's still out there, biding her time.'

'Best left alone then. That's what my old Scots gran used to say about beasties and bogles and things that go bump in the night. You don't bother them and they won't bother you. See you upstairs, mebbe.'

He stood up. Penn said, 'You've forgotten your book.'

He opened the paperback, scribbled in it and handed it to Dalziel.

The Fat Man moved away, squeezing between the crowded tables. He expected Penn would follow his progress out of the café, but when he looked at the reflection in the glass wall which marked Hal's boundary, he saw the bearded face buried deep in a book once more.

Wonder what language he thinks in? thought Dalziel.

Outside, he opened the book. The printed dedication was in German.

An Mai – wunderschön in allen Monaten!

Dalziel's German was up to that. 'To May – beautiful in every month!'

But he didn't need linguistic skills to interpret the message which Penn had scrawled beneath the title *Harry Hacker and the Ship of Fools*.

Bon voyage, sailor!

He laughed out loud.

'Charley,' he said. 'I didn't know you cared.'

man cannot live and work in the same town for many years without finding his head and his heart assailed by fond associations wherever he looks, and when Dalziel's route to the reference library took him past the toilet in which the Wordman had murdered Town Councillor 'Stuffer' Steel with an engraver's burin, he went inside for a pee, but stopped short when he found himself looking at a man up a step-ladder screwing a video camera into the ceiling.

'How do,' said Dalziel. 'What's this? Filming Uro-trash?'

'Updating the system, mate. State of the art, that's what they're getting now. Beam a close-up of your bollocks to the moon with this kit,' said the man proudly.

'Oh aye? Mebbe someone should warn 'em at NASA.'

Unfazed by the prospect of universal distribution, he had his pee then went on his way, from time to time observing other evidence of the new installation taking place.

In the reference library he was greeted with the kind of smile that twangs a man's braces and the words, 'Mr Dalziel, how nice to see you!' uttered with evident sincerity by the fine-looking young woman behind the desk.

The Italian strain in the Pomona family might be a couple of generations old, but the genes had come out fighting in Raina of that ilk, pronounce Rye-eena and contracted familiarly to Rye. Her skin had a golden glow and her dark expressive eyes might have sent a more poetic man than Fat Andy in search of images from Mediterranean skies. Her hair was a rich brown, except for a single lock of silvery grey which marked the main impact point of a head injury she had received at the age of fifteen in the car crash that killed her twin brother. Antipathetic at first towards the superintendent, and not encouraged to greater charity by the reports of persecution she received from her incipient boyfriend, DC Hat Bowler, she had relented her attitude in the aftermath of the Wordman case when she had come to see that, no matter what his outward semblance seemed to indicate, Dalziel was deeply defensive of his young officer and determined that no official crap should come his way.

Also, as she had confessed to Hat (causing the young man some perturbation of spirit), there was something sort of sexy about Dalziel, in a non-sexy sort of way. Observing the DC's bewilderment, she had added, 'I don't want to shag him, you understand, but I can see how it might be that he's not short of offers.'

Hat, who had often joined in lewd canteen speculation about the geophysics of the Fat Man's relationship with his inamorata, the not insubstantial Cap Marvell, found himself looking at things from a new viewpoint. Rye often had this effect on him – this was one of the pleasures, and the perils, of getting close to her – but no previous change of angle had been so disorientating as having to regard Andy Dalziel as a sex object rather than a performing whale. Thank God she had put in the disclaimer about not fancying him herself. Even the imagined prospect of such a rival quite unmanned him.

Knowing nothing of the food for thought he'd given the young couple, and careless of it had he known, Dalziel returned the smile and said, 'Nice to see you too, lass. What fettle? Tha's looking well. Helping young Bowler convalesce must be doing you good.'

Did his eyes twinkle salaciously as he said it? Rye didn't mind if they did, being as indifferent to his speculations as he would have been to hers.

'Yes, he's coming along very nicely. You'll have him back later this week, I gather.'

'That's right. Can't wait, from the look of him. He even popped in for a chat yesterday afternoon, just to get the feel of things. That's what brings me here today, summat he said. Not that I need an excuse to want to see you, but.'

He spoke flirtatiously. He'd decided that there was no way to the subject of her burglary save head on. But like in his rugby-playing days, no harm in a gently distracting shimmer of the hips before you ran straight through the bugger standing in your way.

'He told you about the break-in then,' she said, undistracted.

'You don't seem surprised. Didn't you tell him you didn't want to make a thing of it?'

'I heard he'd been asking my neighbours questions. Didn't think it would stop there.'

'You were right. It was his duty to report it in, and he's a good cop,' said Dalziel sternly. Then he added with a grin, 'And likely he also got to thinking if he said nowt, then you got murdered in your bed and he mentioned casually that your place had been turned over a few days back, I'd have sent him to join you.'

'I'm sure you'd have meant it as a kindness. All right. Some idiot got into my flat, left it looking a bit untidy, but nothing damaged and nothing taken. I couldn't see the point of pouring oil on dying embers by letting you lot really mess the place up with fingerprint powder all over the place and God knows what else. I've had enough of questions, statements and creaking bureaucracy in recent times to last me a lifetime!'

'Aye, it's a slow grinding mill, ours, and everyone ends up a bit ground down.'

'Doesn't show on you, Superintendent,' she said.

He laughed and said, 'Nay, I'm part of the machinery. And once I'm set in motion, I've got to clank on till I run down. Any chance of a coffee?'

'Any chance of me saying no? No. Come on through then.'

He went behind the reception desk and followed her into the office.

It was the first time he'd been in here since he'd supervised the search which followed Dick Dee's death. They'd found nothing here or in the man's flat which added much to the case for the Head of Reference being the Wordman, but it hadn't mattered. In retrospect such a long trail of evidence, albeit mainly circumstantial, led to his door that CID had had to field a lot of hostile questioning about how many people had died because they couldn't see what lay under their noses.

Things had changed considerably.

The paintings and photographs of great lexicographers which had darkened the walls had been replaced by some vapid watercolours of Yorkshire beauty spots and the plaster had been given a coat of paint. The furniture too was new, or at least new in here, probably a straight swap with another municipal office organized by someone sensitive enough to guess that Rye might not be too happy to feel that she was sitting on a seat polished by the buttocks of the man who'd tried to kill her.

'Nice,' he said, looking around. 'Lot brighter.'

'Yes. He's still here though.'

'You reckon? That bother you?'

She shook her head.

'No,' she said. 'They asked me that, not directly of course, but they wanted to move me. And I said no, this was where I wanted to be. You see, I always liked Dick. He was kind to me. Except . . . yeah, well. Except. Maybe if I'd never gone out to the tarn that day . . . Maybes, eh? But here in the library, I always remember him as a good friend.'

She busied herself making coffee, but he could see her dark eyes brimming with tears.

Dalziel said, 'He had to be stopped. What happened to you stopped him. Nowt to feel guilty about, luv. But I know how you feel. Couple of times I've had to send someone down that I'd rather not have done. Only a couple of times, you under- stand. Mainly I'm happy to kick 'em down the dungeon steps and slam the door behind them. But with these two, I some- times think that if mebbe I'd done summat a bit different, mebbe looked the other way, I wouldn't have had to . . . Aye, mebbe's not a spot you want to spend a winter's night in. I'll take mine black.'

Rye finished making the coffee and by the time she set a mug in front of him, she was back in control.

'So apart from the fact that I'm a recovered victim and one of your work-slaves' bit of fluff, how come I'm getting the special treatment over a minor crime? From what I've heard, you're stretched enough trying to deal with major ones!'

'We're never so stretched that we can't find time to spread a little comfort and light,' said Dalziel. 'Listen, I reckon I can talk to you straight. Being a victim and surviving doesn't just get you tea, sympathy and congratulation. It can also get you a lot of unwelcome attention from all sorts of weirdos. There's lunatics out there who work out that having been attacked once means you've probably got a taste for it. Or that it's up to them to finish a job half done. Or they just get a kick out of thinking that, because you've been scared shitless once, you're really going to freak out when it happens a second time.'

Rye had frozen with her mug poised a couple of inches from her mouth.

'This is comfort and light?' she said. 'What do you do when you bring bad news? Shove a severed leg through the letter box and yell, "There's been a bit of an accident, luv!"'

'You prefer round the houses, I'll send DCI Pascoe,' said Dalziel. 'I'm not done yet. They're the freaks and I'm glad to say there's not a lot of them around. But there's another bunch. Them as reckon you're not the victim at all but some other bugger is, someone who's either been jailed or in your case killed. They reckon that what's happened to this other bugger is your fault. Stands to reason, don't it? You're alive and he's dead. Sick proboscis.'

Rye interpreted this as *sic probo* but was wise enough not to test whether the variation was ironic or ignorant.

She said, 'Is this other bunch a large bunch or do you have someone specific in mind?'

'More than my job's worth to put names in your mouth,' said Dalziel virtuously. 'But you mention a name and it 'ud be my duty to look into it.'

He liked the way she didn't hesitate.

'Charley Penn,' she said. 'That's who we're sniffing around here, isn't it? Two of my neighbours saw him, or someone who fits his description, but you know that. Well, I'll talk about him, but let's get one thing clear. I am not putting in a complaint about him. And I'll deny all knowledge of this conversation if you try to make this official.'

'What about this tape recorder I've got strapped to my groin?' said Dalziel.

'Here's me thinking you were just glad to see me,' she said boldly.

He laughed and said, 'You've been keeping bad company, lass. So, unofficially, tell me about Charley.'

'What's to tell? He can't get his head round finding out that his old schoolmate and best buddy was a serial killer. End of story.'

'End of opening para,' said Dalziel. 'What's he said to you?'

'Not much directly. Just sits out there and glowers. I feel his eyes on me all the time.'

'That all? Didn't he used to send you poems or summat?'

'Sort of, in the old days . . . I mean, before all this happened. Thing was, he used to fancy me. At least I think he did, or maybe it was just some silly game he got off on. Anyway, you know these German poems he's been working on for the past thousand years or so?'

'Heinkel,' said Dalziel.

'Heine. He'd leave the odd love poem lying around where he knew I'd find it. He'd pretend it was accidental, but in that leering way he has which made it clear it wasn't.'

'Can't blame the bugger for trying,' said Dalziel.

'Can't you? All right, it wasn't major harassment, but it became irritating and I might have said something if he hadn't been . . . if . . .'

'If he hadn't been such a mate of Dee's,' completed Dalziel. 'But he's not been sending you these billy-doos since Dee snuffed it?'

'No, at least I'm spared that. Though maybe it was better having him leering at me lecherously than glaring at me as if he'd like to . . . I don't know what.'

'So you feel threatened, then your flat gets broken into, and there's a message on your computer which is a straight link to Heinz . . .'

'Heine. You work that out for yourself, or did your pet bloodhound sniff it out?'

Dalziel said gravely, 'Listen, luv, sometimes what a cop needs to do 'cos he's a trained sniffer dog and what he needs to do 'cos he's a love-sick puppy turns out to be one and the same thing. What you grinning at?'

'Trying to see you as a love-sick puppy, Superintendent.'

'I like my tummy scratched as well as the next man,' said Dalziel. 'Just takes a stronger woman, that's all. Point I'm making is, in this case it weren't a matter of professional versus personal. Brains and bollocks, they all told young Bowler he had to have a word. Now that's sorted, let's get back to onions. Charley Penn's scaring you, the break-in suggests a link with Charley, why aren't you screaming for police protection?'

She ran her fingers through her thick brown hair so that the silver blaze rippled like a fish in a peaty stream.

'I don't know,' she said unhappily. 'I suppose I wanted it to be all over, you know, draw a line and say, that's it, new start. They wanted me to have counselling, all that crap, but I said no. Watching Hat get better, and helping him, that was like a kind of surrogate healing for me. And this weekend we've just had, well, it was great. I felt really happy. Then we got back and I saw the flat and I didn't want to let it register, I suppose. I just wanted to tidy up and carry on like nothing had happened.'

'I can understand that. How do you feel now? Ready to make it official?'

She laughed and said, 'You don't give up, do you? All right. I'll make it official my flat was broken into. But I'm not pointing a finger. You want to talk to Penn, that's up to you. He was in his usual spot earlier, but I expect he's gone down to Hal's for a coffee.'

'Aye, he has. That's where I saw him on my way in.'

She stared at him assessingly then said, 'You've spoken to him already, haven't you? All this stuff about needing me to give the go-ahead was bollocks!'

'Nay, lass,' said Dalziel soothingly. 'I had an unofficial word, that's true. All you've done is make it official. It's just a question of labels. Talking of which, you didn't come into work on Friday carrying a suitcase with a lot of labels on, did you?'

'Sorry?'

'You went off for the weekend Friday evening with young Bowler, right?'

'That's right. But I went home first to pick up my bag then drove round to Hat's.'

'Anyone shouting "Enjoy your weekend away! Give him one for me!" as you left?'

'I don't remember, might have done.'

'And was Penn in the library on Friday?'

'Ah.' She had got his drift. She frowned and said, 'Yes, he was. But I can't swear that anything was said then that indicated I was going to be out of my flat till Monday. Will you want to look around now it's official?'

'Your flat? Not worth it if you've cleaned it up. You might think about improving your security, but. Talking of which, I'm glad to see they're spending a bit of money on a decent system to protect their staff round here. Better late than never, eh?'

The absence of a decent security system in the Centre had been one of the obstacles to an early solution of the Wordman case. By an irony not unremarked by his civic colleagues, Stuffer Steel had been the man mainly responsible for the penny-pinching approach which had led to the installation of the Centre's original bog-standard basic CCTV system.

'I don't think it's their staff they're worried about,' said Rye. 'Heritage is displaying the Elsecar Hoard next month, and it was a condition of getting it that our security was right up to date.'

'Poor old Stuffer must be spinning in his grave,' said Dalziel.

Councillor Steele, when news of the controversy about the Hoard first hit the headlines, had opined that the remaining Elsecars should be sent down the mines (if a mine could be found for them to be sent down) and their Hoard sold and the money distributed among the poor and oppressed of Yorkshire.

Andy Dalziel, no great lover of the councillor, for once agreed with him.

'Yes, I suppose he must,' said Rye.

There were tears in her eyes again and Dalziel cursed himself for his insensitivity.

He said, 'Better be off now. Take care, lass. And don't be too hard on young Bowler. But I'd not be too soft either! Cheers.'

On his way out of the library, he met Penn coming back in.

Dalziel took the book out of his pocket and flourished it.

'Nice one, Charley,' he said. 'Can't wait to read it.'

Penn watched him go, then made his way to his usual place and sat down.

Rye was back behind the counter.

Their gazes met, and locked.

It was Rye who broke off first. She grimaced as if in pain, put her hand to her head, then retreated into the office, kicking the door shut behind her.

Charley Penn smiled a wintry smile.

'Gotcha,' he mouthed. Then he turned to his books.

n Wednesday morning, despite the early hour, the passengers on the overnight flight from New York to Manchester strode into the public arrivals area with the sprightly step of the born-again who'd not only survived six hours trapped in a tin can but had passed through the Green Channel without some fish-eyed customs official attempting to investigate their private parts.

One, an attractive athletic-looking young woman with a papoose harness tied tightly against her breast so that it didn't impede her from pushing her luggage trolley, scanned the crowd waiting along the barrier eagerly as if in search of a familiar face.

She didn't find it, but what she did see was a man in a sober grey suit holding up a piece of white card bearing the name CARNWATH.

She went to him and said, 'Hi. I'm Meg Carnwath.'

'Hello,' he said. 'I'm Detective Sergeant Young, Greater Manchester CID.'

'Oh God. What's happened? Has Oz had an accident . . . ?'

'No, no, he's fine, really. It's this case he's a witness in . . . he's told you about it?'

'Yes, he has. He rang up yesterday to say that it had been put back till this afternoon, but he'd still have plenty of time to meet me and drive me back home.'

'How'd he sound?'

'A bit nervous. He said he'd be glad when this first stage was over. After that he thought he'd be OK, like a first night.'

'Well, he's right to be nervous. We got a whisper there might be an attempt to bring pressure on him via you. Probably nothing in it, but for everyone's sake, it made sense for us pick you up and keep you nice and safe till Mr Carnwath has given his evidence.'

'Oh God,' exclaimed the woman, wide-eyed. 'Oz said this guy who killed the girl was pretty heavily connected, but this is like something out of the movies.'

'We'll try to keep the car chases within the legal limit,' said Young, smiling. 'Anyway, even if there was anything to worry about, there isn't now. Here, let me take that.'

Pushing the trolley he led her out to the waiting car which was a big Mercedes.

'Well, this is nice,' she said. 'Didn't realize the police were so upmarket.'

'We didn't want to draw attention,' he said. 'Escort you to a police car and everyone would have you down as a drug smuggler! Besides, you deserve a bit of comfort after being squashed in a plane seat so long. There's a baby harness in the back if you want it.'

'Later maybe. He yelled all the way across then went out like a light when we landed, so I'll let sleeping dogs lie as long as he stays that way.'

She climbed in and made soothing clucking noises into the papoose hood while Young put the cases in the boot.

'Husband not with you this trip?' he said over his shoulder as he drove slowly and carefully through the morning traffic building up around Manchester.

'Partner. He's coming on later. I wanted to get here early and have some time with my brother, show him his nephew, they've not met yet.'

'That'll be nice,' he said.

There was a little more desultory conversation, but when the car left the suburbs behind and began to climb eastwards over the Pennines, Young saw in his mirror that the woman's eyes had closed, so he stopped talking and concentrated on driving through a mist which grew thicker as they got higher. After about twenty minutes he turned the car gently down a side road without disturbing his passenger, and some minutes later turned again along a narrow rutted track which the Merc's suspension negotiated without causing more than a restless shifting.

Finally he brought the car to a halt before a low stone-built farmhouse whose tiny windows, too small to admit a sufficiency of daylight in good weather and useless in these murky conditions, were ablaze with light.

The cessation of movement woke the woman.

She yawned, peered out of the window and said, 'Where are we?'

'Here,' said Young vaguely. He picked up the car phone, pressed some buttons, listened then handed it to her, saying, 'Thought you might like a word with your brother.'

'Oz?' she said into the mouthpiece.

'Meg? That you? Are you OK? Where are you?'

'I'm fine. Not sure where I am though, looks like a scene from a horror movie. Where did you say we were, Sergeant?'

'One of our safe houses,' he said.

'A safe house? I thought we were heading straight for home.'

'Well we are, but not quite straight. Few hours here till the committal proceedings are over, then we'll be on our way. It's OK, Mr Carnwath knows all about it, ask him.'

'Oz,' she said into the phone, 'Sergeant Young says I've got to stay here, wherever here is, some safe house, till the proceedings are over. He says you know about it.'

There was a pause then Oz Carnwath said, 'That's right, Sis. You sit tight till this thing's finished. It won't take long.'

'If you say so, Bro. You're OK, are you?'

'Oh yes, I'm being well looked after.'

She handed the phone back to Young. The farm door opened and another man came out and walked towards them, a slightly menacing figure silhouetted against the rectangle of orange light. She tried to open the car door, but found she couldn't move the handle.

Young said, 'Sorry. Force of habit,' and pressed the lock release.

The new man held open the car door for her. He was young, leather jacketed, with the bold eyes and leering smile of one who imagines himself irresistible to women.

'Get the luggage, Constable,' said Young.

'Luggage? I'm going to be here long enough to need luggage?'

'Stuff for the baby, maybe. He's very good. Wish I could say the same for mine.'

'You've got children, sergeant? How many?'

'Two. For God's sake, be careful, Mick.'

The leather-jacketed man had opened the boot and begun to lift out the cases. As he swung them over the boot's lip, one of them burst open, spilling its contents to the ground. His leering smile vanished to be replaced with the uneasy perplexity of a cabinet minister faced by an ethical policy.

On the ground lay three telephone directories, a Tesco bag full of stones, and a grey blanket clearly marked as the property of Mid-Yorkshire Constabulary.

The woman unclipped her papoose basket, and tossed it to Young, saying, 'Look after baby, will you?'

He wasn't ready for it. It bounced off his hands and turned upside down and only a desperate panic-driven lunge got it into his grasp a few inches from the ground. From inside came a piercing wail of 'Mummy!'

Young looked up in shock to discover the woman was paying no attention to him.

From her pocket she'd taken a small aerosol tube. She was pointing it at leather jacket and giving him a quick squirt. He fell back, cursing and clawing at his face. Young began to rise. The spray turned in his direction. He raised the papoose basket in an effort to protect himself but it was too late. The fine jet hit him right in the eyes. As he twisted away crying out in pain, a plastic doll fell out of the basket, squeaking, 'Mummy!'

The woman picked up the doll and spoke to it.

'Novello here,' she said. 'Think you can come and clear up now.'

eter Pascoe watched with interest as Oz Carnwath gave his evidence that afternoon, but it wasn't the witness's face he watched, nor that of the accused, though it might have been entertaining to see his cocky anticipation turn to shocked incredulity as instead of the expected hesitations and uncertainties, he heard firm and confident affirmations that he, Liam Linford, had driven his Lamborghini out of the car park on the night in question.

It was Linford Senior, sitting in the body of the court, that Pascoe watched. His expression of barely contained fury did more for Pascoe's festive feelings than any number of Christmas cards. Marcus Belchamber did all his considerable best to dent Carnwath's certainties, but hardly left a smudge let alone a scratch on them. It came as no surprise to anyone when the presiding magistrate committed Linford Junior for trial in the Crown Court in February. But the journalists present pricked up their ears when, after Belchamber's application for bail had been heard, the prosecuting lawyer stood up to oppose it on the grounds that there had been a serious attempt to interfere with a witness. The magistrate required a full report as soon as possible and ordered Liam Linford to be remanded in custody till she got it.

Wally Linford proved harder to lay a finger on. Taken in for questioning as he left the court, he had Belchamber by his side from the start, and simply denied any knowledge of the plan to kidnap Meg Carnwath. The two false policemen and the other two men who had intercepted Oz on his way to Manchester Airport also denied any connection with Wally, but claimed they were old acquaintances of Liam who had been overcome by indignation at what looked like a potential injustice. They had certainly been well schooled as nothing on the recording from the wire Oz had worn, or from Shirley Novello's, actually constituted a direct threat. Belchamber, after studying the account of what had happened to Novello, offered as his opinion that if he were advising the false police officers – which of course he had no reason even to contemplate doing – he would probably suggest an action against the WDC for assault. In the meantime, if they had nothing more to ask his client, he thought it best to bring the interview to a close.

Pascoe switched off the recording machine and said, 'Something you should understand, Wally. You've tried to fix Oz Carnwath and failed. His evidence is on record. Your attempt is on record. Anything else that happens to that lad, threats, accidents, even dirty looks, will be noted and reported and investigated. And I'll make sure every bugger connected with this case from the judge to the jury knows about it and believes it's down to Liam direct. And I reckon that will mean years on his sentence. Ask Mr Belchamber here if you don't believe me.'

Belchamber pursed his lips and said, 'This is a conversation I shall of course need to report to your superiors and the CPS, Chief Inspector.'

'What conversation, Mr Belchamber? I heard no conversation. You hear any conversation, Constable Novello? Sergeant Wield?'

His colleagues shook their heads.

'There you are. Three to two. In a democracy, we must be right. So watch it, Wally. After all your big-time stunts, it would be a shame to go down for a domestic, wouldn't it?'

After the lawyer and his client had left, Novello said admiringly, 'Nice one, sir. That made the bastards squirm. Real hairy-chested stuff.'

It was a genuine compliment. Novello liked her men muscular and hairy. The willowy Pascoe-type did nothing for her.

'Not the point,' said Pascoe wearily. 'I just wanted to warn them off Oz and his family. And talking of hairy chests, that trick of yours with the CS-spray, I've written it up as reaction to direct and sudden threat, which is the only way to justify it when you hadn't told them you were a police officer and issued a warning. The only true words Belchamber spoke were when he said they could be entitled to bring an action against you. What were you thinking of? You didn't even try to sound threatened on the tape!'

'Well, I felt it. And it wasn't my fault the case burst open,' protested Novello.

'Fault doesn't come into it. Cop on the spot gets the glory and the crap. All we've got is a couple of guys impersonating police officers. No threats, no holding against your will, no direct link with either Linford. I'm very doubtful we'll have enough to persuade the beak to turn down Belchamber when he requests a review of the remand in custody order. So we'll have Liam out and about, all down to you, Novello. Take heed. You've been backed up once. Don't expect it again.'

With the blank expression which conceals high dudgeon, Novello left.

'Was I too hard, Wieldy?'

'On Linford and Belchamber? Not enough. On Novello? Just about right.'

'Thanks. So, this informant of yours came up trumps. Looks like you've got yourself a winner there. Better sign him up official, quick as you can.'

'Not interested,' said Wield.

'Who? Him or you?'

'Him, of course,' said Wield, meeting Pascoe's eyes straight on.

'Fine. But be careful.'

It was conventional CID wisdom that there was no such thing as a free tip-off.

'Yeah. So we'll be taking this Praesidium thing a bit more seriously now?'

'I expect so. Let's go and see the Mighty Kong.'

'OK. But, Pete . . .'

'Yes?'

'I'd like to keep in the background on this one. I mean, sitting in on the interview with Linford's one thing, but I don't think I should be in the front line if we set up an op on the Praesidium tip.'

'You think it might help someone make a connection between your informant and us if it looks like you're calling the shots here?'

'It's possible.'

'OK. No problem. You'll miss out on the glory though. Could tell against you when you're on the short-list for Commissioner.'

'It's a risk I'll just have to take,' said Wield.

In the criminal's Advent calendar, each window opens on a new opportunity.

Huge truckloads of consumer desirables crowd the road en route for city centres. Shop shelves groan with goodies. The malls are packed with shoppers whose purses are packed with cash. The tills ring merrily all day and much of the night and large sums of money have to be transferred with forecastable regularity to the banks. The average house soon has several hundred pounds' worth of easily portable presents 'hidden' in the garage or the cupboard under the stairs. In the non-average house, their value might run into thousands. The party season starts, at home and in the workplace. The provident smuggler is ready to supply the huge appetite for cheap booze and fags, while the happy toper is morally susceptible to a whole range of no-questions-asked deals and physically susceptible to anyone who fancies his wallet.

To an ambitious policeman, keen to pack his CV with collars felt and cases solved, Advent windows also open upon golden opportunity. Here is the devil's plenty. Here is the year's late harvest. The art is to recognize what's ripe for reaping and what's going to prove indigestible, and with resources stretched to the limit, there is little time for careful consideration. So Pascoe found he had all the encouragement in the world to pursue his resolve to put Franny Roote out of his mind and get on with the job of making sure the better part of Mid-Yorkshire had a happy and crime-free Christmas.

But God's a merry fellow who once He has set a jest in train doesn't care to see its object drift off the pre-ordained path.

After the accuracy of Wield's information in the Linford case, it had been decided to take the Praesidium tip seriously. This didn't mean they could offer blanket coverage, but everyone agreed with the sergeant's assessment that the small firms wages delivery was the most likely target, so that's what they focused on. When told of Wield's desire to keep in the background to protect his snout, Dalziel had taken a deep breath, raised his eyebrows and pursed his lips, giving the effect of a monkfish that had just swallowed an electric eel, but he hadn't argued, and it was Pascoe who found himself put in charge.

'Thanks, Pete,' Wield said. 'Not that it should cause you much bother. My estimate is they'll hit it early while it's still carrying most of the cash and you'll have the rest of the day to do the paperwork and still be home in time for a late tea.'

Of course it hadn't worked out like that.

The DCI and his team had crawled along the narrow country roads after the van all morning, their hearts sinking with each delivery, for they knew that as the money went down, so did their chances of getting a result. A less conscientious officer might have called things off with a couple of calls still remaining. The villains would not only have to be unambitious, they'd need to be downright stupid to risk hitting the van with a prospective share-out of only a few hundred pounds. But Pascoe had stuck it out to the bitter end. Only when the last drop had been made on the northernmost boundary of his patch did Pascoe say to his dispirited men, 'Right, that does it. Let's go home.'

Half a day wasted with no result. These things happened, policemen got used to them, but such philosophy did not dilute his intention of being seriously sarcastic with Wield.

He saw him on the phone as he entered the CID room. The sergeant made a summoning gesture, then said into the phone, 'He's just come in.'

'Who?' mouthed Pascoe as he approached.

'Rose,' mouthed Wield in return, giving Pascoe a moment of fright as he wondered what crisis had got his young daughter ringing him at work. Then Wield, who missed little, saw the reaction and expanded, 'DI Rose.'

This, though a relief, meant nothing, till he took the phone and said, 'Pascoe.'

'Hi there. Stanley Rose.'

'Stanley . . . ? Stan! Hello. And DI! When did this happen? Many congratulations.'

The last time he'd talked to Rose, the man had been a DS in South Yorkshire and the occasion had been the case which brought Franny Roote back into his life.

Looking at people who might think threatening Ellie was a good way to pay old scores, he'd liaised with Rose when he discovered Roote was living in Sheffield. It had all been done by the book, but when Pascoe had turned up to interview Roote, he'd found him lying in his bath with his wrists cut. In fact, the cuts were not very deep and he was more likely to have died from hypothermia than blood loss, but naturally rumours of undue pressure had circulated and for a while both Rose and Pascoe looked susceptible to charges of harassment. But Roote was (in Pascoe's eyes) far too subtle a serpent to risk all on a single strike. So he had made no complaint, but his silence was, (to Pascoe's ears) the silence of the snake lurking in the long grass.

So, no official action or come-back. But in the ledgers of CID, to go on to someone else's patch and cause them embarrassment left you with a debt to pay, and Pascoe guessed it was being called in now.

'Beginning of the month,' said Rose. 'They must have been wondering what to give me for Christmas and I'd been dropping hints all year.'

'I'm delighted. Long overdue,' said Pascoe. 'Remind me to buy you a drink next time we meet. So what can I do for you, Stan?'

On the surface it was a simple request for liaison and co-operation. Rose had got a whisper from a snout of a job that was being planned in the New Year. The information was vague. The forward planning suggested it was big, as did the fact that it involved the recruitment of a top driving and muscle team – which was how the snout had got the whisper. And though the organizational nerve centre was in South, word was that the job itself could be over the Mid-Yorkshire border.

'Sorry it's all so waffly,' concluded Rose. 'But it occurred to me that you might spot a few straws in the wind your side, and they might not seem worth much by themselves, but together . . . well, maybe we could make a brick.'

So, there it was, a more or less token request, a formality which if not quite empty would in the vast majority of cases prove lamentably unproductive.

But Pascoe, because he owed Rose and because he could recall those early days after he had taken that large step from sergeant to DI, read the sub-text.

Rose wanted to make a good early impression. He'd been delighted when his snout was the first with this sniff. Probably he'd made rather more of it than it merited at that stage and when, after a couple of weeks, nothing more had been forthcoming, he'd begun to feel rather foolish. Certainly his colleagues in the rough and ready ethos of the CID wouldn't be backward in asking him how the great crime of the new century was coming on! Perhaps he'd been provoked into once more overselling what remained an insubstantial maybe. So he looked around for help. Who owed him? DCI Peter Pascoe, one of the famous Andy Dalziel's brightest and best, who happened to work on the patch mentioned as a putative location for the putative job, that was who!

So it was worth a punt calling in that debt which, furthermore, would be understood to include the major share of credit should anything ever come of this business.

Pascoe asked questions, made notes and encouraging noises.

'OK,' he said finally. 'I'll pull out all the stops, Stan, believe me.'

'I'm grateful,' said Rose. 'This is really good of you.'

'Self-interest,' laughed Pascoe. 'If we don't help each other, we'll be a long time waiting for any other bugger. You see a Samaritan coming towards you these days, it's probably because he fancies putting the boot in.'

These were Dalziel's views rather than his own; indeed it was possibly the Fat Man's very phraseology. But he felt few qualms about voicing them. Just as Wield had kept his gayness under wraps in order to survive in his chosen profession, so Pascoe had recognized early on that educational achievement and liberal humanism were not exactly episematic qualities in the still very traditional police force. A common soldier may have a field marshal's baton hidden in his knapsack, but he was never going to get the chance to wield it if he didn't learn the language of the barrack room.

'You're right there,' said Rose. 'Things don't go away either. I was just telling your Sergeant Wield, that student he was asking about a while back in connection with a possible suicide . . .'

'Sorry?' said Pascoe. 'I don't recall . . .'

But of course he did. Roote's tutor at Sheffield University, Sam Johnson, had (according to rumour) made his move to Mid-Yorkshire as a result of his reaction to the sudden death of Jake Frobisher, a student he'd put under pressure to bring his work up to date or be sent down. When Johnson himself died in suspicious circumstances, Pascoe had used the possibility that he'd committed suicide to instruct Wield to check up on Frobisher's death, allegedly with a view to providing the coroner with a full picture of the lecturer's state of mind. But he knew, and Wield had guessed, that his real hope had been to find some link, however remote, between Franny Roote and both tragedies.

'Jake Frobisher. Some link with that lecturer who was one of your Wordman victims.'

'Of course. Yes, I remember. Turned out he was popping pills to keep himself awake to meet some work deadline, wasn't that it?'

'That's right. Accidental death, clear cut. Only complication was, when his gear was sent to his family, his sister started asking questions about some expensive watch she said was missing, implication being that one of our lot had nicked it. Well, it all got sorted, no evidence, no case, his mum didn't want a fuss, in fact she didn't even recollect the watch in question. End of story, right?'

'Should be,' said Pascoe neutrally, letting his gaze drift towards Wield, who was peering into a screen as if he saw his future there. 'But I'm not going to bet on it.'

'Wise man,' said Rose. 'Sophie, that's the sister, started here as a student in September, and lo and behold, end of last term she got pulled in with a bunch of other kids all high as kites on speed. Must run in the family, eh? We found a great stash of the stuff in her room, which incidentally is in the same house her brother died in – how's that for morbid? Anyway, the little cow, instead of putting her hand up, starts claiming it was planted there so we could get our own back for her daring to accuse us of nicking her brother's watch! Case came up yesterday. The bloody magistrate lets her ramble on through the whole sad story, wipes a tear away from his eye, glowers at me on the witness bench, and gives her a conditional discharge! I told her afterwards she was lucky and she'd better be careful or she'll end up like her brother. Having my watch nicked, you mean? she says, and gives me the finger, then takes off with her mates, laughing. It's a great job we've got, isn't it?'

'Yes,' said Pascoe thoughtfully. 'Yes, I believe it is. I'll be in touch, Stan.'

He put down the phone and stared at Wield until the sergeant's head turned, as if compelled by the force of Pascoe's gaze.

The DCI jerked his head in summons and went through into his office.

The sergeant followed, closing the door behind him.

Succinctly, Pascoe filled him in on the day's debacle.

'So thanks a lot for that, Wieldy,' he concluded. 'Nothing I like better than a scenic tour of the county in mid-winter instead of wasting my time doing useful things.'

'Pete, I'm sorry. I'll talk to my informant and see . . .'

'Yeah yeah,' said Pascoe impatiently. The failed job had dropped a long way down his priority list of things to be pissed off with Wield about. 'Forget it. But there's something else. Remember when Sam Johnson died, I asked you to check out that student death in Sheffield, boy called Frobisher, the one people seemed to think had upset Johnson so much he made the move here to MYU?'

'I remember,' said Wield.

'And you told me it was all done and dusted, accidental overdose, no loose ends.'

'That's right.'

'What about this missing watch? I don't recollect you mentioning that in your report. That not a loose end?'

'Didn't look like one to me,' said Wield. 'In fact it looked like it was probably nowt at all, not worth mentioning, just a young lass being silly.'

'Even young lasses get over being silly,' said Pascoe. 'Not this one though, eh?'

He hadn't wanted to sound confrontational, but the sheer unreadability of the sergeant's face was a provocation to provocation. For the first time he understood how it must feel to be sitting opposite Wield in the interrogation room.

The reply came in the quiet reasonable voice of a patient father explaining life to a recalcitrant son.

'If you remember, the reason you gave for being interested in Frobisher was it might be relevant to Johnson's state of mind if it turned out he'd topped himself. By the time I got the details of Frobisher's accidental overdose, we knew that Johnson had been murdered by the Wordman, so there was no way for the lad's death to be relevant, not even if it had had more loose ends than you'd find at a monk's wedding.'

The tone remained constant throughout, but the concluding Dalzielesque image sent a message of strong feeling which Pascoe gleefully registered as a minor victory, of which he was almost simultaneously ashamed. Wield had been then, and was now, trying to save him from what he and probably everyone else regarded as a dangerous obsession.

But they were wrong, Pascoe assured himself. Not that he was absolutely, bet-the-deeds-of-the-ranch certain he was right. But obsessions were irrational and as he wasn't going to do anything that couldn't be tested by reason, this was no obsession. As for danger, how could this particular pursuit of truth be more dangerous than any other?

The only real danger he would admit was that of falling out with those he loved most.

He said gently, 'Sorry, Wieldy. I'm being a plonker, but everyone's entitled this time of year. Rose tell you what he was after? No? Ah, well, it's me he feels owes him.'

He quickly ran through Rose's request for help.

'Not much,' said Wield.

'Not much is overstating it. Still, he's a good cop, so let's pull out the stops. Any sniff of anything big going down on our patch, I want to know. Pass the word.'

'Even to Andy? He'll not be chuffed at you paying off old debts on company time.'

'He's going to be even less chuffed if something big did happen and South were sitting there smugly saying, "Well, we did warn you!"'

Wield gave a small nod which might have meant anything from he was totally convinced to he was totally unpersuaded, but Pascoe watched him go, certain that his instructions would be carried out to the full.

He took off his overcoat, hung it up, then sat at his desk and on a piece of paper wrote *Sophie Frobisher*. Then he added a question mark.

What the question was he wasn't certain, nor indeed whether he'd ever ask it.

One thing was certain, thank God, and that was that he needn't make any decision about it till next month when the new university term began.

Perhaps by then Roote would have faded to distant irritation. Perhaps the last letter in which he said goodbye to England would prove to be a farewell letter in every sense.

And perhaps Christmas would be cancelled this year!

Pascoe laughed.

Dalziel said, 'Glad to see you're in such a good mood.'

Shit? Is there a secret passage he uses to get into my room? wondered Pascoe.

'I was just coming to see you, sir. Dud tip, I'm afraid, complete waste of time . . .'

'Half right,' said the Fat Man. 'About the waste of time, but not the tip.'

'Sorry?'

'I've just had an angry call from Berry at Praesidium. Says he thought we were taking care of his wages van today.'

'Yes, sir, and we did until it made its last drop . . . Shit, you're not saying . . . ?'

He was.

The Praesidium security men, after a day spent in the expectation of imminent attack, had felt they deserved a soothing cup of tea on the way back, to which end they had pulled into the lorry park of a roadside cafe on the bypass just north of town. As they got out of the van, they were jumped on by a bunch of masked men armed with baseball bats and at least one sawn-off shotgun. Surprised in every sense, they put up no resistance and were left unharmed, locked in a white transit van, tucked away in a remote corner of the lorry park where they might have remained a lot longer if Morris Berry, the Praesidium boss, hadn't noticed his van suddenly vanish from the screen. He'd sent someone to investigate at the last known location and they'd heard noises from the transit. By the time Pascoe arrived on the scene, he found the security men enjoying their now even more necessary soothing cup of tea and sufficiently recovered to be much amused at the image of the thieves' gobsmacked expressions when they found they'd got a vanload of nothing.

Pascoe didn't share their amusement. This might be a cock-up for the crooks, but he knew that it was going to register as a cock-up for the cops also. When the story was told in the canteen and the papers, the joke was going to be on him. And in the annual list of crime statistics, this day's work would show as a security van hijacked despite a tip-off and an expensive escort operation.

Suddenly Franny Roote was relegated to the very bottom of his piled-up troubles and when at last he returned to his office, he swept the piece of paper bearing Sophie Frobisher's name into his waste bin without even reading it.

The Temptation

Fichtenburg-am-Blutensee

Aargau

Monday Dec 17th (Midnight!)

Dear Mr Pascoe

My mind's in a turmoil so here I am writing to you once
more. Let me skip over my nightmare journey here.
Suffice it to say that my efforts at economy were rewarded
by *two* train breakdowns and I ended up reaching
Manchester Airport only five minutes before my departure
time, and I still had to collect my ticket! No way could I
do that and run the gauntlet of baggage and security
checks in less than half an hour, I thought. Oh dear.
Linda, who likes her arrangements to stay arranged, would
not be pleased.

But I needn't have worried. Even Linda's organization
is like a dry reed beneath the brutal tread of the airlines.

My flight was delayed ... And delayed ... And
delayed ...

Finally we took to the air. Clearly they hadn't let the
delay interfere with their catering schedule. What arrived on
my plate made the Chapel Syke cuisine look attractive. And I
was seated next to a fat talkative estate agent with a bad cold.

Nor did my problems end when we landed in Zurich.

My case was the very last to appear on the carousel, a neanderthal customs officer could not be persuaded that I wasn't a Colombian drugs baron, and when I finally emerged into the public concourse, nowhere amongst all the attendant banners bearing strange devices did I see one with my name on it.

Some time later, I almost literally stumbled across my taxi driver snoozing in the coffee bar. Only the fact that he'd placed the sheet of paper bearing an approximation of my name (Herr Rutt) over his eyes to keep the light out gave me the necessary clue. He seemed to resent being woken and set off into what looked to me like an incipient blizzard without more than a guttural grunt in my direction, but after the estate agent's mucous maunderings, I was not too sorry about this.

(I seem to recollect saying I was going to skip over all this, but it's too deeply impressed on my psyche to dismiss so easily! Sorry.)

Linda had assured me that Fichtenburg was within easy driving distance of Zurich but not, I felt, in this weather or with this driver. It seemed to take forever. In the end my fatigue overcame my fear and I dozed off. When I was awoken by the car coming to a halt with a suddenness which threw me forward quite violently, my first thought was we'd had an accident. Instead, as I recovered my senses, I realized the driver had placed my luggage outside the taxi and was standing holding the passenger door open, not, I hasten to add, in any spirit of flunkeydom but merely to expedite my exit.

Still half asleep, I staggered out, he slammed the door, climbed into the driver's seat, slammed that door also and roared off into the night without so much as a *Leb'wohl!*

It was snowing gently. I strained my eyes to pierce the curtain of flakes. All I could make out in vague outline was rank upon rank of tall fir trees.

The bastard had dropped me off in the middle of a forest!

Alarmed, I span round. And with infinite relief my eyes, now adjusting to the darkness, this time made out the solid-faced and sharp angles of a building. I let my gaze run to the left and couldn't find its limit. To the right the same. I leaned backwards to look up and through the floating veils of snowflakes I glimpsed turrets and battlements.

Fichtenburg!

'Oh my God!' I said out loud.

My school German has almost vanished, but I seemed to recollect that *Fichten* meant pine trees and I was certain *Burg* meant castle.

I had assumed this was just some fancy name Linda's chums had given to their holiday chalet. I should have known better.

Fichtenburg was exactly what its name stated – a castle among the pines!

And, what was worse, apparently a deserted castle.

Feeling like Childe Roland when he finally made it to the Dark Tower and started to wonder if it had been such a great idea after all, I advanced towards what looked like the building's main door. Constructed of heavy oak planks bound together with massy plates of iron, it had clearly been designed by a man who didn't care to have his relatives dropping by unexpectedly.

A bolus of metal attached to a chain hung from one of the granite doorposts. I seized it and pulled. After a while, somewhere so distant it might have been in another world, a bell rang.

In a Gothic novel, or a *Goon Show* script, the next sound effect would have been a slow shuffle of dreadful feet growing louder as they approached.

I was almost glad when my straining ears detected nothing.

Almost, for now the possibility that there'd been some misunderstanding and I wasn't expected and there was no one here to greet me began to loom frighteningly large. My knowledge of Switzerland derives largely from early

213

nineteenth-century literature in which it figures as a confusion of towering mountains, huge glaciers and snowy wastes. Since the airport, I had seen little to correct that impression. Even when I turned my back on imagination and applied to common sense, the answer I got was scarcely more reassuring. People who built castles rarely did so within striking distance of neighbours to whom they could apply for the loan of a barrel of boiling oil if ever they ran short.

The alternative to trudging off into the snow in search of help was to break in.

Now with your average suburban house, this (my acquaintance at the Syke assured me) normally involves little more than putting your elbow through a pane of glass and unlatching a downstairs window.

Your average castle, however, is a horse of a different colour. For a start, and indeed for a finish, the only windows I could see through the drifting snow were well out of my elbow's reach and protected by bars.

It would be easier to break into Chapel Syke!

My one remaining hope was that in a building of this size, there might be a servants' quarter round the back, full of life and warmth, with a TV set playing so loud that the doorbell went unnoticed. Such hopeful fantasies crowd thick upon a desperate man. In any case, any movement seemed preferable to standing here and freezing to death.

I set off along the front and then down the side of the castle, following the twists and turns of its coigns and embrasures, till I had no idea whether I was still at the front or the side or the back! The snow had stopped falling and slowly the cloud was beginning to break up, allowing occasional glimpses of a nearly full moon. But its beams brought little comfort, showing the solid unwelcoming stonework broken only by barred and darkened windows.

In despair, I turned my back on the castle and strained my eyes outwards into the crowding forest.

Was it rescue? Was it an evil delusion? For a second, I was sure I saw a distant light! Then it was gone. But welcome or will-o'-the-wisp, it was all I had and I rushed in the direction I'd seen it, even though it meant leaving the guiding wall of the castle behind me and heading into the forest, all the while slipping and floundering in deep folds of snow, and shouting, 'Help! Help!' then, recalling where I was, *'Zur Hilfe! Zur Hilfe!'*

Finally and inevitably, I fell flat on my face in a drift. When I pushed myself upright and looked around me (the breaking of the clouds giving me the full benefit of the moon at that moment), I saw that I was in a clearing in which stood a building. For a second I had hope that this might be the source of the light I had seen, but as I moved nearer, I saw that it was a ruined chapel. Strange how powerful the human imagination can be, isn't it? You'd think that sheer physical fright at the prospect of dying from exposure in this cold and inhospitable terrain would have left little room for any more metaphysical fear. But as I examined that place, all my awareness of mere bodily discomfort and peril was subsumed in superstitious terror! It wasn't just the post-Romantic knee-jerk reaction to a Gothic ruin in a wild and remote setting. No, what really broke me out in a sweat despite the temperature was what I saw painted on the chapel's internal walls. The plaster had fallen completely in many areas and where it remained it was cracked and flaking, but I had no doubt what it was the artist had depicted there.

It was the Dance of Death.

A grisly enough subject, you are probably thinking, and not one a chap in young Fran's situation would wish to dwell upon, but why should it affect him so strongly?

The answer is this. In Beddoes' *Jest-Book*, that most terrifying scene in which the Duke, hoping to raise his wife from the dead instead resurrects the murdered Wolfram, is set before a ruined Gothic church on whose cloister wall is depicted the Dance of Death. My quest for Beddoes had brought me to this place, and now he seemed to be saying in that typically sardonic way of his, *If you want to see me plain, this way lies your route!*

I know it sounds silly. After all, unlike the Duke, I have no murdered rival whose resurrection I need fear, have I?

And in any case my God-given reason tells me, as it told Beddoes, *there are no ghosts to raise, Out of death lead no ways.* Oh, that there were! How I would labour to raise dear Sam. But what horror if instead of Sam I found myself confronted by . . . some less welcome *revenu!*

What nonsense this seems in broad daylight.

But there in the dark forest close by the ruined chapel, I have to admit, Mr Pascoe, that both innocence and rationality failed me and I closed my eyes and said a prayer.

When I opened them, I saw that some god had heard me, but whether in the Christian heaven or some darker colder Nordic place, I wasn't yet ready to say. The light I had seen before showed itself again, much nearer this time, and approaching! I could see it intermittently among the trees, moving with a serpentine motion, now visible, now masked by the long straight trunks of the pines, a circle of brightness growing larger as it neared, putting me in mind of that shining sphere which marks the arrival of Glenda in *The Wizard of Oz.*

It was a happy comparison, for as – guided I presume by my almost hysterical shouting – it emerged from the forest into the clearing, I saw that it was the headlight on one of those snow buggies, and though the goggled and furred creature that bestrode it was sexless to the eye, I knew she was my Good Fairy when she spoke and said, *'Herr Roote? Willkommen in Fichtenburg.'*

This, God bless her, was Frau Buff, the housekeeper, a woman it emerged of few words, and all of those German, but one whose good sense and ratiocinative powers make you understand why the Swiss lead the world in the manufacture of timepieces.

Mind you, it did occur to me as she indicated I

should climb up behind her (she'd already found my luggage at the castle entrance) and we set off along a winding track through the dark pine trees, to wonder if she might not be a good fairy after all but the Snow Queen, and I, like little Kay, was being abducted to her ice palace at the North Pole.

No ice palace this, I'm glad to say, but a warm and comfortable and roomy cabin with all mod cons! This was the chalet Linda had referred to, belonging to the castle and used, I presume, to accommodate visitors like myself who for whatever reason were best kept separate from the beau monde in the big house. Frau Buff had been waiting for me here. When I didn't arrive at the expected time she'd made enquiries and discovered my plane was delayed. When I still hadn't appeared by the revised expected time, she contacted the taxi company and was told their driver had reported dropping his passenger at the castle some minutes earlier. She, deducing that the Dummkopf had dumped me at the wrong place, had come looking for me.

All this I pieced together with my slowly resurrecting schoolboy German and her sparing replies.

She was, God bless her, much more interested in feeding me than conversing with me. Fortunately, what she'd been preparing was one of those all-inclusive casserole dishes which, unlike airline food, only gets better the longer it stays in the oven.

Once she saw me tucking in, she indicated apologetically that she was leaving me to my own devices. I tried to say that it was me who should apologize for taking up so much of her free time, and I must have got my message across because as she furred herself up preparatory to stepping out into the cold night, she seemed to my slowly adjusting ear to say it wasn't her own pleasure which was taking her away but getting rooms ready in the castle for Frau Lupin.

Thinking I'd got her wrong, I said in my fractured German, 'But Frau Lupin isn't coming till next week.'

And as she went out of the door she tossed something over her shoulder which froze my forkload of delicious stew in mid-air.

'*Nicht Frau sondern Fraulein Lupin. Ihre Tochter.*'

Not Mrs but Miss Lupin. Her daughter.

Perhaps I had misheard!

I broke the spell and rushed out after Frau Buff. She was already on the snow buggy.

'*Fraulein Lupin,*' I cried to her. '*Wann kommt sie?*'

'*Morgen,*' she called. '*Um Schnittschuhlaufen!*'

That baffled me. What in the name of hell was *Schnittschuhlaufen*?

'*Was ist das?*' I shouted as she started up and began to move away.

She pointed away from the chalet with her right hand.

'*Auf dem See!*' she tossed over her shoulder. Then she was gone.

On the sea? I stood there baffled. Then for the first time I noticed the snow had stopped, the clouds were breaking up and going about their business, leaving the sky to a scatter of diamond dust such as those of us in city pent never see, and a slice of moon hung there, bright enough to light up before me a level meadow almost perfectly round.

Except it wasn't a meadow! It was a small lake. Idiot! This must be the *Blutensee* which *Fichtenburg* was *am*, frozen over and besprinkled with snow. (*See* only means 'sea' when it's feminine; I once got my knuckles rapped for forgetting that!)

Skating. *Schnittschuhlaufen* was skating. Emerald was coming here in the morning for the skating!

Now my ever-optimistic mind was racing. Was this coincidence, I asked myself, or was it planned? Could Emerald have learned her mother's plans for me and decided to cut in? Or was I being absurdly arrogant to even imagine that it might be so?

These things distracted me so much that on my

return inside I hardly noticed the delights of Frau Buff's casserole or the smoothness of the bottle of excellent burgundy I had chosen from a well-stocked wine rack. And I have even postponed the plateful of scrumptious-looking *Sahnetorte* the good woman has left for pudding so that once more I can write to you, my friend, my spiritual father, to clear my mind and remind me that in the midst of no matter what fiery turbulence of spirit I can always find a small circle of coolness and calm, like the lake outside my window, to bring me peace.

Well, it's worked. Now I feel ready to face the future – and to enjoy my *Sahnetorte*.

Thank you.

Franny

n England on the whole even criminals celebrate Christmas, but rest for the wicked does not automatically mean rest for the law's guardians also. The crimes of greed which are proper to Advent may fade to nothing on the day itself, but they are more than compensated for by those crimes of new rage and old resentment which spring naturally from the close confinement, with large supplies of alcohol, of blood relations who have had the good sense to keep far apart for the previous three hundred and sixty-four days.

So as Pascoe hastened home on Christmas Eve, bearing with him gifts for Rosie which several of his generous colleagues had placed on his desk, he also bore the fear that the two days off he had won after much hard wheeling and dealing could be interrupted by a phone call saying, Sorry, but there's so much domestic mayhem going on we can't cope, and could you come in and give us a hand, please?

Or, if it were Dalziel calling, scrub the question mark and the please.

As he put his key into his front door lock, he looked at the brass lion's-head knocker which Ellie had 'rescued' from a derelict farmhouse up on Greendale Moor and waited to see if it would turn into the Fat Man's face.

No change, so maybe he was going to be spared a haunting.

But when he went in and saw on the hall table where Ellie left his personal mail an envelope with a Swiss stamp on and the address written in what was becoming a familiar hand, he felt he'd relaxed too soon.

He would have thrown it in the fire except that Ellie would

have known, and he'd resolved to try and keep to himself just how much these letters bothered him.

But he did manage to ignore it till he'd embraced his wife, thrown his daughter into the air, persuaded her fiercely protective dog, Tig, that this was not a form of personal assault, got into his comfortable, back-flattened, dog-chewed slippers, which he did not doubt would be replaced tomorrow by a new stiff pair which he and Tig would have to start working on immediately, and taken a long pull at a long gin-and tonic.

'See you got some more Fran-mail,' said Ellie.

'I noticed. So what's it say?'

'How should I know?'

'You mean you haven't steamed it open?'

'If I were that keen to read it I would rip it open,' said Ellie. 'But I don't deny I'm mildly interested to see how he's getting on hobnobbing with the idle rich.'

'It's their nobs that are likely to get hobbed,' said Pascoe.

He opened the envelope, scanned through the letter then tossed it across to his wife.

She read it more slowly, then turned back to the beginning and started again.

'Hell's bells,' he said. 'It's not Jane Austen.'

'Oh, I don't know. Hero and heroine meet, exchange yearning glances, part perhaps for ever, then by a strange turn of fate are thrown together in a remote Gothic setting. Not a million miles from *Northanger Abbey*,' said Ellie.

'When Roote's involved, there's a good chance the Gothic stuff will turn out to be really supernatural,' said Pascoe.

'No. He's a realist at heart. An explanation for everything. Except that thing about having a vision of you. Very odd. I mean, the Virgin Mary's one thing, but you!'

'You won't laugh when I'm a cult,' said Pascoe negligently.

He hadn't told Ellie about his own vision of Roote by St Margaret's Church at the same time the man was allegedly seeing him. One thing being a policeman taught you was that the world was awash with coincidences. In fact it often seemed to him when critics moaned about a book relying too much on them that usually the false note was struck by writers refusing to admit just how large a part they did play in our day-to-day existence.

So he persuaded himself he had a rational argument for saying nothing. But he found himself childishly eager to have her approve his reaction to the letters in some degree.

'You've got to see he's taking the piss,' he urged.

'Have I? So what precisely do you think he's mocking you about?'

'You see the way he compares the Duke's desire to raise his dead wife with his own longing to resurrect Sam Johnson? Instead, the Duke gets this rival he's murdered. And I ask myself, where do I find a dead rival of Roote's? All over the place, that's where! Albacore for a start. Then there's that student in Sheffield, Jake Frobisher, the one who overdosed himself trying to catch up on his work, the one whose death was responsible for Johnson's sudden move to Mid-Yorkshire Uni.'

'The one whose death you had Wieldy double-check with no result? Come on! At the very worst Franny might be gently mocking your obsession with dragging him into your investigations, but I defy you to point to anything that even a fully paid-up paranoid like yourself can take as positively threatening.'

'What about the bit about envying my domestic bliss?' said Pascoe stubbornly.

She checked it out, looked up at her husband and sadly shook her head.

'He tells you you're lucky to have such a lovely wife and delightful daughter, and you think that's a threat? Come on!'

'Well, how about all that crap about me providing him with a circle of peace and calm. You've got to admit that's just a bit weird,' said Pascoe, annoyed that he'd let himself be drawn into an argument about the letter in spite of all his resolutions.

'Maybe. But you've been elected his guru, his spiritual father, remember? You can't blame an orphan boy with growing pains for turning to his wise old spiritual daddy!'

This might have provoked an outburst most unfitting for the eve of this great family festival had not Rosie come into the room at that moment, yawning widely and demanding to know if it wasn't past her bedtime. This being akin to the Prince of

Darkness suddenly expressing a desire to close down Hell and open a care home, her parents burst into sadly unsympathetic laughter and then had to repair the damage done to her tender sensibilities.

There is a story somewhere of a man in his last night in the condemned cell trying to pretend he is a child waiting for Christmas in order to turn his haring hours into those tortoise-paced minutes of childhood. Fast or slow, good or bad, all things come in the end, and the following morning it took only a paler shade of blackness in the eastern sky to have Rosie bursting into the parental bedroom demanding to know if they intended lying there all day.

After that things proceeded more or less according to her timetable, with Pascoe made to feel that his insistence on having coffee and toast before starting to open the presents was a manifest offence against the European Declaration on Human Rights.

The pile of parcels beneath the tree was large, not because the Pascoes were over-indulgent parents, but because their daughter had a strong sense of equity and insisted that everyone else should have as many parcels to unwrap as she did, including the dog.

Her unselfish delight in watching her mother and father in receipt of their gifts more than compensated for the strain on Pascoe's dramatic abilities as he declared with rapture that a pair of electric blue cotton socks was all he needed to make his life complete.

Of course others of his gifts were more luxurious and/or more interesting.

'Let me guess,' he said to Ellie hefting a book-shaped parcel. 'You've bought me a Bible? No, it's too light. The Wit and Wisdom of Prince Charles? No, too heavy. Or is it that intellectual treat I've been after for ages: *The Pirelli Calendar: the Glory Years?*'

'Don't get your hopes up,' said Ellie.

He ripped off the wrapping paper and found himself looking at a book with a jet black jacket design broken only by a small high window of white which bore the title *Dark Cells* by Amaryllis Haseen.

'I saw it in that remainder shop in Market Street,' said Ellie. 'And I thought, if you're going to be hung up on Roote, you might as well read what the experts have got to say.'

'Well, thank you kindly,' said Pascoe, uncertain how he felt about it. Then he caught Rosie's gaze upon him and was reminded. 'That's absolutely marvellous. I've been looking for a copy everywhere, how clever of you to find one, and so heavily discounted at that.'

Satisfied, Rosie turned her attention to Tig whose pleasure at his prezzies, as long as they were instantly edible, was genuine and unconfined.

Finally the ceremony was over. Rosie now had the difficult task of deciding which of her many gifts to concentrate on first. Her pecking order, which Ellie was glad to see had nothing to do with expense, placed equal top a trace-your-ancestors geneal-ogy kit and a silent dog whistle which the instructions assured her would provide instant control of her pet over distances up to half a mile. Finally, because as she said it was Christmas for Tig too, and ignoring the disincentive of a biting east wind, she opted for the whistle and took the dog out into the garden to change its life. Ellie went upstairs to ring her mother who was coming to them tomorrow but insisted on spending Christmas Day itself with her Alzheimer-stricken husband in his nursing home. To her daughter's proposal that they would all make the two-hour drive to join her there on Christmas afternoon, Mrs Soper had replied briskly, 'Don't be silly, dear. I know you feel guilty, but you really mustn't let your guilt spoil things for others. It's a bad habit I hoped you'd got out of.'

When Ellie had protested, her mother had reminded her of a ruined Christmas Day when, aged twelve, Ellie had decided she was going to send all her presents plus her Christmas dinner to Oxfam.

'That was only one of many times,' she'd concluded. 'Your father's right out of it now. It's my place to be with him on Christmas Day. It's yours to be at home.'

Good for her! Pascoe had applauded internally. But he had tried not to let it show.

Now seated alone with another mug of coffee, he glanced at

his watch, groaned to see that though his body-clock told him it must be dinner-time, its hands told him it was still only nine forty-five, then reached out and picked up *Dark Cells*.

He skipped through the introduction in which the author assured him that this was a serious in-depth analysis of the relationship between penological theory and the practicalities of incarceration, a claim somewhat at odds with that made on the jacket sleeve where he was invited to be titillated by *a riveting account of evil unmasked and a disturbing analysis of the failure of our prison system to contain it. Do not read this book unless you feel strong enough to meet some of the worst men in our society. Be prepared to be shocked, to be scandalized, to be terrified!*

A perfect antidote to Christmas, he thought. He went out to the hall and from a shelf in the cupboard under the stairs he took his private Roote file. Dalziel's gaze had noted it on his office desk, and doubtless noted too the drawer into which he'd slipped it. The drawer had a sturdy lock as did the office door, but Pascoe would not have bet sixpence against the Fat Man breaking through. So that same day he had brought the file home.

He sat down again and from the file he took Roote's first letter and glanced through it. Here it was . . . *I am Prisoner XR pp193–207* . . .

He picked up *Dark Cells* and turned to page 193, where sure enough the author began her case history of Prisoner XR.

After giving details of crime and sentence, Ms Haseen got straight down to her sessions with Roote.

> *His recorded responses during the investigation, the psychological assessment prepared in concurrence with his trial, and the whole raft of subsequent and consequent reports I had read of his reactions and behaviour since sentence all contained significant indices that here was a highly intelligent man sufficiently in control of himself to use that intelligence to make his stay in prison as comfortable and as short as possible, and, though I am very aware of the need to proceed with great caution in matters of analysis, in his case I felt within a few minutes of our first meeting*

fairly sanguine that the proposed course of analysis would affirm the accuracy of those advance impressions.

God, this was turgid stuff! No wonder the book had been remaindered!

From the start he was keen to demonstrate, and to underline in case I missed the point, that he was accepting these sessions absolutely on my terms. Unlike many of the others (see Prisoner JJ pp104 ff and Prisoner PR pp184 ff) he never showed any overt sexual awareness of me, nor when my investigation touched on matters pertaining to his sexuality did he see this as an opportunity to indulge in self-titillating sex talk (see Prisoners AH and BC pp209 ff). Yet despite this strict propriety, I often felt the atmosphere between us was highly charged, sexually speaking.

You can bet your sweet ass it was! thought Pascoe.

This fitted in very well with my developing judgment that Prisoner XR was going to be a difficult case to put under the magnifying glass of detailed analysis. He was clearly determined to provide me with no insight into his psyche that might be at odds with what he saw as the only truly important objects of our sessions viz. his rapid transfer from Chapel Syke to an open prison, and subsequently his early parole.

She may be a lousy writer, old Amaryllis, thought Pascoe, but at least she got that right. Let's see if she managed to get under his guard at all. Though, remembering that it was Roote himself who'd drawn his attention to her book, it didn't seem likely.

Our first few sessions therefore were in the nature of pre-liminary skirmishes whose main function in his eyes was to establish that he was in charge while I endeavoured to persuade him that I was unaware of his efforts so to do. Once past that point, though he always remained on a high level of vigilance, I was able to utilize his greater relaxation to make contact with him at a deeper level than hithertofore.

Hithertofore! He smiled, then, recalling what a sad Christmas this must be for the woman, he stopped smiling and read on.

Lot of background stuff. No names or identifying details, of course, but he fitted these in from his own researches.

Family background: mother and stepfather; the latter a well-heeled businessman called Keith Prime who married Mrs Roote when Franny was six and clearly didn't take long to decide it was worth spending a little of his wealth on keeping his stepson out of his hair.

Boarding schools from age seven – first a prep school, then Coltsfoot College, a progressive public school near Chester. At some point, apparently for business reasons, the Primes had set up home in the Virgin Isles and most of young Franny's vacations were spent staying with friends in England, a practise continued when he went to Holm Coultram College of Liberal Arts where his and Pascoe's paths had first crossed.

Thereafter the vacation problem was solved by residence at HMP Chapel Syke.

His mother, according to Pascoe's own records, had visited her son once during pre-trial custody, thereafter pleading poor health as reason for not attending the trial. Prime had never appeared. There was no record of the mother ever visiting her son in the Syke, but her claim to physical debility was supported the hard way when she died during his second year of detention. She was buried in the Virgin Isles. No application was made by Roote to attend the funeral. No contact with Keith Prime was recorded.

It was evident that Amaryllis Haseen had been fascinated by the relationship between Roote and his mother and father and stepfather, which must have made it easy for him to jerk her around with fictitious memories of the father he couldn't recall at all.

> *XR was clearly father-fixated to a degree which must have been psychologically disabling till he developed techniques of control, though not without detriment to other more conventional emotional procedures. His obviously enhanced memories of incidents involving his father all tended to stress qualities which made the dead man a worthy object of admiration and affection, yet underpinning them always*

was that syndrome in which the subject's sense of being abandoned by the object, even though the cause of abandonment is death, manifests itself in angry and abusive resentment.

An example of the exaggerated memory was the following, being an account of an incident when the subject was four or five years old.

XR: we were walking through the park one day, me and my dad, when this big guy jumped out of a bush brandishing a knife. He grabbed me by the hair and put the knife to my throat and said to my dad, 'Here's the deal, give me your wallet and the kid lives.'

And my dad reached into his jacket and pulled out this huge pistol and he said, 'No, here's the deal, let go the kid and you live.'

And the big guy said, 'Hey man, no need to get heavy,' and let me go. And my dad jumped forward and smashed him across the side of his head with the gun, and when he fell down my dad stamped on the hand carrying the knife till he dropped it.

And the big guy lay on the ground screaming, 'I thought we had a deal, man!'

And my dad said, 'The deal was, you get to live, but I didn't say anything about you living healthy.'

That an incident occurred in which the subject as a small boy was frightened in a park and was defended by his father is possible. In this and other recollections the father is always referred to as 'my dad', the possessive and the familiar abbreviation being together indicative of a deep sense of loss and an almost painful desire for repossession. The gun-toting Dirty Harry accretions have probably been developed over many years of creative recollection and it is likely that the subject is by now completely persuaded of the truth of this version. It is interesting to note that the qualities this embellished narrative stresses have less to do with the kind of story-book heroism which might have appealed to a young boy and more to a cold and calculating self-sufficiency. It *would have been interesting to hear the version of this story that the subject was telling at the ages of, say, ten, and then again at fifteen.*

Alongside this let us set the subject's response when it was suggested to him that he must have missed his dead father greatly.

> *'Miss him? Why the fuck should I miss him? He never earned any more than kept us out of the gutter. Useless bastard, getting himself killed like that. We were better off without him even though he didn't even leave us a pension. Fortunately Mother found herself this drooling dickhead who was so loaded we could afford to buy ourselves all the stuff we wanted.'*

Subject's attempts to reduce his bereavement to economic terms are a typical grief-controlling stratagem in which the discomforts of poverty are substituted for the pain of loss. Accusations of selfishness aimed at the dead for dying appear in this light to have a real and computable base, and the return of prosperity can then be projected on to the subject's ego-view as a healing of any wounds the bereavement may have caused.

At the same time the source of the new prosperity is likely to be viewed with suspicion, or indeed as in this case contempt verging on hatred. I could discern little trace here of any Oedipal jealousy – subject always refers to his mother simply as 'mother', never using 'mum' or any other diminutivization, or employing the possessive pronoun, and never offering any anecdotes in which she features other than as a functional presence – so the unfailing choice of pejorative descriptions for his stepfather must be ascribed to subject's appreciation of his stepfather's wealth as a criticism of his real father's failure to provide for his family and his determination that the newcomer is never going to get close to taking the dead man's place.

There was a lot more like this and soon Pascoe was yawning. What was it the blurb had said? *Be prepared to be shocked, to be scandalized, to be terrified.* It hadn't mentioned the danger of being bored out of your skull.

The author blurb seemed to indicate that Haseen had a good track record as a serious academic psychologist, but even this seemed non-proven to Pascoe in the light of the way she swallowed hook, line and sinker everything that Roote dangled in front of her about his memories of his father.

'I'm glad to see that at least one of my gift choices has not been in vain,' said Ellie, who'd returned undetected.

'It would be a comic masterpiece if it wasn't dull,' said Pascoe. 'How's your mum?'

'Fine. At least she says she is. Celebrating Christmas surrounded by people most of whom can't even remember who they are let alone what day it is can't be a bundle of fun.'

'It's happening all over the country,' said Pascoe. 'Sorry. You're right. It can't be. Still, she'll be with us tomorrow. We'll see she has a great time. Your dad, is he . . . ?'

'No miracle cures, Pete,' she said. 'Or, if there are, they're going to be too late for him, I fear. It's really pissy, isn't it? Losing someone without being able to grieve properly because they're not officially dead.'

'I know, I know,' said Pascoe. He stood up, poured a drink and took it to Ellie. But before he gave it to her, he put his arms round her and pulled her close. After a while she moved away, took the glass and said, 'Thanks. That helped. This too.'

'Part of the service,' he said lightly. 'But do me a favour, any time you think of getting real help, don't apply to Ms Amaryllis Haseen!'

'No? And apart from her sex, what objective evidence do you have for that slur on a well-respected professional woman's competence?'

Pascoe tried to detect how much self-mocking irony there was in Ellie's reaction, found no clue in her expression and decided to play it straight.

'Maybe I'm being a bit hard,' he said. 'Lots of bright people have been given the run around by our Franny. Listen to this. *Subject evinced a comprehensive mental blinkering with regard to interpretation of his father's evidently increasingly eccentric behaviour.*

He said, 'Mother never gave my dad credit for anything he did, in fact she'd deliberately take things the wrong way. When he was away from home on dangerous missions he couldn't tell us about, she got very angry and talked about him going off and enjoying himself boozing with his fancy woman. She even refused to go down to London with him when he was being awarded a medal. He wanted to take me but she wouldn't let him, I don't know why.' And Ms Haseen takes all this as gospel! I know how good Roote is at pulling people's strings, but surely a pro should be able to see through him.'

'But what makes you so sure he's pulling her strings?' asked Ellie.

'What? Ah, you think that Roote Senior might indeed have been an MI5 undercover agent who died bravely in the line of duty? Well, let me disenchant you.'

He picked up his file and riffled through the papers.

'Here we are, Roote's father was a civil servant who died when his son was two years old. Confirmation of what Roote himself says in his letters several times, that he lost his father so early he has no memories of him whatsoever.'

'What is that, Peter?' said Ellie, staring at the file.

'This?' said Pascoe, suddenly remembering that Dalziel's were not the only sharp eyes it was sometimes wiser to keep things hidden from. 'Oh, just some notes about Roote I had lying around. Seemed a sensible place to keep these letters in.'

'Looks a bit bulky for just some notes,' said Ellie. 'And that note you were extracting that stuff about Roote Senior from . . . ?'

'Well, actually it's a copy of Roote's college file, just background details . . .'

'Holm Coultram College, you mean?' said Ellie. 'Those files were confidential!'

'Come on! He was a suspect in a serious investigation.'

'Oh yes. You don't happen to have a copy of my file there too, do you?'

'No, really subversive material I keep in a safe down the nick,' said Pascoe.

She smiled, with just the slightest sign of effort as if it had occurred to her that it was after all Christmas Day.

'Enough shop talk,' she said. 'I thought we'd get the troughing over early so that we can walk it off together while there's still some light in the sky, OK?'

'Fine,' said Pascoe. 'I'll pop out and work up an appetite with our two monsters.'

'Take Rosie a woolly, will you? She's beginning to look quite blue out there, but don't tell her that or she'll just insist on stripping off to show she doesn't feel the cold.'

'Can't think who she gets it from,' said Pascoe.

He rose with *Dark Cells* in one hand and in the other the file which he shook at her as he headed for the door, saying, 'See? Next to nothing in it. I know I may be just a bit obsessive about the guy, but doesn't it make sense to keep some sort of track on him now he's elected me his number one correspondent?'

To his surprise, Ellie said, 'You may be right, love. Listen, last word on the subject today, OK? Either drop the whole thing or do the job properly. Dig deep as you can into Roote's roots; and while you're at it, before you go around badmouthing Ms Haseen, why not check her out professionally with someone like Pottle? Rosie, luv, what's up?'

Their daughter had burst into the room wearing her best exasperated look.

'It's this whistle,' she said. 'I think it's broken.'

'Why's that?'

'I can't hear it.'

'But you're not meant to be able to hear it.'

'But I don't think Tig can hear it either. I blow and I blow and he pays no heed at all.'

Ellie shot a warning glance at her husband, who was grinning broadly, and said, 'I know exactly what you mean, darling. But it doesn't mean Tig can't hear it. It's just that male dogs can be very stubborn, and sometimes you've got to work really hard to get them to do the simplest things. Why don't you get your dad to help you? I think you'll find he's a bit of a specialist.'

232

at Bowler, not being a particularly literary sort of chap, though he was making efforts in that direction to keep pace with Rye Pomona, might have found it hard to offer a detailed gloss of the phrase *hoist with his own petard*, but he knew exactly what it meant.

Christmas had posed a problem. His parents were expecting him home. The only unmarried one of four children, he'd been looking forward to at last quieting their unease at his continued lack of attachment by showing off Rye, who, admitting to no family of her own, might have been expected to jump at the chance of Yuletide with the Bowlers.

Instead she had turned down the invitation flat. At first he had taken her refusal as tactical, a (he hoped) Parthian shot in the bad time she had given him for going against her wish not to make the break-in official. So he had waited till they were emerging from a moment of maximum closeness and repeated the invitation.

She rolled away from him and said, 'Hat, don't you listen? I said, no thanks, I'm just not up for a big family Christmas, OK? But I understand how much your parents and your brothers and sister and their offspring will be looking forward to seeing you. And I'll look forward just as much, or even more, to seeing you when you get back. Don't try to turn me into a little Orphan Annie out in the snow while everyone else is in the warm having a good time. I shall be perfectly happy celebrating Christmas by myself.'

He was coming to recognize the note of finality in her voice and he'd protested no more. But he had gone away and brooded and determined that it was time she too discovered he could take a stand. Take away one member of a large family having a good time and what was left was still a large family having a good time. Take away one lover from a pair of lovers and what was left was two unhappy people.

So he crossed his fingers and, before he could change his mind, pausing only to check that he had the CID room to himself, he took out his mobile and rang his parents' number.

As he spilled out his carefully prepared lie about losing out in the Christmas leave lottery, he could feel his mother's huge disappointment even before she tried to hide it, and by the time he put down the phone, he felt like the worst kind of criminal low-life who deserved everything a gouty judge could throw at him.

And it seemed that God agreed.

'Well, that's good,' said Sergeant Wield's voice behind him. 'Here's me just heard Seymour's down with flu, so having to decide whether it's you or Novello gets pulled in to fill the gap on the Christmas roster, and what do I find but a volunteer? Well done, lad.'

'Come on, Sarge,' said Hat desperately. 'At least ask Novello. She might prefer New Year.'

'Nay, good Catholic girl like her 'ull want to be off at Christmas.'

'Good Catholic! You know she's been going out with that big bearded sergeant in the Transport Police and he's married with four kids.'

'That's between her and Father Kerrigan, who no doubt gets a blow-by-blow account at confession, so let's not be having any religious prejudice here, eh?'

'But, Sarge . . .' Hat began to plead. Then he looked into that rocky landscape of a face and realized there was nothing for him here but a hard landing.

He kept his come-uppance to himself, accepting DC Novello's gratitude at his reported volunteering with a self-deprecating grimace and Rye's sympathy with a philosophic shrug. For a moment when she pulled him down on the sofa to show how far her sympathy went, he started feeling guilty again, but not for long.

Christmas morning itself was so quiet that he didn't even have the consolation of usefulness to salve his disappointment at not being with Rye.

About eleven o'clock Dalziel came wandering in, softly whistling 'God Rest Ye Merry, Gentlemen'. He nodded approvingly when he saw the amount of paperwork Hat had shifted and said, 'That's it, lad. Improve the shining hour.'

'Yes, sir. Nothing for us yet then?'

The Fat Man laughed, scratched his crotch like a boy scout trying to start a fire, and said, 'Don't worry, lad. Early days. There's lots of folk out there have travelled many a weary mile just to put themselves in striking distance of their nearest and dearest, and it's getting near kick-off time. Prezzies opened, irritations building, down the pub for a few soothing bevvies, back an hour later full of good cheer, turkey burnt, pudding hard-boiled, kids fratching, in-laws sniping – it's a powder keg, and anything can be a spark. Had a chap couple of years back slit three throats with the carving knife just because his missus told him he were making a mess of the bird and why didn't he let her dad do it?'

'Even that's not exactly demanding, is it? I mean, it doesn't take much real detective work.'

'Like in the whodunnits? Shouldn't pay too much heed to them poncy writers, lad. What do they know? Most on 'em 'ud honk their rings if they saw a bit of real blood.'

Hat's acquaintance with poncy writers was limited to Ellie Pascoe and Charley Penn. His dislike of the latter was strong enough to discount his liking for the former, so he nodded enthusiastic agreement which probably wasn't a bad career move anyway.

It occurred to him to wonder how come the Fat Man, who cracked the whip and sent all the animals galloping round the ring, should have ended up stuck in the empty Big Top on Christmas Day. A disaster in his private life? Or a sudden rush of altruism to the head? On the whole, Hat thought it wise not to push his luck by asking.

In fact neither mischance nor nobility had played a part in the Fat Man's decision to take Christmas duty. Amanda 'Cap' Marvell, his inamorata, was spending the holiday with her son,

Lieutenant Colonel Pitt-Evenlode MC (the Hero, as Dalziel called him), who had finally found himself a woman sufficiently unimpressed by his heroics to contemplate becoming his wife. Dalziel wasn't invited.

'Worried I'll frighten her off?' Dalziel had asked.

'More likely worried I'll drink too much bubbly and start feeling you up under the table and that frightens her off,' said Cap, who had a nice way of putting things.

'Save the bubbly for Boxing Day,' he'd replied, then told his senior officers they could spend Christmas with their families as he was coming in and he was worth any six of them.

He returned to his office now, opened the huge jar of pickled walnuts he'd found in one of his socks that morning, poured himself a healthy slug from the bottle of Highland Park he'd found in the other, and settled down with *The Last Days of Pompeii*, with his radio monitor bubbling softly in the background. The minutes ticked by, the pages turned, the whisky and the walnuts sank, and, as he'd forecast, the radio-recorded tide of merry Christmas mayhem rose as the Queen's Speech sailed majestically nearer.

The mayhem so far had all remained at the 'domestic' level, which meant it hadn't risen above bruising and cutting with the occasional breaking of bones, all of which fell within the proper purlieu of Uniform, who were getting more stretched by the minute.

Then like a hooked fish the Fat Man felt his attention jerked from first century Campania to twenty-first century Mid-Yorkshire.

'Disturbance at Church View House, Peg Lane. Informant Mrs Gilpin, Flat 14. Sounds like another drunk. Can anyone take it?'

Dalziel laid down his book, scooped up his radio and said, 'Tommy, that Peg Lane call, I'll take it.'

'You will?' The sergeant couldn't hide his amazement. 'It's just a D and D, sir ...'

'I know, but it's the season of goodwill, and I can tell your lads are getting a bit overstretched, so have this one on CID. Unless you're too proud, that is ...'

'No, sir. It's yours and welcome. Cheers!'

Dalziel switched off and bellowed, 'Bowler!'

Five seconds later Hat appeared round the door just as Dalziel came through it.

He leapt aside, then fell into step behind the Fat Man as he raced down the stairs.

'Sir,' he gasped. 'What have we got?'

'Probably nowt, but I could do with a breath of fresh air. You drive.'

In the car, Hat said, 'Where to?'

'Peg Lane.'

'Peg Lane? That's where Rye lives!'

'Aye. And it's Church View we're heading for. Disturbance. Informant your friend Mrs Gilpin. And I'm just wondering if the disturber could be our old friend, Charley Penn. Christ, lad, this is the town I live in you're driving through, not Le Mans!'

But Hat wasn't listening. He sent the car hurtling through the thankfully empty streets recalling that other mad drive only a couple of months before when he'd gone rushing to Rye's rescue. Could lightning strike twice? Could the second strike be fatal . . . ?

Peg Lane was fairly central so the journey took less than five minutes, though to Hat it felt like an hour. The narrow street running between the terraced houses and the eighteenth-century church which gave Rye's building its name was still as an unused film set. Remove the parked cars and you could have shot an episode of *Emma* here.

An upstairs window opened and a woman wearing a red and yellow paper hat leaned out and said, 'I'm not coming out. It's gone very quiet, but he hasn't left.'

'Who?' demanded Dalziel.

'Him. The mad-looking one your lad asked about who was here before.'

His lad, Dalziel now realized, had already vanished into the building.

With a mild oath at the impetuosity of youth, Dalziel followed. On the flat over short distances his bulk was little impediment to velocity, but uphill he went steady, not caring to arrive wheezing like a badly maintained set of bagpipes.

He paused on the first landing. Above him he could hear a thunderous knocking and Bowler's voice crying, 'Rye! Rye! Are you there?'

Groaning gently, Dalziel resumed his ascent.

When he reached the next landing, he saw Charley Penn sitting slumped against the wall beside a door which Bowler was bouncing off like a demented squash ball. Fearing that Penn might have been put there by Bowler's fists, he took hold of the writer's shag of greying hair and raised his head. To his relief the slack and dull-eyed face showed no sign of physical assault and every sign of alcoholic impairment.

He caught the DC on his next bounce and held him tight.

'You'd do better using your head, lad,' he said. 'Your lass changed the lock, right?'

'Yes, and it's locked and bolted, which means she's in there, doesn't it?' cried Hat.

'Aye, and she's probably terrified 'cos this idiot's been banging and shouting out here on the landing. So what makes you think she's going to open up straight off when some other idiot starts banging and shouting?'

It was a good point and Hat seemed to be taking it on board till Mrs Gilpin's door opened revealing the red and yellow hat.

'Is it safe now?' said Mrs Gilpin. 'I told them when I rang, I thought they might need an armed response team, he was making such a racket. You've not shot him, have you?'

'Just the anaesthetic dart, luv,' said Dalziel.

Hat cried, 'It was you who rang, not Rye?'

And started bouncing himself off the door again till Dalziel got him in a neck lock.

'Missus,' he said. 'Would you mind tapping at that door and telling Ms Pomona who you are and asking her if she'd mind opening up? Thank you.'

Moving gingerly around the slumped form of Penn, Mrs Gilpin did as she was asked.

After a long pause, they heard the lock click and the door swung slowly open.

Rye stood there, and Dalziel's first thought was maybe she'd been attacked after all.

She was wearing a bathrobe and so far as he could see not much else. Her face was deathly pale except for the twin black pits out of which her eyes peered like those of a prisoner who does not know if she's been called forth to freedom or execution.

Then they registered Hat and her features were suffused with such joy that even Dalziel's hyperborean heart had to admit a respondent glow.

He relaxed his grip on the boy and watched with sad envy as he rushed forward to fold his arms round the girl.

'I knew you'd come,' she said, collapsing against him. 'Such dreams I was having . . . horrid, horrid . . . but I knew you'd come . . .'

'I always will,' said Hat fervently. 'Let's get you inside, shall we?'

He half carried her into the flat.

'Story of my life,' said Dalziel to Mrs Gilpin. 'I take the call, someone else gets the girl. Thanks for your help, luv. You can get back to your party now. Merry Christmas.'

Reluctantly the woman retreated behind her door, which she left slightly ajar till Dalziel glared it shut. Then he turned to Charley Penn, who was showing signs of revival. Dragging him over to the stairs, the Fat Man cuffed his left hand to the metal balustrade.

As he straightened up he heard footsteps on the stairs. He looked down to see a woman ascending. She was in her thirties, with fashionably short hair and a pleasant round face well suited to show concern, which was what registered there now as she took in the manacled man and his menacing captor.

'Police,' said Dalziel. 'Who are you?'

'Mrs Rogers. Myra Rogers. I live there –' She indicated the door on the other side of Rye's from Mrs Gilpin. 'What's going on?'

'Just a drunk causing a fuss. You heard nowt?'

'No. I've been out . . .' Her gaze went to Rye's open door. 'Is Miss Pomona all right?'

'I think so. This man look familiar?'

'Vaguely. He could be the one I glimpsed that morning the nice young officer asked about, Rye's boyfriend, only I didn't know that till later. You're sure she's all right?'

'Aye, she's grand,' said Dalziel. 'Young Hat's in with her now. You know her well?'

'Quite well ... not that I've known her long ... in fact just since that same day, you know, when she came back and there'd been the bother ... it's good for us both, I think, women alone, to know we've got a friend next door ... just for reassurance ...'

More reassuring than Mrs Gilpin, Dalziel guessed. There was beneath her diffidence an air of competence about Mrs Rogers. Widow? Divorced? Didn't matter. On her own long enough to know she could hack it. Not that she'd be without offers. Hers wasn't a face to stick in your mind – though there was something familiar about her – but close up, those gentle brown eyes and smoothly rounded features were rather attractive.

'There's nowt like a good neighbour for reassurance,' he said. 'Nice to meet you, missus. Merry Christmas.'

The woman came on to the landing, skirted Penn fastidiously, and went into her flat.

'Don't go away, Charley,' said Dalziel.

He went through Rye's door.

There was no sign of disturbance here, confirming his belief that Penn had never got inside. Hat had placed Rye on a sofa and was trying to pour a full bottle of vodka into a wine glass. The girl had recovered sufficiently to make a protective adjustment to her robe under the Fat Man's appreciative gaze.

'Not to worry, luv,' he said. 'When you've seen one you've seen two. Thanks, lad.'

He took the glass from Hat's hand, emptied it with a shudder, and said, 'No wonder them Russkis talk mush. Get the lass a cup of tea, will you? Strong, lots of sugar.'

For a second Hat looked insubordinate, but a narrowing of Dalziel's eyes was enough to send him into the kitchen.

'Right, Ms Pomona,' said the Fat Man, helping himself to another slug of vodka. 'Just a couple of quick questions. Has Charley Penn been inside your flat today?'

'Penn?' She looked bewildered. 'No. Why?'

'That was him banging at your door. You did hear someone banging at your door?'

'I was asleep ... I didn't feel so good this morning, I had this

240

dreadful headache, and I took some tablets and went to bed. There was a lot of noise, but I thought it was in my dream . . . I was dreaming about being back out at Stang Tarn . . . it was all mixed up, the noise and everything . . . even when I woke up I didn't know if I was only dreaming I'd woken up . . . then I heard Mrs Gilpin . . . it was Mrs Gilpin, wasn't it?'

'Aye. So, you weren't feeling too well, went to bed, had a nightmare, that sum it up?'

She shook her head to clear it, not in denial, and said in a stronger voice, 'Yes, I suppose it does. Mr Dalziel, it's always good to see you, but why are you here?'

She was definitely coming out of it.

Hat reappeared with a steaming mug.

Dalziel said, 'Young Bowler will explain. I've got someone waiting for me outside.'

Hat looked gratefully at the Fat Man who mouthed at him, 'Five minutes,' then left.

Outside he found Penn had been sick on the landing.

Uncuffing him from the balustrade, Dalziel half led, half dragged him down the stairs. In the street the bitter east wind hit the novelist like a bucket of ice water. He swayed for a moment then stiffened himself against the blast.

Dalziel nodded approvingly and said, 'Back in the land of the living, Charley?'

'Heading that way. You wouldn't have a flask in your pocket, would you, Andy?'

'Aye, and it's staying there.'

'Can't we get in your car at least?'

'With honk all down your gansy? You must be joking.'

'You're not arresting me then?'

'You done owt I should arrest you for?'

Penn tried a laugh, it changed to a cough, then a bout of dry retching.

'How should I know?' he gasped. 'Don't remember much since lunch.'

'Which you had where?'

'None of your business.'

'No? Let me guess.'

It wasn't too difficult. Penn's mother (original name Penck) lived in a grace-and-favour cottage on Lord Partridge's estate at Haysgarth. She felt her son had betrayed his Teutonic heritage, he resented the way she bowed and scraped to the Partridges.

Dalziel went on, 'You had a good old traditional *Weinacht* with your good old traditional *Mutti* out at Haysgarth, but the only way you could block out the sight of her kowtowing to Budgie Partridge and the sound of her going on about your dad spinning in his grave to see how completely his son has gone native was to get pissed out of your skull on schnapps or some such muck. Then you headed back here to pass on a bit of your misery to some other bugger. We won't go into how you got here, though if I hear of any corpses, human or animal, on the road between here and Haysgarth, I'll be jumping up and down on your belly till you bring up your ribs. How am I doing, Charley?'

'Nice story, pity about the style. Andy, if I'm not under arrest, I'll be on my way afore I freeze to death.'

'Long as you understand there's no one would give a toss, Charley, except mebbe your publishers, and they'd just be thinking of their profits. Even your old *Mutti* would likely just set about transforming you into one of them dead Kraut heroes, my son the Teutonic bard who's up there in Valhalla, serenading the gods. That's what you sentimental Krauts do with dead folk, isn't it? Turn them into summat they're not when they're too dead to answer back. Get it into that thick noddle of thine, Charley. Your mate Dick Dee was a sick, evil bastard and if you can't get your head round that, you'd best stand out here till you catch pneumonia, then go and ask him yourself.'

Penn shivered and pulled his jacket closer around him.

'You done?' he said.

'For now.'

'Thank Christ for that. What's happened to you, Andy? Always thought of you as vulgar and violent. But never verbose. Tell you what I think. You're too wise an old porker to believe you're going to get anywhere grunting at me. So just who are you trying to convince with all those words? Yourself mebbe? Worried about how it's going to look if the truth comes dropping through your letter box one fine morning? Or rather not *if*. *When!* Watch this space, Andy. Watch this space. I'm off. Merry fucking Christmas.'

He turned and walked away across the road rather unsteadily. When he reached the small back gate which led into the churchyard opposite, he pushed it open, raised his right hand in derisive farewell without looking round, and vanished among the gravestones.

Dalziel stood in thought for a moment, then shook his head like a man dislodging a bee, glanced at his watch, stooped to the car, reached in and leaned on the horn.

Upstairs, Hat heard the noise and guessed its source.

So did Rye. She said, 'Better run.'

'No hurry,' said Hat bravely. 'He can wait till I'm sure you're OK.'

She looked better but was still very pale. She said, 'I'm fine, really.'

'You don't look fine. Have you had anything to eat?'

'What had you in mind? Roast turkey and the trimmings? No thanks!'

'I could rustle you up . . .'

He paused while his mind scanned his limited culinary range. The horn sounded once more.

Rye said, 'I don't know if I'm ready for the Bowler book of boy nosh. Go, go.'

Still he hesitated. There was a tap at the door. He looked round and saw Myra Rogers. He'd met her a couple of times in the last few days. Rye seemed to have taken a shine to her and Hat had been delighted to know she had a neighbour she felt she could turn to. Inviting Mrs Gilpin into your life would be like volunteering to go on *Big Brother*.

Mrs Rogers said uncertainly, 'I'm sorry, I just wanted to see if you were all right . . . I've been out and when I came back and saw that terrifying man on the stairs . . .'

'It's all right, he's too drunk to do any harm,' said Hat.

'Yes, well actually, I meant the policeman. I'm sorry, I just wanted to say, if there was anything I could do, but I don't want to intrude . . .'

She looked as if a blink of the eye would send her running.

The horn again, this blast long enough to summon Charlemagne back to Roncesvalles.

Rye said, 'Myra, don't be silly. Hat's got to go, and I'll be glad of the company. Hat, give me a ring later, will you? I think we both need to rearrange Christmas!'

Relieved, even though he suspected Rye may have invited the woman in to make it easier for him to go, Hat ran down the stairs.

Outside he found the Fat Man sitting on the bonnet of the car, which gave it a very lopsided look, and regarding him grimly.

'I hope you've not been shagging,' he said. 'Bad manners to shag and shog off.'

'She's got someone with her, Mrs Rogers from next door ... Where's Penn?'

He'd just registered that the writer wasn't in the car.

'Gone.'

'You let him go?'

'Aye. Here's a tip, lad. Always keep in with your custody sergeant. You never know when you'll need a favour. And one certain way to make a custody sergeant your enemy for life is to turn up on Christmas Day with a drunk who's not got blood on his hands.'

Hat was regarding him with a lack of gratitude bordering on insubordination.

'What if he comes back? At the very least shouldn't we put a watch on Rye's flat?'

'Taken care of, lad,' said Dalziel.

He waved up at a second-floor window where a red and yellow party hat was visible.

'Now let's get into the car and back to the station afore my bollocks drop off and crack the pavement,' said Dalziel.

Fichtenburg-am-Blutensee

Aargau

Tues Dec 18th

Dear Mr Pascoe,

I must have been exhausted by yesterday's adventures as
the sun was shining brightly when I was woken by the
sound of activity somewhere in the chalet. I emerged from
my bedroom to find a young woman with bright red
cheeks and wearing what I presume is some version of
traditional costume, a combination giving her the look of
an animated doll, making my breakfast. None of your
muesli either but a substantial British fry-up!

My Coppelia chatted incessantly, and
incomprehensibly, till, as she was leaving, she pointed at
the letter I wrote last night and said, '*Post?*' I quickly
scribbled your address (excellent quality stationery, don't
you think?) and off she went with it.

After breakfast, I decided to get my bearings and,
wrapping myself up well, I went for a stroll around the
policies.

The grounds of the castle are extensive and lovely,
and made even more so by last evening's snowfall and this

morning's frost. But my appreciation that I was in a wilderness of groaning glaciers and towering Alps has proved quite false! True, looking to the south or west I can see the white swell of the Jura, but in the other direction the land is much flatter and predominantly pastoral. Nonetheless to one whose boundaries were for so long prison walls and security fences, this sense of space and distance was exhilarating. I strolled without plan, drinking in the beauty of the frost-laced landscape where every tree seemed festooned with glittering diamonds which seemed to my suddenly poetic mind to harbinge the arrival of that still fairer jewel, the lovely Emerald!

What pickleheads love, or lust, makes of us rational thinkers!

Eventually, shame at finding myself behaving more like an adolescent boy than a rational adult made me force my mind back to the real purpose of my presence here. I recalled my feelings of the previous night when I found myself confronted by those weird paintings which reminded me so much of Beddoes' play. The circumstances and my state of mind had been peculiarly Gothic, of course, and probably in daylight there would be very little correspondence.

I decided to test this out and, more by luck than judgment, found my way back to the ruined chapel.

I saw at once that I was right and my impressions of the night before had been considerably distorted. In daylight the chapel was much smaller than I had recalled and thus even further removed from the 'spacious Gothic cathedral' of Beddoes' play. Nor was there anything there to correspond to the sepulchre of the dukes of Munsterberg from which the resurrected Wolfram emerges. As for the frescos, there seemed to be much less to see by daylight than moonlight. Any fancy I may have entertained that perhaps Holbein or one of his pupils had popped across from Basel to try out designs for his Dance of Death soon evaporated. The style of these is pretty crude, completely lacking the Holbein wit and energy my imagination had given them the night before.

Yet I found myself thinking that Beddoes lived in north Switzerland for some time. And doesn't Gosse say in his memoir that when he fled from Zurich after the troubles of 1839, he went to the neighbouring canton of Aargau, which is where I am now?

Brooding on these matters, I strolled away from the chapel not paying much heed to my direction, till finally I came out of the forest at the crest of a gentle rise overlooking the castle. Distantly I saw a car crawling up the snow-covered driveway towards the main entrance, and all thought of Beddoes and rationality went clean out of my mind.

This had to be the car bringing Emerald to Fichtenburg. Without conscious decision, I was running down the slope, driven by my desire to be the first person to greet her as she stepped out. I believe I even had some crazy notion of throwing my cagoule on to the ground before her, so that her dainty feet wouldn't have to touch the snow.

Well, naturally I paid for my impetuosity, and instead of the perfect gentle knight greeting his lady with due courtesy, the first glimpse the inmates of the car had of me was more like a court jester desperate for laughs, rolling down the slope in a human snowball.

By the time I picked myself up and brushed off the worst of the snow and made my way to the forecourt, the new arrivals were already unloading their vehicle and Frau Buff was standing in the doorway of the castle to greet them.

One glance told me that Emerald was not among them. How could I have imagined she might be travelling in a battered VW Estate with snow chains!

The party consisted of three young women, all strangers to me, though the smallest of them did have something familiar about her.

This familiarity and the nature of the huge

misunderstanding I had been labouring under became clear when we exchanged introductions.

The small woman was Musetta Lupin! This was the *Tochter* Frau Buff had been preparing for. A moment's thought should have told me that the divine Emerald in search of winter sport wouldn't waste her time and beauty on a little pond like Blutensee; she would be adorning some fashionable resort where the beautiful people strut their stuff.

Naturally I was at pains to conceal my disappointment, but when the girls (for that is what they are; all under twenty and none of them, I suspect, much experienced in life) invited me to share the lunch that Frau Buff had prepared for them, I refused politely and returned to the chalet to nurse my wound. And to seek solace in starting this letter to you.

How lucky I am to have someone like yourself I feel I can turn to in my troubles, though I sometimes suspect that my good luck may be based on your bad luck. What I mean is, I would have anticipated that a man of your ability and amiability would have flapped his wings and flown far afield during the years following our first encounter.

Please don't be offended. I'm not belittling your achievement. For many officers, being a Detective Chief Inspector at your age would seem pretty fair progress. And you were very lowly (meaning highly!) rated in the Syke; a clever, sharp player, one not easily deceived, and offering you a bung was a waste of time! Your one perceived weakness was your reluctance to cut corners. Not that they rated you soft. Oh no. Hard as nails and a terrier once you took hold. I didn't need anyone to give me chapter and verse on that!

The main hope of the MYCF (the Mid-Yorkshire Criminal Fancy!) was that you'd soon take off, leaving space for someone more malleable, and I doubt if anyone would have put money on you still being in your present job these several years on.

So why are you, I ask myself?

Could it be that, like an elegant schooner sailing in the lee of a huge battle-scarred man o' war, you have been both protected from the weather and at the same time had some of the wind taken out of your sails? In other words, is it the Good Ship Dalziel which in some way has hindered the fair and speedy voyage which all have mapped for you?

This is not to aim any sniping criticism at the dear Superintendent. What use to snipe at Juggernaut? He is, you will not be surprised to learn, the Public Enemy Number One of the MYCF, their Hound of Heaven, the man they most love to hate.

Oh, do not let yourself be hidden too long in his huge shadow, dear friend, condemned to do the flitting of the bat. Rather let yourself be the rapid falcon who perches on the fabled roc's shoulders until those mighty pinions have carried him as high as they can – then at last launches himself into blue empyrean!

But I fear I have let enthusiasm carry me into impertinence, and, worse, euphuism. My apologies. I shall not send this letter till I have pondered whether I have earned the right to speak to you with the frankness my heart so desires between us.

Fri Dec 21st

I don't know whether I've earned that right, but if I haven't I must purchase it on credit for once more I find myself in emotional turmoil and, like an addict turning to his drug of choice, I find my hand reaching out for my pen.

Let me take you back to that first day at Fichtenburg.

I wasn't left alone for long to brood over Emerald's non-arrival. Early in the afternoon I heard a knocking at my door and I found the girls had come down to skate on the lake, which I only now noticed someone had swept clear of snow during the morning. How rich a man must be to employ so many silent workers to keep him comfortable! Shyly, the girls asked whether I would mind if they used the chalet verandah for putting their skates on. Naturally I said of course not, feel free to use all its facilities. Then they said they'd brought a spare pair of skates and would I care to join them? I replied I didn't skate. And they giggled like Yum-Yum, Pitti-Sing and Peep-Bo and said it was a doddle.

It wasn't! But it was good knockabout fun. They were all pretty expert and each took it in turn to act as my tutor and, more importantly, supporter while the other two whizzed around with vigorous grace. There is nothing like making a fool of yourself for breaking the ice (not quite literally) between young people, and nothing like being *in statu pupillari* for making you feel young! So by the time we all retired to the chalet for in their cases a cooling and in mine a warming drink, we were chatting away like any bunch of kids.

It turns out that they are all teachers at the International School in Strasbourg. Zazie is (guess!) French, Hildi is Austrian, and Mouse is of course English, but they're all fluent in each other's languages and pretty hot, so far as I can make out, at many others. Zazie is by far the prettiest, full of vivacity and natural grace, definitely the girl to take to the ball. Hildi is stocky and muscular. I suspect she never misses her daily work-out in the gym, and from one or two things that were said I gather she is a top-notch cross-country skier. If I get lost in a blizzard, it's Hildi I want to come looking for me! As for Mouse, well, she isn't pretty, that's for sure. In fact she's plain plain, with many of her mother's features but none of that dominatrix edge which can provoke a sexual shiver. And she's almost as timid as her sobriquet. I'm sure she's great with young kids and it's probably my childish antics on the lake that made her relax with me.

It seems she's spending Christmas here with her

mother's party and her friends have just come for a few days of pre-festive frolics. It was a subject of some mirth that Linda's approval of their visit had been qualified by a warning not to disturb the guest in the chalet, whom they'd pictured as some ancient scholar, impatient of company, interested only in his books and in need of absolute silence.

Well, during the next couple of days there was practically no silence, lots of company and not much scholarship, though I did make use of their linguistic skills. I showed them the chapel and explained my interest in it. Hildi, who had a genuine rather than a casual interest in antiquities, said I should ask Frau Buff about it and volunteered to interpret, so off we all went to beard our chatelaine in her den. Buff's knowledge of the family history was extensive if anecdotal, and she shared this with us as she took us on a tour of the castle, including the unused apartments which take up more than half of it.

Johannes Stimmer (she told us), the founder of the family's fortunes, was a mercenary soldier whose military talent gained him rapid promotion and who managed the difficult balancing act of both amassing considerable wealth, surviving the country's many political changes, and preserving his reputation as a social radical during the last quarter of the eighteenth century. After Waterloo, he decided for reasons ranging from status to security that it was time the family had its own personal fortified seat and purchased Fichtenburg from its previous owners, who'd managed to back every wrong horse that had run across Switzerland in the past fifty years. (His descendants had clearly moved far enough away from old Joe's radicalism to gain admittance into Linda's circle of friends, I observed slyly, and to my delight, Mouse laughed.)

Frau Buff also provided two explanations of the name *Blutensee* (bleeding lake). One is that at certain seasons the last rays of the setting sun catch it in such a way as to turn the waters red. The other is that during the long independence struggle against the Habsburgs in the fourteenth century, a marauding troop of Leopold's cavalry surprised the castle during a wedding celebration, massacred everyone they could lay sword on, and threw their bodies in the lake. Naturally (like Beddoes, I'm sure) I prefer the latter!

As we were walking through one of the unused rooms whose walls were lined with murky oil paintings, something must have registered in that corner-of-the-eye way and at the door I turned back to view the pictures again.

There it was, a modestly sized pen-and-ink wash of three young men, posed in front of what looked like the ruined chapel, and wearing Elizabethan doublet and hose.

Two things hit me. The first was the artist's name, scrawled rather modestly and obscurely in the bottom left-hand corner. It read *G. Keller*.

Now the only Keller I have heard of is Gottfried of that ilk, the Swiss writer. You probably know his autobiographical novel, *Green Henry*, whose hero, like Keller himself, trains as an artist but ultimately, recognizing his lack of real talent, turns to literature. Well, the picture certainly suggested that, if G did stand for Gottfried, he'd made the right decision! But more interesting to me was the recollection that Beddoes had been acquainted with Keller, who shared his radical views, and that, according to Gosse, it was in Keller's company that Thomas had fled from Zurich to Aargau.

The second thing was the figure on the left, slight, with an oval face and big brown eyes that looked out at us with a somewhat sardonic expression.

There is only one known portrait of TLB, a painting done by one Nathan Branwhite when Tom was eighteen or nineteen. The original has vanished, but a photograph of it still survives which shows a somewhat introverted face staring out at the world through what we are assured were large, clear, decidedly brown eyes with an expression between natural reserve and weary scepticism. And, this, I swear, was the same face I was looking at!

So, three young men passing the time doing theatricals (could they have been acting out one of Beddoes' own plays? I fantasized) and caught forever, not as they would have been a century later by someone snapping them with his Kodak, but by the then equivalent, a quick sketch worked up later into the picture I saw before me.

This was exciting. I made a note to ask Linda to get her friends to permit a proper examination of the picture, and then, feeling virtuously that I hadn't after all allowed myself to be seduced totally from my task, I resumed the much more interesting business of having that time of my life which my new friends seemed determined I should enjoy!

Just how far that determination went, I was soon to discover. It was the third day of our acquaintance when it happened.

The girls had left the chalet after their *après-skating* drinks. I'd just got into my shower when I heard someone call from the main room. I wrapped a towel round me and went out to find Zazie there. She said she'd left her gloves, which we found without much difficulty. Then she looked at me, sighed enviously and said she'd love a really hot shower too but the boiler in the castle was playing up and the water was running lukewarm. Uncertain how to take this, I said she was very welcome to use mine after I'd finished, which wouldn't be long. I then returned to the shower, and all uncertainties vanished a moment later when the glass panel slid open behind me and Zazie stepped in.

No details, except to say that I rapidly revised my initial judgment, in her case at least, that here was someone not very experienced in life.

No harm done, I thought afterwards, and a great deal of pleasure taken. Zazie, like Hildi, would be heading off in a day or two to spend Christmas with her own family.

I'd probably never see her again and all I'd be left with (and her too, I hoped) was a happy memory of a lively jig arranged for two players! And if she'd enjoyed it enough to desire a reprise, then I was very happy to make my instrument available again.

That was yesterday. Today I was pleased to see that Zazie showed none of that post-coital possessiveness which might have sounded a jarring note in our now very well-tuned quartet. But, I wondered as I got ready for my shower this afternoon, did this mean it was after all a one-off performance?

Then I heard a noise in the next room and joyfully headed through to greet her.

Only it wasn't Zazie but Hildi.

As I hadn't bothered with a towel this time, the way my thoughts were tending was obvious. Unabashed, Hildi said something in German which I could translate roughly as, 'Seems a pity to waste it,' and next thing . . .

Well again, no detail, but those hours in the gym certainly hadn't been wasted.

I still hadn't quite caught on to what was happening here, but a suspicion was tickling the inside of my brain as I lay on the rugged floor like a defeated wrestler and watched Hildi dress, blow me a kiss, and leave.

After a moment I rose and stretched and was about to return to the shower room when I thought I heard a voice calling outside.

I went to the window and looked.

Out on the frozen lake were Zazie and Mouse. They must have put their skates on again after leaving the chalet to take a last spin round before the daylight went. Hildi was standing on the edge calling to attract their attention. And when they turned and saw her, she clenched both fists and punched them in the air with thumbs upturned.

And then I knew. These charming 'inexperienced' girls had decided to liven up their stay and mine at Fichtenburg by each having me in turn!

And how did I feel about that? Flattered? Outraged? Amused?

None of these. What I felt was afraid.

Two down, one to go, and that one was Mouse.

Mouse who wasn't going to vanish in a couple of days but would be around all through the holiday. Mouse who in my judgment had little talent to deceive. Mouse who was, according to Jacques, the apple of her mother's eye.

My conclusion, which may sound a tad ungallant, was that if we'd been talking about Emerald, who knows? But when it came to Mouse, nothing she seemed likely to have to offer was worth risking even the merest shadow of Linda's disapproval for!

Yet rejection seemed potentially just as dangerous. How would she react if she turned up tomorrow to bring this jolly girls' game to its triumphant conclusion and then had to go out to her friends with her thumbs turned down? Would she be able to laugh it off? Or would she be distressed? Angry? Humiliated? Vengeful?

I don't know. Whatever I do, I can see trouble. You can see why I wish I had you here by my side so I could lay out the situation before you and beg for your wise advice. But I can't, so I've decided to do what any sensible man would do in such circumstances.

I'm going to run.

Not far and not for long. It's Saturday tomorrow. On Sunday Hildi and Zazie are heading off to join their families for the festive season. And on Monday, Christmas Eve, Linda and her cronies will arrive at Fichtenburg. So tomorrow's the real danger point. I suppose I could find an excuse for keeping out of the way, but I've learned from experience that no risk is negligible. Elimination is the better part of avoidance!

So I've packed a bag, written a note to Frau Buff asking her to make my apologies, and tomorrow first thing I'm going to start doing what I came to Switzerland to do in the first place. I'm off to Zurich to pursue my researches into Thomas Lovell Beddoes, and I shan't come back to Fichtenburg till Monday, when hopefully her mother's presence and her friends' absence will combine to keep Mouse in her right senses.

Ihrer guter Freund

Franny

I n the no-man's land between Christmas and New Year, a deathly stillness falls across the ravaged landscape with devastated survivors picking their way carefully round the shops exchanging rubbish they have been bought for rubbish more to their taste, while in empty offices telephones shrill their urgent summonses in vain. It's as if the great heart of the city has paused to breathe, and even crime itself has taken a rest.

It is a lull which policemen take advantage of in many different ways. Andy Dalziel used it for a bit of deep thought, which might have surprised the casual spectator, for in his work as in his play on the rugby fields of his younger days what caught the eye was the sheer brutality of his approach.

But there was more to him than just destruction. Not for him the expense of energy in vain pursuit of the fleet young gazelles behind the scrum. Instead he sent his mind after them, plotting the likely progress of a move on the basis of what he knew of his opponents, what he saw of the conditions. He wasn't always right, but at the end of a game many an opposing winger wondered how it was that after jinking his way round the full back, instead of open countryside ahead, he had found himself, like Childe Roland, suddenly confronted by the Dark Tower.

For Dalziel this calm between the two great orgies was time to sit and read the game.

There was a smell of danger in his nostrils and he didn't yet know precisely where it was coming from except that it had something to do with the Wordman case.

The case was officially resolved and he had the plaudits to prove it. What was more, it had been resolved in the best possible way. Not only had the perpetrator been caught in the act, he'd been killed in the act, thus at the same time providing incontrovertible evidence of his guilt and depriving all those arty-farty-Number-10-party, greenery-yallery-play-to-the-gallery lawyers of any opportunity to controvert it.

Of course only the Law could decide a man's guilt, but you can't libel the dead, and the papers hadn't held back from doing what the courts couldn't by crying *Gotcha!* and proclaiming Dick Dee *Guilty as not charged!*

A good story. But how much better a story it became, now that everyone except those most personally involved had forgotten the triumphing tabloid headlines, if one of the same papers could dig up evidence to suggest a doubt.

He thought of Penn's crack about the truth dropping through his letter box some morning. *Watch this space!* he'd said.

And hadn't Pascoe's chum, Roote, said that Penn was mouthing off about getting help?

That dangerous smell had a strong reek of investigative journalism about it.

This was bad news. Nowadays investigative journalism wasn't just some nosey reporter wanting to make a name, it was big business. If a paper felt there was something to get its teeth into, there would be no shortage of money, expertise or advanced surveillance equipment. And they didn't play by the rules.

He'd thought Dee's death had blown no-side on the Wordman game, but now it looked like somewhere out there the ball might be back in play.

A lesser man might have expended emotion agonizing over the possibility that the police had got it wrong, and wasted his time going over the whole investigation with a fine-tooth comb in search of flaws. Not Andy Dalziel. OK, he'd put someone on it, but meanwhile his place was not at post mortems. Out there on the field was where things got settled. Be first at the breakdown and make sure that after all the shoving and wrestling and kicking and punching are over, you're the man who comes up with possession.

And the best way of doing that was to be the man who hit the bastard with the ball in the first place. So, who to hit?

Not Charley Penn. He'd hit him already and it was clear Charley was indestructible in his conviction that Dee was innocent. Didn't matter. Charley was a nuisance, but writers weren't newsworthy, not unless they were very old, very rich, or very obscene. No, the guy who needed chopping off at the knees was the sodding journalist.

He'd be out there somewhere. And he wouldn't be coming at you like good old Sammy Ruddlesdin of the *Gazette*, fag on lip, notebook in hand, asking where you'd buried the bodies. Nowadays the sting was the thing; they donned disguises, got you relaxed, listened sympathetically as you talked, and all the time the little recorder they'd got taped to their dick was whirring away. Or to their tit. Let's not be sexist about this.

Targets? They'd want a cop. Bowler was an obvious choice. Key witness to Dee's murderous attack on Rye Pomona, plus he was young and impressionable. Definitely the tit-tape there. Rye herself. Get her to admit what Dalziel had gleaned from her tearful ramblings while Bowler lay at death's door – that she had been stripped off, all systems go for a bit of bump and grind with Dirty Dick before the cavalry came on the scene. By the time she was fit to make a written statement, he had nudged her into several small shifts of emphasis so that her readiness to perform had been reduced to a pleasant relaxation induced by wine and warmth from an open fire. Her voluntary nudity was nowhere mentioned. In the confrontational atmosphere of a criminal court, there was no way she could have got away with such fudgings, but the gentle questionings of a sympathetic coroner had sketched a picture of a modern young woman believing her boss was making a play for her and trying to turn him down, when suddenly to her horror it became clear that it was a knife Dee wanted to stick into her, not his knob.

Clearly the version of the incident which Penn would have been urging on his tabloid accomplice was that, having been led to the very brink of passion's pool by this prick-teasing tart then told he couldn't drink, Dee had reacted like any normal stallion and kicked out in fury and frustration. Enter jealous boyfriend, and battle was joined. As for Dee's knife, well, he was going to make toast, wasn't he? And when the big boys arrived on the scene and realized that one of their own had been in a fight and a member of the public lay dead, they'd set about rearranging the facts to make it look like a good killing.

Dalziel was uncomfortably aware that the tidying up he'd done both of the scene and of both Rye's and Hat's account of events would provide some sustenance for Penn's version. His motive had been to protect his young officer from accusation of undue force and the girl from any hint that she was no better than she ought to be, and everything that he'd said or done had been underpinned by his utter conviction that Dick Dee was the Wordman. But he didn't think the tabloids would be much interested in making fine distinctions between a tidy-up and a cover-up.

So, apart from Hat and Rye, what would an investigative journalist go after?

The transcript of the inquest proceedings was in the public domain, so they'd already have that. But there were other things the bastard would be eager to get his hands on. Like police and medical records, particularly the PM on Dee. And CPS records. Dan Trimble, ever a belts-and-braces man, had wanted a CPS opinion to back up the assumption of Dee's guilt. What the CPS had replied was that their business was with realities not hypotheses, but all things being equal maybe there was just a chance that a prosecution could possibly have been successful ... perhaps ...

Par for the course, Dalziel had growled. And now he groaned at what the Sunday Smear or the Daily Dirt might make of all those hesitations and qualifications.

Frankly, but, it didn't matter what they made of it. It was, from their point of view, such a very good case, weird, bloody, baffling, terrifying and at times grimly comic, that even though the dust had hardly settled, already it must feel ripe for a re-run, and if some smart hack could make a story out of Penn's half-baked allegations, let's go for it!

So, how to proceed? Cover everything was the textbook policy. He'd worked out the road he thought this still-hypothetical hack would take, so warn those who needed warned, and send one of your own down the same road. Preferably a new face, fresh eyes.

He picked up his phone, pressed a number, said, 'Ivor there? Send her in, will you?'

Detective Constable Shirley Novello had been *hors de combat* during most of the Wordman investigation. When she returned, Bowler had been on convalescent leave. Now he was back too, it was evident to the Fat Man's sharp eye that a healthy rivalry for top DC status existed between them. Meaning, given the right direction, both would go the extra mile in the hope of impressing their lord and master.

Yes, Ivor would do very nicely as a key figure in defence.

But this didn't effect Dalziel's gut feeling that this wasn't one to counter with subtle defensive tactics, this was one to hit in mid-flight with a hospital tackle!

Such was the conclusion he reached after long dark brooding, and now the light of action came back to his eyes, and he rose like that famous bull from the sea summoned by Theseus to destroy his own son as he fled from the scene of his monstrous crime.

Of course, Hippolytus was completely innocent, but Theseus didn't know that, and it made not a jot of difference to the bull.

Peter Pascoe had pondered long and hard Ellie's well-reasoned assertion that the best way to deal with his Franny Roote 'obsession' was to test it to destruction.

His own conclusion, reached with impeccable male logic, was that when the woman whose body you worship and whose wisdom you respect above all others takes time off to analyse your problems, the only thing to do is prove she is completely wrong.

Roote, he told himself, was not a problem either to resist or resolve. He was a minor irritation which if ignored would eventually go away.

On the twenty-sixth he returned to work, refreshed and ready to make huge inroads into the paper mountain that towers on the desk of most modern CID officers. He did well and didn't think about Roote more than three times. Or four if you counted the time the phone rang and for nearly a minute he didn't pick it up, convinced it was Franny ringing from Switzerland, but it turned out to be DI Rose from South Yorkshire just wondering if maybe he'd got a whisper about the Big Job which he was sure was on, not because he'd heard anything more but because his snout had mysteriously gone missing . . .

Of course while Rose wasn't Roote, the connection was there (making a fifth time) and had to be broken again after he'd assured the DI that Edgar Wield was burrowing away on his behalf even as they spoke.

But he went home pretty pleased with himself on the whole and he woke up the following morning convinced he'd heard the last from Roote and certain that today would see him well on the way to that most desirable of states – a clear desk for a New Year.

Then in the hall he saw the envelope with the familiar handwriting and a Swiss stamp.

From the car on the way to work he rang Dr Pottle to make an appointment and was told he could come instantly as the doctor's first two patients that morning had cancelled as a result of a Yuletide suicide pact.

Pottle, Head of the Central Hospital Psychiatric Unit, parttime lecturer in Mid-Yorkshire University and adviser to the police on matters where his discipline and theirs overlapped, was Pascoe's occasional analyst and sort of friend, meaning Pascoe liked him on the possibly irrational ground that he resembled the kind of psychiatrist you might meet in a Woody Allen film, with sad spaniel eyes and explosive hair whose luminous greyness was in fetching contrast to an Einstein moustache stained a gingery brown as a result of the endless chain of cigarettes depending from his nether lip.

Patients who objected were told, 'I'm here to help with your problems. If my smoking figures among them, leave now and I'll bill you for solving one of them.'

Pascoe showed him the letters. He didn't have to explain about Roote. They'd talked about him before.

Pottle read the letters as he read everything at an amazing speed which Ellie suspected was spoof and done simply to impress. But Pascoe knew she was wrong. Pottle in his consulting room was the Sibyl in her cave, a mortal conduit for the voice of a god, and it was the god's eyes that scanned the words at a rate beyond a human's.

'Should I be worried?' asked Pascoe.

'Should you be asking me that question?' said Pottle.

Pascoe considered, rephrased.

'Is there anything in the letters which you would interpret as concealing, or containing, or implying a threat to me or to mine?'

'If you are threatened by mockery, certainly. If you are threatened by dependency, perhaps. If you are threatened by sheer incomprehension, I can't help you, as I do not have sufficient data fully to understand the letters myself.'

263

'Yes, but should I be worried?' repeated Pascoe impatiently.

'There you go again. Do you want me to try to understand you, Peter, or do you want me to try to understand Mr Roote?'

Another pause for reflection then Pascoe said, 'Roote. Me I can cope with. Him I've no idea about, except that I don't think he's up to any good.'

'So what do you think he's up to?'

'I think he's enjoying trying to screw up my mind. I think he's probing all the time for weak points. And I think he's getting off on telling me about illegalities he's involved with in such a way I can't do anything about them.'

'Examples?'

'The assault in the shower at Chapel Syke, he admits to that. And then at St Godric's, I think he set fire to the Dean's Lodging, and I've got a strong suspicion he assaulted Dean Albacore and left him to die.'

'Good lord. When I read about it, I saw no reference to the possibility of foul play.'

'No, you wouldn't. That's my point.'

'Sorry, I missed that. Evidence?'

'Nothing outside the letters, except a bit of circumstantial with regard to Albacore.'

He spelt out his theory.

'And is this suspicion shared by your colleagues in Cambridge?'

'They're thinking about it,' said Pascoe evasively.

'I see. This probing for weak points – what would they be exactly?'

'He's telling me that maybe I took the wrong path becoming a cop instead of heading into academe. He's showing me that time in jail can move you on a lot further than time in the police force. He keeps drumming on about me being a sedate old married man whose willpower he admires and whose advice he desires while all the time he's trying to make me envious of him being fancy-free, with girls falling into his bed more or less ad lib.'

'Wow,' said Pottle. 'And does he make you envious?'

'Of course not. Most of the stuff he writes is fantasy anyway.'

264

'Except the bits you want to believe where he seems to be admitting to some crime?'

'No, I mean yes . . . Look, I thought you were going to concentrate on Roote not me?'

'It's proving hard to separate the two. Anything else you want to tell me, Peter?'

'Such as?'

'Anything about this vision of you he claims to have had, for instance?'

Pascoe blinked then said quietly, 'Why do you ask that?'

'Because the letters are full of interesting things, but not many truly odd ones. The vision, however, was very odd indeed. And the omission of it from your catalogue of complaints strikes me as odd too. I mean, you clearly want to think that Roote is mentally unhinged, yet you make no reference to the only piece of prima-facie evidence that he may be two groats short of a guinea. So?'

Another blink, then Pascoe said helplessly, 'I saw him too.'

He told the tale. Pottle said, 'Interesting. Let's turn to his sessions with Ms Haseen.'

'Hey, what happened to my visionary moment?'

'Whereof one cannot speak, thereon one must keep silent. You've read her book?'

'Yes; well, the relevant bits.'

'The relevant bits,' echoed Pottle. 'Indeed. Interesting how our friend gave you the precise reference to save you the bother of ploughing through all that clayey prose and making educated guesses. Let me see . . .'

He reached to the bookcase behind him and plucked a black-jacketed volume which Pascoe recognized off a shelf. Then, without reference to the letters, he flicked to what Pascoe could see upside down was the right page and did his speed-read trick again.

'Poor Amaryllis,' he said. 'She is pretty well the opposite of dear Goldsmith who, you recall, according to Garrick, wrote like an angel and talked like poor Poll.'

'You know her,' said Pascoe interested.

'We have met professionally. Indeed, should be doing so again next month when the Winter Symposium of the Yorkshire Psychandric Society, of which I am the current Chair, takes place in Sheffield. Amaryllis Haseen is scheduled to give a paper.'

'But surely in view of what happened, she'll be cancelling?'

'I suggested so in my letter of condolence. She has replied that on the advice of her analyst she is minded to keep the date. She is a woman of great resilience.'

'Evidently,' said Pascoe. 'So how do you rate her? I mean, if you've invited her to address your society, I presume you don't think she's a dud?'

'Far from it,' said Pottle. 'What you're really asking is how much notice you should take of what she says about Roote in her book. I would advise you not to disregard it. She is, as you would see if you'd read the whole book rather than just the bits Roote directed your attention to, a meticulous worker, capable of great insight and not easily fooled.'

'And yet,' said Pascoe, 'in the question of Roote's relationship with his father, she has had the wool pulled completely over her eyes. The man died while he was still a babe in arms. All these so-called memories are pure invention.'

'Is that so? You surprise me.'

'If you'd met Roote you wouldn't be surprised,' said Pascoe fervently. 'He's the great deceiver.'

'Except in your case? Perhaps, Peter, you should retrain as a psychiatrist.'

'Maybe I will. And maybe I'll come along to your Symposium if I'm free.'

'Be my guest,' said Pottle. 'Indeed it might be doubly worth your while for, by one of those coincidences which people only object to in detective novels, another of our speakers is this chap Frère Jacques that your friend Roote refers to.'

'I didn't think your members would have much interest in all that hippy-happy stuff.'

'Peter, I hope you won't be offended if I point out that from time to time you sound disturbingly like your lord and master, Mr Dalziel. Man's relationship with death is a very proper area of study for people in my profession. Indeed you might argue that in some ways it is the only thing that we study. Frère Jacques, though far from free of religion's tendency to poetic waffle at the expense of systematic rigour, has many interesting things to say. We are fortunate to get the chance to listen to him. Also, as he's touring the country promoting the book, we are fortunate to get him for free and his publishers even cough up for a small amount of relaxing booze.'

'Cheap and cheerful then,' said Pascoe. 'So when exactly is this knees-up?'

'Saturday January nineteenth,' said Pottle. 'Your motive in attending would be . . . ?'

'To see for myself a couple more experts whose strings Franny Roote is pulling.'

'Ah. I see. The open-mind approach then. Peter, don't rush to judgment. Read Frère Jacques' book. He has a fine perceptive mind, not easily fooled, I'd say. And, like I said before, read Haseen's book all the way through.'

'And if I do, will I find any mention of the way he more or less blackmailed this objective professional into recommending his transfer to Butlins?' asked Pascoe cynically.

'Peter, once again you're cherry-picking. If you distrust parts of Roote's letters then you must distrust the whole, until you have evidence to the contrary. A common feature of the obsessive personality is a belief that everybody else has got everything wrong.'

Pascoe's face assumed what Ellie called his sulky look, which he himself, if pressed, might have described as the politely stoical expression of one who has heard all the arguments to the contrary but prefers to trust his own judgment.

He glanced at his watch. He should have been at work fifty minutes ago.

'So, bottom line, how do you read Roote's motives in writing these letters?' he asked.

Pottle did the little piece of legerdemain which turned the glowing cinder at his lip into a whole new cigarette and said, 'Difficult. I think he has motives which he knows, and motives which he believes he knows, and motives which he is only dimly aware of. Perhaps your best approach is to simplify matters. To this end, I would advise that you ask yourself why he wrote to you in the first place. Then ask yourself why he wrote to you in the second place. And then in the third place. And so on, till the picture is complete.'

He clapped his hands together then threw them apart in a gesture which momentarily cleared the veil of smoke that hung before his face.

Pascoe knew from old experience that this signalled the end of the session and for a second he felt some sympathy with Andy Dalziel's most printable reaction to trick cyclists and their works. 'Any other bugger made my brain hurt like that, I'd kick him in the goolies till his eyes popped out of their sockets.'

But only for a second.

'Thank you kindly, Doctor,' he said. 'That's been a great help. I think.'

'Good. Till next time then, when perhaps we can start looking at you.'

The Queen

The Queen

fter its terrible start, Hat Bowler's Christmas had really taken off.

He had rung Rye later on Christmas Day as promised, expecting to find she'd taken to her bed once more. To his surprise and delight, she greeted him brightly and in the background he could hear music and voices.

'You having a party?' he asked.

She laughed and said, 'No, idiot, it's the TV movie. It turned out Myra was on her own too, so when she said she'd better be getting back to her own flat, I asked her what she was going to do, and she said watch the movie probably, so I said . . . Why on earth am I going on like this? I think it's just because I feel so much better.'

'Great. You had anything to eat?'

'God, you're a real mother hen, aren't you? Yes, I have. We each applied our special talents to preparing a Christmas meal. To wit, I opened a bottle of wine, two in fact, and Myra made cheese omelettes, really great, the best I've had in ages, so you needn't worry that I'm dying because I turned down your offer of beans on toast.'

Hat didn't recall specifying beans on toast, but he was too glad at the improvement in Rye to protest. With Myra Rogers on one side and Mrs Gilpin on the other, Rye now had a double line of defence in the event piss-artist Penn returned to the fray.

When he got to see Rye again on the evening of Boxing Day he'd found the recovery was complete and all the delights of Christmas, traditional and individual, that he'd been looking forward to tasted all the better for being delayed.

'This is all I want, Hat,' she whispered as she clung on to him after they made love. 'This is where I want to be, here, you, me, warm, snug, safe, forever.'

She lay across him, her arms and legs grappling him to her in an embrace so tight it was painful, but nothing in the world would have made him admit that pain. He had known from early on in their acquaintance that she was the one. Without her, life would be . . . he had no words to describe what life would be. All he knew was that whatever she wanted from him was hers without question. Even when she fell asleep she did not slacken her grip on him, and when she awoke in the small hours of the morning and began to explore his body again, she found his limbs locked in cramp.

'Jesus,' she said. 'Hat, love, what have I done to you? Why didn't you push me off?'

'Didn't want to,' he assured her. 'I'm fine. Oh shit!'

This in reaction to the stab of agony that followed his attempt to stretch his left leg.

She flung back the duvet, climbed astride his body and began to give him a comprehensive massage, which brought first relief then arousal.

'Here's a bit that's still stiff,' she said, running her hand down to his groin. 'That's going to need some real work.'

'Yeah, that's been bothering me for years,' he said. 'Don't think you'll have much luck there, Doctor.'

'At least we can wrap it up and keep it warm,' she said. 'Like this . . .'

And Christmas was merry all over again.

Rye was back at work the next day. While many employers bow to the inevitable and close down for the whole of the holiday period, Mid-Yorkshire Library Service was of sterner mettle, recognizing that after the penal sociability of Christmas, many people would be keen to get back to the solitary confinement of books.

On the twenty-seventh the reference library was fairly busy, but there was one notable and unregretted absentee. Charley Penn.

But midway through the morning, the door opened and Penn came in. He headed for his usual seat but without giving her the benefit of his usual glower and after five minutes looking at an unopened book, he rose and came to the desk.

Without preamble he said, 'Wanted to say I'm sorry about kicking up that fuss on Christmas Day. I were right out of order. Won't happen again.'

'Fuss?' she said. 'Oh yes, someone did say something about a drunk on the landing. I didn't actually notice, but I'm glad to hear of your resolution to reform, Mr Penn. Is that with immediate effect or do we have to wait till the New Year?'

Their eyes engaged, hers wide and candid, his deep-set and watchful. Neither blinked, but before it became a playground contest, Penn said, 'Work to do,' and turned away.

Behind him Rye said, 'Going well, is it?'

If he was surprised, it was hidden by the time he turned back to her.

'Two steps forward, one step back, you know how it is with research,' he said.

'Not really. I suppose I've never been interested enough in a complete stranger to want to know everything about him.'

'You don't start with a stranger. You start with someone you're acquainted with, if only through their works. That's the contact makes you want to know them better. And sometimes they turn out very different from what you imagined. There's the fascination.'

'I see. And is it harder or easier if they're dead?'

'Both. They can't answer questions. But they can't lie either.'

She was silent long enough for him to wonder if this unexpected exchange were at an end, then she said, 'And they can't object to someone sticking an unwanted nose into their private affairs. That must be an advantage.'

'Think you might be confusing my line of work and your boyfriend's,' said Penn.

'Parallel lines that sometimes intersect, aren't they?'

'That's a bit too clever for a simple soul like me,' said Penn.

'Simple, Mr Penn? With all those books to your name?'

'There's nowt clever in making things up about folk you've

273

invented,' he said with the harsh dismissiveness of success.

'But you haven't invented Heine. And I hope you're not making things up about him.'

'No, he's real enough. But finding out the truth about him doesn't need cleverness, just hard work and a taste for truth.'

'And translating his poems?'

'The same.'

'You surprise me. I never seem to see any of your translations any more, Mr Penn. There was a time when I was always coming across them.'

She spoke gravely, with no hint of mockery, but they both knew she was referring to a period when the writer had paid oblique court by leaving translations of Heine's amatory verses where she would chance upon them. When she made it plain she wasn't interested, the poems continued to appear but with a mocking irony colouring his choice. Dick Dee's death brought a halt to all such games.

'I didn't seem able to get down to it for a while,' he said. 'But I'm getting back into the swing now. Hold on a sec. There's something here I'd value a reaction to.'

He went to his cubicle and returned with a sheet of paper which he laid in front of her. It contained two verses side by side.

The rock breaks his vessel asunder
The waves roll his body along
But what in the end drags him under
Is Lorelei's sweet song

But when in the end the wild waters
Plug his ear and scarf up his eye
I'm certain his last drowning thought is
The song of the Lorelei.

She read them without touching the paper.

'So?' she said.

'Two versions of the last verse of Heine's "Lorelei" poem, you know, the one that starts *Ich weiß nicht was soll es bedeuten Daß ich so traurig bin.*'

'I've come across it.'

'Both very free. I give a parallel literal translation, but in my metrical version I try for the spirit rather than just the plain sense of the original. My dilemma is, does Heine want us to think that Lorelei deliberately sang to destroy the boatman? Or

274

simply that it's her nature to sing and the boatman destroyed himself by listening? What do you think?'

'Don't know,' said Rye. 'But I don't much care for "waters" and "thought is".'

'An aesthetic rather than a moral judgment? Fair enough. I'll go with the first.'

He nodded, turned on his heel like a soldier and went back to his seat, leaving the sheet of paper on the desk.

A woman who had been observing this scene from the doorway now advanced to the desk. Rye Pomona looked up and saw a youngish female, rather stockily built, wearing no make up and a rain-spattered, mud-coloured fleece open to show a baggy grey T-shirt whose folds did nothing for her figure and whose colour sat uneasily against her dark complexion. She was holding a Tesco carrier bag and Rye snap-judged her as housewife who'd had kids early, let herself go a bit, and today, with the longueurs and rigours of Christmas behind her, had come to the library determined to seek some educational route to a life less tediously forecastable than her current prospects seemed to offer.

Must be Hat's influence, she told herself. I'm turning into a detective. Which thought, and the thought of Hat himself, brought a smile of such warmth to her face that the woman responded in kind, making her several years younger and three times as attractive.

'Hi,' said Rye. 'Can I help you?'

Making sure her body screened out any observation from the library, the woman slid an ID card across the desk.

'Hi,' she said. 'DC Novello. Maybe Hat's mentioned me?'

In fact Hat, to whom love meant no no-go areas, had talked about his colleagues and his work and himself with a complete but subjective openness. His account of his arch-rival, Shirley Novello, had created in Rye's mind a picture of a smooth svelte sophisticated creature, mobile glued to her left ear, organizer welded to her right hand, each colour co-ordinated with her designer power suit. It took a moment to readjust from both that false impression and her equally flawed attempt at detection and Novello said reassuringly, 'It's nothing heavy. Mr Dalziel asked me to look in to see you were all right.'

What the Fat Man had actually said was, 'Let her know to be careful about some slimy sod oozing his way into her confidence. At the same time, do a bit of oozing yourself and make sure she doesn't have owt to hide.'

'What a kind man Mr Dalziel is,' said Rye. 'As you can see, I'm fine.'

'Oh good. Wasn't that Mr Penn who was talking to you just now? I heard what happened on Christmas Day. He wasn't bothering you, I hope?'

'No, not in the least. We were just discussing a point of literature.'

Novello's gaze dropped to Penn's sheet of paper. Rye slid it away but not before Novello had read the lines of verse upside down.

'Lorelei,' she said. 'Wasn't that what you found on your computer after the break in?'

Done your homework, thought Rye. This was more in accord with Hat's picture.

'Yes,' she said.

'And you're sure Mr Penn wasn't bothering you?'

'Honestly, I know when I'm being bothered,' she smiled. 'I'm sure this was just coincidental. He came to apologize. I don't think we're going to be best friends, but if he wants things quiet, I'm not going to quarrel with that.'

'He may have his own reasons for wanting things quiet,' said Novello.

'Meaning?'

'Mr Dalziel thinks he might have decided he was getting nowhere barking himself, so he's decided to find himself a dog.'

'To bark louder at me?' said Rye, amused.

'More sniffer dog than barker,' said Novello. 'Press.'

'A journalist? But that's stupid. What would I have to say to a journalist?'

'Nothing, I hope. But as you've probably gathered, Mr Penn thinks that you ... that all of us are hiding something. If he's managed to persuade a journalist there could be a story ... point is, it won't be someone coming at you asking for an interview, it's more likely to be someone coming at you sideways. Like here at the library, say. Some fellow asking for your help with something, then striking up an acquaintance . . . it can happen.'

She'd taken the brief smile which touched Rye's lips as scepticism, but it was caused by her memory that this was how Hat Bowler had first attempted to get to know her.

'I'll be on my guard,' she promised.

'So it's not happened yet?'

'No. I think I'd have noticed.'

Novello said gently, 'With these people, the art is making sure you don't notice.'

'Oh dear. Now you're frightening me. But in any case, I've got nothing to hide so what can they hope to get out of me?'

Novello said, 'Can we go into your office for a moment?'

She glanced towards Penn as they went through the door behind the desk, but the writer seemed deeply immersed in his work.

Closing the door she said, 'They'll have the public records. Mr Dalziel thought it might help if you took a look at the inquest transcript.'

She produced a file from the Tesco bag.

Rye said uneasily, 'Is it OK to do this?'

'Of course it is. It's like a copper looking at his notebook in court. No one can remember everything exactly. And if someone did ask you questions, you wouldn't want to give them anything to worry at just because something slipped your mind, would you? They're experts at making owt from nowt.'

Dalziel had said, 'Make sure she understands that what she said to the coroner is all she needs to say.'

And Novello, who had not been made privy to anything but the official picture of what Pascoe and Dalziel had found when they arrived on the scene, nor anything the girl had said outside her formal statement, didn't ask the question forming in her mind, 'And could she say anything more, sir?' because she was beginning to suspect that this ignorance was part of the reason she'd been given this job. Reading everything she could find on the Wordman case had taken up most of her free time since Dalziel gave her the assignment – just because he gave you a job that took up twenty-three hours of the day didn't mean he didn't expect you to fit the rest of your work into the remaining hour.

There was a ring from the enquiry desk bell.

'Look, I've got to go,' said Rye.

'Fine. Keep this. Read it at your leisure. Nothing to worry about, we just don't want you being harassed. I'll keep in touch, if that's OK? Maybe a coffee some time?'

Rye thought then nodded and said, 'Yes, I think I'd like that.'

She ushered the WDC out of the office. Standing at the desk was a tall, blond young man looking like Arnie Schwarzenegger's handsome young brother. Novello gave him a look which was at the same time assessing and admiring. In reply she got a smile which kept up the Hollywood connection by being borrowed straight from Julia Roberts.

Half blinded by such dental effulgence, she glanced at Rye and twisted her mouth into a get-a-load-of-that! expression.

'Take care,' she said.

'You too,' said Rye with a grin.

And as Novello walked away she thought, if that hunk does turn out to be an investigative journalist, then he can investigate me to his heart's content!

t the same time as Novello left the library, about a hundred feet over her head a scene was unfolding which in prospect most investigative journalists would have given their editors' eyeteeth for.

Sergeant Edgar Wield was approaching the top floor of the Centre car park where he had a secret assignation with the teenage rent boy who was madly in love with him.

At least this was how it might be written up by some of these investigative journalists, thought Wield. Which was why, one way or another, he was going to get things sorted between Lee Lubanski and himself today.

After a dodgy start, Edgar Wield had had a very good Christmas.

His partner, antiquarian book dealer, Edwin Digweed, had turned out to be a traditionalist in matters yulic. At first Wield had looked for an element of piss-taking as the familiar outlines of their cottage vanished beneath a folly of furbelows and he found himself sharing their small sitting room with an outsize fir-tree whose apogean fairy bowed gracefully from the waist because her head pressed against the ceiling. On a shopping expedition to a hypermarket, which during the rest of the year Digweed referred to as Hell's Cathedral, he had watched in bewilderment as their trolley piled up with crackers and baubles and puddings and pies and jars of pickled walnuts and yards of cocktail sausage and samples of every kind of exotic confectionary and savoury on display. Finally he had enquired politely if the Red Cross had perhaps warned Edwin to expect a flash flood of starving but picky refugees in remote Eendale.

Digweed had laughed, a sort of jolly ho-ho-ho which Wield

never heard him use at any other season, and continued down the aisle, humming along to the piped carols.

Ever a pragmatist, Wield had decided to relax and enjoy it, and discovered rather to his surprise that he did. Even his initially reluctant attendance at the midnight service had been a pleasure. The whole village had been there, and as Corpse Cottage, the Wield/Digweed residence, now festooned with winking fairy lights, snuggled handily under the churchyard wall, it seemed natural that most of the villagers should drop in for a festal warmer on the way home, and very quickly huge inroads were made into what had seemed their excessive provision.

'I was very pleased to see you at the service,' said Justin Halavant, art collector and critic in whose medieval hand a poppy or a lily would not have looked out of place. 'It's so important to demonstrate the solidarity of our faith, don't you think?'

'Oh aye?' said Wield, a touch surprised as he'd have put Halavant down as an aesthetic rather than a devout Christian. 'Look, don't be offended, I enjoyed it, but I'm not what you'd call a true believer . . .'

'My dear chap, what's that got to do with anything?' laughed Halavant. 'All I meant was, anyone who doesn't show up in the church at Christmas is likely to end up in the Wickerman at Beltane. Lovely candied kumquats, by the way. I may have some more.'

Later he'd shared the exchange with Digweed, who'd laughed, not his ho-ho-ho but his usual dry chuckle, and said, 'Justin likes his jest. But he's right. Enscombe takes care of its own, one way or another.'

Christmas morning had been going well till among the presents beneath the tree Wield had found a padded envelope marked *Not to be opened till Xmas day* in a childish scrawl.

'Came with the post yesterday,' said Digweed with an over-studied lack of interest.

Wield opened it to find a card with all the most sucrose elements of Christmas greetings combined in one glutinous design and something wrapped in tissue paper.

The card was inscribed *To Edgar the best from your friend Lee.*

He unwrapped the tissue to reveal a pair of silver cuff links engraved with his initials.

Edwin asked no questions, but questions hung in the air so Wield gave answers in his most brisk and precise style.

Digweed listened then said, 'You did not think to mention this boy to me earlier.'

'It was police business.'

'So,' said Digweed, glancing at the links and the card, 'it would appear. Isn't there a name for gifts that policemen receive from criminals?'

Oh dear, thought Wield. To a cop, family squabbles leading to domestic violence were a commonplace of Christmas Day. He hadn't anticipated getting personally involved.

'He's not a criminal,' he said. 'But I'll be giving it back to him anyway.'

'And break the little darling's heart? Don't be silly. If you don't want the links, I'll have them. I'll tell people the initials stand for Eternally Worried, that's me.'

He turned away, his shoulders shaking as if at some barely restrained emotion.

'Edwin, there's no need for you to worry . . .'

Digweed turned to face him, still shaking but now the emotion was clear and audible.

'My dear Edgar, what do you take me for?' he said, laughing. 'I may shoot you but I will never play the sulky jealous type. And besides, you say this young man is nineteen but could pass for ten or eleven? I can see you looking appreciatively at a good-looking yunker, but I have never detected the smallest morsel of paedophilia in your make-up. Also, in my experience, cuff links are not the kind of gift a lad gives to his lover. They are more what a son gives to his dad. So, no jealousy, believe me. But some concern. You may not be attracted to young Lubanski, but you are sorry for him and, to a man in your position, that can be more dangerous than sex. You will take care, won't you?'

'He's at risk.'

'No. You are. Don't confuse the apparent child with the real adult. But that's for the morrow. *Carpe diem*, dear Edgar. And here's a little something to help preserve it too.'

He tossed over a package which Wield ripped open to reveal a mini camcorder.

'Jesus,' he said with real feeling. 'Thanks a million. This must have cost a fortune.'

'Self-interest,' said Digweed. 'I understand that you with your computer expertise will be able to make films of me, then doctor them so that I look and move twenty years younger. I can hardly wait for the experiment to begin.'

And after that Christmas had been everything Lee's card claimed it should be.

Wield could not remember a time in his life when he'd been happier. And because he was happy, he wanted everyone else to be happy too, but this he knew was not even a possibility in that other uncontrollable world that lay in ambush for him whenever he ventured east of Eendale. So now as he approached his rendez-vous, his mind filled with foreboding as he spotted the pale-faced boy who stood in wait for him like Cathy waiting for Heathcliff, outlined against the scudding clouds of a wild and wintry York-shire sky.

He had changed their meeting spot partly because regular encounters even somewhere as anonymous as Turk's could draw attention, but mainly because he didn't want any audience if Lubanski got upset with what he was about to hear.

For this was definitely their last meeting.

Dalziel, impressed by the accuracy of the tips so far, had urged Wield to get his new informant signed up properly. Wield knew this wasn't going to happen, but he didn't mind making the proposal because he reckoned this would draw a line under their relationship. The idea of simply continuing to take advantage of the boy's vulnerability and emotional instability filled him with revulsion. Before they parted, he would do his best to persuade Lee out of the dangerous and degrading life he was leading, though, being a realist, he had little hope of success. But no way was he going to let the boy's evident misconceptions about their current relationship continue.

Now Lee turned and saw him, and his change of expression from abandoned puppy dolour to here-comes-master delight struck Wield to the heart and turned the stern words he'd prepared bitter in his mouth, and he heard himself saying, 'Hi, Lee. Good Christmas?'

'Yeah. Made a bundle.'

'I didn't mean trade, Lee,' said Wield, thinking what a stupid question it had been. 'Listen, I've got something to say to you.'

'Me first,' said the youth. 'There's something real big going down in the New Year.'

'Lee,' said Wield, steeling his resolve. 'It's time we put a stop . . .'

'No, listen, this is really good. I made some notes after. I've got them here.'

Proudly he handed over a sheet of cheap writing paper covered with a childish scrawl.

Tear it up, Wield told himself. Tell him you don't want to know, it's all over, you're washing your hands of him. He's got his own life to live and if you can't make it any better, the least you can do is not make it any worse.

But even as the voice of the man inside spoke these words in his head, the eyes of the cop outside were reading the words on the paper.

> *B said that things were OK and man in sheffield shuddunt worry and man in shef said that was for him to deside and there's been plenty to worry about already how did B explain that. And B said coincidence and it hadn't made a difference had it and everything was on as planned for January and the upfront mony would be deposited as arranged. And man in Shef said it had better be and he rang off.*

Now Wield was all cop.

He said, 'This B . . . he's your source for these tips, is he? You do business with him?'

'Yeah, that's right. Regular. He really goes for me. And he's got one of them speaker phones and he seems to like talking to people while we're, like, doing it . . . not about it, though he does that too on the net, but real business talk, and the others've got no idea that I'm there doing it . . .'

Oh God. The Oval Office syndrome. Some guy full of a sense of his own importance and getting a kick out of . . .

His imagination shut out the picture of the act just as Lee's misplaced delicacy had refused to put it into words.

He said, 'So this man in Sheffield, there was no name mentioned?'

'No. Well, not really.'

Something there? Maybe. But concentrate on facts before you start chasing fancies.

'How do you know he was in Sheffield?'

Lee screwed up his eyes in thought then said, 'Because Belchy asked if he was still in Sheffield and he said yes.'

Belchy?

B for Belchy.

Oh shit. If what he was thinking was true, there was no way Andy Dalziel was ever going to let this boy go.

Grasping the nettle at once he said, 'Belchy would be Marcus Belchamber, right?'

Lee didn't answer but he didn't need to. Alarm was twisting his boyish features.

'Right?' insisted Wield.

'I didn't tell you that!'

Wield felt a mingling of pity and exasperation. The stupid boy thought it was safe to pass on information as long as he didn't name names. As if it would make the slightest difference to Belchamber that his name had been guessed rather than betrayed. But it clearly made a difference to Lee, and that was something a good cop could play on.

Despising himself, Wield said reassuringly, 'Of course you didn't, Lee. Whatever happens, we'd make that quite clear. We've known all along, you see. It's always that way, we know a lot more than we ever let on.'

The upside of giving an impression of omniscience, besides calming the boy's fears and making him more malleable, was that it might make him start thinking of Wield as a part of the huge legal machine rather than an individual.

'So you knew all this stuff I've given you?'

'Most,' said Wield. 'But what you told us was great for tying up loose ends. In fact, I don't know what we'd have done without it. You've done really well.'

284

The boy looked so pleased that Wield felt his old guilt well up. However this played, this was definitely the last time, he assured himself.

But he was getting way ahead of the game.

He said, 'So, no names, you say? What about when they said cheerio?'

'The man in Sheffield just hung up. Then Tobe got on the net . . .'

'Tobe? Who the hell's Tobe?'

'It's Belchy's web name, the one he uses when he talks to his mates on the net.'

'How do you know that?'

'Sometimes he's been online while we're . . . you know. Likes to send messages to say what's happening.'

Belchamber, you are a nasty piece of shit! thought Wield.

He said, 'This is a chat room he uses then?'

'Yeah, but it's real complicated to get in, passwords, and all kinds of shit. You want me to find out more about it?'

'No,' said Wield firmly. 'You mustn't do anything that makes him suspicious. So when he went online was this something to do with the call to the man in Sheffield?'

'I think so. I saw this message he left on the noticeboard. *LB call Tobe.*'

'*LB?*'

'Yeah, it's one of these pervs in the chat room, but this one Belchy knows personal and sometimes he'll just leave a message there.'

Someone whose line he doesn't trust to be secure, thought Wield.

'And did this LB ring?'

'Yeah. A bit later. Didn't need to make a note of that, it were really short. LB said what? And Belchy said he'd told his mate the money was through and was it? And LB said he always did what he said he'd do and mebbe Tobe should remember that. End of call.'

'Doesn't sound very friendly.'

'No,' said the boy. 'Come to think of it, when I've heard 'em before, Belchy and LB, I mean, they've always sounded a lot more friendly.'

'And the man in Sheffield didn't sound like a close friend either from what you say.'

'Him? No, definitely not.'

'But you said that Belchamber talked about "his mate's money" when he was talking to LB. Why should that be, do you think?'

'Don't know. Yeah, it is a bit funny. I mean, old Belchy's really posh. Not the kind of guy goes around calling people mate, know what I mean? But he did call the Sheffield guy mate a couple of times. Mebbe he was trying to suck up to him, do you think?'

'Yes,' said Wield softly. 'Maybe he was. Lee, you've done well, picking all this up.'

The boy's face lit up.

'You reckon? Well, you know. Keeps your mind off the job, doesn't it?'

'And how long have you been working for old Belchy?'

'Few weeks now. Real regular. It's good money and no hassle.'

'You sound like you sort of like him?'

Lee looked at Wield blankly and said, 'Like him? He's a punter. I mean, someone like you I can like, but not a punter . . . liking don't come into it . . . and he treats me like a kid . . .'

'Sorry?'

'Well, he goes on like I'm just a kid, you know, ten or eleven or such. He's got these clothes he likes me to put on, school uniform, green blazer with yellow edging, grey shorts and a cap, all that crap, and he gets narked if I say owt that a grown-up would say. Other times he dresses up like them soldiers in that film *Gladiator* and I've got to run around bare arse like I'm a slave or summat. Still, it's his money and you gotta give what you get paid for, that's how things work, right?'

'I'm afraid it is, Lee,' said Wield with infinite sadness. 'I'm afraid it is.'

et me get this straight,' said Dalziel. 'While this lad's under the table chewing his dick, Belchamber's chatting away with his dodgy clients on the phone? Or else he's on his computer giving a running commentary to some other sad shirt-lifters? God, that makes the bastard thick and sick!'

'Wouldn't call him thick,' said Wield. 'It's a power thing. The lad doing this to him is a Roman slave. Or else he's a ten-year-old schoolboy. That uniform Lee mentioned sounds like Thistle Hall Prep School to me. I checked. That's where Belchamber went. Mebbe something bad happened to him there.'

'Not bad enough. He's a disgusting excuse for a human being,' said Pascoe fervently. 'I've never liked him. It will be a pleasure to send him down.'

'Hang about,' said Dalziel. 'Let's not get ahead of ourselves. OK, one reading of this is that Belchamber's put a toe over the line and may be acting as a bagman for one of his dodgy clients, though I can't for the life of me understand why he should. In fact it seems so unlikely that I reckon we take a long cold look at things afore we go steaming in on the basis of some scribbles that a rent boy has given to Quentin Crisp here.'

One thing about the Fat Man, he didn't wrap things up in fancy paper.

Or perhaps (mind-boggling thought!) he believed he did.

Pascoe said, 'Let's wire Lubanski up, get something we can produce in evidence. In any case it'll be better if we can assess what's being said for ourselves.'

'No,' said Wield very firmly. 'I'll not have that.'

'Oh?' said Pascoe, taken aback. 'Do you intend arguing that or merely asserting it?'

Dalziel looked from his sergeant to his chief inspector and for a moment thought about settling back to enjoy a rare public confrontation between them.

Then both personal regard and professional responsibility kicked in and he said dismissively, 'Doesn't need arguing. Lad's got to strip off to change into his school uniform. I bet the Belch watches, so while he's running around in the buff, where's he going to keep a wire hidden? Could try for a phone tap, but doubt we'd get it. Things go wrong, no one's going to fancy having Belchamber shitting on us from a great height. No, we'll have to stick with the lad. What's his motive giving you this stuff anyway, Wieldy?'

It was with great reluctance that Wield had let Lee get into the Fat Man's rattle-bag. Though even Dalziel probably found the notion of sex slavery abhorrent, he drew the line at human rights for snouts. Belchamber's involvement plus his sense that this latest bit of info related to something really big had made it impossible to preserve the boy's anonymity. But no way was he going to discuss the true nature of Lee's motivation. He tried to imagine the landslip of emotion running down that Beachy Head of a face if he replied now, 'He wants me for his dad.' Almost worth it just to see. Almost.

He said, 'He hates Belchamber's guts.'

It wasn't true. In fact Lee seemed almost as indifferent to Belchamber as a human being as the lawyer was to him. But it would do for the Fat Man.

'Does he now?' Dalziel shuddered. 'Jesus! If you ever get a notion that I'm letting some bugger who hates my guts get his teeth anywhere near my dick, be sure to let me know! So let's see what we've got. Mate. You think this guy in Sheffield could be Mate Polchard. Rings a bell, we were talking about him just the other day, weren't we?'

'Was in the Syke with Roote. They played chess together,' said Pascoe, who suspected the Fat Man remembered full well and was merely testing his reaction.

'That's it. Don't think young Franny could be masterminding

this job, whatever it is, do you, Pete?' said Dalziel with heavy
jocularity. 'Fits your Mr Big profile to a T.'

'I'll wait till we're certain that it is Polchard who's involved
before making up my mind, sir,' said Pascoe, po-faced.

'Good thinking. Wieldy, you've checked Polchard out?'

'Christmas at his cottage in Wales. Left on Boxing Day. Spotted in Sheffield the week before Christmas.'

'Spotted where? Doing what?'

'The shops,' said Wield. 'Christmas stuff. Nothing furtive.
Looked like he was shopping till he dropped, then off back to
the countryside for Christmas.'

'So he'd have been around same time as this DI Rose was
getting a sniff of a big job overspilling on to our patch. Pete?'

'I've spoken to Rose. Low key. Didn't want to get him too
excited.'

Which had been difficult. His sense of exultation had come
bubbling down the line and Pascoe had had to work very hard
to keep the cork in.

'Listen,' he'd urged, 'this could be nothing. My advice is, don't
go shouting round the office. If it comes to nothing, you'll look
dafter than before. If it comes to something big, then someone
bigger than you will lift it out of your lap. Good security too.
Fewer people who know, less chance of some idiot blowing
things. Walls have ears, remember?'

This argument seemed to impress. Perhaps Rose had suffered
from idle gossip.

'You're right there,' he said. 'Round here they've got bloody
tongues too!'

'Anything more from your snout?'

'Still no sign of the bugger. His cronies say he's still in London,
but nobody has an address. I bet he's too scared to come back.
Someone's really put the frighteners on him.'

'Someone like Mate Polchard?' suggested Pascoe.

'That kind of strength, yeah.'

They left it that Rose was going to put out cautious feelers
to check if Polchard was back in town and, once found, mount
a distant surveillance on him.

'It's all owt or nowt,' said Dalziel fretfully. 'This other guy,

LB, the one your snout thinks must be one of his creepy computer chums, how's that working out, Wieldy?'

'I'm working on it,' said Wield. 'But these closed chat rooms aren't easy. Lots of checks, codes and passwords. And once you're in, everyone uses screen names.'

'Like Tobe? What sort of fucking name's that?'

'A rather obvious sort, I'd have said,' declared Pascoe. 'I'd guess he calls himself Toby, in reference to Sir Toby Belch in *Twelfth Night*. Can't work out LB though.'

'Better revise your Shakespeare then, hadn't you?' growled Dalziel, who didn't mind showing off himself but deplored it in his underlings. 'This chat room, all else fails, can we do the slimy sod for that?'

'Not unless they're using it to download obscene material under the Act,' said Wield. 'Or procuring minors for illegal acts. But if they're just a bunch of like-minded souls who want a place where they can let it all hang out and talk dirty, it's hard to touch them.'

'If he's into this, isn't he likely to be into one of the big hard-core rings?' said Pascoe.

'Possibly.' Wield hesitated, then went on, 'My reading of Belchamber, though, is that he's too careful to let himself get into something like that which he can't really control.'

'Not so careful if he chats on the phone with a rent boy dangling from his dick,' said Pascoe.

'I think that's all part of it,' said Wield. 'To a lot of people, danger's an essential part of sex. We've all got extremes we like to go to. If we're lucky, we find someone else willing to make the trip. Belchamber wants the danger, wants the extremes, but he's a lawyer. Maximize the professional profit, minimize the personal risk. That's what he likes so much about Lee. He looks like he's ten, and Belchamber makes him act like he's ten, but in fact he's nineteen. If it all went pear-shaped, what have we got? No law against sexual relations with a nineteen-year-old. So Belchamber gets the paedo's kick without the risk. And doing business while he's getting a blow job is the same. It feels really wild, but he thinks he's too powerful relative to the boy to be in any danger of disclosure.'

Pascoe was used to listening to Wield's cool, detailed analyses of situations and cases, but though the tone was as dispassionate as ever, there was some pulse running beneath the surface here that he'd rarely detected before.

Dalziel said, 'Another possibility. We're sure, are we, that this kid, as well as sucking Belchamber's plonker, isn't pulling yours?'

For a moment Pascoe thought the Fat Man was questioning Wield's relationship with Lubanski, then he made the shift from the literal to the figurative.

'Certain, sir,' said Wield. 'And after the Linford case and the Praesidium thing, he's got the track record to back it.'

'The security van thing, tell us about that again. Seems funny for old Belchy to be mixed up with such a bunch of losers.'

'They may be losers, sir,' said Pascoe. 'But we haven't had a sniff of them since. Even the van's vanished off the face of the earth.'

'They'd want something for their efforts, wouldn't they?' growled Dalziel. 'Either it's being gutted and the bits sold off through some dodgy dealer, or maybe they shipped the whole thing across to Ireland and it's running around Dublin as we speak. But what's Belchamber's connection?'

'Don't know. Lubanski came in from the shower – Belchamber likes him clean and smelling of carbolic soap – and just caught the end of a conversation. Belchamber said, "and the Praesidium van?" and the other guy said, "we'll hit it Friday".'

'Not a lot,' said the Fat Man. 'Was this other voice the same as the man in Sheffield?'

'I asked. Lee couldn't say.'

'Could be the aim of the Praesidium job was to bankroll the big job,' said Pascoe.

'Failed miserably then.'

'So maybe Polchard's had to go elsewhere for the money, which might explain how Belchamber got involved.'

'No, he must've been involved already if he were talking to someone about the van before it got hit,' objected Dalziel. 'Look, until we've got a better idea what we're dealing with – and it could turn out to be a bag of bones after all – let's proceed with caution. Wieldy, I'll leave this lad in your tender loving care for the time being, but if ever I feel the need, I'll pick the young sod up myself and shake him around till I'm sure there's nowt else to come out. Now bugger off, the two of you. We've got nowt but mustard seeds here. I'm relying on you pair either to water them or piss on them pretty damn quick.'

At the door Pascoe paused.

'Sir,' he said.

'What? Unless it's about Roote, in which case sod off, I'm busy.'

'What's Novello doing with her nose stuck in the Wordman file?'

'She's doing what she's been told off to do, lad, and a bit more besides. I'd watch that lass. I reckon she's after your job.'

'And welcome to it most days. Shall I ask her direct then?'

With a sigh, Dalziel explained what he was up to, most of it anyway.

'So how's she doing so far?'

'She's spoken to Pomona, put her on guard.'

He gave Pascoe a quick summary of Novello's account of her visit to the library.

'And Penn was showing Rye bits of the "Lorelei" poem? Isn't that as good as an admission he was the one did the break-in?'

'Not so. I'd mentioned Lorelei to him and he's sharp at putting things together, is Charley. Couldn't resist stirring the pot a bit, but I reckon the significant thing is Charley apologizing and being what passes for conciliatory in a tyke-bred Kraut. I reckon that Christmas Day really was just down to too much sauce and he regretted it later. He wants Pomona lulled so's his tabloid wolf can gobble up little Red Riding Hood unawares.'

'I see,' said Pascoe. 'Sir, it is going to be all right, isn't it?'

Pascoe, though he hadn't opposed them, had never been totally happy about the liberties they'd taken with the official version of events that day out at Stang Tarn.

'Worried about your pension?' laughed the Fat Man. 'No need. If it comes to that, you can share mine.'

The laughter still echoing in his ears, How come it's only my pension that's at risk? wondered Pascoe.

* * *

292

Down in the canteen, Shirley Novello and Hat Bowler were looking into the future but with no thought of pensions.

It had been Novello who proposed a chat over a cup of coffee and it hadn't started well.

'I was at the library this morning,' said Novello. 'Had a talk with your girl.'

'What the hell for?' said Hat fiercely.

'Just to see she was all right.'

'Oh yes? And what business is that of yours? Mebbe you should keep your nose out.'

Oh shit, thought Novello. When love came in the window, reason went out the door. Time to summon the bogeyman.

'It was Mr Dalziel's idea. You want I should tell Mr Dalziel to keep his nose out? Or would you rather do it yourself?'

For a moment Hat looked as if he might be seriously contemplating this, then reality set in and he said, 'So what did he tell you to do?'

Novello explained. She held nothing back. Dalziel had told her to handle things in her own way and that didn't include risking alienation of a colleague she might have to depend on at some future juncture.

Bowler seemed determined to be stupid.

'So he thinks that Penn's trying to get the papers interested in a scandal, only there's no scandal to get them interested in, is there? How much time and money are they going to waste on that, do you think? No story, end of story.'

'You're not looking at this straight on, Hat,' she said. 'Think of it this way. We collect evidence of what we think is a crime and we send it off to the CPS and half the time they look at what we think is a water-tight case and send it back saying, "Sorry no can do, won't stand up in court." So, a good case to us looks like crap to them, right?'

'Yeah but . . .'

'The newspapers are to us what we are to the CPS. What looks like crap to us can look like a good case to them. They don't have to worry about proving things in court. Hints, allegations, lots of stuff in quotes, given half a chance they can probably make us look like we're doing more covering up than a drag queen.'

'Yeah, but if no one's done anything wrong, they can't hurt us, can they?'

Could he really be so naive? wondered Novello.

'If they find a story to run they'll run it hard,' she said patiently. 'There'll be questions, maybe another enquiry. You've been through one already, one that was on your side, and you came out a hero. The papers loved you. But love dies. Another scenario, another role. You may come out clean again, but that doesn't mean you won't be damaged. You know how it works, nothing on the record, but at every promotion board, someone asks, wasn't he the one . . . ? Same with Rye. Yes, on paper she's good, but do you recall . . .'

'They still need a story to run,' he said obstinately.

'OK, try this. Librarian screws boss in country cottage. Jealous lover catches them at it. There's a fight. Lover stabs rival to death. Thirteen times.'

'That's a load of garbage!'

'Not the thirteen stabs. I've read the PM report.'

Hat said, 'Listen, Novello, don't you think I haven't been through all this? I was on my back with that bastard on top of me. He'd stabbed me already, would have killed me if Rye hadn't hit him with a bottle. That must've made him drop the knife and he started hitting me with this heavy glass dish and would probably have finished the job with that if I hadn't got hold of the knife somehow and stabbed him with it.'

'Yeah. Thirteen times. Mainly in the back, though you did manage to get him a good one under the ribs too. That would probably have been enough without the other dozen.'

For a moment it looked as if he was going to explode in resentful anger. Instead he closed his eyes tight and knotted his fists tighter, then slowly forced himself to relax.

'We were fighting, him for his freedom, me for my life,' he said quietly. 'We rolled around a bit, I suppose, but mainly he was on top of me with my arms round him, so his back was the easiest target. I don't remember much. I was losing consciousness. All I knew was while I still had an ounce of strength left, I had to use it against him.'

'And of course you were defending your girl's honour,' said Novello lightly. 'Real picture-book heroics.'

To her surprise he grinned at her mockery.

'That's how it started maybe, but not how it finished. In the end it was all about me being scared shitless. Literally, I gather. I was convinced I was going to die and I was terrified. You must know the feeling, Novello. You've been there.'

Her hand went to the shoulder where she'd taken the bullet that had come close to killing her.

'Not straight off,' she said. 'For a time I was out of it. Still breathing, still moving, but too shocked to feel much. Later though, when it looked like all of us were going to end up dead and I was too weak even to think about resistance, then I got scared.'

'Shitless?' he said.

'I may have pee'd myself, but we ended up so wet there was no way of telling,' she said smiling at him in a sharing moment. Then the smile faded and she said in a businesslike voice, 'OK, however you finished, you started off being a hero. In your statement you say that when you burst into the cottage, you found Rye and Dee struggling, both naked, lots of blood. And you assumed . . .'

'I assumed nothing! I saw he was attacking her. And it wasn't just sexual, though that was bad enough. The bastard was trying to kill her!'

'Because of the knife, you mean? And because you'd worked out that all the evidence pointed to Dee being the killer known as the Wordman? If there hadn't been a Wordman connection and you'd come across the same scene, what would you have thought?'

'The same,' he said promptly. 'OK, different motivation. He'd wanted sex, she'd turned him down, he'd got nasty, tried to force her, and when she fought back, he lost it.'

'Right,' she said thoughtfully. 'But even given his sole aim was to kill her, there must have been some sexual element in the attack all the same. I mean, in your hospital statement you say she was naked, right?'

'Yeah. He must have torn her clothes off her, obvious.'

'Fair enough. No mention of this in the inquest evidence though.'

'No need. It wasn't down as an attempted rape.'

'No, of course not,' she said. 'Then there's Rye's injuries. It's on record she needed treatment, but mainly for shock. Physically there was nothing but a few scratches and a little bruising. No need for this to figure in the inquest record either, nor in the enquiry report. She was attacked, she was terrified, that was enough.'

'What's your point?' said Hat. 'In fact, what's the point of any of this? Like I say, I've been through it all before, with Mr Dalziel and with the enquiry. So why the hell do I have to sit here being interrogated by someone who knows nothing about the case and whose only claim to seniority is that she's been a DC a few months longer than me?'

'Do I have to explain it all again?' she said wearily. 'Mr Dalziel, and the enquiry team too, they had the same aim, to clarify the truth, but they had a bloody good idea what the truth they wanted to clarify was. Dee, the psychopathic serial killer, had been prevented from carrying out his last murder by the intervention of Bowler, the modest young hero. That is the gospel truth in the authorized version. Only there's Penn's revised version, which Fat Andy thinks he's persuaded the forces of Anti-Christ, better known as the tabloid press, to take an interest in. We can assume the cunning bastards will get hold of everything I've got hold of. And what we've got to ask ourselves so that we can be ready for it, is what are they likely to make of things like the thirteen stab wounds on Dee's body? The fact that they were made by the deadly weapon with which he was attacking Rye, indicating clearly that he'd been disarmed when he was killed? The absence of any significant and life-threatening wounds on Rye's body?'

She could have added Rye's nudity and the lack of any forensic evidence indicating that her clothes had been removed by force, but she felt she'd gone far enough. Hat, she observed with a pang, was looking worse than he had at any time since his return to duty. Then, apart from a little pallor, he had shown no signs of his illness, but had moved and behaved with all his old ebullience. Now he looked careworn and a decade older.

'So what do you make of it, Shirl?' he asked.

She hated Shirl, didn't much care for Shirley, was happy to be simply Novello which had a neutrality to match her work clothing. But Bowler's rare use of her first name signalled dependency rather than condescension.

'Not much, and I doubt they'll make much either, not without they get something else, like a few good quotes from you or from Rye,' she said reassuringly. 'So take care.'

'You bet,' he said, getting up. 'Back to the grind. See you upstairs.'

She watched him go. She had no special feeling for Hat, but there was a quality of brightness and bounce about him which it was hard to resist, and she wasn't happy to have a part in snuffing it out. She hoped she'd been telling the truth about the likely tabloid reaction, but she doubted it. If, as Dalziel suspected, one of the papers had already committed an undercover investigative reporter to the case, they weren't going to step way from it without at the very least a mud-stirring article. There was enough material here already for that and she'd barely got going on her devil's advocate assignment. But of course, it wasn't just that which would be bothering Bowler. He too was a detective and she doubted if she'd asked any questions he hadn't already asked himself. She just hoped to God that he'd have the nous not to ask Rye. She herself hardly knew the woman, thought her interesting, and was certain there was a lot more to her than met the eye. If that lot more had included opening her pages to her librarian boss, that was her business and Hat would be well advised not to make it his.

But if it made a tabloid headline, it would take a stronger will than she guessed he possessed to keep his lips glued.

ffichtenburg-am-Blutensee

Aargau

Wed Dec 26th

My dear Mr Pascoe

Have you had a good Christmas? I have, in fact so good
that only now does it seem I've had time or energy to sit
down and write to you. Perhaps you'd have preferred it if
I hadn't bothered? I hope not, but in any case it's no
longer a matter of choice. They say in China that if you
save someone's life then it becomes your responsibility. In
a way you may have saved mine by putting me in the
Syke, so now you're having to pay the price.

Last time I wrote I was on my way to Zurich.

God, what a wonderful city! You can almost smell the
money! But that I know will be of little interest to one so
unmaterialistic as yourself, so let me hasten to matters
more to your taste, such as art, history, and the pursuit of
knowledge.

From the point of view of new material, my short stay
was as unproductive as I anticipated. To dig up anything
new from ground already carefully riddled by Sam and
Albacore, I would have needed a vast supply of serendipity,

298

and I'd already used mine in making a possible connection between Beddoes and Fichtenburg. But good biography is as much concerned with getting inside the mind of its subject as establishing external facts about him, and I think I got a great deal out of simply strolling around the city, imagining I was that other lonely, disaffected and unattached exile, Thomas Lovell Beddoes.

You, of course, by instinct and training, are expert at tracking motives. How much easier would it be with you at my side for me to understand what made Beddoes, shortly before his twenty-second birthday and shortly after having taken his degree at Oxford where he had begun to establish a reputation as a poet, decide to leave England and spend nearly all the remainder of his life in Germany and Switzerland? In particular, how could someone who so clearly loved the English tongue as much as he did have pretty well relegated it to his second language by the time he died?

Sam's theory is that everything can be traced to the boy's early exposure to the brutal realities of death, and to the devastatingly early loss of his powerful father. If we look at the three main energy centres of Beddoes' life, we can see how they all relate to his father, and how they're all preoccupied with man's struggle against the ultimate enemy.

Through medicine he seeks for ways to understand and conquer it while at the same time looking for any evidence in flesh, blood and bone of the existence of the soul. While he does not seem inclined to follow his father in channelling his medical skills into improving the health of the underprivileged (Beddoes Sr founded the quaintly named Institute for the Sick and Drooping Poor!), Thomas Lovell actively supports – sometimes at personal risk – what today we would call human rights movements throughout Germany. And, of course, through the creative power of his imagination he attempts to grapple hand to hand with the Arch-Fear.

So why come to Germany? The answer lies in what

I've just written. Here he could be at the cutting edge (ho ho) of medical research; here there were strong undercurrents of social revolution such as only rarely made themselves felt in dull, complacent little England; and here with its dark forests and dramatic castles and sweeping rivers and turbulent mythology lay the true Gothic heart of Europe which, since the Jacobeans, the British had only dabbled their toes in.

But in the end he sees that his attack has failed on all three fronts.

I visited the site of the old town theatre which Beddoes hired for a night in a last sad attempt to pluck some morsel of comfort out of his disintegrating life by dressing young Konrad Degen up in hose and doublet and putting the poor lad on the stage as Hotspur.

Sam muses that perhaps Beddoes saw Hotspur, an uncomplicated, impulsive, brave, honourable, poetry-mocking, life-loving man of action, as the kind of son who wouldn't have let his father die. Or perhaps the only way a man can really bring a father back to life is to become him by having a son yourself.

Poor Beddoes. For a moment I slipped out of my skin and time into his and felt his pain, and felt too, what is worse, his faith that the future must be better than the past and that by the time we reached, say, the twenty-first century, the world would have taken large steps towards Utopia.

But enough of these dolorous imaginings! The festive season was waiting for me back at Fichtenburg. Let me tell you how I have celebrated it.

On my return to the castle early in the evening of December 23rd, I found Linda and her party had arrived that morning. She greeted me warmly with her version of the Continental kiss. One of the most popular videos on offer in the Syke was called *Great British Sporting Moments* (Dr Johnson was right; if you want a patriot, look in the jails!) and one of the Moments which got a particularly loud cheer was the old black-and-white footage of Henry

Cooper flooring Cassius Clay, as he still was then, with a left hook.

Linda's bruising buss to the point of my cheekbone had much the same effect. I was still reeling from it as she followed it up with close enquiry into the progress of my researches. I got the impression she knew all about the pattern of my first couple of days there – Frau Buff, probably – and regarded my rather abrupt departure to Zurich as a pleasing demonstration of my capacity to put duty before pleasure. No hint she knew the form that pleasure took, thank God!

She took the coincidence of the Stimmer connection with Beddoes in her stride, very much a Third Thought reaction. God's hand is in everything; we should marvel all the time, not just on the odd occasion when our spiritual caliginosity clears enough for us to glimpse Him at work. She has no real interest in Beddoes. She is backing me because by doing so she disobliges a lot of poncy academics, and also because (I make the point objectively not vaingloriously) in some as yet undefined way she likes the look of me.

She foresaw no problem in getting the Stimmers to permit examination of the Keller painting. That's her real strength. She simply doesn't admit the possibility of failure!

But I could tell she was genuinely pleased by my progress, for suddenly she apologized – with that brusqueness you encounter in people who are not used to apologizing – for a regrettable but necessary interference with my scholastic privacy. It seems that her party has swollen some way beyond its opening numbers (politicos love a freebie!) and pressure on room space has necessitated putting someone in the chalet's second bedroom.

The good news was that it was Frère Jacques.

I said, 'That would just be Jacques by himself, would it?'

She took my point immediately and said, 'Yes.

Doleful Dierick's back at the Abbey, making sure the Brothers don't enjoy Christmas too much. But I should warn you, he's threatening to join us for New Year.'

Well, sufficient is the evil, etc, and I said I'd be delighted to have Jacques' company, and I meant it. A chaperon was just what I needed. Timid and naive Mouse might be, but she's her mother's child, and Linda is a woman who hates to leave a job undone.

I met Mouse on my way down to the chalet. She greeted me with what looked like unfeigned delight, reproached me for my abrupt disappearance, and said that Zazie and Hildi had told her to wish me a very merry Christmas on their behalf.

Carefully I looked for hidden meaning. With relief, I found none.

In the chalet I discovered Frère Jacques sitting at the kitchen table writing.

He too expressed great pleasure at seeing me and also tried to apologize for breaking in on my scholarly privacy.

I told him I was delighted to have the company, and hoped he didn't mind being separated from Linda's main party.

'Good heavens, no!' he laughed. 'They seem as boring a bunch of politicos as you could hope to find outside of your House of Commons tea-room.'

'No plans to seduce them to Third Thought?' I said slyly.

'That might be a problem, as a Third Thought clearly requires two other thoughts to go before it,' he replied gravely. Then he grinned and said, 'But you can't be a Christian without believing six impossible things before breakfast, so I'm calmly optimistic.'

Now this was unbuttoning with a vengeance! Again that hesitant, doubtful part of my mind, always looking at the shadows in the sunniest scenes, made me recall that old stratagem of Machiavelli's, that the best way to get a man to let you into his confidence is to offer him the illusion of free admission into your own first.

What a trouble to me is this inability to give my trust without stint, but I did feel easy enough with him to ask outright what he was doing spending Christmas at Fichtenburg when I should have thought a man in his line of work might have found the season making other calls on his time.

He said, 'Do not imagine because I mock these politicos that I despise them. For Third Thought to prosper, it can't be seen as a refuge for oddballs. We must appeal to ordinary people, and if they see people they trust trusting me, then they have taken a large step towards us.'

'You think people trust politicians?' I said. 'You know that Linda is known as Loopy Linda in the British Press?'

'You think that people trust the British Press?' he countered. 'Of course with her surname she was bound to be called Loopy. Most of your papers, like Shakespeare, would sell their souls for a bit of word-play! Whenever I get mentioned in your press, few of the journalists can resist the temptation to make a *dormez-vous* or *sonnez les matines* joke. If Linda reverted to her maiden name of Duckett, I dread to think what might ensue.'

This set the tone of the relationship between us and by the time the festivities were over, we were very good chums. He was sharp enough to notice how I avoided the company of Mouse and I countered by comparing her unfavourably with Emerald.

'Yes,' he said. 'I thought you were somewhat struck with Miss Emerald.'

'Funny,' I said. 'I thought much the same about you.'

Which made him laugh, but I felt those keen blue eyes checking me out for hidden meanings as he laughed.

I'm really getting to like this guy. But I still made sure I kept the innermost casket of my soul firmly locked. It's only with you, Mr Pascoe, that I feel able to reveal everything. Frère Jacques might wear the religious robe but it is you who are my sole confessor.

So we had a great time. Even the religious bits were fun. Jacques presided at a decidedly ecumenical service in the music room on Christmas morning. His sermon was short, eloquent and entertaining, one of the politicos (a German) proved to be a dab hand on the piano, and both Linda and Mouse turned out to have very nice voices, the latter soprano, the former mezzo, which combined most pleasingly in a Bach anthem. They sang again, making a fair shot at the "Flower Song" in *Lakme* after the superb Christmas dinner which Frau Buff and her team of Coppelias provided, and each of us was then invited in turn to contribute to the entertainment. I felt a bit like poor old Caedmon as the foreigners did their various things very competently, and might have snuck off back to my cowshed if Linda hadn't fixed me with her dominatrix gaze and said, 'Franny, let's have one for England, eh?'

Reluctantly I stood up. The only thing that came into my panicking mind was a comic poem of Beddoes, "The New Cecilia". His sense of humour is a mix of the dark surreal and the medical robust, and in this poem he tells of the alcoholic widow of St Gingo, who denies her dead husband's capacity to work miracles with the words –

> *He can no more work wonder*
> *Than a clyster-pipe thunder*
> *Or I sing a psalm with my nether-end.*

And she immediately pays the price.

> *As she said it, her breakfast beginning on*
> *A tankard of home-brewed inviting ale,*
> *Lo! the part she was sitting and sinning on*
> *Struck the Old Hundredth up like a nightingale.*

And so it continues for the rest of her life, leading to the moral –

> *Therefore, Ladies, repent and be sedulous*
> *In praising your lords, lest, ah well-a-day!*
> *Such judgment befall the incredulous*
> *And your latter ends melt into melody.*

As I launched into this, suddenly the huge inappropriateness of what I was doing struck me like a pink blancmange at a funeral feast. Here was I on Our Lord's birthday in front of my devout patroness, her spiritual guru, and an audience of her distinguished friends reciting a poem about a saint's widow farting psalm tunes!

But, like the Widow Gingo, I could find no way to interrupt my flow.

I dared not look at Linda. As I finished, I heard a choking sound come from her direction which at first I took for the beginning of an explosion of inarticulate rage. And then it matured into a long macaw-like screech of laughter. She laughed until the tears ran down her face. Most of her guests roared their approval too, and those who had to have Beddoes' nineteenth-century idiom and sometimes convoluted syntax explained to them demanded a repeat performance which I embellished with a bit of body language which also went down very well. But when they urged me to give some further examples of Beddoes in merry mood, I modestly demurred. Leave 'em laughing when you go was always a good maxim in the music halls.

It occurred to me that it might also make a good motto for Third Thought, but I'd taken enough risks for one day so I kept it to myself!

But life is real, life is earnest, and I'm beginning to feel the need to get down to some work on the book, so tomorrow I'm borrowing Linda's car and heading off to Basel.

Why Basel? Because that's where poor Beddoes ended his life in January 1849.

Despite being a doctor, his suicide was a long drawn out business, its first stage being a self-inflicted wound in his right leg in July 1848. It's ironic that after a couple of decades of active involvement in radical politics, Beddoes should have sunk to this pitch of despair in the very year when most German states were in a ferment of revolution. Initially it looked as if the radical cause was winning. In Frankfurt a German parliament was trying to draft a new liberal constitution uniting the whole of Germany, yet it was this same city that Beddoes left in the spring with his young friend, Konrad Degen, to wander through Germany and Switzerland for several weeks without showing the slightest interest in the fascinating new political situation.

According to Beddoes' cousin, Zoe King, Beddoes had been very depressed as a result of an infection contracted through a cut in his own skin while dissecting a corpse. Also, for reasons we do not know, he believed his republican friends had deserted him. His life must have seemed utterly empty when, after the failed theatrical debut of Konrad in Zurich, the friends quarrelled and the young baker headed back home.

So Beddoes moved to Basel and wounded his leg. Perhaps he intended to sever an artery and bleed to death. Strangely off target for such a devoted student of anatomy, he was taken to hospital where he attempted to finish the job by deliberately letting the wound become infected, he hoped fatally. Again he was only partially successful, the part in question being his right leg below the knee, which was amputated in September of that year after gangrene set in.

By January, apparently recovered in spirits and reconciled with young Konrad who'd been installed in lodgings nearby, he was fit enough to make excursions from his hospital room. On one of these he obtained poison of some kind – not difficult if you were a doctor – and that was that.

How sad – not that he should die, for we all must come to that – but that he who had such talent, such intelligence, and such opportunity, should have ended up so depressed and disappointed and disillusioned that life lost all meaning for him.

He left a note, addressed to one of the two important men in his life, both of them lawyers. He was articled for a while to the first of these, Thomas Kelsall, a Southampton solicitor. The law career came to nothing, but a friendship was formed which remained one of the few constants in Beddoes' existence. Without the correspondence between these two we would know even less of Beddoes' life than we do, and without Kelsall's unselfish enthusiasm for the poetry, very little of it might have survived.

The other lawyer, to whom the note was addressed, was a man called Revell Phillips of the Middle Temple who seems to have become Beddoes' consultant on financial matters, though, as with Kelsall, there was clearly something much deeper in the relationship. Together, Sam speculates, these two lawyers may have provided in some wise the substitute he was always seeking for that father he lost so young.

In the note Beddoes writes the phrase which provided Sam with the title for his book.

I should have been among other things *a good poet.*

And typically he ends with a macabre jest.

Buy for Dr Ecklin [his attending physician] *one of Reade's best stomach pumps.*

Knowing, of course, that next time Ecklin sees him he'll be dead from poisoning!

It's a letter that makes me cry every time I read it. And smile too. He was truly a merry mad tragic figure.

But I mustn't end on a melancholy note this letter which has been concerned with this most merry of times! I hope you and yours have had as good a Christmas as I have.

Yours fondly

Franny

ascoe frowned as he read the letter, then tossed it across to Ellie who read it and laughed out loud.

'What?' he said.

'The farting poem. I begin to warm to Beddoes. Who on earth is St Gingo, or did he just make him up for the rhyme?'

'Wouldn't be surprised. Making things up to suit his own weird purposes, sounds just the sort of thing that would appeal to Roote.'

'And what precisely do you think he's making up here?'

Pascoe thought, then said, 'Himself. He's making himself up. This jolly, sociable fellow who gets on with people and has serious conversations with his spiritual advisor and goes off to work out of sense of duty. He's telling me, "Look, Mr Pascoe, I can be anything I want to be. Try to get hold of me and you'll find yourself clutching air."'

'Ah, now I'm with you. He's telling you this in the same way he told you he'd just bashed Albacore over the head and left him to burn to death in the Dean's Lodging?' said Ellie. 'Peter, I suggested you got this business sorted, but I meant by doing your job. All you seem to be doing is diving into Roote's letters like some religious fanatic reading Nostradamus's texts and finding in them whatever fits his particular world-picture.'

'Yeah? Well, Nostradamus was mad too,' said Pascoe stubbornly. 'And Pottle agreed there was something seriously disturbed about the guy when I showed him the letters.'

'Yes, and didn't he say that Haseen was a psychologist of good standing in the trade, not the idiot you took her for?'

'Just shows how clever Roote is, doesn't it?' said Pascoe. 'All that crap about his father, she swallowed it hook, line and sinker.'

Ellie shuddered at the confused image and said, 'So how about maybe it's you who swallowed the crap?'

'Sorry?'

'What do you really know about Roote's childhood and early family background? I mean, where did you get it from?'

'I don't know, the records, I suppose.'

'Right. But where did the stuff in the records come from? Maybe that's the crap and Franny put it there. Maybe Ms Haseen was good enough to dig some of the truth out of Fran and, when he saw it in her book, he was really pissed off at how much he'd let slip.'

'Yes, but it's Roote in his letters that draws my attention to this. I mean, he's not mentioned by name in *Dark Cells*, is he? I'd probably never have known about the sodding book if he hadn't referred to it.'

'Yes, but he knows you're a clever clogs, Pete. OK, he may overdo the admiration for you, but my reading is, he's only exaggerating what he really feels. In his eyes, you'd have no difficulty in tracking down the book and his part in it. So he makes a pre-emptive strike and draws your attention to it and his cleverness in deceiving Haseen about the father he never knew. Because that's what he wants the world to think, that he never knew his father, that he never had this close worshipping relationship with him and suffered this huge psycho-trauma when he left them and/or died.'

Pascoe finished his coffee and rose from the breakfast table, shaking his head in mock wonderment.

'And to think,' he said, 'you're the one tearing me off for reading between the lines! I may be stretching things sometimes trying to break his code, but you're into astrology!'

He stooped and kissed her and made for the door.

She called after him, 'Don't forget the champagne.'

They had decided to celebrate the New Year at home. They'd received a couple of party invitations, and Fat Andy had assured them that an invite to the Lord Mayor's Hogmanay Hop in the old Town Hall was theirs for the arm-twisting, but they'd turned down everything on the grounds that they couldn't get a baby-sitter. Which was probably true. But in fact Ellie knew she hadn't tried very hard, and Peter hadn't looked at all disappointed. Is this how middle age begins? she wondered. Which gloomy thought had made her insist that staying in didn't mean they couldn't celebrate expansively and expensively.

'And get the real stuff,' she shouted after him. 'None of your sodding Cava!'

'You saying you can taste the difference?' he shouted back.

'Maybe not, but I can read it!' she yelled.

She went up to her study to check on Rosie. The genealogy kit she'd got for Christmas had been a great hit, mainly because of a jocular suggestion in the preamble that a study of your ancestry could reveal that you were in fact really a prince or princess.

'Mum,' she said when Ellie entered the room, 'will I ever see Granddad Pascoe?'

Pascoe's father lived in Australia with his eldest child, Susan. Ellie had met him once when she and Peter were students and she'd stayed overnight at their Warwickshire home. She hadn't cared for the way he brought up his son's plans to join the police force and tried to engage her in his objections against them. The fact that she too thought Peter would be throwing himself away made no difference. Fathers should be concerned about their children, but with warmth and understanding, not with chilly uncaring self-righteousness. She sometimes wondered, but not aloud, how large a part the desire to disoblige his father had played in helping Pascoe make up his mind to join the Force.

It had come as no surprise when she re-engaged with Pascoe to learn that his father had joined his favourite daughter in Australia on retirement. He'd never been back. The loss of one grandfather to Alzheimer's had clearly got Rosie wondering about the other.

'One day, I'm sure you will,' she said brightly. 'And all your Australian cousins.'

Who might be all right. She'd seen photos and they looked

quite normal. Anyway, there was time enough for Rosie to learn that families weren't all sweetness and light.

'How's it going, dear?' she asked. Yesterday she'd got the impression that where dialectics had failed, simple tedium might be succeeding.

'It's all right but I think Tig gets a bit bored,' said Rosie.

Ellie smiled. More and more it was Tig who got bored, Tig who got hungry, Tig who got tired. It was a masterly transference strategy which left Rosie able to assert herself without overt selfishness. Everyone, thought Ellie, should have a Tig.

It was certainly true that the little mongrel sitting under the desk had an air of patient long-suffering which seemed to say, this genealogy's OK, but when does the action start?

Now! was clearly the answer as Rosie's mention of his name brought him to his feet with a tail wag that started at the neck.

Rosie slid off her chair.

'Shall I clear up later?' she said. 'Tig looks like he might want to do a dump.'

Clearing away all her gear had been a condition of Rosie's use of the study, but cleaning up after Tig got precedence.

'I'll do it,' said Ellie, pretty sure she'd been conned again.

She sat down at her desk and began to put together the genealogy pack. It was aimed at the young market, and the introductory blurb urged the tyro genealogist to press older relations for details of family history, adding, 'but be careful. As people grow older, they are more likely to make little slips of memory. So double-check everything!'

Good advice.

More or less the good advice she'd been giving to Peter about Roote.

Would he take it? Maybe. Maybe not.

On the other hand, she thought virtuously, there wasn't much point going around dishing out good advice unless you were willing to take it yourself.

And, because she always found the cloak of virtue a rather itchy cloth, she gave herself a good scratch by adding, and wouldn't it be fun to toss the result of her own researches into Roote's background in front of Peter and say, hey, I think you missed a bit!

She got the pack papers in order and began to read from the beginning.

he Old Town Hall clock, still standing proud despite the fact that its broad face which once enjoyed a clear view right out to the swell of the northern dales now had to squint through a jungle of tumescent modernity, gathered its strength and struck.

The still and frosty air offered such little resistance to the note that even the benighted inhabitants of Lancashire must have been made aware that here in the very middle of God's Own County the Old Year was on his way out and the New on her way in.

For a moment there was no competition, then every bell in the town started ringing, rockets climbed into the air to dim the stars with their cascading colours, car horns sounded, revellers round the equine statue of the Grand Old Duke of York in Charter Park which already bore its traditional embellishment of streamers, toilet rolls, and inflated condoms, burst into raucous cheering while in the more sedate confines of the Old Town Hall itself, the guests at the Lord Mayor's Hogmanay Hop let out a welcoming whoop, then started applying their tongues to the first serious business of the New Year.

One of many things Dalziel liked about Cap Marvel was she gave as good as she got and they might have become linked in a lingual knot it would have taken an Alexander to sever if Margot, the Lady Mayoress, hadn't exercised her droit de seigneuse by tapping him on the shoulder and saying, 'Fair do's, Andy. Save some for old Tom's breakfast.'

'By God, Marge, I'd not have liked to be in thy tag team!' said Dalziel, massaging his shoulder where she'd tapped it.

Not many people dared to call her Marge or make open reference to her former career as a female wrestler, but Margot was not in the mood to be offended. She grabbed Dalziel in a neck lock, gave him a kiss like a hot jam doughnut, said, 'Happy New Year, Andy!' then moved on to perform her consort duties round the rest of the guests.

Dalziel winked at Cap then turned his attention to the age-honoured ceremony of embracing every woman of his acquaintance in turn and wishing them a Happy New Year. The greeting ranged from full-length body hug and mouth contact to a chaste cheek peck, though air-kissing happily had not penetrated the heart of Mid-Yorkshire. Dalziel, who was no grabber of unwilling ass, was usually able to gauge to a T the amount of pressure and skin contact each encounter required, but finding himself suddenly face to face with Rye Pomona, he paused uncertain. He'd been delighted if surprised to see Bowler escorting the young woman into the high-vaulted council chamber (now used solely for social functions since the erection of a modern state-of-the-art Civic Centre a few years back), delighted because Rye looked so much better than last time he'd seen her, and surprised that the young couple hadn't found somewhere noisier, sweatier and younger for their night out. All had been explained when during his welcoming speech the mayor had mentioned their sadness at being without Councillor Steel ('Save a fortune on catering but,' Dalziel had whispered to Cap). 'On the other hand,' continued the mayor, 'it gave him great pleasure to have as his personal guests the young people who had contributed so much to the final apprehension of the monster who murdered him.'

So young Bowler was on a freebie. Couldn't blame him for accepting it, thought Dalziel as he saw the champagne corks flying from the mayoral table. And in fact as the evening went on, the average age of the guests seemed to get lower (or maybe it was just the huge quantities of various elixirs of youth being sunk!) and the band had proved up to anything from Scots traditional through strictly ballroom to dirty disco.

Rye, Dalziel decided, was chaste cheek territory, but as he stooped to administer the salute, she turned her head and kissed him on the lips, not long, but long enough to make him think longer would have been nice.

'I hope you find everything your heart wants, Mr Dalziel,' she said seriously.

'You too, luv. You too.'

His gaze drifted to the woman standing next to her. Bit dumpy, but he liked that. Not bad looking, honey blonde hair over good shoulders, wearing a clinging blue dress cut low enough to show a piste of bosom it would be a pleasure to ski down. He didn't know her though she wasn't totally unfamiliar. There was a man by her side. He didn't know him either, but he looked a bit of a tosser. Narrow, pointed face with restless eyes, one of those linen jackets that looks like it's travelled from Hong Kong scrunched up in the bottom of a rucksack, brightly flowered silk shirt that showed his nipples, and a pair of trousers cut so tight it would take a chisel to get into the pockets which presumably was why he carried a handbag. No doubt there was some modern macho term for the male version, but Dalziel like to call a spade a spade.

'Happy New Year to you, too, luv,' he said, giving her the peck.

'You too, Superintendent,' she said.

'Do I know you?' he asked.

'We met briefly on Christmas Day but we weren't introduced,' she said.

'This is Myra Rogers, my next-door neighbour,' said Rye.

'I remember,' he said. 'Nice to meet you again.'

'And this is Tris, my escort,' said Mrs Rogers.

Tris, the escort! Has she hired him for the night then? wondered Dalziel. Hope she got a money-back guarantee.

The band which had greeted the New Year with a furious outburst of 'Happy Days Are Here Again' now decided that the time had come when the kissing had to stop and, with a bagpipe skirl, they announced the onset of 'Auld Lang Syne'.

Cap appeared at his side as they formed a circle.

'Had a good snog then?' he asked her.

'Bruised but unbowed,' she said. 'Here we go!'

'Should auld acquaintance be forgot and never brought to mind . . .'

They sang it once with feeling, then repeated the chorus at speed, all rushing into the centre of the circle. Dalziel targeted a man in the Social Service Department who'd given him some grief in a recent case and was pleased to see him retire badly winded.

'Well, that was fun, wasn't it?' said Cap.

'It were all right. Only one verse but, and even then they get the words wrong,' said Dalziel, who tended to get a bit SNP at Hogmanay.

'And you know them all, I suppose?'

'Bloody right. Me dad taught me and I've got the bruises to prove it. My favourite verse is second from last:

> And here's a hand, my trusty fiere,
> And gie's a hand o' thine;
> We'll tak a right good willie-waught
> For auld lang syne.'

'Lovely,' she said. 'But what on earth's a "right good willie-waught"?'

'Don't know, but I'm hoping to give you one when we get home. Hello, young Bowler. Enjoying yourself?'

'Yes, sir. Very much.'

'Grand. Don't get a taste for free champagne but. It can come pricey. Here, don't rush off, they've just announced a Dashing White Sergeant.'

'That would be Sergeant Wield, would it, sir?'

'Don't be cheeky. Grab that lass of thine and show us your style.'

'Don't think we can do this one, sir.'

'Then it's time you bloody learnt.'

It was a terrifying experience being in the same set as Andy Dalziel, who moved his great bulk around with what at first seemed like reckless abandon, but quickly it dawned on Hat that the Fat Man was in perfect control. Like Henry VIII shaking a leg at Hampton Court, he was at the centre of all movement, directing by command and example. And if he was the king, Rye was the queen. Hat knew from visits to discos what a natural mover she was, but tonight was the first time he'd seen her in more formal dances and it was a revelation which made him feel gauche and inadequate.

As the music came to an end and the dancers started to move away in search of refreshment, Dalziel clapped his hands thunderously and shouted, 'Nay, lads, we're just getting warmed up! More! More!' Recognizing the voice of authority when they heard it, the band launched into the tune once again, and Hat too reluctantly turned back to the fray. But strangely it was Rye who resisted. Her hand felt cold and limp in his and her body, which a moment ago had seemed to be floating weightlessly, seemed stiff and heavy.

He said, 'Hey, come on, can't let him think he's worn us out, can we?'

She looked at him and tried to smile. Suddenly he noticed how very pale she was.

He said, 'You OK, love?'

She said, 'Yes, fine.' And indeed as she moved back on to the floor, her step seemed as light and graceful as ever.

They took their places, the band started playing, fairly sedately at first but under Dalziel's booming demands that they 'put a bit of oomph into it!' the beat got faster and faster and soon Hat found himself spinning round at a pace that set his head reeling. He abandoned any attempt to put in the steps but simply concentrated on keeping up with the other members of the set, all of whom seemed determined not to let a big fat cop outface them. But it was no contest. Dalziel danced like a man possessed, but also like a man perfectly under control, never off-balance, never missing a step. Only Rye kept up with him without giving any sign she found it an effort. She winked at Hat whenever the pattern of movement brought them together and when she encountered Dalziel, she looked straight into his eyes with a faintly mocking smile on her lips.

The music was now at breakneck speed and only a macho determination not to show weakness in front of the Fat Man ... or Rye ... or maybe both ... kept Hat going. Dalziel had Rye in his grasp, spinning her round then releasing her to the next in line. Like a queen she moved, such balance, such grace, such ... Hat felt a surge of pure pleasure at the notion that she was his ... no, not *his* ... not in any controlling, possessive sense ... but that he and she were ...

His thoughts stuttered to a halt. There was something wrong ... no, not wrong ... it was Dalziel's fault ... he had thrown Rye from him with far too much force ... she was spinning away from the other dancers across the floor ... she'd come to a graceful stop in a moment then return, smiling ... but suddenly there was nothing graceful about the way she was moving ... from Queen of the Dance under perfect control she had become mechanical doll with the spring broken ... still she was turning, but now her arms were flailing the air as if to fight off a swarm of marauding bees ... and then she went down.

The music stuttered to a stop. Hat was running towards that writhing, twisting form which wasn't Rye, couldn't be Rye, mustn't be Rye! He was running with all his power, but it felt as if he were running through water.

Her mouth was open but nothing came out. Her eyes were wide and staring but they weren't seeing anything that anyone else in that room could see. Hat reached her, collapsed to his knees by her side. He was trained to deal with emergencies, but now not a single course of action suggested itself. He could only kneel here feeling a paralysing blackness envelope him, unwilling, unable to let himself admit that everything he loved and thought most lovely in the world could in the twinkling of an eye be reduced to this.

Then Myra Rogers pushed him aside, knelt by the young woman's head and forced open her mouth to check that her tongue wasn't blocking the air passage. She looked like she knew what she was doing. Dalziel was close too, shouting, 'Get a doctor. I've seen at least three of the buggers here. Get to the bar, that's where they'll be.' And Cap Marvell had produced a mobile and was talking urgently to the ambulance service.

Rye had stopped moving now. For a moment beyond definition Hat thought she was dead. Then he saw her chest move. A doctor arrived and began to examine her. Myra Rogers eased Hat upright.

'She'll be OK,' she said reassuringly. 'Probably the heat and all the activity ...'

Dalziel said, 'Ambulance on its way. Can hear it now. She'll be fine, lad.'

For once the Fat Man's reassurance felt light and worthless.

The ambulance arrived. As Hat followed the stretcher trolley out, he glanced upwards. It was a clear frosty night. Stars crowded the dark vault of the sky. Was there life up there? Who gave a fuck?

Somewhere close a raucous drunk yelled, 'Happy New Year!'

Hat climbed up into the ambulance, and the doors closed, shutting out indifferent stars and happy drunks together.

The Drunkards

llie Pascoe's New Year had been rather flat. The most bubbly thing about it had been the two bottles of fizz Pascoe had bought. One was your genuine vintage Widow, the other a supermarket selection Cava, the idea being, Pascoe alleged, to test if they could spot the difference, but really, she guessed, having forked out whatever huge sum had been necessary to get the former, he couldn't bring himself to double it. They had made a thing out of testing each other blind, but the fun had been rather forced and the only significant result of the experiment was to thwart Pascoe's efforts to make love to her on the lounge floor. Whenever drink had disappointed them in the past, they had been able to make jokes about it and find other ingenious things to do, but this time he seemed to take it to heart, and her efforts at jollity came out like the clichés of reassurance.

Happily what drink knocks down sleep builds up and she took advantage of his matutinal stiffie before any memory of last night's fiasco could have an inhibiting effect.

'That was good,' he said, 'though next time I'd prefer to be awake all the way through.'

'I've often wondered what it would be like myself,' she said. 'But make a note for next year. Less champers, more con gas.'

'Yeah, and maybe we'll go to the Hogmanay Hop.'

'Good idea,' she said. But when he rang her later in the morning to pass on news of how the Hop had ended for Rye Pomona, she felt a selfish pang of relief that they hadn't been there to see it. She'd grown very fond of Hat Bowler. He'd gone through a lot, and to see him suffering again just when he must have thought that from now on in it was going to be roses all the way would have been unbearable. As it was, the shock was diluted by the news that Rye was in no danger, and though she had not yet recovered consciousness, it was a deep and, they hoped, healing sleep that encompassed her.

Ellie was a devout atheist, but it wasn't such a clinical condition that she feared the odd tot of prayer would bring about a relapse into full religiosity.

She sat before what was to her non-technical mind the most persuasive evidence of the supernatural she had so far discovered i.e. her computer screen, and said. 'God, if you're in there, spare a thought for Rye Pomona and for Hat Bowler too. Give them the happiness they deserve. OK?'

She stabbed a finger down on the keyboard and watched as the name Franny Roote blossomed on the screen.

Hardly the answer to a maiden's prayer.

So maybe it was as well a maiden wasn't praying.

Meanwhile in a quiet side ward of the Central Hospital Rye Pomona was aghast to find herself once more talking to her dead brother.

What was worse, she could see him quite clearly, and as he listened to her he was irritatedly trying to pick bits of fluff and small shards of china out of his skin.

This was one of the things she and Myra Rogers had been able to laugh at as they celebrated Christmas together. Under the fertilizing influence of a bottle of white wine the seeds of friendship sown at their first meeting in the churchyard had burgeoned rapidly, and a bottle of red had brought it into full bloom.

'You must think I'm really weird,' Rye had said, laughing. 'Drunks banging on my door, me glooming round the churchyard like I was spaced out on dope . . .'

'Well, I've got to admit, that first time I saw you there, I thought, Hello, what kind of company am I getting into here! I never did work out what you were up to . . .'

'It was nothing really . . . just a sort of feeling down, you know . . .' said Rye, a small nugget of caution resisting the solvent properties of the alcohol.

'Hey, listen, none of my business, some troubles are best shared, some are better kept to yourself, don't I know it! What happened to decent reticence? When my husband died, suddenly everyone was a counsellor, wanting me to sit down and let it all hang out, when all I wanted to do was go somewhere quiet and sort things out for myself.'

'Yes, I know. How did he die? Oh God, I'm sorry . . . there I go . . .'

'Don't be silly. Funny, now I'm ready to talk, no one ever asks. It was a car accident. Multiple pile-up on the motorway. Just one fatality. Carl. I felt targeted! Like it would have helped if there'd been dozens dead instead of having to read in the papers what a miracle it was things hadn't been a lot worse!'

And that had been enough, plus another glass or two of wine, to bring it all out, the crash, Sergius's death, the broken vase . . .

'It had been there too long. I don't know which was worse, being aware it was there or forgetting all about it. I'd been thinking about it, now that Hat, that's my boyfriend, and me are . . . an item, you know, it didn't seem right somehow . . .'

'Oh, I don't know. I had a boyfriend once who found it a real turn-on to screw in churchyards. I dumped him after I was having a shower at the squash club one morning and a friend asked me why I had RIP stencilled backwards on my left buttock.'

After they recovered from the outbreak of laughter this brought on, it had been easy to tell her everything – or rather that mangled version of everything which she would have given almost anything to be the truth and which she almost believed much repetition might make so. She had even been able to make a joke of the farcical possibilities of her hoovering if, as the Bible promised, our bodies were reconstituted on Judgment Day. It had been a long time since Rye had talked so frankly with another woman and it felt good. Next morning when she tried to recall cloudily what she had said, it didn't feel quite so good, but when she saw Myra again and found her bright and friendly but with nothing pushy or knowing in her manner, the good feeling returned.

Suddenly with the New Year approaching, the future had begun to seem – not possible – but not impossible either. As if through love and friendship and maybe confession (but, oh, how her heart cracked at the thought of confessing to Hat!), some kind of atonement might be within her grasp . . .

Now here she was on the first day of that bright new year, lying in a hospital bed, talking again to her dead brother.

'Listen,' she said urgently. 'I know you're not there. I know you never have been . . . all that stuff . . . I don't know . . . I don't know . . . it wasn't me . . . someone else . . .'

But it had been her. And Sergius was here, standing before her, silently accusing, but of what? Oh God, no, not accusing her of stopping when she was getting close – not urging her to start again and go on to the bitter end till enough blood had been spilt to give him his tongue – no, she couldn't start down that path again, she would run mad. Perhaps she was running mad . . .

'Sergius, Sergius,' she cried. 'Don't ask me. I can't . . . you're not really here . . .'

And to prove it she reached out her hand, and he reached out his to her and she took it and he squeezed her fingers hard. She closed her eyes and didn't know whether to sing out with joy or cry out in terror. And when she opened them again it wasn't Sergius after all but Hat who was sitting there, holding her hand as if he felt that only his strong grip kept her from plummeting into a fathomless pit. Maybe he was right.

'Oh, Hat,' she said.

'Hi.'

'Hat.'

'You said that. You're meant to say, "Where am I?"'

'Don't care where I am so long as you're here.'

To her distress she saw his eyes fill with tears.

'Don't cry,' she urged. 'There's nothing to cry about. Please. What time is it? Come to think of it, what day is it?'

'Still New Year's Day. Just. They said all the signs were you'd got past whatever it was and gone into a deep sleep, but you've been out of it a lot longer than they thought.'

He kept his tone light, but she could tell how deep his concern went.

'Well, I'm back now. So I've just been sleeping, have I?'

'And talking.'

'Talking.' Now it was her turn to keep it light. 'Did I make sense?'

'About as much as you ever do,' he said, grinning.

'Seriously.'

'Not a lot,' he said. 'You kept on calling me Sergius.'

'Oh shit. I was ... dreaming about ... I'm sorry.'

'What for? In hospital again, the smells, the sounds, it must have taken you back subconsciously to that time after the accident.'

'You work that out yourself, Dr Freud?' she said, striving towards lightness, towards the light. 'Have you been here all the time?'

'Most. And when I wasn't, Myra was. She's been great. I like her a lot.'

'Not sure if I approve of my boyfriend liking a good-looking widow a lot,' she said. 'Do they have doctors in this place or are they all still drunk after last night?'

'I think the ones who matter probably still are. There's this kid looks younger than me looking after you. Whenever I ask him what's wrong, he talks vaguely about tests and talking to Mr Chakravarty, the neuro-consultant. I'd better tell someone you're awake.'

'Why? So they can give me a sleeping pill?'

'So that if there's anything they can start doing to make sure this never happens again, they can start doing it.'

Gently he disengaged her hand and stood up.

She said, 'Hat, I'm sorry. Great way to start the year, yeah?'

He looked down at her, smiling.

'Can only get better. And it will. This is the greatest year of my life, remember. It's the year I'm going to marry you. I love you, Redwing.'

He went out of the door.

Rye turned her head and stared at the uncurtained window against which night was pressing like a dark beast eager to get in.

She said, 'Serge, you bastard, what have you done to me?'

And burst into tears.

*　　*　　*

327

She woke up the next morning feeling, rather to her surprise, much better. Not physically, though it was fair to say she felt as well as she'd felt at any time in the past month, but mentally. She had made no New Year resolutions either this year or any previous year of her life, but it felt as if a resolution had been made for her.

The hours drifted by. Nurses did their mysterious things and promised that Mr Chakravarty would see her soon; her adolescent doctor examined her and assured her Mr Chakravarty was imminent; she had visitors – Dalziel with a large jar of loganberries pickled in Drambuie which he ate with a teaspoon; members of the library staff in their lunch break with books and enough gossip to suggest she'd been away for weeks rather than half a day (New Year's Day being of course a holiday); Myra Rogers with a basket of fruit and, wise woman, a small grip full of clothes and other necessities. And Hat came too, of course, with flowers and chocolates, and love, the only gift which made her want to cry, though she felt a bit weepie as she saw Dalziel finish the last of the loganberries.

She dozed off a little (it was funny how lying in bed all day makes you so sleepy) and woke to see Hat in deep confabulation with a couple of nurses. She felt no jealousy, just a kind of languorous pride in the effect his youthful charm clearly had on the young women.

She dozed again and woke to find she'd almost missed Mr Chakravarty. He was looking down at her from a great height. He was tall, slim, dark, extremely handsome. He might have been one of those Indian princes who, she seemed to recollect, went to the great public schools and played cricket for England back in the thirties. And, like a prince, he stayed only long enough to be adored then went on his way.

She asked the nurses and the adolescent doctor the questions she'd failed to ask him. They talked of tests and scans, all of which it seemed must be delayed till the necessary facilities became free. It sounded as though there were waiting lists to go on waiting lists.

Alone at last about teatime, she lay fully awake and pondered these matters. Several things were quite clear to her.

Whatever needed to be done was going to take time. During

that time she was going to be treated like a poor dependant. And Hat was only going to have to smile for everything concerning her diagnosis to be made immediately available to him.

She got out of bed and took the grip Myra had brought her from under the bed.

The ward sister summoned the adolescent doctor, but Rye simply said, 'I will sign anything you want me to sign as long as I have it before me in the next sixty seconds.'

She then went down to the reception area where there was a large diagram of the hospital, studied it for a while, then strode off with such a certainty of purpose that no one felt it necessary to enquire what that purpose was, not even when she entered areas not accessible to the commonalty of patients.

Finally she arrived at a door with the name she sought printed on it – Victor Chakravarty – and went in. A stout young woman behind a stout old desk viewed her without enthusiasm.

'I want to make an appointment to see Mr Chakravarty,' said Rye. 'My name is Pomona, initial R. He has all my details, or at least they are available to him in Ward 17.'

'You're a patient?' said the woman, as if it were a nasty condition. 'Sorry, but you really shouldn't be here . . .'

'I was a patient. I wish to become a client. A paying client. I understand that there are various tests I may have to undergo. I should like to make an appointment to see Mr Chakravarty fairly early one morning so that, after our consultation, I might undertake these tests and hear his interpretation of their results later the same day.'

'He's really very busy . . .'

'So I've gathered. So I won't be too demanding. It's Wednesday the second now. Let's say the start of next week. Monday the seventh would suit me very well.'

The stout woman, her alarm at being confronted by an NHS patient alleviated, now came briskly to the most important point.

'Do you have health insurance?'

'No. I shall be paying for my own treatment. Would you like a deposit?'

The stout woman's eyes said she reckoned this wasn't a bad idea, but her mouth said, 'No, of course not . . .'

'Good,' said Rye. 'Shall we say nine thirty, Monday morning, January seventh? Here's my home number in case of problems. My work number too. I'll be there between nine and five from tomorrow. Thank you.'

At the door she paused.

'Of course, as a private patient, I shall expect complete privacy. Any leakage of information to anyone – friends, relations, *anyone* – I should view very legalistically.'

She left without waiting for an answer.

n the morning of Saturday January 5th Edgar Wield looked at the over-the-top decorations festooning Corpse Cottage and thought with relief that tomorrow would see the end of them. He'd have had them down after New Year but his born-again-traditionalist partner declared it was well known to bring tremendous bad luck if you laid hands on them before Twelfth Night.

Now Digweed said sadly, 'The place won't be the same without them.'

'You're right there,' said Wield with undisguised irony.

His partner regarded him seriously.

Perhaps, thought Wield, he's thinking that in this relationship he makes all the adjustments and when he asks me to go along with one little thing like having bells and baubles all over the place, I make a big fuss. Maybe I should try harder. I *will* try harder!

'Edgar,' said Digweed.

'Yes?'

'Tonight we're going out.'

'OK,' said Wield. 'Where?'

'Tinks.'

If Wield's features could have shown aghast, that's what they would have shown.

He said, 'You mean Tinks? Krystabel's? The club? At Estotiland?'

'As always you are right in every respect. Tinks, the night club.'

Wield still couldn't believe it. Digweed was even less of a

hot-spot night-owl than he was. In his own case, professional discretion played a large part. But for Digweed it was simply a deep-rooted distaste. And of all the clubs available, Wield would have picked Tinks as the one his partner was least likely to be seen dead in. Whether the Estoti brothers had planned it as a gay club, no one knew. But within weeks of its opening in Estotiland, its street name had changed from Krystabel's to Tinkerbell's, whence Tinks, and the management seemed set on running it as almost a parody of what straights thought a gay club ought to be. All this Wield knew by report. If he'd anticipated visiting the place, it seemed likely it would be in the line of duty. Never in his wildest fantasies had he thought he and Edwin would go there as customers.

He said carefully, 'Are you sure this is a good idea? It's a night club, yes, but perhaps not in the way you remember them.'

'And what way is that, pray? Discreet lighting, dinner jackets, a string trio to dance to, and perhaps the Western Brothers or Inkspots as cabaret? I assure you, I am completely *au fait* with modern trends.'

'In that case, why . . . ?'

'My good friend, Wim Leenders, is celebrating his fiftieth birthday there, and he wants me to join his party, and he said I've been hiding your light under my bushel for far too long and insisted I bring you. And if he hadn't insisted, I would have done because you cannot imagine I could contemplate entering such a place without your moral support.'

This, as well as being a nicely turned compliment, explained everything.

Since they got together, Wield had met several of Digweed's friends. Most of them he liked very much, and generally they seemed to like him, but he avoided getting too close. Over the years, like a lot of his straight colleagues, Wield had learnt to be careful about his choice of friends outside the Force. He'd been upfront with Digweed about his reluctance to be swamped by a whole new circle of acquaintance, vicariously acquired, and usually he'd met his partner's chums singly or in pairs.

Wim Leenders was a six and a half foot, sixteen and a half stone, chisel-bearded Dutchman who'd moved to England

332

twenty years ago because he liked to climb rocks and walk uphill. He collected early books on mountaineering and fell walking, which was how Digweed had come to know him. He seemed to have rather more money than his outdoor-gear shops might be expected to generate, but a careful check by Wield (memory of which filled him with shame) had turned up no hint of naughtiness. Most of the time, as if self-conscious about his physical presence, he was a very quiet-mannered, self-effacing, gently courteous kind of chap, but when he let his hair down, he became a runaway juggernaut. Wield had seen something of this side of him at a funeral wake. What he was going to be like at his own fiftieth didn't bear thinking of. This made his choice of Tinks a damage-limitation tactic which said much for his basic good sense. But Wield still couldn't quite grasp why Edwin hadn't simply made an excuse when he got the invitation.

So, because he believed in openness in a relationship, he asked the question direct.

Digweed said, 'Wim helped me out of a rather tricky situation a few years back, long before I knew you. Of course my first reaction was to say no to his invitation, but he has been most pressing and I've brooded on the matter for some days and come to the conclusion it would be – how to put it? – pusillanimous of me to refuse. But I really do need what you would call back-up, Edgar.'

'Of course I'll come,' said Wield. 'On one condition.'

'And what is that?'

'There is going to be jelly and cream, isn't there?'

Digweed laughed, then said seriously, 'Thank you, Edgar. I appreciate it.'

Which made Wield feel good, though the feeling had not developed into any lively anticipation of enjoyment as through the taxi window bearing them south about nine thirty that night he saw a serpentine neon sign wriggling the name *Krystabel's* across the dark winter sky.

But life is full of surprises.

As they got out of the taxi, the club doors burst open and a burly man in a long mohair overcoat emerged. He had a mobile phone pressed to his ear and his face was deathly pale. Behind him appeared a young man with a fashionably shaven head and wearing a tight black T-shirt which showed off his muscular torso.

'Come on, LB, it'll be OK, don't let him snarl you up like this,' he called. 'Hey, would you like me to come with you?'

The burly man showed no sign of having heard and strode off towards the car park.

Wield, who had retreated into the taxi, now got out. He didn't watch the departing man but concentrated on the other who, becoming aware of this, said 'You'll know me again, funny face,' before twisting round and going back inside.

'Yes, I will,' Wield told himself.

'Friend of yours?' said Digweed.

'The night is young,' said Wield, smiling.

Suddenly he felt like a party.

arlier that same evening, Liam Linford too had felt like a party.

The police had used every delaying tactic possible and, despite Marcus Belchamber's best efforts, the young man had eaten his Christmas dinner in custody. Released in time for New Year, his first impulse had been to tear the town apart and make sure those he held responsible for his misfortunes got what was coming to them.

His father had other ideas.

'You keep your head down, your nose clean. I'll get this business sorted, right?'

'Yeah, like you got Carnwath's sister sorted, you mean?' sneered the young man. 'Let's face it, Dad, you couldn't sort washers. If you'd let me break his legs like I wanted, I'd not have spent the holidays in that shithole . . . Jesus!'

He found himself sitting on the floor, nursing a bruised jaw, looking up at Wally Linford in a mood he'd never seen him in before.

'You talk like that to me, you're out of here,' grated the older man. 'You step out of line by half an inch and you're on your own. So help me God, Liam, I'll throw you to the wolves. Couple of years inside might be just what you need. Make up your mind. Do this my way, or do it alone.'

And Liam, who didn't know much but knew that without the clout derived from being Wally's son and heir he was nothing, had seethed with resentment but obeyed.

Hogmanay he'd celebrated quietly at home. But a week into the New Year and he was opining that he might as well have stayed inside, there was probably more fun to be had there. But his father's threats had kept him on the leash till that Saturday night when he saw Wally Linford leaving the house, heading off to find whatever it was passed for fun in his weird world. Liam waited till his car was out of the drive, then got on the phone and rang his closest friend and chief supporting witness, Robbo.

Robbo might have had plans of his own but he knew better than to object. He turned up at the Linford house twenty minutes later and found Liam waiting. When he opened the door of his Porsche to let his friend in, Liam showed he'd absorbed some of his father's lesson by saying, 'No way. The Filth would love to get me and you for drunk driving. I got a taxi coming. Here it is now. Right, mate, this is a whole night job, they told you that? Great. First stop, Molly Malone's!'

By eight thirty they were getting very drunk and the pub was getting crowded.

'Fuck this,' said Liam. 'Let's go to Trampus's, I fancy cunt. And if that other cunt Carnwath's still working there, I'll mebbe tell him I fancy him too.'

Robbo was still sober enough to wonder if this was such a good idea, but he was shouted down and moments later they spilled out into the car park.

'Mr Linford. Over here,' called the driver of a taxi parked a little way away from the pub door.

'Thought it was a fucking car before,' said Robbo as they got into the vehicle, which was a traditional London taxi.

'More room in this, sir,' said the driver, huddled in his seat, woollen hat pulled over his ears and scarf wound round his neck against the dank chill of the night. 'Where to?'

'Trampus's club,' said Liam. 'And get a fucking move on!'

The driver seemed to take the instructions to heart and soon they were bowling along at speed to satisfy even their drunken impatience to be where the action was.

Soon the windows steamed up and when Robbo tried to wind one down to let some cool air in, nothing happened.

He rapped on the security panel separating passengers from driver and yelled. 'Here, mate, let some fucking air in!'

The driver didn't respond and Liam said, 'Give it a rest,

Robbo. They lock the doors and windows so's we can't fuck off without paying. As if we would.'

He followed this with a burst of raucous laughter at memories of past occasions when they'd bilked some unfortunate taxi driver.

Robbo, who was rubbing at the steamed up window didn't join in.

He said, 'Where's this mad fucker taking us? We're out in the fucking country. Hey, you, where the fuck are we?'

He banged on the panel again and the driver said, 'Short cut.'

Now Liam too rubbed a spyhole in the condensation. Outside there was nothing but darkness with occasionally a glimpse of trees or hedgerows blurring past.

'Short cut?' yelled Liam. 'Shortcut where?'

The driver turned to look at him. His face was a skull.

'Shortcut to hell,' he said.

He dragged the wheel over, the taxi went through a hedge, down a steep embankment, and turned upside down as it plunged into a river.

In the rear the two men, bleeding and battered into sobriety, were screaming as they wrestled with the locked doors. For a moment they were suspended in a cocoon of air. Then in the front the driver wound down his window to let the water in.

Soon the screaming stopped.

ook who's here! Ed and Ed! Now truly my cup is full and runneth over!'

Any hope Wield had nursed of taking a back seat vanished when Wim Leenders' voice boomed out across the room as they entered and they were ushered to a table of at least twenty already merry partygoers who were urged to shift along so that the newcomers could sit to the right and left of their jovial host.

He put his arms round them both and invited them to sample the very best that Tinks could offer.

That the champagne was the best Wield took on trust, never having learnt how to distinguish between bubbles. But he drank his share with no discernible effect, toyed with a taco, shuffled a few circuits of the dance floor, and applauded a comic who made Andy Dalziel sound like a Sunday School teacher. After an hour or so he found he was really enjoying himself. Then it came to karaoke time and when Wim started looking for recruits for his famous Village People turn, he slipped off to the loo.

They didn't pipe the music from the club in here, thank God, and he sat in comfortable silence, thinking how great it was to see the usually staid and controlled Edwin letting his hair down, and how lucky he was to have somehow got all the disparate elements of his existence into such a perfect balance.

When he emerged, he could still hear the joyous chant of 'In the Navy' coming from the main room, so he stepped outside for a moment to get a breath of fresher air and almost bumped into the muscular young man in the black T-shirt.

'Sorry,' said Wield.

'Hello, funny face,' said the man. He looked rather pale and

338

there was a whiff of a sweet vomit smell on his breath. Drunk too much and gone out to be sick, Wield guessed.

He said, 'Wally not come back then?'

'No. Don't expect him.' Then a suspicious look. 'You know him?'

'Wally? Yeah, from way back. Mind you, it's a long time since I saw him. I'd have said hello earlier, but he didn't look in the mood to chat. Worried about his lad, I expect.'

'Got cause, hasn't he,' said the young man moodily. 'Should have left the selfish bastard in jail. Ruined my fucking night, hasn't he?'

'How's that?'

'Had himself another accident or something. Little shit. Should have thought, with his trouble, no one would have let him near a car. One yell, and Wally goes running.'

'He is his dad,' said Wield. 'Heard you call him LB, what's that all about?'

'Thought you knew him.' Suspicious again.

'Way back, like I said. It was just plain Wally then.'

'It's just a net name he uses. Lunch box. LB. Linford. Gerrit?'

'Got it,' said Wield. 'Funny.'

'Yeah,' said the young man, looking at Wield assessingly. 'You been dumped too?'

'No, my friend's in there karaokeing. Not my scene. Sorry.'

The young man went back inside. Wield pulled out his mobile and dialled.

'Pete, it's me,' he said. 'What's this about Liam Linford in an accident?'

'Thought this was your night off,' said Pascoe. 'He was in a taxi that went into the river. A driver in another car saw it happen so help got there quick, it was too late. Liam's dead, plus that guy Robson who was his witness. And the driver.'

'Shit,' said Wield. 'Act of God or . . . ?'

'Depends how you look at it. The driver was John Longstreet. That's right. The widower. And when they pulled him out, he was wearing a plastic Hallowe'en mask in the form of a skull.'

After his call was finished, Wield stood outside a while longer. His elation at discovering that Belchamber's LB was Wally

Linford, underwriter of serious jobs requiring a lot of cash to set them up, was totally extinguished, though no doubt it would delight Andy Dalziel. But the Fat Man hadn't seen the father's face as he got the news about his son. Not that it would likely have made much difference.

Pondering these things, he re-entered the club room and walked past the momentarily silent karaoke set-up without paying any attention to a young man with electric blue hair and a matching silk shirt open to the waistband of a pair of trousers cut so tight it made your eyes water to look at them, who stood there, mike in hand, waiting his turn.

He glanced round, saw Wield, his eyes opened in delighted surprise and he leapt forward to grab the sergeant's hand.

'Mac!' he cried. 'It really is you. Hey, this is great. I'm on next. Come and give me some backing.'

It was Lee Lubanski.

Not the pale waif whose vulnerability plucked Wield's heart strings, nor yet the streetwise kid whose cynical view of life so depressed him. This was Lee in his party pomp, Lee hyped up on something, Lee so desperately having a good time, so genuinely delighted to see him there that Wield didn't think to resist till it was too late.

The music began. Wield recognized the song. The old early eighties hit 'Total Eclipse of the Heart' and thought, oh shit.

He could see Wim and his guests out there, faces wreathed in delight, hear them urging him on. He caught Edwin's gaze, saw him drop his jaw in mock gobsmacked mode, then give him an encouraging smile. If he pulled free now and walked off, it wouldn't look like stage fright, it would look like a lover's quarrel.

'*Every now and then I get a little bit nervous that the best of all the years have gone by,*' sang Lee.

He had a good voice for this, a real Bonnie Tyler rasp, and as he approached the big belt-it-out section of the song he urged the still silent Wield to join in.

'*For I need you now tonight and I need you more than ever . . .*'

Fuck it, thought Wield. In for a penny, in for a pound. And he started to sing, or at least to growl out the words in a voice as cracked and fractured as his features.

'. . . *forever's gonna start tonight* . . .'

As the final '*Turn around, bright eyes*' faded away, applause broke out, enthusiastic generally and riotous from Wim's table with everyone on their feet, clapping and cheering.

'That was great, Mac,' said Lee, his eyes shining. 'What shall we do for an encore?'

'Got to get back to my friends, it's a birthday party, sorry,' said Wield.

The look of hurt disappointment that switched off the light on the boy's face stabbed right through him.

He squeezed his hand then let go.

'Hey, Happy New Year, Lee,' he said. 'Good to see you. Keep in touch, won't you?'

And it was almost as painful to see the way in which this small sop of kindness brought back the light.

'Yeah, sure, Mac. See you soon. Enjoy your party.'

In the taxi on the way home, Digweed said, 'Let me guess. That was Lee Lubanski?'

'Yes. Sorry if it embarrassed you.'

'What's to embarrass in the sight of a dad and his lad having a laugh together?'

'Dad and lad,' echoed Wield. 'Isn't there a poem about dads fucking up their lads?'

'Poetry now, is it? I'll have to take you out more often. "They fuck you up your mum and dad. They may not mean to, but they do." That the one you're thinking of?'

'That's the one. It happens, I've seen it. And that's what bothers me, Ed. I'm scared I'm going to fuck the lad up.'

Digweed put his arm round Wield's shoulders.

'Just so long as he doesn't do it to you first, Ed. So long as he doesn't do it to you.'

The Friar

Fichtenburg-am-Blutensee

Aargau

Mon Dec 31st

Dear Mr Pascoe,

Safely back in Fichtenburg, thank God. The weather was
pretty foul in Basel and if Beddoes experienced anything
like those conditions, I don't blame him for being suicidal,
and I could well understand how Holbein came to design
his Dance of Death there. Or perhaps the real gloom was
in me. It's curious. I have always been a person happy with
his own company, but the fun I'd had with the others over
Christmas seemed to have affected me in a strange way,
and for the first time ever I felt really lonely.

I could have come back after twenty-four hours
without much loss to my researches, but I was resolved
not to give in. My hopes of a career depend very much on
the job I do with Sam's book and I'm determined not to
let the chance pass. Nor was it a complete waste of time.
While I found little to add to Sam's own researches in
Basel (oh, for your detective skills, that can take you in an
empty room and let you emerge with clues to the
perpetrator of some long-forgotten crime!), I confirmed

345

some of his speculations and I came away with a sense that he (and dare I say it? Beddoes too!) approved of the progress I was making in my quest.

But I confess I hurried back here today, looking forward to company other than my own, and with lively anticipation of a *Silvesterfest* (Hogmanay!) to match our *Weinachtfest* (Christmas!)

Imagine then my gloom when the first person I saw on my arrival was Frère Dierick! He greeted me civilly enough and confirmed what I'd feared, that he was joining Jacques and myself in the chalet. Well, you're not sharing my room, not even if Linda commands it! I assured myself.

Jacques too seemed to have lost his taste for communal living, and it emerged that Dierick was going to bed down on the living-room floor for the couple of nights before the house party broke up. There was a perfectly good sofa he could have used, but he clearly thought the hard floor would be better for his soul.

My slight depression of spirits rapidly vanished when, for the first time since coming here, I checked my answer phone back home. The only reason I've got one is because Linda tried to ring me once and couldn't get through, which seriously pissed her off, so the royal command came to get some kind of answer service and put it down on my research expense tab. With her in my view, who else was going to be ringing me?

But someone had! Professor Dwight Duerden no less. Twice! He asked me to call him as soon as I could. Naturally I rang immediately, and all I got was his answer service. It was New Year's Eve over there also, so presumably he'd gone away to do whatever Californians do to mark the end of the year.

I left the chalet number, telling him that I'd be here for the next three days, after which I'd ring him from my next destination.

I keep telling myself it must be good news else why would he bother to get in touch? Or perhaps he's just a very polite man and feels he ought to let me know that St Poll Uni Press reckon a book about a poet not many people have heard of by a dead academic ditto, brought to conclusion by an ex-con student double ditto, is exactly the kind of thing they'd pay good money *not* to be involved with!

But next time I write, maybe I'll have something really exciting to tell you.

Now I must get ready for the party.

Tues Jan 1st

My dear Mr Pascoe, here I am again. And a Happy New Year to you and yours!

I ended above saying I might have something really exciting to tell you, and in a sense I have. But it isn't that I've heard from Dwight. Seven or eight hours behind us in California, he's probably still welcoming in the New Year. Ah well. Patience is the virtue of the temperate man.

But excitement there's been – or perhaps I should say excitation!

The party was really jolly, lots of music, games, dancing, with everyone showing off the local customs peculiar to their own country or background.

I was tempted to introduce them to some of the more arcane customs of the Syke, which involved getting blind drunk (sometimes literally) on a potato-based distillation liberally laced with medical spirit, but decided against it! On the stroke of twelve we popped champagne corks and exchanged hugs and kisses all round. I was expecting another bruising blow to the cheek from Linda. Instead to my surprise she aimed right at my mouth and followed through with what felt like six inches of strenuous tongue. Still reeling from this, I was very glad to note that I got nothing but a chaste peck from Mouse.

But, as perhaps you've guessed, it didn't end there.

I finally took my leave in the early hours and started

back on the five-minute stroll to the chalet. The weather here had been the same as in Basel for the past few days, murky and wet, and skating had been banned as the *See's* icy surface became unstable. But tonight the frost had returned, and the air was bright and clear, a joy to be out in after the heat and fumes of the party in the castle. The leperization of smokers is by no means as advanced on the Continent as it is at home and even the men who didn't smoke seemed to feel that *Sylvesternacht* would not be complete without setting light to a huge tube of tobacco and sticking it in their mouths.

I stood and drew in mouthfuls of fresh air. To liken it to champagne sounds like a cliché, but truly that was how it felt, great draughts of coolth which bubbled along the arteries and invigorated the mind.

I heard the crunch of snow behind me as someone else came out of the castle. It was Linda. She said, 'God, I thought I'd smother if I stayed much longer in there.'

'Yes,' I said. 'But it's been a great night though.'

'You've enjoyed yourself, have you, Franny? That's good. I was worried you might be bored among all us politicos.'

'No way,' I assured her. 'It's been great.'

She looked really pleased and, slipping her arm through mine, she said, 'I'll walk through the forest with you a little way till I get cooled down.'

And so we strolled companionably through the pine trees and I can honestly say I've rarely felt more at peace with myself and the world than I did at that moment.

Eventually we reached the ruined chapel that had filled me with such superstitious fear on the night of my arrival. Here we paused. Suddenly Linda shivered, whether because of the setting or simply because the cold had struck deep, I don't know. But it seemed perfectly natural for me to unlink my arm and put it around her shoulders and draw her close to share my warmth.

Well, it was like pressing that button in the Pentagon which starts World War Three!

She turned towards me and next thing that tongue which I had felt at the back of my throat as the clock struck twelve was now trying to lick my brain cells out of my skull. We span round and round among the ruins like a pair of drunken waltzers till we fetched up against the cloister wall. Somehow during this mad motion buttons had got unbuttoned, zips unzipped and hooks unhooked, and suddenly I was feeling the heat of her bare bosom burning against my chest and the savage teeth of sub zero air biting into my buttocks! It was, I thought, like having your haunches in Dante's Cocytus while you dipped your member into Phlegethon. And if such infernal images seem ungallant, I can only justify myself by the context, for over her shoulder as we coupled I could see a whole wallful of frescoed figures who seemed to be engaged in much the same activity. Indeed, as I climaxed noisily, it seemed to me that one of these figures, cowled and sinister, detached itself from the fresco and moved shadowily away into the trees.

Afterwards, we got dressed silently and with a speed that had as much to do (I hope) with cold as with regret. Then she reached out her hand, touched my cheek and said, 'Happy New Year, Franny. Sleep well.' And set off back to the castle.

I watched her go then went towards the end of the wall and looked down at the snow.

I saw the fresh prints of a rope sandal. Only one person at Fichtenburg wore rope sandals.

Frère Dierick.

I hurried back to the chalet. Jacques, who'd escaped the party straight after midnight, was on his mobile when I entered. He brought the call to a rather rapid conclusion. Could it be Emerald on the end of the line? I wondered. No sign of Dierick. Jacques looked as if he'd have liked to sit and chat with me, but I excused myself on the grounds of tiredness. He's sharp of eye and apprehension and though he's possibly in no position to cast stones, I still didn't want him to know that I'd been at

349

it with our patroness on what for all I knew was still consecrated ground. I had a feeling that Dierick wouldn't be rushing to tell him either. Info like that was best stored up and kept for a rainy day.

To my surprise, I slept like a top and woke without a hangover, either alcoholic or psychological. It had been, I assured myself, a one-night stand. Linda had too much sense of her own dignity to risk any hint that she had got herself a toy-boy (OK, I'm not that young, but young enough for the chattering classes of Westminster and Strasbourg to have a good chortle over at their cocktail parties). Once assured that I wasn't about to make a big thing out of our brief encounter, we would resume our old relationship, only enriched by that extra closeness which such a shared memory always brings. As for Dierick, if he started hurling accusations around, it would be Linda he'd be taking on, and she could eat squirts like Dierick for breakfast!

But I must admit I was distinctly uneasy until I'd strolled up to the castle and joined Linda and the others for a cup of coffee. My prognosis seems to be right. She greeted me warmly, but not too warmly. Like me, she seems to have survived the celebrations with little after-effect, and as we looked over the wrecked politicos beached all around us, we were able to share a superior smile.

No sign of Dierick. Skulking bastard! I suspect even Jacques shares my distaste. Certainly he's not quite the same easy, outgoing companion he was before the little squirt arrived.

Anyway, I'm going to end my last full day here relaxing, and keeping my fingers crossed for that call from sunny California!

Wed Jan 2nd, 8.30 a.m.

All good things come to an end, and this for me has been very good indeed. What a change there's been in my life. I look back only a couple of months and find it hard to recall that so recently I was a penniless student with no assured future. And of course I don't have to look much further back to see myself as a convicted criminal paying his debt to society. And then with Sam's tragic death, I hit rock bottom.

Of course I'd give it all up to have him still alive, and if I shared Charley Penn's belief that in fact his killer was still undetected, I think that the desire to make good what the law has failed to address is the one thing that might tempt me back to criminality. But there's no escaping the fact that, from that low point, I've been soaring upwards ever since.

I've had several strokes of luck, giving me hope that rather than just being as it were a midwife to Sam's great brainchild, I may really be able to claim a small part in its parentage. And I'm delighted to say that I have made many excellent new contacts among Linda's politicos.

So, dear Mr Pascoe, everything seems for the best in the best of possible worlds!

But I have to stop now and get my gear packed. The party's breaking up. Not even Dingley Dell can keep the real world at bay for ever. The politicos are getting back on their respective gravy trains. Jacques, accompanied by Dierick, is touching base at the monastery then heading back to the UK to resume his promotional tour.

As for me, it had been proposed before New Year that I should travel back with Linda and Mouse to Strasbourg and stay there a few days before going on to Frankfurt and Göttingen, both of which played a large role in Beddoes' European life. At the time the only thing which made me hesitate about instant agreement was Mouse. By herself she may have reverted to the quiet and shy little creature she really is, but Zazie and Hildi could be waiting back home, eager for a progress report, and ready to urge her back into the fray. I'm probably flattering myself, of course, but now that Linda has put herself in the frame too, I shudder at the picture of myself lying in my bed in the Lupin guestroom and both mother and daughter tiptoeing in to say Hello Sailor!

Why is my life so complicated? What wouldn't I give to be more like you, Mr Pascoe, so well organized, with my life under perfect control, but, alas, those genes were not tossed into my cradle by whatever Fairy Godmother attended my birth. My mother knew what she wanted and set out to get it, so I reckon I must have inherited my chaotic make-up from the father I never knew. From what my mother said about him, which wasn't much, he was wild at heart and not one whom fortune favoured. All I can hope is that I might get some of the luck he never did.

I am sitting writing this as I finish off the coffee at the breakfast table. Frère Jacques and I discovered one of many things we have in common is an internal alarm clock set for early rising, the result of our shared experience of the life cellular! Dierick is an even earlier riser. No sign of him this morning, and, to give him credit, no sign of his overnight presence on the sofa. When I met him yesterday, his manner to me was unchanged, distrustful neutrality! So I think I've read that situation right.

Penologists might like to note that in many ways the monastery has left Jacques a lot more disciplined than the Syke left me. His bag is already packed and standing in the entrance porch, and he has just set out to walk up to the castle and make his farewells. I meanwhile, not yet packed, linger here, pinned down by an irresistible urge to bring you up to date with the course of events since last I wrote and a superstitious feeling that by staying close to the phone I may persuade Dwight Duerden to ring. After all, it's still not midnight in California and I did say in my message that I'd be leaving here today. You must think me pathetic to be clutching at such straws – oh god there it goes!

* * *

Oh god! indeed. Thirty minutes have passed, one thousand eight hundred seconds, and in that time fortune, who doesn't care to be taken for granted, has raised me up and then shown me how easily she can cast me down!

It was indeed Professor Duerden. He said he'd spoken to various people as soon as he got back to St Poll and they were hugely enthused by what he told them. They are all desperately keen to meet me and find out exactly what it is I've got to offer. I had to keep reminding myself that he was ringing from Southern California where most people speak English, a lot speak Spanish, but everyone speaks hype. But when he finished by inviting me out there as a guest of the university, all expenses paid, I couldn't help catching some of his excitement. No, let me not be too English about this. I was bubbling fit to burst! I heard myself asking, idiotically, what the temperature was out there. To tell the truth, I was getting just a bit tired of invigorating frosts. A man can only be braced so far before he busts. Disappointingly he said it was about forty-eight degrees outside at the moment, then he laughed and went on, 'But it is nearly midnight! During the day, when the sun shines, we get in the high sixties, maybe even higher with a bit of luck.'

That will suit me nicely, I thought. Then something occurred to me which sent my spirits diving. I am, you may recall, a convicted felon. Didn't the US immigration authorities have strong feelings about that? Haltingly I put the objection to Dwight. He said, yes, he was aware of that, but dispensations could be made and he'd had a word with an old chum of his in Washington and another with a former pupil currently in their London Embassy, and it seemed that as long as I'd kept my nose clean since release and Dwight guaranteed to take responsibility for me while over there, I would be admitted as it were on sufferance. All I had to do was send off a formal visa application and then present myself at Grosvenor Square for interview when required. Was that OK?

My spirits were rocketing again! I said it was more than OK, it was great! And he said he thought so too and he'd expect to see me some time towards the end of January.

I must admit I put the phone down and punched the air like a celebrating footballer!

While we were talking I'd thought I'd heard the front door of the chalet open and shut, which I put down to Frère Jacques returning. I had to share my exuberance with someone and I rushed through into his bedroom, only to find it empty. I must have been mistaken, I thought, and needing exercise to work off the joyous rush of energy surging through my body, I went into my own room to pack.

There was a head on my pillow, two eyes looking at me rather nervously, a mouth essaying an inviting smile.

It was Mouse.

I stopped dead in my tracks, then took half a step backwards.

Perhaps fearful that I was going to turn and flee, she threw the duvet back to reveal she was stark naked. The way she did it, a quick spasmodic movement rather than a tantalizing unveiling, plus the tension visible in every muscle and the way she kept her legs pressed tightly together, showed me how nervous and uncertain she was.

I should, of course, have turned away and left the room. But, having overcome God knows what crises of mind and spirit to bring herself to this point, how would such a rejection have affected poor Mouse?

Sorry, that sounds like I'm trying to justify my actions. I freely admit that, without that phone call from Dwight, I would have been out of there so quick, she might have thought I'd been a mirage! But like I said, I was bubbling with a delight I wanted to share with everyone and without a first let alone a second thought (and certainly not that Third Thought which is my grave!) I was out of my clothes and into my bed.

Perhaps my sense of joy was infectious for she very

quickly relaxed, though there must have been some pain in it for she was as inexperienced as she looked. But the strange cry she uttered as I entered her (which sounded to my admittedly not very attentive ears like *wununredunAAAYtee!*) seemed more triumphal than distressed.

From my own selfish point of view, I enjoyed it very much, certainly a great deal more than I might have anticipated. But *post coitum timidum est*, and as rapidly as the physical pleasure faded from my nerve ends, the possible consequences of my action came swarming into my disanaesthetized mind.

The first and most immediate was that Jacques might return at any moment, and in my haste to oblige Mouse, I now realized I hadn't even shut the door! I began to roll off the bed but we were still tangled up and she seemed inclined to hang on, resulting in a not unstimulating bout of wrestling which might have made me forget about the open door if out of the corner of my eye I hadn't glimpsed a figure standing like Death on the threshold.

It was Dierick. He smiled, the first time I'd seen him smile. It wasn't a pretty sight. Then slowly he closed the door.

Mouse hadn't seen him. Firmly I disengaged myself and got off the bed and, trying not to show an ungentlemanly haste, I pulled on my clothes. After a moment Mouse followed my example. Fully clothed, we stood on either side of the bed and looked each other straight in the eye.

I felt I had to say something, preferably something at the same time wise and affectionate and maybe a bit conciliatory, but all I could manage was, '*Danke schön.*'

She said, '*Bitte schön.*'

And we both laughed.

Then she left.

So what am I to do now, dear Chief Inspector? Once more I am in desperate need of your good advice. I know how much you must disapprove of what probably seems to you my libidinous nature. How feeble I must sound if I plead strong temptation and very weak flesh! Someone so physically attractive as yourself must have had – must still have – endless opportunity to indulge his baser passions, but I am sure your sense of probity and power of will are both strong enough to make sure you never stray. But that is why I, the weak, must always be turning to you, the strong, in search of strength.

Dierick is the key, of course. I looked for him to open negotiations, but he was nowhere to be found. So I'll have to sweat on it, but I've resolved on one change of plan.

I will finish my packing now, then go and tell Linda that I will not after all take up her invitation to visit Strasbourg but instead will complete my researches in Zurich and Basel, then move on to Frankfurt and Göttingen prior to heading off to sunny California.

Ain't I the laid-back jet-setter then! Ain't I the Citizen of the World!

Of course, even without the threat of Dierick, if Mouse gives Linda any hint of what has just taken place, it may be that I shall no longer have any reason to jet anywhere except home. My claim to be Sam Johnson's literary executor only exists through her goodwill, which might survive or indeed be increased by the memory of our New Year celebration. But the idea that just over twenty-four hours later I'd extended the courtesy to her favourite daughter was not going to go down well.

Once more I ask you to wish me luck.

Dear God, how soon fate exacts payment! Truly no man can call himself happy till he takes his happiness to the grave with him. My visit to Fichtenburg, so successful in many ways, now looks like it might end as badly as it began.

Let me put my thoughts in order.

I went up the castle, as explained above.

On my way there I met Jacques returning to the

chalet. We took our farewells as, with a two-day drive ahead of him, he wanted to be off as soon as he could.

In the castle I found no such haste, however. There seemed to be a general reluctance to break up such a successful house party.

Linda expressed what seemed like genuine disappointment when I said I'd have to skip Strasbourg this time round, but it was balanced with huge delight at my news from America. Mouse came in as we were talking and listened with apparent indifference as her mother relayed my news, but I was perfectly content with indifference. Things move on. Perhaps defloration isn't the big thing in a girl's life it used to be!

Finally I said goodbye to Linda, promising to keep in close touch. Incidentally, her parting kiss, much to my relief, had nothing of strenuous tongue in it but was back to full-blooded Henry Cooper hook mode.

Mouse shook my hand. No significant pressure, nor anything in her tone as she said, 'Goodbye, Franny. I'm pleased things are going so well. I do hope you can keep it up.'

Then she winked at me!

And suddenly it felt like I was the late virgin being encouraged on his way by the voice of old experience.

Perhaps that's what gave me the stimulus to work out what I'm sure your professionally incisive mind spotted instantly, my dear Chief Inspector, to wit, the significance of Mouse's strange cry as I penetrated.

One hundred and eighty!

The triumphal cry a darts scorer sends up as the third dart enters the treble twenty.

'What are you two grinning at?' asked Linda. But her tone was indulgent.

So, nothing to fear from Mouse. Which only left Dierick, who, I thought with relief, was probably on his way north with Jacques by now.

Then Jacques came into the room and asked impatiently if anyone had seen him.

At first the guy's absence was just a cause of irritation. But soon, when he couldn't be found anywhere, it became a matter of real alarm.

Concern that he might have slipped and hurt himself sent us out into the pine forest, looking for tracks and calling his name. We all tried to recall when last we'd seen him, and established that since Jacques and I said goodnight to him in the chalet the previous evening, nobody had had sight of him. Except of course me, and I could hardly explain about that. The weather, after the brief interlude of clear frosty skies we had on New Year's Eve, has returned to low cloud and swirling mist and temperatures high enough to turn the snow soft and mushy. Darkness will be upon us even earlier than usual this afternoon. It was time, Linda decided, to call off our amateur search and inform the authorities. So now I'm back here in the chalet, turning to you for comfort again, Mr Pascoe. Everyone else is back in the castle, waiting for the police. Only Jacques is still out there with a couple of local forestry workers, refusing to give up the search.

I can hear shouting outside, perhaps they've found him, I hope to God they have.

This is truly dreadful. I went out and saw that the disturbance was coming from the lake shore. Jacques was in the water up to his waist and the forestry men were having a hell of a job to drag him out.

It seems one of the men spotted tracks leading out on to the ice and, without a thought for his own safety, Jacques had rushed out there. The ice, weakened by the thaw, soon gave way. Jacques, thank heaven, is safe and well. We got him into the chalet and dried him off. Half an hour later the police arrived with proper equipment. As they started work, the snow stopped and the clouds thinned enough for the dying rays of the declining sun to cast a sickly pink patina across the lake's surface. *Blutensee*, I thought. At that moment I knew the worst, and a minute or two later, the cries of the leading policeman confirmed it.

A little beyond where Jacques had reached, only a few inches beneath the water, rested the body of Frère Dierick.

What had induced him to walk on the lake we can only surmise. Perhaps in the swirling snow he wasn't even aware he was walking across ice. I feel full of guilt lest it was the sight of Mouse and myself naked on the bed which had so distracted him he did not pay heed where he was going. But I comfort myself with the memory of his smile, and his careful closing of the door, neither of which suggested any great mental distraction.

Whatever, it is another tragedy. How they seem to follow me around. Or perhaps it is Thomas Lovell Beddoes they follow. Remember Browning's strange superstitious fear at the prospect of opening the Beddoes box? Perhaps he was right. Could it be that Death, who was such a close and well-loved companion of Beddoes for so many years, still stays close to those who would uncover his friend's secrets, and that his company is the price that must be paid for understanding?

But enough of horrors. There will be an enquiry, of course, and we shall all have to make written statements, but I do not doubt that the combined weight of authority to be found in Linda and her guests will expedite matters and we should all be on our way tomorrow at the latest.

I'll write again soon. And, by the way, if you get any enquiries from the CIA or FBI or whoever does the immigration checking at the US Embassy, I know I can rely on you of all people to assure them that I'm leading a blameless life!

Yours fondly

Franny

llie Pascoe didn't know whether to feel happy or sad as she opened her front door. January 7th, first day of waking to a Christmas-free house after the traditional Twelfth Night clearance, and also the first day of the new term. So now the place felt empty in every way as she returned from dropping Rosie off.

She stooped to pick up the mail from the hall floor and sorted through it quickly. There was one with a Swiss postmark. She made a face as she put it on the hall table with the rest of Peter's mail. Despite her public indifference to, tinged with amusement at, the Roote letters, she wished they would stop. To see a rational man irrationally troubled was a trouble. Plus, the longer they went on, the more she began to question Franny's motivation.

What was he getting out of writing them? At first she'd seen them as a snook-cocking joke. But now the joke was wearing thin, and when Roote talked about the correspondence becoming a necessary part of his life, she half believed him. So now she had two cases of obsessive behaviour to be concerned about.

Perhaps, being further removed from it, she would have a better chance of understanding Roote's than her husband's.

She looked down at the letter, felt tempted to open it, resisted. Women who opened their husband's mail deserved everything they read. She knew how she'd react if she found Peter had been at hers. If she were going to do anything, best to throw it in the fire. But no doubt there'd be more and there was no way to guarantee she'd get to the others first.

In any case, that was almost as bad as opening them.

She checked her own three letters. Two were charity follow-ups. Nowadays no one wrote just to say thanks, they wrote to say thanks but it's not enough.

The third had an official but non-charitable look.

She opened it as she went through into the kitchen, read it quickly on the move, then sat down and read it more slowly a second time.

Her intermittent researches into Roote's genealogy had quickly run into the sand. Using as a starting point Franny's assertion in his first letter that he had been born in Hope, she had looked up the name in her Ordnance Survey atlas and been a little taken aback to discover half a dozen places called Hope and as many again which had enough of Hope in their name to make the young man's jest allowable. She'd written to all the relevant registrars' offices with the information she had and their replies had been trickling in over several days. They ranged from the formal to the friendly with one thing in common: no child with the name Francis Xavier Roote had been registered inside the given time-frame.

Soon she was down to her last Hope, a Derbyshire village in the Peak District, not far out of Sheffield, and it was the County Registrar's letter she had in her hand now.

She read it a third time. Yes, it said, there was an entry for the name and date specified. Address 7 Post Terrace; mother Anthea Roote née Atherton, housewife; father Thomas Roote – and here came the bit that made her sit and read it a third time – police officer.

She reached for the phone to ring Peter. But to tell him what? Surprise surprise ... but being surprising wasn't the same as being helpful. Did it really matter? Wasn't she by doing this merely feeding his obsession when she should have been starving it?

She went back into the hall and looked again at the letter with the Swiss stamp.

Sod it, let Roote decide. If this was as innocuous as the last with its account of Christmas fun, why keep the pot boiling? It might even be a farewell ... *Dear Mr Pascoe, my New Year resolution is to write to you no more. Sorry for any trouble I've caused. Yours etc.*

She ripped it open. No point pussyfooting. If a woman was going to open her husband's mail, sod steaming kettles. Let him see you might be nosey but at least you weren't sneaky!

When she'd read it, she said, 'Oh shit.'

Another death. Another death which advantaged Roote. Truly the guy was either very lucky or . . . No! That was like jumping into quicksand to save a sinking man.

But she could almost hear Peter's reaction to the account of Frère Dierick's death.

Knowledge is power. She'd let herself be talked once again into going shopping in Estotiland with Daphne Aldermann. Daphne, an unrepentant shopaholic, had a theory that the first Monday in January was the time to go to the post-Christmas sales. 'In the early days,' she said, 'there are so many people, they turn into a kind of lynch mob and you can wake up next morning aghast at the memory of what you did the day before. So wait till the crowds have gone, bearing with them most of the chronic sales junk, and step in when they're putting out real bargains to tempt the discerning customer.'

Ellie had let her arm be twisted and now she was glad. Estotiland was a large step on the way to Sheffield, the other side of which lay Hope. So an hour's shopping with Daphne, then off south, and tonight with luck she'd be able to amaze Peter with more than a mohair sweater in the kind of bold design she loved but he hated.

In fact the visit to Estotiland was quite useful for another reason. In a couple of weeks' time Rosie was going to her friend Suzie's birthday party in the Junior Jumbo Burger Bar. Ellie had promised she'd help. At the same time her early-warning system had gone on to red alert at the mention of burgers and this trip today gave her the chance to check the kitchens for potential sources of salmonella, E. coli, and CJD.

Daphne gave a long-suffering sigh, but as she'd resolved long ago never to let Ellie have the satisfaction of seeing her embarrassed, she strode boldly with her into the kitchen where they were greeted with great courtesy and invited to examine whatever they wanted to examine and ask any questions they wanted to ask. All the meat was local, they were assured, an assurance backed up with written details of provenance. Standards of hygiene were exemplary, and supervision of the young staff was militarily strict.

'Told you,' said Daphne as they left. 'Estotiland is Paradise Regained. Now, let's go and pluck ourselves some apples!'

A couple of hours and as many mohair sweaters later, they reached the upper retail floor and Daphne turned instinctively towards the lingerie department. Whether it was Daphne or her husband, Patrick, who got off on silk next to the skin, Ellie didn't know, but she saw that glazed look come into her friend's eyes as they entered. Then she paused, wondering if the condition was contagious, as everything seemed to tremble in front of her as though somewhere deep beneath them an underground train had gone rushing by.

'You OK?' said Daphne.

'I think so. Just something walking over my grave, you know. Something big.'

'Probably that fat bastard poor Peter works for. Let's go and find a seat, get a coffee, or take lunch early. Did you eat any breakfast this morning?'

Touched by her friend's willingness to turn away even from the gates of Paradise to offer comfort, Ellie said, 'No, really, you go on. But I think maybe I have had enough. I'll skip lunch, if that's OK, and head off. I've got something I need to do in Sheffield.'

For some reason she didn't want to give chapter and verse on Roote, maybe because it would have been hard to explain without inviting comment on Peter's obsession.

An hour later she found herself standing on the doorstep of 7 Post Terrace in Hope talking to a woman called Myers who'd bought the house three years ago from a couple called Wilkinson and had never heard of anyone called Roote.

As Ellie turned away in disappointment, she heard an eldritch screech. She'd often wondered what one of these would sound like, but she recognized it as soon as she heard it. Its source seemed to be a neighbouring window, which Ellie had noticed was wide open despite the cold, dank weather.

Peering in, she discovered that the reason for the open window

363

was to ensure as little as possible of anything interesting was missed by an aged crone in a rocking chair who without preamble told her that Mrs Atherton-who-used-to-live-there-before-the-Wilkinsons' daughter Anthea had married a man called Roote and, if Ellie cared to step inside, all would be made clear.

Ellie was in like a shot and soon discovered that her informant wasn't quite so ancient nor so crone-like as at first appeared. Her name was Mrs Eel and she made a nice cup of tea and a lovely Victoria sponge, and what was more she'd lived there all her life and what she didn't know about Hope simply wasn't knowledge.

From a somewhat rambling narrative Ellie extracted a classic plot line.

Anthea Atherton's parents had skimped and saved to give their attractive daughter the kind of education which fitted her to move in circles full of rich young men who spoke proper, lived in big houses, drove Range Rovers, and wanted only the company of a beautiful and intelligent young spouse to make their comfortable lives complete.

Then she'd thrown it all back in their faces and married a cop.

Mrs Eel pronounced this punchline with all the revulsion of Tony Blair discovering that one of his cabinet was a socialist.

'How dreadful!' said Ellie. 'I knew a girl who did the same. It never works. And this policeman, was he local then?'

'Oh no. That would have been bad enough. But this 'un worked down South.'

More shock-horror. Ellie tried for detail but it soon emerged that while Mrs Eel was needle-sharp on Hope, she was a bit vague on South, which began immediately after Bradwell two miles away. But she knew the cop's name was Tommy Roote and he was a sergeant and how they'd met was there'd been some bother at the posh boarding school Anthea went to, and the sergeant had been part of the investigating team, and Anthea was only seventeen then.

'Taking advantage of a child, there should be laws against it,' concluded Mrs Eel.

'I think there are,' said Ellie.

'Likely, and him being a cop, he'd know about 'em, which is why the cunning devil waited till Anthea reached eighteen afore he married her.'

News of this event was greeted by such cries of rage and despair from the Atherton household they were, according to Mrs Eel, audible in Bradwell if not Beyond.

The story now skipped a couple of years to the day when Anthea returned home for the first time since the wedding, pregnant and alone. Her parents took her in and after a while gave out the story that her husband was engaged in some special operation and that Anthea was very keen her child should be born a Hopeite. Mrs Eel was not deceived. Her diagnosis, borne out by subsequent events, was a deep malaise in the marriage.

The child was born prematurely before Anthea could be loaded into the ambulance summoned to take her to hospital (so Franny was being strictly accurate when he said he was born in Hope, thought Ellie). Shortly afterwards, Sergeant Roote appeared on the scene and bore off child and wife to his den in the South, thus apparently confirming the official version of events. But Mrs Eel still was not deceived.

'I knew it 'ud end in tears,' she declared. 'The lass kept coming back more and more frequent, always with the lad, but never with the policeman. I think she wanted a divorce early on, but her mam and dad were dead against it.'

This puzzled Ellie until Mrs Eel revealed the Athertons belonged to some fairly fundamental nonconformist sect to whom a foolish marriage might be an offence against your family, but a fractious divorce was an offence against God. So now it was the parents who attempted to keep things going. All the reward they got was that when some professional disaster hit Sergeant Roote's career, their daughter had to share in it. Exactly what form it took Mrs Eel had to admit she didn't know, but she knew it was bad enough to get him chucked out of the Force without a pension, after which it was all downhill, and when in a short time he died (drink or suicide, Mrs Eel theorized) Anthea was left destitute.

At this point Mrs Eel's direct knowledge of what happened became fragmentary, but she was clearly a great snapper-up of indiscreet trifles and she was able to provide Ellie with enough bits and pieces to add to her own knowledge of the subsequent course of Franny Roote's life for the construction of a convincing mosaic.

She laid this out before Pascoe that night, jumping straight in once the anticipated explosion of 'The bastard's been at it again!' after he read the letter had faded away.

He had listened with close attention but without any of the ooh's and ah's of wonderment and admiration she felt her researches deserved.

But in for a penny, in for a pound.

'I'll leave you to find out what this career-ending disaster might have been,' she said. 'What I think happened after his death was that Anthea, faced with the prospect of vegetating gently in Hope, decided to put the expensive education her parents had given her to practical use. She re-established contact with old schoolfriends. I would guess that to them the sight of a beautiful, wilful, and probably rather condescending old school chum being forced to admit she'd got it all wrong and her life was an unmitigated disaster was irresistible. Soon she was moving once more in their elevated circles. Mrs Eel certainly recalls young Fran (whom she describes as a strange, solemn child, a bit fey) being looked after for increasingly long periods by his grandparents. Ultimately of course Anthea showed her friends the error of their charitable ways by plucking from under their noses the prize plum of the rich and attractive American bachelor who became her second husband. But it seems that Franny did not form part of the deal. He looked like becoming a permanent fixture at his grandparents' house in Hope, then Mrs Atherton died of cancer leaving Mr Atherton too frail and distraught to look after the boy alone. And so, I surmise, began that long involvement with the British boarding school system which has produced such a fine crop of crooks, psychotics and prime ministers.'

'Roote did well then. Two out of three's not bad,' said Pascoe. 'Your conclusions? I can tell by your flaring nostrils that you have conclusions.'

'Surely here we have the perfect explanation of Franny's love/

hatred relationship with his father? He's a hero to the boy – that story of the attack in the park is almost certainly based on truth, if perhaps a little coloured by memory. But his failure to provide for his family led to Fran's neglect and stressful upbringing. He tried to write him out of his life by claiming almost complete ignorance of the man, but Ms Haseen got through his guard. And his obsessive relationship with you derives largely from the fact that you are another cop who has had a tremendous influence on his life, bad in that you got him locked up in the Syke, but good in that everything now seems to be falling right for him. Also he's desperately in need of a living father-figure. And of course your obsession with him must have made him believe that you too felt a special relationship here.'

'The bastard's got that right then,' said Pascoe feelingly.

'Come on, Pete. Give him a break. I'm not denying there's an element of mockery and teasing in these letters, but can't you see there's much more?'

'Like threats, you mean? And hints at crimes committed which I can't touch him for?'

'No. Like . . . need.'

'Ellie, if you're going to say they're a cry for help, I may puke.'

'Shut up and open the prezzies I bought you in the sales,' she commanded.

He tore open the tissue paper and looked in horror at the mohair sweaters in the bright colours and bold designs she believed suited him.

'I may puke anyway,' he said.

hirley Novello was a good Catholic, if Catholic goodness means believing all the rules and keeping as many as you can without bursting. The one she had most problems with was the one that says sex outside marriage is sinful, which was perhaps why, as she once tried to explain to Father Joseph Kerrigan, she got involved with a married man from time to time, as in a way that was sex sort of half in marriage, wasn't it?

Father Joe had shaken his head and said, 'If the SJ's took women, I'd enter you straight off. Next time you feel the urge coming on, pray for strength to resist. Miracles do happen. And while you're at it, make the sign of the cross, but make it with your legs.'

In fact a miracle had happened at Christmas, that most miraculous of times. It had started well. Her Transport sergeant had managed to spend the morning with her using the pretext of a duty-sharing roster, which, considering that there were no trains on Christmas Day, meant his wife must be pretty thick. He'd given Novello a digital camera which must have cost an arm and a leg, so in return she'd given him both her arms and legs and every other part of her anatomy she could bring into contact with every part of his she could reach. How he explained the exhausted state in which he returned home she did not know, but when she next saw him, the day after Boxing Day, she found that memory of their festive fuck plus a vast excess of family festivity had combined to make him start talking seriously of escaping to the wildwoods with her and building a willow cabin or some such nonsense.

Now the miracle occurred.

In the twinkling of an eye he was transformed from a strong handsome interestingly hairy lover in the prime of life to a middle-aged beer belly with the beginnings of a bald patch and four noisy, ill-mannered kids. She gave him his marching orders and even thought of returning the camera, but in the end thought what the hell! she'd earned it.

So Novello had begun the New Year as New Years should be begun, with a clean slate and a whole cageful of lively resolutions. They beat their wings at the bars in vain till a Twelfth Night party from which she woke with the certain knowledge that they'd all flown the coop, though in what order she could not say. But the experience, she seemed to recollect, had been splendidly epiphanic. In other words her head felt fuzzy but her body felt great.

She rolled out of bed – her own – checked that no one was crapping in her bog or cooking in her kitchen – they weren't – complimented herself on having a great time without paying the high price of conversation over breakfast, and knocked back her usual hangover cure of a fried-egg sarnie and a litre of coffee black as a Unionist's heart.

Then she noticed the digital camera next to her party clothes on the floor.

She checked the pictures, didn't, thank God, find anything too naughty, but did come across a snap of a good-looking guy with a nice crinkly grin sitting on her sofa. She couldn't put a name to him, but his face sent a distinct mnemonic tremor through her erogenous zone.

She wanted a close-up, but when she tried to feed it into her computer she found the bloody thing was knackered. Never mind. The station was full of bloody things.

Then she set out for work. She was proud of her fitness and she jogged to the station every other day. This was an other day. A lesser woman might have chickened, but not Novello. She'd woken up at her usual time and she was resolved to follow her usual routine. Sticking a change of clothes plus her camera into a small rucksack, she got into her tracksuit and set off.

Since Dalziel had given her the special assignment, her chosen route usually took her along Peg Lane.

Her task of making sure Rye Pomona wasn't being harassed by investigative reporters was either very easy or quite impossible, depending on how you looked at it. The impossible bit was sticking with her twenty-four hours a day. On the other hand she'd been put on her guard, she was an intelligent woman (formidably intelligent, in Novello's estimation) and quite capable of taking care of herself. So the active part of the assignment had soon diminished to a daily check with her for oddities plus the occasional morning diversion just to make sure there wasn't some low life waiting to buttonhole her at this hour most favoured by police, bailiffs and buttonholers generally.

After the events at the Mayor's Hogmanay Hop, it had seemed that even this small routine wouldn't be necessary for some time, but last Thursday Hat had turned up at work, full of joy, to announce that Rye had rung him the previous night to say she'd been discharged from hospital with a clean bill of health and this morning she'd gone back to work.

Novello, guessing that Dalziel would expect her to know all the ins and outs before he'd even heard the substantive news, headed straight round to the library for a chat.

Rye had greeted her like an old friend. To Novello's enquiries after her health she'd replied that the hospital staff hadn't been able to assign any specific cause to her collapse, suspected it might be viral, had given her a couple of shots of God knows what, and sent her home with instructions to make an appointment with her GP.

Novello had been unconvinced. She had a sharp female eye and a proper detective scepticism, both of which detected telltale signs of worry and debility. Had she been a closer mate of Hat Bowler's, she might have looked for a diplomatic way of hinting her concern, but even then his boundless relief and joy at Rye's return home could have made her hesitate. As it was, with their uneasy relationship, any hint of reservation on her part was likely to be regarded as peeing on his parade.

Her relationship with Andy Dalziel had no such ambiguities. If he gave you a job, even if you thought it was a complete waste of time, you did it, and you didn't skimp. She'd read every syllable of the Wordman archive twice. Asked for her conclusions, she'd taken a deep breath and told the Fat Man, 'If Dee hadn't been caught in the act of attacking Pomona, there's not enough evidence against him to get him community service let alone a conviction for serial killing. And if he hadn't been killed resisting arrest, which is how we sold it, I can think of half a dozen stories he might have told which would have made CPS very unhappy about charging him.'

'Them dozy buggers got hold of Hitler, he'd have pled down to a misdemeanour,' said Dalziel, but without any real force.

'So if there is a journalist on the case, all he has to do is find some way of picking holes in the Pomona attack and after that it's straight through to the goal mouth. Tabloids twenty. Police nil.'

'Play a lot of soccer, do you?'

'Six-a-side down the gym,' she said.

'Don't know what the world's coming to. OK, you've not told me owt I don't know. You could make an old man very happy by pointing out some loose end in the killings that we could tie round Dee's neck.'

'Only loose end I could see was that chap Pyke-Strengler who was found shot and decapitated out at Stang Tarn. There was some blood on one of his fish-hooks, human, group AB. Not Pyke-Strengler's, but not Dee's either, and not belonging to either of the other two suspects, Penn and Roote, who, to be honest, sir, look about as suspicious as the Pope. How they got in the frame beats me.'

'Wishful thinking,' growled Dalziel. 'You'll do more of it as you get older. So one loose end you can't tie up except to say it definitely doesn't point to Dee. That it? Nothing you can cheer me up with by saying, "Please, sir, here's something no one can argue with 'cos you definitely got it right?"'

'Yes, sir, there is something . . .'

'Spit it out.'

'I think you're definitely right to be worried if it turns out there is an investigative journalist on the job.'

He stared at her till she began to regret her boldness, then said, 'Nay, lass, I'm not worried about that, 'cos I've got this smartass cop on his case who's going to find him for me before he prints a word.'

'Yes, sir. And then . . . ?'

'Then I'll kill him,' said Dalziel. 'But if the first I hear of him is when I open my Daily Crap, then I'll have to find someone else to kill.'

So at eight twenty this Monday morning, Novello was jogging down Peg Lane.

Its once fashionable Victorian townhouses were now given over to multi-occupation and small businesses. There were no garages (presumably the fashionable Victorians kept their broughams in some nearby livery) so the house as opposed to the church side of the street was lined with parked cars for its full length. She slowed down as she passed Church View. The usual cars stood outside. The front door seemed firmly closed. It tended to be left ajar during the day which wasn't very good security. Open or locked, it made no difference to Novello as she'd checked out the lock and got herself a suitable key from the vast selection on offer in CID's boy scout (i.e. be prepared) cupboard.

So all quiet on the Peg Lane front. With a feeling of duty done, she speeded up again. And almost missed them.

Right at the end of the Lane where it went into a bit of a chicane an old white Merc was parked. There were two people in it, a man and a woman. And the man she recognized as Charley Penn.

They were deep in conversation. Or something. They didn't even glance her way as she passed. She crossed the road, ran back a bit till she reached the old wall running round St Margaret's, and scrambled over it.

Here she had a good view of the Merc. She wished she'd got a camera, then remembered that she had. Gleefully she dug it out. There were Dalziel Brownie points to be had here, and an ambitious girl snapped these up avidly.

The woman got out of the car. It didn't seem all that amicable a parting, but at the last minute Penn said something and they exchanged a peck. Then he drove off towards town and the woman started walking in the other direction.

Novello kept pace with her, popping up to take the occasional snap. The woman seemed too preoccupied to notice.

Then she reached the steps of Church View, turned up them, pushed the door open and went inside.

Novello vaulted over the wall with the explosive speed which had made her a sprint champion in her school days. She had her key at the ready but the door hadn't shut properly so she didn't need it. She could hear the woman's steps on the stairway above.

As she began to mount towards Rye's landing, it occurred to Novello for the first time to wonder what she was supposed to do now. Journalists, particularly investigative journalists, are not the kind of people it's advisable to arrest without good reason. In such a situation, Dalziel no doubt had many tried and tested techniques at his disposal. Like grievous bodily harm. Pascoe's diplomatic skills would probably come into their own. And Wield would merely stare for a while then say 'Boo!' to get a result.

But how could a young ambitious WDC deal with the situation without getting herself the kind of bad press which got your card marked by the Chief Constable?

And a little way behind these somewhat selfish thoughts came the question, what the hell was this woman up to anyway?

She reached Rye's landing. It was empty. Shit! Had she had time to ring Rye's bell and talk her way into the flat? Novello didn't believe so. Maybe Rye had coincidentally opened her door just as the woman arrived and been pushed back inside. But such behaviour from a stranger would surely elicit protest. She pressed her ear to Rye's door and heard nothing. What now? Ring the bell and check all was well inside? Or continue her pursuit up the next flight of stairs?

A voice said, 'Can I help you?'

Startled she turned to see a bright-eyed foxy-faced woman of indeterminate age peering at her from the next door to the right.

This made up her mind.

'No thanks. Just visiting Ms Pomona,' said Novello, pressing the bell.

A long minute passed before the door opened.

Rye stood there wearing only a cotton wrap. She looked terrible. Either, thought Novello, casting an expert eye over the deep shadowed eyes, the pallid cheeks, the hunched shoulders and the lifeless hair, she'd been at a Twelfth Night party even wilder than the one she herself didn't remember attending, or she was sick.

'Hey, I'm sorry, have I got you out of bed?'

'No, I was up.'

'Can I come in?'

Rye looked as if she'd like to say No, then glanced at the still-spectating neighbour and said, 'Morning, Mrs Gilpin. Yes, come in.'

Unless as well as admitting the suspected journalist, Rye had also hidden her in the bedroom, it looked as though she was alone.

'So what do you want . . . nothing's happened to Hat, has it?'

For the first time some spark of life touched the lacklustre eyes.

'No, nothing to do with Hat. He's fine.'

Relief, then the light died. No need to worry her with anything else, not till she'd got the photos developed and had a word with King Kong.

'No, I was just passing and thought I'd say hello, check that everything was all right.'

'Yeah, fine. Why shouldn't it be?'

'You know, what we talked about, journalists and such. There hasn't been anyone bothering you?'

Rye said, 'How could anyone bother me?'

Strange answer, but she was a strange girl. And not a well girl by the look of her.

'Sorry to bother you then. I'll let you get back to bed.'

'Bed? No, I'm getting ready for work.'

'Work?' said Novello. Then, catching the echo of her own incredulity, she went on rapidly, 'Monday morning's are hell, aren't they? Especially if you've been partying over the weekend. You should have seen me an hour ago. Coffee and a spot of breakfast's the thing for getting back on track. You had any breakfast yet? Let me give you a hand. I could murder another cup of coffee.'

'No thanks,' said Rye. 'I'm not hungry. Bit of an upset tummy.'

Hell, thought Novello. Has Hat got carried away, put her in the club? Stupid sod! Or maybe (don't rush to judgment in this

374

world 'cos you surely won't want to be rushing to judgment in the next, as Father Kerrigan was forever telling his flock) it was planned, what they both wanted, only as always the woman gets the shit, the man gets the cigars.

'Look, none of my business, but are you sure you're OK? You look, well, not a hundred per cent . . .'

'Is that right? How much would you say then? Ninety-five per cent? Fifty? Less?'

That was better. Spark back in her eyes, bit of a flush in her cheeks.

'Sorry,' said Novello. 'I'll be off then, let you get dressed. Take care.'

'Yes. Thank you for calling.'

Again a strangeness of phrase and intonation, this time sounding like Eliza Doolittle reciting some newly learned social mantra.

Novello left. No sign of Mrs Gilpin, thank God. She ran lightly up the next flight of stairs. The top landing was empty. The woman must have heard her pursuing feet and continued up here, listened to the exchange below, then slipped back down and away while she was wasting time in Pomona's apartment. So, a bad decision, she didn't doubt that was how the Fat Man would see it, though she still didn't know what she was supposed to have done if she had confronted this putative journalist.

At least he wasn't going to be able to say she took her time facing the music. As soon as he came in she was knocking at his door. In her hand she held her camera.

'What's this then? Want me picture for your scrapbook?'

Quickly she explained what had happened, playing up her foresight in having the camera, playing down her failure to keep track of the mystery woman. As she spoke she hooked up the camera to the computer which stood on a side table in the superintendent's office, like a memorial to futurity.

When the woman's face came up, he crashed a great fist down on his desk. Novello, anticipating this was the first salvo in a full-blooded assault on her performance, winced. But all he said was, 'Can I send this down the tube so it comes out at the other end?'

'Yes, sir,' she said. 'But I'll need an address.'

'Commander Jenkinson, Scotland Yard,' he said.

There was a service directory by the phone. She picked it up, thumbed through and said, 'Would that be Aneurin Jenkinson? Media Division?'

'That's the bugger.'

'And a message, sir?'

He thought a moment then dictated *Nye – who she? – luv Andy*.

She typed the message, attached the photo and sent it.

Dalziel twisted the screen round so that he could see it.

Novello recalled a story told by the nun who taught deportment at the convent school she'd been expelled from. It concerned Queen Victoria attending a banquet hosted by the Empress Eugenie in Paris. Taking her seat at the dinner table, the Empress momentarily glanced down as most people do to make sure the flunkey was manoeuvring her chair into position. But to the French guests' huge admiration, Victoria seated herself without hesitation or downward glance, as if completely confident that, should the flunkey be remiss in his duty, God Himself would move the chair forward to receive her royal behind.

So, it seemed to her, the Fat Man glowered at the computer in the God-underwritten certainty that his message would receive an instant reply.

It took only a couple of minutes, but that great slab of a face was already beginning to darken with impatience.

She Mai Richter German journalist. CV follows. Watch your balls. She bites. Nye

She printed off the CV, handed it to the Fat Man and read it on the screen herself.

Mai Richter was thirty nine years old, set out to be an academic, had her proposals to do a thesis on American political patronage in the post-war era blocked, dug into the reasons for this and found that certain very senior state officials who controlled the university purse-strings had made it clear this was not an area they cared to see put under the microscope, got her findings published in a national paper, was sued, fought the case to a draw, found that her academic career was on the rocks before it had left harbour, so directed her talent for digging beneath the surface of things to journalism instead.

A list followed of her investigations, mainly in Germany but with some forays into France and the Netherlands. She was an accomplished linguist with perfect Dutch, English, and French. She worked freelance, selling her stories to the highest appropriate bidder. She wasn't a member of any political party but had strong left-wing radical sympathies. She trod a narrow line of legality which, it was theorized, she probably crossed far more often than the couple of times when she'd been caught, which occasions justified her inclusion in international police records. Another reason was that there had been death threats made against her and at least one known attempt.

'Seems to be a dangerous trade, hers,' said Novello.

'She'll find out just how dangerous next time I get my hands on her,' growled Dalziel. 'Let's have another look.'

'Next time . . . ? There's been a first time, sir?' said Novello, bringing the image back up.

'Oh aye. I've danced with her and given her a big wet kiss,' said Dalziel. 'This cow calls herself Myra Rogers. She's Rye Pomona's next-door neighbour and best mate!'

Novello's surprise was diluted with relief. She hadn't cocked up after all. That's how she'd disappeared, simply by going into her own apartment.

The Fat Man dictated another note.

So she bites? Well, I'm used to that, you Welsh git! And I've still got the scars to prove it. How about a spiky-haired runt, answers to Tris, face like a fucked-up ferret, tanned like an old pub ceiling, dresses like a Polynesian pox-doctor and carries a handbag?

This reply was even quicker.

At least you can show your scars. If I start flashing the stud marks where you stomped me, I'll get arrested! Your ferret (very apt) sounds like Tristram Lilley which probably means there's some serious hi-tec surveillance going on.

377

And if he was carrying a handbag, you're probably on Candid Camera! Sounds interesting. Anything we should know about?

Dalziel's reply read Just a little local difficulty. Thanks, mate. I owe you a pint. Hwyl fawr! Andy

'So she simply went into her flat,' said Novello, thinking there was no harm in underlining her innocence.

'Aye. Let that be a lesson. Don't look for magic when the obvious is staring you in the face.'

The Fat Man spoke without force, or at least not with a force aimed in her direction. He brought up the woman's image again (he was, noted Novello, despite his assertive Ludditism, a quick learner) and sent his mind back to his encounter with Charley Penn in Hal's. As he'd approached the writer's table, a woman approaching from the opposite direction had veered off. She had been unmemorable – except as a niggle which made the unremarkable face of Myra Rogers ring a very faint bell when he first met her. Man who didn't listen to bells could end up late at his own funeral, he told himself scornfully.

Another thing popped into his mind, the dedication in the Hacker novel he'd bought – *An Mai – wunderschön in allen Monaten!* – and Penn's suspicious glance as he saw which book it was. Bugger must have thought I was on to him! Well, I am now, Charley!

Novello picked up the CV print-out which Dalziel had dropped on to his desk and read it again. Then she said thoughtfully, 'Funny, though. This doesn't look like her kind of story at all, does it? It's the big political stuff she usually goes for, cock-ups in Cabinets, corruption in high places. *Mid-Yorkshire CID might have got it wrong* isn't exactly going to be syndicated round the world, is it? So why put in so much time and effort when there's not much in it for her, even if she does find out whatever there is to find out?'

It was Dalziel's turn to shoot a suspicious glance but she met it boldly. She wasn't about to ask him direct what it was he didn't want anyone to find, but after a lot of deep thought she'd come to the conclusion there had to be something and she'd made a pretty good guess at what it might be. Being on Dalziel's team meant you often had to put up with being treated like a personal slave, but the upside of this was that his pride of possession was second to none, and if anyone tried to mess with one of his cubs, they found themselves messing with Daddy Bear too. Finding a wounded officer and dead suspect after a struggle, and being persuaded the suspect had it coming, Fat Andy wouldn't hesitate to tidy things up to remove any ambiguity about the killing. She'd now looked at every photo and read every bit of paper relating to the affair, and marvelled at how cleverly the selections offered to first the coroner then the Board of Enquiry had underlined the proper roles of the trio involved – Maiden in Distress, Noble Rescuer Sorely Wounded and Foul Fiend Slain With a Single Blow. Had a case ever come to court, then a good defence counsel would surely have picked up on this manicure job. But dead men didn't get tried.

'So what do you think got Richter interested, clever clogs?' he growled.

'Money? Penn must be worth a bob or two, all this telly stuff.'

'She sound to you like someone who'll do owt just for the brass?'

'Not really,' admitted Novello.

'Look at her list of publications.'

Besides her major investigative articles, there were several books listed on what seemed to be social or socio-literary topics. The title of one was translated as *Heine's Apostasy: the German Choice*.

She said hesitantly, 'Isn't Penn doing a book about someone with a name like that?'

Dalziel looked upon her with the approval he saved for those of his staff whose minds weren't cluttered up with all kinds of art-farty lit. crit. nonsense.

'Aye. This Heinkel or whatever his name is. I'll lay odds they've met before and when Charley started getting these daft ideas in his head about digging up some dirt, he thought of Fraulein fucking Richter straight off!'

'But it still doesn't explain . . .'

'Does if they'd had a roll in the hay first time they met,' said

Dalziel. 'Nay, don't look surprised. I know he's no oil painting, but there's no accounting for taste, is there?'

She looked at the huge bulk slumped before her, thought of Cap Marvell, and said, 'No, that's right, sir,' realizing too late she'd not slammed down the visor over her thoughts quickly enough.

He gave her a promissory glare, then said, 'I reckon she'd spent the night at Charley's place, sorting out his irregular verbs, and he were dropping her off so she could become dear Myra, best mate, again.'

She said, 'Looked as if they might have been having a bit of a row.'

'Good. Mebbe she's decided there's nowt in it for her and is giving Charley his cards,' said Dalziel. 'Off you go, lass. Got no work to do?'

She felt dumped. At the door she paused. Nothing like a Parthian shot, was there?

She said, 'One thing, sir. How long has Rogers been living next door to Rye?'

'At least since a week before Christmas. Why?'

So, three weeks at least. And she'd stayed around over Christmas too. Either her passion for Charley Penn was very strong. Or she thought she was definitely on to something worth spending a lot of time on. She thought of saying this to see if she could get a flicker of unease into those relentless eyes. But was it worth the effort?

She didn't know much about the Parthians but she had an impression that despite all their farewell shots, they'd never made the World Cup finals.

'Just wondered, sir,' she said, heading for the door.

'Don't forget your camera. Here, I didn't realize you knew Sol.'

'Sol?' She turned, puzzled, then saw that the image now showing on the screen was the man in her flat with the nerve-tingling smile.

'Aye. Sol Wiseman. Rabbi at the Progressive Synagogue on Millstone Road.'

'Rabbi. A Jewish Rabbi?' said Novello, gobsmacked.

380

'A lot of them are,' said Dalziel, eyeing her sharply. 'Known him long?'

'No, not really . . . hardly at all . . . just trying out the camera.'

She was thinking with horror of her next confession. 'Father, I've screwed a rabbi . . .'

Dalziel grinned suddenly as if she'd spoken her fears out loud, unplugged the camera and handed it to her.

Once more she headed for the door.

As she opened it, his voice said, 'Another thing, Ivor. You keep this quiet. And I mean quiet. No exceptions, not even Father Joe. Right?'

'Yes, sir.'

She went out into the corridor and was shutting the door when, without looking up, he added, 'Nice work, lass. You did right well.'

Suddenly things didn't seem so bad after all.

Biting her lip to stop herself grinning like an idiot, Novello went on her way.

ye Pomona watched out of her window as Novello drove away.

Her appointment was at nine thirty. At nine forty a grim-faced man came out of the consulting room.

'Do we need another appointment, Mr Maciver?' asked the receptionist.

'What for?' he snarled. And left. A great start.

Chakravarty appeared in the doorway, casually dressed in a shirt so white it dazzled the eye and knife-edged cream-coloured slacks. All he needed was a bat to be opening in a test match. He ushered her in, full of apology and charm.

Rye listened to him stony faced, then glanced at her watch and said, 'So let's not waste any more time.'

He blinked as if a bouncer had just whistled past his nose and said, 'Of course. I have your records here. The tests are scheduled. But first let's see things from your point of view.'

He was a good listener, and a good questioner, though after half an hour Rye felt slightly irritated that he seemed to be focusing less on what in her eyes was the most significant event of her medical history, the accident which had killed her brother and left her with her silver blaze, and more on the events out at Stang Tarn the previous autumn which had left Dick Dee dead.

Suspecting his interest was merely prurient, she said dismissively, 'I don't see how this can be relevant. I only suffered a few minor injuries.'

'So I observe, it must nevertheless have been a tremendous shock to your system. And it would seem your symptoms have appreciably worsened since that event.'

'Aren't you jumping the gun?' said Rye. 'You're talking as if everything you've asked about or I've mentioned is part of a single syndrome. Surely until you've examined the results of all the necessary tests, this is mere hypothesis?'

'I prefer to think of it as diagnosis,' he said with a quick flash of the charming smile. 'So far you've given me a history of severe headaches over many years increasing in frequency, occasional bouts of dizziness or disorientation also becoming more frequent, and mood swings if not violent enough to be called manic-depressive, certainly remarkable enough for you to feel they were worth a mention. These begin to form a pattern which may give a pointer to what I should be looking for in the test results.'

'So why don't we get down to the tests?'

He blinked again. Probably every blink means another hundred on his bill, thought Rye. Well, that's what the private patient paid for, the right to be ruder than the doctor.

She'd come as clean as she could in answering his questions, stopping short of telling him about her conversations with Serge, of course, and not getting within screaming distance of her involvement in the Wordman killings. She had told him about her sense of responsibility for the accident that had caused Serge's death, though without admitting that she was indeed responsible. And she'd gone on to describe how, after her recovery, lines she knew by heart had vanished the moment she set foot on a stage, thus bringing to an end her hope of an acting career. She'd been worried in advance that baring so much of herself to an impersonal expert might tempt her to go the whole confessional hog and let everything spill out. But in fact she was finding that the process was causing a distancing between herself and the self who'd done those dreadful things, turning that other into the killer you read about in the paper or see being taken into court on the telly, then you close the paper or switch off the set, and though you my retain a residual impression of the monster for a while, it isn't strong enough to spoil your dinner or trouble your sleep.

Only the sepulchral confinement of the brain scanner brought it all back to her, brought Sergius too, his flesh disintegrating as it strove to rid itself of all that fluff and dust, his eye accusing, as if all her efforts to contact him had only heaped purgatorial coals upon his spirit. As she rolled back into the by comparison cathedral vastness of the hospital room, she wondered how her turbulent mental activity had registered on the scan. Would it be possible for the expert eye to read a full confession in the message scrawled by all those electronic impulses on the wall of the brain?

After the initial consultation and examination, Mr Chakravarty had vanished, presumably to see another lucrative private client, or maybe glance at a dozen or so National Health patients, while she spent the rest of the morning undergoing tests, some of which she understood, others of which were impenetrably arcane.

Finished, she was told that she should present herself at the peacock throne again at four thirty, by which time Chakravarty, his busy schedule permitting, should have had time to make some preliminary assessments of the test results.

She had no desire to go back to her flat. Hat was working today, but that didn't mean he wouldn't bunk off at some point to visit her at the library. There he would be met by the story she'd fed her colleagues, that she was taking the day off to do the January sales in Leeds. Being a cop, and knowing her attitude to sex and shopping was that they were fine except for the shopping, he might be a little more sceptical than her colleagues and head straight round to Church View. To head him off from doing something stupid like kicking her door down, she'd confided in Myra Rogers who'd promised to listen out for any visitors and confirm that she'd seen her friend set off, hopes high, in search of bargains first thing that morning. Worried that she'd be keeping Myra stuck in Church View, she'd been reassured that her bookkeeping work could for the most part be as easily done at home as in her clients' often cramped offices.

It seemed a good idea too to avoid the chance of an accidental encounter in the town centre so when she got into her car, she drove out into the country. Whether directed by accident or by subconscious choice, she did not know, but she suddenly realized she was driving along the Little Bruton road, and there ahead was the tiny humpback bridge where she'd broken down and sat in despair till she saw the yellow AA van driving towards her like the answer to a prayer. Here it had all started, here the first of her victims had died – no, not a victim, not this one ... his death had been an accident ... an accident which she had interpreted as a sign ...

She stopped on the bridge. Time had stopped for her on that occasion and all those subsequent occasions when deaths had occurred which by no stretch of the imagination could be called accidental. She'd told Chakravarty something about these timeless episodes, not with any detail, of course, but just in an effort to convey her feeling of separation from the chronology of everyday life, her sense of otherness. Now she longed for the experience again ... time slowing ... stopping ... only this time when the flow started again, perhaps instead of the AA man lying dead in the water, he'd be climbing into his van and driving merrily on his way ...

But nothing happened. She stood on the bridge and looked down over the shallow parapet. The stream flowed, and so did time. She got back into the car. The past was past and never changed. The dead were dead and the only way to see them again was to join them. Her eyes filled with blinding tears. She kept on driving, faster and faster, but when her eyes cleared, she was still alive, still bowling along this narrow bendy country road as if hands other than hers were turning the wheel.

At four twenty-nine she was back in Chakravarty's office. At four thirty prompt he appeared. So she'd taught him one lesson. But when he didn't make any charmingly humorous reference to his good timekeeping, she guessed he was not the bearer of glad tidings.

She said, 'Mr Chakravarty, before you begin, please understand there is no need to wrap things up. I require clear explanation. No jargon, no concealing technicalities and certainly no euphemism.'

A blink.

'Fine,' he said. 'Then I am sorry to tell you that you have a brain tumour. This is the cause of your recent headaches and of the convulsive episode you suffered at New Year.'

He went on talking, smoothly, eloquently. She registered the drift – that he was advising immediate hospitalization and the commencement of a vigorous combination of radiotherapy and chemotherapy – and she got the message – that the tumour was inoperable and treatment likely to be merely palliative. But she wasn't really listening. Out on the Little Bruton road she had longed for a return of that sense of timelessness, and now she had it. She felt as if she could stand up and take her clothes off and dance on the consultant's desk then get dressed and resume her seat, and all the time he would go on talking, unaware that she had escaped from the dimension that he was trapped in. Or perhaps, being a wise and experienced doctor who had spent too much of his life looking into the human brain and the human psyche to be easily deceived, he knew very well that she had left him and was elsewhere and elsewhen, and was merely talking on and on to fill the time until she, as she must do, rejoined him in the cage.

One thing she knew now for certain. She had to re-enter at the same point as she went out. There was no escape to the past.

She sighed and stepped back into the middle of one of his well-balanced sentences.

'How long will I live without treatment?'

A blink. Not an indicator this time of an increase in his fee, she gauged, but perhaps a mental bookmark to remind his secretary to make sure Ms Pomona's bill was placed in her hands immediately.

'At best months, but it could be much less. Tumours of this kind are very fast-growing and . . .'

'With treatment, how long?'

He looked at her, looked down, took a breath as if in preparation for a long speech, looked into her unblinking eyes again, and said, 'Longer.'

'Much longer?'

'Who knows?' he said. He sounded unhappy. Was it because of her future or his ignorance? 'Long enough to . . . do things.'

'Like what?'

'Like prepare yourself for . . . I mean, it might not happen . . . so quickly, I mean . . . and there are things, practical and personal . . . nowadays there's a whole raft of strategies . . . it's possible to be ready . . .'

386

Strange how her insistence on directness should in the end drive him to hesitant obliquities.

'Ready for death?'

He nodded.

'Death?' she repeated determined to make him say it.

'Death,' he said.

'OK. You haven't said anything about my old injury.'

He looked bewildered, then relieved. He was being offered an escape route from her short future into her slightly longer past.

He said, 'Well, I thought about it, of course, in terms of the whole range of symptoms you described. Indeed, I had a chat with a colleague of mine who specializes in neuropsychology and has produced a couple of highly regarded papers on various categories of psychiatric disorder which can occur as a long-term result of brain injury. Not that I was thinking of you in terms of serious psychiatric disorder, of course, but merely exploring the possibility that some of your physical symptoms might be explicable in terms of some minor affective disorder . . .'

He was getting away from her again behind those defences of verbiage and syntax which must have done such sterling service for him over the years.

Rye said, 'So what did he say, your colleague? Just the gist will do.'

'Of course, yes. Though you realize this is not at all relevant to your current condition.'

'The tumour that has been giving me headaches and made me have a fit and is eventually going to kill me, you mean? Yes, I realize that, and I understand that once you knew about the tumour you would naturally lose interest in my old head injury. But seeing as you did include it initially in your hypothesis . . . sorry, diagnosis . . . I might as well get full value for my money, mightn't I?'

'Well, there is a wide range of categories of psychiatric disorder which can occur after a brain injury such as you clearly experienced when you were fifteen. I mentioned affective disorders, which include conditions like mania and depression, plus obsessive compulsive and panic anxiety disorders. Associated with these may be arousal and motivational disorders. Psychotic disorders may also present, and there can be an associated inclination to violence and aggression, but none of this really has any relevance to your condition, Miss Pomona . . .'

'Bear with me. This is really fascinating stuff,' she said. 'I know how busy you are, but if I could just take up a little more of your time while I get myself together . . .'

It was a good tactic.

He smiled and said, 'Of course.'

'These psychotic disorders, what sort of thing's involved there?'

'In general terms, hallucinatory experiences, visual and/or auditory . . .'

'Seeing people who aren't there and hearing their voices, you mean?'

'Yes, that sort of thing. This can be associated with delusional belief, that is an apprehension of situations and relationships which is based on a false premise which resists all contra-evidence. Thought disorders linked to problems of language function or information processing . . .'

'Could not being able to remember my stage lines fit in here?'

He looked at her curiously and said, 'Yes, I suppose it could.'

'How fascinating,' she said. 'Just one thing more. My tumour . . .'

She found she quite liked the possessive. My flat. My books. In my opinion. My boyfriend.

My tumour.

'. . . is it in any way, could it be in any way, related to that old brain injury?'

He frowned as if feeling it was unfair of her to remind him she was going to die, then said, 'Actually, I don't have the faintest idea. Seems unlikely, but lots of things we now take for granted once seemed unlikely.'

She nodded as if to reassure him that this was the kind of frankness she wanted.

'But, like an accidental brain injury, is a tumour also likely to cause psychiatric disorders? Or have any effect on the way that the mind functions?'

'Well, certainly, but I really don't think you need to start worrying about that.'

'Because it is going to kill me too quickly for any behavioural changes to become significant, you mean?' she said solemnly.

He frowned again. She gave him a quick grin.

'Not all bad then!' she went on. 'But it could be having some effects on my behaviour and thought processes, right? In which case, it could be that some of these new effects might actually counterbalance or negate some of the old effects of my head injury, right?'

He shrugged helplessly. He looked almost vulnerable.

'Anything's possible,' he said, 'but honestly, I don't think there's much point in concerning ourselves with effects when what we need to do is –'

She stood up, saying, 'Thanks a lot, Mr Chakravarty. You've been really helpful.'

' – deal with causes,' he concluded, determined to get back to the consulted/consulting relationship. 'Miss Pomona, about your treatment . . .'

'No time for that,' she said crisply. 'Don't worry. I'll pay your bill by return of post.'

Then, feeling that he hadn't really deserved such a parting sting, she smiled and said, 'And I'm really grateful. Take care now.'

She went out to the car park. It was curious. She'd been condemned to death and yet what she felt was the kind of euphoria you experience as you leave the dentist's!

It was five thirty. She didn't want to go home yet. She wasn't ready for Myra's sympathetic questioning and even less ready for the possibility of finding Hat sitting on her doorstep. She turned on the car radio and listened to some Country and Western for a while. Its unsophisticated emotionalism seemed just about right. At six o'clock she drove to the Centre. Most of her colleagues would be homeward bound by now and, in any case, as far as they were concerned, she'd spent the day shopping.

She made her way to the Centre theatre. Its director had been one of the Wordman's victims. No, one of my victims, she corrected herself. She didn't know if she could bring herself to confess her sins but at least she could confront them. One of the core members of the company, a young woman called Lynn Crediton, had been appointed as stand-in director and, if the current holiday production of *Aladdin* was anything to go by, the Council might do worse than to make the appointment permanent.

In the little theatre there was the usual bustle as they got ready for the evening performance in just over an hour. Rye spotted Lynn in the aisle, checking some lighting adjustments. She waited till she'd finished shouting her instructions, then went up to her.

They'd met a couple of times before, and Rye's association with the Wordman case underlined the encounters.

'Hi,' said Lynn. 'You an early punter, or do you fancy being the back legs of a camel?'

'Both, maybe,' said Rye. 'Look, it probably sounds daft, but I used to do a bit of acting and I wondered if I could try out a few lines?'

'You want to audition?' The woman regarded her doubtfully, then said, 'Sure, why not? Can you come along say tomorrow morning, about ten?'

'Well actually, I wondered if I could just go on stage now and do a bit? Just thirty seconds, honestly. I can see you're really busy, but it's just that I feel really up for it. No one has to stop doing anything, then I'll be out of your hair.'

Lynn shrugged.

'OK, help yourself. But I can't promise I'll be able to listen, even for thirty seconds!'

Rye smiled her thanks and stepped on to the low stage.

She stood there for a moment looking out into the theatre. They came back to her, those days before . . . before Serge died, this is what it had been like, standing in the light, looking into the dark.

Now here she was again.

Standing in the light, looking into the dark.

She cleared her throat, then opened her mouth with no idea what, if anything, was going to come out.

She heard herself begin to sing.

Come away, come away death,
And in sad cypress let me be laid.
Fly away, fly away breath,
I am slain by a fair cruel maid.
My shroud of white, stuck all with yew,
O prepare it.
My part of death no one so true
Did share it.

When she started the theatre was full of noise and her soft voice was like the song of a lark above a cattle mart. But by the time she finished, every other sound had stopped, and all eyes were fixed on this slim young woman stock-still at the front of the stage.

Not a flower, not a flower sweet
On my black coffin let there be strewn.
Not a friend, not a friend greet
My poor corpse, where my bones shall be thrown.
A thousand thousand sighs to save
Lay me O where
Sad true lover never find my grave,
To weep there.

She finished. There was silence.

Then Lynn Crediton began to applaud and soon everyone else joined in. Flushing, Rye clambered down off the stage.

'That was great,' said Lynn. 'Maybe not quite the mood for *Aladdin*, but you got pretty close to the day!'

'What? Oh, Twelfth Night, you mean. Don't know why I chose that. It was just something we did at school.'

'And you played Feste?'

'No. I loved the play so much I think I had the whole thing by heart. I played Viola, who found her lost brother. Maybe I should have played Olivia who knew how to mourn hers.'

'Lots of time for that. Like I said, can you come tomorrow morning . . . are you OK?'

She was looking with concern into Rye's eyes, which were brimful of tears.

'Yes, yes, never better … happy and sad … lost and found … I'm sorry, I've got to go.'

She hurried away towards the exit. Lynn called after her, 'You'll come in the morning then for a proper audition?'

Over her shoulder Rye cried, 'No. Sorry. No more auditions, no more acting. Sorry.'

And ran through the exit door, leaving the director uncertain whether she had just played a small role in a comedy, a tragedy, or simply a pantomime.

n Tuesday morning Pascoe, after several unsuccessful attempts to hack into the Central Police Computer in search of information about Sergeant Thomas Roote, disgraced, deceased, did what any sensible man did when matters of high technology were concerned, he went to see Edgar Wield.

Usually when faced with such special requests, the sergeant's mosaic features underwent a small rearrangement which experienced Wield-watchers took to indicate a certain degree of pleasure at being given another opportunity to go places that neither Dalziel's strength nor Pascoe's subtlety could reach. Today, however, as soon as Pascoe said, 'Can you do me a favour, Wieldy?', he rolled his eyes and ground his teeth and looked unambiguously pissed off.

'Something bothering you?' asked Pascoe.

'Just get the impression sometimes that no bugger round here thinks I've got owt better to do than hack into places I shouldn't be,' he replied.

'Himself, you mean? As well as myself, of course.'

'Aye, he's on my back to dig up all I can about some guy called Tristram Lilley, but without letting anyone know we're taking an interest. I ask him why he's after this guy and he just growls like a bear that's swallowed a hornets' nest! So it's me fishing blind again, and if I wake some sodding great shark, it's only me that'll get bitten!'

'Come on, Wieldy, you can't say that. You know full well we'd come and visit you in the prison hospital,' said Pascoe. 'So what have you found out about this Lilley?'

'That if you want your computer hacked, your phone tapped,

393

your bank account audited and your intimate moments on video, he makes me look like an amateur.'

'Interesting. But Andy often plays his cards pretty close to his chest till he's ready to thump his Royal Flush on to the table. So why does this one get up your nose so much?'

Wield looked at him speculatively then said, 'I'm getting as secretive as he is. There's more. He's got me checking on a German called Mai Richter a.k.a. Myra Rogers.'

'That rings a faint bell.'

'It should. Myra Rogers lives next door to Rye Pomona and from what Hat's said they've become good mates. He told me not to bother with her official check sheet, so presumably he's got that already. What he wants is how she came into the country, when she changed from Mai to Myra. Well, I took a look at her sheet anyway. She's a journalist, Pete. A ferret. Got some big stories to her credit on the Continent. So what's she doing here, cosying up to the girlfriend of one of my lads, that's what I want to know. That's what I think I'm entitled to know!'

'Me too,' said Pascoe feelingly. 'And I'm going to find out.'

He turned for the door.

Wield said, 'Pete, what was it you came to see me about?'

'Hardly dare mention it,' said Pascoe. 'At least it's no secret. Roote. And before you start lecturing me, it's not Franny, it's his father and it's something Ellie found out.'

He explained.

'Now that is interesting,' said Wield. 'I'll get on to it. For Ellie's sake, you understand. I still reckon the less you have to do with that fellow the better.'

'Me too,' said Pascoe. 'But we all have our albatrosses. You seen Lubanski yet?'

It was a low shot but it hit. Wield, slightly hungover, had attended a conference with Dalziel and Pascoe on Sunday to discuss the implications of the confirmation that Linford, or LB, was backing whatever job Mate Polchard was planning. The Fat Man's reaction to the death of Liam and the others had been, as Wield had anticipated, good riddance. He'd been more interested in the possible effect of the tragedy on the relationship between Belchamber and Linford. 'He'll be looking for some bugger to blame. He had Belchy in his sights already and he'll not be in the mood to take a new aim.'

'How can he blame Belchamber for getting his son out on bail, which is what he must have been screaming at him to do ever since the committal?' asked Pascoe.

'Fathers, sons, logic goes out the window, specially when they're dead,' said Dalziel. 'Wieldy, set up a meet with young Lochinvar, see if he's heard owt.'

'Yes. sir. Can be a bit hard to get hold of,' said Wield, who'd thought it wiser not to mention that he'd sung a karaoke duet with Lee a few minutes after hearing about Liam.

'Hard to get hold of? He's a rent boy, for fuck's sake!' said Dalziel.

All of which helped explain the sergeant's state of pissed-off-ness with the Fat Man.

Now he said to Pascoe, 'Haven't been able to contact him yet.'

'No?' said Pascoe. 'Wieldy, none of my business, but you're not letting yourself get too close to this lad?'

For a moment it looked like Wield might explode, then he took control and said, 'I'd like to help him, if that's what you mean, get him out of the life he's leading . . .'

'But he's not interested?'

'No, it's not that. In fact I think I could get him to make a change but only at the expense of letting him think there was something between us. Not sex, I can deal with that, you learn over the years, but some kind of commitment. I'm not sure exactly what he wants me to be, but I know I can't be it. It would be wrong of me to lead him on, only it can't be right to let him stay like he is if I can do owt about it . . .'

'You try to explain any of this to him?'

'What's the point? The more personal I let things get in the way I talk, the more he takes it as a signal he's making progress. So all I can do is fall back on being a cop, tell him not to waste my time till he's got something really solid to tell me. Now I wonder if that's not just inciting him to take unnecessary risks.'

He sounded so unhappy, Pascoe touched his shoulder and said, 'Come on, mate. What's to risk? If Belchamber catches him poking around, all he's going to do is kick him out, which is what you'd like! Don't think Fat Andy would be very happy, though.'

'That bugger's happiness isn't high up my priority list at the moment,' retorted Wield.

Pascoe went looking for Dalziel but discovered he'd gone out, no one knew where. He retired to his office, leaving the door slightly ajar to make sure he didn't miss the crash of those mighty footsteps, but the Fat Man still hadn't returned an hour later when the door swung open and Wield came in bearing a sheet of paper and a folder.

'Thomas Roote,' he said without preamble. 'Good old-fashioned copper from the sound of it. Started in the Met. Couple of commendations for bravery. CID, then got moved into the Drug Squad. It was a drug scare at Anthea Atherton's school in Surrey that got the two of them involved. Reason the Squad was called in, dad of one of Atherton's posh chums was a distributor in the Smoke and there was a strong suspicion she was keeping the family tradition going in the school. Nothing came of it except Roote got involved with Anthea. Question, would collaring the suspect dealer have meant laying hands on Anthea too? Answer, not proven. But you can be sure when the sergeant married the girl soon as she turned eighteen, there'd be a query set against his name.'

'So, not a good career move,' said Pascoe.

'No. He'd made sergeant early and looked like he was set to move smoothly up the ladder. But now he stuck. Could also have been that things were on the change way back then and the PR boys were getting control of the Force. Not the kind of approach Tommy Roote seems to have favoured. Complaints now instead of commendations. Beat up some guy who grabbed a hold of his son in the park. Lucky to get away with an admonishment . . . that mean something to you?'

'Might do,' admitted Pascoe reluctantly. 'So Sergeant Roote was living dangerously.'

'That's right. Reading between the lines, he was getting increasingly bolshie at work while at home his marriage was in a tail spin. He was also drinking heavily. Crisis point reached when he was so heavy handed on a big bust that another sergeant reported him. When Tommy heard about it, he went for the guy in the locker room. A DI stuck his nose in and asked what the hell was going on. Roote told him to mind his own fucking business and when he didn't Roote decked him. That was that. Rolled into his hearing drunk and bolshie and sent any chance of being retired early with his pension intact up in smoke. After that it was downhill all the way. Guy like him had plenty of enemies outside and, without the protection of his badge, he was easy meat. Ended up in an alley behind a pub, his ribs kicked in. Choked on his own vomit. Death by misadventure. It's all here.'

He dropped the sheet of paper face-down on the desk.

'Hell's bells. That's a terrible tale,' said Pascoe.

'Yeah. Explains a few things about Roote, maybe.'

'Like why he hates the police, you mean?'

'Like why he's so mixed up about his father, I meant. I think it's back.'

Along the corridor echoed the tread of mighty footsteps and a discordant whistling of something which to Wield's sensitive ears might have been 'Total Eclipse of the Heart'. A moment later Dalziel filled the doorway.

His two subordinates stared at him so unwelcomingly that he took a step backwards and said, 'Ee, I've not been met with looks like that since my dear wife left me. What have I done? Left my dirty socks in the bidet again?'

'More like dirty fingerprints on the polished table, sir,' said Pascoe, going straight on the attack. 'What's all this about Mai Richter? Or Myra Rogers? More to the point, what's it all got to do with Rye Pomona?'

Dalziel's response was to advance towards Wield and hold out one huge paw.

'Before the cock's crowed thrice, eh?' he said, shaking his head sadly. 'That for me?'

Silently Wield handed over the folder containing his findings on Richter and Lilley.

'It was me who asked Wieldy what he were up to,' said Pascoe.

'Oh aye? Ask him what he were up to at Tinks last weekend and he sings a song, does he?'

397

'I just think that anything to do with Rye Pomona and Bowler, I'm entitled to know.'

'And why's that then?'

'Because I was with you when we interfered with a crime scene and when we edited Pomona's statement,' said Pascoe baldly.

The Fat Man backheeled the door shut with a slam that had constables in the canteen three floors below bolting their scalding coffee and heading back out several minutes early.

'Nay, lad, you weren't with me,' he said fiercely. 'Except maybe in your dreams. And I'd keep quiet about them, even when you're letting it all hang out on yon Pozzo's couch.'

Jesus, thought Pascoe. Has he got me bugged?

Wield was staring out of the window at the cloudy sky with an intensity that suggested all his senses except for sight were disengaged.

Dalziel suddenly relaxed and smiled ruefully, shaking his great head.

'My torture!' he said, using a strange oath allegedly passed down from his Highland forebears. 'You're getting me as daft as yourselves. Mebbe I should have put you in the picture, but it didn't seem that important. All that's happened is I were told a foreign national might be living on our patch under an assumed name. You know what them sods at Immigration are like, so I thought it best to get ahead of the game and take it seriously.'

'Well, that's awfully conscientious of you, sir,' said Pascoe. 'Can't have anonymous foreigners getting up to their disgusting tricks in Mid-Yorkshire, can we? So tell me, Wieldy, what have you found out about this wolf in sheep's clothing?'

'Born 1962 in Kaub in the Rhine-Palatinate,' recited Wield in an old-fashioned schoolroom voice. 'Studied at Heidelberg, Paris and London. Freelance journalist, concentrating on political corruption stories at a national and local level with a special interest in environmental affairs. Convictions in Germany for breaches of the peace, obstruction, possession. No UK convictions. No warrants outstanding . . .'

'Yeah yeah,' said Dalziel, holding up the folder he'd taken from the sergeant. 'Got all that without wasting your precious time. Hope there's summat a bit more useful in here.'

'Can't say, as I don't know what you want to use it for,' said Wield.

Dalziel gave him a glower and Pascoe hastily interposed his own body, saying, 'Kaub. That's on the Rhine, I recall. Few miles south of the Lorelei.'

'Is it now?' said the Fat Man. 'You been there?'

'Yes. Did a Rhine tour a few years back. Lovely spot. Very romantic, in every sense.'

'One sense at a time is as much as I can manage,' said Dalziel. 'And seeing as we're in such a sharing mood, anything else I should know about?'

His gaze was focused on the sheet bearing the new info on Roote Senior, which, despite the fact that it was face-down on the desk at a distance of several feet, he looked to be reading like a billboard poster.

'No, sir,' said Pascoe firmly.

'And you, Wieldy. Owt more from Boy George?'

'No, sir.' Equally firmly.

'Grand. Then we can all get down to some work, can't we?' He left.

'Why is it that I feel like I've been told, "You scratch my back or I'll have the skin off yours"?' said Pascoe.

'Me too,' said Wield. 'It's like having a pet bear. A lot of the time it's all warm cuddles, then suddenly you realize the bugger's crushing you to death!'

ai Richter dreamt she was back in her home town of Kaub, standing in Metzgergasse, its lovely main street, looking towards the town tower, silhouetted against a ghastly sky. Higher still, a looming presence on even the sunniest days, was the bulk of Gutenfels with its restored ruins reminding those beneath where the real power in this land once lay.

But Mai Richter's gaze was fixed much lower. Before the tower a bonfire raged, its teeth of flame ripping through the ribs of pinewood which formed its frame to reveal the orange heart pulsing within. Figures danced around, cloaked and hooded, with just enough firelight stealing beneath the cowls to reveal pallid faces and staring eyes and mouths twisted in terrible pleasure. They were hurling books into the fire's maw, which received them greedily, devouring whole volumes in a second. She knew that these were her books, books she had written with sweat and tears and love and devotion, all the copies of all her books, every word she had ever written, reducing to ashes before her eyes, vanishing forever from libraries and bookshops and, worst of all, from her mind.

What use to think of books when she knew beyond doubt that when they'd burnt all her words, it would be her body they turned to next. Already she could feel the heat of the ravening flames, yet she had no power to flee or to resist. Somewhere close she could hear the pulse and the roar of the mighty Rhine but its cooling waters offered no relief.

And now its sound was changing, still as powerful and as pulsing as ever, but now something more, something else …

and suddenly she recognized the dark and terrible music of Siegfried's funeral with a shock of fear that woke her.

The dancing shadows of the bonfire were replaced by the still white walls of her bedroom and its searing heat by the sharp chill of an English January night.

But the music remained. Those shuddering glooms of sound which roll down the margins of mortality into the underworld still reverberated in her mind. And in her ears.

She sat up.

Still it was there.

Slowly she got out of bed, fumbled in her bedside drawer, found what she was looking for, and moved towards her bedroom door. Beneath it she could see a line of light, red and faintly flickering as if the bonfire she had dreamt about lay just beyond this portal.

Dauntless, she took the handle, turned it and pushed the door open.

From her tape deck the music boomed, while from her gas-fire the flickering orange flames cast just enough light to trace the outline of a monstrous figure whose bulk spilled over the edge of the old armchair in which it sat.

Her nerveless fingers sought but could not find the light switch.

'Who's there?' she demanded shrilly. 'Who is that? I warn you, I have arms.'

'Good job I'm 'armless then,' said the figure. 'It's all right lass, it's only me, the Ghost of Christmas Past. Come in and shut that door. There's a hell of a draught.'

And the figure leaned forward till she was able to recognize the unwelcome welcome face of Detective Superintendent Andrew Dalziel.

Dalziel relaxed in his chair and watched the woman as she busied herself round the room, turning the music off and the lights on. The round anonymity of her face, which must be so useful in her line of work, had somehow vanished. Perhaps it was the shock of sudden awaking to this strange invasion or the absence of make-up or the fact that her hair was no longer neat and carefully coiffed. Her round features now seemed sharp and well defined. She slept in nothing but a thin white T-shirt and it could be that the new awareness this gave him of her sexuality aided the defining process. He noted that, despite her delaying tactics, she made no attempt to get a dressing gown. Bright lass, he thought. Gets herself together, but reckons there might be some advantage in distracting me with her tits.

Finally she sat down opposite him, very demurely, pulling the T-shirt over her knees.

'So,' she said, 'Superintendent Dalziel, you have broken into my flat at one o'clock in the morning. You are drinking my whisky, which is theft, and as you've gone through my tapes, I presume you've performed an illegal search. Or is there something I have missed?'

'Nay, lass, that just about wraps it up. Nice whisky too. Was a bit worried you might have nowt but schnapps or some other Kraut firewater. Going to join me?'

She smiled and leaned forward to fill a glass and said, 'I'm really interested to know why a senior policeman should put his career at risk in such a way.'

'Aye, that's the tie-break question, isn't it? To tell you the truth, all I really came for was to find out why you are leaving.'

'Leaving?'

'Come on, luv. You don't imagine someone with your record can book plane seats without half the police forces in Europe knowing.'

This was a lie. In the three days since getting Wield's report, the Fat Man had certainly spent a lot of time planning his strategy with regard to Richter, but he'd had no idea of her plans to return to Germany until he'd found the plane ticket in her desk drawer. It was for tomorrow, it was one-way, and it was first class.

His conclusion had been that she felt her job here was either over or getting nowhere and he'd been tempted to steal away as silently as he'd come, but only for a second. It was, he'd discovered in the course of a life packed, both professionally and personally, with problems, a delusion that they ever went away.

And Charley Penn certainly wasn't going away.

She said, 'So you have also been illegally accessing computer databases?'

'Not sure what that means, but I dare say you're right. So let's get down to it, Fräulein Richter. Here's what I know about you and what I want from you. You're an old mate of Charley Penn's, on good shagging terms, from the look of things. You came here at his instigation to see what you could sniff out via Miss Pomona about the circumstances of Dick Dee's death. Now, what I'd like for you to do is tell me what you imagine you've found out, then we can all get into our beds. All right?'

She shook her head in not altogether affected amazement.

'Charley told me about you, Mr Dalziel, but I did not altogether believe him. Now I realize he got it wrong. He told me you were arrogant and ruthless, but he did not tell me you were also stupid. Do you really think you can break your English law and violate my rights in this way and get away with it? You say you've studied my background. You must know I've helped put more powerful and important men than you behind bars.'

'I'm sorry, luv,' said Dalziel, deliberately misunderstanding. 'My dad told me never to contradict a lady, but I've got to say that, when it comes to putting buggers behind bars, I reckon I can give thee half the Sudetenland start and still be in Prague afore ye. But why make such a pother? It's tit for tat, you help me, I'll help you, can't say fairer than that.'

'What could you help me with?' she asked mockingly. 'Are you going to fix a parking ticket, perhaps?'

'I can manage that too, but I were thinking more of keeping you out of jail,' said Dalziel, leaning forward to help himself to more whisky.

'Jail? For what?' she demanded.

'You got no laws in Germany then? Well, we've got enough to go round. First off, personation, forgery and deception. You took this flat telling the estate agent you were English and called Myra Rogers, and handing over a set of references to show what an upright British citizen you were. Want more? You've got a bagful of interesting-looking white powder in your fridge. And while you may have a licence back home for that natty little gun

403

you were waving just now, I can't find any trace of anything which makes it legal here. Want more? You've employed Mr Tristram Lilley to introduce illicit surveillance equipment into a private dwelling which involved illegal entry. Yes, I've had a word with him and, being a self-centred little scrote, he's talking so fast, his own equipment can't keep up. Want more? I haven't even started with the stuff I can heap on top of you yet.'

'These are empty threats, Superintendent,' she said calmly. 'I have been hounded by experts and threatened with physical violence, death even, and I am still here. I know lawyers who will get me out of your clutches without even leaving their offices.'

'I can believe it. They ought to geld one a day to encourage the others. Aye, the law's an ass, all right, but the good thing is it's a broken-winded and spavin'd ass. Now I'd guess that maybe one thing that's helped you decide to leave first class is someone back in Kraut-land has offered you a real job setting the world to rights.'

She was good at hiding, but he was better at seeking and saw he'd scored a hit.

He went on, 'I think I can guarantee you'll stay banged up long enough for your friends back home to find themselves another Mata Hari. And I'll make sure that you get such publicity all over Europe, you'll need to wear a beard next time you go undercover.'

She thought for a moment then she smiled at him.

'Perhaps you're right,' she said. 'Tell me what you want and I'll see if I can help you.'

Then she shivered and went on, 'It's so cold in these English flats, don't you think so? In Germany we know how to keep warm.'

As she spoke, she half turned to the gas fire and arched her body towards it as if in search of heat, hitching the T-shirt up as she did so.

Dalziel relaxed in his chair, nodded approvingly and raised his glass.

After a moment, Richter pulled her T-shirt back over her knees.

'Nice try, lass, but I've got one of my own at home that I'd like to get back to,' said Dalziel. 'Save it for Charley. Though I can't understand what you see in him myself. Thought you lot liked a bit more meat on your men.'

'Charley is a good man,' she said seriously. 'And not a stupid one. When he told me his story and asked for my help, I admit it did not seem like my kind of thing.'

'Which is political corruption on a big scale, right?'

'That sort of thing,' she smiled. 'This sounded, personal, petty. At best, if Charley had got it right, it was about some insignificant provincial bobbies covering their tracks. It might make a little stir in the English papers, but anything makes a stir here. But Charley is an old friend, and it suited me to rest quiet a few weeks away from home. So I came.'

'Saw, and conquered. You certainly seem to have conquered little Miss Rye,' said Dalziel. 'So what have you found out?'

She hesitated and he growled from deep in his chest, 'The truth, remember.'

She said, 'I am not thinking of a lie. No, it is the truth that I have to work out, for to tell the truth I don't know what I have found. Except that Rye is very disturbed, and distressed. Her boyfriend, the young policeman, he makes her very happy, but he is also the cause of much of her unhappiness too. All this I have found hard to understand. When I first spoke to her she was scattering the contents of a vacuum cleaner into the churchyard. I later found when we became friends that it was the ashes of her dead brother which had been spilt during that strange burglary she had.'

'Strange? How was it strange? It was Charley Penn, wasn't it?'

'No. Not so. Charley was here that morning because he spent the night with me. No danger, we knew Rye was away, just like you know she is away tonight, I presume, else you would not have played the music so loud.'

'Aye, she's round at young Bowler's,' said Dalziel. 'So what happened?'

'I don't know. We heard a crash, like something breaking. It seemed to come from next door, but we knew the flat was empty. Charley went out to listen at the door. That's when Mrs Gilpin saw him, so he didn't come back in to me but went home.'

'You sure it weren't you?' said Dalziel doubtingly. 'Some bugger left a message about Lorelei on her computer. Right up Charley's street, that, and not far from the bottom of your street back home, if my information is right.'

'You've been digging deep, Mr Dalziel,' she said. 'Yes, she told me about the message when we became friends. Very odd, especially because of the link with Charley. Another odd thing was the quiet.'

'Sorry?'

'She said her flat was a mess, things knocked over, drawers emptied. Yet apart from the one crash, I heard nothing. Also odd is the other bug.'

'Eh?'

'Did not Tris tell you when you spoke to him?' she said, giving him a sharp look which Dalziel received with apparent complacency. The truth was he'd never talked to Lilley. The man lived in London and it would have been difficult to roust him out without reference to the Met. He wanted to keep his interest in Lilley and Richter low profile. But from what he'd read and seen of the man, he got the impression that he'd be quick to do a deal to save his own skin, and Richter clearly found this easy to believe too.

So, this other bug Lilley was likely to have mentioned . . .

He said, 'Oh aye. That. He did say summat, but it's yours I'm interested in.'

She let out a burst of triumphant laughter.

'Because the other bug is your own, right? And, let me guess, it has not been working properly? Perhaps Tris did something to it when he found it.'

She'd noted his hesitation, but jumped to the wrong conclusion. That's the trouble if you spend your life looking for conspiracies, you start seeing them everywhere!

'Always said you can't trust this modern technology,' he said, trying to sound sheepish but not too much.

'Tris says so too. One bug is never enough. You must ask for a bigger budget.'

'Oh, I shall. But let's concentrate on what you've got, shall we? Bugs are all right, but there's nowt like a close friend for getting to the heart of things.'

She didn't blush but she looked distinctly unhappy. Could journalists feel guilt? Why not? They were only human. In some cases, only just human. But Richter's motivations in the past seemed to have more to do with moral principle than personal profit. And now, if she thought the police had planted this other bug, she could be seeing him as a fellow investigator rather than an object of investigation.

He said, 'I know it's hard when you like someone. I like Rye, too. And I like my lad Bowler. And I want to do what's best for both of them. But I can't do that without I know what's going on, can I?'

He sounded so serious and sincere, he could have sold himself insurance.

She nodded and said, 'OK. I think Rye is troubled because perhaps she knows more than she has said about this Wordman. It is very personal to her. She talks sometimes when she has drunk a lot of wine as if he had something to do with her brother, which cannot be as he died when she was only fifteen. But these things have got mixed up in her mind. She blames herself for the death of her brother, I think, and perhaps somehow she blames herself for the death of this Dick Dee also. She liked him very much, that is clear. And if once you get it in your head that being close to you is what has killed people you love, then you are on the way to breakdown.'

'But why should she blame herself for Dee's death?'

'Perhaps because she'd begun to suspect he was the Wordman but wouldn't let herself believe it. Perhaps she engineered a situation in which he would have to reveal the truth and it all went wrong. And because the truth was never revealed clearly and unambiguously, his death troubles her. What if he were innocent?'

'She's said that, has she?' asked Dalziel. 'She thinks Dee were innocent?'

'She said to me one night, "What if the Wordman wasn't dead, Myra? What if he was still out there, checking out his next victim? What if he's just waiting till everyone's guard is down, then it's all going to start again?' I asked her if she had any reason for thinking this. All I wanted to do was comfort her, but I owed it to Charley to ask.'

'And her answer?'

'She fell asleep in my arms, so I put her to bed,' said Richter tenderly.

'Didn't jump in beside her?' enquired Dalziel casually. Women could do whatever they wanted in his book, so long as they didn't do it in the street and frighten the plods. Or unless one of them was as good as engaged to one of his DCs.

She grinned at him, looking wickedly sexy, and said, 'No, I am aggressively hetero, Mr Dalziel. But you're going to have to take my word for that.'

'Missed the bus, eh? Story of my life. But I never like to climb aboard unless I'm sure I can afford the ride. On you go with your tale.'

'There is not much more to tell,' she said. 'On the tapes I have of her alone, sometimes there is sobbing. Sometimes there is the sound of her pacing around in the night. And sometimes she talks aloud, to her dead brother, often very angrily, as if she blames him for her unhappiness. Also to Hat, full of love, and regret, and apology. More like someone taking leave than someone talking to the person she wants to spend the rest of her life with. But this was before . . .'

'Before what?'

She emptied her whisky glass, filled it up again, emptied it again.

'I do not know if I have the right to tell you this, and I do not think I could tell you this if I was going to stay and be her friend as she believes I am. And I believe it too, or believe it could be so, which is why I am leaving and why I will never see her again, and also why I am able to break the word I have given.'

'Slow down, luv,' said Dalziel. 'That Scotch is turning you German. Breaking confidence is like taking off a sticky plaster. There's only one way, short and sharp.'

She nodded, took a long slow breath, then said, 'On Monday she went to the hospital for tests. She has a brain tumour. She is going to die.'

'Well fuck me rigid and sell me to the Tate!' exclaimed Dalziel, who had let his mind rehearse half a dozen possible revelations without getting close. 'Can't they do owt?'

'She does not want anything done,' said Richter.

'Shit. Someone's got to talk to her,' said the Fat Man agitatedly. 'These days they can cure owt save foot and mouth and politicians. Does Bowler know?'

'No one knows. Except me. Now you. So now it is your responsibility not mine to decide what to do. This is why I am glad to go. My job, which was never a job I should have undertaken, is done. Now I can go to a real job.'

'Run away, you mean, and leave the poor lass to suffer all this alone, after you've weaselled your way into her confidence? Jesus! What they say about you bastards doesn't tell the half of it!'

His contempt left her unmoved.

She said, 'You mistake, Superintendent. If she was as unhappy as I would be in her situation, then I doubt if I could have decided so easily to go. No, the thing that makes me go is that the news has not made her miserable, it has made her happy! She acts as if she had gone along to the hospital anticipating confirmation that she had cancer and instead been told that she was free! I can offer comfort to despair. I cannot try to bring despair to joy. Now I think I have said all that I want to say to you, Superintendent. *Aufwiedersehen*, but not too soon, eh?'

Dalziel finished his drink and said, 'Just one thing afore I go. If you'd not mind taking off that nightie or whatever you call it . . .'

She looked at him, puzzled, then smiled, stood up and pulled the T-shirt over her head.

'Turn around,' he said.

She obeyed.

'Right,' he said. 'You can put it back on.'

'For a moment I thought you'd changed your mind,' she said, parodying a disappointed pout.

'Nay, don't take it personal, lass,' he said, rising. 'Just making sure there was nowt but flesh to see. And very nice flesh it was.'

She smiled at him as he went to the bureau, picked up her gun, examined it, put the safety catch on, then slipped it into his pocket.

'You couldn't take it out of the country,' he said. 'Not legally, anyway. So best I take care of it.'

'I am being permitted to leave then, am I?'

'Can't see why not. One thing more, but. Just in case you're hoping this tape you switched to record when you came in might have summat on it that would embarrass me, don't be too disappointed when you find I disconnected the recording switch. Just as well, eh, else you'd have ruined old Wagner.'

He reset the deck and once again the doom-filled music rolled around the room.

'What would I have used it for anyway?' she said indifferently. 'Tell me, Mr Dalziel, why did you choose this music?'

'Don't know. Why do you ask?'

'There are some who say that it contains all that is best and worst in the German psyche,' she said. 'I thought perhaps it was some kind of statement, a bit racist, even.'

'Racist? Me?' he said indignantly. 'Nay, lass, I just dearly love a catchy tune, even if it were written by a dead Kraut. You'll be seeing Charley afore you go?'

'Yes.'

'What will you tell him?'

'As much as he needs to know,' she said.

'A man can't ask more than that from his woman,' said Andy Dalziel.

A few miles away, close entwined by choice and by necessity in the narrow single bed, Rye and Hat lay in the dark.

'You awake?' said Hat.

'Yes.'

'Not worried about anything, are you?'

'What should I worry about when I've got everything I want? Do I look worried?'

'Well, no . . .'

In fact during the past few days she had seemed to exude happiness. It was true that sometimes when he glimpsed her without her knowledge, he thought she looked paler and the shadows beneath her eyes looked darker. But the moment she

410

became aware of his presence, she glowed with a joy that made such thoughts seem a blasphemy.

He ran his hands down her body and said, 'Not losing a bit of weight, are you?'

'Perhaps. After Christmas I like to start the New Year with a diet to get rid of all those chocs. But I've noticed that cops seem to prefer their women with a bit of weight.'

'Not me,' said Hat fervently. 'But I don't want to feel I'm going to bed with a xylophone – ouch!'

She had rammed a finger up his backside till it hurt.

'My body's my business,' she said. 'You'll just have to learn to play the xylophone. And if you keep on living off junk food, I'll just have to learn to play the bagpipes.'

'We'd better get a house in the country or else the neighbours'll be complaining every time we make love. Talking of which . . .'

'So soon? Are you taking something?'

'No, I meant talking of a house in the country . . . when are we going to move in together? I mean permanently, not turn about, your place and mine. In fact, I mean really permanently. How do you feel about getting married?'

She didn't reply and after a while he said, 'You thinking about it, or just thinking how to say no?'

'I'm thinking about it,' she said. 'Best advice seems to be it's not such a good idea marrying a policeman.'

'You've been taking advice?' he said, faking large indignation to conceal small hurt.

'Of course not, but I read a lot of books, and wherever there's a cop there's usually a marriage in trouble.'

'Books! What do these writers know? They should get out more instead of spending all their time at home inventing stuff.'

'But it's true,' she said. 'It's a demanding job. And it's dangerous.'

She pushed herself away from him as far as she could, which wasn't far without falling to the floor, and said, 'That's one thing that does worry me, Hat. Your job is dangerous, and it's getting more so. I just don't know what I'd do if anything happened to you.'

'Don't be daft,' he said. 'Chances of anything like that must be ... I don't know what, but they've got to be longer than winning the lottery.'

'It almost happened, remember?' she said. 'I came close to losing you.'

'OK, but lightning doesn't strike twice, so that makes it even less likely it could happen again.'

'I wish I could believe that. All I know is, if anything did happen that would be the end for me. Of everything, I mean. My life would be over too. There'd be no point in going on.'

'No, you mustn't say that,' he urged fiercely. 'Look, nothing's going to happen ...'

'But if it did?'

'Then you'd have to bear it, I suppose ...'

'No way.'

'Yes, you could. You're strong, Rye. Stronger than me. I think you could come through anything if you put your mind to it.'

'I wouldn't want to put my mind to it.'

'You'd have to. Promise me!'

'What? That I'd throw roses on your grave then head down to the singles club?'

'No, don't be silly. That you'd give life a chance.'

'That sounds like something off a calendar!'

'I'm sorry I don't have some Fancy Dan way of putting it. It's just that I think these days everyone seems so concerned with getting ready for death. It's all about hospices and such things. Well, death's not that much of a problem, it seems to me, and if it is, it soon gets solved. Living's the hard thing to get right. Living's the important thing.'

He fell silent. She put her hand on his face and traced his eyes and his mouth in the darkness.

'That's a good calendar you've got,' she said. 'OK, I'll promise. Only you've got to promise too.'

'Eh?'

'Fair's fair. If anything should ever happen to me, you've got to promise that you'll practise what you've just been preaching, that you won't confuse grief with despair, that you'll mourn but not forever, that you will never forget me, but you'll never forget this promise that you made to me either. That you understand I won't be at rest till you are happy again. Can you promise that? If you can't, I won't.'

He put his hand up to take hers.

'I promise,' he said.

'OK, then so do I.'

He drew her to him. Her softness, her scent, her warmth enveloped him like the air of lost Eden, but he frowned into the dark as he tried to analyse a strange feeling that something had happened which he didn't understand.

Rye lay with her head pressed against his chest and her lips were smiling.

The UNIVERSITY of SANTA APPOLLONIA Ca.

Guest Suite No 1
Faculty of Arts

Wed Jan 16th

Dear Mr Pascoe

What a week this has been! What a rare mood I'm in!
You cannot believe how much I'm enjoying America. It's
been like stepping into a movie and finding I was a star!
Have you been here? I'm sure you have – a cultured,
well-rounded man like yourself will not have been content
to take the rest of the world on report. You will have
travelled everywhere, observed, sampled, judged. My
exuberance probably strikes you as ingenuous, perhaps
naive, even jejune. But remember, this brave new world is
indeed new to me. All my acquaintance with it hitherto
has been through the cinema, so no wonder I saw and felt
it as a movie set!

Of course my good impression of this bright sunlit
world was helped by the contrast with what I had left
behind. Frankfurt was wet and windy, Göttingen locked in
ice and snow. Anyone wanting to understand the Gothic
glooms of the German character should spend a winter
there! Not that I suffered any particular discomfort, being
able to afford, at Linda's insistence, decent lodgings. But I
made no noticeable advance in my researches in either
place. I did track down some people called Degen in
Frankfurt who may or may not be of the same family as
young Konrad, the baker whom Beddoes lived and
travelled with and attempted to turn into a Shakespearean
actor. But they had no papers or artefacts that could be

linked to their distant relative and I got the impression
that their few alleged family memories of the man were in
fact gleanings from various predecessors (including Sam
himself) who had come here on Beddoes' trail. (Though
there was a young blond Degen who fluttered his silky
eyelashes at me ... ah, the things we biographers do in
search of empathy with our subjects!)

As for Göttingen, it's a pretty enough little town,
much of which has survived intact since Beddoes' day. My
hopes soared, but, apart from viewing his name in the
university records, I could find nothing to add to what his
own letters tell us of his life there. Sam wrote one of his
'Imagined Scenes' in which Beddoes and Heine, both
students at the university and sharing an interest in poetry
and radical politics, met and quarrelled, but the dates
don't really fit and eventually Sam scored through it on
the grounds that even imagination's wings need at least
one feather of fact to achieve lift-off.

So all in all, what with the foul weather, the lack of
progress, the weighty *echt Deutchheit* of everything, I grew
daily duller and more stupefied, and time seemed to crawl
by as if I'd been put into an uncomfortable seat between
two fat men with BO at the start of one of Wagner's
longer operas sung by an amateur music society and
accompanied by a school band, and told there weren't
going to be any intervals.

At this juncture I thought how wise you had been, dear
Mr Pascoe, to eschew the life academic in favour of the life
detective. The mean streets your work takes you down
seemed as nothing compared to the gloomy avenues I found
myself lost in. No wonder that poor Beddoes with his death
fixation opted to spend most of his adult life here. Even now
in this age of universal light when it's possible in England or
America for a child to grow up in a big city without ever
having noticed a star, shades and miasmas and Gothic
glooms are available on tap out here. What it must have
been like in the early eighteen hundreds pains the
imagination! Beddoes sought enlightenment through

medicine, that most socially beneficial of sciences, and through support of radical egalitarian movements, but each of these avenues led him back to the same conclusion, that man was a botched creation whose proper domain was darkness and whose only salvation was death.

The longer I stayed there, the closer I could feel myself coming to agreeing with him!

Happily at this juncture the US Embassy in London, with whom I had been in close correspondence since talking to Dwight, now summoned me for interview, so I took my congé with considerable relief!

Not that things improved in England. The weather was foul and the Embassy officials treated me like their Public Enemy No.1, bent on bringing down the Republic. The only good thing was I once again found Frère Jacques in residence at Linda's Westminster pad, and this time, having become such chums, neither of us objected to me bedding down on the couch for a couple of nights. It turned out he was heading north on his promotional tour and, as I wanted to touch base back in Mid-Yorkshire before heading off into the west, he offered me a lift in his hired car as far as Sheffield.

It was an interesting trip. I got the feeling that something has changed for him. Perhaps Frère Dierick's death has something to do with it. I'm sure the man and the monk in Jacques must always have been in delicate balance, and with the removal of that death's head reminder of his commitment to the life celibate, the man is very much in the ascendancy. He talked of Emerald, and I have a strong suspicion that in the very near future he might be contemplating the huge step of changing his vows monastic for vows marital! (I must confess, shame-faced, that I also for a moment entertained a very faint suspicion that perhaps Jacques knew more about the circumstances of Dierick's death than he should do . . . But I soon thrust this aside. Ungrounded suspicions are a mental cancer. We should trust our friends absolutely, don't you agree, Mr Pascoe?)

What Linda will make of it, I don't know. We shall see.

My stay in M-Y was brief, all too brief, alas, for me to make contact with you. How good it would have been to see you face to face and get direct assurance of the rapport I am psychically convinced my letters are building between us. But I had news of you from one or two common acquaintance, and it was generally good, though dear old Charley Penn, who'd glimpsed you in town, thought you were looking just a little bit peaky. Do take care of yourself, my friend. I know your job necessarily involves irregular hours and takes you out in all weathers, but you're not getting any younger and you mustn't let the indestructible Dalziel overstretch you.

Back to my Great Adventure. At last I left these clouded hills behind and, after an interminable passage through fog and filthy air followed by an even longer passage through the morass of US Immigration, I was greeted by a young god and goddess wearing baseball caps and beaming smiles (literally beaming; dear old Apollonia clearly knows how to honour her devotees!) and waving a banner bearing my name. They turned out to be Dwight's teenage twins, whom he'd sent to meet me, and all my troubles seemed to drop away as they led me, blinking, out into the bright sunshine, and drove me to their lovely home which stands on stilts rising out of a beach of golden sand running down to the deep deep blue of the Pacific ocean. Stout Cortez, I get the message, man!

I spent the first couple of days relaxing and acclimatizing in the bosom of Dwight's family – not literally; this was strictly hands-off territory, though the kids' fondness for skinny-dipping with their friends kept temptation before my eyes. Happily, despite a pleasant air temperature when the sun shines, the ocean is still pretty cold at this time of year and that kept my interest from becoming embarrassing, though maybe Dwight's sharp eye detected something, for once I'd got over my jet lag and was ready to strut my stuff before his publishing friends, he suggested that, now that term was beginning (bit of an earlier start out here than you were probably used to at Oxford – or was it Cambridge? I can't recall), it might be more convenient if I had a room on campus. Nice to think even a modern West Coast liberal academic dad keeps an eye on his kids' virtue.

Being on campus is great, especially as I'm occupying one of the faculty guest suites – not quite as impressive historically as the Quaestor's Lodging at God's, but a lot more user-friendly – and I've been introduced around as a distinguished academic visitor. Dwight got me to sit in on a couple of his classes, then persuaded me to do a seminar on Beddoes' poetry with a specially selected group of students and a few faculty members. It went really well and the students seemed to take to Beddoes in a big way and soon I was getting invitations to talk to all kinds of groups. Dwight was delighted, so long as they didn't get in the way of his own programme, whose purpose I quickly gathered was to do such a good PR job on me that when I finally made my pitch to the top men at the St Poll University Press. I would make my entrance on a wave of golden opinion.

I went along with this, did the parties, pressed the flesh, talked the talk and walked the walk, but I really got a lot more enjoyment out of being with the students. How reluctantly do we all admit that we are taking leave of our youth! With what slow steps and fondly lingering backward glances do we move onward! When at last you begin to understand the truth of Byron's lines 'There's not a joy the world can give / Like that it takes away' then you know you've started the long goodbye. Being with these kids reminded me of the way I felt in those few days at Fichtenburg when I skated and tobogganed and drank sweet coffee and ate cream cakes with Zazie, Hildi and Mouse, pleasure without responsibility, time without definition, world without end. Perhaps the cruel suddenness with which my own student days hit the rocks (yes, yes, my own fault, no resentment, no reproach!)

makes me all the more desperate to clutch at these straws floating round the wreckage. Did you ever feel like this Mr Pascoe? You will be well past such immaturities, I know, but was there ever a time, even after your marriage perhaps, with your lovely daughter still little more than a voice and an appetite in swaddling clothes, when you felt a yearning to be as you had been age eighteen, nineteen, twenty, when nothing you had now seemed worth the loss of those boundless horizons, that unfathomable joy? Or even later, when your little girl lay desperately ill, or when your beloved wife was under threat, did it ever flash across your mind that if you had known it was going to be like this, you'd never have given such hostages to fortune?

Probably not. You're not like me, weak and worldly, though I like to think that in some ways we are very close. And will be closer, I hope and pray.

Anyway, like I said, I met with young people and in their company I felt young again. It is, I think, a canard that American students age for age know less than European students; but it's certainly true that they are much more eager to know more! They lapped up what I told them about Beddoes, and when (because it was easy to move from his obsession with death to my chosen way of dealing with it) I went on to tell them about Third Thought, they lapped that up too. They know nothing of the movement here, it seems, and Frère Jacques' book has not yet found a publisher in the States. I suspect that America in general and California in particular is so awash with home-grown mystic, metaphysical, quasi-religious trends and sects and disciplines that they don't feel much need to import them! But this one really appealed, perhaps because I was able to present it in truly American terms such as, How to live with death and be happy ever after! Soon we were having regular meetings which always began (my idea!) with a chorus of 'Happy We!' from *Acis and Galatea*. (The lyric is, of course, amatory, but this only underlines the relationship with death that Third Thought aims at. And if my suspicions about Jacques are right, how

apt!) Then I'd read a passage from my copy of Jacques'
book, and soon photocopied extracts were being passed
around like *samizdat* literature in the Soviet Union. It
made me realize that, do what we will with technology,
there is no substitute for direct human contact. Soon the
word spread around the campus, aided by the new
in-greeting between initiates – *Have a nice death!* (One of
mine too. Though I confess it owes not a little to
Beddoes' jest of leaving champagne 'to drink his death in'.)

A spin-off of this was, by the time I was finally
summoned to make my pitch to the Uni Press people,
rumours of Third Thought had reached their ears too and
they seemed as interested in Jacques' book as they were in
mine (or rather Sam's, though the way Dwight had sold it,
my part loomed disproportionately large, because, as
Dwight put it when I made some mild protest, 'You're
hot, breathing, and here!')

Anyway, they were very interested in both books, and
by the time we'd finished talking, they'd made an offer on
Beddoes and wanted to get in touch with Jacques. I got
straight on the phone to Linda, who was delighted, and
she got Jacques to ring me, and the upshot is I have been
given full authority to act as I see best on both their
behalves.

So there it is. Triumph. I came, saw, overcame. But I
don't feel I can take any credit. Recently I seem to be on a
roll. Question is, who's loading the dice? Initially I
approached Third Thought in a pretty sceptical frame of
mind. It was interesting, but no more interesting than a
whole lot of weird metaphysical stuff I'd been into in my
teens, with the disincentive it didn't throw in sex or drugs
as part of the deal! Linda's involvement gave me a reason
for sticking with it, but the more I've had to do with Frère
Jacques, the more I've come to believe that there really
might be something here for me.

I'm not certain where you stand on religion, Mr
Pascoe. Somehow I can't see your good lady . . . but there
I go, making assumptions. Bad habit. It really would be

great to talk to you about this, and so many other matters, face to face some time. In the past our meetings have always had – how shall I put it? – a legal agenda. But over the past few weeks as I've been writing to you, I've had such a strong sense of us coming together that I have to believe, or at least very much hope, that you have felt this too.

So perhaps when I get back to Mid-Yorkshire we can meet and by the fire help waste a sullen day, or something? Please.

By the way, Dwight has told me to make full use of the mail services open to senior faculty members, so I'll send this off Express Delivery, otherwise I could get home first!

See you soon!

Yours ever

Franny

P.S. I really do like St Poll. Much more my kind of place than plashy old Cambridge! I've taken the chance whenever possible of drifting off by myself and strolling the streets – yes, it's that rarity in American towns, a place where you can actually walk for miles without exacting the interest of the local constabulary! So much to see. It's got big modern shopping malls, of course, but away from these, lots of small, very individual outlets survive, delis with delicious food, antique shops where you can still unearth a bargain, and bookshops ranging from the uni store where you can enjoy a coffee and a bagel as you read, to lovely atmospheric second-hand and antiquarian dealers.

By one of those coincidences which make life such fun, I was peering in the window of one of these when it dawned on me the name was familiar. I searched my memory and drifted back to that evening at God's when

Dwight assured poor Dean Albacore that he knew a book dealer in St Poll who could put a price on anything, even something as priceless as a copy of Reginald of Durham's *Vita S. Godrici*. His name was Fachmann. Trick Fachmann. And that was the name I was looking at!

On a whim I went inside and introduced myself.

What a fascinating man he is. Transparently thin with piercing bright eyes, he comes across as so erudite, so scholarly, and at the same time so worldly wise. Only in America do I think you could find such a combination. I know the UK academia is full of would-be Machiavels – Albacore was such a one – but Mr Fachmann could at the same time have been a medieval ascetic and the modern *consigliore* to some great Mafia godfather.

I told him how come I'd heard his name, and I made enquiry, just to amuse myself, whether he could justify Dwight's boast and put a price on an original copy of Reg of Durham's *Vita S. Godrici*. Without hesitation he said, 'No problem.' I said, 'So what might it be?' He said, 'That depends whether I'm selling or buying.' I laughed, but he said, 'I'm not joking. There's a market for everything. There's two kinds of possession. The common one is the conspicuous. When you've got it, baby, flaunt it! The other is private, when you both possess and are possessed by an object. You don't need the world to know as long as you know you've got it.'

I said, 'And you know the market?' to which he replied with a smile, 'Know *of* it. To use it would of course be illegal. It's like any other market, full of bustle and stallholders shouting their wares. That amuses you? Listen, any movement of antiquities of any kind anywhere and ears prick. It's like the stock exchange. Movement means availability. I know antique dealers round here who get a dozen enquiries every time the Getty down at Malibu makes a purchase. There's some big deal just gone down for some Brit collection. Once it's in the Getty, forget it. But to get here it's got to be on the move, so the market stirs.'

I presume he meant the Elsecar Horde, which us who live in Yorkshire know all about. He sounded serious too, so perhaps you'd better keep your eyes skinned, Mr Pascoe! (Teaching my grandmother – sorry!)

Anyway, Trick and I talked at length and I told him all about myself. When I mentioned Beddoes, he went to his shelves and came back with a copy of the 1850 Pickering edition of *Death's Jest-Book*. Very few were produced, even fewer survive. I took it from him and held it, which was fatal. I felt that burning lust for possession whatever the cost, which I'm sure a man of culture like yourself must understand. I did not dare ask the price, but my eyes must have spoken the question for he said as if we'd been bargaining, 'OK, here's my final offer. You keep hold of this and send me a signed first edition of your Beddoes book and of every other book you subsequently produce. Deal?'

What could I do but stammer my thanks? I am beginning to discover, as you have always known, that even in these most wicked and selfish times, there are still to be found huge reserves of unselfish goodness and loving kindness. Talk again soon.

Yours ever

Franny

ou see what he's saying?' said Pascoe urgently.
'Please, tell me you see it too.'

'I think it might speed things up if you tell me first,
Peter,' said Dr Pottle with some sign of irritation.

Pascoe had turned up without an appointment,
brushing aside Pottle's secretary's objection that he was far too
busy working on his opening address to the Psychandric Society's
Symposium which was taking place the following day.

'He'll see me,' declared Pascoe, making it sound like a threat.
'I just want two minutes. Ask him.'

And a short time afterwards he was ushered in to be assured
by Pottle that, if he was still there after one hundred and twenty
seconds, the secretary would call security.

'He's saying that when he set fire to Albacore's study to destroy
the man's research papers, he also took the opportunity to help
himself to the copy of the *Libellus de Vita Sancti Godrici* which
he'd seen earlier that night.'

'Knowing, of course, that it would be assumed to have been
reduced to ashes in the fire?'

'That's right,' said Pascoe triumphantly. 'You've got it. You're
beginning to see just what this bastard is capable of.'

'Well, I can at least say I can see why you should be convinced
of this.'

Pascoe studied this answer which fell a long way short of the
hoped-for endorsement.

'Why's that?' he asked.

'Because, having convinced yourself he's guilty of arson and
attempted murder, you're hardly going to strain at a little matter
of theft.'

'A little matter? This thing was invaluable!'

'And that makes a difference?'

Pottle made a note on the pad before him. Upside down, it looked like a meaningless squiggle. Pascoe had once taken the opportunity offered when Pottle was called out of his office to have a quick glance at this pad and found that, right way up, his notes still looked like meaningless squiggles. Perhaps that's all they were, but it felt like the psychiatrist was noting every twist and turn of Pascoe's attitudes to Franny Roote.

'Anything more you have to tell me before you leave?' said Pottle, looking at his watch.

The bugger knows there is, thought Pascoe.

He thought of saying no, but that would have been silly. Pointless having a dishwasher and doing your own pots.

He said, 'Rosie got one of those trace-your-family-tree kits and Ellie got the notion it would be interesting to check out Roote . . .'

'Really? Bit of an odd idea for someone as rational as Ellie to get, isn't it?'

'You think my wife is rational?' Pascoe looked at Pottle with serious doubt.

'You don't?'

'I think she has her reasons that reason wots not of,' said Pascoe carefully. 'Anyway, these are the results of her investigation.'

He passed over a file containing the information Ellie had given him, plus the results of his own follow-up.

Pottle read through it and whistled.

'Was that a Freudian or a Jungian whistle?' asked Pascoe.

'It was an unsophisticated expression of amazement that one irrational woman could so easily discover what a well-organized CID seems to have overlooked for many years.'

'We accepted the records. Only it seems that the information on which they were based was fed into the system by Roote himself. At an early age, it should be said.'

'Meaning he decided very early on that his memories of his father, good and bad, should be completely private. Whatever the truth of Mr Roote, he undoubtedly presents a fascinating object of study. I can see why Haseen got so interested in him. Ellie's findings seem to suggest that, far from being deceived, Haseen got him to open up more than he'd ever done before. It's the stuff in the letters about not remembering his father that's a lie.'

'Didn't I always say you can't trust the bastard?' said Pascoe. Then, sensing an irrationality here, he went quickly on: 'It certainly underlines his reasons for hating the police, who he thinks treated his father so badly. Which all goes to show how right I am in being suspicious when he smarms up to me.'

'That might be a case of throwing out the baby with the bathwater,' said Pottle. 'His reasons for lying to you about his father may have changed from desire to keep your long nose out of his business to a confusion of your function and the dead man's. His memories of his father's standing as a policeman, able to deal with all threats that came to his family, are very powerful. And it's clear he has a huge respect for you as a professional . . .'

'Come on! He's taking the piss, isn't he? He's such an arrogant sod he thinks he's brighter than all the rest of us put together.'

'I think you're wrong. Once he may have felt so, but getting caught and ending up in the Syke made him realize that he wasn't Supermind. Realizing how much Haseen had managed to get out of him must have come as a shock too. His respect for you made him think it likely that not only would you read Haseen's book, but that you would identify his disguised presence in it too. So he pre-empts this by drawing your attention to it en passant and boasting about the way he put one across on Ms Haseen by feeding her duff sensational memories of his father. Would you have read the book, incidentally?'

'No way,' said Pascoe. 'Even if I had come across it by chance, half a para of her turgid style would have made me close it fast. He's been too clever by half.'

'Only because he thinks you're too clever by three-quarters.'

'That's right. He thinks I'm clever enough to read between his lines and get the real messages, but powerless to do anything about them! All the pleasure of boasting, none of the penalties of confession. But he'll over-reach himself one day and I'll have him!'

'But so far you haven't come close?'

'No, but one day ... there has to be something ... maybe that dead student of Sam Johnson's in Sheffield ... he keeps glancing at that ... I'm sure there's something there ...'

'Perhaps. But, Peter, motive is not a constant, you must have observed that. The reason for starting something is often not the same as the reason for continuing to do it. It works in both directions. The penniless man who steals out of necessity may turn into the wealthy man who steals out of greed. Or the ambitious politician who does charity work because it looks good on her CV might end up as a passionate advocate of some particular charity despite the fact that it's having an adverse effect upon her career.'

'And the objective psychiatrist can end up getting religion,' said Pascoe. 'I reckon my two minutes are up. Sorry to leave before the end of the service, but I enjoyed the sermon.'

'A polite man's rudeness is like a summer storm; it refreshes the flowers and settles the dust,' murmured Pottle.

'Freud?'

'No, I just made it up. Peter, read this letter again, read them all again, and try to look for patterns other than the one printed on your eye.'

'If I were you, I'd stick to the day job,' advised Pascoe. 'Gotta dash.'

He left. A moment later his head reappeared round the door.

'Sorry,' he said.

'A rude man's apology is like winter sunshine ...'

'Go screw yourself,' said Peter Pascoe.

arlier that same Friday morning a large container lorry had rolled off the Dutch ferry at Hull dock. The driver handed over his papers to be checked, then swore in exasperation as the officials invited him to drive his vehicle into a remote examination bay where a full team of searchers stood waiting with their equipment and dogs.

'Poor sod,' said the driver of a refrigerated lorry which was next in line. 'Looks like that's his morning gone.'

'More than his morning if what we hear is true,' said the man examining his papers. 'OK, Joe?'

'OK,' said the officer who had been giving the lorry a going-over.

'Safe journey, mate.'

The refrigerated vehicle moved out of the dock complex with the ease of familiarity and was soon on the motorway heading into Mid-Yorkshire. The driver took out a mobile phone and rang a pre-set number.

'On my way,' he said. 'Worked a treat. No bother.'

He spoke too soon. Half an hour later he noticed his oil-warning light blinking intermittently. He banged the instrument panel and it stopped. Then it shone bright red.

'Shit,' he said, pulling over on to the hard shoulder.

Then, 'Shit shit shit!' he added as he slid out of the cab and saw a motorway patrol car a few hundred yards behind him closing fast and flashing to pull in.

'Trouble?' said the police officer who got out of the passenger door.

'Yeah. Oil pressure. Probably nothing.'

'Let's take a look, shall we?'

As they took their look, the police car's driver wandered round the back of the truck.

'Ah,' said the truck driver. 'Think I see what it is. Get that fixed in a couple of minutes. Thanks for your help.'

'You sure?' said the policeman.

'Yeah. No sweat. Twenty minutes tops.'

'Great. We're due off in half an hour, so it'll be someone else's problem if it turns out more complicated than you think.' said the policeman, grinning.

'Harry. Got a minute?'

It was the other policeman.

His colleague went to join him.

'Listen. Thought I heard something.'

'Like what?'

'Like a sort of scratching.'

They listened. The driver watched them for a moment then climbed into his cab.

'There. You hear it?'

'Yeah.'

The cop moved swiftly along the truck and hoisted himself on to the cab step.

The driver had picked up his mobile. He flashed an unconvincing smile and said, 'Just thought I'd better ring my boss, tell him I'd had a little hitch.'

The policeman reached forward and took the phone and looked at the number displayed. Then he switched the phone off.

'Tell you what,' he said. 'Let's not bother him till we see just how little your hitch is.'

Fifty miles away and an hour later, Wield was sitting in Turk's.

When Lee had rung him and asked for a meet, the sergeant had suggested the multi-storey again but the youth had said, 'No fucking way. Froze my bollocks off last time and the weather's even colder today. Turk's.'

He's calling the shots, thought Wield uneasily. Which was bad whatever their relationship was. What did he mean, *whatever*?

Lubanski was an informant, period. Cops who started acting like social workers were asking for trouble. And whatever he looked like, he wasn't a child at risk but an adult in need of protection only if he asked for it.

But now, sitting opposite him and feeling himself drawn willy-nilly into the undisguised pleasure the boy took in his company, Wield saw the scene as it might look to a passer-by whose sharp gaze penetrated the steamed-up window. Uncle and nephew off on a day-trip together. Father and son even. This was the first time they'd met since the karaoke. Dalziel happily had seemed preoccupied with something else and Wield had found it easy to find excuses not to make the effort.

Lee was looking straight at him and, despite his certainty that his face gave nothing away, Wield hid his expression behind the mug of foul coffee which the freezing day had driven him to.

'So what you got?' he asked brusquely.

'You're in a hurry. Got a date or something?' said Lee. But not aggressively, not even provocatively. Just a relaxed joke between friends.

'I've got work to do, yes,' said Wield.

'Get a coffee break, don't you? Anyway, I expect you put this down as work.'

He wants some kind of denial, however qualified.

'That's right,' said Wield brusquely. 'And I hope it's productive. What have you got?'

The hurt in the boy's eyes brought the protective mug up again.

'That guy rang last night,' he said sullenly.

'Which guy?'

'The one he calls Mate.'

'What did he say?'

Lee produced a scrap of paper and began to read.

'He said it were all fixed his end for next week but where was the money? And Belchy said not to worry, it would be there. Then he rang the other guy . . .'

'LB? Thought you said he didn't ring him direct?'

'Usually he don't. But it sounded like he'd been hard to get hold of on the net.'

Understandable. Grief was a great antaphrodisiac. And a great enemy of rational thought. Possibly Linford was blaming Belchamber for getting Liam out on bail now.

'And he made contact?'

'Yeah. And I'll tell you something else. I know who LB is now. He's Wally Linford, dad of that wanker Liam who got himself killed last weekend.'

This was said with such triumph Wield hadn't the heart to reveal he knew it already.

'How do you know?'

'Said "Linford" when he answered the phone. And Belchy called him Linford from then on. They had a right row. Linford was yelling. Belchy never yells, but I could tell he were getting really uptight. His dick went soft.'

Wield felt Lee watching him closely as he said this.

He's sussed how it bothers me when he refers to what he actually does to Belchamber, he thought. And me being bothered implies a relationship. Not good. But he kept his tone level and neutral as he asked, 'What were they quarrelling about?'

'Money. Belchy was worried about some payment he had to make and Linford was yelling he couldn't be bothered with all this crap just now and Belchy said mebbe he should be bothered 'cos his mate were going to be very bothered if he didn't get the next lot of upfronts and Linford said it had nothing the fuck to do with him what this mate felt, he was just an investor and kept a good safe distance away from his fucking clientele, like a fucking lawyer, things went pear-shaped he walked away from the shit, no skin off his nose, so stick that in your crown and wear it, your fucking majesty!'

This sounded like it was verbatim. Wield's mind was racing. Linford, still hugely disturbed at his son's death, was taking it out on Belchamber for the want of anyone else. And it wasn't just a case of a client sacking his lawyer. Their suspicions that for some reason Belchamber had crossed the line were obviously right. He was involved here, not as a lawyer hovering in the background ready to step forward only if things went awry, not even as a reluctant bagman, but as a principal, an initiator. But of what? And why the hell should he be taking that dangerous step across when staying on the legal side must be second nature to him?

And what was all that 'your majesty' business?

Just a joke? One queen to another maybe? Or . . .

'That any good then?' said Lee.

'What? Sorry. Yes, it's very helpful. Any more?'

'No, that's it for now. Don't worry, I get owt else, I'll be right on to you.'

Wield said, 'Lee, I think maybe it's time you stopped dealing with Belchamber.'

'Yeah? Why's that then? You trying to save my soul again, Mac?'

He spoke with a knowing cockiness that grated.

Wield said, 'Not your soul. Your body maybe. If he got wind that you're passing stuff on to me . . .'

'No chance! All I do is listen. Not breaking into safes and such. Anyway, I can take care of Belchy. He's soft as pigshit.'

'Maybe. But there's people he's mixed up with who aren't, and they're twice as nasty.'

'You reckon? Well, I meet lots of nasty people, Sergeant Mac. No need to worry about me.'

'But I do worry, Lee.'

'Really?'

'Really.'

'Yeah, well, you'll be the first.' He spoke with an attempt at throw-away bravado.

'I shouldn't think so,' said Wield. 'Your mam must have worried.'

'Mebbe. And my dad too. He'd probably have worried if he'd known.'

He's still hanging on to the idea that it was ignorance rather than indifference which made his father dump his pregnant mother, thought Wield.

He said gently, 'I'm sure he would have, Lee.'

'Yeah. I wish I'd got a picture of him or something. Mam didn't have anything. Not that he were owt much to look at, she said. In fact most folk reckoned he were a right ugly bugger. But she said looks aren't everything, he were right sexy and she knew he were the one for her first time she saw him. They were just kids, younger than me, I think, so he'd just be in his thirties now. Wherever he is.'

Oh Christ, thought Wield aghast, suddenly recalling the young man's interest in his possible hetero experience. Edwin had warned him that Lee might be seeing him as a father substitute, but for once those sharp old eyes hadn't looked deep enough.

It's not a substitute the poor little sod's after; he's looking to cast me as his actual sodding father!

Lee had brought his wandering gaze to bear full on Wield's ravaged features. His expression was defiant but not despairing. Hope is a persistent virus. Vaccinate yourself against it all you like, it still clings on.

Wield said, 'Look, Lee . . .'

Then the door burst open and several uniformed policemen rushed into the cafe.

One stayed by the door, two went behind the counter and grabbed hold of Turk with rather more force than his unresisting demeanour merited, two more vanished into the rear of the premises while another addressed the half-dozen customers.

'Stay in your seats, gents. We'll need your names and addresses, just as witnesses, you understand, then you can go.'

Lee was now glaring accusingly at Wield, who said, 'It's nowt to do with me, lad.' Obviously unconvinced, the boy began to rise when a hand clapped on his shoulder and a voice said ponderously, as if the words were being prised out of mud, 'Keep sat down.'

Oh shit, thought Wield, recognizing the voice before he took in the face. It belonged to PC Hector, the albatross round Mid-Yorkshire Constabulary's neck, the mote in its eye, the pile on its rectum. He was, Dalziel opined, the most reliable officer in the Force – he always got it wrong. If he survived long enough he might outdistance the Fat Man himself as a source of amazing anecdote.

Now his gaze, which had focused with grave suspicion on Wield's black leathers, moved up to take in the sergeant's features. There was a moment of mental perturbation, then

433

recognition came up like thunder out of China 'cross the Bay, and he said in stentorian tones, 'Hello. It's you, Sarge! What you doing here? Undercover, is it?'

Behind him, Wield saw Turk register the words, saw his gaze flicker to Lee.

He rose and put his face close to Hector's and said in a low voice, 'I'm having a cup of coffee, which is just as well, 'cos if I were on a job, you'd have just blown it.'

Hector looked so crestfallen it was almost possible to feel sorry for him then, and said in the kind of whisper which echoes round the gods, 'Sorry, Sarge, I never thought.'

'There'll be a first time, maybe.' Then turning to the officer who'd addressed the cafe clientele, none of whom showed the slightest interest in what was happening, he said, 'Johnstone, what's going off?'

'Truck broke down on the motorway coming from Hull. Two of our lot stopped to give assistance and heard noises. Turned out it was full of illegals. The driver tried to make a call but got stopped before he got through. This was the number he was ringing.'

'I see. Got a search warrant?'

'One's on its way, but we thought we'd best make sure of getting Sonny Jim here.'

'Yeah. Well, I'd get yon pair out of the back till it arrives, so that if you do find anything, it will be admissible.'

'Yeah, right, Sarge.'

Wield turned back to Lee, who was on his feet and looking anxious to be elsewhere. It came back to him now that on their first encounter the youth had made some crack about Turk's sandwiches containing the remains of illegals that hadn't made it.

'You know anything about Turk being in the people-smuggling business?' he asked.

'I'd heard a buzz, that was all.'

'And you didn't think it was worth mentioning?'

'No. It's not like real crime, is it? Just a lot of poor sods wanting in. Christ, think what it must be like where they come from if they think it's going to be better here!'

This was matter for an interesting discussion on comparative sociology which would have to wait till some other time.

He led Lee to the door and said to the guardian constable, 'This one can go. I've got his details.'

The man stood aside and Lee headed through the door like a canary out of a cage.

'I'll be in touch,' Wield called after him.

''Scuse us, Sarge,' said a voice behind him.

He turned, then stepped aside to let Turk and his pair of close escorts pass.

His gaze and that of the cafe proprietor met. All he saw there was the same blank indifference with which the man dispensed his unspeakable coffee.

No harm done, Wield reassured himself as he watched the police car pull away. So now Turk knew that he was a cop. Presumably he already knew that Lee was a rent boy. God knows what he might speculate about their relationship, but so what? Anyway, he was going to have other more serious matters on his mind.

But still Wield felt uneasiness working like dyspepsia in his gut.

He stayed a little longer to make sure that everything was by the book then left. Part of his mind had never stopped working at the new info Lee had given him and now he gave it his full attention. There was something there that meant something to him. That stuff about *crown* and *majesty* . . .

Unlike most minds in search of something only dimly remembered, Wield's didn't work by turning to something completely different in the hope of stumbling across the desired item by chance, as it were. His relied more on the computer principle. You fed the information into a program, pressed *search*, and waited for results.

The answer came two minutes later as he sat with idling engine waiting for the traffic lights to change.

He was in the right-hand lane. As the lights showed red and amber, he accelerated left across the bows of a stately old Morris containing three old ladies in fur hats on their way to lunch with the bishop, who with a synchronicity worthy of the Beverley Sisters gave him the finger and screamed, 'Asshole!'

t was forty minutes later that Wield pulled into the police station car park.

Proximity to the seat of law being no guarantee of security, he squatted to wrap a length of chain around the rear wheel and pillion, and as he did so he noticed a big black Lexus in one of the public bays.

Its number plate read JUS 10. There was a man in the driver's seat talking into a phone, difficult to identify through the tinted glass. But as Wield snapped his lock shut, the man got out and headed into the building and there was no mistaking that Roman head, those sculpted locks.

It was Marcus Belchamber.

Straightening up, Wield once again felt that acid uneasiness in his gut.

Belchamber had disappeared by the time he reached the front desk. Des Bowman, the duty sergeant, looked up and said, 'How do, Wieldy. What fettle?'

'Grand, Des. Weren't that Belchamber I saw just come in? What's he doing?'

'He's acting for Yasher Asif, you know him? Runs that caff called Turk's by the station. They brought him in for questioning about some illegals-smuggling racket.'

'Thanks, Des. Let me through, eh?'

The sergeant released the security lock and Wield went through the door and hurried up the stairs to CID. He glimpsed Pascoe through the open door of his office and went in.

The DCI was studying a letter whose handwriting Wield identified at a glance. Franny Roote's. Shit, he thought, is the silly sod still letting himself be distracted?

Before he could speak Pascoe looked up and said, 'Wieldy, what do you know about the Elsecar Hoard?'

It was like having his mind read.

'A lot more now than I did an hour ago,' said Wield. 'Why do you ask?'

'No reason . . . just an idea . . . oh shit, what am I tiptoeing around for? It's something Roote says in this letter.'

'Giving you tips now, is he? I thought it were all hidden confessions.'

'I think I may have got another of those too,' said Pascoe grimly. 'But that's between me and him. Anyway, he mentioned the Hoard apropos a conversation he had with what sounds very like a high-class fence. And I got to thinking. It's in Sheffield at the moment and it's coming here soon . . .'

'The twenty-sixth, week tomorrow,' said Wield.

'You're well informed.'

'Some of us get places by honest police work that other idle sods reach by imaginative leaps,' said Wield. 'If you're talking about this job Mate Polchard's planning, that is.'

Now it was Pascoe's turn to feel mind-read.

'What else? Tell me about this honest police work. You interest me strangely.'

Quickly Wield filled him in on his conversation with Lubanski.

'It was this bit about the crown that got me thinking. That and wondering why the hell Belchamber should have got so personally involved in this job. Then I remembered seeing a poster at the Centre about the Hoard being on exhibition in January. And I recalled there was some article fulminating over the sale that Belchamber had written in the *Gazette*. Didn't read it myself, but Edwin gets hot and bothered about such things and he kept quoting bits at me over the dinner table till I told him that the moral indignation of a dipstick like the Belch weren't good for my digestion. Anyway, I went down to the reference library to look it up in the back numbers. Took a closer look at them posters too. They've got Belchamber giving a lecture on the Hoard on the exhibition opening day. Odd that.'

'Why? He's really involved. I saw him on the telly the other week. He might be a shitbag, but he knows his Medes from his Persians.'

'It's odd because of the way he's blown hot and cold. I'll show you what I mean. Yon lass of Bowler's was very helpful. Hadn't seen her since that scare at New Year.'

'How'd she look?'

'Bit pale maybe, but full of the joys of spring otherwise.'

In fact, Rye had greeted him rather frostily till it was established that his motive in appearing there had nothing to do with her. Then she had thawed and to his enquiry after her health, she'd replied, 'Never better. Just some virus that's going around, but I'm over it now. How about you, Mr Wield?'

'I'm fine. At least nothing that a bit of spring sunshine won't cure. Roll on, eh?'

'Yes,' she said. 'I can't wait.'

Which for some reason she seemed to think of as funny and her laughter was so infectious, he found himself joining in.

'This article . . .' prompted Pascoe.

'Articles. There were two of them. It was Rye put me on to the other which appeared way back when Belch were on better terms with the Elsecars. I've got copies. This is the earlier one.'

He handed it over. Pascoe scanned it quickly then read it again at a more leisurely pace.

This described a visit Belchamber and other officers of the Mid-Yorkshire Archaeological Society had been permitted to make to view the Hoard. It was fulsome with expressions of gratitude to the Elsecars for their kind condescension in allowing the visit. The style when he described the content of the Hoard was scholarly and objective, but later it became personal and familiar as he started theorizing, or perhaps romancing was a better word, about the provenance of various items and the background of their owner and the circumstances of their loss.

> *Readers of some previous pieces of mine on Roman Yorkshire may recall that on one occasion I traced my own ancestry back, reasonably legitimately, to the fifteenth century and then, rather more fancifully, to Marcus Bellisarius, an official of the Provincial Governor's commissariat, briefly*

mentioned by Tacitus. Now when I was permitted to hold the
serpent coronet (or Cartimandua's Crown as the Victorians
mistakenly dubbed it) I must confess to feeling a thrill at my
contact with the smooth twists and folds of gold that seemed
more than just the natural pleasure of an amateur of ancient
history. The thought popped into my mind: suppose the collec-
tor of these wonderful things was in fact my putative ancestor
Marcus Bellisarius? Suppose the serpent coronet came to him
as part of the dot of the Brigantian princess that he married
(such alliances were not uncommon in the older Romano-
British families), and suppose that, though the Hoard was lost
beyond recall in flight from God knows what peril, he or his
children survived and flourished and founded the family of
which this undeserving scion, sixteen centuries later, was per-
mitted to hold this symbol of that union?

  Then someone took the coronet from me and I was back
in the world of reality.

'Two snakes intertwined. Good symbol for the Belchamber
family,' said Pascoe.

'You see how completely obsessed he seems to be with the
Hoard and in particular the coronet?' said Wield. 'So it's no
surprise to find him really pissed off when he hears it's going
to America. Here's the second article, the one that got Edwin
going.'

Pascoe scanned it quickly. In measured prose whose orotundity
did not disguise real feeling, it expressed huge indignation that
a weak and time-serving government should allow such treasures
as these to leave the country. It concluded:

My professional work brings me in contact with all sorts
and conditions of men who have committed all sorts and
conditions of crime, but rarely have I confronted an action
as criminal as this. As a lawyer I must take care how I
describe the family who propose it and the politicians who
permit it, but I will say that, though of course I subscribe
to that basic tenet of our legal system that every accused is
entitled to a defence, I think that I personally would draw
the line at defending such as these.

'That's really telling them,' said Pascoe.

'It certainly is. Which makes it odd that he's made it up with the Elsecars since then. Giving lectures and helping them arrange this tour.'

'The aim of which is to help raise enough money to keep it here,' said Pascoe. 'Which is what he wants.'

'Oh aye. That's what he wants right enough,' said Wield. 'But anyone who can add up knows there's not a cat in hell's chance of making enough from admission fees to get anywhere near the Yanks' price.'

Pascoe hid a smile, recognizing that what he was now alleging everyone knew the sergeant had probably not even thought of until a couple of hours ago.

He said, 'So what you're saying is, the reason Belchamber threw his weight behind this tour is because he wants the Hoard out in the open where he can get his hands on it? That's a big leap, Wieldy. This is Belchamber we're talking about, the guy who doesn't fart without studying precedent.'

'Guy gets an obsession, he'll do anything,' said Wield a little pointedly. 'And he's an arrogant bastard, that's clear. Put the feeling you get in both those pieces with his change of heart, then add what Lee overheard . . .'

'You could be right, Wieldy. If so . . . Look, has Lubanski told you everything, do you think? Or is he holding something back to get more Brownie points from you later?'

'I think he's told me everything,' said Wield, his worries reawoken by mention of Lee's name. 'You know that Belchamber's here?'

'Yeah. I met him outside, brought him in. We had a nice chat, but I don't think he's forgiven me for what I said to him after young Linford's committal. Seems he's representing some guy Uniformed just brought in on a smuggling illegals charge.'

'I know. Asif. He runs Turk's caff. I was there when they nicked him.'

'You mean, with Lubanski?'

'Yeah.'

Pascoe digested this, saw the worry in Wield's eyes, guessed its source.

441

'Ah. But this Asif doesn't know you're a cop, I presume?'

'Didn't till Hector opened that great gob of his. Yon bugger's not fit to be let out!'

It was rare that Wield expressed his opinion of a fellow policeman so forcibly.

'But is there anything to make you think Asif might know of the link between Lubanski and Belchamber? Not likely, is it?'

The phone rang. Pascoe ignored it. Sorting Wield was his priority at the moment.

Not that Wield looked ready to be sorted.

'You know as well as I do, Pete, that a lot of stuff we have to pay good money for can be common knowledge if you move in the right circles. Lee knew Turk was into smuggling illegals, for instance. No, he didn't give me a tip, it was just a joke he made that I took no notice of. He assumed everyone knew! Pete, just now you said you met Belchamber and escorted him in. But I saw him a few minutes ago in the car park . . .'

Pascoe picked up his phone and spoke briefly to the desk sergeant.

Putting the receiver down he said, 'Yes. They're waiting for some hotshot to arrive from Immigration. Belchamber had a couple of minutes alone with Asif then came out. Seems he'd left something in the car. Went out for it, came back. That's when you must have seen him.'

Wield digested this, didn't care for the flavour.

'The bastard was on his car phone. Shit, I don't like this.'

Pascoe, concerned to see his usually phlegmatic friend so agitated, said, 'Come on, Wieldy. Don't make something out of nothing. What do you think happened down there in the cells? Asif said to Belchamber, "Oh, by the way, putting aside my natural concern that I am in deep shit here banged up on suspicion of a serious offence which is why I called you, thought you might like to know I've seen that kid who sucks your dick cosying up to a cop in my caff a few times." Then the Belch takes off to his car and rings some hardmen he knows and says, "I'd like to fix up a hit on Lee Lubanski, action immediate." Is that what you're thinking, Wieldy?'

If he'd thought to mock the sergeant out of his concern, he'd miscalculated.

'You're a mind-reader, Pete,' said Wield savagely. 'Tell me why I'm wrong.'

'Because this is Mid-Yorkshire, not the Mid-west. Because a guy like Belchamber might not be too chary about the way he makes his money, but the civilized, respectable face he shows is more than just a face. He may do a lot of things, but I doubt he's capable of having another human being killed!'

'Pete, you're missing the point. Men who use boys the way Belchamber uses Lee don't think of them as human beings. They're toys. That's how he feels able to carry on talking about his business on the phone with Lee there. He's negligible. He has a function and outside that function he doesn't exist. And if it turns out he does, then all that that means is this particular toy is broken, so you throw it away and get a new one!'

Wield's voice had climbed close to shouting level by the time he finished and Pascoe was staring at him in alarm when Dalziel's voice boomed from the doorway.

'What's all this then? Lovers' tiff? Have some consideration, eh? There's folk trying to sleep in this building.'

Quickly Pascoe explained.

The Fat Man listened intently then said, 'So what are you hanging around here for, Wieldy? Go and find the lad. Offer him protection, and if he don't want protected, put him in protective custody and bring him in. Off you go, chop-chop.'

Wield didn't hesitate. It wasn't permission he needed, just affirmation that he wasn't letting his emotions run away with his reason.

Dalziel closed the door behind him and turned to Pascoe.

'I hope this lad's worth all the bother. Come up with owt interesting this morning, did he?' he asked.

Pascoe filled him in and showed him the two articles. The Fat Man read them with little sign of interest then said, 'So what garden path's this stuff leading us up then?'

Pascoe, knowing from experience that Dalziel's dumb-ox reaction was usually a provocation to precise exposition, marshalled his thoughts and said, 'We have two things. DI Rose's tip that something big is being planned which straddles South's patch and ours, and Lee Lubanski's report of stuff he's overheard while servicing Belchamber. Conversations involving possibly Mate Polchard and certainly Linford also point to something being planned which may well be the job in question. Puzzle: why is Belchamber involved at the criminal end instead of merely standing by in readiness in case he's needed at the legal end? Possible answer: because he himself initiated the job.'

'The job being heisting this Hoard thing 'cos, like a good little patriot, he wants to save it for England?' said Dalziel, sounding like the Pope being told God was a woman.

'I'd say from these articles that that was certainly his initial reaction. Something had to be done, anything was worth doing, to keep the Hoard in the country. But at some point, perhaps as he began to realize the appeal to the country for money and to the Elsecars for patriotic sacrifice was going to fail, he began to ask himself, does the country deserve to have the Hoard saved for it?'

'And his answer was . . . ?'

'No, it doesn't because it doesn't value its heritage sufficiently. I, on the other hand, do. So why not save it for myself? But how to do it? And now his years of crawling in the mud with the pondlife come in useful. He needs experts, he knows where to find them, and he knows how the system works.'

'Which system's that?'

'The finance system,' said Pascoe impatiently. Sometimes the Fat Man took his dumb elenctic act too far. 'He needs the best. Also he wants to keep control. He's not offering a share of profits. This is not a profit-making job. So this means paying top dollar. I don't know what level of remuneration gets Polchard out of bed these days, but I expect it's a little over the National Minimum Wage. And, profits or not, Mate will be well aware of the notional value of the stuff he's being asked to heist.'

'So why not go for it himself?'

'Because he's a cash man. Because he knows how hard it would be to move stuff like this. And also because he knows that Belchamber's often been the only thing between him and a lot more years in the Syke.'

'Gratitude, you mean?' said Dalziel sceptically.

'No. Chess. Sacrifice everything except your queen.'

'So why bring in Linford? Belchamber must be pretty well heeled.'

'Certainly. But with most of it well tied up. Also, he doesn't want to draw attention to himself by the sudden realization of assets. So he turns to Linford, who is expert in the supply of large quantities of used banknotes.'

'He'll want payback with interest.'

'He'll get it from the profits.'

'Thought you said there weren't going to be any profits? Thought the idea was Belch would keep the Hoard in his cellar and go down there and have a wank from time to time.'

'No. If you read his articles, the first one, a large part of the Hoard consists of golden coin, hugely valuable but by its nature hardly unique. I don't think he'd have any problem moving most of this. Also I suspect that, in terms of personal ownership, what he really lusts after is the snake coronet. A lot of the other stuff he might be very willing to share with similar bent collectors for a price.'

'And you and Wieldy got all this from someone making some crack about the Belch wearing a crown?' said Dalziel sceptically.

'There's also the fact that the Hoard Exhibition is currently in Sheffield on DI Rose's patch and it's transferring up here to the Centre on January twenty-sixth.'

'It's still a hell of a leap,' said Dalziel.

'You got a better shell-hole in mind, why don't you just jump into it?' snapped Pascoe.

The Fat Man grinned with satisfaction.

'Nay, lad, you believe in it enough to get stroppy, that's good enough for me.'

There was a tap at the door and Novello's head appeared.

'Ah. You're both here,' she said.

'Isn't that what I always say about Ivor, Pete? Smart as a whip,' said Dalziel.

'Sergeant Bowman downstairs has been trying to get hold of one of you. Some Immigration official's turned up,' said Novello.

'Oh aye. Tell 'em to sit him down and fetch him a cup of tea.'

The Fat Man grinned. 'Better still, tell Bowman to get Hector to fetch him a cup of tea.'

'Yes, sir.'

Pascoe said, 'Shirley, I seem to recall you're an expert on saints.'

Novello remembered Sister Angela who wielded a ruler edge-on like a broadsword if you got a detail wrong.

'Know a bit, sir,' she said.

'Saint Apollonia. Any connection with teeth?'

'Yeah. She had all of hers knocked out or pulled out during her martyrdom. She's the one to pray to if you've got toothache.'

'Thanks, that's very helpful.'

Novello left.

Dalziel said, 'That got owt to do with owt, or have you just lost a filling?'

'Just something I was curious about.'

'Curious is right,' growled the Fat Man. 'I hope you're not on the turn, lad. One practising Catholic in the squad's quite enough.'

'Hadn't you better go and see this Immigration chap? He's probably hopping round with a scalded crotch by now.'

Dalziel boomed a laugh and said, 'We can live in hope. If plonkers like him showed a bit more common humanity then mebbe there'd be fewer poor bastards thinking the only way they can get into the country is curled up in a truck with a lot of frozen ham. Why are you walking funny? Hurt your ankle?'

'No sir,' said Pascoe. 'Just trying to avoid stepping in this milk of human kindness someone's spilt all over the floor.'

'Ha bloody ha. That's the trouble with you poncy liberals. Think you've cornered the market in heart.'

'Talking of which, sir, do you really think Wieldy's right to be concerned about Lubanski?'

'Shouldn't imagine so,' said Dalziel.

'Then why did you send him to look for the lad?'

''Cos if we're going to start taking this Hoard thing seriously, I wouldn't mind half an hour with the little scrote myself, see what he really knows. This seemed as good a way as any to get Wieldy to bring him in without coming over all maternal. Can't

446

abide to see a grown man crying, that's always been my trouble. So stop worrying, he'll be back with his likely lad in half an hour and then I'll really give the young sod something to suck on!'

ut for once Andy Dalziel was wrong.

More than an hour had passed before Wield returned, and he was alone.

'He wasn't at his address, I checked out all the other likely spots and there was no sign. Someone thought they might have seen him getting into a car, but couldn't be sure.'

'There you are then,' said Pascoe reassuringly. 'Off with a punter.'

'It's the middle of the sodding day!'

'Come on, Wieldy! What's that got to do with anything? OK, maybe it was a mate who picked him up. Your witness said "getting into a car", not "being dragged" into it. So wherever he is, he's gone willingly and I don't doubt he'll be back in his own good time.'

Dalziel returned from dealing with the happily unscalded Immigration official.

'Not a bad fellow,' he opined. 'Mad eyes and shoulders on him like an ox. Don't know if that influenced Asif, but he were real co-operative. Put his hand up like teacher's pet. Likely that call Belch made from his car were to whoever's behind Turk. Belch and him had had a word, Turk wanted to know what the deal was if he took the rap, Belch passes the word. Up goes Turk's hand and the buck stops there.'

Wield said, 'Let's hope you're right.' But he didn't sound very hopeful.

And when six o'clock arrived with still no sign of Lubanski, he re-embraced his first theory with renewed passion.

'I think it's time we had a word with Belchamber,' he said forcefully.

'And what's he going to say? Yes, I fixed for Lee to be kidnapped? Get real, Wieldy.'

'Depends how you put the question,' said Wield grimly.

Pascoe and Dalziel exchanged glances.

The Fat Man said, 'I can see it's an attractive notion, Wieldy, taking Belch somewhere quiet and kicking his guts till he spills them. But you'd have to go all the way and kill him 'cos if there's one person a good cop doesn't want coming after him with a complaint, it's Marcus Belchamber.'

Pascoe, seeking a less basic appeal, said, 'More importantly, if you're wrong about this, and Belchamber's got no reason to think Lee has been grassing him up, you could be dropping Lee right in it, plus we'll have shown our hands in a big way.'

Wield considered this then said, 'Let's say you're right. So why's Lee vanished?'

'Simple,' said Dalziel. 'You warned him that what he was doing could be dangerous, right? Told him to take care.'

'Yes, but he wasn't taking a damn bit of notice,' said Wield.

'Might give that impression, kids like him live on bravado, eh? Show you're scared in the streets and you're knackered. But he trusts you, Wieldy, everything you've said about him shows that. So you say something, it'll have sunk in. Then what happens? He's sitting with you in Turk's and suddenly the place is full of cops. I know you explain it's nowt to do with you, but even if he believes you, it's a reminder. You may be a wise old father-figure, but you're a cop as well, and he's been cosying up to you in public, and God knows who's been watching. So maybe it's time he took a little holiday. Business has been good, he's got a bit in the bank. Wouldn't surprise me if he wasn't on his way to Marbella this very moment.'

It was logical, it was persuasive. Pascoe could see Wield setting the Fat Man's hypothesis alongside everything he knew about Lubanski and getting a good match.

Also it gave him real hope and that's a bait it takes a Beckett to spit out.

'All right,' he said. 'You could be right. But if you're not . . .'

He left his threat unspoken, or perhaps he simply hadn't yet worked out the details but knew it would be the terror of the earth.

'You really think he's on his way to Spain, sir?' said Pascoe after Wield had left.

'Fuck knows. But for the sake of argument, let's assume he's been kidnapped. Why? 'Cos someone got worried about what he's been telling Wieldy about Belch's plan. What has he been telling Wieldy abut Belch's plan? Not a lot. Most of what we think we know about it is loaves and fishes, a big meal based on a few scraps. But if they tret him like yon Saint Aspidistra you were asking Ivor about and pulled his teeth out to find out what he'd said, all they'd hear about were the scraps. And, not knowing what active imaginations Wieldy and you have got, they likely think they're still in the clear.'

'So if we are right and it's the Elsecar Hoard they're after, which is being transported here next Saturday, a week from tomorrow, that doesn't leave much time.'

'No it doesn't, but it's still not a lot to go on,' grumbled Dalziel. 'What we need is some silver-tongued bastard full of low cunning who can go down to Sheffield tomorrow morning and sell them this notion in such a way that, if it turns out a dud, it's all their fault, and if it turns out a winner, we get most of the credit.'

'That would indeed take a huge length of silver tongue and a dizzy depth of cunning,' said Pascoe. 'Have you anyone in mind, sir?'

'Belt up and bugger off,' said Dalziel.

The Pedlar

ascoe liked Sheffield. Everyone with an eye for beauty, a nose for excitement, a taste for variety likes Sheffield. Built on seven hills like Rome, it is possible to pass from spring in its valleys to winter on its heights without ever crossing the city boundary.

Perhaps it gets its peculiar buzz from being a frontier town, for this is where Yorkshire in particular and the North in general end. After this, wrap it up how you will, you're into the Midlands. The White Peak bits of Derbyshire may have something of the North in them, but it's hilly landscape stood on its head. You are looking down from edges rather than staring up at heights.

DI Stan Rose was certainly looking down rather than staring up. His lost snout had been picked up in London trying to use a dodgy credit card. Rose had gone south to see him. He'd found a very scared man, showing signs of a recent severe beating.

As Pascoe heard this, he thought uneasily of Lee Lubanski. Mate Polchard didn't have a reputation for gratuitous violence, but he was up for anything that the situation demanded. And God knows what kind of mindless muscle he was employing.

Then Rose, unprompted, mentioned the Elsecar Hoard, and his concern for the missing rent boy evaporated.

Strong hints that further info on the Sheffield job could persuade Rose to put in a word when the Met came to decide how to proceed in the snout's present difficulty had at first produced only the eloquent comment that he might be better off inside. To which Rose had replied that, in that case, he would make sure he got a conditional discharge, then let it be known around Sheffield that he'd been down for a chat.

Even then, all he got was a date. January 26th, a week from today, the day the Hoard was being transferred from Sheffield to Mid-Yorkshire.

'But what made you think of the Hoard as a target in the first place?' asked Pascoe.

'Polchard's record made me think it might be a security-van hit, so I researched a list of all possibles this month,' said Rose proudly. 'When I saw the date matched the Hoard transfer day, I got all the museum security tapes and went through them. And you know what, Polchard's visited the exhibition twice at least. Coat collar turned up, hat pulled down, but it was definitely him.'

'Perhaps he's just interested in Roman history,' said Pascoe drily. 'You were going to tell me all this, weren't you, Stan? I mean, we are talking about next Saturday, right?'

'Of course I was. I've been putting some ideas together, just wanted to run them by my boss, he's been off with this Kung Flu, just got back today, so I was planning to ring you. Anyway, it's still all a bit speculative, isn't it?'

'I think it's a bit more than that, Stan,' said Pascoe.

As he explained the reasons for his visit, Rose had the grace to look positively embarrassed at the contrast between Pascoe's speedy sharing of new information and his cards-close-to-the-chest approach.

'Pete, this is really good. This is all I need to get the go-ahead on my . . . on our op.'

'I'm pleased for you. Though of course if, as seems likely, they're planning to make the hit during transfer, it's as likely, in fact more likely to take place on Andy Dalziel's turf.'

He paused a moment just to let Rose contemplate the life-threatening perils of a power struggle with the Fat Man, then went on, 'But the guy who takes the call calls the shots, isn't that what they say? It's your show, Stan. You'll get full backing from our side of the fence – just as long as we're getting full intelligence from yours.'

'Pete, that's great. Thanks a bunch. Look, I've got a lot of ideas for this oppo. I'm calling it Operation Serpent, by the way. Thought that fitted.'

He spoke almost defiantly and Pascoe concealed his amusement.

'So why don't we get down to some hard planning while you're here,' the DI continued.

'To be honest, I'd rather get down to the museum and see what all the fuss is about,' said Pascoe.

He had seen photographs of various items in the Hoard, but they hadn't prepared him for its full splendour. It wasn't a huge collection but it had clearly been put together by a man with an eye for beauty who must have approved the care which had been taken in setting his pieces out on display. Rings, bracelets, brooches, necklaces, each was shown to its best advantage on slowly rotating stands covered with black velvet and lit by shifting lights which moved from the full glare of sunshine to the soft glow of candleshine. At the very centre, set on a fibreglass ovoid, which though faceless somehow invited you to see whatever features you found most beautiful there, was the serpent coronet.

For a moment as he studied it, Pascoe almost understood Belchamber's desire for possession. And he could certainly share his indignation that this treasure was being allowed out of the country.

They saw the Exhibition Director and questioned him about the transfer arrangements at the end of the exhibition. They kept the tone as low-key as possible, stressing that these were just the routine security enquiries any movement of so valuable a cargo would require. Prevention might be better than cure, but neither of them had any desire to alert the gang to their suspicions and warn them off. As Dalziel once put it, with hard-bitten pros, the only true crime prevention was prison. Anything else was mere postponement.

One piece of information caught Pascoe's interest. The transfer was going to be done by Praesidium Security.

Rose, with a sensitivity to reaction which boded well for him in his career, noted the flicker of interest and brought it up as they left the Director's office.

Pascoe told him about the earlier attack on the Praesidium van and of the link with Belchamber.

'So you think this could have been some kind of rehearsal?'

'Could be. It would certainly explain why they weren't that much interested in the money that had been on board. Though I must say if they think the crew ferrying the Hoard are going to stop at a caff for tea, they must be seriously thick.'

Pascoe paused as they passed through the main foyer. On a noticeboard a poster had caught his eye. It advertised the one-day conference being held at the university by the Yorkshire Psychandric Society – and of course today was the day. He wondered how Pottle's opening address had gone down.

He went closer to check the details.

Amaryllis Haseen had been on that morning, so he'd missed her. But Frère Jacques, Roote's guru, was on after lunch, talking about Third Thought and his new book.

Back at Sheffield HQ he met Rose's boss. He didn't look well and, despite his assurances that he was no longer infectious, whenever his chain smoking brought on a bout of ferocious coughing, Pascoe tried to keep to the windward.

He was less convinced than his DI that Pascoe's news meant there was definitely a heist attempt in the offing, but he questioned him closely about Andy Dalziel's attitude. Obviously the Fat Man's opinions carried weight everywhere. Finally he gave Rose that conditional blessing which Pascoe well recognized. Interpreted, it meant: your triumph is ours, your cock-ups are your own.

But Stan Rose was delighted. Outside the smoky room, he said, 'Pete, let me buy you some lunch. Least I can do. I owe you.'

Pascoe said, 'Thanks, Stan, but there's something I need to do up at the university. Talking of which, there is something . . . Remember that boy Frobisher, the one Sergeant Wield asked you about way back in connection with that lecturer's death on our patch . . . ?'

'Yeah, I remember him. Accidental overdose trying to stay awake to finish his work.'

'That's the one. Look, while I'm here I'd like to poke around the house he lived in, have a word with any of his mates who are still there, nothing heavy – but if anyone got stroppy, it would be good to say I'd checked it out with you.'

Rose was regarding him like a poor relation who'd suddenly mentioned money.

'This anything to do with that fellow Roote?' he asked.

'Distantly.'

'Pete, this is a non-suspicious death, all done and dusted.'

'From what you said, his sister didn't think so.'

'What are sisters for? Pete, it's a waste of time.'

'You're probably right. And I realize I should be devoting all my energies to assisting you in this Hoard oppo . . .'

He slightly stressed *assisting*.

Rose sighed.

'Be my guest, Pete. I can always say you pulled rank on me.'

'That was my next move,' grinned Pascoe.

t the university, Pascoe entered the lecture theatre just as Dr Pottle was concluding his introduction of Frère Jacques. The front rows were full but there were plenty of empty seats near the back. Perhaps the flu bug was to blame. Pascoe seated himself in the rearmost row alongside a trio of world-weary female students who looked like they'd only come in to get out of the cold. Pottle finished and stepped down to take a seat at the front. A woman next to him turned her head to speak and, though he'd only seen a book jacket photo, Pascoe thought he recognized Amaryllis Haseen.

Frère Jacques was a surprise. With his cropped blond hair and his tight-fitting black turtleneck, which showed a muscular torso with no sign of fat, he looked more like a ski instructor than a monk.

'Well, hello sailor,' said one of the girls sitting near Pascoe. 'Wonder if he's got a dick to match?'

It came out perfectly natural, on a par with a young man's *not many of them in a pound* on sight of a big-breasted woman. Was this an advance to equality or a backward step? wondered Pascoe.

Jacques began talking. His English was structurally perfect with just enough of an accent to be sexy. He talked easily of death, his own experiences as a soldier, his belief that Western man's growing obsession with longevity and wonder cures had foolishly made a foe out of the one fact of nature we couldn't hope to defeat.

'*Pick your friends carefully* is a wise motto,' he said. 'But pick your enemies even more carefully is a wiser one. Losing a friend is much easier than losing an enemy.'

His ideas were carefully couched in the language of psychology and philosophy rather than of religion. Only once did he stray in the direction of Christian dogma, and that was when he referred with an ironic twinkle of those luminous blue eyes to the unique comforts of the English Prayer Book 'which assures mourners at a funeral that "man that is born of woman hath but a short time to live and is full of misery. He cometh up and is cut down like a flower." No wonder the tradition has grown up after a funeral of heading back to a house or pub and downing as many drinks as are necessary to blot out this cheerful message!'

A thread of humour ran though all his exposition of the stratagems and disciplines by which Third Thought aimed to make its practitioners more comfortable with that awareness of death which he argued was essential to a full life. But there was never anything frivolous or factitious or tinged with mere bravado in his talk. He ended by saying 'It is commonplace, as many great truths are commonplace, to talk of the miracle of life. But being born is only the first of the two great miracles which humanity is involved in. The second is of course death and in many ways it is the greater. The fine Scottish poet Edwin Muir understood this, as expounded in the opening verse of his poem "The Child Dying".

> *Unfriendly friendly universe*
> *I pack your stars into my purse*
> *and bid you, bid you so farewell.*
> *That I can leave you, quite go out,*
> *Go out, go out beyond all doubt,*
> *My father says, is the miracle.'*

He sat down. The applause, led by the three no longer bored girls, was enthusiastic. Pottle stood up to say that Frère Jacques would now take questions and afterwards would be happy to sign copies of his new book.

The questions were as usual led by the tyro academics eager to count coup. One quoted with heavy irony from a later stanza of Muir's poem which referred to 'the far side of despair' and 'nothing-filled eternity' and wondered what the good Brother's religious superiors thought of this alternative to the Christian heaven he seemed to be promising his proselytes. One of Pascoe's neighbours said very audibly, 'Dickhead!' but Jacques needed no external shield, parrying the blow easily with the assurance that the questioner, whether atheist or Christian or anything else, need not fear his beliefs were being challenged as Third Thought was non-secular, non-proselytory, and concerned only with the living.

The girl who'd said, 'Dickhead', then asked very seriously what part sex with its 'little death' played in Third Thought philosophy, to which Jacques replied equally seriously that if she cared to read chapter seven of his book, he was sure she'd find her question answered. As he finished speaking, he smiled, not at the questioner but at someone seated at the other end of Pascoe's row. He leaned forward to look and saw a stunningly beautiful blonde-haired young woman smiling back at the monk.

Afterwards Pascoe bought a copy of the book and was wondering whether to join the signing queue (which included all three of his young neighbours) when Pottle tapped his shoulder and said, 'Peter, how nice to see that the policeman's pursuit of enlightenment doesn't stop in the forensic laboratory. Let me introduce you to Amaryllis Haseen.'

As he shook hands with the woman, Pascoe thought that Roote's description had been a bit over the top but not much. She was definitely sexy in a slightly overblown and garish kind of way. He could see how she might provoke many stirrings and rustlings and scratchings in the wainscot of St Godric's SCR.

He said, 'I was very sorry to hear of the death of your husband, Ms Haseen. Sir Justinian will be a great loss to scholarship.'

Englishmen are notoriously bad at offering condolences and Pascoe thought he'd done it rather well, but the woman regarded him with unconcealed scepticism and said, 'You knew my husband, Mr Pascoe?'

'Well, no . . .'

'But you know his books? Which one impressed you most?'

Pascoe glanced appealingly at Pottle who, smiling faintly, said, 'In fact, Amaryllis, you and the Chief Inspector do have a common acquaintance, I believe. A Mr Franny Roote.'

Grateful for both the change of subject and the opening,

Pascoe said, 'I read with great interest what you said about him in *Dark Cells*, which I was really impressed with, by the way. Fine work. If you've got a moment to talk about him, I'd really appreciate it.'

His attempt at diversion by flattery failed miserably.

She said coldly, 'I cannot talk about my clients, Mr Pascoe, none of whom was identified in the book anyway.'

He said, 'No, but Franny identified himself to me in a letter. Prisoner XR, if I remember right. So perhaps the rules of confidentiality no longer apply. He was certainly very open about his sessions with you and the debt he feels he owes you for supporting his transfer from the Syke to Butler's Low.'

'If you've got a whip,' said the Gospel according to St Dalziel, 'just a little crack will usually do the trick – so long as they're convinced you're willing to draw blood.'

Pascoe fixed her with what he hoped was a stare full of Dalziel-esque conviction.

Get 'em in a corner then show 'em a get-out, was another of the Master's tips.

'But you met him again recently at St Godric's, I believe, long after he'd ceased to be a client, so no ethical problems talking about that, are there? I know it must be a very painful memory to you, that conference. But at the same time it must have been a source of great pleasure seeing someone you'd helped as a prisoner receiving the applause of a distinguished academic audience for his paper. Weren't you impressed?'

'By the paper, no. Like most literary analyses, so called, it was big on waffle, low on psychological rigour. Hardly worth rushing lunch for. But of course it wasn't Roote's work, was it? I was rather more interested in his relationship with the late Dr Johnson.'

'You must have known Sam when Sir Justinian worked at Sheffield?'

'Oh yes. We met.'

He said, 'I knew him too. Very bright, very attractive guy, I thought.'

'You found him attractive?' She gave him an assessing glance.

'Yes, I did. I gather there was some kind of falling out with your husband.'

She shrugged and said, 'On Johnson's part, perhaps. A certain type of character always comes to resent those who have helped them as much as Jay helped Johnson with his Beddoes book. For some people it is easier to quarrel with the helper than to acknowledge the help. I did not know him well, but he always struck me as a very volatile, perhaps even unstable character. I was not surprised when I heard of the circumstances of his departure from Sheffield.'

'The death of that student, Jake Frobisher, you mean?'

'You know of that? Of course, you would. Again the closeness followed by the rejection, the same pattern as with Jay, except of course the closeness in this case was sexual rather than academic collaboration. I think Johnson's death may have been a lucky break for Roote, in more ways than one.'

'I'm not sure he sees it like that. And certainly he doesn't see the rift between your husband and Johnson in quite the same light,' said Pascoe, finding in himself the beginnings of a serious antipathy to this woman.

He guessed she wasn't exactly crazy about him either, and now she proved it.

She said, 'You name is Pascoe, you say? That name rings familiar. Wasn't one of the policemen who helped put Roote away called Pascoe?'

'That was me,' said Pascoe.

'And he's writing to you, you say?' She smiled with evident satisfaction. 'That must be a source of concern to you, Mr Pascoe.'

'Why?'

'Because whenever he spoke of his trial, though he claimed to have sublimated any thought of revenge into other areas, particularly his academic research, I still detected an undercurrent of resentment and a feeling of having been ill done by. Of course, this was years ago, and time does, in some few cases, bring about changes . . .'

'Indeed,' interposed Pottle. 'And Mr Roote, some of whose letters I have seen, wrote specifically to the Chief Inspector to assure him he had no thought of revenge.'

Amaryllis smiled again, like a Borgia hostess seeing her guest holding out his wine-glass for a fill-up.

'Well, that's all right then. If someone as devious, as complex and as clever as Franny Roote tells you that he doesn't want to harm you, what have you to worry about? If you'll excuse me, I'm heading back to Cambridge today and I need to get packed.'

She moved away.

Pascoe said to Pottle, 'That sounded to me very like a vote for my interpretation of Roote's motives. She doesn't go out of her way to be charming, does she?'

Pottle smiled and said, 'Peter, you were aggressive, indeed threatening, and hinted all kinds of criticism of her recently dead husband. What makes you think that psychiatrists are above feelings of resentment and thoughts of revenge? I see you have the good Brother's book. Would you like to get it signed? I think he might welcome being rescued.'

The book-signing queue had diminished to the three female students, who were crowding round Jacques apparently hanging on to his every word and looking ready to hang on to anything else of his they could get hold of. Standing a little to one side, watching with a quizzical smile, was the beautiful blonde.

The predatory trio looked up resentfully as Pottle and Pascoe approached.

'Sorry to interrupt, but you have an appointment to keep, Brother. Ladies, I'm sure you'll find a chance to continue your conversation later in the day.'

Jacques said goodbye to the girls, who retreated, comparing inscriptions.

'This appointment . . . ?' he said to Pottle.

'With Mr Pascoe here,' said Pottle. 'Chief Inspector Pascoe who, among other things, would like you to sign his book. Let's find somewhere a little more private.'

As he led them away, Jacques shot an apologetic glance at the blonde. Pottle showed them into a small empty office, closing the door behind them.

'Pascoe?' said Jacques musingly. 'Tell me, you're not Franny Roote's Inspector Pascoe by any chance?'

'Depends in what sense you use the possessive,' said Pascoe.

'In the sense of being the policeman who forced him to con-front his anti-social behaviour, understand his motives for it, pay the necessary legal penalty for it, and ultimately become the better, more mature person he is now.'

'That seems to me to be stretching the sense quite a bit,' said Pascoe.

'Yes, he told me you had some problems with coming to terms with your role in his life,' said Jacques.

'I had problems!' Pascoe shook his head vigorously. 'Believe me, Brother, the only problem I've got is dealing with Roote's problems!'

'Which are?'

'Basically that he's a sociopathic fantasist whose unpredictable behaviour makes me very uneasy about my own welfare and that of my family.'

As he spoke, Pascoe was asking himself, What happened to my plan of having a quiet chat with this guy about his crazy chum during the course of which I'd glean many interesting ears of information without him suspecting the true nature of my interest?

'These seem large judgments to make on the basis of a few presumably non-threatening letters.'

'What makes you presume that?' demanded Pascoe. 'And how do you know he's been writing to me anyway?'

'Because he told me so. And as I imagine that written threats to a policeman from a former convict would rapidly result in apprehension and charges, I presume no such threats were made. In any case, Mr Pascoe, I hope it will reassure you to learn that whenever he mentioned your name he did so in terms of great respect and admiration, bordering, I felt, on affection.'

'So you talked about me.'

'He talked, I listened. The impression I received was of someone exploring his feelings towards someone else and being rather surprised at what he was discovering. I am not a psychologist – Dr Pottle might well be worth consulting on this matter – but my instinct suggests that Franny matured intellectually at an early age, but emotionally and morally is still in late adolescence.'

He regarded Pascoe for a moment as if to assess how he was responding to this analysis, then went on, 'You are perhaps tempted to retaliate by quoting from his letters some deprecating comment he has made about me. But I would suspect that his initial attitude, that I was some kind of – what is your expression? – some kind of religious plonker worth being polite to for the sake of keeping in with his patroness, Mrs Lupin, has moderated somewhat. You see, one thing my line of business has made me expert in is spotting the difference between lip-service and genuine commitment. Franny, I believe, has made a genuine movement.'

'Franny's expertise lies in making people feel what he wants them to feel,' said Pascoe coldly.

'Perhaps. Shall I sign your book, or was that merely your ticket of entry, Chief Inspector?'

'No, please sign it,' said Pascoe, feeling he'd been ungracious enough for one day.

The monk took the book, opened it at the title page, scribbled a few words and handed it back.

Pascoe looked at what he'd written. It was his signature followed by *Thessalonians 5, 21*.

He said, 'OK, you got me. Save me having to look it up.'

'"Prove all things: hold fast that which is good."'

'That's nice, but for a cop it works out slightly different,' said Pascoe. 'Prove all things: then hold very fast that which is bad. Thank you, Brother.'

He opened the door. Outside he saw the blonde beauty waiting, Suddenly he knew who she was.

'You've made up your mind about Miss Lupin then?' he said. Jacques didn't look surprised.

'Yes, I have made up my mind.'

'Congratulations. I hope all goes well for you both.'

'Thank you. Franny is right, you are a sharp man, Mr Pascoe. We would prefer for the moment to keep our news to ourselves. Until people close to us have been told. My Brothers, Emerald's mother.'

'Will this effect your Third Thought work?' asked Pascoe.

'Why should it? I have never ignored the existence of the two other thoughts.'

'Well, good luck. And take care.'

'You too, Mr Pascoe. And God bless you.'

Outside he nodded pleasantly at Emerald and went to find Pottle.

'So what did you get?' asked the psychiatrist.

'I got blessed. In both our languages,' said Pascoe.

466

he house in which Jake Frobisher had died was a large semi-detached building in monumental granite which age and atmosphere had darkened to mausoleum grey. Situated on the edge of the Fulford suburb of the city, its small front and side gardens were sadly neglected by comparison with others in the road, and the paintwork on the doors and windows was cracked and flaking too.

Pascoe, ever ready to put two and two together, read its history as rich tradesman's dwelling slowly declining towards multiple occupation till it became either by purchase or long lease wholly a student residence, which was probably something of an irritant to the inmates of these neighbouring properties which looked to have reverted to one family occupation as the area swung back up to something like its original status during the closing decades of the last century.

There was a line of bell-pushes on one of the door columns. They didn't give much promise of working. Pascoe peered down a weathered list of names and made out the name Frobisher against number 5. He guessed this was unchanged since last summer when the unfortunate youth had died. He pressed the button, heard nothing, and was about to try other buttons when the front door opened and a young man pushed a bicycle out. Pascoe held the door to assist and got a cheerful, 'Thanks, mate' in exchange.

He went inside.

The smell brought back his student days, not so long ago in terms of years but, oh, an ache of lifetimes away in terms of memory. There was curry in it and other spices, a hint of vegetable decay, a touch of drains, a soupçon of sweat, a curl of joss-sticks and a wraith of dope. Trapped in the refrigeration unit of the unheated hall and stairwell, it didn't assault the nostrils and tear at the throat, but he was glad it wasn't midsummer.

He went up the stairs and found a door marked 5 on the first landing.

It was slightly ajar.

He tapped at it and when there was no reply, he pushed it open and called, 'Hello?'

No reply. In fact, unless there was someone concealed in the big Victorian wardrobe or, even less likely, under the unmade futon, there was no possible source of answer.

He stood in the doorway and tried to . . . what? He'd no idea what he was looking for here, couldn't begin even to imagine what he might hope to find. OK, a few months ago a boy had died in this room, but in a house this old, it must be almost impossible to find a room in which at some point someone hadn't died.

So what was he expecting? Some message from the grave? Lines from the poem in the Beddoes collection open by Sam Johnson's side when he found the lecturer's body came to Pascoe's mind:

> *There are no ghosts to raise;*
> *Out of death lead no ways.*

So, just a room. He stepped inside as if to affirm his dismissal of the possibility of any malign or supernatural influence. His foot caught on something. He stooped to unhook whatever it was and came up with a flowered bra whose blues and reds had blended in with the patterned carpet which covered most of the floor. He saw now there were other female garments strewn on the crumpled duvet that covered the futon.

Time to retreat and knock on a couple of doors, see if he could find someone who remembered Frobisher and was willing to chat.

'Who the fuck are you?' said a voice behind him.

He turned to see a young woman in the doorway. She was wearing a Japanese robe and drying her long blonde hair with a towel. She looked as unpleased as she sounded.

468

She also looked as if the slightest wrong move would have her yelling for help.

Pascoe smiled and made a reassuring gesture, which turned out to be a bad idea as it only drew attention to the bra he was holding.

'I'm sorry,' he said. 'I didn't realize that . . .'

That the room was occupied? That it was occupied by a female?

He changed direction, heading for firmer ground.

'I'm a policeman,' he said, reaching for his warrant card, which gave him an excuse to casually drop the bra.

He opened the card and held it up without moving towards her.

She peered at it then said, 'OK, so you're a cop as well as a pervert. I believe your type gets really well treated in jail.'

'Look, I'm sorry. I shouldn't have come in here. And I stuck my foot in your bra . . .'

'Well, that's novel,' she said. 'That *will* sound interesting in court.'

This was not going well. It was time to be blunt.

He said, 'I don't know if you know, but last summer there was a death in this house. A student called Frobisher . . .

She said with renewed fury, 'What the hell are you talking about? What kind of cop are you? Let me see that warrant again!'

He produced his card once more and this time took it towards her.

She studied it closely and said, 'Mid-Yorkshire? You're a long way off your ground, aren't you? You got permission?'

'Yes, of course. DI Rose . . .'

'That wanker!'

'You know him?'

'Oh yes. Useless bastard.'

She pushed by him and went to sit on a rickety stool in front of a matching dressing table and began to comb her hair.

'If you know DI Rose, then surely you must know about Frobisher's death . . .'

'Yeah, all about it. But it wasn't in this room.'

'I'm sorry, it was the name by the front door . . . ah.'

It dawned, so obvious that he felt embarrassed.

'You're Jake's sister,' he said. 'Sophie.'

'That's right.'

'But this wasn't his room . . .'

'Of course it wasn't. Listen, I loved my brother and he'd arranged for me to have a room in this place when I started in the autumn, but you don't imagine I was going to take the same room he was killed in, do you? That would be real bloody macabre!'

'Yes, of course, I'm sorry. And I'm sorry for intruding like this, Miss Frobisher . . .'

'You could be a lot sorrier if I make a complaint,' she said. 'Trespass and sniffing around my underwear, that could be a bad career move.'

'I'll take my chances,' he said, still uncertain how best to go forward. It would be easy enough to get her on his side by indicating he was still not satisfied with the inquest verdict on her brother, but having her proclaim him as an ally might be an even worse career move than letting her accuse him of being a pervert.

'So what the fuck do you want, anyway?' she demanded.

Time to show your colours, Pascoe, he thought.

He said, 'Just now you said, "the room he was killed in". What did you mean by that?'

She turned to him with the comb halfway down her long wet tresses.

'What's it to you what I meant?' she said.

It sounded like a real question, not a snarl of defiance.

He said carefully, 'I would just like to be sure myself of the circumstances of your brother's death.'

'Is that right? I need a bit more than that, Inspector. Sorry, Chief Inspector. I mean, it's understandable for me, just a silly young woman and Jake's sister to boot, to get all uptight and hysterical about his death, isn't it? I bet that's what DI Rose says about me, when he's being polite, that is. But you, a high-ranking gumshoe from another division, what brings you around all this time on asking questions?'

The best way of hiding the whole truth is with a bit of the truth, as any lawyer knows.

Pascoe said, 'One of Jake's tutors, Sam Johnson, died in suspicious circumstances on my patch last autumn. At first it seemed possible it was suicide and, because he'd moved to Mid-Yorkshire rather precipitously after Jake's death, we had to look at the possibility that there was some connection. You know, state of mind and that sort of thing. Later we discovered Dr Johnson had been murdered so the connection with your brother no longer seemed important. But for some reason I kept on thinking about his death . . .'

It sounded feeble but the girl's eyes were shining as she said, 'You mean, like Johnson's death turned out not to be suicide but murder, you think Jake's might be the same? Not accident but murder? The same person who killed Dr Johnson maybe?'

'Definitely not that,' said Pascoe imagining Trimble's reaction, not to mention Dalziel's, at seeing the headline STUDENT DEATH PROBE – ANOTHER WORDMAN KILLING? 'There really is no way there can be a link between the deaths, believe me.'

Except of course Roote . . .

But he wasn't going to mention Roote either which made it a bit difficult to explain when Sophie Frobisher said irritably. 'So what the hell are you doing here then?'

'I was in Sheffield on another matter and DI Rose told me about your reservations about the way your brother died. And about the missing watch. And because I was involved before, I thought it might be useful to have a chat with you. To tie up loose ends, so to speak.'

This was even feebler than before, and provably so inasmuch as it must stick out like a sore nose that he hadn't come here with the intention of seeing her.

But she seemed satisfied and said, 'OK, start tying.'

'Why are you so certain Jake didn't in fact accidentally overdose in his efforts to keep himself awake to finish his work assignments?'

She was looking at him obliquely now through the mirror in which she was combing her hair.

She said, 'It was just . . . well, you'd have to know Jake. First off, he always seemed so laid back about his work. I used to come up and stay with him sometimes and I don't think I ever saw him write a word. It's all sorted, he'd say. Decks cleared so I can entertain my little sis! As for drugs, he did the usual stuff, yeah, but he was really careful. Had to know the ins and outs of where it came from. He was always telling me if I wanted E's to come to him, not to risk picking up something dodgy from a guy dealing in a disco bog. He was the last guy on earth to go over the top by accident.'

'The nature of drugs is that they affect the judgment,' said Pascoe. 'You can start off taking care but once you're under the influence . . .'

'Score a lot, do you?' she said scornfully. 'I know my brother . . . knew my brother . . .'

Tears came to her eyes and she began to drag the comb through her hair as if trying to pull it out by the roots.

'Maybe it did happen that way,' she said, half sobbing. 'Maybe I just don't want to accept he's dead . . . he's dead . . . I don't really understand what that means . . . dead . . .'

Words of consolation and reassurance crowded Pascoe's tongue but he didn't utter them. If this woman was getting to some kind of acceptance that her brother's death was accidental, it would be selfishly wrong to let his obsession with Roote get in the way.

Looking for a diversion in facts, he said, 'Tell me about the missing watch.'

She rubbed the back of her hand across her eyes and said, 'It was something he got given, don't know who from, but they must really have fancied him. It was a big chunky one, just his style, an Omega I think, gold bracelet – well, I don't know if it was real gold, but it certainly looked the job. And it had an inscription on the back.'

'Didn't that tell you who it was from?'

'Not really. I asked him, but he just laughed and said, "Little sister, big nose, the more she sniffs the bigger it grows!" That's what he always used to say when we were . . .'

The tears were back.

Pascoe, trying to stem them, asked, 'This inscription, can you remember what it said?'

'I can show you,' she said. 'It was quite long, little letters, and done in a circle to fit the back of the watch, so it wasn't easy to read. So I did a rubbing, like I used to do with coins when I was a kid.'

She went to a drawer, poked around for a moment, then handed him a sheet of paper.

She was right, it was hard to read, with the words so close engraved in a fancy script it was hard to tell where one ended and another began, and being in a circle didn't make it any easier. He took the folding magnifying glass he always carried out of his pocket, assembled it, then peered at the lettering again.

It took a little effort to work out, but he finally got it sorted into:

YOURS TILL TIME INTO ETERNITY FALLS OVER
RUINED WORLDS

He said, 'Can I hang on to this?'

She looked at him doubtfully.

He said, 'I'll get it photocopied, send it straight back.'

She said, 'Why not? Makes a change to have someone interested.'

'Yes, I'm interested. But please don't get your hopes up. When was the last time you saw your brother?'

'Three weeks before he . . . died.'

'And he had the watch then?'

'Definitely. God, it really pisses me off to think some plod helped himself to it. And his stash too. That not strike anyone as odd? Just a couple of loose pills found?'

She glared at him accusingly.

'How did he seem that last time you saw him?' he asked 'He must have known he was in trouble about his work assignments by then.'

'He seemed fine. One of his mates said something which made me think he might be in trouble, but Jake just laughed as usual and said, "It's sorted, Sis." Like he always did.'

'I see.' Pascoe sought for an exit line which wouldn't leave hope, because he didn't have any to leave. He was himself clutching at straws, or rather the shadows of straws, and suppose he did by some miracle find that the death of Jake Frobisher had somehow involved foul play, what comfort could there possibly be in that for Sophie?

He said, 'I might as well look at Jake's room while I'm here. What number was that?'

'Eleven. Upstairs. But there's somebody in it.'

'Fine. Thank you very much, Miss Frobisher. Look, like I say, I don't really expect there's going to be anything new here, but either way, I'll be in touch. So, take care, eh? And I'm very sorry about your loss.'

'Me too,' she said.

She fixed all her attention on the mirror. She seemed to have shrunk within the robe and to Pascoe as he left she looked not much older than Rosie, dressed in her mother's dressing gown, playing at being grown up.

The door to Room 11 was opened to his knock by a young man with the build of a rugby forward which, from the boots slung into a corner and the hooped jersey draped over a radiator, he probably was, though why he wasn't running round a freezing field with all the other muddied oafs this Saturday afternoon wasn't clear.

It became clear when the young man spoke.

'Yeah?' he said, in what at first sounded like a thick foreign accent. 'Help you?'

The two further words revealed the truth. Not foreign but true Yorkshire, going into or coming out of a severe bout of the dreaded Kung Flu.

Averting his head, Pascoe introduced himself. Risk apart, the flu bug did have one positive benefit in that the young man, who said his name was Keith Longbottom, expressed no curiosity about his desire to look at the room but merely said, 'Help yourself, mate,' and collapsed on his unmade bed.

Pascoe looked. It was a pointless exercise. What was there to see?

He said, 'Did you know Jake Frobisher?'

Longbottom opened his eyes, walked mentally round the question a couple of times, then said, 'Yeah. Living in the same house, you get to know who's who.'

'You lived here last year then?'

'Yeah.'

Pascoe digested this, then went on, 'But not in this room, obviously?'

'No. I mean it were Frobisher's room, weren't it?'

'Yes. Of course. So how . . . ?'

'How did I get it? Well, it's bigger than my old room, which was down in the basement anyway, so when this fell vacant I thought, why not? Felt a bit spooky, but my girl said not to be daft and go for it. Like she said, it weren't as if I really knew the guy. Nowt in common. He were a bit arty, doing English or something, you know the type.'

The long answer seemed to exhaust him and the eyes began to close again.

'And what are you studying, Mr Longbottom?'

Geography, he guessed. Or Sport Injuries. Get a degree in anything these days!

'Maths,' said the youth.

You patronizing plonker, Pascoe reproved himself, his gaze now going beyond the sport kit to the books lying on the table and standing along the windowsill.

The door opened and a young woman came in unbuttoning her coat.

She stopped in the doorway when she saw Pascoe, and Longbottom said, 'Hi, luv. Didn't expect to see you till to-night.'

'Can't make it. Got to do an extra shift,' said the woman, taking her coat off to reveal a nurse's uniform beneath. 'So I thought I'd best pop round and see if you're still living. God, this place is a sty!'

She began tidying up, shooting suspicious glances at Pascoe.

Longbottom said, 'This is Jackie, my girlfriend. Jackie, this is Inspector Pascoe. He were asking about Frobisher, you remember . . .'

'I remember,' she said shortly. 'I thought that were all done and dusted.'

'It is really,' said Pascoe. 'Just a loose end or two to tie up.'

'You know his sister lives here now?' said Longbottom.

'Yes, I've been talking to her.'

'Not been upsetting her, I hope?' said Jackie, filling an electric kettle at the hand basin.

'Tried not to,' said Pascoe. 'Mr Longbottom, the night it happened, I don't suppose you recollect anything unusual? I expect some one asked you this at the time.'

'Yeah, the pi-, the police talked to us all. No, I heard nowt, saw nowt. Like I say, we were down in the basement then.'

'We?'

'Aye, me and Jackie.'

Pascoe looked at the nurse who was, he noticed, making coffee for two. Just as well. He didn't fancy using any cup that might have got near Longbottom's lips. Perhaps nurses developed a natural immunity.

She said, 'I sometimes stay over.'

'And you stayed that night?'

'Yeah,' said Longbottom, smiling reminiscently. 'It were a good night, I recall. We got some pizza sent in, drank a bottle of vino, listened to some tapes, then we . . .'

'I don't think the Inspector needs the details,' said Jackie.

'No,' said Pascoe, giving her a smile she didn't return. 'Anyway, clearly you were far too busy to have heard anything or seen anyone hanging around. Well, thank you for your time. I'll get out from under your feet now.'

He'd opened the door when the woman said, 'There was someone.'

He stopped and turned.

She said, 'I didn't stay all night. I was on early shift and needed to get back to the Home to get changed. I woke up about half one and thought I'd best not go back to sleep or I'll likely sleep in. No use relying on him to wake me, he's like a log once he's gone.'

Longbottom nodded complacently.

The nurse went on, 'So I got up and got dressed and headed off out. I'd just got outside and was going to start up the steps from the basement when I heard the front door open and I saw this guy come out. Thought nowt about it. It weren't all that late and, in his business, there's no opening hours.'

Longbottom had a violent bout of coughing and the nurse looked at him with concern changing to indifference as, like Pascoe, she spotted this was signal rather than symptom.

'His business?' said Pascoe, recalling what Sophie had said about Jake's stash going missing, nothing but a few loose tabs lying around, about getting her E's from him . . .

'He peddled dope?' he said. 'He was a supplier?'

'You didn't know? Jesus, where do they get you guys?' said the nurse in disgust.

'Big time?'

He looked at Longbottom, who said dismissively, 'No. He just had connections, could always get you sorted.'

'Yes, I see.' But Sophie was right, there'd have been a stash, unless he'd taken the lot himself, which hardly seemed likely. Which meant it had gone somewhere.

'Did you ever say anything about this man you saw leaving to any of my colleagues?' he said to Jackie.

'No. Why should I? No one ever asked me. I mean, I wasn't around when they found the poor sod. In fact I knew nowt about it till days later. It were a right busy time for us, I recall. Don't see how it matters anyway. Unless you know something you're not telling.'

A sharp young woman, thought Pascoe.

He said, 'Nothing, I'm afraid. And you're probably right. It doesn't matter. This guy you saw leaving, was it someone from the house?'

'No, definitely not.'

'You knew all the residents well enough to be sure?'

'No, not all of them.'

'Then how can you be sure he wasn't a resident?' he asked, puzzled.

''Cos I knew the guy I saw. Not personally, but I'd seen him around at work.'

'At work? At the hospital, you mean?'

A wild hope was squirming in Pascoe's belly. He crossed his fingers and said, 'What hospital do you work at, as a matter of interest?'

'The Southern General.'

477

Where Franny Roote had worked as a porter during his time in Sheffield before he moved back to Mid-Yorkshire.

'And this man you saw, what did he do at the hospital? Nurse? Doctor?'

'No, he pushed trolleys around. He was a porter.'

'You don't know his name by any chance?'

'Sorry. And I've not seen him around for months now, so he must've moved on.'

'But you're sure it was the same man?'

'Oh yes. Couldn't mistake him. Dead pale he were, and always dressed in black. Someone once said he looked like he should have been on the trolley himself, not pushing it. Dr Death, the youngsters used to call him.'

Dead pale, dressed in black.

Dr Death.

Oh, thank you, God, exulted Peter Pascoe.

The Child

he Burrthorpe canal, constructed in the age of Victoria to bring the coal from the mines of South Yorkshire to new industries springing up further north, had been one of the first to fall victim to the competition of improved roads, mechanical trucks and developing rail services after the turn of the twentieth century. Because of this it was in an advanced state of decay when the age of canal refurbishment came, and the fact that it was relatively short and did not link up with any navigable river meant that it had little attraction as a recreational waterway, so it lay neglected except by a few hardy fishermen who dreamt of monstrous carp lying in its weedy depths.

The towpath had long since vanished, the banks were overgrown and the only evidence remaining to show that this was a work of man not of nature was the Chilbeck Tunnel not far over the border into Mid-Yorkshire. Drilled through a low mound (which was in fact a Bronze Age barrow, a fact known only to the engineer who shored up the evidence behind his shiny brick walls without compunction rather than risk a delay in the completion of his contract) it ran for a distance of less than thirty yards, but its interior proved so attractive to small boys and others with troglodytic tendencies that the ends had been boarded up in the interests of public safety.

But nails rust and wood rots, and when two hardy Sunday anglers whose boast it was that not even the foulest January weather could keep them from their sport saw the skies darken and the rain come down at a rate beyond even their tolerance, they pulled aside a dislodged board and stepped into the tunnel for shelter.

When their eyes had adjusted to the gloom, one of them noticed a rope floating in the water. To an angler any line is an object of interest, particularly if one end dives steeply into the depths. Using his rod, he hooked the rope to the edge and began to haul it in.

After a while it stuck.

'Gie's a hand here,' he said to his friend.

And together they hauled at the rope.

Whatever was on the end of it was heavier even than a big carp.

And certainly heavier than a pair of trainers, which were the first things they saw breaking the surface.

Then another heave revealed that the trainers still contained feet, and the feet were attached to legs . . .

At this point one of them let go and the other made only a token effort to retain his grip. Heedless now of the rain they hurried out of the tunnel to ring the police.

An hour later, with several police cars and an ambulance pulsing their lights into the teeming rain on the road a hundred yards away, the body of what looked at first glance like a child was laid on the canal bank. The rope was bound tight around his ankles.

The police doctor declared what no one doubted, that death had taken place. Photo flashes lit up the scene both inside and outside the tunnel. Radios crackled. Rain hissed.

Then a new sound was heard, the roar of a powerful motorbike engine being pressed hard.

It skidded to a stop on the wet road, the rider dismounting as it did so and letting the machine come to rest against a hedge. He pulled his helmet off and at the sight of his face the officers advancing to remonstrate fell back.

He pushed his way past them, slithered down the slope into the field and stumbled across the tussocky grass to the canal bank.

There he stood for a moment looking down at the small young face at his feet.

Then he moved through the broken board into the tunnel and a second later all work stopped as a cry like the rage of a wounded Minotaur came trailing out of the dark.

* * *

It was not till the following morning that Pascoe learned of the grim discovery. Sunday he'd spent down in Lincolnshire on a visit to Ellie's mother. He'd faxed in a digest of the official part of his Sheffield visit to the Fat Man and suggested they meet first thing on Monday morning to examine the implications. A trip into outer space wouldn't have prevented Dalziel from tracking him down if he'd wanted an earlier consult, but the discovery of the body had kept that great mind occupied.

'Definitely Lubanski,' said Dalziel. 'Dead for a couple of days at least. Being in the water makes it hard to be precise.'

'How'd he die?' asked Pascoe.

'Drowned. But there's evidence he took a beating first. After that it looks like someone tied the rope round his ankles and tossed him into the cut, then dragged him along a bit afore hauling him out. Several times maybe.'

Pascoe grimaced, then said, 'Asking questions, you reckon?'

'Could be.'

'So it could be they didn't mean to kill him, just went too far?'

'Or that they heard all they wanted to hear, so dropped him in and left him to drown. Either way, it's murder in my book.'

'Mine too. How's Wieldy taking it?'

'How do you bloody think?' snarled Dalziel. 'I just about had to tie him down to stop him heading straight off to kick the shit out of Belcher.'

'Doesn't sound such a bad idea,' said Pascoe.

'Oh aye? Old Mr Human-rights Pussyfoot has suddenly become an expert on kicking shit, has he? Well, I've got gold medals and, believe me, this isn't an option. Belchamber gets warned off, Wieldy gets locked up, how's that help anything?'

'If they made Lubanski talk, won't they be warned off anyway?'

'Depends. If all he knew was what he told Wieldy, that was fuck all, wasn't it? Any road, from what Wieldy said about the lad, I wonder if he told them owt, except maybe that Wieldy was a punter after his arse. Easy enough to credit. I don't doubt Belchamber knows Wield's gay. Gay cop in tight black leathers rides into Turk's with a rent boy in tow, what's the criminal mind to think but he's a bent cop in every way, using his clout

483

to get freebies. No, I reckon that's the tale the lad would stick to.'

'You think someone like Lubanski was capable of that sort of resolution?'

'*Someone like Lubanski?* Hark at you, Chief Inspector. OK, if you won't give the little scrote credit for any noble feelings, how about self-interest? Some psycho's asking you if you've been grassing him up to the pigs. Tell him yes, and you're absolutely certain you're going to die. Keep telling him no, and perhaps, just perhaps, you'll make it. Didn't work out, that's all. Either the psycho miscalculated or he's a real psycho. Either way, it don't matter. Here's how we play it. For the papers, body found in the cut, identification difficult because of deterioration in the water, enquiries proceeding.'

'And Wieldy, is he going to play along?'

'He'd better. I sent for yon Digweed to take him home and keep him there for now, even if it means chaining him to the bed. Yon old fart's likely got the chains anyway.'

Did he actually say that to Digweed? Pascoe decided he didn't want to know and remarked, 'Wieldy won't be happy.'

'Don't want him happy. Just don't want him doing owt that'll make him look like anything but a bent cop shit scared 'cos this lad he's been forcing to give him freebies has turned up dead. That should convince Belcher's boys that Lubanski's told us nowt.'

Pascoe considered then said, 'You've been persuaded that this idea that Belchamber's planning to heist the Elsecar Hoard's got legs, have you? You were a bit sceptical on Friday. My trip to Sheffield persuaded you, did it?'

Dalziel grinned.

'It helped, but it was the phone ringing with news of a definite ident on the body that did it. There's an upside to everything, Pete. Lubanski alive and feeding Wieldy with titbits because he liked to see him smile meant nowt. Lubanski tortured and dead means there's definitely something going off and most likely it's Belchy trying to get his hands on the Hoard. So God bless the lad, eh? But don't tell Wieldy I said that!'

Pascoe looked at his boss with a distaste he made no effort to disguise. From time to time he had tried to persuade Ellie that most of the Fat Man's callousness, not to mention his occasional racism, sexism, and general political incorrectness, was deliberately provocative rather than deep engrained.

'Or maybe it's a safety valve to help him deal with the crap, like a surgeon making bad jokes as he carves open a patient,' he theorized.

'Or maybe you thinking like that is your technique for stopping you kicking the fat bastard in the balls,' said Ellie.

'Probably break my foot if I did,' said Pascoe.

But listening to the Fat Man now made him think it might be a risk worth taking.

On the other hand, his own reaction might have less to do with the natural sensitivity of his soul than with (a) guilt that his own attitude to Wield's relationship with the youth had been pretty ambivalent, and (b) the fact that he'd had a lousy night and was feeling a bit under the weather. It was two days since his trip to fluey Sheffield, just about the right incubation time, and he'd breakfasted on orange juice and some proprietary brand anti-flu capsules which consumer tests showed were less effective than simple aspirin, though costing six times as much, but in whose efficacy he had an almost superstitious trust.

Dalziel glowered back at him and said, 'What's up wi' thee? Ellie kick you out of bed last night?'

'I'm fine,' snapped Pascoe. 'By the way, am I ever going to get to hear what's going off in regard to that German journalist and Rye Pomona? Or is it a national security matter, for your eyes only?'

'Could be. Like you and Roote maybe.'

It was a telling counterpunch. He'd kept very quiet about his continued concern with and about Franny Roote, and he was sure that Wield wouldn't have engaged in a deliberate act of delation over his researches into ex-Sergeant Roote's background. But it was difficult to do anything in this building without twanging one of the threads that ran straight to Shelob's lair.

'If you show me yours, I'll show you mine,' he said.

'You think that'll be a fair swap?' said Dalziel doubtfully. 'I reckon I'd need change. But all right. Two cocks are better than one, as the actress said to the Siamese twins.'

Despite his show of reluctance, it was, Dalziel had to admit to himself, a relief to share the details of his interview with Mai Richter. In the week since, he'd looked at what he'd learned from every which side and found he'd no idea what it meant. He'd already contemplated laying it out before Pascoe, but whenever he thought he'd made up his mind, the counter-argument had come surging back, that this was merely the indulgence of weakness, off-loading on to someone else a burden he'd wilfully hoisted on to his own shoulders, and anyway the woman was long gone back to the land of Siegfried and Lorelei.

But one of his strengths was he was aware of his weaknesses, which happily were to some degree Pascoe's strengths. All right, sometimes he went out of his way to get up that narrow sensitive nose, like when he'd sounded off about Sore Arse and Rusty Bum and the Aral Sea. The difference was that while he knew poetry by rote, he knew nowt about poetry, what made it work, what it was for. Pascoe knew these things. Sensitivity, intuition, imagination, these were the gifts tossed into the infant Pascoe's cradle which had maybe been crushed in his own by the weightier prezzies of a cast-iron gut and sledge-hammer will. No escaping it, Pascoe was a useful, perhaps a necessary complement. Thank God after a sticky start, he'd actually grown to like the bugger!

So now it was with relief that he shared everything he'd done and discovered.

Pascoe listened intently. Physical unwellness, as long as it didn't involve active pain, always seemed to hone his mind to a more than usually keen edge. The Fat Man offered little explanation of his own thought processes, but Pascoe filled out the bald description of events easily, recognizing and being touched by his boss's willingness to accept total responsibility for the 'tidying-up' (or 'cover-up' as it would no doubt have appeared in the tabloid headlines) of Dick Dee's death, both at the scene and in the subsequent witness statements. But the risk of that kind of accusation seemed to have passed, leaving a very different problem, and Dalziel's implied acknowledgement that he needed help and perhaps comfort here was even more touching.

Not that it came very close to being openly implied.

'So there it is,' he growled in conclusion. 'What do you make of that, clever clogs?'

'Forget it,' said Pascoe.

'What?'

'That's the clever clogs answer. Be ready to collect Bowler's pieces and try to put them back together when Rye dies, but till then forget it. There's going to be grief to spare when that happens. Why go looking for more in advance?'

Tables turned, he thought. Here's me being pragmatic, down-to-earth. And there's him, wrestling with doubt and maybe even conscience!

But he knew what Dalziel was really wrestling with because it was the thing which, despite all differences, united them – the need to know the truth.

'Except . . .' he said.

'Might have known there'd be an except,' said Dalziel.

'Except it's no use us forgetting it unless everyone else is forgetting it too. This woman, Rogers/Richter, how'd she look to you?'

'Nice tits,' said Dalziel reminiscently.

Pascoe resisted the bait and said, 'You think she's going to drop it?'

'Aye. Not her cup of tea. Also she got to like Pomona and started feeling guilty. Plus there's this feminist solidarity thing, sisters, sisters . . . weren't there a song?'

Fearful that Dalziel was about to burst out singing once again, Pascoe hurried on.

'Tick her off then. Charley Penn?'

'Charley 'ull never shut up, but he's like a clock. People will only take notice when he stops ticking.'

'Which still leaves the other eavesdropper. The second bug, remember? Where was it by the way?'

'In the bedroom behind the headboard. I went in and had a look afore I left Church View. According to what Lilley told Richter, it was self-powered, voice-activated, range of mebbe fifty yards tops, and likely to have run out of gas after a fortnight. So the bugger could listen in from a car parked in Peg Lane.

487

Or, if he didn't want sit around there all night, he could have had a radio cassette tuned in and left somewhere handy. There's St Margaret's churchyard opposite, lots of nice overgrown tombstones to hide summat like that under. I had a poke around but didn't find owt. What's up wi' thee?'

Pascoe had jumped up and grabbed at the phone on the desk between them.

He dialled, listened, said, 'Hi, it's Chief Inspector Pascoe. I need to speak to Dr Pottle. Yes, urgent police business. Or clinical business, whatever gets him to the phone.'

A pause, then Pascoe spoke again, 'Yes, sorry, I'm making a habit of it, aren't I? Listen, all I want is Haseen's mobile number. No, I won't tell her how I got it.'

He scribbled on the desktop, dialled again.

'Ms Haseen, hi. It's DCI Pascoe, we met in Sheffield on Saturday. Sorry to trouble you again, but there was something you said when we were talking about Franny Roote . . .'

Dalziel groaned, rolled his eyes and generally did his *How long, o lord, how long?* act.

'No,' said Pascoe. 'Nothing personal or private. It was just that you said when talking about listening to him delivering Johnson's paper on the laughs in *Death's Jest-Book*, it wasn't worth spoiling your lunch for. But in the conference programme, Roote was scheduled for nine o'clock on Saturday morning . . . yes . . . yes . . . that's fine. Very helpful. Thank you very much, sorry to have troubled you.'

He put the phone down and turned triumphantly to Dalziel, who said, 'Don't tell me. You've found a way of dragging Roote into this. Jesus, Pete, you'll be telling me next he were Jack the Ripper, after he finished killing the princes in the Tower, that is.'

'His conference session was rescheduled from nine a.m. at his request because he developed terrible toothache the evening before and managed to arrange an emergency appointment for first thing on Saturday morning. Professor Duerden, who had the one thirty session, was pleased to do a swap. I bet Roote was touchingly grateful! But Amaryllis was pissed off because in order to hear Roote, which she wanted to do either for her own professional reasons or because hubby wanted her expert opinion on his state of mind, she had to duck out halfway through a posh lunch someone else was paying for.'

'Pete, I don't know what the fuck you're talking about,' said Dalziel.

'I saw him that morning, in St Margaret's Churchyard. Bang on nine. I thought it was some kind of optical delusion, or even worse, some kind of psychic apparition when I got that letter in which he claimed he'd had a vision of me as he started to give his address at nine a.m. But the bastard was just covering his tracks, don't you see?'

'Hang about. You're saying that Roote were here early that morning . . . how?'

'He drove.'

'Weren't one of them letters you got written on a train? And weren't his car in dock?'

'You do pay attention, sir,' said Pascoe. 'So he hired a car . . . no, wait a sec, Blaylock, that Cambridge DI, he said something about some absent-minded academic reporting his car stolen that morning then finding he'd parked it on the other side of the college. Roote stole it, drove up, got here about half seven maybe, did what he had to do, drove back . . . he could make it by half ten or eleven, plenty of time to show his face and be ready for his post-lunch session.'

'Why?' asked Dalziel.

'Because he's listened to Penn banging away so much about Dick Dee being innocent that he's begun to wonder if maybe he could be right, maybe the guy who really killed his chum Sam Johnson is walking free. So he decided to check out Penn's theory of a police cover-up himself. He knew Rye was away that night, he realized being down at the conference gave him an alibi if anything went wrong, so he thought, here's a great chance to have a poke around her flat and also to plant a bug. He must have just hidden the cassette when I saw him. He probably picked it up last time he came back. It all fits!'

Except for one or two holes, such as, why did he turn the place upside down when bug planters traditionally took care to leave no trace of their passage?

Dalziel didn't look for holes, merely shook his head wonderingly, and said, 'Don't know if you're right or wrong, lad, but it makes no difference. What you're saying is, if there's some other bugger out there still sniffing around, it's up to us to find out afore he does where the smell's coming from.'

'Or put him somewhere that his nose can't bother us,' said Pascoe.

He related his latest discoveries in Sheffield.

'So he killed this Frobisher 'cos he were jealous of his relationship with Johnson?'

'He's killed before. For less reason.'

'Mebbe,' said Dalziel. 'And your evidence for this is what? Something a nurse going on early shift might have seen? After a night spent on the nest, she were probably too knackered to tell which way were up on a bedpan!'

'There's the missing watch. And the missing drugs.'

'Oh aye? Which Roote stole? Why?'

'Drugs, obvious. For use or profit. The watch because Johnson had given it to Jake Frobisher as a love token. Roote took it as a trophy, maybe.'

'Maybe. You got this inscription there?'

Pascoe had photocopied it and sent the original rubbing back to Sophie Frobisher as promised. He now produced the copy with his own transliteration underneath.

'More sodding poetry,' said Dalziel gloomily.

He reached into his desk, found a jeweller's eyeglass and peered at the rubbing.

'Reckon you got it wrong,' he said, not without satisfaction.

'Wrong? How so?'

'I'd say it isn't *YOURS TILL TIME INTO ETERNITY FALLS OVER RUINED WORLDS* but *TILL TIME INTO ETERNITY FALLS OVER RUINED WORLDS YOUR S*'

'Let's have a look,' said Pascoe.

He peered through the glass and said, 'I think you're right. That just makes it even more definite it was a gift from Sam!'

'Or Simon, or Syd or Santa fucking Claus.'

'No, it has to be Sam Johnson. I checked out the quote, or rather I got Ellie to check it. It's from *Death's Jest-Book*, that's a play by Beddoes whose Life Sam was researching. That's the Life that Roote has been given the job of finishing by Linda Lupin. She's . . .'

'Please, God, no more! My brain feels like someone's stirring it with a porridge ladle. I give in. The watch was a prezzie from Johnson to Frobisher. Right, but what's it prove? I reckon we'll have a long day in the outfield if we rely on you getting enough evidence to put him back in the Syke. We're pissing in the dark here. Best thing if we don't want to end up with wet boots is for me to have a heart-to-heart with little Miss Pomona, find out exactly what's going off. And even if she's not talking, I might get a hint how soon it'll be afore she takes whatever she thinks she knows to the grave!'

Pascoe shook his head in disgust.

'There you go again,' he said. 'Same as with Lubanski. To you death's just another policy tool, isn't it? These are real people we're talking about!'

'No,' said Dalziel. 'Not Lubanski. He's a dead person, Pete. Not real any more. Where he was is a space. That's what Wieldy's so cut up about. We go, and despite all the memorial services and monuments and pious crap about living on in memories, we have ceased to exist. Where we were is a space an elephant could fart through and we'd never notice the smell. It's like losing a tooth. It hurts for a bit, then we notice the space for a bit, then we start chewing on our gums or the other side of our mouth, and soon both tooth and space are all forgotten. End of sodding sermon. I'll talk to the lass, do the old paternal act. They all love their daddies, ain't that what Freud says? Now to more important things. This DI Rose, you rate him, do you?'

'Yes, sir. I think he's OK.'

'Well, I've got my doubts about anyone who can come up with a name like Operation Serpent. Watches a lot of movies, does he? All right, all right, I accept your judgment. It's his show. But it's us as will take the crap if it goes wrong on our patch. I'll be seeing Desperate Dan shortly and if I'm to get his go-ahead, it'll be because I'm telling him I've got you overseeing the job. Thinks the sun shines out of your backside, does Dan.'

'That's nice,' said Pascoe.

He stood up and swayed slightly but not so slightly Dalziel didn't notice.

'You sure you're OK?' he said.

'I think so.'

But he was lying. He'd spent much of Saturday sharing air with Kung Flu germs and he knew for certain now they were advancing on him with wild Asiatic screams, chopping and stabbing and kicking.

But he wasn't going to give in! No way ... no way ... no way ...

ife is nothing without death, for it is death that defines life, giving it meaning even when it seems completely meaningless. Ask yourself, what could be more meaningless than a life without death?

Peter Pascoe, lying on a bed of pain, was absolute for death. Every bone in his body seemed to have its peculiar ache. He'd never before been so conscious of himself as an osseous being, an articulated construct. It seemed very odd to him that in art Death should be so often figured as a skeleton. It was in his bones that life persisted, painful miserable unbearable life. His flesh and his mind and his soul were all desperate to wave the flag of surrender, but these insurgent bones persisted in defying Death's violent engines. He lay like Leningrad under that siege, kept alive by the sheer pain of the assault that was aimed at destroying him.

Not that his bones were good for anything other than aching. He had crawled out of bed on Tuesday morning, dismissing as female fuss all Ellie's attempts to persuade him he was unfit even for Dalziel's company. He had got into his car and sat there for a little while feeling that something was not quite right but unable to put his finger on it. The main problem seemed to be finding somewhere to insert his ignition key. Gradually it came to him that he was sitting in the rear seat. It was during his attempt to rectify this error that the unreliability of his limbs made itself absolutely clear, and Ellie, who had been watching his contortions from the house with growing concern, emerged to half lead, half drag him back inside.

Death is our constant companion from the moment we are

> *born, never more than a heartbeat away, and yet we make*
> *a stranger of him, a dangerous stranger too, a bitter enemy.*

Not me, said Pascoe fervently. Not me. Come on, mate. I'm all yours, let's be off, over the hills and far away!

He heard Rosie on the landing being refused admittance by Ellie.

'Why?' she asked. 'Is Daddy dying?'

'Of course not,' said Ellie. 'He's just got the flu.'

Why did she lie? You shouldn't lie to your kids. Tell them the truth. Of course he's dying! Could a man feel like this and not be dying? Most of his body knew it. If only these bloody bones, the incorruptible, the immortal part, would accept the majority vote and let him die in peace! At least his daughter understood how serious his illness was.

'If Daddy does die before Saturday, would that mean I'd miss Suzie's party at Estotiland?' said Rosie anxiously.

'Not necessarily,' said Ellie. 'I'm sure we could find a corner of the bouncy castle to lay him out in.'

> *When the sun shines and the sky is blue and our hopes are*
> *high, then we give thanks to God for life. It is only when*
> *the storm clouds blot out all light and hope lies crushed that*
> *we turn to death with pre-emptive thanksgiving. But it is*
> *in that glorious morning that we should be giving thanks*
> *for death also.*

Later of course when he recovered, the memory of his wimpish self-pity filled him with shame. At what point he had picked up Frère Jacques' autographed book from his bedside table he didn't know, but from time to time he dipped into it at random, hoping to light upon a strategy for dealing with these Kung Flu assailants.

> *While we are living, every third thought should be our*
> *grave, but when we are dying every third thought should*
> *be our life.*

He tried that and he found that the plural possessive was very apt, for the feverish nightmarish world which he inhabited for much of the time was lit by brief flashes of total awareness in which he knew everything that was going on. Perhaps he picked up hints from things Ellie said, as well as from the brief distance-keeping visits of Dalziel and Wield, back at work and, apparently, back in control.

He knew for instance that Dalziel had talked to Rye Pomona because Dalziel was telling him this during his visit, but somehow he found himself experiencing their conversation rather than just listening to a précis of it . . .

'Time for a quick word, luv?' said Andy Dalziel.

'For you, Superintendent, always,' said Rye.

Dalziel looked at her and thought, she knows why I'm here.

Here was her flat. He'd visited it once before, illegally, after his illegal entry into Mai Richter's apartment next door. Light and her welcoming presence made it look different now. She looked different too from the last time he'd seen her. She was definitely thinner. And paler, but her pallor disguised by a light that seemed to shine through her translucent skin. This light, her lively movement, her gay manner, all disguised or at least distracted the eye from the fact that she was beginning to look seriously ill.

He sat down opposite her and they locked, or rather engaged gazes, for there was nothing of strife or opposition in the way they looked at each other.

He heard himself saying, 'Myra Rogers, her next door, she were really Mai Richter, an investigative journalist. I expect you knew that?'

'I guessed it. Or something like it. But only after she left. She said she'd got a job offer down south, but I knew there was more to it. More to her.'

'She liked you. She couldn't bear to hang around after you told her you were going to die and not let anyone do anything about it.'

He hadn't meant to say any of this, or at least he hadn't planned to say it in this way, but to keep as long as he could the advantage of knowing more than she did.

'I liked her.'

495

'Me too,' admitted Dalziel. 'I know how she felt. I'm not mad about sitting around doing nowt while you snuff it.'

'Unless you plan to hold me down while you operate, I don't see there's much you can do about it,' she said, smiling.

'What about young Bowler? How's he going to feel?'

'As bad as anyone can feel and still go on living,' she said sombrely. 'But he will go on living. I'm glad you know the truth, Mr Dalziel, because you'll be ready to help Hat. You and Mr Pascoe. He thinks you're both marvellous. This is your chance to prove he's right.'

He thought of all the arguments he could put forward to make her change her mind, and dismissed them. In the interrogation room, he generally knew after a couple of minutes when there was no point going on. He knew that now.

He said, 'You'll do what you want, lass. In my experience that's what lasses usually do. One thing, but – are you planning to leave any little billy-doos behind you?'

'In my experience, you can be a bit more direct than that,' she said.

'All right. There's buggers like Charley Penn and maybe others who don't think the Wordman's dead. I'm not interested in what you and Dee were getting up to that day out at the Stang. But I'd like to know what you think, Is the Wordman dead?'

She thought about this long enough to make him feel uneasy. Then she said in a low voice, 'Yes, I believe he is. And I'm sure that when he looks back at what he did, whatever pleas there might be in mitigation, he is filled with a horror that makes death welcome. But Charley Penn is right. Dick Dee was a lovely man. Charley's right to remember him like that. When we die I don't think anything matters much, but if anything matters a little, it's how our friends remember us. Goodbye now, Mr Dalziel.'

She watched him go. And Pascoe through his feverish gaze watched him go too at the end of his sick-room visit and found he was watching through Rye Pomona's cool brown eyes and thinking what she was thinking, which was so unthinkable that he twisted in his turbulent thoughts like a drowning man and struck out wildly for some impossible shore and found himself in the middle of Edgar Wield's pain . . .

'I'm sorry,' Wield said. 'This is stupid. I shouldn't be like this. It's worse than stupid, it's unfair. I shouldn't be doing this to you.'

'And who else should you be doing it to?' said Digweed. 'So shut up and eat your *frikadeller*. They are, though I say it myself as shouldn't, being the one who has slaved away in the kitchen to produce them, quite perfect.'

Wield, who found them indistinguishable from frozen meatballs cooked in the microwave, dutifully put one in his mouth.

'I don't know why I should feel like this,' he said, chewing. 'There really was nothing between us, Edwin, you know that, don't you?'

'Oh yes there was,' said Digweed. 'He must have been a remarkable child. I told you at Christmas he was looking for a dad, and, against all the odds, I think he succeeded. You're not acting like a bereft lover, Edgar, but a bereaved father. Which is fine. Odd but fine. But for once I agree with that stuffed cloak-bag of guts, that roasted Manningtree ox, Superintendent Dalziel. What you mustn't act like is an avenging fury. No man can profit from assaulting a lawyer. Besides, from what I know of Marcus Belchamber, he seems unlikely to have countenanced this brutal assault.'

'He's countenancing what could turn out to be a brutal assault on some security guards,' retorted Wield.

Usually he was as discreet as a confessor about the details of his job, but grief and anger had unlocked his lips.

'At a distance, in pursuit of an obsession, and on people he doesn't know,' said Digweed. 'I dare say this has given him pause. Shock at Lee's death plus fear of what he may have revealed to you could well result in the whole thing being cancelled.'

'I hope not,' said Wield. 'Because if we can't get him for this, I'll need to go round to his office and punch his lights out.'

He spoke tough but he didn't feel tough. Vengeance was for heroes. He did not feel heroic. Nothing he could do to anyone was going to remove either of those memories which would forever have the power to leave him feeling weak as a tired child trying to weep away this life of care. The first was of that other tired child's battered, drowned face looking up at him on the canal bank. The second was of that same face, smiling encouragingly, lovingly, as it belted out the words of the song on the karaoke screen.

I really need you tonight ... forever's going to start tonight ...

Perhaps Pascoe had picked this up from Wield's monosyllabic references ... perhaps the sergeant had opened up to Ellie with whom he'd always been very close ... but there were other projections which were much harder to explain ...

In the comfortable study where Lee Lubanski had visited him so often, Marcus Belchamber sat and tried to recapture the sublime thrill he had felt when he held the serpent crown. And failed. All he could see was Lee's slim body being hauled out of the cold murky waters of the Burrthorpe Canal. He had never felt anything for the boy. He was a whore. You rented his body like a hotel room, looked to find everything there that you'd paid for, made yourself perfectly at home in it, but you never thought of it as home. At the end of each rental period you left without a backward glance. And yet ...

If the boy had died in a road accident, he wouldn't have thought of it other than as an inconvenience. Like your hotel burning down. You have to find another place to stay.

This was different. Though he refused to accept responsibility, he could not deny that between himself and that sordid death ran an unbroken chain of causality. It was not his fault that the boy was dead. But he was attainted by the death in too many ways.

His first reaction had been to talk of cancelling the whole job.

Polchard had smiled his cold smile and made it clear that he and his team would still require payment in full. Already because Linford in his grief had reneged on the further payments which had fallen due, Belchamber had had to promise Polchard a large portion of the monies projected from the sale of the disposable part of the Hoard. That was bad enough, but worse was the fear that now that the initial agreement had been broken by Linford's default, Polchard might simply take the lot, ruthlessly melting down individual items to make them more easily disposable.

Or perhaps the crown would suffer the fate of so many stolen works of art and end up as permanent collateral in a series of squalid drug deals.

He couldn't bear the thought of that.

In the end he had to accept Polchard's assurance – no; not assurance; the man didn't feel the need to reassure, simply to assert – that all he wanted was his agreed cut. Which made it easier to accept his further assertion that Lee's death had been caused by an overenthusiastic minion and that to the end the youth had insisted that his relationship with the ugly cop was purely professional. In other words, the dirty little scrote had been giving freebies in return for protection. So fuck him. No problem.

So he gave the go-ahead, trying to retain the illusion that he was still in charge. And he sat in his study trying to recall the thrill he had felt when he held the serpent crown.

And failed . . .

Death is a very great adventure, but to many people, especially to those who find the experience of going on a package holiday traumatic enough, the idea of embarking on an adventure is completely horrifying. Yet with holiday trips, most of us enjoy ourselves when we get there. And at a distance, are we not all full of delighted anticipation?

An unexpected visitor to Pascoe's sickbed had been Charley Penn, or rather he'd come to see Pascoe not knowing he was sick. Why he came wasn't clear . . . something to do with Rye Pomona . . . or maybe with Mai Richter . . . or maybe because his search for answers had left him uncertain of the original questions he'd been asking . . .

Charley Penn sat in the library and tried to concentrate on the poem he was working on.

It was called *Der Scheidende*, literally 'The Parting One' which he'd translated as 'Man on his way out', though perhaps he should try to preserve that idea of parting in the sense of division, which he was sure must have been in the mind of dying Heine with his *doppelgänger* obsession.

He'd done the first six lines while Dick Dee was still alive.

> *Within my heart, within my head*
> *Every worldly joy lies dead,*
> *And just as dead beyond repeal*
> *Is hate of evil, nor do I feel*
> *The pain of mine or others' lives,*
> *For in me only Death survives.*

But since Dick's death, he hadn't been able to return to the poem. Not till now.

Why had Mai gone so abruptly?

She'd said it had all been a waste of time, there was nothing to find, he should forget his obsession and get on with life. But it hadn't rung true.

Somehow Pomona had magicked her. Mai was the clearest-minded woman he knew. He respected her hugely, which came as close to love as he'd ever felt for a woman. But she'd let herself be magicked.

He twisted in his seat and looked towards the desk.

She was there in her usual place, apparently absorbed in what-ever she was doing. But after only a second she raised her eyes to meet his. Once he had been proud of what he thought of as his ability to make her aware of his accusatory gaze, but in the past few days he had found himself wondering if perhaps these eye encounters might not owe more to some power she had of precognition rather than any he had of will.

He broke off contact and returned to the second part of the poem.

> *The curtain falls, the play is done,*
> *And, yawning, homeward now they've gone*
> *My lovely German audience.*
> *These worthy folk don't lack good sense.*
> *They'll eat their supper with song and laughter*
> *And never a thought for what comes after*

A bit free but it got the feel, which in a poem is the greater part of sense. He looked at his draft of the final six lines. Did it matter that he'd changed Stuttgart to Frankfurt because the Main suited his rhyming better than the Neckar? He hadn't been able to find any evidence that the inhabitants of Stuttgart had any particular reputation for Philistinism. Frankfurt on the other hand was certainly a great German metropolis even in the 1850s. Goethe called it 'the secret capital', though Heine's short work experience there, in banking then grocery, hadn't been very happy. What the hell, if some scholar somewhere wanted to write to him after the book's publication and explain the special significance of Stuttgart, it would give the pedant pleasure and himself enlightenment!

He made a couple of minor changes then began to write a fair copy.

> *He got it right that man of glory*
> *Who said in Homer's epic story*
> *'The least such thoughtless Philistine*
> *Is happier living in Frankfurt am Main*
> *Than I, dead Achilles, in darkness hurled,*
> *The Prince of Shades in the Underworld.'*

He turned and looked towards Rye again. This time she was watching him already. Her face was surely a lot paler than it had been, even the natural Mediterranean darkness of her colouring couldn't disguise that, and her eyes, always large and dark, now looked even larger and darker. But this seemed less the pallor of sickness than that cool radiance the Old Masters gave to saints at their moment of martyrdom.

Or something, he added to himself in reaction against the weirdly fanciful thought. But there was something about the girl that encouraged a man's mind down such exotic avenues, an otherness, a sense of disjunction giving you vistas over altered landscapes which returned in a blink to what they'd always been, leaving you doubtful of the experience.

What the future might hold for her and Hat Bowler, who struck him as an uncomplicated young man inhabiting a world of straight lines and primary colours, he could not guess. He had a feeling that they were players in some drama in which his own pain at Dick Dee's death no longer had a major role.

She had a faint gentle sweet smile on her lips. Was it for him? He wasn't sure, but he found himself hoping so.

Perhaps he was being magicked too?

Mist rolling down the hills, a still sea silvered by a rising moon, silence and loneliness in a populous city, eyes meeting strange eyes in the Tube then breaking off but not before a moment of recognition, the feeling of what now? after the applause for your greatest achievement has died, your dog suddenly no longer a puppy, a line of melody which always twists your heart, a ruined castle, casual farewells, plans for tomorrow: the list could go on forever of the prompts to think of death that life never tires of giving us. Don't ignore them. Use them. Then get on with living.

Late on the evening of Friday January 25th Peter Pascoe broke the surface of the surging ocean of strange dreams and visions he had been floundering in for three days and thought of a hot Scotch pie with peas and Oxo gravy and, for a whole five minutes before he closed his eyes again, wondered, almost disappointedly, if perhaps he wasn't going to die after all.

Judgment Day

n Saturday the twenty-sixth of January, Rye Pomona woke on the floor of her bathroom. She recalled feeling sick in the night and climbing out of bed, but she recalled no more.

She stood up and realized she had fouled herself.

Stripping off her nightgown, she stepped into the bath and turned the shower full on.

As the icy blast slowly turned warm, she felt life return to her limbs and her mind. She found herself singing a song, not the words but the catchy little tune. This puzzled her, as recently she'd found no problem in recalling anything, even things from her very earliest years.

Then it came to her that she couldn't recall these words because she'd never known them. Even the tune she'd only heard once. It had been sung by the boy with the bazouki in the Taverna, the Greek restaurant in Cradle Street. Of all the songs he had been asked to sing that night, this was the only one which sounded authentically Greek. The words she didn't understand, but the rippling notes created an impression eidetic in its intensity of blue skies, blue waters and a shepherd boy sitting under an olive tree on a sun-cracked hillside.

She got dressed, tidied up, left everything as she would have liked to find it on her return, locked the door carefully behind her.

Mrs Gilpin was coming up the stairs with her morning milk.

'Off to work then,' she said.

'No, I'm not working today,' said Rye smiling. 'I've been admiring that lovely window box of yours. It's so clever of you to get such colours in the middle of winter, and I thought I'd drive out to that big garden centre at Carker and see if I could pick up anything as nice.'

Mrs Gilpin, unused to her neighbours being happy to exchange more than the briefest of greetings with her, flushed at the compliment and said, 'If you want any help, don't hesitate to ask.'

'Thank you. I won't,' said Rye.

She ran down the stairs, happy in the knowledge that every word of the exchange would be imprinted on the magnetic tape of Mrs Gilpin's mind, and a little bit sorry that she had never gone out of her way to show the woman a friendly face before.

Until she met her neighbour, she hadn't had the faintest idea where she was going, but now she knew. And she knew why, though it wasn't till she crossed the town boundary and set her car climbing sedately up the gentle slope which led to the brow of Roman Way that she formulated the knowledge. At the top, she pulled on to the verge and waited.

Below her stretched the old Roman road, running arrow straight down an avenue of ancient beeches for nearly all of the five miles to the village of Carker. Down there she had sat in wait for the boy with the bazouki, watching as the light of his motorbike raced towards her, then switching on her own headlights and driving into his path.

Of all her victims, he perhaps was the one she regretted most. He had been young, and innocent, with no guile in his heart, and music at his fingertips. She hadn't killed him, but she had caused his death and in her madness read that as her licence to kill.

If she could bring someone back to life . . .

The thought made her feel disloyal to Sergius, her brother whom she'd also killed with her driving, though not deliberately, simply by selfishness and neglect.

But he would understand.

She waited till the road ahead was empty. In her mirror she saw a distant vehicle coming up behind her. Could it be . . . ? Yes, it was!

A yellow AA van.

What more fitting witness could she ask!

But a witness to what? Here was a problem. How could you have an accident on a perfectly straight and traffic-free stretch of road?

Yet somehow it didn't feel like a problem.

She set off down Roman Way, her foot hard on the accelerator.

As her speed increased, she felt time slowing, so that the beech trees which should have been blurring by her were moving in sedate procession. This was part of that aura which had preceded her terrible deeds, the same kind of aura which in clinical terms often preceded the onset of epilepsy or other kinds of seizure. In her present case it could be either, the tumour at its destructive task or the harbinger of her final killing. She would on the whole prefer her medical condition not to be a factor in her death. She couldn't imagine it being a comfort to Hat to know he would have lost her anyway, and she could imagine how he would feel to learn she had been hiding the truth about her health from him.

But if it had to be, it had to be.

Then she saw the deer heading towards the road across the field to her left.

It was, she presumed, moving very fast, but to her leisurely gaze it advanced at a slow lope.

She recalled driving with Hat to Stang Tarn when a deer had appeared on the road ahead of them, sending his little MG skidding on to the grass verge and triggering memories which had come bubbling out, bringing her and Hat dangerously close, making her contemplate for the first time ever – and already too late – the possibility of happiness.

Happiness she had had, however brief, however tainted.

A deer had started it and now a deer would end it.

This was good. Hat would remember, and such patterns of fate are a comfort to the stricken. We grasp at anything to give us evidence that what seems meaningless has meaning, what seems final is only a pause before a new beginning.

The deer reached the hedgerow and flew over it in a movement of such beauty her heart stopped at the achieve of, the mastery of the thing!

Then it was on the road. She swung the wheel over, touched

the brake lightly to give a touch of evidential authenticity to the AA man who was now within sight, and careered towards the far side of the road with scarcely any loss of speed. Yet in her time-out world, the approach to the tree that was to kill her felt so slow that she could make out clearly its bruised and scarred trunk and knew with a burst of joy that here was the very same beech beneath which the bazouki boy had died.

Even the dying which the coroner would describe as instantaneous took long enough for her to see the line it was necessary to cross. On one side knelt Hat looking pale and stricken and on the other stood Sergius and the bazouki boy, overlapping and melding, smiling in welcome.

Then it was dark, and in the control room of Praesidium Security where Hat had been posted to follow the progress of the van dispatched to collect the Hoard, everything went dark too.

'What's up with you?' demanded Berry, the manager, looking with concern at the young DC who had risen from his chair and was clasping both hands to his pallid face.

'I don't know. Nothing. Didn't the power fail?'

'Eh? I think I'd have noticed.'

'No, look there was something . . . see there! The signal's gone.'

Berry glanced at the computerized map, smiled and started counting.

'. . . fourteen, fifteen, sixteen, seventeen . . . there it is!'

A flashing light had appeared on the screen heading south.

'It's the Estotiland underpass,' he said. 'Shields the signal. Usually takes between twelve and twenty seconds, depending on traffic. Any road, no need to get your knickers in a twist. It's on the way back with the Hoard on board that these master criminals of thine are going to strike, not on the way down with an empty van. Didn't they teach you owt at police college?'

Hat didn't answer. It felt like something had been snuffed out in his mind. Was it possible to have a stroke at his age? But there was no paralysis of one side of his body, no twisting of his mouth, no sense that the link between thought and speech had been lost.

Yet something had been lost.

'You don't look so grand,' said Berry, observing him more closely. 'Sit down, lad, and I'll bring you a cup of tea. You've not been near anyone with this Kung Flu, have you?'

'What? Yes. The DCI's got it.'

'That'll likely be it then. How old's your DCI? I've heard it can be a killer.'

But Peter Pascoe in fact was feeling much much better.

For the first time in five days he'd woken up without feeling he had been unwillingly summoned from the grave, and the only trace his mind held of the troubled visions of the past few days had something to do with a Scotch pie.

He had been sleeping alone, for his comfort and Ellie's protection. He pushed back the duvet and swung his legs over the edge of the bed. Excellent. No dizziness, no sudden overheating of the body.

The door opened and Ellie came in with a tray.

'Well, hello, Lazarus,' she said. 'What's this? Urgent call of nature?'

'Something like that. What did you feed me last night? I've got dim recollections of a Scotch pie. I think there's been a miracle cure.'

'Scotch pie? No, you're still delirious. Stand up.'

He stood up and fell over.

'Just a little miracle then. Do you want a lift into bed or are you going to levitate?'

Sulkily he crawled back beneath the duvet.

'But I really do feel much better,' he protested.

'Of course you do. Why is it your bouts of illness always follow such a hyperbolical parabola? A simple cold takes you from death's door to the Olympic stadium in one mighty leap.'

'A simple cold? Bollocks. And hyperbolical parabola sounds tautologous to me.'

'I know you're getting better when you start sneering at my style. And I'm glad of it,' said Ellie, setting down the tray. 'It means I can leave you with a clear conscience.'

'Leave me? I know you writers are sensitive, but that's a bit extreme, isn't it?'

'Leave you to your own devices while I try to stop your power-mad child from hijacking Suzie's birthday party at Estotiland.'

'Typical. Gadding off enjoying yourself while I'm lying on a bed of pain,' said Pascoe.

'What happened to the miracle? And if you really want to change places . . .'

Pascoe closed his eyes, imagined the party – the noise, the violence, the vomit – and said, 'I think I'm having a relapse.'

But later, after he'd heard the front door close behind Ellie and his wildly excited daughter, he climbed out of bed again and this time, not needing to impress with his returned athleticism, he was able to stand upright and take a few tentative steps with little more counter-effect than a drunken stagger.

He put on his dressing gown and went downstairs. As he made himself a cup of coffee he switched on his official radio. He no longer took sugar, but what better sweetener does a man at home need than to eavesdrop on his colleagues hard at work?

Not a lot on the general frequency. Shoplifting in the town centre. Bit of strife outside the railway station as visitors arriving for that afternoon's football match were fraternally greeted by home supporters. And an accident on Roman Way. Only one car involved and they were still cutting the victim out of the wreckage.

He tried the frequencies that CID normally occupied and on the second of them heard Dalziel's voice asking for a report from Serpent 3. Operation Serpent. He'd forgotten all about that. Funny how a virus could reduce matters of seemingly vast importance to vanishing point. Bowler, who must be in the Praesidium control room, reported that the pick-up van was inside the Sheffield city boundary. Pascoe felt a pang of guilt. It should have been his job to make sure that Mid-Yorkshire's share in the operation was trouble free. At the very least he ought to have rung Stan Rose and wished him luck. He could remember his own first big job after he'd been promoted to DI, how eager he'd been to get things right, to reassure everyone – and in particular Fat Andy – that he could hack it. Too late to get involved now, but he'd make a determined effort to be first with his congratulations.

The telephone rang.

He went through to the lounge and picked it up.

'Pascoe,' he said.

'Mr Pascoe! How lovely to hear your voice!'

He sat down. It wasn't a voluntary movement and fortunately there was a chair conveniently placed for his buttocks, but he'd have sat down anyway.

'Hello? Hello? Mr Pascoe, you still there?'

'Yes, I'm still here.'

'Oh good, thought I'd lost you for a moment there. It's Franny, Mr Pascoe. Franny Roote.'

'I know who it is,' said Pascoe. 'What do you want?'

'Just to talk. I'm sorry. Is this a bad time?'

To talk to you? Every time is a bad time!

He said, 'Where are you, Mr Roote? America? Switzerland? Germany? Cambridge?'

'Just outside Manchester. I got back from the States this morning. Plane was late. I felt a bit knackered, so I hung around and had a shower and a hearty breakfast, and now I'm on my way home. Look, Mr Pascoe, I wanted first of all to say sorry about all these letters I've been bombarding you with. I hope you haven't found them too much of a nuisance, but I realize I've never given you the chance to say so. Maybe I was scared to. I mean, if you didn't tell me direct that you were pissed off with getting letters from me, then I could imagine maybe it was OK, maybe you even quite enjoyed reading them and looked forward to them ... OK, that's probably going too far, but writing them has been important to me and I'm sure you can't do your job without understanding how ingenious human beings are at justifying doing the things that seem important to themselves.'

'I understand that very well, Mr Roote,' said Pascoe coldly. 'I think the most persuasive line in self-justification I ever heard came from a man who had just dismembered his wife and two children with a meat cleaver.'

There was a pause. Then Roote said, 'Oh shit. You really are pissed off, aren't you? I'm sorry. Listen, no more letters then, I promise. But won't you at least talk to me?'

'That's what I seem to be doing,' said Pascoe.

'Face to face, I mean. It's amazing, I feel I know you really well, like a . . . really well. But if you think about it, just about all the times we've talked face to face have been when you came looking for me officially. There's not a lot of scope for conversation in those circumstances, is there? All I ask is one meeting, it would mean a lot to me. I could call round to see you . . . no, maybe that's not such a good idea. Invasion of personal space and all that. Maybe you could come round to see me. You know where my flat is, don't you – 17a Westburn Lane. Any time to suit yourself. Or just drop in. I'll be spending most of my time there when I get back. I've really got to get down to some hard work on Sam's book. There's a deal of editing to do, a couple of chapters to write more or less from scratch, and I've even been trying my hand at a few of his 'Imagined Scenes', you know, imaginative reconstructions of events and conversations. It's a device to use with great care, of course, but, as you know yourself, Mr Pascoe, when not a great deal of physical evidence exists, you've got to use all your professional skill to put together a plausible picture of events. Oh God, I'm rabbiting, aren't I? If you could come to see me, I'd be more pleased than I can say. And if I happen to be out, don't disappear. I'm never far away. There's a spare key with my neighbour, Mrs Thomas, she never goes out, arthritis, tell her Francis says it's OK, she always calls me Francis, so if you say that, she'll know you've spoken to me. I'm ringing off now before you can say no. Please come.'

The phone went dead.

Pascoe sat in thought for a long moment. He had, despite himself, been touched by what sounded like a note of real pleading in the young man's voice.

But that was his deceptive art, wasn't it? That was what pleasured the cunning bastard. He'll be sitting there now, that pale face blank as ever, but inside he'll be grinning like a death's head at the thought of the little seeds of fear and uncertainty he's planted in my mind.

He stood up with sudden resolution that seemed to send new

strength surging along his arteries to revive his weakened limbs.

'Thanks for the invitation, bastard,' he said. 'Don't worry. I'll come!'

He went upstairs and got dressed. If he'd gone back into the kitchen he'd have heard Edgar Wield, code sign Serpent 5, sitting astride his Thunderbird on the South and Mid-Yorkshire boundary line, reporting to Serpent 4 (Andy Dalziel) that he'd just had word from Serpent 1 (DI Rose) that transfer was complete and the Hoard was on its way north out of Sheffield.

And if he'd turned back to the first channel he'd have heard that the registered owner of the crashed car on Roman Way was a Raina Pomona and that the corpse of a young female, presumed to be Miss Pomona, had just been removed from the vehicle.

But Pascoe had ears only for the voices in his own head.

he party in the Junior Jumbo Burger Bar was going a treat.

Ellie, on the excuse of going to the loo, had double-checked the kitchen to reassure herself there hadn't been a switch from fresh local produce to reclaimed gunge since her previous visit.

Satisfied, she returned to the party just in time to nip in the bud an assault spearheaded by Rosie on a neighbouring bouncy castle occupied by a tribe of little boys who had been foolish enough to opine that girls were stupid and should be permanently banned from Estotiland.

The boys screamed their delight at the enforced retreat. Then suddenly delight turned to shock as their bouncy castle started to deflate and Ellie found herself with no justification whatsoever staring accusingly at her daughter.

'I just *wished* it,' said Rosie defensively.

Oh God, thought Ellie. Don't tell me I've got one of *them!*

Ten miles away the Praesidium security van bearing the Elsecar Hoard was moving steadily north, followed, though not too closely, by an unmarked car containing DI Stanley Rose and four of his South Yorkshire colleagues. Also moving north on by-roads and side roads were various other police vehicles, staying roughly parallel to the main highway so that major reinforcement was never more than a few minutes away, and in the event things went pear-shaped, all escape routes could be rapidly blocked.

A few days ago Edgar Wield would have strongly opposed

these tactics. In his book, prevention was always better than cure. OK, it made a better statistic and certainly put a bigger feather in the police cap, and in Stan Rose's cap in particular, if they got a positive result by taking Mate Polchard's gang in the act. But no matter how fast they moved in on trouble, there was always a chance the security guards could get hurt. Better by far in his opinion to have flashing lights and screaming sirens before and after the van, sending all the low-life scurrying back to their murky crevices.

But that was before the discovery of Lee's corpse.

Now as he tracked the South Yorkshire car on his Thunderbird, he was longing for the expected ambush to occur, to put bodies in reach of his stick and his hands.

Ahead a huge sign with a direction arrow said *Estotiland – Visitors* and a quarter of a mile further on the slip road slid away to the left. Good planning that, he approved. The complex itself was five miles further, but feeding the visitors off so early considerably reduced the chance of a tailback extruding dangerously on to the main highway. Even as he let these thoughts of traffic control flow across the surface of his mind, he knew he was trying to damp down what the Estotiland sign really said to him. *And I need you now tonight . . . and I need you more than ever . . .* and the foul canal water forcing itself down Lee's throat and into his belly, his lungs . . .

He shook his head violently as though shaking it free of water and forced his attention back to Operation Serpent, scanning the way ahead for the first sign of danger.

Peter Pascoe stood on the threshold of Franny Roote's flat.

Getting the key had been easy. Getting away from Mrs Thomas, the key's keeper, had been more difficult. But after suffering a lengthy and seamless encomium of her lovely young neighbour, Francis, who was such a parcel of virtues you could have sent him as gift-aid, he had finally been released by the announcement of the next horse-race on her television set.

Now as he stood there looking into what he thought of as his enemy's lair, he wondered once more, not with self-doubt but with amazement at the gullibility of his fellows, why it was that he always seemed to be swimming against a tide of Rootophilia.

He also wondered what the hell he imagined he might gain by coming here.

Indeed it occurred to him that the mention of the spare key might simply be a lure to make him waste his time, the kind of stratagem the youth loved.

Well, if he was going to waste time he might as well waste it quickly!

He stepped inside and began a methodical search.

Marcus Belchamber stood before one of the most treasured items in his study – a life-size model wearing the uniform and equipment of a military tribune of the late empire.

On his desk stood a high-powered radio illegally tuned in to police frequencies through which he had surfed until he hit the one that interested him.

Operation Serpent! What dull plod had thought that one up? It was like saying, if you want to keep track of our anti-heist plans, here's the channel you should be listening to.

It did mean, however, that either the Sheffield grass or poor little Lee had said enough to alert even a dull plod.

But according to Polchard it didn't matter that they knew. In fact the plan was always going to assume they knew anyway. But not of course everything.

He was, for such a terrifying man, comfortingly reassuring.

For all that, Belchamber had a packed bag in the boot of his Lexus and a plane ticket to Spain in the glove compartment. When trouble comes, the professional criminal rings his clever lawyer. But who does the clever lawyer ring? No, at the first sign of things going wrong, he was going to vanish and oversee developments from a safe distance.

The uniform was necessarily eclectic; a bit here, an item there, put together over many years and at the expense of many thousands of pounds. Only the cloth and the fine purple plume in the helmet weren't original. He was particularly fond of the helmet. He liked to put it on at moments of crisis. When he was alone, of course. The only person who ever saw him wearing the uniform in part or whole was the dead boy.

Don't think about him.

With the helmet on, he sometimes had the fancy he was that hypothesized ancestor, Marcus Bellisarius. Certainly he seemed to see things more clearly when he wore it, perhaps with the ruthless eye of the military tactician, balancing so many men lost against so much ground gained.

He took the helmet down now. Was something happening? The voices on the radio no longer sounded quite so bored and routine.

He raised the helmet high and placed it on his head.

Stanley Rose was beginning to sweat. He hoped his colleagues wouldn't notice, but when you've got five big men packed together into a medium saloon, sweat is hard to hide. If they did notice, they'd know the reason. And behind their grimly blank faces, they'd be grinning. When Operation Serpent got the go-ahead, he'd revelled in being The Man and he hadn't been able not to let it show. Try as he might, he knew that at briefings he'd come on strong, always having the last word, making sure everyone knew whose show they were in. Christ, when he'd gone to the bog, if there'd been any of the team there, he'd even pissed with more authority!

Logically, if the Hoard got safely delivered to Mid-Yorkshire, that was a job well done. But it wouldn't read like that back in Sheffield. If he'd been a little more tentative in his approach, he might have got away with some heavy ribbing. But when you'd strutted your stuff as The Man, a no-show with its expense of time and effort and manpower was going to be chalked against you almost as heavily as a successful heist.

They were approaching the Estotiland underpass. Another twenty minutes beyond that would see them home.

Polchard! he screamed mentally. Where the fuck are you?

* * *

517

A hundred and fifty yards ahead, Mate Polchard looked back at Rose's car through the mirror of the Praesidium security van.

The pigs were still keeping their distance. He'd banked on this. Not for them the plain fare of successfully escorting the Hoard to the Mid-Yorkshire Heritage Centre. No, they wanted to dip their snouts in the great steaming trough of arrests, and bodies in cells, and headlines in papers. But they hadn't thought to escort the empty van down from Mid-Yorkshire. Forcing it to divert into the Estoti service area off the underpass had been easy. And while the strong-arms in his team dealt with the driver and guard, the substitute vehicle, its call-sign signal carefully adjusted, emerged from the southern end of the underpass.

Reversing the process required a bit more guile.

'Keep it steady,' he said to his driver.

They'd gradually diminished their speed for the past quarter-hour so that now they were barely doing forty-five. Were the pigs suspicious? Why should they be? In any case it was too late now, he thought, focusing his gaze beyond the trailing car.

The pantechnicon coming up fast in the outside lane had no problem in getting past the police car just as the van began its shallow descent into the underpass. Signs warned, no stopping or overtaking, but the pantechnicon flashed its indicator after passing the police saloon and began to pull in front.

'Plonker!' yelled Rose. 'Get past him, for Christ's sake.'

His driver began to flash to pull out, but there was a white transit van slowly overtaking him now, blocking the manoeuvre.

Polchard watched all this in his mirror, then said 'Go,' when the saloon was completely out of sight.

The driver rammed down the accelerator.

Ahead was a sign with an arrow pointing off left, saying ESTOTILAND SERVICE AREA – AUTHORIZED VEHICLES ONLY. The security van roared along the slip road. Further on, down the exit slip road from the service area, the original Praesidium van joined the underpass road at a sedate pace.

'It's all right, guv, he's turning off,' said Rose's driver reassuringly. as the pantechnicon began to move over on to the exit slip road. 'No need to worry. There's the van up ahead.'

'Where the fuck did you expect it to be? Vanished into thin

air?' snarled Rose, annoyed to have let his anxiety show so clearly. 'Close up a bit, will you? And try not to let any other fucker get between us.'

'. . . fifteen, sixteen, seventeen, eighteen . . . there they are,' said Berry as the blip reappeared on the computer screen. 'Not long now. Beginning to look like much ado about nowt, isn't it?'

'Yeah,' said Hat Bowler. 'Nowt.'

This oppo couldn't finish too early for him. Though the extreme effects of whatever malaise had hit him over an hour ago hadn't been repeated, he still felt somehow physically cold and mentally spaced out. Another reaction had been a desire verging on a need to hear Rye's voice, so when Berry was called out of the control centre for a few minutes he'd taken the chance to ring the library, only to be told that Rye wasn't due in today.

This had surprised him. When he'd told her he was going to be tied up on Saturday, he'd got the impression she was working too. He then rang her flat. Nothing but the answer machine.

So she was out. What did he expect her to do when he wasn't around? Sit at home and mope?

But he felt uneasy though he knew no reason why.

The door of the control room opened.

'Hello, Superintendent. Come to check up on things?' said Berry. 'Must say you lot are taking this very seriously, but it's all going like a dream so far.'

Hat didn't turn from the screen. All his earlier symptoms were back mob-handed. He knew it wasn't Dalziel who'd come into the room, it was Death.

Death that master of role-play who was yet always himself. For he could come garbed as a nurse, or a close friend, or in the cap and bells of a jester, or as a great fat policeman, but the cavernous eyes and grinning jaw-bone were still unmistakable.

So he sat and stared at the light pulsing like a heart across the screen.

'Hat,' said Dalziel, 'could you step outside for a moment. I need a word.'

'Watching the van, sir,' said Hat stiffly. 'Won't be long now till it gets to the museum.'

'Mr Berry will watch for us,' said Dalziel gently. 'Come on, lad. We need to talk. Your office all right, Mr Berry?'

By now the manager too knew that a darkness more than the semi-dusk of a grey January day had entered the room.

'Sure,' he said.

Hat rose and, still without looking at the Fat Man, went out of the room.

'Will he be back?' said Berry.

'No,' said Dalziel. 'I don't think he will. You can manage here, I expect?'

'What's to manage?' said Berry, glancing at the screen. 'I reckon it's all over now.'

'I think you're right,' said Dalziel. 'It's all over.'

Pascoe was beginning to wish he'd stayed in bed.

He sat on a chair and looked uneasily round Franny Roote's flat.

Normally he was the most meticulous of searchers, missing no possible hiding place in his pursuit of whatever it was he was pursuing, and just as assiduous in leaving no messy traces of his searching. In fact it was a standing joke among his less particular colleagues that if you wanted to give a room a good tidying, you got Pascoe to search it.

But something had gone wrong today.

Roote's flat looked like it had been done over by a disturbed juvenile on his first job.

With no effect whatsoever, except to waste so much energy he'd broken out in a muck sweat. He took off his jacket and wiped his brow.

What to do? he asked himself desperately.

Flee, and hope it got put down to said disturbed juvenile?

Stay and brazen it out if and when Roote turned up?

Or try to tidy things up and cover all traces of his passage?

That was going to be hard, he thought as he looked around. He'd made a real mess and he knew he couldn't put it all down to his illness. He'd often looked at the after-effects of a destructive burglary and wondered why it was that as well as stealing the thief had needed to wreck what he left behind. Now he began to understand. For some people it wasn't enough simply to rob; they had to hate and even blame those they robbed.

He'd found nothing to use against Roote, but by God! he'd let the bastard know what he thought of him!

It was a shameful thing to have done, quite inexcusable.

Though, thank God, there were limits.

There was a bookcase against one wall, serviceable rather than ornamental and stained a funereal black. The only things he hadn't laid violent hands upon were the books.

And, though there'd been nothing conscious in the omission, he thought he knew why.

He went to the case and took a book down. He'd been right. The name on the fly cover was Sam Johnson. These were part of Roote's inheritance from his old friend and tutor. If there was anything at all about Roote that Pascoe trusted, it had to be the genuineness of his grief for Johnson's death.

And, of course, it helped that his theory that Roote was involved in Jake Frobisher's death depended on the existence of a love for Johnson that led to a murderous jealousy.

But it made him feel a little better to think he hadn't reached the point where true pathological hatred would have started, the destruction of what the object loved the most.

There was a two-volume edition of Beddoes' poems he thought he recognized, quite old with marbled paper boards. He took down one of the books and opened it. Yes, it was the Fanfrolico Press edition. This was Volume Two, the very book that had been found open on the dead academic's lap.

He started to replace it carefully, and only then saw there was something behind it, a narrow package wrapped in a black silk handkerchief, rendering it almost invisible against the dark wood.

He took it out and carefully unwound the silk.

It contained an Omega watch with a gold bracelet, very expensive looking.

He turned it over and looked at the back of the watch.

There it was, a circlet of writing, which had been easier to make out on Sophie Frobisher's rubbing than on this shiny surface, but he knew it off by heart anyway.

TILL TIME INTO ETERNITY FALLS OVER RUINED WORLDS YOUR S

Well, time into eternity had fallen for both of them now, leaving, like all deaths, ruined worlds behind.

And now at last, he thought with less glee than he'd imagined he'd feel at this moment of justification, he had it in his power to ruin forever the world of Francis Xavier Roote.

Behind him the door opened.

He turned so quickly that his Kung Flu dizziness hit him again.

When his vision cleared, he was looking at Franny Roote.

'Hello, Mr Pascoe,' said the young man, smiling. 'I'm so glad you could come. Sorry the place is such a mess. Hey, you look a little pale. Are you sure you're all right?'

When the pantechnicon pulled in front of Rose's car, Wield's instinct had been to pull out straightway and overtake, but he too found himself blocked by the white transit.

He finally managed to squeeze by through the narrow space between the vehicle and the central reservation barrier just as the pantechnicon began to turn into the slip road. A long way ahead he glimpsed the rear of the security van.

A very long way ahead.

Perhaps it had speeded up. But why should it? The natural thing to do if you momentarily lost sight of your escort in your rear-view mirror was slow down.

He accelerated till he got close behind it. The transit had speeded up too and went by him. Some drivers are like that, hate to be overtaken, especially by a superannuated rocker in black leathers with EAT MY DUST in silver studs on his back. The guy in the passenger seat wound down his window as he went by and Wield half expected to get the finger. But the gesture when it came wasn't the finger, it was a thumbs-up.

And it wasn't aimed at him, it was directed at the Praesidium van as the transit went rushing past it.

What the hell did that signify? Could be nothing more sinister than the camaraderie of the road, one working lad greeting another, as you might nod and say How do? to a stranger encountered on your way to work in the morning.

But as the van rejoined the inside lane ahead of the security vehicle and slowed to match pace with it, his heart misgave him.

Suddenly he was recalling Lee Lubanski's tip about Praesidium which had ended in the fiasco of the only thing going missing being the van itself. They'd all laughed at this new evidence that most crooks were a full stop short of a sentence, but suppose that in fact things had gone perfectly to plan and all they wanted was the van? Which could mean . . .

He slowed till Rose's car was overtaking him, then speeded up again to keep pace, mouthing urgently at the DI in the passenger seat.

Rose wound down the window.

'What?' he yelled.

'I think they've done a switch,' shouted Wield. 'I don't think that's our van.'

It was like knocking at some poor bastard's door and telling him his wife has been in a crash. Rose's face went white as he struggled to resist the words.

This was the young DI's big test. Now he could get angry, refuse to believe it, carry on as though nothing had happened. Or . . .

'Don't be daft,' he yelled scornfully, desperate not to see Operation Serpent swallowing its own tail.

'Ours is back at Estotiland,' cried Wield urgently. 'The decoy'll lead you into town, stop at lights, the driver and his mate'll get out, go round a corner and get into that transit.'

He wasn't sure, he couldn't be sure, but he knew he had to sound sure if Rose was to summon up the cavalry.

They were out of the underpass now. Estotiland was falling behind. They were back at ground level, the road curving between shallow embankments running up to fields.

Time for decision, not debate.

'I'm going back,' he yelled.

He hit the accelerator and sent the bike across the hard shoulder and bucketing up the rough grassy slope.

'By God, he can handle that machine,' said Rose's driver with untroubled admiration. He could afford to be calm. All he had to do was what he was told, no come-back.

In the same spirit, the three men crushed together in the back looked at their leader with blank expressions which said, This where you earn your pay, guv.

'Shut up the lot of you,' said Rose savagely. Then grabbing the radio, he said, 'Serpent One to all units . . .'

'It's over, Franny,' said Pascoe wearily.

Roote smiled with pleasure.

'I think that's the first time you've called me Franny,' he said. 'What's over?'

'The games,' said Pascoe. 'This is the closing ceremony.'

'Surely the awards come first,' said the young man. 'Would you care for a drink? Have to be a tea-bag. I seem to be out of coffee.'

He was looking ruefully at the heap of grounds Pascoe had emptied out of the jar into the sink.

'I'll leave awards to the judge,' said Pascoe.

'Please, don't tell me you've found something else you imagine I've done,' cried Roote. 'I thought we'd put all that behind us. No, I see you're serious. All right, let's get it out of the way, then we can really talk. So what is it this time?'

He didn't look or sound in the least worried, but then when did he?

Pascoe gathered his thoughts. The clever thing would be to get him down to the station and sit him in an interview room properly cautioned with the tapes running.

But you didn't get anywhere with Roote by being clever. So be open, tell him what you've got, get a preview of how he's going to play it so that you're at least partially prepared to counter his tactics when things get official.

He let his mind run over everything he suspected. None of that stuff from the letters was any good here. Roote himself had planted it in his mind and was no doubt fully covered. Hit him with the unexpected.

'You burgled Rye Pomona's flat,' he said.

'That's right,' agreed Roote without hesitation. 'Though I think burglary implies felonious intent.'

'Which you didn't have? I don't think you can deny criminal damage though.'

'Well,' said Roote, looking around his wrecked room with a smile, 'I bow to your expertise there, Mr Pascoe.'

Pascoe flushed and said, 'So what was your intention, if not to steal?'

'I'm sure you've guessed. It's dear old Charley Penn, really. He went on so much about his chum Dee being innocent that in the end he got me wondering. I don't give a toss about Dee, but if it were true that he wasn't the Wordman, this meant the guy who did kill Sam Johnson was still roaming free. Of course Charley's obsessed and a man with an obsession tastes with a distempered appetite, as I'm sure you are aware, Mr Pascoe. I must say I have always sensed something . . . different about Ms Pomona, an odd sort of aura. Anyway, without having the slightest idea what I might be looking for, I thought I owed it to Sam to have a poke around.'

'And you chose a solitary woman's flat to have a poke around in?'

'Where else to start, Mr Pascoe? Charley was full of police conspiracy theory. I knew of course that, as far as you were concerned, that was out of the question, and I certainly didn't fancy breaking into Mr Dalziel's house. But young Mr Bowler, one look tells you he'd sell his soul for the sake of Ms Pomona. So she had to be the starting point. I knew she was going to be away that night, I had an excellent alibi in the conference. My session was a bit early, but it was easy to get it changed. It was a bit of a shock to run into you, I must admit. You looked like you'd seen a ghost, so I thought maybe I could persuade you that in a sense you had. Hence my second letter. Would I have written it if we hadn't encountered? I don't know. My first letter was genuinely intended to clear the air between us. But after the second, I found I was really enjoying having someone I could unburden myself to. In a sense, I regard our encounter as a nudge from God. But I'm sorry if the letters have caused you any distress.'

If he sounded any sincerer, I'd buy his old car, thought Pascoe savagely.

He said, 'So you found there was nothing to find, but left a bug anyway?'

'You found that? Clever. My intention, of course, was to leave no trace of my passage. But I accidentally knocked a vase over, which turned out to be a funerary urn. This confirmed my sense of Ms Pomona's otherness. People who keep dead people in their bedrooms are, you must admit, different. No way to clear it up, so I set about making it look like your normal burglary, rather as you have done here, Mr Pascoe. Then as I was leaving I took the precaution of peering through the peephole, and who should I see lurking on the landing but Charley Penn! That gave me the idea of leaving something on her computer which might make Charley suspect number one.'

'Lorelei,' said Pascoe.

'You picked it up. Good. Then I went into the churchyard to plant my receiving cassette under the eave of a rather vulgar tomb, and that's when I saw you. Waste of time, by the way. A few sound effects and a little pre- and post-coital converse, then the useless thing packed up. So you've got me bang to rights for that. On the other hand, will Mr Dalziel be all that keen to force me to explain my behaviour in detail under the public gaze in open court? Perhaps we'd should move on. I presume from the way you are clutching that watch that there is more?'

Why do I always feel like I'm speaking lines he's written for me? thought Pascoe desperately. Why can't I be a good old-fashioned dull unimaginative cop who at some point would give him a good old dull unimaginative kicking and send him on his way? What am I doing here? There's all kinds of places I'd rather be. Home in bed. Chasing around the county on Operation Serpent. Even, God help me, watching twenty little girls creating mayhem in the Jumbo Burger Bar at Estotiland!

Why in the name of sanity am I here?

For a while as the kids tucked into their Jumbo burgers, there was relative peace. Even Rosie found it difficult to talk with her teeth sunk deep into a succulent wad of prime beef and chopped onion, crimson with ketchup. Ellie nibbled at hers, admitted its excellence, then took another long draught of the black coffee which fell some way short of the standard set by the burgers but would have to do as a restorative till she could get within annihilating distance of a big gin and tonic. Some of the other mums were still trying to be sparkling and sprightly, but Ellie could read the tell-tale signs.

Rosie finished her burger, washed it down with a quarter pint of something which was fluorescent mauve in colour and looked as if it could strip wallpaper, then approached her mother and said, 'Can I go with Mary to play on the Dragon?'

The Dragon was a feature of the play area which in Ellie's view could have been marketed as a pervert's sex-aid. Made of soft but tough plastic in vomit green and arterial blood red, the creature crouched menacingly with its head on the ground. You entered it via its anus and clambered up through its guts to emerge at the top of its spine. Then you slid, legs astride, down its neck over a series of savage bumps, till your weight triggered off some mechanism which produced a climactic roar and an orgasmic jet of scarlet smoke as you shot over its gaping mouth into a sandpit.

Rosie loved it.

Ellie shot a glance at Mary's mum, who shot a glance back. Both nodded and a moment later the two girls rushed out, screaming with anticipation.

Ellie watched them fondly and sipped her coffee. She heard the roar of an engine and saw a motorbike go shooting by on the walkway. Some moron in black leathers. Where the hell was Security? Anywhere near the children's areas was designated a completely pedestrianized zone. Worth an angry word to someone, she noted. But not now. Rest while you could. And besides, the bike was long gone.

Wield had cut across a couple of fields till he joined the Complex approach road. There was a small queue of traffic at the main entrance. He wove his way through it at speed till an irritated-looking security man blocked his passage.

Happily it turned out he was ex-job. He recognized Wield's warrant at a glance and reacted to his terse summary of the situation with equally concise directions to the main service level. He was already on his radio by the time Wield sent the mud-spattered Thunderbird racing forward.

The man's directions were good and within a minute he was on a curving ramp which took him down to the lower service deck. At the extreme point of the first curve his heart leapt as he glimpsed below the unmistakable shape of a Praesidium security van.

But had they had time to transfer the Hoard to another vehicle and escape down the slip road to the underpass?

He tail-skidded round the final curve and saw with relief that he was in time. Two figures wearing the Praesidium uniform were in conversation with an Estotiland security man. He brought the bike to a halt about thirty yards away and assessed the situation.

The pantechnicon was parked alongside the security van. Two other men, one short and square, the other tall and well muscled, were carrying a crate from the van to the larger vehicle. Both men wore navy blue overalls and woollen hats pulled low over their brows. Wield guessed the Complex security man had noticed the presence of these unaccounted for vehicles and come to ask what the problem was. They wouldn't be looking for trouble if it could be avoided and so far the conversation looked pretty amicable. But any second the security man's radio could sound an alert and then things might get nasty. They needed bodies down here fast. What was DI Rose doing? Did he have the bottle for this? Where was the cavalry?

Above all, where the hell was Andy Dalziel when you needed him?

Andy Dalziel stood with his arms locked around Hat Bowler's body. Whether he was offering comfort or applying restraint he didn't know. He was experiencing a very odd feeling. Utter helplessness.

Later when he gathered together every scrap of information on the circumstances of Rye Pomona's death, he would be able to put them together with all those other scraps and hints and intuitions which added up to a conclusion too monstrous to articulate, and tell himself, this way was best. This drew a necessary line under everything.

But there in that untidy office with the boy in his arms, his body feeling as lifeless as that other sad corpse now lying in the mortuary, he would have given anything to have the power to breathe life back into both of them.

His mobile started squeaking like a bat in his pocket.

He ignored it.

The squeaking went on.

'Answer it,' commanded Hat.

He thinks it might be a message saying it's all been a dreadful mistake, thought Dalziel. In a life with too many deaths in it, he had come to understand at what pathetically flimsy straws desperate fingers may grasp.

He removed one arm from its embrace and took the phone out.

'Dalziel,' he said.

Hat's ear was pressed close so that he could catch the voice coming out of the mobile.

'Guv, it's Novello. I've been trying to get you. Serpent's gone pear-shaped. They've done a switch out at the Estotiland complex. No one seems sure where the Hoard is . . .'

'Jesus wept!' exclaimed Dalziel.

He let Hat go and headed back to the control room.

Berry looked up from his newspaper.

'Nearly there,' he said cheerfully, nodding towards the screen where the flashing light was just crossing the city boundary. 'Going to join the welcome committee, are you?'

'Wanker!' snarled Dalziel.

He went out again and met Hat coming out of the office.

'Where do you think you're going?' he demanded.

'To the hospital, where else?' retorted the young man.

One straw crumples, you grab at the next.

'I'll come with you.'

'Don't be stupid,' said Hat savagely. 'You've got work to do.'

He pushed the Fat Man aside and ran down the stairs.

Dalziel watched him go, that unfamiliar feeling back with reinforcements.

Then he put the phone to his ear again and said, 'Ivor, you still there?'

'Yes, sir.'

'I'm on my way. Listen, you get yourself down to the hospital morgue. Bowler's on his way there. I want you to stick to him like shit to a blanket, OK? Don't let him out of your sight. If he goes to the bog, count ten then kick the door down. Got that? Good.'

He thrust the phone into his pocket and headed down the stairs at a speed to match the young DC's. This was feeling like a very bad day indeed.

At least there was no way he could see for it to get worse.

Pascoe said, 'Yes, there's more and it gets more serious. Jake Frobisher. You remember him?'

Roote's expression turned solemn.

'Yes. I knew him vaguely. A bright young man. Tragic accident. Greatly missed.'

'Especially by Sam Johnson.'

'Indeed. Sam was very close to Jake, and naturally he was cut up when it turned out Jake had overdone it, popping pills to keep him awake to catch up with his course work.'

He enunciated the words carefully, like a kid reciting a lesson.

'Yes, I understand that was the official verdict,' said Pascoe. 'And I can see why, in the circumstances, Sam should feel so cut up he couldn't wait to get away from Sheffield. Which explains his rather precipitous move to MYU, with all its sad consequences. Funny that. You could say, if Jake hadn't died, Sam would still be alive too.'

That got to you! thought Pascoe gleefully as for a second pain fractured the mask of polite interest on Roote's face.

'I've often thought the same,' said the young man quietly.

'I bet you have,' said Pascoe. 'I bet you could write a nice little paper on tragic irony, couldn't you, Mr Roote? Tragic irony and the eternal triangle, by F. X. Roote MA. A new research topic after you've finished exploring Revenge.'

'What are you getting at?'

'Let me spell it out. Sam and Jake were lovers. That got right up your nose. You alone wanted to be Sam's best boy. You chummed up with Jake and waited your chance to break up the relationship. Maybe you even encouraged the boy to believe that his closeness to Sam put him above the uni's normal academic demands. Whatever, it finally came about that the Academic Board forced Sam to wield the big whip and tell Jake, either this course work gets done or you're out. Mission accomplished, you must have thought, except that either it seemed possible Jake might indeed get the work done, or you simply didn't trust Sam not to give him a bunk-up with his grades. So, under pretence of helping Jake out, you sit in his room the night before the deadline, feeding him uppers to keep him mentally right on top of things, only God knows what else you slip in there till finally the boy collapses. Plenty of choice, him being a pedlar in a small way. Then you slip away. Only you made two mistakes, Franny. One, you were seen by a witness who can positively identify you. Two, you couldn't resist taking his drug stash and, more tellingly, this love token, which it must have torn your guts to see Jake flashing around.'

He held up the watch.

He didn't expect Roote to start like a guilty thing surprised, but the youth was full of surprises. His face crumpled and tears came to his eyes as he looked at the watch. Could this at last be confession time? Pascoe asked himself.

The security man's radio crackled. He lifted it to his mouth, pressed the Send button, and said, 'Yes, over.'

Then he listened.

Wield couldn't make out the words but he didn't need to. Body language told all.

The security man took a step back from the Praesidium men.

The radio was still pouring urgent words into his ear.

Don't be a hero, urged Wield, letting the bike move gently forward.

The man pressed the Send button and began to speak.

The taller of the other men reached into the cab of the pantechnicon. When he straightened up, he had something in his hands.

Wield, because he had that kind of mind, identified it even from this distance as a Mossberg 500 ATP8C shotgun.

He sent the Thunderbird raging forward.

The big man pushed between the Praesidium pair, pointed the gun at the security man, and fired.

The man staggered back drunkenly, took a few steps sideways, then collapsed.

Wield had to swerve to avoid his body and felt the machine going from under him. His loss of control probably saved his life. The big man had swung the gun to cover his approach and now he fired again. Wield heard shot pellets ricocheting off concrete, felt a spatter of them bed themselves into his leathers. One of the Praesidium men was yelling angrily, but his words were drowned by the noise of a fast-approaching siren. At the same time, several more security men came racing down the ramp.

Wield hadn't stopped rolling till he fetched up against the front wheel of the van. He came to his feet in a single movement and scrambled through the open door, pulling it shut behind him as the next shot ploughed into the armour-plated side. The key was in the ignition. He turned it on, pressed on the accelerator and swung the wheel over hard, swinging the vehicle round till it crashed into the front of the pantechnicon.

'Get out of that if you can,' he mouthed at the big man, who sent another ball of shot crashing into the van's window, which bulged and crazed but didn't give.

A police van was coming fast up the slip road.

The heisters seemed uncertain what to do, all except the big man, who had seized the crate from the back of the pantechnicon and was now dragging it, screaming at the others for help, into the loading bay, heading towards the service lift.

The others began to follow him. Police officers and security men began to run forward. One-handed, the big man sent a shot towards them. It didn't find a target, but it was enough to discourage heroics and send the pursuers diving for cover.

The four fugitives and the crate disappeared into the lift and the doors closed.

Up above, aware of the sound of police sirens but happily

ignorant of the drama going on beneath her feet, Ellie Pascoe grimaced as Suzie's mum, the founder of the feast, acknowledged that the partygoers had eaten as much as they could contain. Next on the agenda was the Punch and Judy show, a sore test of political correctness but a good way of channelling the little buggers' newly refreshed energies and aggressions.

Leaving the other mums to get the kids into a rough kind of line, Ellie went outside to summon Rosie and her friend. Little Mary came instantly, but Rosie yelled, 'Just one more go,' and vanished into the Dragon. The sound of sirens was nearer, coming from all sides. Along the walkway beyond the play area, Ellie saw four men running, two of them in some kind of uniform. One of the uniformed men and a short square man in overalls were carrying a crate between them. The other uniformed man was jogging alongside another man in overalls who was huge and carried something in his right hand.

It looked like a gun.

'Oh Jesus,' said Ellie. Then she screamed, 'Rosie!'

Her daughter had appeared on top of the dragon. She waved at her mother and launched herself down the switchback neck. The beast roared, the crimson smoke belched, Rosie vanished into it and, when she reappeared through the fumes, she was caught up under the big man's left arm.

'Mum!' yelled the little girl.

Ellie began to run forward. Their paths must intersect. The gun began to wave in her direction but she knew it didn't matter. It would take more than a gun to stop her now.

But before her suicidal bravado could be put to the test, there was the sound of a siren behind her and a police car came round the side of the Jumbo Burger Bar.

The fleeing men changed direction, now heading away from the play area towards the crowded commercial shopping area of Estotiland.

Ellie went in pursuit, but as they disappeared through a sliding glass door, she felt herself seized from behind.

She turned on her captor, swinging her fists, but stopped struggling when she saw the unmistakable features of Edgar Wield.

'They've got Rosie,' she sobbed.

'It'll be OK, Ellie,' he said urgently. 'There's nowhere for them to go.'

She wanted to believe him, she wanted to run after her daughter, she wanted . . . above all – fuck feminism – she wanted her husband.

'Wieldy,' she said. 'Get Peter, for me. Please. Get Peter!'

t's funny,' said Roote. 'You know where the quotation comes from?'

'*Death's Jest-Book*,' said Pascoe. 'What's so funny about that?'

'Just the context. A message of love from Sam. But if you look at the context of the quote, we're back with that tragic irony you were talking about, Mr Pascoe. Here it is.'

He took down the other volume of Beddoes' works and opened it at a page which was marked by what looked like a sheet of writing paper.

He said, 'Athulf, the Duke's son, is talking to his brother, Adalmar. He says "I have drunk myself immortal." His brother replies, "You are poisoned?" And Athulf says,

> *I am blessed, Adalmar. I've done't myself,*
> *'Tis nearly passed, for I begin to hear*
> *Strange but sweet sounds, and the loud rocky dashing*
> *Of waves, where time into Eternity*
> *Falls over ruined worlds.*

Beautiful, isn't it?'

'I'm not here to discuss aesthetics,' said Pascoe wearily. 'If you've got a point, make it, then I'll arrest you.'

'Yes, I'm sorry. My point is . . . I think you'd better read this, Mr Pascoe.'

He removed the bookmark and handed it over.

Pascoe now saw that it was indeed a sheet of writing paper which was enclosed in a piece of transparent plastic through which he could see writing.

He looked up at Roote, who nodded encouragingly. And sympathetically.

Don't read this, Pascoe told himself. It's another spell this evil sorcerer is laying on you. Take him in, hand him over to Fat Andy, the Witchfinder General!

But even as he told himself not to read, his eyes were taking in the scrawled words.

> *Darling Sam its all too much its not just the work though thats more than I can get through without the help you promised me its what you said to me I thought you loved me more than that Im looking at the watch you gave me as I write well my worlds really broken now why did you do this to me youve been carrying me for two years now you always said that as long as you were around I didnt need to worry about grades or anything whats changed Sam except that you stopped loving me or maybe all I ever was to you was an easy way of getting your gear theres no other explanation and I cant bear it I wont bear it Jake*

'What's this supposed to be?' said Pascoe, trying for mocking scepticism and failing. In any case Roote looked beyond reach of such weak weapons as he began talking in a rapid low drone, as if returning somewhere he didn't want to be and wanting out fast.

'I was round at Sam's that night, it was supposed to be a review session on my thesis but he wasn't in any state to review anything except his own psyche. He drank and rambled about Jake and what he meant to him. There are plenty of nasty people around in the academic world, Mr Pascoe, and when it became known that Jake's assessment work was way behind schedule, it was made clear to Sam that this new deadline was absolute and unextendable, and if there were the slightest hint that Sam had been offering any special assistance, either by way of writing the assignments or grading them, it wouldn't just be Jake's head on the block. So he'd given him a real talking to and tried to shock him into a realization that he had to find his own salvation. Now he was beginning to feel he'd gone too far. You should never talk to someone you loved like that. He wanted to go round and see Frobisher and apologize. What did a stupid degree matter anyway? They could set up house together, Jake could act as his research assistant, happiness ever after was still a possibility, lots of maudlin crap like that.'

'I can see how it would have touched your heart,' said Pascoe sarcastically.

'I'm not pretending I was sorry to see the relationship heading for the rocks,' said Roote. 'I stopped him going out, he kept on drinking and in the end I put him to bed about midnight. Then the phone started ringing. I answered it. It was Frobisher. He just assumed I was Sam and started off with all these incoherent ramblings. I remember thinking, Christ, I just get shot of one self-absorbed monologue, and now I'm right into another. Then what Jake was actually saying began to get through. He'd taken something, lots of things from the sound of it. My first reaction was, good riddance! I'm not proud of it, but there you go. Finally he stopped speaking, and then I got to thinking what this really meant. And I knew I had to go round there.'

'To make sure he'd done the job properly?' said Pascoe.

Roote smiled wanly but ignored the crack.

'I got round there, found his door unlocked and him lying on the floor. He was dead.'

'Well, that was handy.'

'It was disastrous,' said Roote coldly. 'I found this note. I knew that Jake's suicide would devastate Sam. Plus the knives were out for him in the university, and the reference to Frobisher supplying him with dope would finish him professionally. So I had to do whatever I could to tidy things up. I sat Jake at his table and dug out all his unfinished work and set it round him, making it look like he'd been really trying to get it into shape. Then I put the jug and glass by his hand. I put some pill bottles there too, empty of everything except a few uppers. I checked I'd done everything I could to make it look accidental, and left. I took the note for obvious reasons, and the watch because I didn't want some smart cop making connections with Sam, and the drug stash to stop awkward questions being asked around the house. The rest you know.'

Pascoe sat in silence for a long while. Once more it seemed he was cast as Tantulus; the closer to the prize he came, the more bitter the pain of seeing it snatched away.

He said, 'And you kept the note because . . . ?'

'Because if it ever emerged that I had been there that night, I needed something to back up my story. You can check it's Frobisher's handwriting, and of course it'll have his fingerprints all over it. As I'm sure you'd agree, Mr Pascoe, without it, I might have a problem persuading some people that all I did was help a friend in need.'

'That's true,' said Pascoe, looking at the note thoughtfully.

Roote smiled.

'Another man, Mr Dalziel, say, might be tempted to lose this note. Or burn it.'

'What makes you think I'm so different?'

Roote didn't reply but took the note from Pascoe's unresisting fingers and removed it from its plastic cover. Then he rifled through the contents of a desk drawer which Pascoe had deposited on the carpet, came up with a cigarette lighter and flicked on the flame.

'What are you doing?' said Pascoe unnecessarily. He knew what was going to happen but he had no strength to stop it.

'Just clearing up,' said Roote.

He held the flame beneath the paper till it shrivelled up and fell away in ashes.

'There,' said Roote. 'Now you can proceed without any risk of contradiction, Mr Pascoe. If you are so convinced of my guilt, the way is clear. You've proof I was there. I admit I interfered with the scene. As for the rest, it's just the word of a convicted felon. Sounds like you've got a pretty good case. Shall we go down to the station now?'

It's always me being judged, me being tested, thought Pascoe desperately. Shall I call his bluff, if it is a bluff? Could be the real reason he burnt that note is that now no one can ever check the writing and the prints. Could be he wrote it himself against this eventuality, and now I'm the only living person who can vouch that it ever existed!

His head felt muzzy and heavy. He should still be in bed. He was in no state to be making this kind of decision. What to do? What to do?

Somewhere a phone rang.

'Aren't you going to answer that?' he demanded.

'I think,' said Roote, 'it's yours.'

Pascoe reached into his pocket and took out his mobile.

He didn't want to talk to anybody, but anybody was better than talking to Roote.

'Yes,' he croaked.

'Pete, that you?' said Wield's voice.

'Yes.'

'Pete, I'm at Estotiland. We've got a bad situation here.'

Pascoe listened. After a while his legs gave way and he sat down heavily. Questions crowded his mind but he couldn't find the words for them.

He said, 'I'm coming.'

With difficulty he stood up.

Roote looked with alarm at his colourless face and said, 'Mr Pascoe, are you ill?'

'I've got to go.'

'Go where? Please, sit down, I'll call a doctor.'

'I've got to go to Estotiland. My daughter . . .'

He began to move to the door like a man walking on Saturn.

'You can't drive,' said Roote. 'Not without your car keys anyway.'

He picked up Pascoe's discarded jacket, felt in the pockets, produced the keys.

'Give them here,' snarled Pascoe.

'No way,' said Roote. 'You'll kill yourself. Tell you what, though, I'll drive you. Deal? Come on, Mr Pascoe. You know I'm right.'

'You always are, Franny, that's your problem,' said Pascoe, not resisting. 'You always fucking are.'

540

oote drove as Pascoe, if he'd been in a state to notice, would have expected him to drive. Smoothly, efficiently, never taking obvious risks, but always first away at lights, slipping into the narrowest of gaps at intersections, overtaking slower vehicles at the earliest opportunity, so that they were out of town and hurtling down the road to Estotiland in the shortest time possible.

As he drove he asked questions. Pascoe, using all his will to hold himself together mentally and physically, had none left over to resist interrogation and answered automatically. The whole story unfolded. Only once did Roote make any attempt at conventional reassurance and that was when Polchard was mentioned.

'Mate?' he said. 'Then there's nothing to worry about. Necessary violence only. He'll know there's no benefit in hurting your daughter.'

'Where was the benefit in drowning Lee Lubanski?' replied Pascoe dully. 'He did it all the same.'

As they approached the Complex, Roote said, 'Looks like wall-to-wall fuzz ahead. You got one of those noddy lights? Else we're going to take forever getting through.'

Pascoe reached in the back and found the lamp. He hadn't used it since that morning he'd raced along the bus lane to get Rosie to her clarinet lesson on time, the same morning he'd had his apparent vision of Roote.

Even with the lamp flashing, a couple of cops seemed inclined to check their progress but rapidly hopped aside as Roote wove his way through the scatter of cars with undiminished speed.

'We've got to find out where to go,' said Pascoe, reaching for his phone.

'It's all right. I'm following Mr Dalziel.'

Pascoe had been aware of a car ahead of them, but now for the first time he realized who was in it.

As he watched, it skidded to a stop by a side door in the structure holding the main shopping mall. The Fat Man got out and headed inside. Pascoe reached over and leaned on the horn. Dalziel paused, looked round, then waited for them to get out and join him. His gaze touched curiously on Roote but his main concern was for Pascoe.

'Pete, you look like shit. But I'm glad you're here for Ellie's sake. No change as far as I can make out. Let's get inside and check.'

They went inside. A few steps behind, Roote followed.

They climbed a flight of stairs till they reached a door marked SECURITY – NO ADMITTANCE WITHOUT PASS. A uniformed constable stood outside. For a moment he looked inclined to hinder their progress, but one look at Dalziel's face changed his mind.

Inside they passed through a large office into an even larger control room with TV monitors banked up an entire wall. There were several people here, including Wield and DI Rose. And Ellie.

She saw her husband and came to him in a rush. They embraced like lovers on a sinking ship, each other's last hope in a disintegrating world.

Dalziel said, 'Situation?'

He spoke to Wield, not to Rose.

The sergeant said, 'There's four of them. They're on the top floor, back of the building, lingerie department.'

'Lingerie!'

'No significance. Just happens to be the section you arrive at if you keep heading up towards the roof, which was what they were after, I reckon. It's a flat roof with several fire escapes. By the time they showed there, we'd got the escapes covered, though. DI Rose's quick thinking saw to that.'

For the first time Dalziel looked at the South Yorkshire DI.

'Stan, isn't it?' he said. 'Stan the Serpent. How do you see things, Hissing Stan?'

Poor sod, thought Wield. He's tracked dirt on to Andy Dalziel's carpet and he's going to have his nose rubbed in it.

Rose said, 'We've got an Armed Response Unit in position, all exits covered, Inspector Curtis in charge, he's out there doing a recce at the moment.'

Pascoe and Ellie had broken apart now.

Pascoe said, 'What about contact? Have they made any demands?'

He was still looking like shit, thought Dalziel, but not such bad shit. Nothing like being at the front to stiffen the sinews, summon up the blood.

'Not yet. There's a phone up there. We keep on ringing but no one's picked it up yet.'

'Can we see anything on the closed circuit?' asked Pascoe staring desperately at the wall of screens.

'Sorry. Those two there, B3 and 4, cover that area of the top floor.'

'Shot them out, did they?'

'Don't think so,' said a man in a black suit. 'I'm Kilroy, Head of Security for Estotiland. I think they've got someone who knows his electronics. I think they simply disconnected them.'

Ellie said to Pascoe, 'But they saw them arrive before the monitors went. Rosie was with them, she looked OK, isn't that right?'

She was asking for a repeat reassurance for herself as much as for her husband.

One of the security men monitoring the screens turned round and nodded reassuringly.

'Yeah, she was walking with one of them, he was holding her hand, but she didn't look distressed or owt. In fact she seemed to be talking away ten to the dozen.'

'That's my girl,' said Dalziel. 'She'll be grand.'

Ignoring him, Pascoe said, 'Any other hostages? The place must have been packed with people.'

'We sounded the fire alarm,' said Wield. 'Got everyone out

double quick. We'd no idea where they were headed and it seemed best just to clear the whole complex.'

'Drills worked a treat,' said Kilroy. 'Everyone safely out in eight and a half minutes.'

'Nice to know your fire drills work so well,' grated Dalziel. 'Likely you'll get a bonus.'

'Sir, one of Mr Kilroy's men's in hospital, critical,' said Wield warningly.

'Is that right? I'm sorry for it, Mr Kilroy.'

The radio Wield was holding crackled into life.

'Control to Serpent 5.'

Dalziel seized it and said, 'Fuck serpents. Dalziel here. What?'

'We've got all four now, sir. You know we picked up the first two when they dumped the security van . . .'

'Don't waste my time telling me things I bloody well know!' roared Dalziel.

'Sorry, sir. The pair in the transit spotted the arrest and took off. Pursued them for fifty miles, then crashed on the A1, no serious injuries.'

'More's the pity. That it?'

'Just hearing from Sergeant Bowman and the team that went round to interview Mr Belchamber. Bit odd.'

'I like odd,' said Dalziel. 'Patch me through. Bowman, Dalziel here. What's the situation?'

'We're outside Belchamber's house. His car's here, open. There's a bag in it with a bunch of money and a plane ticket for Malaga. OK to break the front door down, sir?'

'With a bulldozer if you like,' growled Dalziel.

He looked at the others. He could see on the Pascoes' faces the thought that this was an unnecessary diversion. He wasn't about to tell them it was necessary for him, to give himself time to work out what the hell to do next.

'Sir, Bowman here. We're inside. We've found Mr Belchamber, He's wearing fancy dress. Some sort of Roman soldier's outfit, I think. And he's got a sword stuck in his belly. Ambulance on the way.'

'Not dead then?' said Dalziel.

'Not yet, but it don't look like it's going to be long, sir.'

'Oh, tell him to take as long as he likes,' said Dalziel. 'Keep me posted.'

He tossed the radio back to Wield and said, 'All right, Mr Kilroy, you're the on-the-spot expert. How do you see the situation here?'

'From the point of view of containment, we've got them bottled up,' said the security man. 'No way out. But no easy way in either to take them by surprise. Defensively, they've picked the best spot in the complex.'

'He's right,' said a new voice.

The door had opened and a man in ARU gear had come in.

'You Curtis?' said Dalziel.

'Yes, sir.'

'So what's the problem? There's only four of them, right?'

The newcomer, a crop-haired man who looked like he worked out between work-outs, glanced frowningly at Ellie.

'It's all right,' said Dalziel. 'You can talk in front of Mrs Pascoe. She's one of us.'

Meaning, thought Wield, if I could think of any way of getting her out of here, I would, but I can't, so let's get on with it!

'Four's enough, depending on how many of them are armed,' said Curtis.

'Only saw one weapon,' said Wield.

'You want to bet money they don't have more?'

Wield shook his head.

'Me neither. The point is, where they are there's no windows. There's an office with one door on to the retail floor. Behind the office there's a series of stock rooms with a service lift. They've immobilized the lift, so our only approach is full frontal on the office door across the display area, which we reckon they've got full CCTV coverage of.'

'All retail sections have their own monitors for on-the-spot surveillance for shoplifters and so on,' explained Kilroy. 'All they had to do was disconnect our link.'

'We could cut off power, but the one thing we've heard from them was someone yelling out, "Anyone touches the electrics and we come out shooting with the little girl leading the way."'

He glanced apologetically at Ellie.

'So they can see us but we can't see them? Bloody marvellous,' said Dalziel. 'So what are your recommendations, Inspector?'

'Limited options, I'm afraid. Either the long game or direct assault full frontal . . .'

'You mean stun grenades and CS gas?' said Ellie. 'Andy, for God's sake, tell them!'

'It's OK. We'll do nowt that will risk harming Rosie,' assured the Fat Man. 'What about listening devices? Photo optics? We need to know what's going on in there.'

'We're working on it,' said Curtis. 'Like I say, it's hard getting any kind of access.'

'He seems to be managing,' said one of the security men before the monitors.

Everyone looked. On one of the screens a figure was striding boldly through a display of men's outdoor clothing towards a line of lifts. A man in plainclothes intercepted him and spoke. He took something out of his pocket, showed it, said a few words, then entered one of the lifts and the doors closed behind him.

'Christ almighty, it's Roote!' exclaimed Dalziel. 'Who's that plonker he spoke to?'

'He's one of mine,' said Rose, pulling out his mobile.

He did a quick dial. The man on the screen took out his phone and put it to his ear.

'Joe,' said Rose, 'that guy you just let get into the lift . . .'

He listened then said, 'He says it was DCI Pascoe. He showed him his warrant.'

Pascoe slapped his hand to his pocket.

'Shit!' he said. 'The bastard had hold of my jacket.'

'Where's he going?' said Dalziel.

'There he is, top floor. Looks like he's heading for the lingerie department,' said Kilroy.

'We'll soon stop him,' said Curtis raising his radio.

'No!' cried Ellie.

Curtis looked at her, looked at Dalziel.

'Andy,' said Ellie, 'he's doing something. Nobody else is.'

The Fat Man said, 'Pete?'

Pascoe rubbed his hand across his face. Pale before, now all colour seemed erased by the movement.

He said, hopelessly, 'Let him go. Why not? Perhaps . . . Let him go.'

'Inspector, tell your men not to get in his way,' ordered Dalziel.

'Your decision, sir,' said Curtis, in a tone which said just as clearly, And your career.

He spoke into his radio. They watched as Roote walked off the edge of the monitor.

'He's into the area covered by the dead cameras,' said Kilroy.

Curtis, his radio clamped to his ear, said, 'Sir, my men have him in sight. He's standing looking towards the door of the stock area like he wants to be seen. Now he's walking across the display area. He's at the door. It's opening. He's gone inside.'

'So what do we do now?' said Stan Rose.

They all looked at Dalziel.

He scratched his left buttock like the Count of Monte Cristo beginning to work on the walls of his cell.

'We wait,' he said. 'Pete, lad, you always said yon Roote could talk a rabbi into sharing a packet of pork scratchings. Let's hope that for once you're right about the sod!'

ranny Roote! It really is you. Here, what do you think?'

Mate Polchard was sitting behind a desk on which he had placed a travelling chessboard with magnetic pieces.

On the floor, seated against an open packing case, was Rosie Pascoe, eating a chocolate bar. On her head rested a cirque of gold in the form of two snakes. She glanced at the newcomer, decided he didn't look much fun, and returned her full attention to the chocolate. Nearby a short squat blockhouse of a man in blue overalls was watching a couple of security screens on which the lingerie retail floor could be seen in its entirety. Of the other two gang members, there was no sign.

Roote advanced and looked at the disposition of pieces on the chessboard. It was an early middlegame situation, the pieces developed, no losses yet on either side, but Black had a bit of a problem in the centre.

'Samisch – Capablanca 1929,' he said. 'Black's knackered.'

'Bit early to be saying that, isn't it?' said Polchard, frowning.

'That's what Capablanca thought. Played on for another fifty moves. He still lost,' said Roote. 'He'd have done better to give in gracefully and go off for a bit of shut-eye.'

'That's how it looks to you, is it?'

'That's how it is, Mate,' said Roote. 'Like you once said to me, the thing about chess is it teaches you to see things that have happened before they've happened.'

'I said that? Must be true. How've you been, Fran? Never came to see me in Wales.'

'You know how it is,' said Roote. 'Out on license, they see

548

you associating with the king of crime, they don't listen when you say we're just playing chess. Then, later on, I got a new life going. I'm an academic now. A teacher, sort of.'

'I know what a fucking academic is,' said Polchard.

'Do you? Wish I did,' said Roote placatingly.

'Much money in it?'

'If you know where to look.'

'That's the secret, isn't it? Knowing where to look. That kid there, she's got more money on her bonce than you'll ever see, I'd guess.'

'I get along,' said Roote with a serene smile. 'You know who she is, do you?'

'She keeps telling us her dad's some VIP and he's going to come along and whip our arses. She can certainly talk, I'll give her that. Couldn't think how to shut her up till I found that whoever uses this desk is a chocoholic. Fancy a Mars Bar?'

'No thanks. She's DCI Pascoe's daughter.'

'Is that right?' said Polchard indifferently. 'Bad choice then. Could have been worse, though. Could have been that fat bastard's lass.'

'Still not good, Mate. The security guard that got shot's still alive, by the way.'

'Glad to hear it. Nothing to do with me though. You can't get the help these days.'

'No? This the same mad bastard who topped the kid in the canal?'

'You know a lot,' said Polchard, looking at Roote speculatively. 'That was definitely nothing to do with me. What are you doing here anyway?'

'Helping out a friend. Two friends, if I include you, Mate. Think about it. Good lawyer, few years improving your chess, no sweat.'

'Good lawyer.' Polchard smiled wanly. 'Used to have one of those. Reckon I might be needing another now. What you got in mind for the endgame, Franny?'

'I walk out of here with the girl, tell them you're coming out too. Couple of minutes later, you show; the hard men with guns do a lot of shouting but no shooting, and before you know it, you're nice and comfy where you don't have to worry about the taxman.'

Polchard bent his head over the board for a long moment. Then with his forefinger he flicked the black king off its magnetic base.

'Off you go then,' he said.

'Right,' said Franny. 'How about the guns? You want I should take them too?'

Polchard laughed.

'There's only the one, and I knew nothing about it till it went off. No, Franny, leave the gun to me. I really don't think you want to hang around and try to persuade your old chum to hand it over to you, do you?'

'My old chum?' said Franny, puzzled.

For the first time Polchard looked surprised.

'You don't know? Well, well. And here's me thinking you were really brave! He's wandering around looking for a way out.' Polchard glanced towards the stock-room door and lowered his voice. 'I'd push off before he comes back if I were you.'

'But who . . . ?'

'Go while you can!'

When Polchard spoke with that degree of urgency, even the screws at Chapel Syke had jumped.

He went to Rosie and offered her his hand. She stood up. Her mouth was stained with chocolate. The serpent crown which was too big for her slim head slipped to one side. She looked like a tipsy cupid.

'Your dad sent me,' he said.

She looked at him assessingly. He had seen the same expression in her father's eyes. This time it was followed by belief and acceptance, which had never happened with Pascoe.

They walked hand in hand to the door. He opened it slowly and stood there a moment just to make sure the watchers on the far side of the display area registered who it was.

It was a moment too long.

'Roote! It is you! Roote, you fucking bastard! I've been waiting a long time for this! Bring the kid back inside.'

Franny's brain, always hyperactive behind that calm front, had already worked out who Polchard had to be talking about. It wasn't hard. All he had to do was run a finger down the list of people he'd met in the Syke, looking for the kind of madman who'd disobey even the great Mate's instructions and smuggle a gun on a job and use it.

He reached down and took the serpent crown off the girl's head and said in a low voice, 'Rosie, when I say run, run! But not straight. Run right. OK?'

'OK,' said the little girl, deciding she'd been wrong and maybe he was fun after all.

Slowly Roote turned and faced the man who stood in the stock-room doorway.

He was big, very big. He had a black woolly hat like a funeral parlour tea-cosy pulled very low over his brow. And he was holding a shotgun.

Seeing he had Franny's full attention, he took one hand off the weapon and tore off the hat to reveal a bald head tattooed with an eagle whose talons were poised over his eyes.

Roote's face split in a broad grin.

'No, Dendo, you didn't ... it's real, is it? You got yourself tattooed in loving memory of poor old Brillo! Now that's really touching. You make a great tombstone!'

'Get inside! Brillo would want this to be slow!'

'Of course he would,' said Franny Roote, stepping forward so that his body was between the gunman and the girl. 'He needed everything slow, didn't he, the poor bastard. Run!'

Rosie set off right. Roote sent the serpent crown spinning towards Bright then hurled himself left. The first shot ripped along his shoulder but he kept running. Bright came to the doorway, his face mottled with such rage it was hard to see where the tattoo ended and unsullied flesh began. And then a fusillade from the waiting marksmen punched a new and final pattern into his body. But he still managed to get off one more shot.

Roote felt a blow in the middle of his back. It didn't feel all that much, the kind of congratulatory slap one overhearty sportsman might give another to acknowledge a good move. But it switched off the connection between his brain and his limbs and he went down like a pole-axed steer.

Men in police combat gear carrying guns came running across the floor to the stock room. Rosie Pascoe leapt into Ellie's arms with such force they both collapsed to the ground and already, even as they lay there locked together, the girl was describing her wonderful adventure. Dalziel took possession of an unresisting Mate Polchard. Wield stepped over Dendo Bright's body like it was a dog dropping and stooped to pick up the serpent crown. He saw nothing of its beauty. To him it was a bit of bent metal which wasn't worth the loss of a single second of Lee Lubanski's life.

And Pascoe, after sinking his face briefly in his daughter's hair, left her to her mother and went straight to Franny Roote.

He put his arm round him to make him more comfortable and felt the warm blood oozing between his fingers.

'Medics!' he screamed. 'Get some help here, for fuck's sake!'

'Made up your mind yet, Mr Pascoe?' said the youth in a voice scarcely louder than a whisper. 'Going to put me on trial? No, of course you're not. It's not in you . . .'

'Don't be too sure. I can be a right bastard when I try,' said Pascoe with an effort at lightness. 'We'll talk about it when you're convalescing.'

'Convalescing? I don't think so.'

His eyes clouded for a moment then cleared again and he seemed to take in his surroundings and began to laugh, painfully.

'Remember that inscription I told you about? Need a change now. Franny Roote . . . Born in Hope . . . Died in Ladies Underwear . . . even better, eh?'

A paramedic arrived and knelt down beside the wounded man. Pascoe tried to move aside but Roote's fingers found strength from somewhere to hold him back.

'Know what the date is?' he said. 'January the twenty-sixth. Same day Beddoes died. Funny that.'

'Don't talk about dying,' said Pascoe sharply. 'You can't die yet. It's not your time.'

'Want to keep me alive, Mr Pascoe? It would be a good trick. For all his talk of death, I sometimes think Beddoes would have liked to master it. But why should you want me alive if you're not going to try me?'

'So I can thank you, Franny,' said Pascoe desperately. 'So you can't die.'

'You know me, Mr Pascoe ... always looking for someone who'd tell me what to do,' said Roote smiling.

The paramedic was doing what he could, all the while talking urgently into his lapel radio, demanding to know where the hell the stretcher was and saying they needed a chopper here, an ambulance would be too slow. Franny showed no reaction to the sound of his voice or the touch of his hands or the prick of his needle. Still he kept tight hold of Pascoe's hand and never once took his eyes off his face, and Pascoe locked on to the young man's gaze as if by sheer force of will he could hold it steady and bright.

All around them was noise and bustle, people moving swiftly, men shouting orders, radios crackling, distant sirens wailing; but for all the heed either of them took of this, they might have been a pair of still and isolated figures sitting under the solitary moon in the hush'd Chorasmian waste where the river Oxus flows on his long and winding journey to the Aral Sea.

Imagined Scenes

from

AMONG OTHER THINGS:
The Quest for Thomas Lovell Beddoes

by Sam Johnson MA, PhD

(revised, edited and completed by Francis Xavier Roote MA, PhD)

It is January 26th, 1849. In the Town Hospital of Basel, Thomas Lovell Beddoes awakes. It is early. The large garden overlooked from his window is still in darkness and the birds that winter there have not yet unlocked the first notes of their aubade.

He feels a stab of pain in his right leg, just beneath the knee joint. He grimaces, then smiles as the pain fades. The ghost of a poem in the comic macabre style flits though his mind. In it the amputated limbs tossed into the furnace of the hospital mortuary sing their resentment at this enforced exile from their proper sphere and send farewell messages to the bodies that have betrayed them.

He shifts in his bed and a book falls to the floor. He shares his bed with numerous volumes which range across all his interests, from medical treatises through modern German novels and translations of the classics to a new collection of Goethe's letters to Frau von Stein. Absent only are the radical tracts of earlier days. He has said goodbye to all that.

He lies there with his eyes staring into the dark until light begins to seep through the edges of the heavy curtains, then he throws back the coverlet in a torrent of books and rolls out of bed.

With the aid of a crutch he has achieved an agility which is the wonder of Dr Ecklin and Dr Frey and all the hospital attendants. His generally lively demeanour gives them hope of a matching mental recovery and if his jokes have something of a macabre cast, then they always did.

Later in the day, as he moves rapidly out of the hospital grounds, he returns cheerful greetings to those he encounters who often pause to watch his progress with admiration.

On his way into town he passes the house where Konrad Degen is lodged but he does not pause. That too is over. Degen has been persuaded by mutual acquaintance to return from Frankfurt to Basel to aid his old patron's recuperation. But a true friend would have needed no persuasion. And a son would have crawled over hot coals to comfort his stricken father.

In a quiet side street he pauses a while to make sure he is unobserved by anyone of his acquaintance. Then he enters an apothecary's shop where he is greeted deferentially as Herr Doktor Beddoes and offered a chair in which he sits and chats about his medical researches while his required prescriptions are made up.

Back at the hospital, he tells his attendant that his excursion, though enjoyable, has fatigued him and he is now going to rest for a few hours.

Locking his door, he takes from his pocket the drugs he has obtained. Only one of them does he have any use for. He mixes it in a glass of heavy Rhenish wine, sips, makes a wry face, adds a little more wine, sips again, then sits down at the table which stands before the window and sharpens a pen. His mind meanwhile is running through a list of possible correspondents. His sense of drama, though it falls well short of that necessary to a practical rather than a literary playwright, is refined enough to know that more than one last letter is a profligacy which risks touching the absurd.

His choice is made. Phillips, a good and noble man, head of a happy family and a pattern for fathers everywhere.

He scrawls across the head of his paper *To Mr Revell Phillips, The Middle Temple, London*, and begins to write, pausing from time to time to sip his wine.

Outside the day is dying young.

My dear Phillips,
I am food for what I am good for – worms.

Food for . . . good for . . . I could use that. Make a note?
Hardly worth it! The echo of Hotspur's dying speech makes
him think of Konrad. He pushed the thought aside.

I have made a will here which I desire to be respected, and
add the donation of £20 to Dr Ecklin, my physician.
W. Beddoes must have a case (50 bottles) of Champagne
Moet 1847 to drink my

He pauses. My health? Hardly. Then he smiles and starts
writing again.

> *death in.*
> *Thanks for all kindness. Borrow the £200. You are a good &*
> *noble man & your children must look sharp to be like you.*

Yours,
if my own,
ever,
T. L. B.

He throws down his pen.
It is over.
But the retiring actor does not leave the stage without
many a backward glance and the retiring singer can never
resist one last reprise, and no real writer ever truly retires.
So he takes up his pen again and scribbles a few more
lines.

Love to Anna, Henry, the Beddoes of Longvill and Zoe and
Emmeline King –

Anyone missed out? Of course, the most important of them
all.

also to Kelsall whom I beg to look at my MSS and print or
not as he thinks fit. I ought to have been among other things
a good poet. Life was too great a bore on one peg and that a
bad one.

Bit self-pitying that? Perhaps. End on a jest, that's the true way of death! He winces as he feels a spasm in his gut from the poison. Then he smiles again. A little medical joke to finish with.

Buy for Dr Ecklin above mentioned one of Reade's best stomach-pumps.

Perhaps he should elaborate on this but now the pen feels heavy in his hand and his lids feel heavy on his eyes.

He sets the pen down, takes up the note and carefully pins it to his shirt. He drains the wine-glass and hops across to his bed across which he sprawls supine.

By now it is quite dark outside. Or is the darkness his alone? He does not know. His mind ranges across his life, his huge hopes – for himself, for mankind – and their huge failure, which somehow at this moment of departure does not seem quite so huge. Fantastic images spin across his brain and instinctively he reaches out to them and tries to trap them in a net of words. Now he is seeing death, not on the slab, not on the stage, not on the printed page, but real and active and standing before him, rendering all those thousand of words he has used to describe it sadly inadequate – shards of a broken glass, ashes of an incinerated painting, echoes of a distant music. If only he could raise his pen now, he might after all be more than a good poet, he might be a great one.

Is it too late? Who knows? Can death take a joke as well as make one?

His lips part, his collapsing lungs strive to uncrease themselves and take in that rich and healing air which he knows can revive him, but his strength has gone. Death's jest is complete.

So Thomas Lovell Beddoes exhales his last breath bearing his last words.

'Fetch the cow . . . fetch the cow . . .'

The End

Censorship in Britain

Paul O'Higgins

Censorship
in Britain

'The condition upon which God hath given liberty to man is eternal
vigilance; which condition if he break, servitude is at once the
consequence of his crime, and the punishment of his guilt'
JOHN PHILPOT CURRAN, *Speech delivered before the Irish Privy
Council*, 1790.

Nelson

Thomas Nelson and Sons Ltd
36 Park Street London W1Y 4DE

PO Box 18123 Nairobi Kenya

Thomas Nelson (Australia) Ltd
597 Little Collins Street Melbourne 3000

Thomas Nelson and Sons (Canada) Ltd
81 Curlew Drive Don Mills Ontario

Thomas Nelson (Nigeria) Ltd
PO Box 336 Apapa Lagos

Thomas Nelson and Sons (South Africa) (Proprietary) Ltd
51 Commissioner Street Johannesburg

© Paul O'Higgins 1972

This book first published 1972

SBN 0 17 138022 0

Printed in Great Britain
by Richard Clay (The Chaucer Press), Ltd.,
Bungay, Suffolk

Table of Contents

Preface

This book is not intended as an exhaustive account of censorship in Britain. To write such a book is probably beyond the powers of a single person, if only because the forms of censorship are so infinitely varied. It is hoped, however, that it has been possible to indicate some of the main forms that censorship takes in Britain. The main aim of this book is to make people aware of the different kinds of censorship operating in Britain; and to suggest that censorship poses a number of basic problems for those who are concerned to maintain and increase the area within which freedom of thought and expression operate in the community. Above all, the object has been to persuade the reader to accept the basic principle that no form of censorship is acceptable unless it can be rationally demonstrated that some social or individual good deserving protection can be safeguarded only by its imposition, and that the social or individual good being protected in this way outweighs any restriction, detriment, loss or inconvenience caused thereby to individuals or groups.

The recent establishment of three official inquiries into the operation of section 2 of the Official Secrets Act 1911, and into the law of defamation and the law of contempt, will, it is hoped, make this brief examination of the way these and other rules and practices are utilized for purposes of censorship, particularly relevant.

I am indebted to the Leverhulme Trust for a grant to make a study of the history of theatrical censorship in this country. Some of the fruits of that research are reflected in this book.

As this book is not intended to be a work of 'academic' scholarship, footnotes have for the most part been excluded. At the end of the book, there is both a select bibliography, for those who wish to read further in this field, and also an indication of the authorities relied upon in the writing of the different chapters, for those who would like to examine some of the evidence for themselves.

PAUL O'HIGGINS

Christ's College, Cambridge
March 1972

Acknowledgements

I owe a special debt of gratitude to my friends Bob Hepple, Fellow of Clare College, Cambridge, who kindly read the manuscript of this work and made a number of valuable suggestions for improvements; Martin Partington, of the School of Law, Warwick University, who gave me the benefit of some of the information he has collected regarding the scope of local legislation in this country; and Mrs Dorothy Tanfield, who patiently made sense of a manuscript which would have daunted all save the most skilful and intrepid of typists. Peter Ford has given me help and encouragement for which I am most grateful. A number of people have patiently responded to requests for information, and to these I express my gratitude. Rachel, Maeve and Siobhan O'Higgins have all helped me in various ways and, as always, I am in their debt.

I am grateful to the Controller of HM Stationery Office for permission to quote from Crown Copyright material.

1 Introduction

'Assassination is the extreme form of censorship'
George Bernard Shaw

There is a curious coyness in Britain about the whole subject of censorship. Most discussions of this topic fail to give any clear indication of what is meant by the term; indeed, very many deny that censorship exists in this country at all. Huw Weldon, Managing Director of BBC Television, has stated that 'in the normal sense of the word there is no censorship in BBC Television'. In a publication on *Human Rights in the United Kingdom*, issued by the official Central Office of Information, it is stated, 'There is no Government censorship [of the press], except in wartime on security grounds, and no Government control'. Sentiment and wishful thinking is often the only basis for the expression of such beliefs, for no one should now be unaware of the extent of censorship and control which presently exists. Sometimes reality does break through, however, as when in 1961 Lord Radcliffe, a judge who used to sit in the House of Lords, admitted that 'we are surrounded on all sides by censors of a kind and must necessarily remain so under the conditions which now govern the dissemination of ideas and information'.

The *Oxford English Dictionary* is uncharacteristically unhelpful when it comes to a definition of censorship, thus reflecting the fact that censorship in Britain is not a topic to be discussed. It offers a choice of two meanings: (a) the office of a Roman censor (the Roman censor was an official who drew up the register of citizens and had supervision over public morals); and (b) the office or function of an official, a censor, 'in some countries', whose duty it is to inspect all books, journals, dramatic pieces, etc., before publication, to secure that they shall contain nothing immoral, heretical or offensive to the government. If we forget the Roman official who is not relevant to Britain today, we are left with a very limited definition.

An American authority on the subject of censorship many years ago defined it in a rather different way. 'Censorship,' said Harold Laswell, 'is the policy of restricting the public expression of ideas, opinions, conceptions and impulses which have or are believed to have the capacity to undermine the governing authority or the social or moral code which that authority considers itself bound to protect.'

Even this is too narrow a definition, and seems to ignore a number of important aspects. In contrast with earlier definitions, for present purposes censorship is used to describe the processes *whereby restrictions are imposed upon the collection, dissemination and exchange of information, opinions and ideas.* Although this definition is enormously wide and includes aspects of the subject which are not the immediate concern of this book, it is essential to be aware of the very wide range of ways in which restrictions are in fact imposed upon the expression and exchange of ideas and information.

Censorship as defined takes a number of different forms. Since the subject of censorship is one which is rarely discussed, there is no agreement on the terminology to be used, so we have to invent our own terms.

First of all, there is what may be called *autonomous* or *self-censorship*. This is used to describe the processes whereby such factors as greed, fear, ambition, self-interest and other conscious or unconscious motives lead to an individual refraining from the expression of opinions or ideas; or lead him to express them only in a distorted or even perverted way.

Secondly, there is *social censorship*, which may be used to describe ways in which groups, or society as a whole, discourage the expression of particular opinions and ideas. A full understanding of social censorship, which includes education in its broadest sense, is dependent upon one's view of the nature of society. If one believes that a certain dominant group or groups or classes ultimately determine and influence ideas and opinions in society in a way favourable to their own interests, then at bottom one will regard social censorship in Britain as having a function to protect the existing order of things and, in particular, the interests of the dominant groups.

Thirdly, *legal censorship* is a special form of social censorship, wherein the rules determining what may or may not be freely expressed are embodied in rules enforced by policemen, courts and other similar institutions. Legal censorship is itself usually regarded as taking two forms. First of all, there is *pre-censorship* (sometimes called *prior censorship*), under which legal rules confer authority on some person to examine the text of what is proposed to be said, published, performed or distributed, and only after receiving the licence of such authority is the dissemination of the information concerned lawful. Dissemination without licence is itself a legal offence, even if the content of what is disseminated is quite harmless and not in itself unlawful. The second form of legal censorship is *punitive* or *penal censorship* (sometimes referred to as *subsequent censorship*). In this case legal rules do not require authorization before the matter is disseminated, but impose penalties, fines, prison, deprivation of civil rights or damages upon the persons responsible for the dissemination of material which contravenes certain limits, usually extremely vague, laid down by the law.

Fourthly, there is *extra-legal censorship*, by which is meant a large number of practices not expressly authorized by the law used to effect censorship. These include such aspects as the system of bluff and bluster whereby pressure is exerted by the police and others in authority to discourage the dissemination of certain material by threatening to take legal action against the disseminator – often in cases where legal action would certainly fail. They also include much more sophisticated and institutionalized systems, such as D Notices.

Fifthly, *voluntary censorship* describes the process whereby an individual (or it may be a company or institution), without any legal authority to do so imposes upon others restrictions as to what ideas or information they may express without suffering disadvantage. Such voluntary censorship may often be institutionalized, as in the case of the Press Council, or it may involve the action of a single employer. Of course, voluntary censorship is based largely upon the acceptance of a shared set of beliefs, or code, as to what are or are not permissible opinions. Recognizing this, Alexander Cockburn wrote recently: 'Of course, the British have devised a code system in the ideological area to stop contamination creeping in. Unemployment will dog the wouldbe teacher who is "doctrinaire" or "biased". Imprisoned in his ideology, he will be unable to lecture "objectively", will misinform his students, hence betray the principles of academic freedom, and thus quite reasonably be refused a job in the first place.'

Finally, *subterranean censorship* has been used as a term to describe the situation where open intervention by government or other public authority is avoided, but either a public authority, or sometimes even a private person, uses its powers (given for some purpose other than explicit censorship) to effect censorship instead. One example would be the refusal of a bookseller to stock certain books because he disapproved of their content.

Before we commence our discussion of censorship in Britain, certain facts or, if you prefer, assumptions should be made clear, because they have a bearing upon the seriousness with which the reader is likely to view the problem of censorship.

First of all, it is the writer's belief that it *is* possible to suppress ideas and information. This can be done by massacre, as in the case of certain medieval heresies, or by education. Long ago, Bury said that there are not only facts which are capable of demonstration or verification but there are also beliefs which cannot be verified. 'The thoughts of the average man consist not only of facts open to verification' – such as the existence of Napoleon or Paris – 'but also of beliefs and opinions which he has accepted on authority and cannot verify or prove.' It is the great achievement of British education that the historical existence of Jesus Christ is generally accepted as a fact susceptible of verification by ordinary historical methods, whereas it is a belief accepted on authority and cannot in fact be established by ordinary methods of verification.

Then there are certain areas of British life and institutions which are given special protection against criticism, where the views of critics may lead to their suffering disadvantage or simply to not obtaining a hearing for their views. When Malcolm Muggeridge expressed some mildly irreverent views on the British monarchy in the *Saturday Evening Post* in 1958, he was temporarily excluded from appearing on BBC Television. The Christian religion is itself carefully shielded from critical discussion, and the police and the judges are given very special protection from criticism.

Lastly, the importance of censorship is increased rather than diminished by the kind of society in which we live. It may be less obtrusive than in more dictatorial systems, but the system requires censorship to continue to exist.

The more government is recognized to be based upon 'consent', the more essential it becomes that the governed should consent to the will of the governors only. . . . The only difference now is that authority is estopped from brutal frankness. The only change made by democracy is, as Alexis de Tocqueville observed, that it 'immaterializes despotism'. The methods of control become more subtle and complicated and indirect, but they hardly cease. The early dread of education has disappeared as its advantages have been realized: the educated and democratic citizen can be more deftly ordered by reason than the ignorant and brutalized slave was kept to obedience by force. The only result of democracy has been to make the business of censorship vastly more ingenious.

2 Legal Censorship

'In the last analysis all censorship is political censorship'
William Seagle

If we are to understand the special role played by legal rules in Britain in the control of the communication of information and ideas, it is important to understand some basic characteristics of the British system of law. First of all, there is no written constitution covering the whole of the United Kingdom in which could be found enshrined and guaranteed the basic freedoms of the individual, embodying in particular a right to freedom of speech, freedom to communicate and obtain information. The absence of a written constitution also means that, as compared with the United States of America, there is no limit laid down by law as to the restrictions which Parliament may impose upon freedom of communication. In the United Kingdom generally there is no concept of an unconstitutional and invalid Act of Parliament. Whatever the Parliament of the United Kingdom enacts is law, however much that law may interfere with freedom of individuals or groups. Although the absence of a written constitution means that English judges have not got authority from a Constitution to override unconstitutional Acts of Parliament, the absence of a written constitution means that, apart from inconsistent Acts of Parliament, there is no limit on the power of the judges to restrict freedom of communication where, in a case before them, they consider it proper to do so. We shall see this in cases involving contempt of court and the claim of the state that it be not obliged to give the court information relevant to legal proceedings. Unlike judges in certain other countries, British judges have a very wide power to make new legal wrongs which may have the effect of extending or narrowing the area within which freedom of communication may exist without legal restrictions.

Of course, the position is slightly modified in Northern Ireland by the presence there of a written constitution, the Government of Ireland Act 1920, and possibly in Scotland by the Act of Union 1700. But whatever the effect of these two enactments in limiting the power of the state and judges, such limitations are confined to Scotland and Northern Ireland, and the limitations concerned do not have much bearing upon the question of freedom of communication of information and ideas.

The absence of a written constitution guaranteeing certain basic rights means that the individual has no protection under British law against Acts of Parliament, or judicial interpretations of or additions to the existing law. The United Kingdom is, however, a party to the European Convention on Human Rights and Fundamental Freedoms, which does guarantee certain of the basic rights. Those most relevant to censorship are Article 8, guaranteeing the right to privacy, Article 9, which protects the right to freedom of thought, conscience and religion, and Article 10, which protects the right to freedom of expression. (The texts of these articles may be found in Appendix Four.) An individual who feels aggrieved by an Act of Parliament or a judicial decision which violates his rights as embodied in the European Convention, may petition a body, known as the European Commission on Human Rights, and complain against the United Kingdom's failure to give effect to his rights.

It is important not to exaggerate the advantages of having a written constitution. While such a constitution can be helpful, in times of war or social stress – or in cases where the individual or group seeking to invoke the constitution (before courts whose function it often is to uphold the constitution) is one whose opinions or national or racial origins are disapproved of by the judges – the courts will often fail to uphold the constitution, which so comes to afford little or no protection. This can be seen from the cases arising out of the internment in 1942 of American citizens of Japanese origin in the United States. Anti-Japanese hysteria was such that the Supreme Court of the United States decided by a narrow majority that imprisonment without trial of those American citizens was not a violation of their constitutional right not to be deprived of liberty without 'due process of law'. In Britain during the First World War, both Parliament and the courts failed notably to intervene to prevent the unlawful despatch of refugees from Russian anti-Jewish persecution in the first years of the twentieth century back to Tsarist Russia. Of course, there was no constitution they could invoke, but since what was done to them was unlawful, their inability to invoke the law on their side successfully illustrates the same point – namely, that in times of national hysteria the courts may not be effective guardians of the liberty of unpopular minority groups.

The absence of constitutional guarantees of fundamental rights does not necessarily mean that in practice there is no freedom. The existence of freedom in any community depends upon prevailing social and political circumstances. This is equally true of countries with or without written constitutions. However, the legal definition of 'rights' and 'freedoms' in a country without a written constitution is essentially negative when any attempt is made to define these freedoms in legal terms. Dicey, the great Victorian constitutional lawyer, said that 'Freedom of discussion is then in England little else than the right to write or say anything which a jury, consisting of twelve shopkeepers, think it expedient should be said or written.' Put another way, freedom of discussion in Britain is the freedom to write or say anything which is not a violation of the law as interpreted by the courts (sometimes with, sometimes without, the aid of a jury). To define the area of freedom of speech, one has to make a list of the legal wrongs which may be committed by the expression of opinion or the communication of information, and the area which is left describes the area within which 'freedom' of speech and communication exists.

As we shall see, the list of offences which one may fall foul of in the course of expressing an opinion or communicating information is very wide. But, in addition, the offences concerned are often vague and extremely ill-defined, which leaves a wide freedom of choice in the interpretation and application of these wrongs to particular situations.

The vagueness of the offences involved in the communication of opinions and information, which we may loosely refer to as 'offences of opinion', means that the judges play a vital role in the defining of the area of freedom when they give a broad or narrow construction to the legal rules.

Another important characteristic of the British legal system is the social origin of its judges. Since those judges who sit in the most important courts, the High Court, the Court of Appeal and House of Lords (and also the equivalent Scottish and Northern Irish courts), have law-making powers, the manner in which this power is exercised is often largely influenced by the views of the judges concerned on moral, social and political values. In what may loosely be called offences of opinion the judge's own view of right and wrong, his views of what is socially, morally or politically desirable or acceptable has greatly influenced the way in which new legal wrongs, as for example the crime of conspiracy to corrupt public morals, revived by the House of Lords in 1961, or old wrongs interpreted and applied, as with the decision of Mr Justice Birkett in the case of *R.* v. *Caunt* 1947, where the judge narrowed the scope of seditious libel.

Fenton Bresler once gave the following account of English judges in answer to the question as to 'what manner of men' they were. They are, he said:

largely what you would expect: gifted and talented members of the upper classes. England has its normal quota of success stories from rags to riches, its millionaires who started as office boys, its tycoons who sold newspapers on street corners. But no one other than a gentleman, in the class sense of the word, has ever graced the high court bench. Working-class origins are not recommended for anyone with judicial ambitions.

Such is the structure of the Bar from which the judges are chosen, and such is the nature of the education a high proportion of them have received that it is practically inevitable, as is the case, that their views on social, political and moral issues should be conservative.

We must not exaggerate the significance of the powers of the judges to create and interpret the law. These powers are interstitial. The state has enormous reserves of legal powers, for not only are the common law offences of opinion often extremely wide, but there are also in existence many statutes which have created extremely vague and far-reaching offences. Dicey acknowledged this when he said, regarding one among many vague offences of opinion, that 'any one will see at once that the legal definition of a seditious libel might easily be used as to check a great deal of what is ordinarily considered allowable discussion, and would if rigidly enforced be inconsistent with prevailing forms of political agitation'. This was written in 1885. Dicey saw as the safeguard against the wide application of these vague offences the fact that any legal proceeding involved would be before a jury who, he assumed, would apply the vague offence in a sensible way. This faith in a jury is hard to justify, and in any case modern statutes creating offences of opinion usually allow the prosecution the choice of whether the trial be before a jury or before a magistrates' court, without a jury.

Quite as important as the legal rules are the practices adopted by the authorities in the control of freedom of expression and communication. Many of these lack any clear legal authority, but are sanctified by long practice – the power of magistrates, for example, to bind people over to be of good behaviour. Others are the recent invention of the police or other authorities. Some are a violation themselves of the law. Without such practices the British legal system would grind to a halt. We shall illustrate the practices in the course of our discussion (see below, p. 50, for an example).

We will now examine the legal offences most relevant to censorship in Britain, but before doing do it may be worth re-emphasizing that censorship is a subject about which lawyers are so pathologically coy as to lead to a denial of its existence. Thus, in the third edition of the many-volumed encyclopedia of English law, *Halsbury's Laws of England*, there is no entry at all under 'censorship' in the index. Even the official *Index to the Statutes, containing the legislation in force on 31st December 1968*, published by the Stationery Office in 1969, contains only 'Censorship of Plays – see Theatre'.

Defamation

It is a civil wrong to make untrue statements about another person which are defamatory. There is, however, no precise definition of what is meant by 'defamatory'. Various tests exist such as that any statement is defamatory which would lower the person referred to in the estimation of right-thinking people, or which would cause him to be shunned, or which exposes him to hatred, ridicule or contempt. But the tests do not always give the same answer when applied to the same statement. Defamation is further of two kinds: (a) slander, which is transient and temporary; and (b) libel, which is a statement in some more permanent form, e.g. writing, sculpture, pictures and, nowadays, films, television and records. Most civil wrongs require proof that the person who enlists the aid of the court has suffered some damage or loss. In the case of libel, and even in certain kinds of slander, it is not necessary to prove any actual loss. Exceptionally today in civil cases, where juries have virtually been abolished because of the inconsistency with which they awarded differing amounts of compensation for wrongs which are essentially similar, the use of the jury has been specially preserved in cases of defamation. This means that successful claimants may obtain quite large sums by way of damages. Litigation is in any case expensive in this country, but there is no legal aid available in defamation cases. It is up to the person who made the statement to prove the substantial truth of what he said, or, if his statement was a mixture of fact and opinion, he must prove that it was both factually accurate as well as that the opinion element in it was honestly believed in.

A person who claims he has been libelled may not only recover damages, but, in rare cases, may also, while his case is awaiting trial, obtain an order, or injunction, restraining the defendant from continuing to publish the alleged defamatory statement. This latter possibility may cause the publisher considerable loss in a case which could ultimately be decided in his favour.

Because the risks of incurring damages and heavy legal costs are considerable; because of the onus on the defendant of proving positively the truth of what he has said, a publisher of newspapers or books may prefer not to publish material which he knows to be true, but which he could not if challenged substantiate, for various reasons. He may, for example, be unwilling to reveal the identity of the informant who supplied him with the information, or the informant may indicate that he will deny that he ever supplied the information and will deny its truth. Defamation has the effect of inhibiting press comment, and although defamation actions against newspapers in particular are not all that common, this is because newspapers employ lawyers to scrutinize their material so as to remove potentially libellous material before printing. The *Daily Mirror* and *Sunday Mirror* in 1969 employed, between them, 15 barristers wholetime and part-time to keep libel out of their pages. Cecil King, the former Chairman of the International Publishing Corporation, has said that British libel law makes it difficult for any author or journalist to tell the truth.

Yet there are certain limitations upon the law of libel. In particular, there is no liability if a group of people, e.g. a political or religious minority, is defamed, unless it can be shown that a particular individual is so identified with the group that an attack on the reputation of the group necessarily involves also an attack on the reputation of the individual. Also it is possible to defame only the living. So that when in Rolf Hochhuth's play *Soldiers* it was suggested that the late Sir Winston Churchill had been responsible for the death in a flying accident during the war of the Polish leader General Sikorski, no *civil* claim for defamation could be brought in respect of this allegation by any member of Churchill's family. However, the pilot of the plane involved, being still alive, recovered compensation from the lessees of the New Theatre where the play was performed from December 1968 to April 1969.

On the other hand, the law of libel is very wide because it is not only the person who wrote or published the original statement who may be sued for damages, but also the distributor and the bookseller or newsvendor who eventually retailed the book or paper containing the defamatory matter. A limited defence has been given to such 'innocent disseminators' by the Defamation Act 1952, but for technical reasons they may not always be able to claim the benefit of this protection.

An example of where the law of libel has been used to restrain the dissemination of allegations which subsequently turned out to be true, and where such action was brought against a distributor, was the case in 1963, when Mr Profumo recovered damages against a British company for distributing in this country an Italian magazine containing suggestions that Mr Profumo was, or had been, in some improper relationship with Miss Christine Keeler. As we knew, the truth of the allegations led to the leading British political scandal of the 1960s.

It is, in part, due to the law of libel that newspapers may refuse to publish stories which ought in the public interest to be made available to the public. This was so in the Woolf case in 1962, when no newspaper in Fleet Street was willing to publish an account of the very odd circumstances in which a Mr Herman Woolf had died while attended over by the police. *Private Eye*, that journal with an endearing indifference to libel suits, published the story, and almost at once every newspaper took the story up with the result that an official inquiry was set up into the death of Mr Woolf, which exculpated the police. It is no wonder that Wayland Young has referred to *Private Eye* as 'the bravest, and often the most accurate, organ of opinion in the British Press'. There is often some truth therefore in Joseph Dean's aphorism that 'if the pen is mightier than the sword, in England at least the writ is mightier than the pen', and the suppression of truth would be more complete were it not for the continued existence of 'irresponsible' journals like *Private Eye*.

The law of libel may often be used in another way to prevent communication to the public. Thus, for example, the British Board of Film Censors have in the past refused to give certificates to films commenting on current political problems on the ground that their contents might be libellous. This occurred in the case of two films in 1960 which dealt with the activities of German ex-Nazi officers, *Holidays on Sylt* and *General Speidel—the Archives Testify*.

* * *

Most of the other legal rules relevant to censorship are part of the criminal law; that is, they expose people who violate their prohibitions to the risk of fines or imprisonment.

Blasphemy

A statement is blasphemous if it denies the truth of Christianity (no other religion is given the same protection), or of the Bible or the Book of Common Prayer, or the existence of God. In the past, no more than this was necessary to establish liability, but since decisions of the courts, in particular the House of Lords in *Bowman* v. *Secular Society* in 1916, a further element appears to be necessary. Blasphemous words or representations are only punishable 'for their manner, their violence, or ribaldry, or, more fully stated for their tendency to endanger the peace then and there, to deprave public morality generally, to shake the fabric of society and to be a cause of civil strife'.

It is important to note that Bowman's was not a criminal case and the opinions expressed by the judges were strictly what the lawyers call *obiter dicta* so far as the criminal law is concerned, and what they said was inconsistant with the great bulk of earlier authority. As the late Sir Ivor Jennings said in 1959, 'blasphemy is such a wide offence that the older books state that any attack on Christianity is a crime. Later judges have dissented from that view, but the law is so doubtful that an intolerant Court of Criminal Appeal could make what it pleased of it.' Even if, however, it be correct to condense the Bowman principle somewhat and say there is no liability for blasphemy unless the matter concerned is such as to tend to endanger the peace, there remains some uncertainty as to what is the standard by which this tendency to endanger the peace is to be tested. In 1922 the Court of Criminal Appeal upheld a direction to the jury, in a prosecution for blasphemy, by Mr Justice Avory, in which he said to the jury:

What you have to ask yourselves in this case is whether the words which are published, these matters which are published in these two pamphlets are, in your opinion, indecent and offensive attacks on Christianity or the Scriptures or sacred persons or objects, *calculated to outrage the feelings of the general body of the community* and so lead, possibly – not inevitably, but so lead, possibly, to a breach of the peace. You must ask yourselves *if a person of strong religious feelings had stopped* to read this pamphlet whether his instinct might not have been to go up to the man who was selling it and give him a thrashing, or at all events, to use such language to him that a breach of the peace might be likely to be occasioned. . . .

Notice, however, that the two sets of words which have been italicized constitute two separate and quite different standards by which to determine whether the words are blasphemous or not.

Gott's case is of interest because it illustrates the judicial prejudices so often called into play when parties before a court lack religious belief.* In the Court of Criminal Appeal the Chief Justice Lord Trevithin said that 'this was a most dangerous class of crime'. Was Mr Gott not ashamed the Lord Chief Justice asked, to have suggested in his pamphlet that Christ had entered Jerusalem 'like a circus clown on the back of two donkeys'; from which suggestion the Lord Chief Justice appeared to deduce that Mr Gott had been 'unfortunate in his education'. As Clive Bell has commented, had the Lord Chief Justice himself 'been more of a scholar, he must have perceived what is obvious even from a summary report in *The Times*, that Mr Gott was raising an

---

* Cf. Refusal by the Chairman of London Sessions to permit an agnostic witness to affirm, which lead to quashing of a conviction by Court of Criminal Appeal. *The Times*, 13 January 1962. See also editorial in *The Humanist*, July 1961.

interesting point in textual criticism'; for as Mr Bell points out, although Mark 11:7 describes Christ as riding upon a single donkey, Matthew 21:7 reads, 'And [they] brought the ass, *and the colt*, and put on *them* their clothes, and then set Him thereon' – i.e. exactly as Mr Gott suggested, Christ is described as entering Jerusalem on the back of two donkeys.

Successful prosecutions for blasphemy are rare, the Home Office stating in 1966 'it is doubtful whether this offence is ever prosecuted now'. The last successful prosecution appears to have been in 1940, when a Mr Woodhall was sentenced to prison for a month at Jersey Criminal Assizes. Mr Woodhall had produced his passport to the Chief Aliens Officer at St Helier to obtain an exit permit. The passport contained two photographs of Mr Woodhall which showed him lying on a beach wearing bathing trunks and with his arms outstretched. A cross and other marks had been sketched in, making the picture into what the Chief Aliens Officer described as a 'representation of Christ crucified'. One is glad to be able to record that Mr Woodhall was liberated by order of the Home Secretary before completing his sentence.

Yet despite the paucity of recent prosecutions, it is worth noting that from time to time attempts are made to persuade the authorities to take action. Thus in 1963, when Tottenham Hotspur won the European Cup Winners Cup, fourteen Tottenham clergymen and ministers of all denominations asked the Home Secretary to prosecute under the blasphemy laws three gentlemen who had accompanied the winning team on their triumphal tour through north London wearing beards and flowing white robes, carrying placards which bore the words respectively, 'They Shall Reign For Ever', 'Hallowed Be Their Names' and 'Adore Them For They Are Glorious'. The Home Office took no action, but not too much significance should be attached to this as evidence that the Home Office believed that a prosecution would not have succeeded. It has been the traditional policy of the Home Office, under the advice of the Law Officers of the Crown, always to move with great circumspection in considering whether to prosecute persons whose basic offence is to show insufficient respect for established political or religious orthodoxy. Thus in 1851 the Home Office considered whether it might be advisable to prosecute John Mill for having expressed certain mildly agnostic views in a public lecture, and were advised by the Law Officers, John Romilly and A. E. Cockburn, as follows:

We are of opinion that John Mill is liable to prosecution and that it may be either by indictment of information but we think it proper to add that we should in this case consider it highly inexpedient for the Government to institute any such proceedings but that it may be properly left to the magistrates [in Newcastle upon Tyne where the lecture was given] to take such course in this matter as they may consider to be most advisable.

This wise advice has been given over and over again in this kind of case, if not always successfully. But the essence of it is that the law is often wide enough to make criminal quite inoffensive behaviour, though the authorities must before prosecution weigh up the fact that a successful prosecution may lead to demand for a narrowing of their legal powers; an unsuccessful one merely gives wider publicity to the views and opinions of which the authorities disapprove – the lesson of the unsuccessful prosecution of Penguin Books in the *Lady Chatterley* case in 1961.

When in August 1970 Mr Geoffrey Russell complained to Scotland Yard that the play *Council of Love* was blasphemous, no prosecution followed.

Even if blasphemy rarely gives rise to a criminal prosecution it may none the less influence what is permitted in practice. Thus, before 1968, when the Lord Chamberlain was still exercising his powers over plays, a frequent ground upon which he prohibited matter in plays was that the matter concerned was blasphemous. Thus the line 'This is my beloved secret agent in whom I am well pleased' was ordered to be deleted, on the ground that it was blasphemous, from an Edinburgh 'fringe' production, *The Bubonic Plague Show*, the scene of which was set in a germ-warfare situation. The BBC is always very sensitive to criticism that it has in any way blasphemed or ridiculed religion. Thus Lord Normanbrook, BBC Chairman, apologized to Sir Cyril Black MP in 1967 for the use of Holman Hunt's painting *The Light of the World* in the satirical programme *The Late Show*. 'Those responsible for the programme overlooked the fact that many people who care deeply for this particular picture because of its association as part of their upbringing with their religious beliefs extend to the picture itself their respect for those beliefs.'

When the BBC put on John Osborne's play, *A Subject of Scandal and Concern*, as the Sunday-night play in November 1960, the *Listener* apologized for the fact that 'There may be some it [the play] will scandalize.' The play told the story of the imprisonment of George Jacob Holyoake, who was convicted of blasphemy in 1842 for having denied the truth of the Christian religion. So embarrassing did the BBC find the play's subject matter, that it was put on at an hour much later than usual for the Sunday-night play on the ground that 'it was unsuitable for children'.

More seriously, the law of blasphemy lurks in the background because whenever the lawyers who are consulted by the mass media as to whether a particular piece might or might not lead to conflict with the law they, as cautious if not cowardly lawyers will, may say that although it is unlikely that any action will be taken, such is the uncertainty of the law that the expression of certain opinions or ideas *might*, if the court took an illiberal view of law, lead to a successful prosecution for blasphemy. From time to time, the BBC in particular appears to have withheld certain items from viewers for just such a reason.

There are a number of offences related to blasphemy, such as indecent behaviour in church, under the Ecclesiastical Courts Jurisdiction Act

1860. When in 1967 a number of people volubly protested at what they regarded as the hypocrisy of the Prime Minister and Foreign Secretary reading lessons in a Brighton Church, it was for this offence that the offenders were fined and two of them sent to prison. The Lord Chief Justice expressed the opinion that it made all the difference that the words uttered by the defendants were uttered in a sacred place – while they might have been acceptable elsewhere, they became criminal when uttered in a church.

Under the Town Police Clauses Act, 1847, it is an offence for any one to offer for sale or distribute a profane publication or to sing profane songs. Whether *profane* means more than 'irreligious' is difficult to say.

Obscenity

The Obscene Publications Act 1959 lays down that the test of the obscenity of an article is whether its

effect . . . is, if taken as a whole, such as to tend to deprave and corrupt persons who are likely, having regard to all relevant circumstances, to read, see or hear the matter contained or embodied in it.

A person may be guilty of an offence under the Act (as amended in 1964) if he publishes or has in his possession an obscene article intended for publication for gain.

Three kinds of proceedings are open to the authorities wishing to take action in respect of obscene articles. They may prosecute the accused person before a magistrates' court summarily, that is, without a jury, in which case the penalty imposed may be a fine of up to £100 or prison for up to six months or both.* Or the authorities may prosecute the accused on indictment, that is, before judge and jury, in which case there is no upper limit to the fine which may be imposed and the maximum prison sentence is increased to three years. In other words, the prosecution has the initial right to choose whether there shall be a prosecution with or without jury. So much for Dicey's dictum that a man may say what he likes subject only to the limits set by a jury.† A further disadvantage from the accused's point of view is that, if, for example, the police choose to prosecute within the London Metropolitan area, owing to the system of stipendiary magistrates (full-time magistrates sitting alone) attached to a particular area in London, they may virtually pick the magistrate who will try the offence.

The third procedure open to the authorities is to obtain a warrant under Section 3 of the 1959 Act to search and remove obscene articles. Articles seized in this way may be forfeited and destroyed by order of a magistrate after notice has been given to their owner to show cause why they should not be forfeited. Again, in such proceedings no jury is involved.

* The accused may in this case insist upon having a jury if he wishes.
† See p. 16 above.

The 1959 Act is an improvement upon the earlier law in that it grants, under Section 4, a defence of public good.

1 A person shall not be convicted of an offence against section two of this Act, and an order for forfeiture shall not be made under the foregoing section, if it is proved that the publication of the article in question is justified as being for the public good on the ground that it is in the interests of science, literature, art or learning, or of other objects of general concern.

2 It is hereby declared that the opinion of experts as to the literary, artistic, scientific or other merits of an article may be admitted in any proceedings under this Act either to establish or to negative the said ground.

Articles which may be obscene under the Act include anything which can be read or looked at, any sound record, or film, or picture, as well as anything intended to be used for the reproduction of an article as defined, e.g. photographic negatives. It was held in the *Oz* case, by the Court of Appeal, that in the case of a magazine, the test of obscenity is not the effect of the issue of the magazine considered as a whole but is rather whether any item in the issue is obscene, in which case the whole issue becomes obscene.

The fundamental difficulty about obscenity is what is meant by tending to deprave or corrupt. The answer, as Mr Havers, QC, told the Working Party set up by a conference convened by Lord Goodman, Chairman of the Arts Council, to consider the Obscenity Laws in 1968, is that 'Nobody knows what this means'. Can a judge explain to a jury what to deprave or corrupt means? In *The Last Exit to Brooklyn* case in 1968, Lord Justice Salmon, speaking for the Court of Appeal, said:

When, as here, a statute lays down the definition of a word or phrase in plain English, it is rarely necessary and often unwise for the judge to attempt to improve on or redefine the definition. Certainly, in the circumstances of the present case he [the trial judge] cannot be blamed for saying no more than he did about the words 'deprave and corrupt'....

In an effort to define the indefinable, the trial judge had suggested that, 'The essence of the matter, you may think, is moral corruption.' Like many judicial attempts to explain and define obscenity, it was circular and not very helpful. In the end the matter is left to the jury, if there is one, or if there is not to the magistrates, to determine *subjectively* what *they* consider to be obscene. Lord Justice Salmon did not give up without a struggle, however. Towards the end of his judgement he said:

The depravity or corruption may also take various forms. It may be to induce erotic desires of a heterosexual kind or to promote homosexuality or other sexual perversions or drug taking or brutal violence.

But there is nothing unlawful in heterosexual desires, or in homosexual activity between consenting adults; some forms of drug taking are perfectly lawful, as is brutal violence in certain circumstances. A letter from a well-loved but absent wife may arouse heterosexual erotic desires, but does that make it obscene? A letter from a consenting adult with whom one has a homosexual relationship may promote homosexuality. Is it obscene? The advocacy of violence against an enemy may not be obscene. Because these suggestions are so obviously not very helpful, Lord Justice Salmon finally concludes, having particular regard to the defence of public good: 'The jury must set the standard of what is acceptable in the age in which we live.'

There is therefore no clear definition of obscenity. What it is, is to be determined subjectively by the tribunal. As the Arts Council Working Party said in its Report on the Obscenity Laws:

This is the core of the matter; in the last analysis Obscenity Laws are really about conformity and *mores*. That is why Lord Justice Salmon, after a valiant effort to find a more solid basis for them, had finally to retreat from the attempt and admit that all we could, in practice, expect from a jury is their opinion of 'what is acceptable . . . *in the age in which we live*'. That is another way of saying 'what is not shocking to contemporary mores' and its effect is directly to contradict Mr Justice Stable's warning to the jury [in 1956]; 'The charge is *not* that the tendency of the book is to shock and disgust.'

The concept of obscenity is unsatisfactory in a number of other ways. The intent of the author is irrelevant. Evidence of experts that the book is for the public good on some ground if not countered with any evidence in rebuttal does not mean the tribunal must accept such evidence; it may reject the evidence on the experts' part without any explanation. The scope of obscenity moreover is not confined to sexual matters. In 1964, in *John Calder* v. *Powell*, it was decided that *Cain's Book* by Alexander Trocchi could be lawfully regarded as obscene because it advocated drug taking. The Chief Justice, Lord Parker, said, 'In my judgement there is no reason to confine obscenity and depravity to sex . . .' In *D.P.P.* v. *A. & B.C. Chewing Gum* in 1968, it was decided that violence could be obscene, thereby upholding the conviction for obscenity of a company which sold bubble-gum packets containing cards depicting battle-scenes. There is therefore no limit, other than that which the courts may decide themselves to impose in the future upon the subject matter of obscenity.

The bubble-gum case is of particular interest, because there is in existence a statute under which the defendant might have in any case been liable without the invocation of obscenity. This is the Children and Young Persons (Harmful Publications) Act 1955, which forbids the dissemination of harmful publications defined as publications

of a kind likely to fall into the hands of children or young persons and consist wholly or mainly of stories told in pictures (with or without the addition of written matter), being stories portraying –

a the commission of crimes; or

b acts of violence or cruelty; or

c incidents of a repulsive or horrible nature; in such a way that the work as a whole would tend to corrupt a child or young person into whose hands it might fall.

It appears, however, that no prosecution has ever been brought under this Act, but its terms constitute evidence that Parliament, like everyone else, had assumed that obscenity is confined to sex.

The range of objectionable matter which is forbidden by the law, in the area of sexual information, is not confined to matter which is *obscene*, but also includes matter which is *indecent*. Under the Indecent Advertisements Act 1889 it is a criminal offence to display *on* any building or other place (the Act curiously specifically includes urinals), so as to be visible to passers-by, or to give such passers-by, any picture or written matter which is of an obscene or indecent nature. The Act specifically provides that any reference to venereal disease or any other complaint connected with sexual intercourse shall be *indecent*. The Venereal Diseases Act 1917 makes it a criminal offence to advertise any offer to treat or to give advice in relation to the treatment of venereal disease. In 1970, the incidence of venereal disease had reached epidemic proportions in Britain, particularly among the young. In discussing the Indecent Advertisements (Amendment) Bill in the House of Lords on 11 May 1970, Lady Birk, chairman of the Health Education Council, explained the background and objectives of the Bill:

The Health Education Council, of which she was chairman, was set up by the Government as an authoritative health education body. It had a duty to perform in this area. If the council was to carry out its duty effectively it must draw attention to the dangers of venereal disease, the health hazards of promiscuity, and the need to obtain information immediately.

The council had embarked on an anti-V.D. campaign directed at the 13- to 16-year-olds, the age group where the biggest increase had taken place. It consisted of posters and leaflets explaining the facts about the disease.

Every poster and leaflet had to carry a warning that if they were displayed where they were visible to someone passing along the street or public highway or footpath there was a risk of prosecution under the 1889 Act. Without doubt this was a hampering factor in the fight against venereal disease.

A poster might be put up in a library, but if the door was open and someone could see the poster from the street then a complaint could be made. . . .

The only objective of the Bill was to amend the 1889 Act so that advertisements related to venereal disease were not to be deemed indecent *if they were published for a local or public authority or otherwise with the approval of the Secretary of State.* [Italics added.]

The limited alteration proposed became law as the Indecent Advertisements (Amendment) Act 1970 and gives no protection to any private body offering advice to young people. This alteration has not prevented the police on occasion from seizing copies of anti-V.D. posters from a community advice centre in Newcastle-upon-Tyne. The posters were returned when it was discovered that they had been provided by Newcastle's Medical Officer of Health.

The obvious absurdity of the use of these two Acts to prevent action being taken to combat venereal disease has not prevented their invocation by the police to prevent perfectly sensible activity. In May 1970 a prosecution was brought against Mr Richard Branson, Director of the Students Advisory Centre, London, for advertising the fact that the Centre was willing to give advice in connection with venereal diseases. Mr Branson was prosecuted for a violation of both the 1889 and 1917 statutes. The police who had taken the action conceded to the court that the only advice given by the centre was to send the persons concerned to recognized hospitals and clinics. Having heard this fact, the stipendiary magistrate, Mr Rupert Rawden-Smith, dismissed the charge for violation of the 1917 Act, presumably because he liberally interpreted the Act as forbidding only the offer to give advice to undergo unqualified treatment, thereby using common sense to cut down the literal meaning of the Act. None the less, he found Mr Branson guilty of an offence under the 1889 Act, and fined him £7.

Of course the prosecution was an absurdity, as is the law. But it is important to emphasize that there is no obligation upon the police to enforce absurd laws. They have a discretion to prosecute or not to prosecute which is wide enough (it is not, of course, an unlimited discretion) to have permitted them not to prosecute in this case. No police prosecution is ordinarily brought on the initiative of an ordinary police constable; there is control over prosecution policy by more senior police officers. Of course the police are often subject to pressure to prosecute, from many different sources, particularly including vigilante bodies concerned with the suppression of obscenity and so forth. If pressure from any source occurred in this case, it should have been ignored.

The word *indecent* is to be understood in a wider sense than *obscene*. When in 1964 a London housewife was prosecuted for committing an act of indecency contrary to an LCC bye-law of 1900 for wearing a topless dress on Westminster Bridge, the Bow Street magistrate, Mr A. Babington, explained:

I take it that 'indecent' is an act, using 'indecency' in the everyday sense of the word. Indecency is any conduct which offends against modesty or delicacy.

You know as well as I do that in any civilised community at any one time there are certain conventions of decency in public places, which are generally accepted and approved. These conventions must be respected by the individual and they must and will be upheld by the courts of law.

A number of different statutes create criminal offences with regard to indecent *or* obscene matter. For example, the Post Office Act 1953,

Section 11, provides that it shall be a crime for any person to 'send or attempt to send or procure to be sent a postal packet which . . .'

b encloses any indecent or obscene print, painting, photograph, lithograph, engraving, cinematograph film, book, card or written communication, or any indecent or obscene article whether similar to the above or not; or

c has on the packet, or on the cover thereof, any words, marks or designs which are grossly offensive or of an indecent or obscene character.

An offence can be charged under this Act of sending either an *indecent* item or an *obscene* item, that is, obscenity and indecency are not seen as synonymous. This was held in a prosecution under the Post Office Act by the Court of Criminal Appeal in the case of *R.* v. *Stanley* in 1965. Explaining the distinction, the Chief Justice, Lord Parker, said:

The words 'indecent or obscene' convey one idea, namely offending against the recognised standards of propriety, indecent being at the lower end of the scale and obscene at the upper end of the scale. . . . What the jury [at the trial] in fact said was: we find that what happened here, the brochure in the one case and the films in the other, were not offending against recognised standards at the top end of the scale so as to be obscene, but only at the lower end in that they were indecent. As it seems to the court, an indecent article is not necessarily obscene, whereas an obscene article almost certainly must be indecent.

At the trial the jury had been told that indecent 'simply means something that offends the ordinary modesty of the average man', whereas obscene refers to something which 'tends to corrupt or deprave'. The Court of Criminal Appeal did not dissent from this explanation, and in fact approved an example of the distinction given by a Scottish judge, Lord Sands, in 1931:

I do not think that the two words 'indecent' and 'obscene' are synonymous. The one may shade into the other, but there is a difference of meaning. It is easier to illustrate than define, and I illustrate thus. For a male bather to enter the water nude in the presence of ladies would be indecent, but it would not necessarily be obscene. But if he directed the attention of a lady to a certain member of his body his conduct would certainly be obscene.

It was decided by the Court of Appeal in the *Oz* case (1971) and in *R.* v. *Stamford* (1972) that the defence was not entitled to produce evidence from people to show what the effect on them had been of literature which had given rise to proceedings for an offence under the Post Office Act, s. 11 (1) (b) or the Obscene Publications Act 1959. As the Court said

. . . [T]he juries, . . . were themselves the custodians of the standards. They did not need assistance.

There are a number of other miscellaneous acts which are used to control indecent or obscene matter. The Vagrancy Act 1824, Section 4, makes it a criminal offence wilfully to expose to view, 'in any street, road, highway, or public place, any obscene print, picture, or other indecent exhibition'. Section 2 of the Vagrancy Act 1838 extends the 1824 Act to include the exposure 'to public view in the window or other part of any shop or other building situate in any street, road, highway, or public place, of any obscene print, picture or other indecent exhibition'. The Town Clauses Act 1847 makes criminal any public dissemination of profane, indecent or obscene books, and so on or the singing of profane or obscene songs, or the use of profane or obscene language, if done in such a way as to obstruct or annoy other members of the public. The Customs Consolidation Act 1876 permits the forfeiture and destruction by the Customs authorities of goods imported into this country which fall into the following categories:

Indecent or obscene prints, paintings, photographs, books, cards,
lithographic or other engravings or any other indecent or obscene articles.

These provisions are not dead law, but are regularly used by the police, and sometimes by private persons (in Britain private persons ordinarily have the same right to bring a criminal prosecution as the police), to repress matter which is regarded as 'offensive' (under the Post Office Act), or profane (under the Town Clauses Act) or indecent or obscene under all the Acts we have just discussed. This does not exhaust the arsenal of weapons available to the authorities, as there are also common law offences, i.e. offences evolved or invented, and defined, by the judges, which make, for example, the keeping of a booth for the purpose of holding an indecent exhibition, or any 'act of open and notorious lewdness', criminal offences. As the Law Officers of the Crown told the Joint Committee on the Censorship of the Theatre in 1966:

There is some authority for the proposition that 'In general all open
lewdness, grossly scandalous, and whatever outrages decency or is
offensive and disgusting, or is injurious to public morals by tending to
corrupt the mind and destroy the love of decency, morality and good order,
is a misdemeanour indictable at common law.'

Some of these archaic offences are used in particular in the case of art exhibitions. In 1966, Mr Robert Fraser, owner of the Robert Fraser Gallery in London, was fined for exposing to public view an indecent exhibition, contrary to the Vagrancy Act 1838. What was complained of was a number of paintings by the American artist Jim Dine. Also in 1966, Sattssinos Paraskos was fined £5 for exposing to public view two obscene pictures in the Leeds Institute of Art. In the same year police removed a number of reproductions of prints by Aubrey Beardsley from a Regent Street shop. At the same time the Victoria and Albert Museum had put on an exhibition of Beardsley drawings and prints which included originals of the copies seized in Regent Street. A senior museum official denied that some of the drawings had been 'cleared' with the Home Office. 'It is true, however,' he added, 'that we decided not to show half a dozen drawings which we could have had for the exhibition. But this decision was made by the museum.' Then in 1967, the Justiciary Appeal Court in Edinburgh upheld the decision of a lower court that Beardsley prints that had been on exhibition in the Victoria and Albert Museum were indecent, and refused an appeal against a fine of £20 imposed on the seller.

In 1970, summons were issued under another Act, the Metropolitan Police Act 1839, against the London Art Gallery for exhibiting eight indecent prints by John Lennon 'to the annoyance of passengers'. The prosecution was somewhat inept. The prints were not visible from the street, and as the magistrate Mr St Harmsworth pointed out:

As I understand the word *passenger*, it means someone on the move, but people who enter the gallery are not *passengers*; they then finish for the time being *passaging*.

Pending the trial of the case the prints were kept in police custody, thus depriving their owner of an opportunity to display them at his own peril. The gallery's director was reported as saying that the prosecution had cost him about £4,160. And he was not guilty at the end of the day.

Conspiracy to corrupt public morals

Of all the vague offences available to the authorities (and others), the offence of conspiring to corrupt public morals is the one likeliest to catch any conduct or the expression of any opinion which is of an unconventional or controversial nature. This offence was revived in 1961 by representatives of the Crown who wanted to make sure that, if a man who had been involved with the production of the *Ladies' Directory* (a publication giving details of prostitutes for those who wished to locate them after they had left the streets as a result of the Street Offences Act 1959) escaped conviction on the more obvious charge of living on immoral earnings, he should not escape conviction on some other charge. The House of Lords approved and gave the shape of law to the new notion of conspiring to corrupt public morals. The whole approach of the House of Lords to the problem of the right of the judges to create new crimes in the mid twentieth century, when they have had no express authority given them to do this by Parliament, is summarized in an extreme form in the judgement of Viscount Simonds, who said the following:

My Lords, as I have already said, the first count in the indictment is 'Conspiracy to corrupt public morals', and the particulars of offence will have sufficiently appeared. I am concerned only to assert what was vigorously denied by counsel for the appellant, that such an offence is known to the common law, and that it was open to the jury to find on the facts of this case that the appellant was guilty of such an offence. I must say categorically that, if it were not so, Her Majesty's courts would strangely have failed in their duty as servants and guardians of the common law. Need I say, my Lords, that I am no advocate of the right of the judges to create new criminal offences? I will repeat well-known words: 'Amongst many other points of happiness and freedom which your Majesty's subjects have enjoyed there is none which they have accounted more dear and precious than this, to be guided and governed by certain rules of law which giveth both to the head and members that which of right belongeth to them and not by any arbitrary or uncertain form of government.' These words are as true today as they were in the seventeenth century and command the allegiance of us all. But I am at a loss to understand how it can be said either that the law does not recognize a conspiracy to corrupt public morals or that, though there may not be an exact precedent for such a conspiracy as this case reveals, it does not fall fairly within the general words by which it is described. I do not propose to examine all the relevant authorities. That will be done by my noble and learned friend. The fallacy in the argument that was addressed to us lay in the attempt to exclude from the scope of general words acts well calculated to corrupt public morals just because they had not been committed or had not been brought to the notice of the court before. It is not thus that the common law has developed. We are perhaps more accustomed to hear this matter discussed upon the question whether such and such a transaction is contrary to public policy. At once the controversy arises. On the one hand it is said that it is not possible in the twentieth century for the court to create a new head of public policy, on the other it is said that this is but a new example of a well-established head. In the sphere of criminal law I entertain no doubt that there remains in the courts of law a residual power to enforce the supreme and fundamental purpose of the law, to conserve not only the safety and order but also the moral welfare of the State, and that it is their duty to guard it against attacks which may be the more insidious because they are novel and unprepared for. That is the broad head (call it public policy if you wish) within which the present indictment falls. It matters little what label is given to the offending act. To one of your Lordships it may appear an affront to public decency, to another considering that it may succeed in its obvious intention of provoking libidinous desires it will seem a corruption of public morals. Yet others may deem it aptly described as the creation of a public mischief or the undermining of moral conduct. The same act will not in all ages be regarded in the same way. The law must be related to the changing standards of life, not yielding to every shifting impulse of the popular will but having regard to fundamental assessments of human values and the purposes of society. Today a denial of the fundamental Christian doctrine, which in past centuries would have been regarded by the ecclesiastical courts as heresy and by the common law as blasphemy, will no longer be an offence if the decencies of controversy are observed. When Lord Mansfield, speaking long after the Star Chamber had been abolished, said [in a case *R.* v. *Delaval*, decided by Lord Mansfield in 1763] that the Court of King's Bench was the *custos morum* of the people and had the superintendency of offences *contra bonos mores*, he was asserting, as I now assert, that there is in that court a residual power, where no statute has yet intervened to supersede the common law, to superintend those offences which are prejudicial to the public welfare. Such occasions will be rare, for Parliament has not been slow to legislate when attention has been sufficiently aroused. But gaps remain and will always remain since no one can foresee every way in which the wickedness of man may disrupt the order of society. Let me take a single instance to which my noble and learned friend Lord Tucker refers. Let it be supposed that at some future, perhaps, early, date homosexual practices between adult consenting males are no longer a crime. Would it not be an offence if even without obscenity, such practices were publicly advocated and encouraged by pamphlet and advertisement? Or must we wait until Parliament finds time to deal with such conduct? I say, my Lords, that if the common law is powerless in such an event, then we should no longer do her reverence. But I say that her hand is still powerful and that it is for Her Majesty's judges to play the part which Lord Mansfield pointed out to them.

It is important to add that the House of Lords also decided that the Section 2 (4) of the Obscene Publications Act 1959 was inapplicable to any charge for conspiracy. Section 2 (4) had said that the defence provision of the 1959 Act (namely that publication was for the public good) was to apply to all offences whether charged under the Act or not where the 'essence of the offence [is] that the matter is obscene'.

Since the House of Lords invented the new offence it has been used frequently, especially in prosecutions of persons who have shown obscene films. However, it has also been used in the prosecution of Richard Neville, the editor of *Oz*, the underground magazine, and his associates, because of a special 'school kids' issue of *Oz* in June 1970, which 'was put together with the help and inspiration of about twenty young people, all 18 or under'.

It is worth reproducing the actual charge to get its true flavour:

On divers days between the 1st of January and the 8th day of June, 1970, within the jurisdiction of the Central Criminal Court, conspired together with Vivian Laurence Berger and with certain other young persons to produce a magazine containing divers obscene lewd indecent and sexually perverted articles cartoons drawings and illustrations with intent thereby to debauch and corrupt the morals of children and young persons within the Realm and to arouse and implant in their minds lustful and perverted desires.

If one inquires why this odd offence of conspiring to corrupt public morals is used, instead of the offence of publishing an obscene magazine, the answer is probably that this is done in order to deprive the accused persons of the defence to which they would, under the Obscene Publications Act 1959, be entitled if the prosecution were brought merely on the grounds of obscenity.

In November 1970, the publishers of the magazine *IT* were fined £1,500, having been found guilty of (a) conspiring to corrupt public morals and (b) conspiring to outrage public decency. This was based largely upon advertisements which solicited males for purposes of homosexual activity. Homosexual conduct between consenting adult males is not of course, criminal. The editor of the magazine said in evidence:

Our intention was to provide, in good faith, a public service for a minority of individuals who had been continually discriminated against, harassed and victimized.

An important element in this case may have been the allegation that insufficient check was made to ensure that advertisers were over twenty-one.

Seditious libel

Seditious libel is the expression in some permanent form of opinions made

with an intention to bring into hatred or contempt, or to excite disaffection against the King or the government and constitution of the United Kingdom as by law established, or either House of Parliament, or the administration of justice, or to excite British subjects to attempt otherwise than by lawful means the alteration of any matter in Church or State by law established, or to promote feelings of ill will and hostility between different classes.

In the past, seditious libel was interpreted in such a way that it could catch almost any criticism of the established institutions of society. Lord Chief Justice Holt said in 1704*:

If persons should not be called to account for possessing the people with an ill opinion of the government, no government can subsist; for it is very necessary for all governments that the people should have a good opinion of it.

In 1804 Lord Ellenborough said:

It is no new doctrine that if publication be calculated to alienate the affections of the people, by bringing the government into disrepute, whether the expedient be by ridicule or obloquy . . . it is a crime.

No wonder Dicey commented in the nineteenth century on the definition quoted:

. . . any one will see at once that the legal definition of a seditious libel might be so easily used as to check a great deal of what is ordinarily considered allowable discussion, and would if rigidly enforced be inconsistent with prevailing forms of political agitation.

But is the definition now correct? A series of twentieth-century cases fortunately suggest that any seditious offence – for there may be a seditious conspiracy as well as a seditious libel – requires an intention to incite to violence or public disorder, and that proof of intention to promote feelings of ill will between different classes of subjects does not

* Notice the similarity of approach to that adopted by Lord Reid, 1968. See p. 152.

give rise to criminal liability. This was decided by the Canadian Supreme Court in 1951. In 1947 Mr Justice Birkett adopted the same approach in Britain.

It is not enough merely to provoke hostility or ill will, because that may be done by speeches which certainly do not come within the realm of seditious libel. Sedition has always had implicit in the word, public disorder, tumult, insurrection or matters of that kind.

Twentieth-century judges have not always been so unequivocal. Mr Justice Rigby Swift, in summing up at the trial of the Communist leaders in 1925, said considering the alleged seditious nature of certain books:

If they [the jury] found that the books contained nothing but innocent propaganda they would find the defendants not guilty. If, however, they came to the conclusion that there was in their doctrines and statements of objects that which would lead to civil war, or that which implied that it was lawful and commendable to employ physical force against the Government of the King, *or that the language tended to subvert the Government and the laws of the Empire, it would be their duty to find the prisoners guilty*. [Italics added.]

Even if an intention to bring about violence or disorder is an essential element in the offence, any direction from a judge in terms similar to those above, especially using the word subversion (which is conveniently imprecise and ambiguous, covering both violent and peaceful change), is apt to confuse and mislead a jury.

Apart from seditious libel and conspiracy, there are a number of offences usually concerned with the prevention of disorder. Using insulting, abusive or threatening words in a public place or meeting, or distributing written material of the same kind, with intent to provoke a breach of the peace, or whereby a breach of the peace is likely to be occasioned, is a criminal offence under the Public Order Act 1936. It is irrelevant whether or not the words are true, or whether they embody sentiments with which all civilized people must agree, such as, 'Hitler was wrong to slaughter the Jews'. If the audience to which they are addressed contains a bunch of fascists who might be provoked into violence by the expression of such sentiments, the speaker commits a criminal offence. It is an odd paradox that all too many of the people prosecuted under the Race Relations Act 1965 have been members of racial minority groups.

An odd offence is confined to aliens. Under section 3 of the Aliens Amendment Act 1919 it is a criminal offence for any alien who has not been *bona fide* employed in any industry for at least two years to express opinions calculated to cause 'industrial unrest'. An alien who has been eighteen months in this country employed in a non-union factory may commit a crime by calling upon his workmates to strike for higher wages. The Immigration Act 1971, while it amends the 1919 Aliens Act in a number of ways, carefully – and curiously – preserves section 3.

Official Secrets Acts

The Official Secrets Acts 1911, 1920 and 1939 constitute a formidable obstacle to the free communication of information regarding governmental activity and the free expression of opinion thereon. Without freedom to obtain and communicate information, it is impossible to substantiate the expression of opinion on governmental activity. Of course, everyone will agree that there must be certain areas of governmental activity where secrecy will be required under any system – information on military matters in time of war, for example. What other areas of secrecy ought to be given special protection against disclosure remains open to discussion, but the blanket coverage of the Official Secrets Acts can hardly be justified. Ironically, the current body of law, which is largely embodied in the 1911 Act, was passed in a few hours one hot August day, when most Members of Parliament were more pleasurably engaged. Its purpose, as indicated by its own title, 'An Act to re-enact the Official Secrets Act, 1889, with Amendments', and by the statements made by the members of the government when explaining the purpose of the Bill in Parliament, was clear. It was essentially to make it easier for the authorities to catch spies. It did this in a number of extraordinary ways, as by using extraordinarily vague and wide language. Section 1, for instance, makes it a criminal offence to be in a prohibited place for a purpose prejudicial to the interests of security of the state. Moreover, it permits the prosecution to show that one's purpose was prejudicial to the interests of the state by showing one's character and antecedents. In other words, in certain circumstances the onus is on the accused to prove his innocence rather than on the prosecution to prove his guilt.

In 1962, in *Chandler* v. *Director of Public Prosecutions* the House of Lords decided that it was for the government of the day to decide whether or not a particular act was prejudicial to the interests or safety of the state, despite the fact that when Sir Gordon Hewart, the Attorney General, was asked in the course of the Commons debate on the 1920 Official Secrets Bill who was to decide whether or not some particular conduct was prejudicial he had replied: 'The Courts.' Indeed, Hewart had emphasized that the concept of being prejudicial to the interests of the state had reference only to espionage:

The Bill has nothing to do with opinion. It is aimed at spying and the acts of spys, their accomplices and assistants. . . . It could never be contended that in a Bill to amend the Official Secrets Acts 1911, the words 'prejudicial to the interests of the State' refer to something of a different character from that which was being dealt with in 1911, which is the matter of spying. . . . It would be, in my submission, hopeless to maintain that these words had any other or larger meaning.

In fact, the accused may sometimes be denied the right to argue that what he was doing was beneficial to the interests of the state, and he may not be allowed to show that the government is mistaken as to what the interest of the state are.

The breadth of the information covered and the classes of persons who are bound by the Official Secrets Acts is staggering. The 1911 Act, Section 1, makes it a very serious criminal offence 'for any purpose prejudicial to the interests or safety of the State' to make

any sketch, plan, model, or note which is calculated to be or might be or is intended to be directly or indirectly useful to an enemy; or [to obtain or communicate] to any other person any sketch, plan, model, article, or note, or other document or information which is calculated to be or might be or is intended to be directly useful to an enemy. . . .

Anyone can be sent to prison for a *minimum* period of three years for making a note of information which *might be indirectly* useful to an enemy!

Section 1 (2) makes the prosecution's task easier, for it provides that if no particular act tending to show a purpose prejudicial to the interests of the state can be proved against any person, he may still be convicted 'if from the circumstances of the case, or his conduct, or his known character, as proved, it appears that his purpose was a purpose prejudicial to the interests or safety of the State . . .'.

Section 2 (1) makes it a criminal offence for any person in the following classes:

a persons given information in confidence by holders of offices under the Crown, i.e. Ministers, civil servants, judges, policemen;

b persons who themselves hold office under the Crown;

c persons who in contravention of the Act have obtained any information;

d persons who have contracts with the Crown, e.g. someone who supplies stationery to a government department;

e persons who are employed by someone else who holds office under the Crown; or

f persons employed by someone who has a contract with a government department,

who has obtained information in virtue of belonging to one of the above classes of persons, either to communicate such information to some unauthorized person (i.e. to someone to whom he has not got permission to give such information), or to retain such information if reduced to some permanent form (if it is embodied in a sketch or plan) when he has no right to keep it in his possession.

Section 2 (2) makes it a criminal offence to *receive* any information if one knows, or ought to have known, that the communication of the information involved a violation of the Act. The only defence such a person has is to show that the information was communicated to him 'contrary to his desire'. Anyone therefore who benefits from hearing the office gossip which may fall from the lips of a friendly civil servant commits a criminal offence, unless he can show that the information was pressed upon him against his will.

In 1971 a journalist, Jonathan Aitken, and others were prosecuted under section 2 for having communicated a British diplomat's report on the Nigerian civil war to unauthorized persons, including the *Sunday Telegraph*, which published extracts from it. The judge, Mr Justice Caulfield, was so unsympathetic to the patent absurdity of section 2 that he almost interpreted it out of existence, adding for good measure:

This case, if it does nothing more, may well alert those who govern us at least to consider, if they have the time, whether or not Section 2 of this Act has reached retirement age and should be pensioned off, being replaced by a section that will enable men like the defendants and other editors of journals to determine without any great difficulty whether a communication by any one of them or a certain piece of information originating from an official source, and not concerned in the slightest with national security, is going to put them in peril of being enclosed in a dock and facing a criminal charge.

The bringing of this prosecution appears to have been motivated by official pique at the publication of information which threw doubt on the veracity of certain ministerial pronouncements. Its failure led to the establishment of a committee of inquiry into the possibilities of amending, not the Official Secrets Acts, but only section 2 of the 1911 Act.

Section 1 (2) of the 1920 Official Secrets Act makes it criminal, among other things, for any person in possession of an official document to neglect to hand it back to the authorities or to a police constable. In other words, a newspaper which has obtained an official document commits a criminal offence by retaining it.

Section 7 of the 1920 Act also makes it a criminal offence to do any act which is 'preparatory to the commission of an offence' under the acts. If one refills the glass of a garrulous civil servant in the hope that he might let slip some further office gossip, one commits a crime. One even commits a crime by buying the bottle of whisky with which you hope to top up the glass of any garrulous civil servant who may happen to drop in. It is no wonder that Mr David Williams, the leading authority in this field, has commented:

[The law on official secrets] is based on an ill-considered principal act as amended by an oversimplified subsequent statute. . . . Each was undoubtedly either inspired by or endorsed by the War Office and Admiralty. Together they have become one of the most ubiquitous, far-reaching and all-purpose blocks of statute law ever perpetrated in this country.

Despite the enormously wide scope of these Acts, we might well be inclined to argue that no one in their right mind would take advantage of them in such a way as to give rise to reasonable complaint. In no other country in the world has the doctrine of 'leave it to those in authority—they know best' become so widespread. And the fact is that this doctrine is pernicious and undermines any chance of maintaining reasonable standards of behaviour on the part of those in authority. For, of course, power *is* abused, and these Acts have been used and abused extensively.

In 1926, a retired prison governor was fined for having written for the press an account of the last days of murderers who had been in his charge. In 1930, a journalist was sent to prison for publishing details of wills in the probate registry a few hours before they were officially made public. In 1931, George Lansbury's son was prosecuted for publishing a summary of a cabinet paper dealing with unemployment, to which his father had had access when in the Labour Cabinet. In 1937, a civil servant was prosecuted and convicted for having in his possession documents which he had taken home to work on. In the same year, another journalist was prosecuted for having published details of a suspected swindler, which information had been obtained from a police circular. Compton Mackenzie was prosecuted under these Acts when he gave an account of his wartime exploits in his autobiographical *Gallipoli Memories* in 1932.

The worst aspect is the fact that the authorities sometimes arbitrarily threaten a prosecution. When in 1938 Duncan Sandys embarrassed the government with questions directed to reveal what he regarded as deficiencies in the country's defences, the Attorney General threatened him with proceedings. Still more ludicrous, in 1935, when Sotheby's announced that they intended to auction Lord Abingdon's collection, which contained original letters from Lord Nelson and the Duke of Wellington, written to the British ambassador in Paris between 1800 and 1830, the authorities stepped in and prevented the sale of the letters on the grounds of their being 'official secrets'.

In 1958, two Oxford undergraduates were sent to prison for publishing in *Isis* an article based upon information they had acquired while doing national service. It revealed that the British military authorities, to obtain details of Russian armaments, troops, and so forth had indulged in behaviour which was often stupid, frequently dangerous to the peace of the world and on occasion in violation of international law. Clearly, if true, this information was of a kind that it was in the public interest for it to be made known, for how else can public opinion play a part in restraining the lunacies to which governments are so partial? It was, indeed one of the main points made by the article that, 'It is incredible that this should have been allowed, but the irresponsibility bred and sheltered by the Official Secrets Act is uncontrollable.'

Of course, it is not only actual prosecutions which interfere with freedom of expression, but also the threat of prosecution which can be an even more potent weapon. As Lord Tangley said in the House of Lords in 1963, referring to evidence given to the Joint Working Party set up by Justice and the British Committee of the International Press Institute to consider the law of the Press:

There is a tendency, the Press firmly believe – and we had a good deal of evidence on it in our working party – for the Official Secrets Acts to be used for the purpose of muzzling criticism or restraining the passage of information, outside the strict realm of security.

Thus, in 1963, when an organization called Spies for Peace distributed a pamphlet containing information regarding Regional Seats of Government and the government's preparations for nuclear war, the editor and publisher of *Peace News* were visited by two senior police officer when it became known that *Peace News* intended to reprint extracts from the pamphlet, which had been widely distributed. The police officers sought to dissuade *Peace News* from publishing the extracts on pain of being prosecuted. But *Peace News* published the extracts and there was no prosecution.

Contempt of court and contempt of Parliament

Courts of law and Parliament each possess the power to punish any person for contempt who expresses opinion which are derogatory to the dignity of courts or of Parliament. Contempts of court and of Parliament are very similar in some ways, but they also differ, at least in the vitally important fact that there can be no appeal from a finding by either House of Parliament that one has been guilty of a contempt of Parliament.

Contempt of court covers any interference with the proper administration of justice, as by physically interfering with the judge, or by publishing any matter which might prejudice a fair trial. When the *Sunday Times* in 1967 published a photograph of Michael Malik, while he was still awaiting trial on a criminal offence, with a caption which suggested he was guilty of unlawful acts, with which he had not been charged, the newspaper was fined £5,000, but in contrast with some cases in the past the editor was not sent to prison – unlike the editor of the *Daily Mirror* who had been imprisoned in 1949 – because on the facts in this instance it was felt that the editor was unaware of what had happened.

Criticism of a judge may also amount to contempt of court and here it is important to notice that the truth of the criticism is no defence. In 1928 the *New Statesman* commented on the libel action against Dr Halliday Sutherland which Dr Marie Stopes had lost before Mr Justice Avory, and said that 'an individual owning such views as those of Dr Stopes [on birth control] cannot apparently hope for a fair hearing in a Court presided over by Mr Justice Avory' – which was undoubtedly true. Notwithstanding this the editor of the *New Statesman* was found guilty of contempt. The court did not consider the question of whether the attack was justified, this being presumed to be irrelevant.

Modern courts might take a more reasonable view of criticism of judges, and the 1936 dictum of Lord Atkin, that 'Justice is not a cloistered virtue, she must be allowed to suffer the scrutiny and respectful, though outspoken, comments of ordinary men,' is much quoted. But notice the word 'respectful'. In 1967, following the sentencing of a number of political demonstrators 'invading' the Greek Embassy to lengthy prison sentences, the severity of which was largely due to the fact that they had committed political offences in the past, the *Guardian* expressed its disapproval of the sentences, saying *inter alia*: 'If the sentences are not reduced on appeal to ones more appropriate to the actual offence on this occasion, there ought to be more demonstrations.' Lord Parker on behalf of the Court of Appeal went out of his way, although in fact taking no action against the *Guardian*, to issue the following statement.

The Court desires to say that its attention has been drawn to the fact that in one newspaper certain criticisms have appeared of the trial judge in regard to the sentences he imposed. Much more, the writer of the article suggested that if these sentences were not reduced on appeal there ought to be more demonstrations.

. . . It is of course recognized that it is only right that responsible comment and comment unlikely to interfere with the fair hearing of a pending appeal should be permissible.

As was stated on 10 July by the Attorney-General in the House of Commons: 'The press is free to comment responsibly on verdicts and sentences of criminal courts, even where the appeal is pending, and in my opinion this freedom is a valuable safeguard and it should not be curtailed.'

This Court entirely agrees. But the emphasis is on responsible comment and in the respect to which I have already referred this Court is quite satisfied that what was said in the newspaper went well beyond the limits of responsible comment.

What the limits are remain unclear. The *Guardian* returned to the attack and argued that, for an offence of conscience, a previous conviction for another political offence should not determine the length of sentence. '. . . It is wrong to try to cure a man of having a conscience by the same method [one might use to deal with a twice-convicted burglar]. It is not only wrong but pointless.'

A special problem regarding contempt of court has arisen with respect to what has come to be known as 'trial by television' – an interview with some person who may be in danger of legal proceedings to discuss with him the activities which ultimately do lead to him facing trial. Clearly the publication of prejudicial material once a person has been arrested or charged is a contempt, but what about a situation where no charge has yet been made and the person interviewed has come voluntarily to the studio, agreeing to be interviewed before an audience? In 1967, Dr Savundra was tried and convicted of certain criminal offences. He appealed, and among the grounds of his appeal was that pre-trial publicity in the press and on a television programme in which he took part had prejudiced a fair trial. The appeal was unsuccessful, but Lord Justice Salmon had this to say on behalf of the Court of Appeal:

To deal with the first point, in July 1966, a press campaign of considerable magnitude was mounted in relation to the parlous state of FAMIC's* affairs, the disappearance of the appellant Savundra and his past unsavoury record. At that stage there was nothing to suggest that criminal proceedings were even in contemplation. There is accordingly, no question of contempt of court. When an insurance company fails and its policy holders are left stranded, this is undoubtedly a matter of public interest and, indeed, public concern. When in such circumstances the moving figure in the company *is a man with an unsavoury record who appears to have used large sums of the company's money for his own purposes* and disappeared abroad, the matter becomes a public scandal. There is no doubt that a free press has the right, and indeed the duty, to comment on such topics so as to bring them to the attention of the public. It is in the public interest that this should be done. Indeed, it is sometimes largely because of facts discovered and brought to light by the press that criminals are brought to justice. The private individual is adequately protected by the law of libel should defamatory statements published about him be untrue, or if any defamatory comment made about him is unfair. This court does not consider that any real complaint can be made about the press campaign in July 1966, eighteen months before the trial.

But notice what is being said. The moment the press makes the statement in the words italicized, clearly it is the duty of the authorities to investigate and to consider the possibility of a criminal charge. It might appear from this that the mere allegation of criminal activity does not constitute a contempt, provided it occurs well before the trial takes place.

Lord Justice Salmon continues:

The court, however, takes a very different view of the television programme of February 1967, in which the appellant Savundra was interviewed shortly after his return to England. At this time it must surely have been obvious to everyone that he was about to be arrested and tried on charges of gross fraud. It must not be supposed that the proceedings to commit for contempt of court can be instituted only in respect of matters published after proceedings have actually begun. No one should think that he is safe from committal for contempt of court, if, knowing or having good reason to believe that criminal proceedings are imminent, he chooses to publish matters calculated to prejudice a fair trial. On any view the television interview with the appellant Savundra was deplorable. With no experience of television he was faced with a skilled interviewer whose clear object was to establish guilt before an audience of millions of people. None of the ordinary safeguards for fairness that exist in a court of law were observed, no doubt because they were not understood. They may seem prosaic to those engaged in the entertainment business, but they are the rocks on which freedom from oppression and tyranny have been established in this country – as one well known journalist subsequently

* Fire, Auto & Marine Insurance Co. Ltd, with which Dr Savundra was associated.

pointed out in an evening paper. On the other hand, surprisingly and regrettably, virtually the whole interview was reproduced verbatim in one of the Sunday newspapers. The court has no doubt that the television authorities and all those producing and appearing in televised programmes are conscious of their public responsibility and know also of the peril in which they would all stand if any such interview were ever to be televised in the future. Trial by television is not to be tolerated in a civilised society.

But notice that Dr Savundra had gone voluntarily to be interviewed, and he must have known the kind of thing that was in store for him. The interview took place seven days before his arrest. The result of what Lord Justice Salmon has said is to place the burden upon the commentator referring to activities which, by their very nature are capable of giving rise to criminal proceedings to guess how close the authorities are to bringing a prosecution. He may comment upon facts which, if true, amount to the commission of criminal activities without giving any simultaneous right of reply to the person about whom he is writing. But if he confronts him before a camera and gives him an opportunity to explain his point of view, he may commit a contempt of court. It is impossible not to feel that the lack of safeguards involved in a television interview for the interests of the layman, who is in effect being charged with a criminal offence, was the decisive factor in the court's attitude, with the consequence that a further limitation has been placed upon the freedom of the media to discuss with the people most closely involved matters which are of public concern.

Although in contempt of court there are cases which suggest the kind of thing which is likely, in the case of comment, to constitute a contempt, there is no such certainty in respect of contempt of Parliament. Contempt of Parliament is simply whatever either House of Parliament chooses to regard as a contempt of itself, and, for such contempt, there are certain penalties, including imprisonment. Nowadays, so far as commentators outside Parliament are concerned, the likeliest penalty is the inconvenience and obloquy of being hauled before Parliament, and perhaps even of having to make a public apology to Parliament for one's offence. Members of Parliament who are themselves guilty of contempt may be suspended or even expelled, as in the case of Mr Allighan in 1947, who was expelled for making imputations on the sobriety of his fellow members in the columns of the *News of the World*, for casting suspicion upon fellow members of having committed offences of which he himself was guilty and for having taken money for the disclosure of confidential matters occurring in Parliament to an outside body. In 1956 the editor of the *Sunday Express* was summoned to the Bar of the House of Commons and obliged to apologize for a leading article that had appeared in his paper at the time of a petrol shortage during the Suez crisis, and which alleged that it was an injustice that, while ordinary people were rationed for petrol, MPs were getting an unfairly large allocation.

Truth, it should be noticed, is no defence to an allegation of contempt of Parliament. In 1968 a Select Committee set up to report on parliamentary privilege said:

If . . . it is held that, even though the allegations may have been true, their real character was that of an improper attempt at obstruction of the House or of a Member or Officer of the House in the performance of its or his functions, we are satisfied that truth alone should not be accepted as a good defence.

The main criticism one would make about contempt of Parliament and contempt of court, apart from their very uncertainty, is the fact that the truth of the allegations may be irrelevant to the establishment of liability. It is doubtful whether judges should be given a special protection against criticism of their judicial activities. Peter Lloyd has cogently argued that criticism of judges should cease to be contempt, and that any judge who feels that he has been maligned should be free to take action under the ordinary law of libel. Parliamentary contempt makes forceful criticism of the activities of MPs hazardous, and it is doubtful whether Parliament deserves special protection from criticism; or, if it does, whether such special protection should be enforced by Parliament itself and not an outside body. Both courts and Parliament require protection from physical interference and from any external pressures that would improperly hinder them from the free exercise of the discretions vested in them, but it would be safer to define by legislation the circumstances in which such interference and pressure should be unlawful rather than to continue to allow the courts and Parliament to make up the law in their own favour as they go along. Such legislative authority is bound to depend in its exercise too much upon the personal idiosyncrasies of the judge concerned.

Local legislation

Local legislation is of two kinds: local Acts of Parliament, some of them over 100 years old, and a mass of bye-laws issued by the numerous local authorities all over the country. Between them, these constitute an enormous mass of law, the bulk of which is uncharted. There is no proper subject index of local Acts of Parliament, and so even if one wished to do so, it would be a task of many years of research to list those provisions in Acts of Parliament which bear upon the question of censorship and applying only in particular localities.

When the Town and Country Planning Act 1947 was passed, the planners wanted to provide a complete code of legislation affecting the poster business. This was never done because it was found that there were so many local Acts that it was not possible to trace them all. They got as far as something like 400 and then gave up.

Local Acts relating to posters are only a small part of the picture of local legislation, but local Acts are also relevant to such things as leafleting, demonstrations, the use of public address systems, and so on and so forth.

To illustrate the importance of the provisions of local Acts of Parliament, some examples may be given. The Beverley Corporation Act 1948, Section 90, contains the following (and provisions of this kind are extremely common):

A person intending to organize or form a public or ceremonial procession or a circus procession or a procession of wild animals through the streets of the borough (other than a public or ceremonial procession which is regularly held through such streets) shall give written notice thereof and of the route proposed to be taken and of the time at which it will take place to the Corporation and to the chief constable of the county by leaving such notice at the offices of the corporation and at the police headquarters in the borough respectively thirty-six hours at least (exclusive of Sundays) previous to the time fixed for such procession to march through the streets.

A small fine is imposed for violation of this provision. Some similar local Acts make it a petty criminal offence to depart from the route proposed in advance. For our purpose, the importance of such provisions is that processions (and other forms of demonstration) are among other things a means of communicating information to other people, and statutory provisions of this kind impose a restriction on such communication.

There is, in general, no legal right to hold or address public meetings in this country, but occasionally local Acts may authorize local authorities to set aside places specifically dedicated to the holding of public meetings, demonstrations, etc. Such provisions are, however, rare, and they may include an express prohibition of such activities in places other than those designated. The Whitstable Urban District Council Act 1948, Section 81, provides

1 Where any part of the promenades . . . has by notices affixed in prominent positions on the promenades been set apart by the Council for the delivery of lectures sermons or speeches –

   a no person shall without the consent of the Council, which consent shall only be given in respect of public ceremonial occasions, deliver any lecture, sermon or speech on any other part of the promenades.

Such provisions are important because of the lack of places ordinarily dedicated to the public delivery of speeches, and so on. The general law of the land, embodied in the Highways Act 1959, as interpreted by the court in *Arrowsmith* v. *Jenkins* (1963), has the effect that the holding of a meeting on any part of the highway is an unlawful obstruction of the highway, notwithstanding that that particular place may have been used traditionally for purposes of public meetings – perhaps so much so as to be known locally as 'Speakers' Corner' – and it is no defence to a person charged with this offence to show that hundreds of other meetings have been held on the spot concerned with the active cooperation of the police. The dedication of land under local authority control to the holding of meetings in virtue of some local Acts, gives some appearance of a right to express one's opinions openly in public before a gathering of one's fellow citizens.

Local acts regulating advertising are, as we have seen, extremely common. The Brighton Corporation Act 1954, Section 33, forbids the use of loudspeakers 'for the purpose of advertising any entertainment, sporting event, or meeting, or trade or business', but also contains a very important safeguard that this prohibition shall not apply to the use of loudspeakers 'for any religious, charitable, or political purpose, or for the purpose of a trade union (as defined in the Trade Union Act 1876)'.

A consequence, unintended no doubt, of the repeal of the 1876 Trade Union Acts, and the new definition of trade unions in the 1971 Industrial Relations Act, is that such provisions giving protection to trade unions will be rendered more limited, with the consequence that the use of loudspeakers for some purposes hitherto regarded as trade union purposes may now be unlawful.

Local Acts confer an important reserve of power on the authorities which has two particular advantages. First of all, since some common-law offences involving the expression of opinion or the communication of information may not always be easy to prove, local Acts, and even local bye-laws, which may make criminal the same physical activity, may make it easier to secure convictions by defining the offence in a simpler way than the common law. Secondly, general statute law, such as the Obscene Publications Act 1959, may confer a defence on persons accused under that Act which may be entirely absent if the local authority or police choose to take action under local legislation which contains no such defence. An example is the Glasgow Corporation Consolidation (General Powers) Order Confirmation Act 1960. Section 162 of the schedule to this act authorizes the issue of a warrant to search 'any house, shop, room, building, part of a building, or other place' for any 'profane, indecent or obscene article, book, paper, print, photograph, drawing, painting, or representation' which is kept 'for sale or for lending on hire or for publication for purposes of gain'. Possession of such items is punishable with a maximum fine of £100 or sixty days in prison. Furthermore, the articles seized *must* be destroyed.

This last example shows that some local Acts of Parliament may impose quite severe penalties, although most of them involve only a small fine. But even in the case of a small fine, it is vitally important to note that it is always open to the police, if more than one person is involved, to prosecute the accused not for the actual violation of the local Act, but instead for agreeing or conspiring together to violate the local Act – in which case there is no limit to the maximum penalty (excluding death) which may be imposed if the accused are found guilty. Prosecutions for such conspiracies still occur nowadays, especially in the case of defendants who were politically motivated in their actions.

Local Acts may not merely impose a penalty upon individuals for behaving in certain ways, but may also impose restrictions upon the activities of the local authority itself. One of the strangest of these provisions is to be found in the Dunoon (Burgh (Pavilion Expenditure) Order) Confirmation Act 1954. In 1949, the Dunoon Pavilion which was widely used for all kinds of public entertainments was burnt down. To enable the local burgh to raise money for replacing the destroyed building, this Act was passed. However, it also provided that the town council should not, unless they had obtained the previous consent in writing of the Cinematograph Exhibitors Association of Great Britain and Ireland, show, among other things, in the new pavilion and entertainment hall any feature film within eighteen months after it was first generally released, or charge less at film shows than was usually charged in local cinemas.

A recent example of a prosecution under a local Act of Parliament is of interest. Peter Wallington, a lecturer in law at Edinburgh University, distributed handbills outside Meadowbank Stadium in Edinburgh during the Commonwealth Games in July 1970. The handbills drew attention to the gross disparity between the money being spent by Edinburgh Corporation on the Games in comparison with its meagre expenditure on social welfare and housing in areas like Leith. He was prosecuted under the Edinburgh (Corporation Order) Confirmation Act 1967, Section 467 (1) (a) (i), which forbids the distribution of handbills not relating to political meetings or political purposes or to trade disputes in the city. He was convicted before the Edinburgh Burgh Court which took the view that the handbills were not for a political purpose. In cases like this, where the fine is often small and the waste of time and money involved in a successful appeal often considerable, many people feel that it is not worth appealing even though they know that an injustice has been done. Mr Wallington was merely 'admonished', but he decided to appeal to the Justiciary Appeal Court, where, of course, his appeal was successful and the conviction quashed.

In addition to local Acts of Parliament, bye-laws made by different local authorities often contain provisions which have a limiting effect on the communication of information and opinions. Unlike local Acts, bye-laws are always limited as regards the penalties they impose, to relatively small fines.

General

The range of legal wrongs which may be invoked to control the exchange of information or the expression of opinion is much wider even than our survey so far would suggest, but most of the more important ones have been discussed. In 1970, a man was fined £5 for having the letters ACAB embroidered on his denim jacket, thereby using insulting words, whereby a breach of the peace was likely to be occasioned. Apparently to the initiated the letters stood for 'All Coppers Are Bastards', although to the rest of the world it could mean all sorts of other things. Mention should also be made, however, of offences under the Public Order Act 1936 and the Race Relations Act 1965.

Particular groups, such as civil or military servants of the Crown, may be subject to special statutory provisions which may limit their freedom of expression in ways which may not apply to the rest of the community. Thus, an extraordinarily severe view was taken in February 1963 of the action of two young RAF junior technicians who were sentenced to eight months' imprisonment to be followed by discharge from the Service with ignominy. They had written letters to *Peace News*, the pacifist organ, inviting pacifists and nuclear disarmers in the services to contact them with a view to the formation of a services Campaign for Nuclear Disarmament group. One young man was nineteen, the other twenty, and both had joined the RAF at sixteen or seventeen, on a twelve-year-engagement. Both had good records in the service, but since joining they had both developed their attitudes and come to object on moral grounds to the use of nuclear weapons. They were convicted of the offence of displaying conduct to the prejudice of good order and Air Force discipline, contrary to the Air Force Act, 1959, Section 69.

The vagueness of the scope of many of the offences we have covered, and their extremely wide possible application, has the practical consequence that, as Dicey suggested in the nineteenth century, if the law should be fully enforced to its widest possible extent, there would be little or no freedom left for the expression of opinion or the exchange of information and ideas. The fact that in practice this is not so at any one moment in time is no guarantee that, in some future or political emergency situation the full rigour of the law might not be enforced. Indeed, in times of no particular stress an officious policeman can invoke some of the more extreme restrictions, and as we have seen this does in fact occur from time to time. The existence of these legal rules in their present form constitutes a serious threat to liberty, not only because of their occasional use to convict some person of unorthodox behaviour or opinion, but also for several other reasons.

First, any prosecution encouraged by these rules which is unsuccessful will still often impose a heavy penalty upon the successful party, because neither in civil nor criminal cases is the winner likely to recover all the expenses to which a successful defence has put him. Costs in criminal cases, where an award of costs against the unsuccessful prosecutor is still too rare, are often a very severe punishment for all save the rich. Secondly, the middle men of the cultural market-place – the printers, the publishers, the booksellers and the librarians – are all too easily frightened by the threat of prosecution, and may decline to disseminate matter which the police have suggested could give rise to a prosecution. Thirdly, since the risks of libel actions or other legal sanctions may be great, the middle-men turn to their lawyers, who, being cautious men, may all too often give advice which amounts to saying, 'Personally I think the chances of a libel action or a criminal prosecution being brought are small, but if one was brought, as the law now stands you would have no defence, and I must add that, although the chances of legal action being taken against you are small, if such action is taken you stand to lose a great deal.'

3 Extra-Legal Censorship

By extra-legal censorship is meant a number of different practices. Some of these constitute a violation of the law. Others are not authorized by the law and so are, in that special sense, unlawful. Still others occur in such circumstances that no legal rule is required to sustain them, and so are not in any sense unlawful. A number of practices, originally lacking legal authority, have in some manner acquired such legal authority with the passing of time. Practices of these various kinds are the essential lubricants without which the British machinery of justice would break down – or so is often claimed by the men who operate them. Some would certainly meet with general approval, if people were aware of them. Others would not.

Many of these practices are found in the area of police action, and have no particular connection with censorship – for example the police practice of detaining people for questioning, which is, of course, quite unlawful. This practice is referred to euphemistically on the mass media when they say that 'a man has been at the *XYZ* police station for the last *x* hours helping the Police with their inquiries'. At all costs, the façade of legality must be preserved. There is, in consequence, a reluctance to discuss such practices in public. Ministers often refuse, for example, to answer parliamentary questions on telephone tapping.

Two practices may briefly be referred to as illustrating the relevance of extra-legal censorship. To ensure a fair, unprejudiced trial for a person charged with a serious offence, the Criminal Justice Act 1967 provides that only limited details of the charge against the accused person should be made public after the magistrates have, at committal proceedings, decided that there is sufficient evidence against the accused to justify him being sent for trial. The Act requires that, after committal, the identity of the accused and the charges on which he has been committed should be displayed in a public part of the courthouse. In cases involving offences against children, especially sexual offences, publicity given to the identity of the children concerned may cause them damage, but according to the law the names of the children should be displayed in the notice as they are mentioned in the formal charge against the accused. The Home Office in 1970 advised clerks to justices to commit a minor breach of the law by not naming such children in the notices displayed.

Another practice of importance is the result of an odd decision of a Divisional Court in *Duncan* v. *Jones* in 1935. Here the court held that the crime of obstructing a policeman in the execution of his duty, which one might suppose meant things like striking a constable while he was arresting someone, was also to apply to the situation where a policeman orders a person holding a meeting in a public place to stop his speech altogether or to deliver it somewhere else. Should the person ordered to desist or to move elsewhere refuse to obey, he commits, said the court, the crime of obstructing a policeman in the execution of his duty. The only limitation is that there must be some grounds on which the policeman could reasonably believe that a breach of the peace might occur, so that his order is to be seen as a means of lessening the possibility of a breach of the peace. The problem is that wherever someone expresses controversial opinions in a public place it will nearly always be reasonable to believe that a breach of the peace *may* occur. It is not necessary for it to be shown that a breach of the peace *is likely* to occur, merely that there is a *real*, as opposed to an *imaginary*, possibility of it occurring. The practice of police interference with the holding of public meetings on this ground has obtained the sanctity of apparent legality as a result of the decision in *Duncan* v. *Jones*, but it is beyond doubt that, when Parliament created the offence of 'obstructing the police in the execution of their duty' under the Prevention of Crimes Act 1871, this is not what was meant by obstructing the police.

Let us now consider some of the more sophisticated extra-legal forms of censorship.

Disclaimers

One of the procedures followed by the police in dealing with obscene literature is the search and forfeiture procedure, under Section 3 of the Obscene Publications Act 1959. That is to say, the police obtain a warrant to search for obscene literature, and seize it when they find it. The *owner* of the books seized may subsequently appear before a magistrate to show cause why the books should not be destroyed as obscene literature. For many years now in the London area, at least, it has become a practice for the police in such circumstances to obtain signatures to the following form from the booksellers concerned:

I .... do hereby disclaim ownership to the above [number] items [shown in a list] of property seized by Police from my bookshop at [address] on the [date].

As the Commissioner of Police of the Metropolis, Sir John Nott-Bower, told a Select Committee of the House of Commons in 1957 in answer to a question, this disclaimer has no statutory authority behind it at all. 'It is really a means of avoiding the time and labour and expense of issuing summonses [on booksellers inviting them to show cause why the books should not be destroyed], if a man says he is prepared to surrender his right to the articles and agrees that they ought to be destroyed.' The committee failed, however, to make any comment on this undesirable practice in their report.

And the practice is undesirable, not only because it amounts to the owner telling a lie, but also because it deprives the bookseller of any right he may have to contest the destruction of the books, for only the owner may do this. The form is not in such terms as to ensure that the bookseller appreciates exactly what he is doing, as it would do if it ran something like, 'I understand that the owner of the books seized has a right to show cause before a magistrate why the books should not be destroyed and I wish to state that I do not intend to exercise any right I may have to contest the making of a destruction order by the magistrate.' But such forms, even if it was clear that the bookseller was aware of what he was doing, are still undesirable because they remain open to abuse. It is not too far-fetched to envisage that a bookseller on occasion being invited to sign the disclaimer in such circumstances that, if he signs, he will have no further trouble, but if he does not, then. . . . This is because there is no reason, as far as the bookseller is aware, why the police should not, instead of seeking for an order merely to destroy the books, prosecute him for the crime of having obscene books for sale. In which case he risks more than the loss of the books, he risks a fine or imprisonment.

Telephone tapping

Telephone tapping is not a precise term, but broadly it covers the situation where any third person listens in to or records a conversation conducted between two other people over the telephone. Such listening in can occur in a number of different ways. What is of concern to us here is that unrestricted telephone tapping may lead to people being penalized, embarrassed or blackmailed because of having expressed an opinion over the phone. Information acquired by telephone tapping may also be put to other improper use by third parties. Our concern should be to remove the inhibitions to which any ordinary person would feel himself subjected if he knew that his phone was tapped.

Is it, in fact, lawful for the police or other public officials to tap telephones? The answer is by no means clear. In 1762 Lord Camden, in the great case of *Entick* v. *Carrington*, laid down certain general principles. (1) A public official may lawfully only do such things for which express authority may be found in some statute or in some common-law rule. (2) The mere fact that public officials have lawful authority under an Act of Parliament or a common-law rule to perform certain acts does not give rise to the implication that they must necessarily have, by analogy, lawful authority to do acts which are very similar to those for which they have express authority. (3) The mere fact that public officials have performed certain activities for a very long time does not make that activity lawful. (4) An act performed by the state does not become lawful merely because it can be shown in some sense to have been in the interest of the state to have performed that act.

Although these principles are admirable, and ought in the interest of liberty to be upheld, it is simply not true that the courts have consistently upheld them. The issue is this: does the state in English law enjoy only the right to do that which is expressly authorized by the preexisting law, or can it not also do any such other act, whether it involves a violation of a legal right or not, which can be shown to be in the interests of the state? Subsequent courts have, in fact, excused unlawful acts by public officials because they could be shown to be in the public interest.

Telephone tapping by the police, by the customs and by the security services has long been practised in Britain. In 1957, following an outrageous occurrence when material obtained by means of telephone tapping was made available in disciplinary proceedings against a barrister, Mr Marrinan, a committee of three privy councillors was set up to consider and report upon the exercise of the executive power to intercept communications, the authority for doing so, the extent of its use and the safeguards subject to which the power should be used in future. This involved an investigation into the legal basis for telephone tapping, and, point by point, by rejecting each of Lord Camden's principles, the privy councillors came to the view that it was lawful. There was no express legal authority for it, but that did not matter. There was implied power to open letters, because the Post Office Act 1953 makes it a specific criminal offence to open a letter without a warrant from the Secretary of State. It should be obvious from this, they suggested, that the opening of letters under the Secretary of State's warrant was lawful. But not at all. The Post Office Act says nothing about the lawfulness of opening letters in general. It creates a special criminal offence, which persons having a warrant do not commit. But the Act is silent as to the *legality* of what they are doing. Furthermore the opening of letters has gone on ever since there was a postal service.

Since the privy councillors' Report suggests the opening of letters under a warrant is lawful, so obviously is the opening of telegrams; it would be absurd to draw the line at that point. Therefore the tapping of telephones is lawful. In any case telephone tapping is a very useful thing for the state to carry out, it leads to the detection of crime and espionage.

Tapping was therefore seen to be lawful at least under a warrant. And the privy councillors were assured, tapping took place *only* under warrant, while the number of interceptions of letters and telephonic communications each year was small. Warrants were issued only after special consideration had been given by the Home Secretary, and warrants were specific and related to the interception of messages to and from specific individuals. Subject to the offence in respect for which the warrant was granted being serious, and normal methods of investigation having failed, and there being reason to believe that interception of communications to or from the individual concerned would lead to a conviction, warrants might be issued by the Home Secretary. The privy councillors therefore felt that the practice should continue, subject to further safeguards. There should be a monthly review of each warrant; no interception should be carried on longer than necessary; warrants should be for a specified period, normally no longer than one month and never more than two, and lastly, transcripts of tapped telephone conversations should not be made available for the purpose of disciplinary proceedings by professional bodies.

The privy councillors, while admitting the possibility of such things occurring in future, finally concluded that all the evidence before them 'was to the effect that there is and has been no tapping of telephones by unauthorized persons in this country'.

In retrospect, it is only possible to be staggered by the *naïveté* of their Report. Deliberately or not, they were certainly misled on the extent of interception in communications, for as was to be disclosed in 1967, every telegram coming into or going out of the country was intercepted by the security services. True, there was a specific legal authority for this in the Official Secrets Act 1920, Section 4, which provides that the Secretary of State, where he considers it in the public interest to do so, may issue a warrant for the production to him of 'the originals and transcripts either of all telegrams, or of telegrams of any specified class or description, or of telegrams sent from or addressed to any specified person or place, sent or received to or from any place out of the United Kingdom by means of any such cable, wire, or apparatus, and all other papers relating to any such telegrams as aforesaid'.

But no reference is made to this statute or to this practice in the privy councillors' Report, even though it would have seemed to be relevant to their business. The fine principles they found to apply to the interception of letters and telephonic communications were shown in 1967 to have no application whatsoever to the interception of overseas telegrams, which has been going on since the 1920s.

Mr Geoffrey Marshall, Fellow of the Queen's College, Oxford, drew attention to certain oddities in a letter to the *Spectator* of 10 March 1967.

Since the Privy Councillors [in 1957] were aware of the power to issue warrants in respect of telegrams in section 4 of the 1920 Official Secrets Act and since they themselves point out that reference to interception of postal packets and letters in the 1953 Post Office Act covers the interception of telegrams, one of the following conclusions must follow: 1. The Privy Councillors were not informed of the existence of an important form of interception; or 2. the figures given in the 1957 report and the implicit assurance that they represent the full range of interception are misleading; or 3. the practice in relation to telegrams has changed since 1957 despite the Prime Minister's assurance that it has been the same for forty years; or 4. there is no such generalised interception of telegrams.

In the light of the Report of the Committee of privy councillors appointed to inquire into 'D' Notice matters in 1967, we know that conclusions (3) and (4) are false. This leaves us with the assumption that the figures in the 1957 Report are false and that the privy councillors in 1957 were not informed of any large-scale interception of telegrams. Someone appears to have deliberately misled or even to have lied to them. The Security Service, as we shall see, does not always tell the truth.

The *Spectator*, commenting on the 1957 Report made perhaps the sanest comment, most others having merely commented that the Report did not go far enough. It stated:

We repeat that there is only one way to prevent continued progress down that road [i.e. the police and security services coming to regard themselves as above the law], and this latest scandal is but further proof of the fact; it is to ban telephone tapping entirely, for whatever purpose, rejecting the 'tiny gains' in order to avoid the 'great losses'.

The scandal to which the *Spectator* referred involved the case in 1959 of a doctor accused before the General Medical Council, which was supplied with a transcript of telephone conversations in connection with charges of unprofessional conduct against him. The telephone had been tapped by the police with the consent of one of the parties to the conversation. The listening in was done at a private exchange on a private subscriber's line. There was *no* warrant for the tapping in this case. The evidence obtained was then made available to a professional disciplinary body, and so all the strictures of the privy councillors had gone for nothing. Those who excused what had occurred argued that what was done was not tapping for it had been done with the consent of one of the parties to the conversation. The privy councillors had not foreseen that the interception of communication would not be interception if it took place with the consent of either of the parties.

On becoming Prime Minister in 1970, Edward Heath reiterated a policy laid down by Harold Wilson. In 1966, Mr Wilson had announced that he had made a change in the practice of telephone tapping followed by governments since 1957. He had apparently forbidden for the future the tapping of telephones of Members of Parliament (this, it was later made clear, applied to the Lords as well as to the Commons). No indication was given of the previous extent of the tapping of Members' telephones, but the indications were that such tapping had occurred. One looks in vain for MPs who were during the period of 1957 to 1964 convicted of criminal offences as a result of tapping, for the privy councillors had stated, and the government had reiterated, the view that tapping should occur only in connection with a serious criminal charge when there was good reason to believe that the tapping would result in a conviction.

The subject of telephone tapping is one which is officially not to be discussed in public, for, as Mr Wilson said in 1966, his announcement on MPs' telephones being immune from tapping was a departure from the normal practice whereby he and the Home Secretary 'were unable to answer questions [in Parliament] relating to these matters'.

According to Professor Street, when in 1965, 'a journalist revealed that some of the Queen's telephone calls were being intercepted: he was threatened with a prosecution under the Official Secrets Act because he allegedly had asked G.P.O. telephone operators whether they ever intercepted telephone messages'. This episode may refer to an article in the *Wiltshire Echo* of 19 August 1965, which reported that telephone operators had listened in to calls going through the Chippenham exchange, including some by the Royal Family, and that telephone calls were 'frequently and consistently tapped'. A Post Office inquiry was held, which denied that there was any evidence to substantiate the allegation that business deals over the phone had become public knowledge.

With regard to the allegation that the staff and supervisors flagrantly listen in to telephone conversations, most telephone calls these days are dealt with by automatic telephone exchanges and STD and this applies to Chippenham.

It is essential that all telephone calls which are passed through the operator, for the telephonist to hear the opening comment of a caller and the response from the telephone number called.

In addition it is an essential part of the telephone operator's duty to check up on a telephone conversation which has been continuing for an unusually long time.

The journalist responsible for supplying the original story commented:

This looks like one big white-washing campaign by the Post Office. Both girls [who gave evidence of listening in] have proof of other girls listening in. At the moment they are not prepared to give names because of the Official Secrets Act, but if action is taken against them they will do so.

The ease with which a phone can be tapped is all too apparent, and consequently tapping appears to be a common enough occurrence. In February 1970, Mr G. K. Young, chairman of the executive of the Society for Individual Freedom, disclosed that he had evidence that calls to foreign embassies in Britain about trade deals had been intercepted and the information obtained passed on to the Board of Trade. 'This seems to me,' he said, 'not to be identified with national security.' Where telephone tapping takes place privately, the Court of Appeal has held in *R.* v. *Senat* (1968) that any evidence obtained thereby is admissible, and that assurances given in Parliament concerning telephone tapping apply only in respect of action taken by the police, security forces and the like.

There has been a significant growth in tapping for purposes of industrial espionage. However, the use of any device attached to some object in the place where the conversation to be overheard occurs, operating by transmitting the conversation to a listener outside by radio waves and involving the use of a wireless transmitter without a licence is a criminal offence under the Wireless Telegraphy Act 1949.

The legality of the use of devices for listening in to people's conversations is often dubious, and their use open to abuse. Yet, it is worth noting that the use of bugging devices by BBC journalists has not been altogether outlawed by the corporation. Indeed, in 1967 the Director-General, Sir Hugh Greene, laid down the following policy regarding their use.

This is a dangerous means of collecting information and should be used only in circumstances which would be extremely rare, if they ever arose, when a story which it was in the public interest to have revealed could only be revealed by these means. . . . Permission would have to be sought from very near the top in the BBC immediately below myself.

D Notices

We now come to a practice which remained hidden from the public view for thirty years before even a whisper reached the public, and for even longer before its general outline was made known in 1962. Following the Official Secrets Act 1911, the hand of the military and their power to control information was strengthened in 1912 by the establishment of the Admiralty, War Office and Press Committee. Its secretary was an employee of the Press Association, and its members included members of the service departments and of the press. It issued 'D' or Defence Notices whose purpose was to advise the press that it would not be in the public interest to make reference to certain matters. During the Second World War, the Ministry of Defence issued 'D' Notices, 'agreed with representatives of the Press'. When the war ended the Committee was reconstituted in its present form, and became known as the Services, Press and Broadcasting Committee. It consists of four government representatives, permanent civil servants and eleven others representing press and broadcasting interests, including the Newspaper Publishers Association, the Newspaper Society, the Scottish Daily Newspaper Society, the Periodical Proprietor Association, news agencies, the BBC and the Independent Television Authority. The committee issues either D Notices or P and C Letters (private and confidential). The latter mention the relevance of old D Notices to new matters about to come up. The D Notices themselves apparently take the following form:

Dear Sir,
    The Services, Press and Broadcasting Committee request that in the interest of national security you will make no reference to the following:

The D Notices are sent to newspapers, periodicals, radio and television. There is no automatic sanction for non-compliance with the terms of a D Notice, although theoretically in some cases a prosecution might be brought under the Official Secrets Acts. But very often the matters covered in the D Notice could not even if disclosed in public give rise to a prosecution under the Official Secrets Acts. The request in the D Notice dated 27 April 1956, for example, that no reference be made to 'Secret intelligence or counter-intelligence methods and activities in or outside the United Kingdom', is so wide as to cover many possible references of a quite harmless character. Such broadly worded D Notices are naturally undesirable, and their application in practice may be determined by mutual understanding between the committee and its secretary and the mass media, so that in real life such a request may not inhibit all reference to intelligence activities. But the very uncertainty of where to draw the line in such a case gave rise to a dispute between the government and a committee of privy councillors (The Radcliffe Committee), set up in 1967 to inquire into allegations of a violation by the *Daily Express* of the D Notice system. The committee found there had been no violation. The government insisted there had.

D Notices are not confined to restraining reference to matters which would involve the disclosure to an enemy or potential enemy of information of which he is unaware. It is unlikely, for example, that the *Daily Express*'s revelation in 1967, that all foreign telegrams coming into or going out of the country were intercepted by the security service, was unknown to the security service of potential enemy countries. During the Second World War, similarly, it would have been no news to the Germans that they were using landmines, but during the course of the war a D Notice was in force against references to these weapons.

The sanctions for non-compliance only exceptionally include criminal prosecutions, but as Andrew Wilson, when he was defence correspondent of *The Times*, pointed out:

... Everybody concerned is aware that there could be serious consequences. For example, as a defence correspondent you could be denied all Ministry of Defence 'facilities', such as visits to military establishments, transport in service aircraft, and most important of all, off-the-record talks in Whitehall. Without these facilities most correspondents would find it extremely hard to do their job.

He added:

From time to time a correspondent must ask whether the system is being used to cover up facts which in his opinion the public should know. Examples could be a particular practice by a security organisation, or performance deficiencies in a weapon system for which Parliament is voting large sums of money.

When that happens, a good newspaperman will obey his conscience. He may then get away with it by a skilful use of words, or conceivably by passing the information to an overseas colleague not subject to D Notices, and reprinting the overseas man's story. (D Notices are automatically lifted when their subject matter has appeared in print.)

But the 'dilemma of conscience' is not always clear cut. It is generally very difficult to know with complete certainty what constitutes a genuine security consideration; while 'the duty to tell the public' can too easily be confused with the urge to get a good story regardless of the consequences.

In these circumstances the D Notice system has served authority fairly well. Apart from the disputed *Daily Express* case there has been only one officially recognised breach in six years.

It could be argued that the system could not have worked at all if many newspaper men had felt that it was being continually abused. Nevertheless, there is a widespread feeling, at least among defence correspondents, that the present body of D Notices is too vague.

In February 1967, when it became known that the *Daily Express* intended to publish an account of the traditional practice of intercepting all overseas telegrams for examination by the security services, frantic efforts were made by the Security Service, government ministers, the secretary of the D Notice committee and others to stop publication. When confirmation was sought from a government department that this practice was being carried on, a flat denial of the existence of the practice was issued on the instruction of the Security Service. When it was clear that the denial was untrue, other efforts were made, but in vain, because the *Daily Express* understood that the relevant D Notices did not apply to this particular practice. When the affair was over, although the government had insisted that there had been a violation, when invited to prosecute anyone under the Official Secrets Act the Attorney-General stated that there was no evidence of the commission of any criminal offence and there could therefore be no prosecution.

The absence of any prosecution emphasizes the fact that the D Notice system, which so effectively enables the government to manipulate the press, rests essentially upon the willingness of the press to be manipulated. As Colonel Leslie Lohan, the secretary of the D Notice committee in 1967, said, for it had come in for much undeserved criticism:

It's all so ironic. I've done my best always to help the Press, yet never embarrass a Minister, and I find myself in this mess. My whole object has been to get people together on a friendly basis. It's worked thousands of times.

No one's mentioned all the successes I've had, *just by knowing the journalists and telling them not to do something*. Because it's fallen down once, it's been blown up into a storm. . . .

Apparently much of the work of persuading journalists not to publish was done very much on an informal social basis without any particular reference to the detailed provisions of D Notices, which gives rise to all sorts of risks, not least of which is widening the area of information which journalists are persuaded not to disclose.

Again discussion of the D Notice system is discouraged. The Radcliffe Committee said that 'the only safe rule if there is to be a "D" notice system at all, is that all notices be treated as confidential documents, guarded with care under editorial control and withheld from publication'. Not only must no reference be made to certain matters, but the very existence of a request, not to refer to intelligence activities in this country for example – is not to be made public. Who is being protected from what? Clearly not the potential enemy. It can only be the public who are being protected from information as to the areas of knowledge which the mass media will not supply him with lest he might be unduly concerned.

Such a system as this is bound to be abused in a way which conflicts with the public interest. It is no wonder that Lord Francis Williams was reported as saying in 1970:

. . . the D Notices warnings were being used to prevent the disclosure of information not because it would be damaging to Britain's security but because it might be damaging to the reputation for efficiency of some civil servants or ministers.

Aliens

Powers of immigration control in this country have long been used to effect purposes which are unlawful; and, in the area in which we are interested, to effect the imposition of penalties upon the holders of certain opinions and to inhibit the exchange of information. Thus, in 1965, the Home Secretary, Sir Frank Soskice, refused to admit spokesmen of the South Vietnam Liberation Front to address public meetings. Explaining this decision, Sir Frank stated that the sole object of the Vietnamese in coming to this country 'was to conduct propaganda justifying armed incursion by the North Vietnamese into South Vietnam'. If one drops the emotive language, he excluded them because he thought that they might explain the policy towards the Vietnam conflict of the group to which they belonged. How many Americans have been excluded because they justified the policy of their government in Vietnam? It is clearly in the public interest of people in this country that both sides should be heard, but Sir Frank was determined that this should not be permitted. In 1963 the Berliner Ensemble was refused permission to attend the Edinburgh International Drama Conference. In the same year, Mr Brooke, the Home Secretary, refused to allow Lenny Bruce, the abrasive American comedian into Britain and had him sent back to the United States, 'because his admission to this country would not be conducive to the public good' – somewhat odd interpretation of the scope of his powers to exclude aliens. It has never noticeably been a condition of aliens seeking to enter this country that their admission should be conducive to the public good. Mr Brooke, it would appear, did not approve of Mr Bruce's brand of humour.

In 1969, James Callaghan used his powers as Home Secretary to deny those members of the Church of Scientology who were aliens permission to remain in or enter Britain for the purpose of studying their beliefs at the movement's headquarters in Sussex. This was done because Scientology was alleged to be harmful. But the fact is that Scientology, however bizarre and irrational its activities may seem to some, is not considered sufficiently harmful to justify its activities being made criminal. If the social harm allegedly involved in the practice of Scientology is sufficiently limited for British Scientologists to be free to exercise their beliefs freely, it seems wrong that, without any public inquiry into the facts, the Minister by a purely administrative measure should penalize the holders of certain opinions by denying them freedom to enter this country to study. As the National Council for Civil Liberties said at the time, the use of administrative measures to obstruct freedom of association and freedom of opinion is 'objectionable in principle and dangerous in practice'. Stung by this and other criticism the government invited Sir John Foster, Q.C., in January 1969, 'to enquire into the practice and effects of Scientology'. Almost two years later, Sir John's report was published in December 1971. It revealed that some people not wishing to work or study scientology in this country had been excluded merely because they were scientologists. Referring to this Sir John said:

. . It seems to me wrong in principle for the Secretary of State for Home Affairs to use his wide powers of exclusion against those Scientologists who happen to be foreigners or Commonwealth citizens, when there is no law which prevents their colleagues holding U.K. citizenship from believing in their theories or carrying on their practices here. If the practices of Scientology are thought to constitute a danger to our society sufficiently grave to warrant prohibition or control under the law, then it is for Parliament to make such a law and for the Executive to apply it impartially to Britons and foreigners alike. But so long as none of our laws are being infringed, the classification of *foreign* Scientologists as 'undesirable aliens' so that they are forbidden entry through our ports . . . seems to me to constitute a use of this discretionary power which is quite contrary to the traditional policy followed by successive Home Secretaries over many years.

The latest example of the use of the administrative powers of immigration control being used to penalize opinion is in the case of Rudi Dutschke, the German student leader and revolutionary, who was admitted to do research at Clare Hall, Cambridge, in 1970. The Home Secretary, Mr Maudling, refused to alter the conditions on which he had originally been allowed to come to this country for purposes of medical treatment and convalescence to allow him to remain for the purposes of studying for a higher degree at Cambridge. Dutschke appealed to an appellate tribunal consisting of members chosen jointly by the Lord Chancellor and the Home Office. The five members were all establishment figures used to understanding the risks of left-wing 'subversion'. They were a former judge in Kenya, a retired army general, two retired members of the Diplomatic Service and a former president of the Law Society – hardly a tribunal in any way representative of a cross-section of the community. In January 1971 the tribunal, having heard evidence in secret from the Security Service, which neither Dutschke nor his lawyers had any opportunity of contradicting or putting to the test in the usual ways known to court procedure, decided to approve the Home Secretary's decision not to allow Dutschke to remain in Britain to study. The tribunal found that Dutschke had not constituted a risk to national security in the past, although there was a risk (unexplained) that he might in future become such a risk. He had taken part in political discussions and meetings. But the aspect of the tribunal's opinion which is of most concern is the assumption that the discussion of political questions is equivalent to 'the planning and organization of political demonstrations:' a remarkable obeisance to the Marxist theory of the unity of thought and action. But there is a difference between talking about political questions and the organization of political action, and it is a vital distinction for freedom of thought. Dutschke himself summed it up.

As a result of this decision it should now be clear to every foreigner that even the ability to think critically and discuss politics is a risk in the eyes of the present government. I have never engaged in direct political or organizational activity in Britain.

. . . Now every critical Englishman and woman could be confronted with the same accusation. 'You think and discuss, therefore there must without doubt be risk.' Is not the greater risk the threat to civil liberties in Britain posed by this government? We will continue to think critically and will continue to live.

4 The Media

'Reade was right, but wrong to say it: the human race must be allowed to keep its illusions'
Winston Churchill, referring to Reade's book *The Martyrdom of Man* (1872).

Books

Books have borne the brunt of prosecutions (and seizures) under the Obscene Publications Act, not to mention seizure by the Customs or prosecutions by the Post Office for being indecent or obscene. Rarely is the actual author of the book brought before the court. Under the Obscene Publications Act, it is the publisher or bookseller who is likeliest to be involved. In the case of Customs seizure or a Post Office prosecution, it is the traveller who has bought a book, or someone who has sent away to a foreign exporter for books or photographic material of whose exact nature he may be unaware; or it may be the seller of such material if he is in this country. The operation of the legal prohibitions against obscenity and indecency are essentially arbitrary. A customs officer may seize a book which is freely available inside the country. One magistrate may decide that a book is obscene, while another in a different part of the country may rule that it is not. Cheap editions of such works as *Fanny Hill* may be declared obscene, while a more expensive edition can be distributed without any interference from the police. While the ordinary reader may be denied the right to obtain from the local library a book which has been the object of a successful prosecution for obscenity, a special library has been set up for Members of Parliament consisting solely of such books. Perhaps MPs, unlike ordinary people, are like the policemen who, it was decided by the Court of Criminal Appeal in *R.* v. *Clayton* (1962), were not susceptible of being depraved or corrupted.

Perhaps the most important point one can make in respect of proceedings against books for obscenity is that, although they may inflict considerable hardship upon individuals, they are irrelevant, if their aim is to prevent the representation of cruelty, violence, perversion and even normal sexual activity, because for every book prosecuted one can match it with scenes equally 'obscene' from other works, not least of all the Bible, and other now accepted works of literature.

The search and forfeiture procedure under the Obscene Publications Act 1959, Section 3, is much disliked because it denies the owner of the books the right to claim a jury trial. Since the unsuccessful prosecution of Penguin Books on account of *Lady Chatterley's Lover*, it is clear that the police generally prefer to proceed in this way, no doubt because the prospects of successful prosecution are greater. The bookseller alone is directly involved, and since the ruling of the magistrate that the book is obscene and should be destroyed affects only that particular bookseller's stock, the publisher may not feel it is in his interest to come to the aid of the defence, which he or the author may do. Until 1967 a private person could bring a proceeding under Section 3, but this possibility is now lessened as a result of a provision in the Criminal Justice Act 1967:

A justice of the peace shall not issue a warrant under Section 3 (1) of the Obscene Publications Act 1959 except on an information laid by or on behalf of the Director of Public Prosecutions or by a Constable.

This provision does not have the effect of guaranteeing a jury trial, as the Home Secretary, Mr Roy Jenkins, said it would in March 1967. All it does is to prevent action by a private individual, without the consent of the Director of Public Prosecutions. But we should take note that it does not require the police to obtain the Director's permission before they act. If the police do act under Section 3, the fact remains, as before, that the owner of the books seized cannot claim jury trial.

On occasion, as a matter of policy decided at the highest level, a decision may be taken to avoid a jury. Thus the Director of Public Prosecutions and, perhaps, the Attorney-General, no doubt chastened by their failure with *Lady Chatterley's Lover* before a jury, took action against John Cleland's *Fanny Hill – Memoirs of a Woman of Pleasure*, under Section 3 of the 1959 Act. As Roy Jenkins, later himself to be Home Secretary, said of the procedure adopted in the *Fanny Hill* and other cases:

The legal authorities of this country can be relied upon to mishandle any issue touching the censorship of books. Unfortunately this record of ineptitude does not make them fight shy of this subject. The Director of Public Prosecutions, aided by that indefatigable scourge of the impure, Mr Griffith-Jones, is usually willing to have a go.

A complaint which has substance in it is that proceedings are often brought against small booksellers, or small publishers, who suffer particularly from the costs of litigation even if they win their action. Cases in which Mr Dobson, the Bradford bookseller, has been involved were reported to have cost him £17,500 (not to mention two periods of imprisonment). Dave Cunliffe's legal expenses in *The Golden Convolvulus* case were £500 (not to mention a £50 fine). Often such persons prefer to cut their losses and plead guilty to a prosecution, or to decline to contest forfeiture proceedings.

When, in 1965, Mr Cunliffe and his partner, the proprietors of a small poetry press in Blackburn, were prosecuted for publishing an obscene book, *The Golden Convolvulus*, an anthology of erotic writing. *The Times Literary Supplement* commented:

But the case ought never to have been brought – and never would have been brought (in this day and age) against a reputable commercial publisher who chose to print the same selection of material.

In 1968, a Brighton bookseller, an American poet, Bill Butler, was prosecuted for having obscene books for sale and convicted. In this instance a *Times Saturday Review* columnist commented:

Butler has been caught in a nonsense. Had his Unicorn Bookshop been in London it is unlikely he would have been prosecuted. This is implicit in the fact that bookshops large and small throughout the country including Dillons, The Times Bookshop and Bumpus, plus many public libraries carry titles for which he was convicted. Even people who share none of the literary tastes of Butler and his customers must see that it is an absurdity that he should be £2,700 down for having tried to make 'an honest statement in bookshop terms of what is actually going on'. In England we are used to some variations in the penalties exacted by magistrates' courts, but for an offence to be prosecuted in one town and not in another is inconsistent to say the least.

Evidence given in this case for the accused distressed the chairman of the Brighton magistrates, Mr H. Ripper, who said:

May I say how appalled my colleagues and I have been at the filth that has been produced at this court, and the fact that responsible people, including members of the university faculty, have come here to defend it.

It is something which is indefensible from our viewpoint. *We hope these remarks will be conveyed to the university authorities* [italics added].

The Golden Convolvulus case also gave rise to problems over the seizure by the police of other material. As Mr Cunliffe and his partner complained in the *New Statesman*:

The police have now prevented us from functioning by seizing all our files and most of our book stock in a police raid on our premises on August 19. They arrived complete with search warrant and conducted a detailed and lengthy probe. They seized all copies of the *Golden Convolvulus*, *Poetmeats 5, 7, 9/10* and a small poetry collection, *Whether you or I love or hate*. They seized all files, invoice-records, mailing lists, etc., relating to our publications and one strictly personal address book. They also took away the original manuscripts and stencils of *The Golden Convolvulus* and *Poetmeat 9/10*, plus correspondence and books from our own private collection.

On 9 March 1967 a similar use of powers of search occurred in the case of the periodical *IT* (*International Times*), whose premises were entered by the police on a warrant authorizing them to seize copies of the journal *IT*. Subscription files were removed, in triplicate, 'and office and private address books – one with £12 tucked inside – taken'. Some time later, no legal proceedings having been taken, *IT* itself threatened legal action against the police and the property was returned in May. This kind of behaviour has the effect of interfering with the freedom of the bookseller or publisher to carry on his business in the normal way, in circumstances where, as it so often turns out, there may be no sufficient grounds to justify the police taking further action, as may have been the case in this instance.

In February 1965, police seized a number of books from a Bradford bookseller, Mr Dobson, including nineteen copies of a book called *Bawdy Setup*. In November 1965, Mr Dobson was sentenced to two years' imprisonment and fined £500 for possessing *other* similar books which were found to be obscene. Shortly afterwards the Director of Public Prosecutions wrote to the Chief Constable of Bradford listing the books regarded as obscene and saying, 'The remaining books, which are considered not to be obscene, can be returned to Dobson'. These included *Bawdy Setup*.

In July 1966, Mr Dobson was freed by the Court of Appeal; two months later, the books referred to in the director's letter were returned to him, including *Bawdy Setup*.

In August 1967, books were again seized from Mr Dobson's shop including *Bawdy Setup*. In February 1969, Mr Dobson was again sentenced to two years' imprisonment for possessing *Bawdy Setup*, which was held to be obscene. (This sentence was to run concurrently with a similar one for possessing the complete unexpurgated edition of *My Secret Life*, by the pseudonymous Victorian author, 'Walter'.)

Sometimes uses of police powers occur, the justification for which is not apparent to the writer, as when the police raided a showing of Andy Warhol's film, *Flesh*, at the Open Space Theatre Club, London, and the organizers were told that the warrant for the seizure had been issued under the Obscene Publications Act 1959. Mr Marowitz, the theatre's artistic director, said:

The police superintendent read out provisions of the Act and told me this was an obscene film. But I gather he has not seen it.

When criticism of the raid was expressed in the House of Commons, the Home Secretary Mr Callaghan replied:

Broadly speaking, I want the House to know that I shall support the police when they act in response to complaints from the public in investigating these matters.

When the Director of Public Prosecutions decided that no action should be taken on the grounds of obscenity, he sent the papers dealing with the case to the Greater London Council suggesting that they consider taking action against the club, and in due course the club was fined for showing a film without a certificate from the British Board of Film Censors (or the Greater London Council) to an audience which included members of the public.

Another ground of complaint is that in obscenity proceedings magistrates are only too willing to ignore the evidence of literary and other experts for the defence. After hearing a parade of literary experts praising the virtues of *Fanny Hill*, in 1964, the Bow Street magistrate, Sir Robert Blundell, said:

I have no hesitation in saying that the order [for destruction as being an obscene work unredeemed by literary merit] should be made.

Reports vary as to how long it took him to reach this decision, which required him to weigh up on the one hand the expert evidence – all on one side testifying to the book's merits – against on the other its tendency to corrupt and deprave. All agree that he took very little time.

Whether the presence of a jury is beneficial to the defence is a moot point. It is clear that many people, including publishers, believe it to be to the defendant's advantage to be tried before a jury. The result of a number of prosecutions of books for obscenity in 1954 led some people, as C. H. Rolph describes it, to accept '. . . the then popular theory – later invalidated by the *Chatterley* case – that if a judge tells an obscenity jury what to do they will do it, while if he sums up impartially they will disagree'.

Experience suggests that this should be qualified to say that the advantage of a jury holds good, subject to the qualification that a mixed jury containing a married woman or two is less likely to be extreme in its hostility to obscenity than is an all-male jury.

In *The Last Exit to Brooklyn* case in 1967, the judge ruled under the Sex Disqualification (Removal) Act 1919 that an all-male jury should hear the case. *The Last Exit* case was also of interest as being the first in which evidence of being detrimentally affected by a book was given for the prosecution. Sir Basil Blackwell, the Oxford bookseller, said:

I feel it depraved me, because I felt that my mind was impaired, vitiated and defiled by the language that I read in the book – much of it new to me – by the conduct in the book – of much of which I was only dimly aware.
I felt I was seriously hurt by the book and wanted to go away and cleanse my mind.

The Rev. David Sheppard, former England cricketer, and later Bishop of Woolwich said:

I am afraid it left the impression that it is pandering to all that is worst in me. . . . I feel I am not unscathed by reading a book like this. I would not like to say I could read a book like this and suffer no damage from it.

But what justification is there for ruining men, for sending them to prison, in obscenity proceedings? Are they being punished for anything more than giving offence to the shockable, or are they being punished for the harm they have done to society? If the former, then the savagery of some of the sentences is inexcusable. It cannot be the latter, because, notwithstanding Sir Basil Blackwell and the Rev. David Sheppard in *The Last Exit* case, we have no cogent evidence that books are an important causitive factor in contributing to social ills. As the Report of the Arts Council Working Party on the Obscenity Laws said in 1969:

It is not for the State to prohibit private citizens from choosing what they may or may not enjoy in literature or art unless there were incontrovertible evidence that the result would be injurious to society. There is no such evidence.

In the absence of such evidence, punishing such behaviour may itself be a social ill. As Professor Bernard Williams commented in 1961:

> The hypocrisy of banning books on the grounds that they do harm, when we can in general have no notion of what harm they will do, to whom, or how, is something that itself is likely to have more serious consequences than the publication of a very great number of dirty books.

Very many people remain convinced however, that obscene books do cause harm. Yet, because of the lack of real evidence that books can do social damage, many of them are apt to fall back upon such mystical phrases as 'damage to the nation's moral fibre'. In 1954, when Vivian Connell's *September in Quinze* gave rise to proceedings for obscenity, the judge, Sir Gerald Dodson, Recorder of London, had this to say when passing sentence:

> It is a very comforting thought that juries from time to time take a very solid stand against this sort of thing, and realize how important it is for the youth of this country to be protected and that the fountain of our national blood should not be polluted at its source.

This kind of approach does not require proof of damage in order to justify the banning of books; it knows instinctively – and irrationally – that certain books, which are readily recognizable, cause harm. As counsel in a case in 1968 said, 'The magistrates will know a dirty book when they see it.'

The problem is not made easier by those who believe that it is possible to distinguish between obscenity, which may sometimes be acceptable, and pornography, which is not. D. H. Lawrence and Sir Alan Herbert are not the least distinguished of those who have believed this. A little reflection would show this is untrue historically, for much that was once condemned as filth for filth's sake has now became part of the world's accepted great literature. None the less, the belief that there is a difference between pornography, or hardcore pornography and the rest, persists and has even found an echo in legislation, as is evidenced by the long title of the Obscene Publications Act 1959:

> An Act to amend the law relating to the publication of obscene matter; to provide for the protection of literature; and to strengthen the law concerning pornography.

Yet the Act makes no further reference to pornography, thereby leaving one to conclude, if one were to take the Act seriously, that articles, above all books, may be divided into three parts:

1 Literature, which may be obscene without being criminal;
2 Obscene books, which are criminal, unless they are literature; and
3 Pornographic books which are criminal because they are obscene.

Sometimes people believe that a desire to make money out of publishing a book is the touchstone of pornography, 'unaware', as Alan Watkins has pointed out, 'that all publishers print books in order to make money'. In 1969, in the prosecution of Mr Dobson for having published an edition of *My Secret Life*, after he had been convicted, Mr Justice Veale addressing Mr Dobson said:

You were not printing *My Secret Life* in order to make it available to professors and students. You were deliberately proposing to make money out of the sale of filth because you thought it had money value.

Given that the rules governing obscenity are so unsatisfactory what should be done about them?

In his book, *Books in the Dock*, published in 1969, that sane legal commentator C. H. Rolph proposed the following reforms in the area of books and obscenity:

1 That 'books' be exempted from the operation of the obscenity laws.

2 That no private person shall have the right to prosecute.

3 That the 'crime' of publishing an obscene article should be abolished, and that any proceedings should be for forfeiture only.

4 That (if the above is unacceptable) the defendant and not the Director of Public Prosecutions should elect the mode of trial.

5 That there should be a right of trial by jury in forfeiture proceedings as well as in criminal prosecutions.

6 That there should be a time limit between 'seizure' of a book and the hearing of the case against it.

7 That the jury should be effectively required to read the book.

8 That the charge of 'conspiring to contravene the Act' should be abolished.

9 That all local Acts and by-laws in conflict with the intention of the Obscene Publications Acts, or covering the same ground, should be repealed.

10 That any criminal trial, and any forfeiture proceedings taken before a jury, should be in two distinct parts; the first to determine the alleged obscenity and the second (if the book is found to be obscene) to decide whether its publication is nevertheless justified.

Mr Rolph's proposals are obviously common sense. Many others have made other proposals for a change in the law, although most assume the continued existence for purposes of the criminal law of the concept of obscene books and articles. Of major importance are the conclusions of the Arts Council Working Party on the obscenity laws, which felt that the obscenity laws, 'while constituting a danger to the innocent private individual, provide no serious benefit to the public'. They therefore recommended a repeal of the obscenity laws *in toto* – with the exception of the Post Office Act 1953, where they wanted an amendment so that it could be invoked to protect the *offended*(!) recipient of unsolicited obscene or indecent material – for a trial period of five years. The force of these conclusions is underlined by the fact that an inquiry in Denmark led to effect being given to a recommendation that the obscenity laws be repealed, and in the United States a Presidential Commission reached similar conclusions (although President Nixon did not act on them). The main points of the Working Party's Report are worth repeating:

1 It is not for the State to prohibit private citizens from choosing what they may or may not enjoy in literature or art unless there were incontrovertible evidence that the result would be injurious to society. There is no such evidence.

2 No crystal ball can tell us dogmatically whether more or less pornography would result from Repeal but in any case there is a complete absence of evidence to suggest that sex in the arts, even when aphrodisiac in intention, has criminal or anti-social repercussions.

3 Though it is sometimes conjectured with no indisputable evidence that heavy and prolonged exposure to the portrayal of violence may not only reflect but also influence the standards of society, violence has been ubiquitous in the art, literature and Press of the civilised world for so long that censorship must by now be recognised as a totally inadequate weapon to combat it. Indeed laws available for the purpose including the Obscenity Acts are virtually never even invoked against it.

4 Since judges have to work in what is in effect a legal vacuum, the prosecution of an occasional book – usually the wrong one – often succeeds only in bringing the law into disrepute, without effectively preventing the distribution even of that book.

5 The very objective of the law is not even established, let alone identified in concrete meaningful terms that could command acceptance. Although judges emphasize that an article cannot be condemned because it shocks or disgusts, in practice that is precisely what happens, since juries have no other criterion to guide them.

6 It is impossible to devise a definition of obscenity that does not beg the question or a rational procedure for weighing depravity and corruption against artistic merit and the 'public good'.

7 When juries and defendants are without a comprehensible definition of the crime alleged, the defendant is left at the mercy of a personal opinion; which is a system of censorship rather than a system of law.

8 It is intolerable that a man should be criminally punished for an action that he has no means of ascertaining in advance is criminal.

9 Incitement to criminal behaviour is sufficiently covered by the ordinary law of incitement. To that extent the Obscenity Acts are redundant. In so far as they add the concept of a mere unintentional tendency toward crime as a punishable offence they are to be deplored.

10 It is an affront both to legal and common sense that incitement to a non-crime should be punishable as a crime; and worse when this doctrine is extended to a mere tendency.

11 No encouragement should be given to the concept of the State as *custos morum* with its corollary that merely to shock is a criminal offence.

12 The proper sanction for breaches of taste or nonconformity with current *mores* should be social reprobation and not penal legislation.

The government has refused to give effect to the Working Party's recommendations, as it has even to many other less radical proposals for reform.

Apart from obscenity, other legal rules may affect the publication of books. In particular, the Official Secrets Acts may limit the freedom of those subject to them. It is, however, noticeable that ex-Ministers are not infrequently guilty of the kind of indiscretion which has, in the past at any rate, led humbler servants of the state into legal difficulties. When, in September 1970, Richard Crossman as Editor of the *New Statesman* disclosed legal advice given to the Labour Cabinet, of which he had been a member, over the 'Concorde' aircraft, no action was taken against him. There is now apparently a practice, brought in to avoid such embarrassments by which all Ministers and ex-Ministers submit proofs of books to civil servants in the Cabinet Office. In Mr Anthony Nutting's book on the Suez affair, *No End of a Lesson*, the names of most civil servants were removed, but, as Mr Hugh Fraser, MP, has commented, 'these omissions heaped maximum and uncensored blame on the politicians'.

Publications by civil servants, which are based on official information, require the permission of the department head concerned. The same applies with even greater severity in respect of people who, having left the armed forces, wish to write of their war-time experiences, and threats of action under the Official Secrets Acts have had to be resorted to bring them to heel.

Ministers who wish to publish books while in office are subject to somewhat vague rules. When Dr Jeremy Bray, Joint Parliamentary Secretary at the Ministry of Technology, wished to publish a book, *Decision in Government*, he submitted the text to the Prime Minister. Mr Wilson apparently 'felt difficulty in agreeing to its publication,' wrote Dr Bray, 'and suggested that to test the temperature I should publish a short summary of the book in *The Guardian*.' This was done 'without any embarrassing reactions'. After this odd procedure, Mr Wilson still required Dr Bray to resign before the publication of the book itself. He wrote to Dr Bray: 'I have no alternative but to uphold the principles which every Prime Minister must retain in relation to the collective responsibility of his Administration.'

When the book was published, it was difficult to see what precise principles Dr Bray's forced resignation was supposed to have upheld. It contained nothing of importance which was not already known outside government. As Hugh Stephenson, reviewing the book in *The Times*, said of this event, it was one of a number of 'inexplicable lapses' by the Labour government from the policy of encouraging more open discussion of public issues. Yet, as Mr Stephenson says, the book itself was 'a remarkably circumspect *critique*, rather than a criticism, of the governmental decision-making process', which included among other things 'a rather simplist description of a day in the life of a departmental Minister . . .'

Publishers obviously exercise a choice in deciding whether to publish a book or not. If we can separate considerations as to the commercial viability of a book, and its literary or scientific merits from other factors, among the other considerations will be such issues as whether the publisher is willing to run the risk of libel actions or criminal prosecutions which the book might involve. Even if there is no such risk, publishers obviously have their own convictions, which may in some cases lead them not to wish to publish books which may conflict with them. Others may take a more detached view and be more largely concerned with either commercial or professional considerations.

An extreme example of the kind of dilemma which may face a publisher was with respect to Anthony Heckstall-Smith's satirical novel *The Consort*. The book is about a Prince who, on a good will visit in a Royal yacht to the 'Backward Islands', falls in love with a local girl and refuses to return to his wife and children. Although far-fetched, the novel contained certain resemblances to real-life personages. In 1963, Mr Anthony Blond, the publisher, got as far as printing 3,000 copies, but he then destroyed them. 'I don't now think,' he explained in 1967, 'that there are any risks involved. That was all a long time ago. We had a solicitor who felt rather stuffy about these things.' In the meantime, the book had become a best seller in the United States, and was even placed on the market in Britain in its American edition.

Sometimes publishers may object to apparently trite expressions of opinions by their authors. In 1963, Richard Crossman, active in British politics for so many years, wrote an introduction to a new edition of Walter Bagehot's classic *The English Constitution*, to be published by Fontana. In the course of his introduction, Mr Crossman expressed the opinion that the British Prime Minister had the power to liquidate the political career of any of his governmental colleagues as effectively as any leader of the Soviet Union could remove his rivals. 'His publishers protested and he removed the observation. In 1967, after three years in the Cabinet, the only thing he regrets about his introduction was the omission of this sentence.'

Publishers may sometimes decline to publish a book for political reasons. When this has occurred, the ultimate possibility of publication may come to depend upon the willingness of the author himself to finance publication of the book. There have been examples of this in recent years. Sometimes the book involved has turned out to be a moderate commercial as well as critical success.

Ethical considerations may deter an author from publishing a book. In the case of Lord Moran's *Diaries*, published in 1966, which suggested that Churchill's medical condition could have affected his political actions, it was felt by some that Lord Moran ought not to have published information of this kind, which he obtained through his position as Churchill's physician. Certainly such publication may offend the more sensitive members of the deceased's family. On the other hand, it is clearly in the public interest that it should be known that politicians do suffer from serious ailments which may well affect their political judgements. The *Lancet* commented:

A doctor, like a lawyer or a priest, does not readily recount his professional dealings with an identifiable person: and the public's trust in the medical profession derives largely from its conviction that what transpires between patient and doctor will not be bandied about. If this confidentiality is owed to the living, it is doubly owed to the dead. Sir Winston may have agreed to the diaries appearing after his death. But that is beside the point. The point is that Lord Moran, by writing publicly about the medical condition of an identified patient, is creating a modern precedent. It is a bad precedent which no one should follow.

Yet it is difficult not to feel that there must be some limit to the protection to be given to deceased politicians, particularly if such protection prevents the disclosure of information necessary for the public to form a realistic opinion of their political judgements, and, by implication, of the political judgements of other elderly politicians still in office who might be subject to the risk of similar pathological conditions. Protecting a deceased Churchill gives unjustified protection to others living.

Ethical considerations of a different kind may arise where a politician comes to be aware of facts which suggest that, on a matter of the utmost national importance, his colleagues have lied and misled the public. Such was the case of Mr Anthony Nutting with his book *No End of a Lesson*, which revealed, contrary to denials by Ministers, that there was collusion and plotting with respect to British action over the Suez Canal, which was based in turn upon prior agreement with France and Israel. At the time, in 1956, Mr Nutting contented himself with resigning. Ten years later, he published what he knew. Breach of his silence he apparently felt to be justified at that late date, because most of the important political figures involved in the 'affair' had retired or left active political life. The issue here was the suppression of information of the utmost political importance, which, if it had been revealed when the matter was still a live question might have changed the political fortunes of a number of individuals. This feeling, that one should not reveal in such a way as to damage them information about the mendacity of one's colleagues which had been acquired through holding political office, goes very deep and has strong traditional roots in British society. Its effect is, of course, to lead to the suppression (sometimes only temporarily) of vitally important information.

When Mr Nutting's information was revealed, it appeared to strengthen the hands of those in Parliament who wanted an official inquiry into the Suez affair. But, by adroit manoeuvring, this never came about. No Minister appeared to be over-anxious to establish a precedent by which, if Ministers lied to Parliament, they would have to fear a public inquiry which could bring public oppobrium down upon them.

People other than civil servants, or publishers, and distributors may seek to influence the content of books to be published. When it became known that Lord Moran was writing his book about Churchill, his widow, Lady Churchill, told Lord Moran that she would rather he did not write about her husband, and expressed her regret that Lord Moran intended doing so. When the book was written she asked Lord Moran to show her the proofs before publication, but Lord Moran refused.

When in 1966 it became known that Mr Leslie Frewin intended publishing *Officer in the Tower*, the autobiography of Norman Baillie-Stewart, the Secretary of the Seaforth Highlanders' Association, Major Wright wrote to Mr Frewin, asking to see the manuscript, as

. . . we are most anxious to preserve the good name of the regiment and would not like there to be in the book any reference to the regiment or to any individual in it with whom Baillie-Stewart might have served which might be of an adverse or derogatory nature.

The request was refused. Baillie-Stewart had become known as the 'Officer in the Tower', when held in the Tower of London for betraying secrets to Germany while serving as a Lieutenant on The Seaforth Highlanders. He was later sentenced to prison for broadcasting for the Germans during the war.

Booksellers are in a similar position to publishers and may decide not to stock or to sell particular books for a variety of reasons including fear of legal action. As a spokesman for Wyman's, a large retailer of books, has said: 'We can't afford to take risks.' Of the retailers, W. H. Smith & Son has come in for most criticism, because it appears that in exercising their freedom to choose to sell or not sell particular books or journals, considerations other than fear of litigation may have prompted them. From 31 May 1940 until some time after the war, the National Association of Wholesale Newspaper Distributors (in which W. H. Smith took a major role) banned the distribution of *Peace News* throughout Great Britain. The magazine *Censorship*, which for a few years struggled to discuss problems of censorship in a rational and factual way, eventually died for lack of support, and not the least of its difficulties had been the refusal of W. H. Smith to sell copies. Among books which W. H. Smith did not stock at all were the Penguin *Private Eye* and *The Profumo Affair* by Wayland Young. Other books which from time to time have not been stocked but have been available only on request – such as Henry Miller's *Tropic of Cancer* and *Tropic of Capricorn*, and William Burroughs's *The Naked Lunch*. Anthony Heckstall-Smith's *The Consort* was sold for a fortnight and then withdrawn.

Another example of the role of a distributor of books can be found in the case of Librairie Française Hachette, probably the leading importer of French books into Britain. In reply to a request from the author in

September 1965, that Hachette obtain for him a copy of a non-fiction work published by the Olympia Press, Paris, he received the reply: 'We beg to acknowledge your communication dated the 28th instant, but regret to inform you that we do not import books published by the Olympia Press.'

It must be asserted unequivocally that when the distribution or importation of books by particular commercial enterprises reaches a situation where particular companies control a large segment of the business concerned, there is then a public interest which requires that they do not refuse to act as purveyors of literature for any reason except that the literature concerned would involve the importer or distributor in a violation of the law; anything less is an abuse of power. The absurdity of the present situation is that it has to be left to the importer or distributor to decide the question as to the legality of the books or periodicals being purveyed – a task for which commercial enterprises are peculiarly unsuited.

Similar problems arise with printers, who may also face difficulties in deciding whether or not to print minority opinions or the literary effusions of the young. There can be few creative literary journals or undergraduate journals, not to mention journals representing minority political opinions, which have not on occasion had difficulty in finding a printer willing to print their material. Examples are journals like *Black Dwarf*, *Solstice*, and many others.

Libraries

For very many people the public library is the channel whereby they gain access to books and periodicals. As regards newspapers, this is particularly true with respect to old-age pensioners and others whose incomes do not allow them to buy one regularly. The extent to which libraries are not selective in their purchase of books and periodicals – except on the basis of satisfying public demands, and the necessity of operating on a limited budget – is extremely important if we are to avoid libraries serving as a barrier between the public and the expression of opinions and the communication of ideas of which library authorities might disapprove. However, the legal position is fairly clear. Public libraries are not authorized to exercise a choice of the material they make available on any grounds, other than those implicit in the idea of providing an efficient library service to the particular locality in which the library is situated.

The Public Libraries and Museums Act 1964, Section 7, lays down the duties of library authorities as follows:

1 It shall be the duty of every library authority to provide a comprehensive and efficient library service for all persons desiring to make use thereof, and for that purpose to employ such officers, to provide and maintain such buildings and equipment, and such books and other materials, and to do such other things, as may be requisite. ...

2 In fulfilling its duty under the preceding sub-section, a library authority shall in particular have regard to the desirability –

a of securing, by the keeping of adequate stocks, by arrangements with other library authorities, and by any other appropriate means, that facilities are available for the borrowing of, or reference to, books and other printed matter, and pictures, gramophone records, films and other materials, sufficient in number, range and quality to meet the general requirements both of adults and children. . . .

But libraries do, in practice, sometimes act as censors. First of all, they may place on restricted shelves certain works to which access will only be granted on request. This is sometimes justified by saying that while the book may be unsuitable for children, it remains freely available to any adult who requests it. Sometimes books may be placed on restricted shelves merely because of complaints received from certain members of the public. This apparently happened in the case of the prize-winning novel, *A Green Tree in Gedde*, by Alan Sharp, the Scottish author, which in 1967 was removed from the open shelves of Edinburgh Central Library and placed in the restricted category. Sometimes a library may withdraw a book altogether. Where the line should be drawn in these two cases (i.e. withdrawing the book altogether, or restricting the class of persons with access to it to adults) may be a matter for discussion, but surely the correct policy on stocking and making available books by public libraries, leaving aside the issue of withholding certain books from ready access by children, has already been drawn up in a rational way by the Library Association.

In 1963, the following statement on censorship was approved by the Council of the Library Association:

The function of a library service is to provide, so far as resources allow, all books, periodicals, etc., other than the trivial, in which its readers claim legitimate interest. In determining what is a legitimate interest the librarian can safely rely upon one guide only – the law of the land. If the publication of such matter has not incurred penalties under the law it should not be excluded from libraries on any moral, political, religious or racial ground alone, to satisfy any sectional interest.

The public are entitled to rely upon libraries for access to information and enlightenment upon every field of human experience and activity. Those who provide library services should not restrict this access except by standards which are endorsed by law.

In 1965, the year in which a local stipendiary magistrate ruled that *The Carpetbaggers*, the *Kama Sutra*, *Tropic of Capricorn* and *The Perfumed Garden* were obscene, the City of Birmingham's Public Libraries Committee set an example of commonsense courage by deciding not to withdraw these books from circulation. Councillor Jonas, a solicitor, and chairman of the Public Libraries Committee, announced that the committee was prepared to take the risk of prosecution, which it in any case believed to be negligible.

If [proceedings] are brought we will defend and seek to show that these books do not tend to deprave or corrupt, and that it is in the public interest that we should continue to issue them.

It is the function of the Libraries Committee to provide the public with the means of access to books and literature, some good, some bad, some great and some not so great.

The Committee has tried to discharge this function to the best of its ability by making available as many different types of books as possible, without acting as a censorship body, but insisting on safeguards.

The safeguards referred to by Councillor Jonas were that the books should come from a reputable publisher and that certain books should not be available to young people. The proceedings before the stipendiary magistrate had been forfeiture proceedings under Section 3 of the Obscene Publications Act 1959, and he had heard no arguments, defence or witnesses. Of the books concerned, *The Carpetbaggers* was on the library shelves in the restricted category, and the other three were kept 'under the counter' and were available to adults on request.

When however, in 1967 Hubert Selsby's *Last Exit to Brooklyn* was ruled obscene by an Old Bailey judge, copies were hastily withdrawn by Birmingham Public Libraries from circulation. Even copies of the book currently on loan to readers were summarily recalled.

Censorship on political grounds is more likely to occur with respect to the newspapers stocked by public libraries, where not infrequently the *Morning Star* meets with difficulties. In recent years there have been examples of local authorities refusing to permit the *Morning Star* to be displayed in the reading room of the local library, because of political considerations. But under the terms of the Public Libraries and Museums Act 1964, any discretion not to display or make available to the public books or periodicals on political grounds, or because the local library authority disapproves of the moral or social tone of the works concerned, appears to be unlawful.

Special problems may arise with the copyright libraries, and in particular with the British Museum. The copyright libraries are those which are by Act of Parliament entitled to receive a free copy of every book published in the United Kingdom. By the British Museum Act, Section 3 (3), it is provided:

It shall be the duty of the Trustees [of the British Museum] to secure, so far as appears to them to be practicable, that the objects comprised in the collections of the Museum . . . are, when required for inspection by members of the public, made available in one or other of the authorised repositories under such conditions as the Trustees think fit to impose for preserving the safety of the collections and ensuring the proper administration of the Museum.

It has been suggested by the courts that making available a defamatory book to a member of the public who requests it could make the library concerned liable for defamation in circumstances where the library knew, or ought to have known, that the work was or might be defamatory. As for liability for obscenity, because the Obscene Publications Act emphasizes as an element in liability for an offence that the article concerned must be intended to be used in some way 'for gain' by the accused person, it is unlikely that a free public library, as opposed to a lending library, charging individuals who borrow books, could be liable to a prosecution. Perhaps because of the risk of legal liability, but often for other reasons, the copyright libraries have from time to time restricted readers' access to certain kinds of book. This is particularly so in the case of the British Museum, where two categories are subject to restriction: (a) those in the so-called Private Case, and (b) the 'Suppressed Books.' Those in the Private Case consist largely of erotica of various kinds, including serious sexological works. In 1967 it was announced that the British Museum was engaged in a change of policy towards those works in the Private Case, which hitherto only the most persistent would-be reader was allowed to see. These, it was announced, were not to be added to, and eventually more than half of those it already contained would be derestricted and placed in the general catalogue.

'Suppressed Books', on the other hand, contains a miscellaneous collection of items. First of all there are those books which have been successfully prosecuted for obscenity. Secondly there are works which have given rise to successful claims for defamation. Thirdly, there are works which are restricted for reasons of copyright, so as to protect commercial secrets. Fourthly, there are works restricted to protect 'official secrets', using that term in a very wide sense. (Although they do not come into the 'Suppressed Books' category, the museum also applies to 'governmental documents' the same period of restriction as does the Public Record Office.) There are other reasons for books falling within the 'Suppressed Books' category, as, for example 'books saying unseemly things about the holy family, or making disloyal revelations about the royal one', works which might be politically embarrassing in certain quarters, and even works critical of the British Museum's own administration. No public record is kept of these works, and no reader, not even the most persistent, is allowed to consult them, so that they remain literally an unknown quantity. Peter Fryer, in his book *Private Case – Public Scandal*, was in 1966 able to guess by an admirable piece of detective work at some of the titles included under the heading 'Suppressed Books'. Again in 1967, the British Museum announced that it was examining works in this category with a view to derestricting some of them. As was explained by a museum official at the time, 'this is necessarily a slow process'. But one can only add that it is traditionally so slow a process that books are retained in the 'Suppressed Books' category long after the secrets they contained or the persons they defamed are in need of any protection.

Films

Oddly enough, there is no direct requirement by law that films should be subjected to examination before public exhibition. What has happened in practice is that the Cinematograph Acts 1909 and 1952 have given local authorities power to impose conditions on the exhibition of films in places to be licensed by them for such exhibition. It is now a universal practice in the licence granted to use premises for the public commercial exhibition of films to impose some conditions of the kind which follow. The following extracts are from the rules to be observed by holders of cinematograph licences made by the Justices of the Peace for the City of Cambridge on 26 June 1970:

3 The licensed premises shall not be opened when the Justices, for the preservation of the peace, may signify their desire in writing to the Licensee, or other person having at the time the care and management of the licensed premises, that the same should not be opened.

4 No film shall be exhibited unless

   a It has received a 'U', 'A', 'AA', or 'X' certificate of the British Board of Film Censors; or

   b It is a current newsreel which has not been submitted to the British Board of Film Censors.

5 No person apparently under the age of 18 years shall be admitted to any exhibition at which there is to be shown any film which has received an 'X' certificate from the British Board of Film Censors.

10 When films have been examined by the Justices they shall be exhibited exactly in the form in which they were passed for exhibition, without any alteration or additions, unless the consent of the Justices to such alteration or addition has previously been obtained.

11 Where the licensing authority have given notice in writing to the Licensee of the premises objecting to an advertisement on the ground that, if displayed, it would offend against good taste or decency or be likely to encourage or incite crime or to lead to disorder or to be offensive to public feeling that advertisement shall not be displayed at the premises except with the consent in writing of the licensing authority. . . .

13 No advertisement displayed at the premises of a film to be exhibited at the premises shall depict as a scene or incident in the film any scene or incident which is not included in the film as certified by the British Board of Film Censors or approved for exhibition by the licensing authority, as the case may be. This rule shall also apply in respect of any advertisement of a film other than at the premises.

14 Where the licensing authority have given notice in writing to the licensee of the premises prohibiting the exhibition of a film on the ground that it contains matter which, if exhibited, would offend against good taste or decency or would be likely to encourage or incite to crime or to lead to disorder or to be offensive to public feeling, that film shall not be exhibited in the premises except with the consent in writing of the licensing authority.

These rules preserve, in effect, the ultimate authority of the local authority.

One of the special features of film censorship in Britain is that, for nearly half a century, local authorities have exercised a right to control the content of films by means of conditions imposed in the licences they issued under the Cinematograph Act 1909. Yet Parliament intended to confer a power only to impose conditions relating to safety, and never contemplated the use of licensing powers to impose censorship. As Dr March Hunnings, the leading authority on the history of film censorship in Britain has said in his book *Film Censors and the Law*:

The Cinematograph Act, 1909, was passed as a result of fears connected with the safety of audiences from the danger of fire. The drafting of the Act makes it clear that it was intended solely to enable adequate fire precautions to be enforced, and this was both stated by the Home Office and embodied in its own Regulations issued on December 21st under s.1 of the Act and which contain no provisions directed to other than structural and safety matters.

The British courts, as they do so often, by interpreting the Act in a way which Parliament never intended, have been able to uphold the validity of the censoring power which the local authorities had usurped unto themselves. But even this usurpation was eventually threatened by the disappearance of inflammable film, because the Cinematograph Act 1909 applied only to film of this type. So Parliament stepped in to save the system of censorship by passing the Cinematograph Act 1952. The test of inflammability was abolished, and instead the requirement of a local authority licence was to apply to all cinematographic exhibitions other than (a) performances to which the public were not admitted (thus leaving a loophole for the club cinema to show uncensored films), or (b) performances to which the public was admitted free, or (c) performances given by certain non-profitmaking bodies. Special provision was made to control films to which persons under sixteen were admitted. A right of appeal was given to anyone who wished to complain of the refusal of a licence or of the conditions under which a licence had been granted. Above all the Act gave the local authorities a wide power to impose conditions on the grant of a licence, thus making lawful what had hitherto never been granted by Parliament – namely, a right to impose the censorship of films.

Local authorities do not themselves ordinarily censor films; this function is, for most practical purposes, delegated to the British Board of Film Censors, whose certificates the local authorities usually accept. The current system of certification, introduced in July 1969, is as follows:

'X Certificate': connotes that admission to view such films is restricted to those over eighteen years of age.

'AA Certificate': connotes that admission is restricted to those over fourteen.

'A Certificate': a special category to warn parents that the film is not suitable for children under fourteen.

'U Certificate': connotes that the film is considered suitable for everyone.

It is of interest to note that, in 1969, when the old classification was still in operation (i.e. 'X' – over sixteen, 'A' for no persons under sixteen unaccompanied by an adult, and 'U' as now), ninety-four feature films were given 'U' certificates, 116 were given 'A' certificates and 220 were given 'X' certificates.

The Board is financially independent, its only source of income being from the fees it charges for examining films. Its chief officers, the president and secretary, are nowadays appointed by means of an informal process, in which the initiative is taken by the Council of the Incorporated Association of Kinematograph Manufacturers in consultation with the principal trade associations as well as the Home Secretary and the principal associations of local authorities.

In the past, the Board has often been subject to forceful and direct pressure from the Home Office. The extent of any such influence today is unknown, however, although the chief officers of the Board strongly assert their independence of any governmental control. Or the other hand, informal links and contacts are maintained by the secretary 'with representatives of the local authorities, the churches, educational and welfare organizations, and the press'. It is also understood the Customs authorities consult the secretary over the seizure of imported films. There are two areas where outside advice is acknowledged to be taken. 'The main one,' said John Trevelyan, who was secretary until 1971, 'is in the psychiatric field. I've got a lot of experience in psychiatry, and I know roughly where there are doubts. In particular I get advice on sexual sadism and on drugs in films which could be regarded as encouraging people to take them.'

'The other main area where I take advice,' he added, 'is on anything to do with the police. We don't protect the police in any way but we have to take precautions on matters to do with crime.'

During his term of office John Trevelyan attached great importance to the fact that the 'British Board of Film Censors has no code of rules or "code", and its policy changes from year to year'. The Board believes that its policy should, as far as possible, 'reflect intelligent public opinion, and this is variable and not static'. Such a pragmatic approach has not always been followed by the Board, and in the 1920s and 1930s an effort was made to apply a 'code', as can be seen from the following list of prohibited scenes and themes published in 1929:

Religion

1 The materialised figure of Christ.
2 Religious rites and ceremonies treated with irreverence, or in any way calculated to bring religion into contempt, and even when the treatment is reverent, exception is taken if the ceremony is of such a sacred character as to be unsuitable for dramatic treatment.

3 Irreverent introductions of quotations from the Bible or Church services to produce comic effects and equally the comic introduction of biblical characters, Angels, Gates of Heaven, etc., which is extremely offensive to a large majority of the audience in this country.

Political

1 Subjects which are calculated to wound the susceptibilities of foreign peoples and especially of our fellow subjects of the British Empire.
2 Stories and scenes which are calculated and possibly intended to foment social unrest and discontent.

Social

1 The nude both in actuality and shadowgraph.

2 Swearing, or language in the nature of swearing, in titles or sub-titles.

3 'Orgy' scenes and similar incidents oft-times incongruous and generally superfluous.

4 Incidents which bring into contempt public characters acting in their capacity as such, i.e. officers and men wearing H.M.'s uniform, Ministers of Religion, Ministers of the Crown, Ambassadors and Representatives of Foreign Nations, Administrators of the Law, Medical men, etc.

5 Embraces which overstep the limit of affection or even passion, and become lascivious.

6 Impropriety of dress and deportment, including suggestive and indecorous dancing.

7 Offensive vulgarity and excessive drunkenness even when treated in a comic vein.

8 Scenes connected with child-birth such as puerperal pains, which is considered too intimate for public exhibition.

9 Subjects dealing with V.D. or any other matters suitable only for Hospital or Medical Lecture Theatre.

10 Stories showing any antagonism or strained relations between white men and the coloured population of the British Empire, especially with regard to the question of sexual intercourse, morals and intermarriage between individuals of different races.

Crime

1 Scenes demonstrating methods of crime which might lend themselves to imitation.

2 Subjects dealing with the 'drug' habit, the Board believing that the exhibition of this vice with its insidious allurements involves the danger of spreading the pernicious habit.

3 Prolonged scenes of extreme violence and brutality.

4 Hanging scenes, and the depiction of actual executions, treated seriously or in a comic spirit.

5 Stories of which the sole or main interest is that of crime and of the criminal life without any counter-balancing element of love and adventure.

6 Themes calculated to give an air of romance and heroism to criminal characters, the story being told in such a way as to enlist the sympathies of the audience with the criminals, whilst the constituted authorities and administrators of the law are held up to contempt as being either unjust or harsh, incompetent or ridiculous.

7 Organized knuckle fights.

Even in 1929, this list appeared absurd to intelligent critics, as must any attempt to codify subjects which may not be dealt with cinematically.

Given the absence in Britain today of any set of rules or code as to what the censor will allow the personal views of the men concerned on how they see their own function is very important. Although Lord Harlech, the President of the British Board of Film Censors, is no mere titled figurehead and is often consulted, the tone of film censorship in Britain has until 1971 been set by the secretary of the Board, John Trevelyan, a former public school and Cambridge trained educationist and administrator, whose urbanity helped to render his censorial role widely acceptable, without in any way altering its fundamental character. Mr Trevelyan has given many different versions of how he saw his role. Sometimes primary emphasis was given to the protection of children and teenagers, and this explanation was used to justify his refusal of any certificate to such films as *The Trip* which might encourage young people to take LSD. As he has said: 'We need censorship for the protection of children. I don't want to overprotect them, but I don't want to expose them too early to certain things in modern life before they are ready to cope with them.' Sometimes the emphasis was upon public taste. 'We act,' said Mr Trevelyan, 'as a barometer of public taste by viewing the products of the film industry and then awarding them certificates.' Or, on another occasion, he explained it thus: 'We are a barometer of public taste, offering the film companies protection. We tell them what is acceptable. If anything goes wrong, we get the criticism, not them.'

A leaflet outlining the Board's work states that it is 'to exclude from public exhibition anything likely to impair the moral standards of the public, by extenuating vice or crime or by deprecating social standards, and anything likely to give offence to any reasonably minded members of the community'. Mr Trevelyan has explained that it would be wrong to take one's standards of acceptability solely through contact with 'what may broadly be described as the class of *New Statesman* readers'.

It may be to protect the public from offence that the Board in 1970 refused a certificate to a film called *The Christine Keeler Story*. Mr Trevelyan explained: 'The film created no censorship problems either visual or verbal under the current policies. But we felt that to grant a licence would provoke strong public reaction. To my recollection this is the first time we have ever turned down a film on those grounds.' (The Greater London Council also refused the film a certificate on the different and conflicting ground that 'taken as a whole, [it] tends to deprave and corrupt persons who are likely to see it'.)

Another function which Mr Trevelyan saw the Board as having was to prevent the exhibition of films or scenes which might give rise to criminal prosecutions. This was the reason, according to Mr Trevelyan, for its refusal to give any certificate to the uncut version of Joseph Stricks film of James Joyce's novel *Ulysses*. 'The Board asked for certain cuts, having regard to the legal position in this country. . . .' Again, in early 1968 at a special showing of the Swedish film *Hugs and Kisses*, Mr Trevelyan explained to the press why he had cut out a fifteen-second shot of an actress which showed her pubic hair. This, he said was because the law of obscenity was so vague that the film might give rise to proceedings, if shown uncut, against its exhibitors and distributors, and even, he suggested somewhat fancifully, against the Board itself. He had consulted Lord Goodman, the chairman of the Arts Council who, although he had not seen the shot concerned, agreed that the law of obscenity was very vague. A few months later, having permitted a display of female pubic hair to pass for exhibition in Lindsay Anderson's *If*, Mr Trevelyan shifted his ground somewhat and explained: 'When my Board asked for cuts in the nude scene in the Swedish film *Hugs and Kisses* we were really testing public opinion. There was no massive outcry one way or the other, and some local authorities even passed the film with the pubic hair left in. So we decided to leave the film *If* intact in this respect.'

Fear lest films might encourage emulation among young audiences has led to the banning of certain films in which the wicked did not meet their just deserts. Thus *The Wild One* was banned for fourteen years, not as the *Observer* film column explained, because 'the then Secretary considered the film immoral or too violent, but because its morality was thought too subtle (the gang was insufficiently punished for their depredations) and in the Teddy Boy era, there was a possibility of local emulation'. Sometimes fear of juvenile emulation leads to the deletion of scenes where at least to the non-religious person, the possibilities of imitation would appear somewhat limited. Thus in Roman Polanski's *Rosemary's Baby*, in 1969, the censor cut a scene in which the heroine enjoys a nude rite with Satan and conceives a child by him. The censor said: 'While the film in general paints an unfavourable picture of people who indulge in this kind of thing, this particular scene is not helpful, since the sexual side is undoubtedly an attraction to some participants or would-be participants.'

Mr Trevelyan once summarized the objects of the Board by giving an account of its origins as follows:

We were set up in 1912 for three reasons. First to protect the cinema from local authority interference. Second to protect the cinema from the courts. Here you have to take into account the fact that even if you win a court case it can still be a very costly business. Although John Calder, for instance, won his appeal in the *Last Exit to Brooklyn* case, it still cost him £5,000. Third, we were set up to protect the industry from public criticism. We act as a barometer of public taste. Whether we are right to do this is another matter.

As history this is not very convincing, but as an account of how Mr Trevelyan saw his role it is important.

The power and influence of the Board is not limited merely to the examination of completed films. Because films represent large amounts of invested capital, film makers are often unwilling to place their money at risk of the whim of the Board denying them the right to put their capital to work by exhibiting it publicly. To forestall unwelcome refusals of certificates, it is common practice for film companies to consult the Board in advance by submitting a script or a synopsis before the film has been made. At that stage the film maker may be willing to accept suggestions from the Board as to how to avoid unnecessary cutting, or even the total banning, of the film in its finished form. This may, in part at least, explain the reference by the film critic Alexander Walker, in his book *The Celluloid Sacrifice*, to the fact that the censor 'can also, if so minded, if he has the will and ability, play an unofficial part in the creative side of film-making'.

The most notorious example of script censorship was the case of the script based on *Spare the Rod*, a novel by Michael Croft, published in 1954, which dealt with the related problems of teaching in a tough, badly run secondary modern school and corporal punishment. Ronald Neame, the director, produced a script with the author, which was submitted for approval to the Board. Back came the response:

An inefficiently run school and the moral deterioration of teachers through their inability to control children are not fit subjects to be debated in the presence of children of school age. It would be highly improper for children who are going to school next day to sit and watch a film about masters who are frankly sadists.

Therefore the film, if made could only be given an 'X' certificate, which, in the days before some 'X' films, at least, became money makers, meant that no backer was available to finance the film's production. At about the same time the Board also turned down a script from Ted Willis (now Lord Willis) which showed a prison officer taking a bribe.

We could not allow a suggestion of corruption on the part of our prison officials. This would be an unmerited slur on the integrity of the Prison Officers' Service.

Ultimately, but some years later, another version of *Spare the Rod* was given an 'A' certificate, although it was in fact more brutal and sadistic than the original script.

It would also be wrong to assume that the Board is only concerned with the effect of the film upon potential audiences. The Cinematograph Films (Animals) Act 1937 makes it a criminal offence, carrying a £100 fine or three months in prison, to exhibit any film, if in connection with its production any scene shown therein was directed or organized in such a way as to involve 'the cruel infliction of pain' on any animal or 'the cruel goading of any animal to fury'. This provision has been the reason for the excision from films like *The Lost Continent* of scenes recording the treatment meted out to animals in other parts of the world. The censor has apparently concerned himself with other things, such as the extent to which the proprieties have been observed by the film makers while making the film. Mr Walker records in his book that Mr Trevelyan, in considering whether the *Amorous Adventures of Moll Flanders* should be passed, was not too bothered by Kim Novak's 'obtrusive charms'. But the 'scene he *did* hesitate over passing was a long shot of Moll emerging from a lake, apparently nude, when surprised by highwaymen. This finally got by on the producer's assurance that all the decencies were observed during the shooting.'

As the ultimate legal power of censoring films rests with the local authorities, the latter are not bound to accept the classification adopted by the British Board of Film Censors. In some areas, synopses of all films given an 'X' certificate by the Board must be submitted to the local authority, who may then refuse to permit the film to be shown in their area. Bedfordshire abolished this system only in 1967, but it is believed still to exist in one or two areas. In 1969 the system still operated in Reading, where the borough council had delegated to the town clerk the task of reading the synopses. If he was satisfied, he could permit the films to be shown; if not then he asked the committee to see them. In London in particular, the local authority has sometimes disagreed on the appropriate certificate, overriding the Board and substituting its own classification.

Over the past year there has, however, been an increase in the number of occasions when local authorities refuse to permit the local exhibition of films which have received a certificate, usually an 'X' from the Board. Thus in March 1972 it was found that at Southend the council's public protection committee reviews every 'X' certificate film, and bans on average one in four. It was the same council which banned *Zabriskie Point*, only to discover that the film having obtained a certificate from the Board had already played at three cinemas in the town and had been booked by a local school for a private showing. The ban was revoked.

It is, however, in those cases where the Board has in the first instance refused to grant any certificate at all that the practical significance is shown of the ultimate censorship authority of the local authorities. In such cases, films can only be shown in an area where the local authority has been persuaded to exercise its right to grant a certificate, entitling the film to be publicly exhibited within that particular authority's jurisdiction. The fact that the local authority has given the film a certificate, does not, of course, ensure that it is exhibited, for local cinema owners may exercise their own special form of censorship by choosing not to exhibit films which they think undesirable on commercial or other grounds. In Beaconsfield the local authority and cinema management are combined, the local cinema being owned by Beaconsfield Urban Council, who have complete faith in their entertainments manager, who operates as a one-man public censor. As one might expect, he objects not only to obscenity, but to other things as well. The Beatles' *Yellow Submarine* was banned. 'Not because,' the then manager explained, 'there was anything naughty in it, oh, there was nothing naughty about it. It was just pure unadulterated rubbish.'

In 1967, when the British Board of Film Censors refused to give a certificate to *Ulysses* unless substantial cuts were made, the distributor, the Columbia Picture Corporation, applied to a number of local authorities for a certificate to allow the uncut film to be shown locally. A certificate of any kind was refused by the following local authorities: Aberdeen, Belfast, Berkshire County Council, Birmingham, Blackburn, Blackpool, Bolton, Brighton, Bristol, Burnley, Bury, Cambridgeshire and Isle of Ely County Council, Cardiff, Coventry, Dartford, Derby, Dorset County Council, Eastbourne, East Sussex County Council, Edinburgh, Glasgow, Heanor, Hereford City and County Council, Hertfordshire County Council, Huddersfield, Ilkeston, Kettering, Leicestershire, Liverpool, Leeds, Long Eaton, Manchester, Newcastle (Staffs.), Norwich, Northamptonshire, Nottingham, Oxford, Portsmouth, Reading, Redditch, Ripley, Shropshire County Council, Solihull, Surrey County Council, Swansea, Thetford, Wellingborough, West Suffolk, Wiltshire, Wolverhampton and Woodstock.

The following local authorities granted the film an 'X' certificate uncut: Alloa, Burgess Hill, Caerphilly, Cambridge, Croydon, Dundee, Essex County Council, Exeter, Blastonbury, Greater London Council, Great Yarmouth, Grimsby, Hawick, Ipswich, King's Lynn, Leek (Staffs.), Llanelly, Nelson, Newport, Nottinghamshire County Council, Newcastle, Plymouth, Stoke-on-Trent, Street, Warwickshire County Council, Wells and Worcester.

The interesting thing about the result was that in many cases where the film was banned in the county town, a bus ride would allow would-be viewers to see it in a neighbouring county. The reasons given for banning it were typified by the comments of Alderman Beardsworth, Vice-Chairman of Blackburn Watch Committee:

We have decided to ban this film because it is obscene. Parts of it are not fit to be heard by anyone, let alone young people. It is just one mass of obscenities. There is hardly a sentence in which there is not an obscene word. If we had allowed this film to be shown it could have had a very bad effect on young people.

In Southampton, the Chairman of the Public Safety Committee, Alderman Michael Pettitt, said that, having read the book about thirty years ago, 'I believe that without its obscenities and blasphemies a film version of *Ulysses* would not be worth seeing anyway.' He further expressed the opinion that he did not think it right for people to 'waste their money on this kind of rubbish'.

In contrast was the attitude adopted by the authorities in Hawick who without seeing the film gave their decision in its favour. Provost

James Henderson said: 'Who are we to set ourselves up as an unofficial Board of Censors?' Senior Baillie Sydney Irvine said: 'I would like to think we are sufficiently broadminded to let the individual decide for himself. We have no right to dictate to 16,000 people.'

Four local authorities – Bradford, Sheffield, Southampton and Wiltshire – banned *Ulysses* without having viewed it. By way of explanation the chairman of Sheffield's licensing sub-committee said: 'We have not seen the film but we did have the observations of the British Board of Film Censors before us at the meeting.' The Board had apparently made available to local authorities the extracts from the script to which it had objected. In Southampton, only these extracts were considered and not the film itself or its script. A storm of local protest at this attitude led to the Public Safety Committee laying down as future policy that, in considering any application to exhibit a contentious film, the committee should obtain the views of the British Board of Film Censors and should also take into consideration the views and decisions of the Greater London Council and any other corporate body which might have a bearing.

Oddities even more extreme than those in the *Ulysses* case occurred in 1965 over a film version of *Fanny Hill*, to which the Board refused any certificate. Local authorities were then approached. The film was refused a certificate in several places, including Chatham, Chester, Dover, Edinburgh, Sheffield, St Andrews, Tunbridge Wells, Whitby, Wigan and Wrexham. Eighteen local authorities, however, gave it an 'X' certificate including Berkshire, Hastings, Pontypridd, Reading, Scarborough, Solihull and Swansea; forty-four gave it an 'A' certificate, including Aston, Banbury, Belfast, Burnley, Bury, Cambridge, Carmarthenshire, Folkestone, Llanelly, Nottinghamshire, Plymouth, Tonbridge, Warwickshire and Worcestershire; and, believe it or not, five gave it a 'U' certificate, indicating that it was entertainment suitable for all ages (i.e. in Birmingham, Coventry, Ilkeston, Kettering and Newcastle-under-Lyne). In 1968, Yoko Ono's film *Number Four*, which concentrated its attention on the human backside and was refused any certificate by the Board, unless certain other portions of the human anatomy were deleted, received an 'X' certificate from the Greater London Council and a 'U' certificate from Birmingham.

Over the winter 1969/70, *The Killing of Sister George*, denied a certificate by the Board because it portrayed lesbianism, received and was refused certificates by local authorities all over the country, producing a result similar to *Ulysses*.

Because the amount of 'censorship' work they became involved in is not very great, apart from the Greater London Council, local authorities do not usually have special committees to perform this function; instead, it is added to the chores of some other committee. In Sheffield, for example, it has been the Finance Committee to whom the task has been allocated, and in Brighton the Fire Brigade Committee (in which case, the local Fire Chief may be invited to the viewing). In other cases it may be the Watch Committee (when the local Chief Constable may be invited along). In Derby the Corporation Estates Committee has performed the job; in Birmingham, the Public Entertainments Committee; in Kettering the Public Health Committee, and in Tynemouth, the Civil Defence and Traffic Committee.

In those towns where the magistrates perform a censorship function, this is because the local authority has delegated its censorship power to magistrates, as is the case in Oxford, where such delegation took place as long ago as 1910 in accordance with section 2 of the Cinematograph Act 1909.

An interesting insight into the views of a councillor, who had taken part in the decision that Sheffield should not allow the uncut version of *The Killing of Sister George*, was revealed in an interview, published in the *Sheffield Star* on 8 October 1969, with Councillor Reg Munn, Chairman of the Licensing Sub-Committee:

I enjoyed the film. It is very good, and Beryl Reid is very good in it. I think it is a pity that the Sheffield public can't see it. It examines a human problem which does exist and which I think they ought to see. It was the film producers who prevented the public from seeing the film. They refused, on artistic grounds, to screen a cut version.

There was just one scene, towards the end of the film, which I would have cut. It showed two women making love on a bed. It began with one woman caressing the breasts of the other – the cameras stayed on the two women right up to the moment of climax. Immediately after this a third women enters the room.

Now I would have cut the film after the scene which showed the caressing and resumed it again with the entry of the third woman. To show the whole love scene would have been, in my opinion, unnecessary to the plot. It was obvious what was going to happen, and I don't think a cut at this point would have detracted from the point of the film.

I was embarrassed by the scene and wanted to look away. Perhaps it was some deep Freudian reflex in me that made me react in this way. But these things are not pretty to watch any more than it is pretty to see someone sitting on a bed pan.

When we watch these films we can't help being very subjective. But when we saw the film as a committee we tried to imagine how the majority of people in Sheffield would have reacted to it.

I am certain that the majority would have preferred not to have seen this particular scene.

I'm all for watching girls dancing round in the nude. But when it comes to watching people making love – no. It's a private matter and I don't think it is necessary to put it on the screen.

But I should say that I am against censorship anyway. I would like to see the British film censor go and I would like to see the cinema made as free as the theatre.

But since there is censorship, we on the Licensing sub-committee have to draw the line somewhere – that is what we are put there for. If the City Council, or the community, don't want this sort of censorship they must say so, and until the law is changed we would give every film automatic approval.

I'm no expert on the cinema – and most of my time on the Licensing Sub-Committee is taken up with dealing with licence applications from taxi drivers, people who want to install one armed bandits, and so on.

But I don't think it is necessary to be an expert for this sort of job. You don't have to have any special qualifications. Almost anybody would do really. It's just people.

Now for a word about the cinema clubs, which under the terms of the 1952 Act are enabled to show uncensored films. These clubs are on the increase, but are subject to restriction in various ways. First of all, they are not immune, nor is any cinema showing an officially censored film, from criminal prosecution by the police, or by private individuals. They are often subjected to police harassment – that is, threats by the police to take action against them, threats issued as a means of persuasion. These clubs also sometimes meet with considerable hostility from local residents.

We have concentrated upon institutionalized systems of film censorship, but these are only one means of controlling the content of films. Sometimes film companies alter the finished film to make its content more acceptable (commercially? morally? politically?). This happened, for example, to the film *Three Into Two Won't Go*, written by Edna O'Brien and directed by Peter Hall (both of whom asked to have their names removed from the refurbished version). Peter Hall told the story in *The Times* of 27 October 1970:

My film, and Andrea Newman's original novel, was about the break-up of a marriage so dishonest that it needed breaking up. The crisis was provoked by the husband's affair with a young hitchhiker. She, observing the double standards of his existence, calls on his wife when he is away, becomes a friend and is invited to stay. She is then as ruthless as a cuckoo in a nest. At the end, the three people go their separate ways, having achieved some measure of honesty. I believe this is what appealed to wide audiences. I have been told that young people like the film because of the merciless candour of the girl. For them it was about the generation gap.

Universal's new picture is about a probation officer's search for a girl who has broken her parole. She is somewhere on the road, hitch-hiking. She left home because she was not loved by her drunken step-father (new scenes, new characters). He is the reason she has gone to the bad, and why she 'has this thing against men'. The probation officer interviews people who have seen the girl recently (new scenes, new characters). A girl is chary of giving help: 'Ever since the trouble I've tried to stay away from her.' A pop singer who was her boyfriend says 'I believe Ella really loved me. But she wanted to destroy me.' The probation officer is clear that if they can only find the girl they can help her. 'She has built up an unnatural antagonism to men,' she observes.

At the climax of the picture, the girl's mother tells the probation officer that she has done what she should have done years ago – thrown the drunkard out. The probation officer is delighted.

My picture ended with the empty house, lights burning. The husband, the wife and the girl have gone. Universal have added another scene. The next morning, the probation officer receives a telephone call. Apparently, it is the girl. 'Oh, Ella,' says the probation officer, 'I'm so glad you called. You won't regret it.' And she rushed out to collect her. The camera holds on the office while an end-slogan is superimposed: 'Filmed entirely on location, in and around Camberley, England.' This scene, like all the interpolations, was filmed in America. But then there was no probation officer in the original picture.

Cutting by film companies may sometimes be for such a narrowly commercial reason as that it is too long to allow for the normal 'candy break'. This was the reason Paramount gave for a fourteen minute cut in Peter Bogdanovitch's film *Targets*.

A more significant aspect, of course, concerns the way stories are selected or rejected for making into films; in this original selection, political, moral and social values play a vital part. Similarly important is the practice of denying completed films a public showing, or of denying them a general release following their completion. There is a limited number of film manufacturers and in Britain the ownership of cinemas remain largely under the control of two large circuits. Unless one or other of these accepts a film for exhibition, it cannot become financially viable. A number of important films have secured only a limited West End release and have not been generally exhibited – for, it would appear, a wide variety of reasons, some of them commercial some of them not. *They were Strangers* (1948), for example, starring John Garfield, Jennifer Jones and Pedro Armendaríz, which was about a revolutionary group in pre-Castro Cuba, received only a limited run in Britain.

Open censorship on political or social grounds appears no longer to be practised by the British Board of Film Censors, as it certainly was in the 1920s and 1930s, though social and political attitudes still appear to colour some decisions. Social and political censorship operates rather more behind the scenes in the manufacture of films. As Dr Neville March Hunnings has said:

The hidden 'censorship' exercised in the offices of film companies themselves would lead to an examination of the financial control of, and the degree of monopoly or oligopoly in, the film industry and thence to a detailed investigation into the whole film-making and financing process.

Theatre

The current law relating to theatrical censorship is largely to be found in the Theatres Act 1968, which came into force on 26 September 1968. Although its long title is 'An Act to abolish Censorship of the Theatre and to amend the law in respect of Theatres and Theatrical Performances', it merely abolishes the system of prior censorship operated by the Lord Chamberlain, an official of the royal household, which had hitherto existed under the now repealed Theatres Act 1843. Plays no longer require a licence before they can be performed, although theatres must continue to be licensed to enable public control to be exercised over them with regard to public health and safety. A number of sections of the Act summarize the legal liabilities to which persons associated with the performance of a play may be subject. The provisions do not apply to the performance of a play 'in a private house on a domestic occasion' (whatever that may mean), or to a rehearsal of a play or to the performance of a play for the purpose of a recording, a broadcast, and so forth. Section 2 places plays in a similar position to obscene articles under the Obscene Publications Act 1959, and gives a defence of public good.

3.—(1) A person shall not be convicted of an offence under section 2 of the Act if it is proved that the giving of the 'performance in question was justified as being for the public good on the ground that it was in the interests of drama, opera, ballet or any other art, or of literature or learning.

Section 2 (4) contains a useful provision to prevent the evasion of these safeguards:

No person shall be proceeded against in respect of a performance of a play or anything said or done in the course of such a performance –

a for an offence at common law where it is of the essence of the offence that the performance or, as the case may be, what was said or done was obscene, indecent, offensive, disgusting or injurious to morality; or

b for an offence under section 4 of the Vagrancy Act 1824 consisting of wilfully exposing to public view an indecent exhibition, including such an offence under that section as applied to Scotland by section 15 of the Prevention of Crimes Act 1871; or

c in Scotland, for an offence under section 380 of the Burgh Police (Scotland) Act 1892, where it is of the essence of the offence that the performance or, as the case may be, what was said or done was obscene or indecent.

A play, for the purpose of defamation, is to be treated as libel. Section 5 makes criminal the incitement of racial hatred by means of a dramatic performance; Section 6 makes it criminal to give a performance of a play involving the use of threatening, abusive or insulting words or behaviour, if this was done with an intention to provoke a breach of the peace, or if the performance, taken as a whole, was likely to occasion a breach of the peace. Proceedings for presenting an obscene play, contrary to Section 2, a play inciting to racial hatred, contrary to Section 5, or a play involving risk of a breach of the peace, contrary to Section 6, can only be brought if the Attorney-General either himself initiates proceedings or gives permission to someone else to do so, thus setting an obstacle in the path of the over-zealous puritan. Unlike the old law, all premises in which the public performance of plays takes place must be licensed by the local authorities, who shall, however, have no authority to impose any conditions on the grant of a licence, except those which are concerned with physical safety and health.

A problem may arise as to who may be prosecuted for a criminal offence under the Act. The answer is anyone *directing* or *presenting* a play. The licensee of the theatre is not necessarily liable unless he *directs* or *presents* the play. Who *presents* the play? Presumably the impresario, if there is one, but the concept of *presenting* a play is left vague because all the Act says about the person *presenting* a play is that 'a person shall not be treated as presenting a performance of a play by reason only of his taking part therein as a performer'. An actor will not ordinarily be liable unless, without reasonable excuse, he acts otherwise than in accordance with the director's instructions, in which case he becomes liable as though he were the director.

Liability remains for certain vague common law offences, which clearly ought to have been removed or dealt with under the Act, remains e.g. for seditious libel, criminal libel and blasphemy. In respect of these offences there would, of course, be no need for a would-be prosecutor to obtain the permission of the Attorney-General.

The Act does not remove the ability of persons to exercise certain private forms of prior censorship. Because the *presenter* may be liable, could a local borough council, a theatre club or a festival committee be made liable under Sections 2, 5 and 6? Even if not the *presenter*, they might be liable for aiding and abetting an offence as being closely connected with the presentation or direction of the play. Because of this risk – surely a hypothetical one – a correspondent in *The Amateur Stage* gave the following advice:

It is possible for the interpretation and business introduced by a director and actors to give a quite different intention than could be seen from the script, read by the festival committee. Because of this it is important that festival organisers should not accept entries without carefully 'vetting' (*this is quite different from censoring*) the plays first. The ideal, of course, is to see the actual production by the society, but this is impracticable in the great majority of cases. In any event, if a festival organiser is at all doubtful about any sections of the script, or the company's interpretation of them, he will wish to take this up well in advance with the company concerned, for no responsible official would wittingly offer to his audience, for example, an obscene performance – whether or not he is likely to be prosecuted for it! [italics added.]

Presenters and *directors* may well act on this kind of advice. There may be other occasions for censorial activity. Thus, in 1957, and again in 1964, ministerial sanction was refused for a grant of £100 which the Deptford Borough Council wished to make to the Unity Theatre, on the grounds that no grant can be made from the rates to anybody whose activities seemed to be directed to party political purposes! In 1968, an attempt was made to secure the withdrawal of Nottingham's grant to Nottingham Playhouse because it had put on Brecht's *Mother Courage* accompanied by a programme note which drew a parallel between the play's action and the Vietnam war. In the same year, the Board of Trade suggested that a play by Ronald Miller, based on William Clark's novel, *Number 10*, should be taken to Toronto for a 'British Fortnight'. An agreement was made for the Board of Trade to contribute to the inevitable expense involved, but the agreement was cancelled, too late for the visit to be called off, by the Commonwealth Office, lest the play give offence to African states.

This kind of thing is not affected by the Theatres Act 1968. Although the Act outlaws the imposition of censorial conditions in the grant of a licence, local authorities may still play the role of censor. In August 1968, when the Waltham Borough Youth Theatre wanted to put on Edward Bond's *Saved*, the local authority refused to provide the grant without which the production was impossible. In May 1970, the borough committee which controls the civic theatre at Wimbledon, without a single one of its eleven members apparently having seen it, banned the musical *Hair*. Councillor Philip Corbishly, Chairman of the Committee, explained:

I do not think it is a suitable show for a suburban theatre. It is not the sort of thing for Wimbledom audiences. It is just not my cup of tea, and as the majority feeling was against the play coming here at all we felt there was no point in even going to see it.

In October 1968, Felixstowe's council-backed drama festival was to open with Harold Pinter's *The Homecoming*, which has as a leading character a reformed prostitute who lapses. It was felt to be unsuitable and was replaced by *The Killing of Sister George*, which deals, of course, with lesbian love.

Despite the way in which plays have dealt with a wide variety of different forms of sexual behaviour since the 1968 Theatres Act abolished the Lord Chamberlain's powers, prospects of prosecutions seem small. Thus the Attorney-General, Sir Peter Rawlinson, has refused to give permission for a criminal prosecution against Kenneth Tynan's revue *Oh Calcutta!*

The freedom conferred by the Theatres Act has enabled very many plays which would have been unacceptable to the Lord Chamberlain to reach the public, e.g. Hochhuth's *Soldiers*, with its suggestion that Churchill had been responsible for General Sikorski's death. It is worth noting that, in 1967, the National Theatre refused for political reasons to accept the play, independently of the Lord Chamberlain. When subsequently performed, it gave rise to considerable controversy culminating in suggestions that the law of libel should be extended to cover defamation of the recently dead.

Before the Theatres Act 1968, police intervention to persuade producers not to persist in the production of a particular play was quite common. Thus, in April 1968, a planned club production of Edward Bond's *Early Morning* was called off after police questioning of William Gaskill, the artistic director of the English Stage Company, and Alfred Esdaile, licensee of the Royal Court Theatre. Such police intervention seems to have been less frequent since September 1968.

Nudity on the stage gives rise to problems for actors, and creates possibilities of abuse. Accordingly, a code of conduct has been drawn up between Equity, the actors trade union, and the Theatres National Committee. The code requires that actors be given advance notice if a production involves their appearing nude. If auditions involve nudity, an official of Equity should be present. The fact that the Arts Council has refused to interfere in disputes between management boards and the directors of subsidized provincial theatres over their choice of plays is a problem which has become more acute with the new wave of nudity and plays on subjects hitherto forbidden.

The Lord Chamberlain's powers were defined by Section 12 of the Theatres Act 1843, which provided that every play 'to be produced and *acted for hire* at any theatre' should be performed only if it had been examined by him and given a licence *before* the performance began. The key phrase was *acting or performance for hire*, and this was defined by Section 16 to include 'every case in which any money or other reward shall be taken or charged, directly or indirectly, or in which the purchase of any article is made a condition of admission of any person' into the theatre, and also 'every case in which any stage play shall be acted or presented in any house, room or place in which distilled or fermented excisable liquor shall be sold'. This meant that every play had to have a licence if either (a) the actors were paid, or (b) some charge was made for admission, or (c) the play concerned was performed in a place where alcohol was sold. Despite this clear provision, the Lord Chamberlain followed the *unlawful* practice of not requiring that any play performed in a theatre club should be licensed. Despite the fact that this was obviously unlawful, it was a useful device and restored some degree of freedom of experimentation to the British theatre. The Lord Chamberlain himself brought an end to this system in February 1966, owing perhaps to his irritation over a series of disputes with the English Stage Company. To put on Edward Bond's play *Saved*, which the Lord Chamberlain had refused to license without extensive changes, the English Stage Company established a theatre club. The Lord Chamberlain took a dim view and instigated a prosecution of the English Stage Company for putting on unlicensed plays. He was at pains to state that he had no quarrel with *bona fide* theatre clubs, but what was involved here, he felt, was not a *bona fide* theatre club; it was merely a device to evade the law. We can only be astonished at the *naïveté* of this approach. The whole phenomenon of theatre clubs represented a device to evade and break the law.

People attending the proceedings before the Marlborough Street stipendiary magistrate, Mr Leo Gradwell, were surprised by the fact that Mr Gradwell seemed to show an unexpected interest in the question of whether alcoholic beverages were sold in the bar of the Royal Court Theatre. The case inevitably ended in a conviction of the English Stage Company, not because they were not a *bona fide* theatre club – for the Theatres Act 1843, knew no such thing – but because they had put on an unlicensed play. At one stroke the unlawful status of theatre clubs – which had always been there for those who could read the Act – was made doubly clear for all to see. The decision met with mixed reaction. After a period of hesitation the Scottish Arts Council decided to renew their grant to the Edinburgh Traverse Theatre Club, notwithstanding that it continued to put on unlicensed plays. The chairman of the British Arts Council, Lord Goodman, announced that

> . . . the Arts Council has no alternative but to refuse to make available any of its funds for so-called 'Club' presentation of plays.
>
> . . . a Club presentation is not now in any way a substitute for the Lord Chamberlain's licence so that a play presented without a licence is a simple illegality. Neither the Arts Council nor any other public body could finance illegalities from public funds. But we do very much deplore that a device that, in the past, has enabled the presentation of a great many plays of high quality to a discriminating public has now been swept away because of a recent judicial interpretation.

Either theatre clubs had always been unlawful beyond reasonable doubt, or, if they were not, it is hard to see why so much sanctity should be attached to the decision of a single magistrate whose rule could, in any case, have application only within that part of London where he exercised his jurisdiction.

Although the Lord Chamberlain's powers of prior censorship have been swept away by the Theatres Act 1968, it is worth considering the ways in which his uncontrolled censorial powers were exercised, because they illustrate the fact that any unregulated system of censorship – and the Lord Chamberlain could not be controlled in his activities by anybody, not by the courts or Parliament – is likely to lead to abuse, absurdity and violation of the law (sometimes, as we have seen, from the best of motives) as well as to gross interference with the rights and freedom of others.

The list of oddities and absurdities associated with the Lord Chamberlain's régime is almost endless. It must be remembered that they often involved the mutilation of someone else's property, denying to the playwright and others concerned, if they wished to do so, the right to put to the test in public the issue of whether the play concerned defamed anyone or involved the commission of any criminal offence which anyone wished to prosecute. It is still worth considering some of these absurdities, if only as a warning:

1 Improvisation was forbidden. This regularly led to persons being prosecuted for not having had their improvisations approved beforehand by the Lord Chamberlain. Thus, in 1958, Theatre Workshop was fined for introducing a skit of Churchill opening a public lavatory in *You Won't Always be on Top.*

2 In *Fings Ain't What they Used to Be* the Lord Chamberlain objected to a ladder being carried at a phallic angle.

3 In Harold Pinter's *The Caretaker*, it was not permitted to say 'Piss off'. The Lord Chamberlain substituted 'Get Knotted'.

4 In Osborne's *Luther* the Chamberlain objected to a reference to 'the Balls of the Medici', and suggested that 'testicles be substituted'.

5 December 1965: the Lord Chamberlain banned *Simple Golgotha*, a devotional play, because it portrayed Christ on the stage.

6 Nudity was forbidden on the stage in a play, but since ballet and dancing was not a stage play, the Lord Chamberlain had no jurisdiction. Therefore without offence to anyone the Senegal Dance Company performed with bare breasts at the Princess Theatre London in December 1962, and *Les Ballets Africains* performed similarly unclad at the Edinburgh Festival in September 1964.

7 October 1962: a sketch about a southern United States segregationist governor was banned in *The Premise*: when he, the governor, died and went to heaven, he found that God (who was not portrayed) was a Negro.

8 July 1962: it was not permitted to portray the living heads of state of foreign countries on the stage, unless they were Communists. The skits on the Kennedys were removed from *The Premise*, an American review, in 1962, even though they had been included in the original when performed in New York, and even though President Kennedy had made it known that he had no objection to the skits being performed in England.

9 February 1964: the Lord Chamberlain insisted that seven lines (including the last five lines) be cut from E. E. Cummings's poem 'I Sing of Olaf', which was included in *The Rebel*, performed by the Royal Shakespeare Theatre Company at the Aldwych. The poem in its entirety had been included in many printed anthologies and was spoken in its entirety on the BBC television programme *Monitor* in 1963 without a single complaint from any viewer.

10 July 1964: in Beckett's *Endgame*, performed by the Royal Shakespeare Company at the Aldwych, the Lord Chamberlain forbad the translation of the line in the original '*Le salaud! Il n'existe pas*' (referring to God), as 'The bastard! He doesn't exist', and insisted that for this there be substituted 'The swine! He doesn't exist.'

11 August 1964: the Lord Chamberlain requested Graham Greene to alter a line in *Carving a Statue* 'because it might cause a prurient member of the audience to snigger'.

12 In 1966: when the script of *US* was submitted to the Lord Chamberlain by the Royal Shakespeare Company, he rang the Chairman of Governors of the company to say that he wished to disallow the show in its entirety, because in his own words, it was 'beastly, anti-American, and left-wing'.

13 In 1966: the Lord Chamberlain granted a licence to Hochuth's *The Representative* only on condition that a view favourable to the Pope's activities during the Second World War was printed in the programme, the play having raised the issue of whether the Pope might not have saved the lives of many Jews had he spoken out against Hitler's extermination policy. He also ordered the removal of the following shots from a newsreel shown in that play:

a A vague, unfocussed shot of a naked woman running.
b All close-ups of naked male and female bodies.
c Shots of corpses being unloaded from a lorry.
d The shot of a female body being tipped into a communal pit.

The fact that the newsreel showed what had happened in Hitler's concentration camps would have been irrelevant to the Lord Chamberlain, for, as he explained to the Joint Committee on Censorship of the Theatre, the function of his censorship was to prevent offence. He expatiated on this:

I am only thinking of making life more pleasant. It can be an awful nuisance if one takes one's family or friends to a play that simply turns out to give offence to them. I am merely thinking of providing a service to playgoers which might be good for the theatre.

14 March 1967: after a sketch had been seen by something like ten million people on television, the Lord Chamberlain, having discussed it with the Boy Scouts Association, banned it. It showed two officers talking during the Boer War. One says to the other that after the war he intends to go camping with the young lads. The other replies: 'Good Heavens, Baden-Powell – you could get seven years for that.'

15 May 1967: the Lord Chamberlain found the word Jesus, used as an expletive in Edward Albee's *Who's Afraid of Virginia Woolf?* 'too blasphemous'. He required that for 'Jesus' should be substituted 'cheeses'!

The maddest episode in the later history of the Lord Chamberlain's career as theatrical censor occurred in connection with Edward German's opera *Merrie England*. When this was revived at Sadler's Wells in 1960, not only had that portion of the plot which showed Elizabeth I mooting the poisoning of a rival been erased, but the episode had had to be revamped so completely as to make Elizabeth herself the victim of the intended plot.

One earlier episode in the career of the Lord Chamberlain as theatrical censor is worth recording, partly because it has not been told in much detail before, and partly because it exemplifies the dangers of abuse inherent in any form of prior censorship. In 1907 *The Mikado*, which had been produced without objection many times over many years, was banned by the Lord Chamberlain because it was thought it might give offence to the Japanese Crown Prince while on a visit to Britain. It is not easy to know who took the initiative to suppress *The Mikado*. It has been suggested that it was the Japanese government, but the evidence points rather in the direction of it being the Lord Chamberlain himself, and a Home Office official reported that, in the Lord Chamberlain's office, 'Great stress is laid on the necessity for the prohibition by the King [i.e. Edward VII] and other members of the Royal Family.' The Lord Chamberlain withdrew the licence he had granted for the performance of *The Mikado* and a number of performances taking place or being rehearsed in different parts of the country had to be abandoned under threat of criminal prosecution as from the date of the revocation of the licence – which was 26 March 1907, the Japanese Crown Prince not being due to arrive until 6 May!

Mrs D'Oyley Carte, who stood to lose a great deal of money over the ban, protested and inquired about compensation for what was tantamount to the confiscation of her property. She was informed that no compensation was payable under the Theatres Act 1843. The Home Office was somewhat embarrassed politically by the high-handed behaviour of the Lord Chamberlain, but Mr Gladstone, the Home Secretary, was informed on behalf of the Lord Chamberlain 'that Mrs D'Oyley Carte was at the present moment in conference with the Examiner of Plays with a view to a detailed alteration and entire modification of the Play which might be submitted to Mr Gilbert in the hope that he would rewrite it, preserving for the public advantage the music and the wit in a manner which could be offensive to no-one'. Mrs D'Oyley Carte having invested a lot of money in the opera, was anxious to get the ban on its performance removed as rapidly as possible. In June 1907 the Japanese Crown Prince had left the country, but the ban remained. The Home Office was informed that the Lord Chamberlain was considering whether the ban should be removed, but in fact it was not withdrawn until the following year.

The effect of protests from foreign governments is difficult to assess where the protest expressly or by implication seeks the suppression of some opinion or statement being made in Britain. It is not possible to assess the extent or effectiveness of such governmental protests on communications today, but in the past they often led to action by the British authorities which lacked any legal authority. Thus, in 1907, the Russian Ambassador asked the British Foreign Secretary to prohibit theatrical performances by a young woman who called herself 'Countess Romanov' and claimed some kinship with the Tsar's family. The Foreign Secretary approached the Home Secretary, who in turn wrote to the Lord Mayor of Manchester where the lady was performing. The mayor got his Chief Constable to act with the result that due to representations made by the Chief Constable a series of engagements that the actress had to appear in the city were cancelled. The lady continued to follow her career in other parts of the country under the title 'Countess Romanov' and the Home Office set the police in motion to stop her, although they were advised that, as a matter of law, there was nothing criminal in her conduct. The Metropolitan Police succeeded in persuading the actress's theatrical agent to refuse to find further engagements for her, as well as procuring the cancellation of a number of London engagements.

It is in the very nature of such clandestine official police activities, whereby pressure is put upon employers behind the scenes, that they should rarely come to light, and when they do, it is often long after the events themselves occurred. We cannot know how far practices of this kind do or do not continue today, but we shall return to this topic again in our discussion of the security services.

Advertising

There is no general statute controlling advertising, but apart from oddities like the Indecent Advertisements Act 1889 and the Venereal Diseases Act 1917, there are fifty-six statutes listed in the *British Code of Advertising Practice* which affect advertising. These statutory provisions cover a wide range of topics, ranging from provisions designed to protect the consumer from misleading descriptions, under the Trade Descriptions Act 1968, and the prohibition, in the interests of safety, of aerial advertising under the Civil Aviation (Licensing) Act 1960, to the regulation of the display of outdoor advertisements, under the Town and Country Planning Acts 1947 and 1962. This latter provision is concerned with 'amenity' and public safety, and not with the content of the advertisements. Flyposting, a form of public advertisement which is of particular importance to politically active groups in the community is now generally illegal under the Town and Country Planning Act 1962 (and it is also more directly prohibited under local legislation such as in the London Metropolitan police area by the Metropolitan Police Act 1839, Section 54).

Besides the statutory control of advertising, there is also a system of voluntary self-regulation and censorship exercised by different sections of the advertising industry, and by the industry as a whole. This is of particular importance regarding the extent to which the expression of views on controversial topics and political and religious opinions is permitted in advertising.

In fact there are a large number of codes or bodies of rules laid down by different sections of the advertising industry. They are laid down and applied by such bodies as the Independent Television Authority, British Transport Advertising Ltd, London Transport Advertising, the Producer House Members of the British Direct Mail Advertisers Association, the Association of British Pharmaceutical Industry, the Display Producers and Screen Printers Association, the Society of Hearing Aid Audiologists, the Farming and Poultry Advertisement Control Board, the Society of Motor Manufacturers and Traders, and so forth. There are also a number of committees which monitor advertisements, or issue guidance; or, in some cases, even approve copy in advance, including the Advertising Investigation Department Co-ordinating Committee of the Advertising Association, the Joint Copy Committee of the Newspaper Publishers Association and Newspaper Society, the Independent Television Companies Association, the Censorship Committee of the British Poster Advertising Association, the Kinematograph Renters' Society, the Proprietary Association of Great Britain, the Panel of Referees of the Institute of Practitioners in Advertising, and the Copy Claims Committee of the Incorporated Society of Advertisers.

The activities of particular segments of the advertising industry do not necessarily accord with the public interest. In 1962, the Joint Censorship Committee of the British Poster Advertising Association ruled against the acceptance and display by association members of posters issued by the Ministry of Health dealing with the dangers of smoking. When asked by Lord Francis Williams in the House of Lords whether the government's attention had been drawn to this event, Lord Hailsham replied '. . . we must stand on the general principle that in Parliament the government do not have to answer for any idiotic decisions except their own'. The government then entered upon an exchange of views with the Joint Censorship Committee, in the course of which the secretary of the committee wrote:

The committee has . . . recently banned three posters issued by the Ministry of Health concerning lung cancer. These all contained the statement that 'cigarettes cause lung cancer'. This is, in the opinion of my committee, undue exaggeration.

They appreciate that a great deal of evidence has been adduced to show there is a link between lung cancer and smoking but they are not aware that there is positive proof that cigarettes cause lung cancer.

They would be perfectly willing to display, as they have done in the past, posters stating that cigarettes *may* cause lung cancer, and naturally they would reconsider their recent decisions if and when positive evidence is forthcoming to substantiate the wording of the rejected posters. Here again, I must point out that no outside influence of any kind has been brought to bear to influence my committee in its decision.

Lord Hailsham replied:

You write that you have knowingly prevented the Minister of Health from communicating the findings of scientific opinion to the public because 'there is no positive proof that cigarettes do cause lung cancer'.

Your terms of reference do not, I note, include the assessment of scientific evidence. Nor am I aware of any qualifications you possess which would enable you to do so.

On the other hand a number of scientifically qualified bodies support the Ministry of Health in their opinion that cigarette smoking is a cause of lung cancer . . .

I know of no scientifically qualified body which has come to a contrary conclusion.

What constitutes positive proof is a matter of opinion, but, in my judgement, to deny a public health authority the right to inform the public of an overwhelming scientific opinion is to be guilty of a grave public disservice.

The Committee's secretary then replied to Lord Hailsham:

Your letter . . . was considered by my committee today. I am directed to say that they are as anxious as anyone to do everything possible to cut the lung cancer mortality rate. However, they cannot ignore certain long-established rules about advertisement copy and design which are adhered to by *all* media owners. In effect, these rules bar copy which is exaggerated or calculated to induce fear. They feel sure that the Ministry of Health and/or their advertising agents must be unaware of these rules or have not interpreted them correctly.

My committee maintain that the phrase 'cigarettes cause lung cancer' is too sweeping and may cause undue alarm. They have to bear in mind that untold millions smoked cigarettes for a great many years before the incidence of lung cancer reached its present proportions: that all the sufferers from the disease have not been smokers and that the word 'cigarettes' used as it is could be taken to mean as few in number as two.

. . . Had the posters contained the statement made in your letter and also in the Report of the Royal College of Physicians that 'cigarette smoking is a cause of lung cancer' they would have been accepted without question.

. . . The committee ask me to say that they consider that the outdoor advertising industry has been pilloried most unjustly in this matter through maintaining a principle common to all media, including the press . . .

Lord Hailsham, in commenting on the difference felt by the committee to be significant between 'cigarettes cause lung cancer' and 'cigarette smoking is a cause of lung cancer', said that it was 'absolutely indefensible, an irresponsible illogical quibbling, and a quite ridiculous position that this body has taken up'.

An interesting aspect of this ban on Ministry of Health posters was that representatives of the British Transport's advertising department were present on the committee which banned the posters, and British Transport, a nationalized public corporation, itself acted in accordance with the ban.

To complete the story, in 1966 agreement was in a sense reached voluntarily between the government and the principal cigarette manufacturers limiting expenditure on cigarette advertising through press and posters. Advertising in cinemas ceased as a result of agreement, and on television as a result of a ministerial order.

Quite apart from the legal rules and the voluntary institutionalized forms of regulation of advertising, individual enterprises carry out their own policy of censorship. Thus, in 1968, Mill & Rockley, owners of a third of Britain's hoarding space, refused to display a Communist party poster, 'Stop America's Brutal War in Vietnam'. London Transport also regularly bans posters for a variety of reasons. In 1960, they banned posters advertising two films dealing with the activities of former Nazi officers during and after the Second World War, *Holidays on Sylt* and *General Speidel—the Archives Testify* – apparently on the ground that the films had been refused a certificate by the British

Board of Film Censors. In 1964, London Transport banned a poster from the Hampstead branch of Amnesty International, a non-political movement seeking the release of political prisoners all over the world. The poster read:

In Prison because they wanted freedom – political or religious; because they disagreed with their Governments and said so. Amnesty International fights their cause: more members urgently needed.

Its display was refused because it did not comply with London Transport's conditions of acceptance, which require that advertisements should not attack a member, or the policies of any government, and should not be of a political nature, beyond providing information about political meetings.

In 1968, however, London Transport refused to display a poster which read 'Vietnam burns – a meeting to challenge the Government's silence, called by the National Vietnam Committee, Chairman: L. Collins, Central Hall Westminster' (followed by date and admission price). The National Council for Civil Liberties had its advertisement of an event in 1969 at the Festival Hall, held jointly with the Defence of Literature Society, banned because one of the human figures depicted revealed 'too much thigh and a suggestion of a nipple' – a reason so absurd when the endless bra and bathing costume ads which line every underground escalator is considered, that one is forced to suspect that the real reason was not unconnected with the fact that the NCCL poster was part of an anti-censorship campaign.

Bans may be imposed not only for political reasons but also because of religious susceptibilities. In 1960, the British Transport Commission ordered the removal of advertisements by the Family Planning Association because 'it was controversial on religious grounds'. In 1967, the London Underground once more dropped advertisements for pregnancy testing for, it would appear, the same reason, although at the same time British Rail were displaying similar advertisements at their stations. In 1970, the Independent Television Authority recommended that advertisements for family planning should be permitted on commercial television provided they were 'official or semi-official'.

But on balance, both public and private enterprises, which control advertising space, exercise control over advertisements and posters in a way which operates to the disadvantage of minority political and religious groups.

In 1962, the Advertising Standards Authority was set up by the industry with the object of 'the promotion and enforcement through the United Kingdom of the highest standards of advertising in all media so as to ensure co-operation with all concerned that no advertising contravenes or offends against these standards having regard *inter alia* to the British Code of Advertising Practice'. Put more sceptically, the Advertising Standards Authority was established to meet the demand by the public for better policing and regulation of advertising in the public interest, and also to exercise very general supervision over the various systems of self-regulation in operation. The Advertising Standards Authority consists of eleven people: five from the advertising industry, five not connected with the industry, and an independent chairman, who is himself appointed by the industry, but who in turn appoints the other ten.

The authority is willing to receive complaints from members of the public, and these are investigated by the Advertising Investigation Department of the Advertising Association, which gives guidance to the industry. In 1965 the Authority 'ruled that advertising for pregnancy testing should not be accepted in the general press'. In 1966, it changed its mind and gave 'its decision that such advertisements may be published in the general press at the discretion of the publishers, subject to a number of safeguards and a prescribed form of advertisement'. The language of *decision* and *ruled* is that used by the Authority, but strictly speaking it has no powers to legislate at all, and its rules and decisions are for advertising agencies, publishers and so forth to accept or not as they please, though in practice they do abide by them.

Closely associated with the Advertising Standards Authority is the British Code of Advertising Practice, which was sponsored by seventeen organizations engaged in the advertising industry, including all those representing owners of the mass media which carry advertisements. The code (reproduced as Appendix 3 to this book) sets the minimum standards to be observed by the industry. It is drawn up by the industry and is policed by the British Code of Advertising Practice Committee, on which the sponsoring organizations are represented. Thus the industry, having drawn up the Code, provides the machinery for its enforcement on a voluntary basis. The Advertising Standards Authority and the Code Committee act in cooperation, and indeed work from the same address. Both operate essentially on the basis of persuading and educating the industry to behave in particular ways. Neither dissent from the discouragement of 'opinion advertising'; neither can nor will seek to recognize a right in an advertiser to have accepted for display any advertisement which does not conflict with the British Code of Advertising Practice. It is explicitly recognized that,

A media owner is free to accept or reject, without reason, any copy offered to him. The fact that the Authority see no objection to the publication of particular advertising does not in any way prejudice the right of the medium owner to refuse it.

Yet the problem is clear. In a community where the mass media are increasingly subject to control by a small number of bodies, and where the communication of information to the public by political, religious or social, or educational groups must very often be through the media, two conditions are essential for the creation of a situation where freedom of expression is to have any real meaning: (a) that no restrictions be placed on political, religious or social opinion advertisements on the ground only that they are opinion advertisements; and (b) that there must be a duty on those few bodies – certain nationalized industries, the press, commercial television, and so on – concerned with the display of advertisements, not to discriminate in their acceptance provided that such advertisements do not violate the law.

Control of the content of advertisements has many different aspects. We might wish to reduce the dependence of advertising on irrational appeals to potential consumers. We might wish to restrict advertising to the mere statement of facts, and to exclude as far as possible any emotive appeal. But two aspects in particular require more positive protection. First, there is the need to protect the consumer from being misled by misleading and false advertising techniques. Secondly, it is necessary to give protection to the right of political and social groups to communicate to the public through advertising. Both raise difficult problems, if only because there is an apparent contradiction between seeking, on the one hand, to restrict as far as possible commercial advertising to the communication of information, and on the other trying to open up advertising to the communication both of facts and opinions in the field of opinion advertising. It would seem clear that the industry itself, whose interests are fundamentally commercial (and, in so far as they are political, they are fundamentally and in the long run concerned with the perpetuation of a state of affairs in which commercial advertising is both necessary and profitable), cannot provide adequate machinery to secure these objectives. It follows that only further statutory regulation of the industry can achieve the desired end.

In 1966, a Labour Party Commission under Lord Reith reported after an inquiry into advertising. The issue of opinion advertising, however, was side-stepped, although the commission did recommend the setting up of an independent public body, the National Consumer Board, with considerable powers to act as a watchdog over the advertising industry. But, as its name suggests, the National Consumer Board was to be concerned almost entirely with the question of consumer protection, which is not the only important issue raised by the operation of advertising.

In 1967, Royden Harrison reported on the results of research financed by all but one of the members of the Independent Television Companies Association into public attitudes to advertising. Among the large amount of information obtained it appeared that out of a sample of 785 people questioned 82 per cent agreed with the statement, 'Advertising should only be allowed to continue if there is some kind of legal control or censorship to guarantee truthfulness and good taste;' 18 per cent disagreed.

The special problems raised by advertising in the press and on television will be considered later on (pp. 106 and 125).

The Press

There is no general press law in this country, although there are a number of statutory provisions which give the press some limited protection against the civil and criminal liabilities to which they might ordinarily be exposed by publishing reports of certain kinds of material. (Some, but not all, of these privileges are shared with broadcasting.) The press is also the beneficiary of certain defences against liability for defamation, which have been provided as a result of decisions by the judges. The most important statutory provisions are to be found in the Defamation Act 1952, the Public Bodies (Admission to Meetings) Act 1960 and the Law of Libel Amendment Act 1888. In addition, the Monopolies and Mergers Act 1964 prohibits the merging of any two newspapers which have a new combined circulation over a certain amount, unless such merger has been first approved by the Monopolies Commission. The prevailing legal rules are based upon two principles: (a) by and large the press ought not to be subject to any greater restrictions or the recipient of greater privileges in respect of matters appearing in its columns than the ordinary citizen, and (b) such is the inevitable operation of the present economy that the law cannot effectively impose any restriction on mergers, windings up of newspapers, and so forth.

The basic facts about newspapers in Britain are that few national newspapers can survive long (except where they cater for a specialized readership), unless they have a mass sale of enormous size, and linked with this is the fact that they are very dependent upon revenue from advertising. Whatever 'freedom of the press' means in this country, it does not mean that every citizen is free to start up his own national newspaper, or even that he is entitled to expect that the existing national newspapers will freely provide a platform for his views. Newspapers are primarily commodities, produced with the object of making a profit for their owners. Other objectives are always in the long run, subordinate to these facts.

Freedom of the press to publish information and opinions is limited by the many legal rules we have considered earlier, of which the most important are contempt of court, the Official Secrets Acts and the law of libel. In 1965, a Joint Working Party of members of Justice (a body of lawyers in this country) and the British Committee of the International Press Institute made the following recommendations:

1 *Official Secrets Acts:* It should be a valid defence in any prosecution under the Official Secrets Act to show that 'the national interest or legitimate private interests confided to the State were not likely to be harmed and that the information was passed and received in good faith and in the public interest'.

2 *Contempt:* Apart from a number of not unimportant tidying-up reforms, the basic safeguard against abuse of proceedings for contempt of court should be that where proceedings were brought against the press this should only occur on the instructions or with the consent of the Attorney-General.

3 *Libel:* A number of detailed proposals were made which would give the press much greater freedom, provided the press had acted honestly in publishing material of public interest. This would mean that to escape liability the press would no longer have to prove the truth of everything printed.

Although a Bill largely based upon these proposals was introduced into Parliament by a private member in 1969 (see Appendix 8), the law remains unaltered.

It would, however, be foolish to base any discussion of the legal restrictions inhibiting the expression of opinion or the communication of information by the press upon the assumption that the press stands eager to speak forth vigorously on many issues, but is debarred from doing so only by these restrictions. Although the press does occasionally help to air an unpopular opinion, or even to remedy a grievance of a minority or to disclose some abuse of power by officialdom, this is not the function for which the present industry is designed. Its primary objective is the selling of commodities, including newspapers.

Advertising and the revenue it brings is a major factor in the functioning of the modern press. The influence of advertising on the content of newspapers is a subtle one. The Royal Commission on the Press found in 1962 no substantial evidence of advertisers exerting pressure on newspapers to influence their opinions. A less clear-cut picture emerged, however, from the Report of the Labour Party's Commission of Enquiry into Advertising in 1964:

... Miss Elizabeth Gundrey, a professional consumer journalist, expressed in evidence the opinion that investigating had failed to find hard evidence of pressure because the 'ordinary journalist is not very likely to speak freely about such things for fear of losing his job, or being very unpopular with his employers', and she explained: 'It is also something on which it is very difficult to obtain specific evidence because for the most part these matters are arranged by word of mouth and not in writing.'

The Labour Party Commission concluded:

... It appears that the extent of political discrimination of the kinds described is small, though it is important to note both that it does happen and that it almost never succeeds in influencing editorial opinions.

Things are different with regard to consumer columns, this is where a journalist is writing about the products which the advertisers are seeking to sell. Here there is far more evidence, some of it of a very subtle and indirect kind. The Labour Party Commission's Report included the following comment:

... Miss Katherine Whitehorn, when Fashion Editor of the *Observer*, confessed to withholding the name of a firm whose goods she criticized when, had she not been so conscious of advertising, she might not have done so: 'The most subtle damage is always done in the journalist's own head.' And Miss Gundrey explained: 'Very often if a writer knows that he is not going to get away with an adverse criticism – it is going to be cut out by the sub-editor or whoever it is – then obviously he would not waste his time writing it. He just skips that bit, knowing it will not get published.'

One oddity in Britain is the way in which advertisements – and the accompanying payments for such advertisements – have been withheld by government departments from the *Morning Star*, formerly the *Daily Worker*, except for a brief period in 1970. But the decision by the Decimal Currency Board in December 1970 not to advertise in the *Morning Star* suggests that the old policy may have been restored. This policy appears to be based upon the close identification existing between the *Morning Star* and the British Communist party.

In any discussion of methods of keeping alive existing newspapers, and in particular of helping to preserve the continued expression of minority political opinion, we must consider, among other things, the role of the state as advertiser. Clearly in Britain, although the global sums involved in state advertising in newspapers may not be enormous, they are still a not insignificant factor in helping to preserve the existence, in particular, of small circulation papers. It may be that more money ought to be distributed in this way to ensure the continued existence of certain newspapers, but in any event it is difficult to justify the exclusion of any newspaper from the state's bounty, so long as the policies and content of that paper concerned do not violate the law.

It is of interest to compare the payments made in the government's campaign in the autumn of 1969 to publicize changes in National Insurance rates and benefits by advertising in the press, and the relevant figures are given in the accompanying table, with the circulation of the

Publication	Circulation	Sum received from government to pay for advertisements		
		£	s	d
NATIONAL				
Daily Express	3,731,673	5,874	0	0
Daily Mail	1,992,591	3,916	0	0
Daily Mirror	4,924,157	7,072	0	0
Daily Sketch	871,041	1,372	10	0
Daily Telegraph	1,380,367	3,546	0	0
Financial Times	172,347	1,243	0	0
Guardian	292,602	904	0	0
Sun	951,132	2,452	0	0
The Times	437,278	2,338	0	0
News of the World	6,227,684	8,544	0	0
Observer	879,024	3,134	0	0
People	5,532,959	5,367	10	0

Continued overleaf

Publication	Circulation	Sum received from government to pay for advertisements		
		£	s	d
NATIONAL				
Sunday Express	4,235,326	8,188	0	0
Sunday Mirror	5,008,731	8,844	0	0
Sunday Telegraph	753,441	1,525	10	0
Sunday Times	1,454,079	3,390	0	0
LONDON EVENINGS				
London Evening News	1,088,638	2,950	0	0
London Evening Standard	583,083	1,800	0	0
SCOTTISH SUNDAY				
Glasgow Sunday Post	1,000,000	800	0	0
PROVINCIAL MORNINGS				
Birmingham Post	69,571	146	5	0
(Bristol) *Western Daily Press*	59,981	81	5	0
(Darlington) *Northern Echo*	113,089	226	0	0
(Ipswich) *East Anglian Daily Times*	34,071	56	17	6
Leamington and District Morning News	11,324	35	15	0
(Leeds) *Yorkshire Post*	117,396	186	17	6
Liverpool Daily Post	95,242	130	0	0
(Newcastle) *The Journal*	115,234	170	12	6
(Norwich) *Eastern Daily Press*	72,532	86	2	6
(Nottingham) *Guardian Journal* (Combined rate with *Nottingham Evening Post*)				
(Plymouth) *Western Morning News*	70,980	81	5	0
(Sheffield) *Morning Telegraph*	64,716	13	15	0
(Aberdeen) *Press and Journal*	103,291	130	0	0
(Dundee) *Courier and Advertiser*	120,482	130	0	0
(Edinburgh) *The Scotsman*	74,124	227	10	0
(Glasgow) *Daily Record*	520,927	414	0	0
Glasgow Herald	83,357	243	15	0
(Cardiff) *Western Mail*	100,407	195	0	0
PROVINCIAL EVENINGS				
(Barrow) *North Western Evening Mail*	29,303	31	4	0
Bath and Wilts Evening Chronicle	32,496	36	8	0
Birmingham Evening Mail	390,105	357	10	0

Publication	Circulation	Sum received from government to pay for advertisements		
		£	s	d

PROVINCIAL EVENINGS

Publication	Circulation	£	s	d
(Blackburn) *Lancashire Evening Telegraph*, (Burnley) *Evening Star*	93,544	130	0	0
(Blackpool) *West Lancashire Evening Gazette*	76,518	87	15	0
(Bolton) *Evening News*	83,718	107	5	0
((Bournemouth) *Evening Echo*	64,042	54	12	0
(Bradford) *Telegraph and Argus* Saturday Weekly	146,820 123,465	254	5	0
(Brighton) *Evening Argus*	99,390	83	4	0
Bristol Evening Post	182,936	196	12	6
Burton Daily Mail	24,484	32	10	0
Cambridge News	45,574	46	16	0
(Carlisle) *Cumberland Evening News and Star*	30,088	30	0	0
Chatham, Rochester, Gillingham Evening Post	42,868	65	0	0
(Cheltenham) *Gloucestershire Echo*	35,000	42	5	0
Coventry Evening Telegraph	137,227	114	8	0
Darlington Evening Despatch	23,288	39	0	0
Derby Evening Telegraph	98,000	78	0	0
Doncaster Evening Post (Leeds) *Yorkshire Evening Post*	287,868	579	2	6
(Exeter) *Express and Echo*	39,502	47	2	6
(Gloucester) *The Citizen*	40,000	36	8	0
Grimsby Evening Telegraph	73,000	118	13	0
Halifax Evening Courier and Guardian	41,834	95	12	6
(Hartlepool) *Northern Daily Mail*	33,412	78	16	0
(Hereford) *Evening News* *Worcester Evening News*	40,152	56	17	6
Huddersfield Daily Examiner	50,486	113	0	0
Hull Daily Mail	133,000	220	7	0
(Ipswich) *Evening Star*	46,802	54	12	0
(Kettering) *Northamptonshire Evening Telegraph*	48,783	54	12	0

Continued overleaf

Publication	Circulation	Sum received from government to pay for advertisements		
		£	s	d
PROVINCIAL EVENINGS				
Leicester Mercury	180,000	156	0	0
(Lincoln) *Lincolnshire Echo*	37,000	43	17	6
Liverpool Echo	389,267	325	0	0
(Luton) *Evening Post* (Reading) *Evening Post* (Watford) *Evening Echo* (Slough) *Evening Mail*	171,717	255	2	6
Manchester Evening News	453,287	406	5	0
(Middlesbrough) *Evening Gazette*	117,824	240	2	6
(Newcastle) *Evening Chronicle*	233,904	452	0	0
(Northampton) *Chronicle and Echo*	55,019	71	10	0
(Norwich) *Eastern Evening News*	71,804	75	8	0
Nottingham Evening Post (combined rate with (Nottingham) *Guardian Journal*		227	10	0
Nuneaton Evening Tribune	16,844	26	0	0
Oldham Evening Chronicle	46,437	57	4	0
Oxford Mail	42,792	65	0	0
Peterborough Evening Telegraph	21,530	32	10	0
(Plymouth) *Western Evening Herald*	69,519	78	0	0
(Portsmouth) *Evening News*	104,292	107	5	0
(Preston) *Lancashire Evening Post*	140,058	162	10	0
Scarborough Evening News	15,695	48	0	6
(Sheffield) *The Star*	202,242	395	10	0
Shropshire Star (Wolverhampton) *Express and Star*	312,864	195	0	0
(South Shields) *Shields Gazette*	36,692	73	12	0
(Southampton) *Southern Evening Echo*	98,903	78	0	0
(Stoke) *Evening Sentinel*	125,000	117	0	0
Sunderland Echo	84,788	137	4	0
Swindon Evening Advertiser	33,768	48	15	0
(Torquay) *Herald Express*	26,942	30	17	6
(Weymouth) *Dorset Evening Echo*	22,934	26	0	0
(York) *Yorkshire Evening Press*	60,399	127	2	6
(Aberdeen) *Evening Express*	72,371	97	10	0

Publication	Circulation	Sum received from government to pay for advertisements		
		£	s	d
PROVINCIAL EVENINGS				
(Dundee) *Evening Telegraph*	65,699	65	0	0
(Edinburgh) *Evening News*	154,247	211	5	0
(Glasgow) *Evening Citizen*	193,010	260	0	0
(Glasgow) *Evening Times*	191,002	208	0	0
Greenock Telegraph	24,360	32	10	0
Paisley Daily Express	17,089	40	12	6
(Cardiff) *South Wales Echo*	146,831	282	10	0
(Newport) *South Wales Argus*	56,492	115	0	0
(Swansea) *South Wales Evening Post*	71,000	141	5	0
PROVINCIAL SUNDAYS				
(Birmingham) *Sunday Mercury*	225,124	156	0	0
(Newcastle) *Sunday Sun*	245,075	195	0	0
(Plymouth) *The Independent*	46,118	52	0	0
(Glasgow) *Sunday Mail*	757,513	338	0	0
OTHERS				
Baner AC Amserau Cymru	—	127	10	0
Herald Cymraeg A'r Genedl	—	124	12	0
Herald Mon	—	124	12	0
Y Cyfned	—	84	0	0
Y Cymro	—	108	0	0
Y Dydd A'r Corwen Chronicle	—	34	10	0
Y Seren	—	84	0	0
Y Tyst	—	26	10	0
Asia Weekly	—	120	0	0
Des Perdes Weekly	—	132	0	0
Janomot	—	90	0	0
Mashriq	—	195	0	0
Punjab Times	—	180	0	0
Garavi Gujarat	—	105	0	0
Aafaq	—	120	0	0
Nai Sadi	—	90	0	0
Jamaican Weekly Gleaner	—	26	8	0

papers concerned. It can be seen from these figures that some minority papers representing minority national groups receive sums which, although small, none the less make a significant contribution to their viability.

The concentration of newspaper ownership as a cause of restriction upon the views expressed editorially, tends to be deftly turned aside as a source of public concern by references to the proprietor's respect for editorial independence. The following revealing remarks by Lord Thomson are worth consideration here. When he was asked to define his attitude towards editorial independence by the Monopolies Commission during the course of its inquiry into the desirability of his acquisition of *The Times* newspaper in addition to the *Sunday Times*, which he already owned, he replied by describing his relationship with Denis Hamilton, the editor of the *Sunday Times*:

We frequently talk together, I have views on various questions and I make sure that he knows them but I never see them appear in the paper unless he agrees with them. We discuss things and he knows that on certain matters I am very concerned in my mind that this is the thing and so on, but he is the Editor and nothing of my views goes in the paper unless they are also his views. No newspaper today, and I think we must recognize this, can operate with an Editor in isolation.

It is not unreasonable to suggest that men do not reach senior positions inside the newspaper business unless they are known to share certain basic social and political assumptions with those above them in the hierarchy; and, in particular, with the proprietor. This phenomenon explains why there should be so little need for formal instructions from on high to adopt such and such an attitude on public issues; with common shared assumptions, those who are in a position of authority in this country tend instinctively to react in a similar way.

The Press Council was set up partly to assuage public anxiety over some of the problems we have discussed. As reconstituted in 1963, the council consists of twenty-six members: an independent chairman, who was Lord Devlin until 1969, when he was succeeded by Lord Pearce; five co-opted members, representing the general public, and twenty others representing the newspaper industry as follows:

5 The Newspaper Publishers Association Ltd (at least two of whom must be editorial – as distinct from managerial – nominees)

3 The Newspaper Society (at least one of whom must be an editorial nominee)

2 Periodical Publishers Association Ltd (including one editorial nominee)

1 The Scottish Daily Newspaper Society

1 Scottish Newspaper Proprietors' Association

2   The Guild of British Newspaper Editors

4   The National Union of Journalists

2   The Institute of Journalists

The Press Council is essentially a voluntary body set up by the newspaper industry itself and possessing no legal powers or authority. It is represented over and over again by its most active supporters as being an alternative to statutory control of the press. This amounts to an admission that there is public concern that the press should behave and be regulated and controlled in a way which takes account of the public interest. But whether the Press Council succeeds as a substitute for proper statutory control of the press is doubtful. Clearly the council can do nothing about the basic economic problems of the industry, the trend towards greater monopoly, the ghastly uniformity of basic outlook of most newspapers. Sir Max Aitken has claimed that 'Reduced a little bit in numbers the Fleet Street newspapers today offer the public a complete range of opinion and expression totally free from outside direction . . .' It would appear that when he spoke Sir Max had forgotten all about D Notices. Richard Boston has commented on his optimism:

A complete range of freedom and expression, in Sir Max Aitken's phrase, would presumably include, say, support for wildcat strikes, the legalisation of marijuana, home rule for Scotland, war resisters who turn to direct action, Jack Dash, Miss Bernadette Devlin, students who try to take over their universities, hippies who take over empty houses and workers who take over their factories. These opinions, and a host of others that diverge from the bourgeois consensus, I do not remember having seen expressed in Fleet Street papers – except perhaps in a context that clearly labels them as crackpot, and that, surely, is not allowing what Sir Max Aitken calls a complete range of *expression*.

A great deal of humbug is talked about British institutions. Phrases like 'freedom of the press', and 'independence of the judges' are such that, while they are constantly bandied about they are clearly never used in any meaningful sense. If freedom of the press includes ensuring that Fleet Street should offer a complete range of opinion, the activities of the Press Council are irrelevant to achieving this end.

The Press Council has been very critical of the fact that the Criminal Justice Act 1967 limits the amount of publicity which may be given in the press to committal proceedings. Committal proceedings are not a trial; they are a preliminary administrative step taken to inquire into whether the prosecution has sufficient evidence to justify an accused person being tried for a serious criminal offence. Because it is not a trial the ordinary rules of evidence, which prevent the giving of prejudicial and irrelevant evidence, do not apply, and sometimes evidence is given in the course of committal proceedings which would not be permitted at the actual trial. The reason for limiting the publicity which can be given to such proceedings – and, for the most part, this would be in the press, usually the local press – is the belief that publicity given to prejudicial evidence – and at the committal proceedings it is usual to hear only the evidence for the prosecution – would create the possibility that the jury which ultimately tried the accused person might, to some extent have made up their minds against him. This belief may or may not be well founded, but it is a sufficiently serious risk to justify limiting pre-trial publicity, unless the accused person himself requests that the limit on publicity be lifted. Oddly enough there is confirmation that the police themselves and the Home Office have long believed that this was a serious risk. Since 1935, it has been the consistent policy of the Attorney-General not to bring criminal proceedings against any member of the police force who has been involved in disciplinary proceedings which have received publicity. Thus, when certain Sheffield policemen applied to the Home Secretary against their dismissal from the force for having allegedly been involved in the beating up of persons in custody, after the report of their unsuccessful appeal had been published in 1963 the Attorney-General ruled that they should not be prosecuted, even although there was overwhelming evidence to justify such a trial. This rule of practice, that in such circumstances the police concerned should not be prosecuted is based upon the assumed practical impossibility of their obtaining an impartial trial before a jury once publicity has been given to internal proceedings against them. This principle, if it is soundly based, would seem to justify secrecy being attached to details of the proceedings before committing magistrates. The Press Council has, however, strongly opposed any restriction on the publicity to be given to committal proceedings, essentially, it is fair to say, on the basis that justice ought to be seen to be done.

Lord Devlin, in his Foreword to the 15th Annual Report of the Press Council (1968), praised examples of editorial courage in publishing material which, in view of the uncertainty of the law, might have given rise to legal proceedings. It is somewhat surprising, seeing such encouragement being given to editors to take risks on the one hand and on the other expressed concern for the need for justice to be done in public that the Press Council holds its own investigations into complaints against the press by members of the public in secret, with neither the press nor the public present. (In committal proceedings, press and public may be present; there is simply a limit to the information which may be published thereafter.) Why this secrecy? Because the Council 'might be involved in heavy damages for defamation. . . . In the circumstances the Council felt that while it had nothing to hide it could not take the risk of conducting its affairs in open session.' Perhaps the Press Council should practise what it preaches. It is worth adding also that the council refuses to permit legal representation in proceedings before it. The proceedings, even though the outcome of an investigation into a complaint is pompously referred to by itself as an 'adjudication', leave something to be desired, and objections have been made that complainants have not had the same opportunity to present their side of the case as has the journalist, or editor of the newspaper against whom the complaint has been made.

But the Press Council is not without its advantages. It has helped to establish certain elementary standards of fair play in limited areas – that, for example, editors should not delete parts of letters they publish without indicating this or consulting the correspondent concerned; that, in many cases, they should be willing to publish factual corrections and even to publish apologies for their own errors. The Council has slowly been evolving general principles of reasonable conduct which have affected the way in which some, or even most, of the national newspapers behave. On the other hand, many of their adjudications are a little surprising and reveal an arbitrariness and unexpressed prejudice, the results of which may be seen in some of their opinions. Thus, when the London *Evening News* in a leading article suggested that a lady who had slapped the face of Mr Jack Dash, the Communist unofficial dockers' leader, at a strike meeting, should be awarded the OBE 'for setting an example of courage and commonsense in a time of national crisis', the council, having heard the Editor of the *Evening News* explain that the article was light-hearted (perhaps in intent, but no one who read it would have known that this was the intent from the words used), announced its 'adjudication':

'The Editor of the *Evening News* was fully entitled to express his views on the dock strike incident. The complaint is rejected.'

In 1968 the Press Council was referred to a Cummings cartoon in the *Sunday Express*,

which depicted a company director interviewing a coloured man attired in flowered coat and sandals with a copy of the 'Race Relations Act Pains and Penalties' in his hat, applying for the post of managing director. An interpreter was quoted as saying 'My friend's qualifications are as follows: he landed illegally, doesn't speak English, can't read or write, has a siesta from 2 o'clock until 6 o'clock and if you don't give him the job he'll have you arrested for racial prejudice.'

One complainant said that the cartoon was offensive to the immigrant community and to British people anxious to see improved relations between coloured and white people in the United Kingdom. Another described the cartoon as 'crass, gross, totally unfunny and a blatant incitement for many people to race hatred'. The editor of the *Sunday Express* described the cartoon as a comment on a topical political issue and he also indicated that he did not accept that the Council had jurisdiction over what political comments a newspaper could or could not make. The Council's 'adjudication' was:

To censure a publication simply on the ground that it is or may be offensive to a part or even the majority of the population would be quite inconsistent with the freedom of the Press. The complaint against the *Sunday Express* is rejected.

One may consult in vain the objects of the Press Council (Appendix 5) for any indication that it has any censorial function, but it has. For example, on several occasions it has notified newspapers of requests from Buckingham Palace that publicity should not be given to certain activities of the Royal Family. When complaints were made in 1969 against the *Daily Express* for having reprinted photographs of the Queen in bed after the birth of her last child, the complaint was rejected, because it would appear that the photographs had been widely publicized already all over the world and the editor of the *Daily Express* had 'acted properly in notifying the Palace of his possession of the photographs'. The 'adjudication' then added: 'If the Queen had directly requested that they should not be published, it would plainly have been wrong of the *Daily Express* to do so.'

In addition to D Notices and threats of prosecution under the Official Secrets Acts, a great deal of information is suppressed by persuasion and other informal means. The persuasion, or – since the persuaders and the persuaded so often share the same social and political assumptions – it may be better and more accurate to refer to it as 'the old boy network', may be institutionalized as in the Press Council or the Services, Press and Broadcasting Committee, or it may remain entirely informal. Where it is informal it is of course difficult to illustrate, but the paucity of examples should not lead one to underestimate its significance. Thus when, in the course of the events leading up to the abdication of Edward VIII Mrs Simpson was divorced in an English court, scant reference was made to this fact in the British press, nor indeed was any reference made to the possibilities of abdication and morganatic marriage, although foreign newspapers devoted a considerable amount of space to these problems. When foreign newspapers containing this information were distributed in Britain the distributors were found to have blocked out the offending passages. No press reference was made either to the historic moment when Prince Philip became an Englishman by naturalization. Informal persuasion does not of course always succeed. Thus, in 1970, when the *People* newspaper received evidence suggesting that British troops in Malaya in 1948 had been involved in an alleged massacre of a number of civilians, the Ministry of Defence asked them to delay publication of the story. The *People* declined to do so.

More formalized are the rules inhibiting the use of information obtained by the group of journalists who associate most closely with Ministers and politicians at Westminster and who are known as the 'Lobby'. The rules governing the use to which information may be used by these correspondents are to be found in 'The Lobby rules' (the 1956 version of which has been published in 1970 by Jeremy Tunstall in his important book *The Westminster Lobby Correspondents*). These 'rules', which have been evolved by a sort of osmotic process between the journalists who belong to the 'Lobby' and members of the government, reflect very clearly the way in which admission to any 'club' is utilized to exert social pressure on those privileged to be admitted not to disclose information to outsiders,* even though outsiders might be considered to have a legitimate interest in the information concerned.

Remember always that you hold a responsible office, and that Ministers, Members and officials have a right to rely on your tact and discretion.

Keep in mind that: (1) while you have complete freedom to get your own stories in your own way, and while there are no restrictions of any kind of [sic, on?] personal initiative, you have a duty to the Lobby as a whole; (2) you should do nothing to prejudice the communal life of the Lobby, or the relations with the two Houses and the authorities; (3) this is in your interest and that of your office, as well as in the general interest of the Lobby.

It has become common practice for Ministers and others to meet the Lobby collectively to give information and to answer questions.

Members of the Lobby are under an obligation to keep secret the fact that such meetings are held, and to avoid revealing the sources of their information.

Sometimes press facilities may be made available by government departments only on condition that newspapers accept certain restrictions. Although journalists may now on occasion visit and describe conditions inside British prisons, they are still forced to submit copies of any articles before publication to the Home Office. The Home Office states that this is 'not to inhibit editorial opinion or to suppress news but to check facts and to prevent identification or embarrassment to prisoners or their relatives'.

The law of libel has been put to some odd uses by the press itself. *Private Eye* has been a constant irritant to the establishment, and some of the more established journals and journalists have been stung into taking legal action against this journal. Having little capital it is not much of a mark for libel action, though it has since its foundation paid out over £25,000 in costs and damages. On the other hand, it cannot successfully withstand too many successful claims for large damages. In November 1967, the editor of the *Daily Express*, Mr Marks, brought a libel action against *Private Eye*. To avoid losing the actual trial and so having a large sum of damages awarded against it, *Private Eye* settled the action for £750 damages plus costs. In addition, the editor of *Private Eye* gave Mr Marks a written promise not to publish in future anything that was 'defamatory of you or the *Daily Express* or *anything which reflects* directly or indirectly on your editorial competence or integrity'.

* Cf. the reaction in certain Cambridge circles when C. P. Snow published his novels *The Light and the Dark* (1947) and *The Masters* (1951), giving a fictional but recognizable picture of the kind of events which may occur inside a club, in this case a Cambridge college. Gentlemen apparently do not disclose to outsiders what may go on inside the club.

In March 1968, Paul Johnson, then editor of the *New Statesman*, with the New Statesman and Nation Publishing Co. Ltd, sued the editor, Richard Ingrams, and the Publishers of *Private Eye*, Pressdram Ltd, for libel. The action was settled, as a result of which the *New Statesman* published a copy of an agreed statement made in open court, the cost of the advertisement being borne by *Private Eye*. The statement in part read:

During the course of the last two years the Defendants have sustained a scurrilous and malicious campaign in the form of a number of gravely defamatory attacks on the Plaintiffs, fourteen of which are cited in the writ issued on the Plaintiffs' behalf. The purpose and effect of this campaign has been to suggest that the *New Statesman* has abandoned its progressive principles and to portray Mr Johnson as a person unworthy to be Editor of the *New Statesman*. It has also been suggested that he has allowed members of the government to interfere with what was published in the *New Statesman* and that he has adopted a fawning attitude towards the Prime Minister. In addition to other matters with which I need not concern the Court it has been suggested that Mr Johnson was inspired to dismiss a senior member of his staff from improper motives.

For a long time the Plaintiffs took the view that these attacks should properly be treated with the contempt they deserve. It has recently become apparent, however, that the attacks were part of a deliberate campaign and that credence was being given to them on account of their reiteration. The Plaintiffs therefore came to the conclusion that such a campaign could no longer be allowed to continue.

As the Defendants now acknowledge, the allegations made against the Plaintiffs in these articles were completely untrue. Furthermore the Defendants now recognise that the stories maliciously published by them in an attempt to portray Mr Johnson in an unfavourable light were false and should never have been published.

I am glad to tell your Lordship that the Defendants attend today by Counsel to express their sincere apologies to the Plaintiffs and they have given a written Undertaking that no more of these attacks will be made in the future. They have also agreed to indemnify the Plaintiffs in respect of the legal costs which they have been obliged to incur.

In addition, *Private Eye* gave a written undertaking '. . . not to publish *anything malicious* or defamatory about the *New Statesman* or its editor'.

In April 1969, the *Spectator* sued and was paid £250 and costs in an out-of-court settlement. An agreement was also made that *Private Eye* 'will not publish any further reports concerning the *Spectator*, Mr H. D. F. Creighton, or its business without the approval in writing of the editor of the *Spectator*'.

It is important to notice that in each case these undertakings went beyond a promise to refrain from committing libel in future. Richard Ingrams made a nice lawyers' point in a letter to *The Times*:

It is not usually understood that the word 'defamatory' is not synonymous with 'libellous'. Almost any criticism or attack on anyone may be defamatory, but it only becomes libellous if it cannot be justified as true in fact or as fair comment in the public interest. A pledge not to print defamatory comments is a pledge, in effect, not to criticise.

He added:

Of course it is 'open' to *Private Eye* to contest these pledges in the courts. Unfortunately, however, a major libel action, if lost, seldom costs less, in legal costs alone, than £10,000.

Even if one contests Ingram's point, the words 'anything malicious' go beyond the protection to which any journalist or periodical is reasonably entitled.

Although libel, the Official Secrets Acts and contempt of court are the main sources of legal rules inhibiting the press, more recently the doctrine of confidentiality has given rise to problems. In *Argyll* v. *Argyll* (1964) it was held by the courts that a partner to a former marriage could obtain an order from the courts restraining the other partner from publishing in the newspapers information acquired during and as a result of the marriage. In *Fraser* v. *Evans* (1968) an attempt was made to prevent the *Sunday Times* from publishing an article based on a report supplied to the Greek government by its public relations consultant in England. The contract between the Greek government and the consultant imposed an obligation that the consultant would not disclose the report to anyone but his client. The report somehow came into the possession of the *Sunday Times*, and they wished to publish it as it revealed methods used by a British public relations consultant to influence British public opinion and Members of Parliament in favour of the foreign government which employed him. The Court of Appeal refused to restrain publication of this information.

... the Court would in a proper case restrain publication of confidential information. The jurisdiction to restrain was widely based not only on property and contract, but also on good faith. No person was permitted to divulge to the world information received in confidence unless he had just cause for doing so. Even if he came by it innocently, once he got to know it was originally given in confidence he could be restrained from breaking that confidence.

But the party complaining must be the person entitled to have the confidence respected, the person to whom the duty of good faith was owed. That was where Mr Fraser's claim broke down. There was no doubt that he himself was under an obligation to the Greek Government. But there was nothing express in the contract which put the government under any obligation of confidence, nor anything to be implied.

The Press Council has expressed its views on confidentiality. Lord Devlin in the 15th Annual Report (1968), wrote:

We have recently been made aware that there is a third area [apart from libel and contempt] in which the obscurity of the law may affect an editor; this is on the question of how far confidentiality can be imposed and enforced. The Press Council has made its attitude on what may be called the 'non-legal' aspects of this last question quite clear. The Council will not accept that when a document contains material of public interest the author can, by rubberstamping it, impose an obligation of confidence on everyone into whose hands it may fall. If an editor comes by it fairly and is not himself bound by the confidence, he must use his discretion about publishing it, satisfying himself first that it really is a public and not a private matter and then asking himself whether its publication would do more harm than good.

The Press Council has, on a number of occasions, upheld the use of documents marked 'confidential' or 'not for publication' by news-papers. This did not prevent Lord Devlin, wearing another hat as chairman of the Joint Board for the National Newspaper Industry, from condemning the 'premature publication in the *Guardian* of parts' of a report on the newspaper industry by the Economic Intelligence Unit prepared for the Board, which contained information received by the unit in the strictest confidence. Lord Devlin complained that the *Guardian*'s report was misleading. The *Guardian* replied in part: '. . . Why, if disclosure is good for other industries, should it be bad in the newspaper industry.'

The press in general, with the exception in the past of *Reynolds News* and the *Daily Herald*, and, today, of the *Morning Star*, have generally been unsympathetic to industrial action by trade unions. A major factor in the build-up of a public opinion hostile to strikers and trade unions, which enabled both the last Labour government to initiate a bill legally restricting the activities of strikers and trade unions, and the present Conservative government actually to enact such legislation, has been the generally unfavourable publicity that strikes have received from the press. That there has been a deliberate emphasis upon strikes as opposed to other causes of lost production can be seen from the fact that, while strikes are constantly in the headlines, an infinitely more serious source of lost production to the country is rarely mentioned and is not a front page issue. This is the growing toll of death and human misery caused by preventible accidents and diseases arising out of employment. News, of course, is selected, but the question remains by whom, and in the interests of whom, is such selection made? A partial answer is that no selection of news on the industrial front is based upon an assessment of the interests of the working population, nor is it made by the mass of persons employed in the newspaper industry. Difficult problems arise for a liberal capitalist society as a result.

In December 1970 there was a strike of workers in the electricity supply industry, and on 9 December production of the London *Evening Standard* was halted because of a dispute over a cartoon. The first edition depicted 'Homo-electrical sapiens Britannicus, circa 1970' by Jak.

The cartoon showed an aggressive cloth-capped individual with his head labelled 'solid bone', eyes 'green with envy', ear 'deaf to reason', mouth 'permanently open', hand 'always out', and a hole where his heart should have been, marked 'nothing here'. In the corner of the cartoon was framed magnifying glass labelled 'to find brain break glass', and in his hand the man held a newspaper headlined 'Blackout Hits Sick'.

When production was stopped by electricians working on the paper the whole of the first edition had been printed. After a meeting with the editor and managing director, union leaders agreed to resume publication as soon as a letter stating their objections could be published prominently near the cartoon.

The *Evening Standard*'s branch of the National Union of Journalists then issued a statement saying:

It was agreed that this chapel will not countenance any censorship of the contents of the Evening Standard by any union. It is, and must be, the decision of the editor what the editorial columns contain.

The chapel protests in the strongest fashion at the action of members of maintenance and production chapels in stopping production of this newspaper. It believes that any objection to matter in the paper should be taken up by officials of these chapels in a proper organized fashion through the chapels. It calls on chapels to resume work forthwith. It draws attention to the precarious situation of the paper in the present circumstances.

Mr Chataway, then Minister of Posts and Telegraphs, commented at once on this episode: 'This is a direct attack on one of the basic freedoms in any democracy, the freedom of the press.'

In November 1970 threat of industrial action by a printing trade union, NATSOPA, prevented the *Observer* from carrying a story about internal disagreements inside a printing trade union, SOGAT, of which NATSOPA was the major constituent. Later Mr Briginshaw, Secretary of NATSOPA, explained:

We objected to something that went into the *Observer* last week, but we did so on the basis of what we considered the industrial unfairness of the employer involved.

We do not consider it our job to interest ourselves in censorship. Secondly, we reckon it is the responsibility on the part of the publishers to avoid direct industrial provocation of their workers.

We say, in addition to this, that we do not professionally or industrially cover the field which covers journalism either positively or negatively.

Later still, irked, no doubt, by the suggestion that the union's threat causing the removal of an item from the *Observer* was undemocratic, he asked: '[B]y what democratic process was the Hon. David Astor elected Editor [of the *Observer*]?'

It is worth adding that, immediately after the defeat of the General Strike in 1926, a collective agreement, dated May 1926, between the publishers and the printing unions provided *inter alia*:

4 The Trade Unions agree that there shall be no interference with the contents of any newspaper, periodical or other matter printed or published by members of the Employers' Organizations.

One possible response to the *Observer* and *Evening Standard* episodes is certainly to condemn the trade-union action on each occasion as an improper interference with the freedom of the press. But this is a somewhat naïve approach unless one is content that in this context freedom of the press should mean only the freedom of those who, by the accident of owning or controlling a newspaper, have the exclusive right to select what they will or will not publish. But there is nothing democratic about this right of selection being conferred solely in virtue of ownership or control. And we know, in any case, that newspapers do accede to pressure from other quarters to suppress information, the only difference being in that kind of case that proprietors and editors are willing to be persuaded, whereas in the case of trade union pressure they are often not. As the electricians of the *Evening Standard* and *Daily Express* said in protest to their editors: 'Does one suppose for an instant that a similar scurrilous cartoon directed against the Royal Family would not have met with instant intervention by the officers of the persons so attacked.'

Does anyone doubt that if such a cartoon had been published that a protest from the right quarter would at once have led to its removal from the columns of the paper? So the discussion turns out, after all not to be about *freedom of the press* – meaning that no pressures shall be exercised against newspaper editors – but rather about what kind of pressures are or are not acceptable in the kind of society in which we live. As, speaking in another context, Mr Donald Thomas has said: 'The relevant question at any stage of human history is not "Does censorship exist?" but rather, "Under what sort of censorship do we now live?" ' Or, adjusting his words to our problem of the freedom of the press, what kind of censorship of the press do we now have and by whom is it exercised? What are the kinds of censorship, and by whom, do we feel in our present circumstances to be illegitimate?

Radio and Television

Radio and television are, of course, like the other media, subject to the general rules discussed in Chapter 2, such as the law of defamation. But they are also subject to a body of special law, to be found in the case of the BBC for the most part in the Wireless Telegraphy Act 1949 and in the BBC's Charter of Incorporation, as well as in its Licence and Agreement with the Postmaster General which lapse in 1976. Under Clause 12 (4) of the Licence, the Postmaster General 'may from time to time by notice in writing require the Corporation to refrain from sending any matter or matter of any class specified in such notice'.

In 1927, a direction was issued requiring the BBC not to broadcast its own opinions on current affairs or on matters of policy – that is, the BBC is not entitled to editorialize on current affairs. In 1964, it was directed to maintain standards of good taste and decency, and high general standards in respect of content and quality of programmes, including a reasonable proportion of British material. It has also to maintain a proper balance and wide range of subject matter. In 1955, the BBC was directed to refrain from sending out controversial party political broadcasts other than those arranged with the leading political parties – the Conservative, Labour and Liberal parties. The BBC has a board of governors appointed by the government, but the day to day running of the corporation is in the hands of the director general.

Where commercial television is concerned, the Television Act 1964 imposes considerable legal control and restriction over the matter allowed to appear. These provisions are of a far reaching kind, and require the Independent Television Authority (ITA) to draw up codes on violence and on advertising, while setting limits to what may be included in programmes and giving the government extensive legal authority to control what is broadcast. It is worth while to set these provisions out in detail.

Provisions applying to all programmes

3·1 It shall be the duty of the [Independent Television] Authority to satisfy themselves that, so far as possible, the programmes broadcast by the Authority comply with the following requirements, that is to say –

a that nothing is included in the programmes which offends against good taste or decency or is likely to encourage or incite to crime or to lead to disorder or to be offensive to public feeling;

b that a sufficient amount of time in the programmes is given to news features and that all news given in the programmes (in whatever form) is presented with due accuracy and impartiality;

c that proper proportions of the recorded and other matter included in the programmes are of British origin and of British performance;

d that the programmes broadcast from any station or stations contain a suitable proportion of matter calculated to appeal specially to the tastes and outlook of persons served by the station or stations and, where another language as well as English is in common use among those so served, a suitable proportion of matter in that language; and

e that due impartiality is preserved on the part of the persons providing the programmes as respects matters of political or industrial controversy or relating to current public policy.

In applying paragraph (e) of this subsection, a series of programmes may be considered as a whole.

3·2 . . . [I]t shall be the duty of the Authority to secure the exclusion from the programmes broadcast by them of all expression of their own opinion as to any of the matters referred to in paragraph (e) of . . . [subsection one], or of the opinion as to any such matters

a of any of their members or officers, or

b of any programme contractor, or

c in the case of a programme contractor being a firm, of any partner therein, or

d in the case of a programme contractor being a body corporate, of any director or officer thereof or person having control thereof.

3·3 It shall be the duty of the Authority to satisfy themselves that the programmes broadcast by the Authority do not include, whether in an advertisement or otherwise, any technical device which, by using images of very brief duration or by any other means, exploits the possibility of conveying a message to, or otherwise influencing the minds of, members of an audience without their being aware, or fully aware, of what has been done.

Provisions applying to programmes other than advertisements

4·1 The Authority:

a shall draw up, and from time to time review, a code giving guidance:

  i as to the rules to be observed in regard to the showing of violence, particularly when large numbers of children and young persons may be expected to be watching the programmes, and

  ii as to such other matters concerning standards and practice for programmes (other than advertisements) broadcast by the Authority as the Authority may consider suitable for inclusion in the code,

and in considering what other matters ought to be included in the code in pursuance of sub-paragraph (ii) shall have special regard to programmes broadcast when large numbers of children and young persons may be expected to be watching; and

b shall secure that the provisions of the code are observed . . .

4·2 The Authority may, in the discharge of their general responsibility for programmes other than advertisements, impose requirements as to standards and practice for such programmes which go beyond, or relate to matters not covered by, the provisions of the code. . . .

5·1 In the case of programmes other than advertisements, the methods by which the Authority discharge their duties under section 1 (4) and section 4 of this Act shall include the consideration of programme schedules submitted by programme contractors to the Authority for approval in accordance with this section; and . . . no such programme provided by a programme contractor shall be broadcast by the Authority unless it forms part of a programme schedule so approved.

5·2 The Authority may give directions, which may be, to any degree, either general or specific and qualified or unqualified:

a as to the exclusion of any item from a programme schedule;

b as to the inclusion in, or in a particular part of, a programme schedule of an item or items, of a particular category; or

c as to the inclusion in a particular part of a programme schedule of a particular item,

and the Authority shall not approve a programme schedule until they are satisfied that it conforms with any directions given under this section. . . .

Advertisements

7·3 It shall be the duty of the Authority to secure that the provisions of Schedule 2 to this Act are complied with in relation to the advertisements included in the programmes broadcast by the Authority.

7·4 After consultation with the Authority the Postmaster General may make regulations by statutory instrument amending, repealing, or adding to the provisions of the said Schedule.

7·5 . . . [I]t shall be the duty of the Authority to consult from time to time with the Postmaster General as to the classes and descriptions of advertisements which must not be broadcast and the methods of advertising which must not be employed and to carry out any directions which he may give them in those respects.

8·1 It shall be the duty of the Authority:

a to draw up, and from time to time review, a code governing standards and practice in advertising and prescribing the advertisements and methods of advertising to be prohibited, or prohibited in particular circumstances; and

b to secure that the provisions of the code are complied with . . .

8·2 The Authority may, in the discharge of their general responsibility for advertisements and methods of advertising, impose requirements as to advertisements and methods of advertising which go beyond the requirements imposed by the code.

Powers of government in relation to authority

18·1 The Postmaster General and any other Minister of the Crown may, if it appears to him necessary or expedient to do so in connection with his functions as such, at any time by notice in writing require the Authority to broadcast . . . any announcement . . .

18·3 . . . [T]he Postmaster General may at any time by notice in writing require the Authority to refrain from broadcasting any matter or classes of matter specified in the notice. . . .

SECOND SCHEDULE

Rules as to advertisements

8 No advertisement shall be permitted which is inserted by or on behalf of any body the objects whereof are wholly or mainly of a religious or political nature, and no advertisement shall be permitted which is directed towards any religious or political end or has any relation to any industrial dispute.

The legal obligations of the BBC and the ITA, leaving aside the special rules relating to advertising, are similar in many respects. Both are under a legal obligation to transmit official government announcements, but the ITA is under a specific duty of political impartiality, as well as a duty not to permit the transmission of programmes which may be offensive to public feeling. It may be because of the absence of this kind of legal restriction that it has in the past been possible for the BBC to transmit political satire, a *genre* noticeably lacking in ITA programmes. The ITA is given specific responsibility to enable it to control the content of programmes transmitted by the programme contractors, that is, the commercial companies to whom the authority has given contracts for the transmission of programmes.

Besides legal rules, there are other restrictions on the content of programmes. In the case of the BBC an agreement known as the *aide-mémoire* was drawn up in 1947 between the Corporation and the Labour and Conservative parties. As a result of this it was agreed that the government should be able to make ministerial broadcasts of a purely factual or explanatory kind, or in the nature of appeals to the public to cooperate in some national policy, such as an appeal for economy in the use of fuel at the time of a fuel shortage. These broadcasts were not 'in the ordinary way' to entitle the Opposition to any right of reply. The absence of a right of reply depends upon the non-controversial nature of the broadcast – if the party whips agree as to this, there is no problem, but if the Opposition Whip feels there ought to be a right of reply to what was, in effect a controversial ministerial broadcast, then the BBC acts as a court of appeal and has to decide whether to permit a reply. The ITA is in a slightly different position as it is under a statutory duty of impartiality, and it must decide for itself initially whether the ministerial broadcast is such as to give rise to a right of reply. For the BBC the *aide-mémoire* also provides for a number of controversial party political broadcasts, the number of such broadcasts to be settled by discussion between the BBC and the main political parties. In practice, the ITA follows the general terms of the *aide-mémoire*.

Both the ITA and BBC are very susceptible to criticism by religious groups, and both regard the exposition of the Christian viewpoint as part of their duties. The Chairman of the Governors of the BBC said, in 1967, following a meeting with the British Humanist Association:

First, the B.B.C. continues to adhere to the policy of according a special position to Christian religious broadcasting.

Second, the B.B.C. does not recognize the Humanist Association as having a claim to a similar position.

Third, it can hardly be contended that humanist assumptions have not been reflected in contemporary broadcasting.

Fourth, I stated, as did my predecessor, that those responsible for general programmes within the B.B.C. would consider with care and understanding individual suggestions as to how humanist beliefs and activities might be presented in ways likely to make good television.

This, of course, still adds up to ensuring a special position, and, indeed, a special protection, for religious opinion belonging to a particular section of religious believers. Sensitivity over the feelings of particular Christian religious groups has caused the BBC to apologize for a sketch on the satirical programme, *Not so much a programme, More a way of life*, which made reference to Roman Catholic fertility and the attitude of Catholic priests to it in Liverpool. Similarly, when Granada TV in 1966 planned to show an edition of *The World Tomorrow* about the wealth of the Catholic church, this was held up by the ITA until there could be included in it a statement by Mgr Bruce Kent, 'a leading cleric from the Westminster diocese'.

The BBC and ITA both operate internal control over the content of programmes. Until 1963, a list of rules were applied by the BBC forbidding references to royalty, religion, politics and sex in light entertainment. These, embodied in a confidential sixteen-page booklet, were abandoned in the light of the satirical programme *That was the week that was*. A BBC spokesman at the time said: 'The tenets of good taste and manner are being observed as they always were. . . .' Every producer, he added, was aware of BBC guidance on good and bad taste, and when in doubt could go for further guidance to the head of the department concerned.

In June 1965, Mr Sydney Newman, head of BBC Television Drama, sent a memorandum to producers reminding them of the need for 'good sense in the treatment of sex, religion and minorities'. According to *The Times*'s summary of the memorandum:

Producers should give careful consideration from every point of view . . . before including in a play scenes of couples in bed, the portrayal of near nudity, and reference to sexual parts. Blasphemy offended religious people and it should be remembered that exclamations or curses such as 'Jesus' and words like 'bloody' were offensive. There were enough words in the English language to provide 'punchy' speech without resorting to blasphemy and obscenity.

In November 1965, Mr Newman sent out another memorandum warning producers to watch the content of plays carefully. He pointed out that it was not a note of chastisement, and that the drama department had done 'extremely well' in observing what had previously been laid down over the presentation of sex, violence and blasphemy. A further memorandum was necessary, however, 'because the anti-B.B.C. hounds are baying more shrilly than ever' (the BBC has been much criticized by certain pressure groups for its moral laxity).

Among subjects to be watched carefully were needlessly lengthy violence, references to sexual parts, underclothes and contraceptives, the showing of near nudity, the physical handling of someone with sex in mind, the portrayal of couples in bed, and the use of offensive words.

In 1967, Sir Hugh Carleton-Greene, then Director-General of the BBC, told senior executives that programmes 'should not express a permissive attitude towards drugs or drug taking'. In 1968, the Governors of the BBC addressed a ten-page booklet entitled *Broadcasting and the Public Mood* to its executives, which said, among other things:

The map is no longer smothered in British red. Young men and women have no Pax Britannica to administer in distant parts. . . .

At all costs and at all times the B.B.C.'s independence from governmental or other external pressures must be maintained. We cannot and will not tailor facts or adapt our policies to meet the wishes, express or implied, of political parties, in government or in opposition. . . .

It is not that we are impartial about everything. We are not impartial about crime or race hatred. The essential point is that we have no editorial policy, no opinion on current affairs. Over a period we are committed to maintain a political balance.

On the subject of drama, it was difficult to assess what is at a particular time good or bad taste. Sex and swearing should be handled with particular care.

Nevertheless the B.B.C. has a definite obligation to the public not wilfully or unnecessarily to depart from a standard of good taste. At the same time, the B.B.C. has a responsibility to achieve for the creative artists the maximum amount of freedom consistent with this. . . .

Goodness may be difficult to portray in dramatic terms. But there is a lot of goodness in the world and it has its place in drama. The seamy side of life is not the whole story.

The document disclaimed any notion that the BBC was destroying established moral values; but, on the other hand, was the BBC bound to urge higher moral standards?

The answer must be that even if we so wished, we are not equipped to define such standards for others. . . . If we do not pursue a traditional line, we should not cultivate or appear to cultivate a 'permissive' one. We cannot be neutral on moral values.

All of which leaves the situation somewhat confused. But clearly, while some of the internal control of the content of programmes derives from the individual sense of the fitness of things on the part of individual producers, and even of the Director-General, the BBC is also motivated to control the content of certain programmes to avoid giving offence to outside bodies, public and private.

Sometimes prudery may outweigh the public interest in surprising ways, as when, in 1969, the BBC refused to broadcast a full description of a mini-van that the police were anxious to trace in connection with their investigation of a murder case. The van was dirty and undistinguished, but it bore a sticker 'Dirty van – a dirty weekend'. The BBC declined to broadcast these words as part of a description of the van being sought by Scotland Yard.

An odd complaint of a failure by the BBC to censor material of public interest was made by the *Observer* when, following the assassination of President Kennedy in 1963, Lyndon B. Johnson became President of the United States. The BBC broadcast in its TV programme *Panorama* an interview which Johnson had given to a local Texas TV station, which showed him in a very relaxed mood when explaining his somewhat simplistic view of the role of the United States in the world. The *Observer*'s complaint was that the interviewing was shown without 'explaining to British viewers that this (interview) was no more representative of his political attitudes than "Housewives' Choice" is of the BBC's musical standards'.

The extent of overt external political pressure on the BBC is difficult to assess. It clearly exists on occasion. Thus, in 1969, a curious event took place when the Secretary General of NATO persuaded Tyne Tees Television, ultimately with the backing of the Minister of Defence, not to show a film made for them.

But it is worth noting the comment in the field of political censorship by J. Denis Forman, Joint Managing Director of Granada, made in 1967:

There remains one major doubt about the independence of television from political censorship, or at least from political influence. This doubt lies in the peculiar English method of censorship by association.

The old Establishment which lives on in the clubs and the great houses has been joined in an uneasy alliance by a new lot which includes politicians of both parties, academics who advise, chairmen of great companies who are consulted, and scientists who can bridge the gap between true knowledge and common understanding.

These are our new aristocracy, or as they would prefer it, meritocracy. Amidst the new nexus of power there has appeared a tendency (so common with the old upper classes) to appoint one of themselves – a 'sound' man, a man who can be trusted to work the machine – in key posts as they fall vacant.

Let me be clear, there is no element of Tammany Hall about this. It is the result of proper and enlightened decisions taken constitutionally by appropriate ministers.

But when the type of appointment is extended to the control of the major means of communication, the result must raise a flutter of alarm in the breasts of independent souls like you and me.

There was a time when Sir John Reith was in charge of the BBC and some years later Sir Kenneth Clark at the head of ITA. Neither owed any allegiance to Westminster. Indeed in the one case the allegiance was only to God and in the other to a most marvellously balanced sense of aesthetic and social values.

The day of the knights, however, has passed and television is now living with lords. We have Lord Hill, appointed to the ITA by Harold Macmillan, reappointed to the BBC by Harold Wilson, and at the same time we have Lord Aylestone (Herbert Bowden to you and me) appointed to head the ITA.

Neither of these noble lords has shown or will show the slightest inclination to allow his background as a professional politician to influence him in the way he discharges his duties. For one thing they are far too good politicians for that to happen.

Yet, nevertheless, television is becoming linked, by way of an old boy network, to Westminster.

It is no good shouting before you are hurt, and we have not been hurt, yet. Least of all has there been any indication of political censorship. The shadow is no bigger than a peer's hand. But it is something to watch, for censorship is never more insidious than when it does not appear to exist.

Disentangling the respective roles of official pressure from outside the BBC and the BBC's own editorial policy (though as Mr Forman implies, the Old (Political) Boy Network means that these two may often be indistinguishable) is not easy. Thus when in 1965 the BBC decided not to put on Peter Watkins film, *The War Game*, which it had itself commissioned, about the effects of a nuclear war on Britain, Sir Hugh Carleton Greene denied that the decision was anything other than the BBC's 'own, independent, decision not to show the programme'. Then, referring to the fact that the film had been shown privately to representatives of the Home Office, he said:

The fact that some people outside the BBC saw the film does not mean that any pressure was put on us. This is a not uncommon form of consultation, as any editor must know, but no pressure at all was put on us.

In 1968, a film on police relations with immigrants, in the series *Cause for Concern*, was withdrawn temporarily after the police had seen a special showing and been given a copy of the script. The police took a very dim view of what they regarded as an unfair and biased attack upon them. After some considerable hesitation, and having delayed it 'on legal and other grounds', the BBC eventually persuaded the police to take part in the programme and in the discussion which followed its showing.

At the time of the Anglo-French attack on Egypt in 1956, the Prime Minister, Sir Anthony Eden, sought to persuade the BBC that what was involved was a national war, and that the BBC should voluntarily submit to censorship of a wartime type. The BBC refused.

Influence of an official character does occur in relation to controversial political broadcasting, in this case over the choice of politicians to take part in such programmes. This is sometimes done within the party by the Chief Whip issuing instructions to individual party members to limit their appearance in particular programmes. In the 1966 election, an instruction was sent out to Labour MPs that if they were invited to take part in radio and television programmes, they should see the Chief Whip first. Mr Woodrow Wyatt, MP, who had been invited to take part in a programme on commercial television during this period was forbidden to do so by Transport House, who informed him that if he persisted 'they would exercise their right to speak to the ITV and, in an election period, I wouldn't be allowed to go on'. In June

1970, Michael Stewart, the Foreign and Commonwealth Secretary in the Labour government was stopped by the Labour party from appearing on BBC television's *Panorama* in a discussion with Sir Alec Douglas-Home. Instead, Mr Denis Healey, Secretary of State for Defence, whom Transport House had insistently asked to appear in the programme, replaced Mr Stewart in a separate interview. It was widely believed that, had Labour won the election, Mr Healey would have become Foreign Secretary in Mr. Stewart's place.

Perhaps the most important external control to be exercised over political broadcasting occurs in connection with electoral broadcasts, where the rules for the allocation of radio- and television-time are drawn up by the government and opposition Whips in consultation with the BBC, without any legal rules to guide them. As *The Times* explained in 1966:

Things are decided by a self-constituted committee of the broadcasting authorities and the three big parties, the former trying to cut down the time and the latter cutting it up. The committee is responsible to no one in particular, and having done its work for the immediate future it dissolves, leaving nothing there to take the rap.

Accepting the importance of electoral broadcasts, and that in the past the self-appointed committee laid down rules which effectively prevented the smaller parties from having any time at all (this situation has since improved), it must remain a matter for astonishment that the rules governing the allocation of electoral broadcasting time should have been left to three of the interested parties to decide among themselves, even if in formal consultation with the broadcasting authorities. There was a chance in 1964 that Parliament might have been forced to examine the role of radio and television in elections, and in the event there would probably have had to have been a Royal Commission or some such inquiry, which might have recommended the enactment of rules to protect minority political interests. This occurred when the poet Hugh McDiarmid, stood under his real name of Dr C. M. Grieve as Communist candidate in the same constituency as Sir Alec Douglas-Home, and sought to have Sir Alec's election declared void on the ground that he had aided and abetted the commission of an electoral offence under Section 63 of the Representation of the People Act 1949. Sir Alec had taken part in an electoral broadcast, and Section 63 (I) provides:

No expense shall, with a view to promoting or procuring the election of a candidate at an election, be incurred by any person other than the candidate, his election agent and persons authorized in writing by the election agent on account –

(c) of . . . presenting to the electors the candidate or his views or the extent and nature of his backing or disparaging another candidate. . . .

Newspapers and other periodicals, but not radio or television, were expressly exempted from the prohibition of incurring expenditure in this way. (This anomalous difference has now been removed by the

Representation of the People Act 1969.) It is clear that by applying ordinary principles for the interpretation of statutes, the BBC and ITA had incurred expenditure in violation of the Act, and by appearing Sir Alec had aided and abetted the offence. However, the Election Court avoided unseating Sir Alec by interpreting the Act as referring to the subjective intention of the BBC and ITA, which was, apparently, to give information to the public, instead of applying the more conventional test of objective intention, which would have been to ask what are the natural consequences of what the BBC and ITA had done were, and to assume that they intended these natural consequences. As Professor Street has said:

The B.B.C. and I.T.A. must have known that, when they put on the broadcasts, the intention was to promote the election of those who took part and their fellow candidates throughout the country; they must have known that it is an advantage to a candidate over his opponents in the same constituency if he is allowed a national broadcast and they are not.

Professor Geoffrey Wilson, another constitutional authority, has also drawn attention to a decision of the Court of Criminal Appeal in 1927 in *R.* v. *Hailwood*, in which that court applied the more usual test in somewhat similar circumstances. Mr Justice Avory said in this latter case:

It is not . . . open to a person charged with the doing of acts forbidden by the statute, who has done acts to prejudice one of the candidates which must and must to his knowledge have the effect of promoting the election of other candidates or one of them to say that he never intended his acts to have that effect.

The absurdity of the decision in Dr Grieve's case is that, as a result of trying to be sensible and avoid unseating a Minister of the Crown, the Election Court, instead of applying the ordinary rules of statutory interpretation, interpreted the Act so as to permit what would otherwise have been a violation of the law, thereby removing an urgent need for a public inquiry into the operation of the rules governing electoral broadcasts. Had Sir Alec been unseated, it is probable that instead of electoral broadcasting time being left to the three main parties to allocate chiefly among themselves, there would now exist a rational body of legal rules to govern this area.

Another area in which outside influences affect political broadcasting relates to the selection of interviewers to interview governmental figures. Mr Wilson always insisted, when he was Prime Minister, that ordinary courtesy required that the BBC and ITN should allow him a say in the choice of who should be permitted to interview him.

The overt banning of music by the BBC may be rare but it does occur. One notable example was with respect to the music of Dr Alan Bush, the English Marxist composer. In 1941, Dr Bush had, along with a number of other people distinguished in the arts, including Sir Michael Redgrave, Arnold Goldsborough and André van Gysegham, associated himself with and given support to the People's Convention. The individuals concerned were informed by the BBC that, unless they stated in writing their withdrawal of support for the People's Convention, they would not be permitted to broadcast again. Mr Duff Cooper defended the BBC's action in the House of Commons, saying:

It is not the business of the BBC to ascertain what are the private opinions of artists. But when artists, apart from their artistic activities, take an active part in political agitation they must not expect to be given the great privilege – it is a privilege not a right – of being employed by the BBC.

Dr Ralph Vaughan Williams, at that time the most distinguished living British composer, then wrote a letter of protest to the BBC which was published in *The Times* on 15 March 1941,

Sir, I learn from *The Times* of March 8 that the British Broadcasting Corporation has banned the musical compositions of Dr Alan Bush on account of his political opinions. So far as I know Dr Bush's political views I am strongly opposed to them. Nevertheless I wish to protest against this victimization of private opinion in the only way possible to me. You may remember that the British Broadcasting Corporation have lately done me the honour to commission from me a choral song. I now bid leave to withdraw my offer of this song to the British Broadcasting Corporation. I return the fee which was paid me and ask you to give directions that all manuscript material of the song be returned to me. I will, of course, be responsible for the expenses incurred in its production. I am sending copies of this letter to Sir Adrian Boult and to *The Times*.

Such was the very widespread public outcry, that the ban was withdrawn, though some of the artists concerned were not, in practice, employed by the BBC for a long time thereafter.

Apart from this exceptional instance of an overt ban on music because of the politics of its composer, the BBC also 'bans' or places on a restricted list certain pieces of music because of the words used in such music. Where a record is placed in the restricted list, this may mean in effect banning it, but if a producer wishes to use it, he can ask for special permission, which may be given. Thus Barry McGuire's protest hit 'Eve of Destruction', was banned by the BBC in 1965. More recently pop records which it was believed might encourage young people to experiment with drugs have been banned, such as the Beatles' 'A Day in the Life', from *Sergeant Pepper*, and the Game's 'The Addicted Man'. Northern Irish susceptibilities have been responsible for the banning of such Irish rebel songs as 'Bould Robert Emmet', 'Father Murphy', 'Johnson's Motor Car', 'The Bold Fenian Men' (where the publishers offered to pay the owner of the copyright £200 if she would agree to allow the substitution of 'mountain' for 'Fenian', so as to make it a song about 'The Bold Mountain Men'), and 'Men of the West'.

The position of the BBC employees is such that they may often be subject to pressure to restrain the expression of their personal opinions. This is partly a reflection of the BBC's policy of itself having no editorial line on matters of current affairs. But it can be taken quite far, as when a disc jockey, Mr Kenny Everrett, was dismissed for making remarks in his programme about Mrs John Peyton, the Minister of Transport's wife, having passed her driving test, and also for remarks criticizing BBC's Radio I. There was apparently a term in Mr Everett's contract under which he agreed to say nothing derogatory about the BBC. When Mr David Dimbleby made some *ad lib* remarks during his commentary on the visit of President Nixon to Britain in 1968, the Prime Minister, Mr Wilson, apparently took a very dim view, and protests were lodged, but no action was taken against Mr Dimbleby.

The BBC's rules governing the content of its programmes are in law, largely a matter for its own discretion, so that while there is a code of practice for BBC television on violence (see Appendix 6) this is not a result of any statutory obligation. On the other hand, the Television Act requires the ITA to draw up codes on advertising and on violence (see Appendix 2). Also, of course ITA and the individual companies engaged in commercial television exercise editorial control over programmes to varying degrees. The ITA is subject to the same kind of political pressures as the BBC. Thus an episode in *The Power Game* in 1966 was postponed because of an election. Social criticism in plays may also cause difficulty, as happened with *The Division*, which showed brutality in a naval approved school. On the ostensible grounds of its having scenes 'of prolonged violence and cruelty', the play was postponed for a period, but then, after persuasion by the Guild of British Writers, was shown, uncut, but with an apologia that the events all happened a long time ago and that things were different now in such institutions. Like the BBC the ITA is often sensitive to outside pressure groups, and efforts are made to reduce grounds for complaint. Directives of the kind sent to BBC executives may also be sent to employees of the commercial television companies, warning against the excessive use of swear words and other matters which could give offence to the prudish.

The showing of old films on television gives rise to a number of problems. The fact is that, whereas television audiences may contain a wide span of ages, many films when licensed for the cinema by the British Board of Film Censors may originally have been given an 'X' certificate. The Government has consistently refused to restrict in any way the freedom of ITA and BBC to show such films, leaving it to the authorities concerned to use their own discretion. This has the consequence that one may see on the television screen material which has been refused a certificate or only been given an 'X' certificate by the film censor. This is clearly anomalous, though the anomaly may be lessened by the fact that such films tend not to be shown at family viewing times. They are usually shown late in the evening. Apart, however, from occasional introductory references to their containing scenes unsuitable for the squeamish, television does not adopt any system of classification which would give an indication to those who wished for it of the suitability for various audiences of films and other programmes.

Because films made for the cinema may not have the standard length required to fit neatly into the ordinary television programme schedule, they are often cut to enable them to be fitted into particular vacant periods. This has led to sharp protests being made to both the ITA and the BBC from many notable British film makers, who have objected to the mangled travesties of their work which have been shown on television.

Similar problems have been met with by script-writers, whose scripts have been mangled in the past, but this problem has in some part been resolved by mutual agreement.

So far as the script-writer is personally concerned, it has been dealt with in a very limited way by collective bargains between the Writers' Guild of Great Britain and the relevant television authorities. Thus in an agreement dated 1 July 1969 between the Guild and fourteen commercial television companies (running from Anglia Television Ltd. to Yorkshire Television Ltd) dealing with original teleplays it is provided in Article 9 as follows:

A company shall be entitled to make such reasonable alterations to a script of an original teleplay as it shall consider necessary in the interests of good television production and such other alterations as may be required to enable it to comply with any official requirement of the I.T.A. to such extent as the writer may be unwilling and/or unable to carry out such alterations himself; provided that the writer, if he objects to the proposed alterations, shall be entitled to buy back his script on payment to the company of 50 per cent of the fee already paid to him, provided that the company has not already incurred a legal obligation to a third party.

The Writers' Guild has also got an agreement, dated 1 June 1968, with the BBC covering teleplays, and this provides in Article 9:

When script alterations are necessary it is the intention of the BBC to make every effort to inform and to reach agreement with the Writer and whenever practicable any necessary alterations (other than minor alterations) shall be made by the Writer. Nevertheless the BBC shall at all times have the right to make

(a) minor alterations and
(b) such other alterations as in its opinion are necessary in order to avoid involving the BBC in legal action or bringing the BBC into disrepute.
Any decision under (b) shall be made at a level not below that of Head of Department. It is however agreed that after a script has been accepted by the BBC alterations will not be made by the BBC under (b) unless (i) the Writer, if available when the BBC requires the alterations to be made, has been asked to agree to them but is not willing to do so and (ii) the Writer has had, if he so requests and if the BBC agrees that time permits if rehearsals and transmission are to proceed as planned, an opportunity to be represented by the Guild (or if he is not a member of the Guild by his agent) at a meeting with the BBC to be held within at most 48 hours of the request (excluding weekends). If in such circumstances there is no

agreement about the alterations then the final decision shall rest with the BBC. Apart from the right to make alterations under (a) and (b) above the BBC shall not without the consent of the Writer or his agent (which consent shall not be unreasonably withheld) make any structural alterations as opposed to minor alterations to the script, provided that such consent shall not be necessary in any case where the Writer is for any reason not immediately available for consultation at the time which in the BBC's opinion is the deadline from the production point of view for such alterations to be made if rehearsals and transmission are to proceed as planned.

There is a similar agreement, dated 29 December 1969, between the guild and the BBC to cover series and serials.

The Writers' Guild, which is the trade union which caters specifically for writers who have obtained 'credits' for film and television scripts, in 1962 set up a Censorship Appeals Committee 'because of mounting resentment among TV members (of the Guild) at the way their work was liable to arbitrary mutilation, emasculation and even total suppression, hardly even knowing who had applied the ban and sometimes being given no reason for it'. The objects of the committee, which is *not* a joint committee of members of the guild and the television authorities, are (a) to inquire into the censorship of films and television; (b) to represent members of the guild in censorship disputes, and (c) to 'evolve some bridge mechanism between censors and writers'. The BBC and the committee made a simple verbal agreement as a result of which it was established that a writer who was censored had a right to be informed of the reasons and to put his case, or to have the Guild's Committee on Censorship put it for him, to whoever was responsible for the cut. In any event, there was a right of appeal to the departmental head concerned, and from him to the BBC Head of Drama.

Since the Independent Television Authority does not make programmes itself, the situation was more complicated, but following a meeting between the Guild's Committee and ITA a procedure with limited scope was agreed. Where a programme company forbad scenes, words and so forth, on the grounds that the ITA would not approve of such words or scenes, the writer concerned should be free to ask the company to justify the ban, or to obtain a ruling from the ITA. Where a ban was, in fact, imposed by the ITA on the grounds of its statutory duty, the ITA authority conceded the principle that, if the programme company concerned wished to discuss the ban, it could bring the writer into the discussion. In fact, the Guild's Committee on Censorship has on occasion approached the ITA direct on behalf of a member, and the procedure is interpreted and applied more liberally than its narrow terms might suggest.

In 1967, Mr Frisby, author of a script for a play commissioned by the BBC, successfully invoked an agreement between the BBC and the Screen Writers' Guild under which the BBC had agreed not to make any structural alterations in any play without the author's consent. The

BBC had wished to delete the line spoken by an unmarried pregnant girl, 'My friend Sylv told me it was safe standing up.' Mr Frisby was able to obtain an injunction restraining the BBC from broadcasting the play without this line, which, in his view, had an important place in the play's scheme. It was accepted that the agreement between the Guild and the BBC applied in this instance.

5 Jobs and Censorship

'If you bring in *Lady Chatterley's Lover* to read at work you'll be dismissed instantly'
Notice to employees in a Nottingham hairdressing saloon (1960).

At first sight it might appear that there is no immediate relationship between employment and censorship, but in fact there is often a very close connection. We have defined censorship very broadly as the processes whereby restrictions are imposed upon the collection, dissemination and exchange of information, opinions and ideas. One of the most potent methods whereby restrictions are imposed on the expression of opinions and the exchange of information is in the employment relationship. The opinions held by individuals, while perfectly lawful, may lead to employers refusing to employ them in the first place; or the political opinions of workers may lead to them being denied promotion. In white-collar occupations, the public service, education and business, a person not regarded as a 'sound man' may find that ordinary avenues of advancement are closed to him. In an *Observer* article discussing the activities of a number of propagandist enterprises, including the Economic League, Paul Ferris reported that prospective employers could obtain from the League information 'about trouble-makers and "subversive elements", in particular Communists'.

Many firms that subscribe to it [the Economic League] insist they know nothing about this side of its work. But one very large company which makes a four-figure donation says flatly that the League 'does a hell of a lot of security vetting for us on political grounds. This is their sole use to us, and for x pounds a year, it's good value for money.'

The existence of black-lists of employees used by employers in certain industries is well known. The legal freedom of the employer to dismiss his employees was traditionally subject to a single limitation in this country, namely that, unless the employee was guilty of serious misconduct, the employer had to give him notice to terminate his contract of employment. If he failed to do this, the worker was entitled to recover wages for the period of notice. Since the period of notice required by law was usually very short, there was no effective safeguard against arbitrary dismissal.

Criticism of the employer has often been a reason for dismissal, as happened to one worker who in 1968 wrote a letter to the local press criticizing his employer. Such criticism may be regarded by the employer as being so defamatory as to justify dismissal. An Indian labourer in Leamington Spa was dismissed after he had made allegedly defamatory remarks while seeking advice from the local Citizens' Advice Bureau. His employer's, the Automotive Products Group, explained that he was 'not dismissed for making allegations concerning bribery or corruption, not for being unable to substantiate these when interviewed by AP Management. He was dismissed for making a defamatory statement about one of the company's senior executives.'

Unlimited freedom of dismissal, and unlimited freedom not to take people into employment, has acted as an important deterrent to the free expression of opinion, especially on politics and religion, by employees. The arbitrary right of employers to hire and fire has had a constant, pervasive and subtle effect on the willingness of employees to express their opinions freely.

The Industrial Relations Act 1971 marks a beginning of the introduction into British law of the idea of job-security.* An employee is not to be deprived of his job arbitrarily. Giving effect in a somewhat half-hearted way to Recommendation 119 of the International Labour Organization, passed by its 1963 Conference with the support of the British government, the new statute protects a worker in a limited way against unfair dismissal, once he has been employed for two years. So, during the first two years, he is largely unprotected against arbitrary dismissal, though after this period he is entitled to compensation if he is deprived of his job for any reason not connected with the operational requirements of the firm which employs him – that is, through redundancy, or his own misconduct, or his lack of physical or intellectual competence to perform the job for which he was employed, or for 'some other substantial reason'. This provides protection against dismissal, with or without notice, on the grounds of his religious, political or social views.

The Act does not, of course, give any protection against workers being dismissed on the grounds that their conduct has involved a breach of contract, and the contract of employment may contain express or implied terms to limit an employee's freedom to express his opinions or to exchange information with others. One increasingly common provision in contracts forbids employees to publish anything, or to publish anything relating to the activity in respect of which they are employed, without first submitting it for their employer's approval. In 1966, the Sussex County Cricket Club reproached Ted Dexter,† former Sussex and England cricket captain, for his oversight in not submitting for their approval the manuscript of his book *Ted Dexter Declares* before publication. Under the rules established by the Advisory County Cricket Committee, cricketers are forbidden to publish public pronouncements about cricket without the prior consent

* The Race Relations Act 1968 protects workers against refusal of employment or dismissal on racial grounds, and is not concerned with opinions or attitudes as a ground of non-employment discrimination.

† Mr Dexter, not being a professional player, may not have been an employee; but this episode is a good example of this kind of contractual provision.

of the club for which they play. The secretary of Sussex Cricket Club explained:

The general committee considered the circumstances in which E. R. Dexter's book came to be printed before it was possible to make certain amendments which the county club thought to be desirable after the manuscript had been perused. The committee have pointed out to Mr Dexter in the strongest terms that his action was contrary to the rules which apply to all publications by registered cricketers and have warned him that loss of his registration would result from any further such breach.

What were the matters to which the club objected? Apparently references to Walter Robbins, manager of the MCC team in the West Indies, might have been 'more happily phrased', hearsay evidence should have been avoided in a chapter on 'throwers', and words 'hired men' in relation to umpires should have been deleted.

The Sussex County Cricket Club accepted Dexter's apology for his offence, but the MCC Executive Committee was not so easily lulled into condoning it. They imposed a suspension of Mr Dexter's qualification to play for Sussex for one month. He himself commented on the episode:

Complete freedom of speech may be a myth, but at least speech is freer in this country than anywhere else. You can curse royal garden parties when you are jammed by traffic in the Mall. You can even stick bills in your car urging support for Rhodesia. And you will hear nothing about it from the Queen or the Prime Minister.

Free speech in cricket however is something you must forego if you want to avoid hearing from the M.C.C. I accepted these restrictive regulations when I wanted to play the game, but I doubted their value then, and now I do so again.

A general term prohibiting disclosure of information received is apparently in the contracts of employment of persons employed by the Royal Family, and such terms have been upheld and enforced by High Court order. This occurred in the case of Mr Leo Groden in 1966. Mr Groden, who had been employed as a chef by Princess Margaret and Lord Snowdon, after he had left their employment published an article in a German magazine – copies of which were imported into Britain – containing information acquired in the course of his employment. An injunction was issued restraining Mr Groden from divulging in future information acquired during his time in the Snowdon household, Mr Groden's contract of employment having included a covenant that

he would not, during or after his service, disclose, publish or reveal to any unauthorized persons any incident, conversation, or information concerning any member of the Royal Family or Lord Snowdon or any of their guests or visitors which came to his knowledge by virtue of his employment.

Quite apart from the use of express terms preventing the expression of opinion or the communication to the outside world of certain information – and such terms have now spread far beyond research workers, people engaged in secret processes, etc, to cover categories of employees where the employer has no possible legitimate interest to protect by gagging his employees (other than a desire to inhibit the expression of opinions of which he might disapprove), the law has always been willing to imply a duty of good faith imposed upon all employees, which has the effect of depriving the employee of the right to do anything which might injure the welfare of his employer's business. Thus the duty of good faith has been held to prevent the employee making a private profit for himself out of information he has obtained in the course of his employment, and which the employer might have used to his own advantage had he been aware of it. The limits to the duty not to make a private profit out of information acquired purely as a result of holding a particular post or office are by no means clear; but one would like to see someone bring an action to recover, for the benefit of the state, the profits earned by former Prime Ministers from writing their memoirs and filling them with information which they have acquired solely as a result of their former public office! It is unfortunately doubtful if the duty of good faith would go as far as to apply in such a case.

An obligation not to disclose information acquired in confidence will be readily implied in a contract of employment, but may also be implied in other relationships, even in the absence of a contract. A wife may, under this doctrine of confidentiality, be restrained by a court order from disclosing to newspapers details of her matrimonial life. A company which has in all innocence received certain information from a worker, who in turn acquired it while in the employment of another company, can be prevented from using this information, if it is of a kind which the worker acquired in circumstances making the information confidential.

This duty of non-disclosure may even continue after the relationship of employment has ended. In such circumstances it is also permissible for the former employer to enforce any express term there may have been imposing a restriction on the use of any such knowledge as could be regarded as equivalent to the employer's property (e.g. a knowledge of customers' names and addresses). But restrictions after the employment relationship has ended will be valid only if they are reasonably necessary and no wider in their scope than the smallest restriction necessary to protect the former employer's property interest. During the currency of a contract of employment, there is no restriction on the express terms restricting the employee's freedom to use such knowledge.

Can the disclosure of secret or confidential information be excused as being in the public interest, so mitigating the implied duty not to make a disclosure of secret information to an outsider? It has been held that a contract whereby the employee agrees expressly not to disclose libellous or other defamatory material confided to him can be upheld by the courts. On the other hand, it is not clear at what point an employee can be freed from the implied duty of non-disclosure. Two main issues arise: (a) what kind of information may he disclose without breach of the implied duty of non-disclosure; and (b) to whom may he disclose it; does the reason for its disclosure make any difference, e.g. if the information is sold for money to a newspaper? In *Initial Services* v. *Putterill*, the Court of Appeal considered these questions. In this instance an ex-employee had passed certain documents and other information on to a newspaper. An article then appeared which was based on this information. The ex-employer sought, among other things, damages for breach of the implied duty not to disclose confidential information. The employee sought to justify his action by claiming that he had disclosed information which showed (a) that his former employer was in breach of provisions of the Restrictive Trade Practices Act 1956, which required him to register a restrictive business agreement to which he was a party; and (b) that the employer had made statements about price increases which were misleading to customers. The court held that, in the circumstances, this information was of a kind that it was in the public interest for the ex-employee to be free to disclose. Lord Denning, the Master of the Rolls, apparently thought on the other hand that such information ought to be disclosed only to the proper authorities – that is, the Registrar of the Restrictive Practices Court – but without expressly saying so, he seems also to have assumed that disclosure to the press was equally permissible. Lord Denning said that the exceptions to the duty of non-disclosure covered not only the situation where the employer was guilty of a crime or fraud, but extended to any misconduct of such a nature that it ought, in the public interest, to be disclosed to others. He then added cryptically:

I say nothing as to what the position would be if he disclosed it out of malice or sold it to a newspaper for money or reward. That indeed would be a different matter. It is a great evil when people purvey scandalous information for reward.

There are certain kinds of employment where the power of the employer to dismiss or control the activities of the employee raise special problems. One of these concerns persons employed in the mass media. In March 1969 *The Times* 'Diary' published the following report:

The B.B.C. has stopped publication of a rumbustious Fabian pamphlet arguing the case against local commercial radio by Mr Phil Sidey, manager of Radio Leeds, one of the B.B.C.'s eight experimental local radio stations.
I understand that the B.B.C. did not dislike the pamphlet. They simply did not want one of their men to be publicly associated with a political group, and are quite willing for it to be published elsewhere.

Mr Kimche, editor for many years of the *Jewish Observer and Middle-East Review*, was dismissed in 1967 after a disagreement over his wish to publish an article on unemployment in Israel. The *Review* commented, after the dismissal:

It may be suggested that the real issue in the present controversy was the resolve of the Board of Directors of the Zionist Review Limited to insist on their freedom to protect the rights of the British Zionist Movement. . . .

Employment by political, religious or other groups is commonly associated with a contractual obligation to submit writings to the group for prior approval, or, with an obligation not to do, write or say anything damaging to the group's reputation. Where there is a contractual obligation of this kind, dismissal may occur on the ground that publication of unauthorized books or articles critical of the employing organization was a breach of the employee's contract. Sometimes, especially where there is no contractual term of this kind, dismissal still occurs because of the publication by the employee of views unacceptable to his employer.

In the teaching profession generally, and particularly in higher education, the need to protect the right of employees to express opinions and communicate information is a vitally important aspect of academic freedom. The Blackburn case at the London School of Economics (when Mr Robin Blackburn was dismissed for having expressed approval of the removal by students of certain gates objectionable to them – approval expressed *after* the event – and for having made a general statement supporting direct action, both of which seem to have been equated with support 'for a policy of violence'), has been followed by a number of other disquieting examples, from which it becomes clear that the opinions of teachers may disqualify them from promotion or even continued employment in the academic field. In 1971 an English teacher, Christopher Searle, was dismissed from his post at a London East End school because he had published some of his pupils' verse. One objection apparently was that the anthology was not 'balanced'. It should have shown the light as well as the dark. As a result of a High Court action the first notice of dismissal had to be withdrawn. The Governors of the school were not deterred by this from issuing a statement of their intention to dismiss Mr Searle, properly, by giving him notice a second time in 1972. (At the time of writing, March 1972, this notice awaits confirmation by the Inner London Education Authority.)

A more subtle form of pressure limiting the freedom of political opinion and action by university teachers and students is to be found in the events at Warwick University in 1969/70. Not only did the vice-chancellor exercise his power to refuse admission to a student, on the grounds, apparently, that his headmaster had sent a further report to the vice-chancellor of the student's 'preoccupation with student politics', but Lord Radcliffe in his first Report into the procedures followed 'in the university with regard to receiving and retaining of information about political activities of the staff and students', suggested that it would be proper for the vice-chancellor, having received complaints about the quite lawful political activities of staff and students from outside sources, 'to take up the complaint with those concerned and ask them whether their line of action is helpful to the university's interest in the long run'. In other words, it is proper for the head of a university to discourage his staff from taking part in lawful political action of a kind which gives offence to local businessmen.

It would be wrong to assume that pressure by academic authorities restricting the expression of opinion by others is confined to restricting the 'politically subversive'. In February 1969, three London University students who organized a petition against the demolition of Woburn Square for redevelopment by the university, received a letter from the Warden of Connaught Hall, Professor D. M. Lang, where they lived. The letter said in part:

The Principal of the University has already asked for a list of the names of the main instigators [of the petition] and the Colleges to which they belong.

As Warden of this University Hall, I must state that this course of conduct constitutes a source of grave embarrassment, both to me personally, and to the University at large.

After the defeat of the motion on preservation of Woburn Square in Convocation last week, I would like to ask whether you are prepared to withdraw the petition which you submitted to the Minister of Housing and Local Government, and to give an undertaking to desist from this form of action in future.

Because the state is the largest single employer in the country, and because it also can influence the employment policy of the nationalized industries – not to mention the policies followed by businessmen who have contracts to supply goods and services to the state – its attitudes are of the utmost importance in the field of what we may call 'job censorship'. In the public service itself, the threat of the loss of pension rights represents one of the most potent disciplinary weapons. It provides forceful backing to restrictions on freedom of expression by public officials. Inside the civil service, well-understood rules prevent, to various degrees, civil servants from participating in ordinary political activity, and there are also restrictions upon their freedom to express opinions on matters of governmental policy in public, and to communicate official information to the outside world. Although, from time to time, lip service has been paid to giving civil servants greater political freedom, there has been remarkably little change over the past few years in most government departments.

One remarkable example of the practical limitation on the freedom of public servants to express opinions freely, even when the public interest demands that they should do so, occurred in the police service in the early 1960s. In 1962, the Royal Commission on the Police reported that opinion within the police force opposed the idea of any alteration to the system whereby the police themselves are primarily responsible for investigating complaints against themselves. But this was only on the surface. In a report of an inquiry, into a police inquiry, by Mr Mars-Jones, QC, published in 1964, it was recorded that a number of police officers had in fact expressed a wish to voice their opinions on a number of matters, including the investigation of complaints against the police, to the Royal Commission on the Police. This, according to Mr Mars-Jones, is what happened:

They consulted various people . . . as to how they could give evidence before the Royal Commission *without prejudicing their own prospects of promotion or risking the possibility of disciplinary proceedings. This problem proved to be an intractable one and it was not found possible to find a means whereby they could submit memoranda or give evidence to the Royal Commission which would not endanger their future or their pensions.* [Italics added.]

A provision commonly found in government contracts, especially in building and construction contracts, is one which allows a government department which has a contract with an outside employer to require the employer to dismiss a named employee. The department does not have to give any reason for its demand, and the outside employer must comply. Section 159 of the Industrial Relations Act 1971 backs this up by providing that, where a worker complains of having been the victim of an unfair dismissal, it is to be a complete defence to the employer if it can be shown that the dismissal was taken to safeguard national security, and a certificate from a Minister is to be *conclusive evidence* of the fact that the dismissal was in the interests of national security. Alternatively, even if the dismissal was not ordered to protect national security, the dismissed worker is still to be denied a remedy if a Minister certifies that information required by the worker to substantiate his claim cannot be revealed because its disclosure would be against the national interests. This right to deny a dismissed worker a remedy is not confined to cases where the state is the employer; it actually applies to dismissal by any employer, whether private or public. The dangers in this kind of statutory provision are underlined in a revelation by the Campaign against Secret Police Powers that the security service do approach employers about the alleged undesirable political opinions of particular employees, with the consequence that such employees may suddenly find themselves out of work. Sometimes the security services make a mistake, and persons who lose their jobs may not in fact hold the 'subversive views' which the security service alleged against them.

A legal restriction on the disclosure of information by employees which has not operated in the public interest can be illustrated by the case of *Bent's Brewery* v. *Hogan*, decided in 1945. Here the court decided that it was a civil wrong for a trade union official, when considering the preparation of a wage claim on behalf of his members, to solicit from them information about the business turnover of their employers. Yet if the unions lack detailed information on the financial state of the employers with whom they are negotiating terms and conditions of employment for their members, realistic and effective collective bargaining is restricted. The Industrial Relations Act 1971, Section 56, now requires employers to disclose to trade union representatives all such information as *both* represents information without which the trade union representatives would be impeded in carrying on collective bargaining, as well as information which it is in accord with good industrial relations practice for the employer to disclose. What is considered to constitute good industrial relations practice in this context will be known only when the Secretary of State for Employment and Productivity has published an amended version of his *Code of Industrial Relations Practice*, under Section 2 of the Industrial Relations Act 1971.

In general, we can see that the pressure exerted by employers, public and private, is in practice a very important means of repressing the free expression of opinion and the communication of information. Because this pressure so often takes the form of it being made clear to the employee that persistence in a particular line of action or thought may operate to his future detriment where promotion, pension rights and so on are concerned it is often extremely difficult to document, but sufficient may have been said here to indicate that 'job censorship' is a significant aspect of censorship in Britain. In the related field of collective bargaining, the restrictive rules concerning disclosures of confidential information by employees to outsiders have, in the past, interfered with the establishment of effective collective bargaining.

6 Official Secrecy

From what has already been said, it will be clear that Britain shows an unusual attachment to the idea that secrecy for official activities is on principle a good thing. Of course, there are secrets which most would agree should, in the public interest, remain secret. But the wider the range of information which is given special protection, the greater the possibility of abuse; and the greater also the risk of secrecy being used to stifle criticisms of official action, thereby lessening the chances of public opinion in any way influencing governmental activity. This chapter will emphasize that the cloak of secrecy in Britain is, in fact, cast over official action in ways which do not always serve the public interest.

Central Government

We have already seen the D Notice system in operation in Chapter 3. Speaking in November 1967, in a talk on press freedom and national security, Mr Chapman Pincher gave as his opinion that what was intended as a genuinely voluntary system, with give and take on both sides, had become an instrument intended to apply on the government's say-so. Leaving aside the abuses of the D Notice system, there was also the occasion when it was revealed that deletions had been requested or suggested by the Ministry of Defence in the Report of the Select Committee of the House of Commons after its visits to chemical and biological establishments. The Ministry comments were made public in a Report of the Committee of Privileges. One paragraph suggesting deletion of a particular passage ran as follows:

There can be no possible objection on security grounds in the normally accepted sense of that expression to publication of this information. Indeed, I think there have been references elsewhere to the university contracts. Our advice would be to publish, but it is for consideration whether the indirect reference to the insecticide firm .... and to universities is desirable in present circumstances when there is a great deal of criticism of Porton (where government research in biological and chemical warfare is carried on).

Governmental secrecy extends far beyond areas in which there can be anything in the nature of a military secret to protect. Examples are abundant. In 1965, teachers attending a conference on English organized by the Department of Education and Science were issued with the following notice:

No account of the conference may be published without the prior approval of the Department of Education and Science.

When Jack Ashley, M.P., asked on 23 November 1971 that the Secretary of State for Social Services should publish information as to the amount spent by local authorities per registered disabled person on services for such persons, he was told that it was 'not possible to provide any figures of expenditure per registered disabled person *without inviting misleading comparisons*, and this I am not prepared to do'. Somewhat disturbed by the implications of this answer – that information will not be given by a Minister if it is open to misleading interpretation – Mr Ashley wrote to the Prime Minister, who in turn stonewalled. Mr Heath wrote in reply that figures previously published had been used to draw unwarranted conclusions about the relative performance of individual local authorities. The decision not to reveal similar figures for 1970–71 was right because they could have been used in the same misleading way, added Mr Heath, although he also insisted that there was 'no question on concealing information of public importance'.

But it is in this area of social security itself that secrecy becomes a significant factor in the operation of the Welfare State. Under the National Insurance Act 1965 and the National Insurance (Industrial Injuries) Act 1965 people who are in need, as a result of such personal catastrophies as widowhood, ill-health or accidents at work, are entitled to a wide range of social security benefits. The law embodied in these two statutes, in their accompanying regulations and in the mass of decisions of courts and National Insurance Commissioners, constitutes what is probably the single most complex area of English law. The civil servants who administer it, and, in particular, the Insurance Officers who make the decisions in case of application for benefit, are supplied by the Department of Health and Social Security with a book which guides them through this maze. This book, which represents the Department's understanding of what the legal rules mean, is a secret and confidential document that is not to be revealed to members of the public.

Similarly under the Ministry of Social Security Act 1966, which provides for supplementary benefits to be paid to those who do not qualify for benefit under the two National Insurance Acts of 1965, the officers deciding the questioning of whether to grant supplementary benefit, and, if so, how much, are supplied by the department with written instructions, in this case telling them how their discretion to grant or withhold supplementary benefit should be exercised. While the guide to the National Insurance Acts explains to the official what the law means, the guide to officials deciding questions of entitlement to supplementary benefit tells them *how* they should exercise the discretion which the law gives them, without the law defining the manner of the exercise in any great detail. Both books are secret, but their non-disclosure to the public raises special problems. Under National Insurance it is of great importance to would-be recipients and their advisers to know how the department interprets the law. Of even greater importance in the case of supplementary benefit – where the legal rules are few – it is essential to would-be recipients and their advisers to know the principles according to which official discretion is exercised. The problem referred to here has been *partially* ameliorated by the publication by the Department of Health and Social Security of the *Supplementary Benefits Handbook* (1970, revised edition, 1971). Without such information, people cannot know what their entitlements are. Without such information it is impossible to know whether or not discretions are being exercised in a lawful or proper manner.

When, in 1967, an official inquiry was conducted into the circumstances of certain families receiving supplementary benefit it was accidently revealed that, when the amount of supplementary benefit was fixed for families in desperate need, a notional deduction of 7s. 6d. was made to represent the amount which the unemployed family breadwinner would have had to spend on travelling to work, had he been going to work. There was no legal provision in the statute to provide for such a deduction, and it was entirely an invention of the administrators. Once revealed, of course, it was forthwith abandoned. We cannot know, as long as the Department's official guide to its own civil servants remains secret, whether or not other unlawful practices are at present being operated.

Local Government

The Official Secrets Acts, and, one assumes, the D Notice system, has no application to the activities of local government. The Public Bodies (Admission to Meetings) Act 1960 makes provision for admitting of the public to meetings of local authorities, and simultaneously authorizes their exclusion.

1 (1) Subject to subsection (2) below, any meeting of a local authority or other body exercising public functions, being an authority or other body to which this Act applies, shall be open to the public.

(2) A body may, by resolution, exclude the public from a meeting (whether during the whole or part of the proceedings) whenever publicity would be prejudicial to the public interest by reason of the confidential nature of the business to be transacted or for other special reasons stated in the resolution and arising from the nature of that business or of the proceedings; and where such a resolution is passed, this Act shall not require the meeting to be open to the public during proceedings to which the resolution applies.

Such right as there is to attend meetings of local authorities does not, with the exception of education committees and joint committees of two or more local authorities, extend to meetings of smaller committees. The exception represents an important safeguard to help the public obtain the information through which criticism and control of local authorities can be exercised, but since it does not extend to smaller committees, it does not offer as much protection as the public interest would seem to require.

The Courts

The courts are given special protection against public criticism by the doctrine of contempt of court. In recent years there have been suggestions that the scope of contempt of court should be extended to include the activities of tribunals of inquiry – bodies set up under an Act of 1921 to conduct public investigations into some matter of concern. After the Aberfan disaster in 1966, for instance, a tribunal of inquiry was set up to investigate the disaster. Sir Elwyn Jones, the Attorney-General, said in Parliament:

The tribunal having been established with wide terms of reference, it is highly undesirable that any comments should be made in the press or on radio or television on matters which it will be the express function of the tribunal to investigate.

This threat provoked widespread protest from bodies including the Press Council, and in 1968 the Bar Council proposed that the publication of information and comment on matters that have been referred to a tribunal of inquiry should not be restricted by the rules of contempt of court. A committee set up to investigate the law of contempt as it relates to tribunals of inquiry urged that freedom of comment should be allowed to press and public alike in investigations by such tribunals. This report awaits implementation by Act of Parliament.

One curious piece of information supplied to judges in criminal cases – in confidence and not to be made public – is a copy of the accused's previous record. This explains in part why the statue of justice on the top of the Old Bailey in London is not blindfolded, as she is in other countries. Justice in Britain is, in this important respect at least, not blind. If the judge in a criminal case wishes to know whether the accused has a previous criminal record, he has only to read the information supplied to him. In one extraordinary instance in 1970, after an accused person had been acquitted of a motoring offence, Mr Justice Bean, of the Manchester Crown Court, turned to the man acquitted and said:

I want you to know that if this jury had found you guilty I would have sent you to prison.
What you and I know but what the jury did not is that this is the fourth time you have been caught driving when you were not qualified to drive. And it is the second time you have driven on after an accident.

An important safeguard for the proper administration of justice in Britain is that justice is administered in public, and, subject to the uncertain scope of contempt of court, the conduct of judges can be made a matter for public criticism. There are, however, a number of important limitations. First, certain proceedings may be held *in camera* – certain parts of the trials of persons accused of offences under the Official Secrets Acts, for example. But such trials from which the public is excluded are very exceptional.

Secondly, there appears to be a widespread practice of preventing the taking of notes during trial proceedings, as happened at the trial of a number of Cambridge students which arose out of a riot in protest against the Greek Government in Cambridge in 1970, held before Mr Justice Melford Stevenson. A number of members of the public were prohibited from note-taking by policemen acting as court ushers. There seems to be no legal authority for such a restriction on the freedom of members of the public, unless, of course, it is to be found in the whim of the judge. But in the Cambridge case it is not known whether or not the ushers acted on their own initiative.

Thirdly, if serious and responsible comments on the conduct of a criminal trial are to be made, it is often necessary for anyone wishing to write such an account or criticism to have access to a transcript of the proceedings. These transcripts are available, but, besides the very substantial fee which is charged for them, they are ordinarily only available to the parties involved in the case and their legal advisers. A journalist wishing to obtain a transcript has to seek official permission to purchase it; and as was shown when Mr Ludovic Kennedy was writing a book on the trial of Dr Stephen Ward, there is no obligation on the Attorney General to give such permission, and in this case permission was arbitrarily refused. Other writers have been more fortunate.

Fourthly, the one body of men and women who need have no fear of contempt of court and who may speak their minds more freely than the rest of the community, namely Members of Parliament, are subject to a rule which in this area takes away that very freedom of comment. No Member of Parliament may raise in the House of Commons any question relating to the conduct of an individual judge, unless it takes the form of moving a motion that the judge should be removed from office for having been guilty of serious misbehaviour. Thus, even though it can be argued that the public criticism of the activities of judges is an essential safeguard for the maintenance of high judicial standards, freedom of comment is, in practice, severely restricted.

A curious example of censorship occurs in respect of persons serving prison sentences. In 1965, rules were promulgated regulating the circumstances in which prisoners and inmates of borstals and detention centres may write books *during their sentences.*

Prisoners or inmates who wished to write a book while in custody may do so and the book may be published after release, provided there is no reference to prison conditions, members of the staff, fellow prisoners, or former prisoners. A manuscript may not be sent out of prison during the writer's sentence.

Books or diaries written by prisoners while in custody are regarded as prison property. This, at any rate, was the reason given for refusing to allow Peter Kroger, convicted as a spy, to take some notebooks with him, when he was exchanged with Gerald Brooke, who, ironically, brought back more than twenty prison notebooks with him on his return from a Russian gaol.

Public records

One important aspect of governmental secrecy, which not only inhibits adequate discussion of public issues, but also frustrates the historian, is the series of restrictions placed upon access to the documents and papers of government departments, and, above all, upon Cabinet documents. No civilized country is as wedded to secrecy for official documents as is Britain. Yet such secrecy is hardly essential to the proper functioning of a civilized country, as can be seen from the example of Sweden, where, in principle, *all* public documents are open to *all* persons who wish to see them subject to certain narrowly defined exceptions. In Britain, in principle nobody is allowed to see any official documents, unless it has to be made public for some unfortunate reason. This attachment to secrecy is not easy to explain, but it is a belief widely enough held to extend to the House of Lords, which in the *Thetis* case (*Duncan* v. *Cammell Laird*, 1942) laid down that there was *a class* of documents whose secrecy was so essential to the proper functioning of the public service that, if the state so wished, it could refuse to disclose the contents of any document belonging to such a class to a court, notwithstanding that the document might be relevant to an issue before the court. The ground given to justify this secrecy was that,

the public interest requires a particular class of communications with, or within, a public department to be protected from production [to the courts] on the ground that the candour and completeness of such communications might be prejudiced if they were ever liable to be disclosed in subsequent litigation rather than on the contents of the particular document itself.

Spurred on by some adroit manoeuvring by the Master of the Rolls, Lord Denning, the House of Lords laid down in 1968 that, in ordinary cases the claim of the state to maintain the secrecy of any document would not be conclusive, but that the court itself would have the right to examine the document, and in the light of that examination, weighing up the public interest in the fair administration of justice against the public interest that documents should remain secret where their disclosure would be damaging to the national interest, to decide whether their contents should be disclosed. But then the House of Lords went on to indicate that there were certain, unspecified, classes of documents, 'which ought not to be disclosed whatever their contents may be', as Lord Reid said. In explaining this, he went on to make some revealing remarks.

Virtually everyone agrees that cabinet minutes and the like ought not to be disclosed until such time as they are only of historical interest; but I do not think that many people would give as the reason that premature disclosure would prevent candour in the cabinet. To my mind the most important reason is that such disclosure would create or fan ill-informed or captious public or political criticism. The business of government is difficult enough as it is, and no government could contemplate with equanimity the inner workings of the government machine being exposed to the gaze of those ready to criticise without adequate knowledge of the background and perhaps with some axe to grind. That must in my view also apply to all documents concerned with policy making within departments including it may be minutes and the like by quite junior officials and correspondence with outside bodies. . . .

No italics are necessary to emphasize the extraordinary nature of what is being said – namely, that there is a public interest which demands that the court shall shield the government from public criticism.

Under the Public Records Acts 1958 and 1967, records of the Cabinet and central government departments are placed in the Public Record Office, where, in general, they are open to public inspection after thirty years have elapsed from the January following the year in which they were first made. This is subject to a power vested in the Lord Chancellor to lengthen or shorten the period of non-disclosure on the request of a Minister. This statement is, however, misleading in several ways. First of all, a constant sieving process goes on inside every government department that involve the destruction of very many of the documents created in the course of government business. The sheer bulk of paper involved clearly necessitates the destruction of a large proportion of the material, because it would be quite impossible to find the space to store it. Indeed, most of it is of no interest to anyone. But we must be aware that this sieving process may also lead to the deliberate destruction of documents* which might either cast a discreditable light upon governmental action in the past, or disclose that governmental methods have been in operation in the past which it would wish to avoid disclosing to the public, in case such disclosure should suggest the possibility that such methods continued in use. It would be naïve to suppose that this has never happened, and those who care to spend time with the public records left behind by the British authorities on their departure from Ireland may find evidence to suggest that there are certain police methods which have been used in the past, and which are in operation today, that no current government, Irish or British, would wish to be disclosed. It is, in fact with respect to police matters, or to issues involving political minorities and rebellions, that one finds a further qualification to the thirty-year rule. The records, for example, of the courts-martial of leaders of the unsuccessful Irish rising at Easter 1916 are subject, as criminal proceedings, to a hundred-year rule.

In 1967 the Lord Chancellor, Lord Gardiner, explained the criteria upon which variations of the basic thirty-year closed period are likely to be made.

* For a suggestion going beyond mere destruction to the possibility of Cabinet records being 'doctored', see J. Barry, "1940: cooking the Records?", *Sunday Times*, 3 January 1971.

Those for which longer periods have been prescribed fall into the following categories: first, those containing information about individuals whose disclosure would cause distress or embarrassment to living persons or their immediate descendants (such as criminal or prison records, records of courts martial, records of suspected persons, and certain police records); secondly, those containing information obtained under a pledge of confidence, such as the census, and various individual returns used in publishing statistical compilations; thirdly, certain papers relating to Irish affairs; fourthly, certain exceptionally sensitive papers which affect the security of the State. In addition certain papers, the ownership of which is shared with "old" Commonwealth countries, cannot be released until all the Governments concerned have given their consent.

One oddity of the British closed-period is that identical information can sometimes be found in 'open' foreign documents, and it is difficult to see why authors should not use such material, subject always to the quirks of the operation of the Official Secrets Acts. But such a situation can be a source of concern to an author. According to 'Atticus' in the *Sunday Times*, in 1966 this problem faced Mr J. Bennett in respect of his book, *British Broadcasting and the Danish Resistance, 1940–1945*. He wished to use two pieces of information which fell inside the British closed-period but were easily available in Denmark. The precaution taken by Mr Bennett is recorded by 'Atticus':

. . . Mr Bennett went to the D Notices committee who look after such things in Britain. They realised that there was not much they could do about it, so they quickly 'declassified' the secrets, which they can do if the secrets aren't against the public interest.

This provides an odd side-light on the way in which informal censorship bodies tend to extend their jurisdiction to matters which appear at first sight to be none of their business, so far as the functions of the D Notice Committee have been explained to the public.

It is, however, only lesser mortals who have to worry about D Notices, Official Secrets Acts, closed-periods for official documents and so forth. In November 1968, Mr Sydney Silverman, M.P., told the Prime Minister that former Cabinet Ministers were able to side-step the bars on publication of official Cabinet documents by talking about Cabinet activities rather than quoting cabinet documents. In reply, Mr Wilson agreed that there were many examples of such evasions of the rules. He then added:

There was one published last year which seriously broke all the conventions of collective responsibility and the usual rules and restrictions applied to this [kind of] publication.

7 Why Censorship?

'[A]n overwhelming case can be made out for the statement that no nation can prosper or even continue to exist without heretics and advocates of shockingly immoral doctrines'
George Bernard Shaw

Censorship – does it exist? After many pages, we come absurdly to this question, because there are still some who deny the existence of censorship in Britain. Speaking in 1967, a publisher and former Governor of the BBC, Mr (now Sir) Robert Lusty, said:

A contagious conspiracy of nonsense on the subject of censorship in general and of the printed word in particular seems regularly to be engendered for the confusion of the public at large. There is such an epidemic at the moment. Apart from a censorship for purposes of national security it cannot be too often repeated that there exists no censorship of the printed word in this country.

The only justification for such a view is that it must be based upon a very restricted view of the term 'censorship'. But as we have seen, if by censorship we mean restrictions placed upon the expression of opinion or the communication of information, censorship in Britain takes innumerable forms. Censorship is to many an emotive word, but in this book there has been no intention to use it in this way, for obviously certain restrictions upon the expression of opinion and upon the communication of information remain desirable, if not essential, to life in a civilized community. But the essence of a rational, civilized society is that restrictions should be imposed on rational grounds, and that any restrictions can be shown to be reasonably necessary for the protection of the interests and values upon which that particular society is based. The problem is where to draw the line, and what sanctions should be imposed upon those who transgress it.

The essence of the rules and practices involved in censorship in Britain is that they have never as a whole been subjected to scrutiny to test the issue of whether or not particular restrictions are socially justified. Indeed, any general scrutiny of censorship in this country has always been carefully avoided. When the author was invited to take part in an unscripted television debate on censorship in the theatre, before the debate began a somewhat embarrassed producer informed the participants that the recording of the debate would not be transmitted later in the evening if the discussion wandered from the field of theatrical censorship to broader issues – in particular, to the topic of censorship on television itself. When both Houses of Parliament set up a committee in 1967 to inquire into theatrical censorship, considerable precautions were taken to ensure that the inquiry did not open up a public inquiry into the overall operation of censorship outside the entertainment industry.

If we are to reply to the question, Does censorship exist in Britain? we have to answer that of course it exists, and that its operation, as we have seen, takes many extraordinary forms. Censorship as practised in this country consists of an extraordinary amalgam of sense and nonsense, of enlightenment and cruelty, of stupidity and absurdity, which could never be justified as a whole by any sensible person. Very many of the restrictions which exist today are a hangover from earlier traditions, and are often based on no rational principle whatever. Many restrictions are based upon irrational motives which are irrelevant as justifications. Other restrictions can find their justification only in the role they have to play in protecting the existing social and political *status quo*, and in shielding it from serious and effective criticism. Others may be justified on the ground that they protect information – public or private – which has to be protected if the kind of society in which we live today is to continue. Yet others, if they are justified at all, find their *raison d'être* in the need to protect the younger and more susceptible members of the community. Yet it is impossible to avoid the impression that a good many of these restrictions are, in modern terms, wholly irrational, and except to the most traditionally minded members of the community, are not truly relevant even to the preservation of the social *status quo*.

A number of institutions are specially shielded from criticism. There are, as we have seen, the police. When Mr Michael Schofield, a member of the Government's Advisory Committee on Drug Dependence, and himself an authority on the problems of young people, contributed an 'afterword' to a book critical of the police treatment of young people accused of drug offences, he was asked to resign from the committee. All groups when attacked or criticized are apt to over-react to the outsider who criticizes them, but over-reaction in the case of the police is specially significant. Not only do the police continue to be responsible for investigation of complaints against themselves, but also their over-reaction makes investigation by sociologists into their activities extremely difficult. It has been a not uncommon experience of research workers investigating the practices of such officials as the police to find that continued cooperation by these officials in future investigations of the same kind is dependent upon their producing reports which are not over-critical of the operations concerned. This can only make informed, dispassionate discussion of the activities of public officials, if it is to be based upon sociological investigation, extremely difficult.

An example of what can happen to material in any way critical of one of these specially protected institutions was reported by the *Sunday Times* of 13 December 1969, dealing with a play that was eventually performed on ITV for the first time on 15 December 1970. This play,

The Day They Buried Cleaver, according to the report, with some exaggeration, 'must be the most-banned play ever produced'.

It was written by Stuart Douglass for Sidney Newman's Armchair Theatre 11 years ago. It was stopped by the ITA of those days who were affronted by any suggestion of bribery in the police force. When Newman went to the BBC he asked the Corporation to put it on, but they said they would lose all their police co-operation with Z-Cars and other such programmes if they did. So Douglass sold it to a film company who, for some reason, submitted it to the Chief Constable of Surrey. He advised strongly against its production, so it was sold to another film company who sent it to Scotland Yard for an opinion: again the answer was Don't Put It On.

At last Granada, in the person of Stables producer Gordon McDougall, recorded it a year ago and it's due to take the air in the final Stables Company production under their deal with Granada. In fairness, one can see what the fuss has all been about: although author Douglass maintains that it's a play about corruption in society in general, it does make one wonder just how many policemen are bent. John Fraser is particularly convincing as a sadistic sergeant; equally impressive is David Langton as the Chief. But the final effect is to give one confidence that any irregularities uncovered in the Force are properly dealt with.

Another institution given special protection in Britain is the monarchy. When the Theatres Act was being enacted in 1968, Mr Norman St John-Stevas, to most people a normally liberally minded man, wanted to make it a criminal offence for a playwright to portray any living member of the Royal Family on the stage. His amendment to this effect was defeated. But his proposal symptomized the seemingly deeply ingrained irrational impulse to protect royalty from criticism, or even from offence. When, in 1963, the proprietor of a West End club said to have royalty in its membership, refused to pay for theatrical costumes supplied to him, he explained that the feathered costumes for his chorus girls were inadequate for his purposes:

I wanted feathers, feathers and feathers. Having the Royal Family I cannot have empty spaces on the body.

When the Queen Mother and other members of the Royal Family attended a performance of the film, *The Prime of Miss Jean Brodie*, an extra cut not required by the film censor had to be made in case the same gave offence.

When, at the National Eisteddfod in 1967, a young adjudicator in the satirical poem competition complained of the subject set for the poem, *The Literary Pavilion*, as being too restrictive, his adjudication was cut in the Eisteddfod's official literary publication. He had had the temerity to suggest that, in the satirical poem section, competitors should have more freedom to write about topical subjects, such as 'The inadequacy of the Secretary of State for Wales' or 'Prince Charles's Liking for Polo'.

The protection of royalty is taken very seriously by British representatives abroad. In 1967, the Bell Telephone Company withdrew an advertisement which used a picture of Queen Elizabeth II and the Duke of Edinburgh as a result of protests by the local British consul-general. In the same year, Pye records restricted the sale of a record, *The Reluctant Patriot*, by the Tinkers, to the Irish Republic, because it contained references to Princess Margaret and Lord Snowdon joining the IRA and to Prince Philip playing polo 'on an ass in Stephen's Green'.

More seriously, when Malcolm Muggeridge consulted an eminent lawyer as to whether he could take action for libel against distorted accounts in British newspapers about what he had actually written about the monarchy in the New York *Saturday Evening Post*, he got a not very helpful answer.

There might well have been libel, he said, pacing up and down his office, but I must never forget that, in view of the circumstances, and the particular matter at issue, I could not count upon a jury or judge taking an unprejudiced view. It was eerie and a little alarming to have the theory of 'People's' justice, as administered in Communist countries, thus expounded by this Dickensian figure – winged collar, dark suit, liability to press his finger-tips together – in the antique quiet and tranquillity of one of London's Inns of Court.

Mr Muggeridge's difficulties did not end there. His club, the Garrick, learning that he had made remarks over American television about the monarchy, had applied to be supplied with a transcript of the broadcast so that the 'propriety of a member of the club speaking against the monarchy' might be considered. Mr Muggeridge resigned, and the committee of the club having examined the transcript, ruled that there was nothing to complain of in it.

Judges, Christianity and other organs of the Establishment tend to be protected from criticism in similar irrational, and sometimes even in rational, ways. Examples of acts of censorship in fields entirely unrelated to the ones we have been discussing also abound. In the two examples that follow, it is not easy to understand the motivation of the persons concerned.

In 1966, it was proposed to issue a series of stamps to commemorate the fact that the final stages of the World Football Cup competition were to take place in Britain. Among the sixteen nations to reach the final stages was North Korea. A new 1s. 3d. stamp was designed for the Post Office showing a football surrounded by the flags of the sixteen countries taking part. The Foreign Office objected to the North Korean flag being represented on a British postage stamp, and accordingly another design was substituted.

In the journal, *The Criminologist*, in 1970, the late Dr Thomas Stowell published an article on the identity of 'Jack the Ripper', the Victorian murderer of prostitutes in London's East End. In it he suggested that the murderer had been a member of the Royal Family, and he was understood by some readers to be referring to the Duke of Clarence.

Shortly after the article was published, Stowell died, leaving behind him a folder containing evidence as to the Ripper's identity. Such apparently was the tenderness felt by Stowell's son for the subject matter, that he destroyed the file unread. Explaining his action, T. E. Stowell said:

I read just sufficient to make certain that there was nothing of importance. The family decided that this was the right thing to do. I am not prepared to discuss our grounds for doing so.

My father left no instructions or request on what we were to do with it. I know that he had been interested in this subject for many years, and that it arose again recently – for what reason I don't know. The case doesn't interest me particularly. It was before my time.

The ugliest manifestation of the irrational is probably in the field of race relations, especially when combined with conventional sexual attitudes. For a very long time – that is up to the mid 1960s – the portrayal of the naked human female was forbidden in the cinema, or apparently so. But a moment's reflection shows this to be quite untrue. For a very long time films were always shown, even in the most puritanical parts of the country, containing an abundance of naked women's breasts, but these were the breasts of non-European women, usually appearing in travel pictures, but occasionally in fictional films as well. The non-European breast was not an object which violated the universal prohibition against nudity. Cedric Belfrage has described the impact of the first American director to discover the (commercial) glories of the naked non-European breast:

The first director to make a film of early native life in the South Seas had been welcomed in Hollywood like a king, because without knowing it he had solved the problem of the hour: the problem of how to put breasts on a screen in a way that escapologist society would accept, that is without appearing on the surface to be indecently motivated.

The director had been signed up at once to make more films of native life, and his new employer, putting his arm lovingly round his shoulder and handing him a cigar, had said:

'Now you get right back to those islands and bring me back a screenful of tits.'

When Hollywood had heard of Bali, where women were said to go around exhibiting the most beautifully developed mammary glands in the world, the race to can them on reels of celluloid for retailing to the boobus Americanus at 25 cents an eyeful was on. It had been an edifying commentary on the sudden interest in Bali that the first of these films to be widely shown was called *Goona Goona*, which means 'Magic' in Balinese, but that within a month or two the term 'Goona Goona' had been incorporated in American slang as a new term for the mammary gland or glands of the human female.

The first American film to break through the American ban on North American female nudity in a major fiction feature film was Sidney Lumet's *The Pawnbroker* in 1964. But, it must be added, the beautiful woman who most prominently bared her breasts was American all right, but she was not white.

More recently, a breakthrough occurred with the use of the nude in advertising. Among the earliest example was the advertisement for Elliott's, the boot people, which showed a young woman wearing nothing except a pair of Elliott's boots. Bob Wright, creative director of Dunn-Meynell Keefe, who dreamed up the advertisement explained:

What we uncovered was a deep-rooted desire that both men and women have to associate themselves with a daring idea projected safely from the unattainable. Of course, no woman is going to walk about wearing only a pair of boots. But buying the boots and wearing them gives an emotional identification with someone who has – in this case the model. The use of a non-European model – her name's Hyette, and she comes from Mauritius – acted as a safety valve, preventing total identification because of the wide gap in physical make-up.

On another occasion he put it more bluntly: 'Non-European models don't count as nudes.'

Established organs of opinion still find it difficult to understand the offence which certain accepted attitudes give to minority groups. For many years now one of the most successful BBC variety shows has been *The Black and White Minstrel Show*. Historically the minstrel show, with white performers blacking up their faces, is a product of the social inferiority of the Negro in North America, combined with his social non-acceptability as a performer, although he already had some cultural things which the white man wanted. In 1967, a petition was presented to the BBC asking for an end to the 'hideous impersonation' of *The Black and White Minstrel Show*. The BBC, of course, paid no attention, and the producer of the show, George Inns, was astonished. 'How anyone can read racialism into this show is beyond me.' *The Times* in an editorial deplored the petition, but not in the main because of its merits. 'The main criticism of the petition is one of timing.' Neither *The Times* nor the BBC seemed to understand that the show was an affront to a racial minority in Britain, and that, in a situation of racial tension, to portray members of a minority group in such a stereotyped manner was socially undesirable, if not downright dangerous.

To paraphrase the late Professor Bury, it is a marked feature of the legal rules enforcing censorship, especially in the case of offences like obscenity, blasphemy, seditious libel and even in cases of violation of the Official Secrets Acts, that the policy of enforcing such laws is very largely only against the poor, the uneducated, the friendless and the socially inferior, or against those who address their words and opinion to the masses. Within the ranks of the establishment far greater freedom is tolerated without problems.

Does censorship matter? This is difficult to answer because it is extremely difficult to estimate its effects. In some areas these are well recognized: the almost complete absence of political satire on the stage has been due to the operation in the past of the Lord Chamberlain's authority. The generally uncritical approach of the British people in this country to officialdom, as well as the deadly uniformity of the mass media, is perhaps a result of the operation of censorship. Professor Bury wrote long ago:

Speaking Out is an intellectual duty. Englishmen have a strong sense of political responsibility, and a correspondingly weak sense of intellectual responsibility. Even minds that are not commonplace are affected for the worse by the political spirit which 'is the great force in throwing love of truth and accurate reasoning into a secondary place'.

Yet it is the very essence of *responsibility*, which is so often invoked, to stifle effective criticism. Judges welcome responsible criticism, and responsible criticism is not a contempt. The sober and responsible discussion of the foundations of Christian belief does not constitute blasphemy. But this approach stifles those who are beginning to think critically. Institutionalized, it becomes the old-boy network, which plays such a vital and sometimes unconscious role in ensuring that criticism of the established order should be simultaneously responsible, muted and ineffective.

Does this mean that censorship ought to be abolished? Since the practices imposing restrictions are often based upon motives explicable only by the psychologist, many of them are not susceptible to abolition by legal amendment, only by education and understanding, which may, in turn, depend upon an alteration in the basic structure of society. But other restrictions imposed by law could be repealed, and the more absurd abuses of the legal machinery could be abolished.

Would the abolition of censorship be a desirable thing? In so far as certain restrictions arise out of the individual unconscious, their removal might or might not be desirable, depending upon their nature and present function. Legally imposed restrictions should be abolished, unless it can be shown that their retention protects some social or individual good. And it is simply not true that many of the existing rules do protect a social good. The alleged *raison d'être* of the retention of film censorship, for example, is the protection of the young, but we do not have sufficient evidence to prove that such censorship in fact achieves its objective. Even if, as may be the case, the belief that censorship protects the young from psychological injury is possibly, or even probably, true, to justify retaining that kind of censorship for this purpose, we must add two qualifications.

First of all, film censorship in fact goes far beyond the protection of the young. If its function is to protect the young, then it has no business to go beyond this, unless, of course, it can be shown that doing more is necessary to protect some other group from *injury*. Secondly, if film censorship, and censorship in other media, exists to protect the young, why is it necessary simultaneously to protect the young from access to the kind of information which they must nowadays have to be adequately protected – namely, information about venereal diseases or contraception. But venereal disease propaganda is inhibited by the existing legal rules, and both film and television censors are apparently afraid of natural and overt references to the practice of contraception.

In 1969 the Film Censor asked for cuts from the Czechoslovak film *The Hurricane,* described by the *Guardian* as 'a domestic comedy and not salacious'. The *Guardian* commented:

All the same, the censor has asked for two scenes to be excised. In both, the wife of the hero is preparing a contraceptive before bed – she goes into the kitchen, fills a syringe, and then the scene is cut to the couple in bed. Is this a new ruling? Is contraceptive equipment forbidden on the screen, even when married couples are involved?

Given for the sake of argument, that censorship may be needed to protect certain social interests, the existing rules and practices at best make a very poor shot at doing this, and at worst stifle the communication of information and expression of opinion necessary to such protection. If the protection of the young is involved, we need to have that discussion of venereal disease and contraception which has not hitherto been permitted brought into the open.

What is necessary today is a thorough and more detailed investigation into the operation of censorship in different sectors of society, as well as some attempt to assess the interests being protected and the impact of the restrictions involved. Simultaneously, and this research has already begun in this country, notably in the work of Dr Himmelweit and Professor J. D. Halloran, we need to know far more about the possibly deleterious effects of the mass media on the minds of the young in particular.

Assuming that it is not possible to show that the very many of the legal rules and practices which today inhibit and restrict the freedom of opinion and communication do in fact protect any valuable social interest worth protecting, how can we ensure that the mass media will in future respect the need for an absence of restriction. The basic problem here remains that the present economic structure of the communications industry necessarily carries with it restrictions on the use which ordinary people, not to mention the practitioners themselves, the journalists, commentators and so forth can make of the vast potential for free expression and communication represented by the mass media. How to make such freedom of expression and communication a reality for the majority in the community is a question which we have hardly begun to explore.

Appendices

Appendix 1

The Earl of Chesterfield's Speech on a Bill to License Dramatic
Performances, House of Lords, 1 June 1737.*

Note: This pamphlet, which is one of the classics of English libertarian literature,
is reproduced here not merely because of the powerful attack it contains on any
system of prior censorship but also because it is a classic which is not nowadays
readily accessible to the general reader.

My Lords,

The Bill now before you I apprehend to be of a very
extraordinary, a very dangerous Nature. It seems designed not only
as a Restraint on the Licentiousness of the Stage, but it will prove a
most arbitrary Restraint on the Liberty of the Stage; and, I fear, it
looks yet farther, I fear, it tends towards a Restraint on the
Liberty of the Press, which will be a long Stride towards the
Destruction of Liberty itself. It is not only a Bill, my Lords, of a
very extraordinary Nature, but it has been brought in at a very
extraordinary Season, and pushed with most extraordinary Dispatch.
When I consider how near it was to the End of the Session, and how
long this Session had been protracted beyond the usual Time of the
Year; when I considered that this Bill passed through the other
House with so much Precipitancy, as even to get the Start of a Bill
which deserved all the Respect, and all the Dispatch, the Forms of
either House of Parliament could admit of, it set me upon inquiring,
what could be the reason for introducing this Bill at so unseasonable
a time, and pressing it foward in a manner so very singular and
uncommon. I have made all possible Inquiry, and as yet, I must
confess, I am at a loss to find out the great Occasion. I have, it is
true, learned from common Report without Doors, that a most
seditious, a most heinous Farce had been offered to one of the
Theatres, a Farce for which the Authors ought to be punished in the
most exemplary Manner: But what was the Consequence? The
Master of that Theatre behaved as he was in Duty bound, and as
common Prudence directed: He not only refused to bring it upon the
Stage, but carried it to a certain honourable Gentleman in the
Administration, as the surest Method of having it absolutely
suppressed. Could this be the Occasion of introducing such an
extraordinary Bill, at such an extraordinary Season, and pushing it in
so extraordinary a Manner? Surely no;——The dutiful Behaviour of
the Players, the prudent Caution they shewed upon that Occasion,
can never be a Reason for subjecting them to such an arbitrary

* Taken from *The E—— of C—— f——D's Speech in the H——se of L——ds,
against the Bill for Licensing all Dramatic Performances* (Dublin, 1749).

Restraint: It is an Argument in their Favour, and a material one, in my Opinion, against the Bill. Nay farther, if we consider all Circumstances, it is to me a full Proof that the Laws now in being are sufficient for punishing those Players who shall venture to bring any seditious Libel upon the Stage, and consequently sufficient for deterring all Players from acting any thing that may have the least Tendency towards giving a reasonable Offence.

I do not, my Lords, pretend to be a Lawyer, I do not pretend to know perfectly the Power and Extent of our Laws, but I have conversed with those that do, and by them I have been told, that our Laws are sufficient for punishing any Person that shall dare to represent upon the Stage what may appear, either by the Words or the Representation, to be blasphemous, seditious, or immoral. I must own, indeed, I have observed of late a remarkable Licentiousness in the Stage. There have but very lately been two Plays acted, which, one would have thought, should have given the greatest Offence, and yet both were suffered to be often represented without Disturbance, without Censure. In one, the Author thought fit to represent the three great Professions, Religion, Physick, and the Law, as inconsistent with Common Sense: In the other, a most tragical Story was brought upon the Stage, a Catastrophe too recent, too melancholy, and of too solemn a Nature, to be heard of any where but from the Pulpit. How these Pieces came to pass unpunished, I do not know: If I am rightly informed, it was not for want of Law, but for want of Prosecution, without which no Law can be made effectual: But if there was any Neglect in this Case, I am convinced it was not with a Design to prepare the Minds of the People, and to make them think a new Law necessary.

Our Stage ought certainly, my Lords, to be kept within Bounds; but for this, our Laws as they stand at present are sufficient: If our Stage-players at any Time exceed those Bounds, they ought to be prosecuted, they may be punished: We have Precedents, we have Examples of Persons having been punished for Things less criminal than either of the two Pieces I have mentioned. A new Law must therefore be unnecessary, and in the present Case it cannot be unnecessary without being dangerous: Every unnecessary Restraint on Licentiousness is a Fetter upon the Legs, is a Shackle upon the Hands of Liberty. One of the greatest Blessings we enjoy, one of the greatest Blessings a People, my Lords, can enjoy, is Liberty; —— but every Good in this Life has its Allay of Evil: —— Licentiousness is the Allay of Liberty; it is an Ebullition, an Excrescence; —— it is a Speck upon the Eye of the Political Body, which I can never touch but with a gentle, —— with a trembling Hand, lest I destroy the Body, lest I injure the Eye upon which it is apt to appear. If the Stage becomes at any Time licentious; if a Play appears to be a Libel upon the Government, or upon any particular Man, the King's Courts are open, the Laws are sufficient for punishing the Offender; and in this Case the Person injured has a singular Advantage; he can be under no Difficulty to prove who is the Publisher; the Players themselves are the Publishers, and there can be no want of Evidence to convict them.

But, my Lords, suppose it true, that the Laws now in being are not sufficient for putting a Check to or preventing the licentiousness of the Stage; suppose it absolutely necessary some new Law should be made for that purpose; yet it must be granted that such a Law ought to be maturely considered, and every Clause, every Sentence, nay every Word of it well weighed and examined, lest under some of those Methods, presumed or pretended to be necessary for restraining licentiousness, a Power should lie concealed, which might be afterwards made Use of for giving a dangerous Wound to Liberty. Such a Law ought not to be introduced at the Close of a Session, nor ought we, in the passing of such a Law, to depart from any of the Forms prescribed by our Ancestors for preventing Deceit and Surprize. There is such a Connection between licentiousness and Liberty, that it is not easy to correct the one, without dangerously wounding the other: It is extremely hard to distinguish the true limit between them: like a changeable Silk, we can easily see there are two different Colours, but we cannot easily discover where the one ends, or where the other begins. —— There can be no great and immediate Danger from the licentiousness of the Stage: I hope it will not be pretended that our Government may, before next Winter, be overturned by such licentiousness, even though our Stage were at present under no sort of legal Controul. Why then may we not delay till next Session passing any Law against the licentiousness of the Stage? Neither our Government can be altered, nor our Constitution overturned by such a Delay; but by passing a Law rashly and unadvisedly, our Constitution may at once be destroyed, and our Government rendered arbitrary. Can we then put a small, a short-lived inconvenience in the Ballance with perpetual Slavery? Can it be supposed that a Parliament of *Great Britain* will so much as risque the latter, for the sake of avoiding the former?

Surely, my Lords, this is not to be expected, were the licentiousness of the stage much greater than it is, were the insufficiency of our Laws more obvious than can be pretended; but when we complain of the licentiousness of the Stage, and of the insufficiency of our Laws, I fear we have more Reason to complain of bad measures in our Polity, and a general Decay of Virtue and Morality among the People. In publick as well as private Life, the only way to prevent being ridiculed or censured, is to avoid all ridiculous or wicked Measures, and to pursue such only as are virtuous and worthy. The People never endeavour to ridicule those they love and esteem, nor will they suffer them to be ridiculed: If any one attempts it, the Ridicule returns upon the Author he makes himself only the Object of publick Hatred and Contempt. The Actions or Behaviour of a private Man may pass unobserved, and consequently unapplauded, uncensured; but the Actions of those in high Stations, can neither pass without Notice, nor without censure or Applause; and therefore an Administration without Esteem, without Authority among the People, let their Power be never so great, let their Power be never so arbitrary, they will be ridiculed: The severest Edicts, the most terrible Punishments, cannot entirely prevent it. If any Man therefore thinks he has been censured; if any Man thinks he has been ridiculed upon any of our publick Theatres, let him examine his Actions he will find the Cause, let him alter his Conduct he will find a Remedy. As no Man is perfect, as no Man is infallible, the greatest may err, the most circumspect may be guilty of some piece of ridiculous Behaviour. It is not Licentiousness, it is an useful Liberty always indulged the Stage in a free Country, that some great Men may there meet with a just Reproof, which none of their Friends will be free enough or rather faithful enough to give them. Of this we have a famous instance in the *Roman* History. The great *Pompey*, after the many Victories he had obtained, and the great Conquests he had made, had certainly a good Title to the Esteem of the People of *Rome*; yet that great Man, by some Error in his Conduct, became an Object of general Dislike; and therefore, in the Representation of an old Play, when *Diphilus*, the Actor, came to repeat these Words, *Nostra Miseria tu es Magnus*, the Audience immediately applied them to *Pompey*, who at that time was as well known by the Name *Magnus*, as by the Name *Pompey*; and were so highly pleased with the Satyr, that, as *Cicero* says, they made the Actor repeat the Words an hundred times over: An Account of this was immediately sent to *Pompey*, who, instead of resenting it as an Injury, was so wise as to take it for a just Reproof: He examined his Conduct, he altered his Measures, he regained by degrees the Esteem of the People, and then he neither feared the Wit, nor felt the Satyr of the Stage. This is an Example which ought to be followed by great Men in all Countries. Such Accidents will often happen in every free Country, and many such would probably have afterwards happened at *Rome*, if they had continued to enjoy their Liberty; but this sort of Liberty in the Stage, came soon after, I suppose, to be called Licentiousness; for we are told that *Augustus*, after having established his Empire, restored Order in *Rome* by restraining Licentiousness. God forbid! we should in this Country have Order restored, or Licentiousness restrained, at so dear a Rate as the People of *Rome* paid for it to *Augustus*.

In the Case I have mentioned, my Lords, it was not the Poet that wrote, for it was an old Play, nor the Players that acted, for they only repeated the Words of the Play; it was the People who pointed the Satyr; and the Case will always be the same: When a Man has the Misfortune to incur the Hatred or Contempt of the People, when public Measures are despised, the Audience will apply what never was, what could not be designed as a Satyr on the present Times.

Nay, even tho' the People should not apply, those who are conscious of Guilt, those who are conscious of the Wickedness or Weakness of their own Conduct, will take to themselves what the Author never designed. A public Thief is as apt to take the Satyr as he is apt to take the Money, which was never designed for him. We have an Instance of this in the Case of a famous Comedian of the last Age; a Comedian who was not only a good Poet, but an honest Man, and a quiet and good Subject: The famous *Moliere*, when he wrote his *Tartuffe*, which is certainly an excellent and a good moral Comedy, did not design to satirize any great Man of that Age; yet a great Man in *France* at that Time took it to himself, and fancied the Author had taken him as a Model for one of the principal and one of the worst Characters in that Comedy: By good Luck he was not the Licenser, otherwise the Kingdom of *France* had never had the Pleasure, the Happiness, I may say, of seeing that Play acted; but when the Players first proposed to act it at *Paris*, he had Interest enough to get it forbid. *Moliere*, who knew himself Innocent of what was laid to his Charge, complained to his Patron the Prince of *Conti*, that as his Play was designed only to expose Hypocrisy, and a false Pretence to Religion, it was very hard it should be forbid being acted, when at the same Time they were suffered to expose Religion itself every Night publicly upon the *Italian* Stage: To which the Prince wittily answered, *'Tis true*, Moliere, *Harlequin ridicules Heaven, and exposes Religion; but you have done much worse – you have ridiculed the first Minister of Religion.*

I am as much for restraining the Licentiousness of the Stage, and every other sort of Licentiousness, as any of your Lordships can be; but, my Lords, I am, I shall always be extremely cautious and fearful of making the least Encroachment upon Liberty; and therefore, when a new Law is proposed against Licentiousness, I shall always be for considering it deliberately and maturely, before I venture to give my Consent to its being passed. This is a sufficient Reason for my being against passing this Bill at so unseasonable a Time, and in so extraordinary a Manner; but I have my Reasons for being against the Bill itself, some of which I shall beg leave to explain to your Lordships. The Bill, my Lords, at first view, may seem to be designed only against the Stage, but to me it plainly appears to point somewhere else. It is an Arrow that does but glance upon the Stage, the mortal Wound seems designed against the Liberty of the Press. By this Bill you prevent a Play's being acted, but you do not prevent its being printed; therefore, if a License should be refused for its being acted, we may depend on it the Play will be printed. It will be printed and published, my Lords, with the refusal in capital Letters on the Title Page. People are always fond of what is forbidden. *Libri prohibiti* are in all Countries diligently and generally sought after. It will be much easier to procure a Refusal, than it ever was to procure a good House, or a good Sale: Therefore we may expect, that Plays will be wrote on purpose to have a Refusal: This will certainly procure a good Sale: Thus will Satyrs be spread and dispersed through the whole Nation, and thus every Man in the Kingdom may and probably will, read for Sixpence, what a few only could have seen acted, and that not under the expence of half a Crown. We shall then be told, What! Will you allow an infamous Libel to be printed and dispersed, which you would not allow to be acted? You have agreed to a Law for preventing its being acted, can you refuse your Assent to a Law for preventing its being printed and published? I should really, my Lords, be glad to hear what Excuse, what Reason one could give for being against the latter, after having agreed to the former; for, I protest I cannot suggest to myself the least Shadow of an excuse. If we agree to the Bill now before us, we must perhaps next Session, agree to a Bill for preventing any Play's being printed without a Licence. Then Satyrs will be wrote by way of Novels, secret Histories, Dialogues, or under some such Title; and thereupon we shall be told, What! will you allow an infamous Libel to be printed and dispersed, only because it does not bear the Title of a Play? Thus, my Lords, from the Precedent now before us, we shall be induced, nay we can find no Reason for refusing to lay the Press under a general Licence, and then we may bid adieu to the Liberties of *Great Britain*.

But suppose, my Lords, it were necessary to make a new Law for restraining the Licentiousness of the Stage, which I am very far from granting, yet I shall never be for establishing such a Power as is proposed by this Bill. If Poets and Players are to be restrained, let them be restrained as other Subjects are, by the known Laws of their Country; if they offend, let them be tried as every *Englishman* ought to be, by God and their Country. Do not let us subject them to the arbitrary Will and Pleasure of any one Man. A Power lodged in the Hands of one single Man, to judge and determine, without any Limitation, without any Controul or Appeal, is a sort of Power unknown to our Laws, inconsistent with our Constitution. It is a higher, a more absolute Power than we trust even to the King himself; and therefore I must think, we ought not to vest any such Power in his Majesty's Lord Chamberlain. When I say this, I am sure I do not mean to give the least, the most distant Offence to the noble Duke who now fills the Post of Lord Chamberlain: His natural Candour and love of Justice, would not, I know, permit him to exercise any Power but with the strictest regard to the Rules of Justice and Humanity. Were we sure his Successors in that high Office would always be Persons of such distinguished Merit, even the Power to be establish'd by this Bill could give me no farther Alarm, than lest it should be made a Precedent for introducing other new Powers of the same Nature. This, indeed, is an Alarm which cannot be avoided, which cannot be prevented by any Hope, by any Consideration; it is an Alarm which, I think, every Man must take, who has a due Regard to the Constitution and Liberties of his Country.

I shall admit, my Lords, that the Stage ought not upon any Occasion to meddle with Politics, and for this very Reason, among the rest, I am against the Bill now before us: This Bill will be so far from preventing the Stage's meddling with Politics, that I fear it will be the Occasion of its meddling with nothing else; but then it will be a political Stage *ex parte*. It will be made subservient to the Politics and Schemes of the Court only. The Licentiousness of the Stage will be encouraged instead of being restrained; but, like Court-journalists, it will be licentious only against the Patrons of Liberty, and the Protectors of the People. Whatever Man, whatever Party opposes the Court in any of their most destructive Schemes, will, upon the Stage be represented in the most ridiculous Light the Hirelings of a Court can contrive. True Patriotism and Love of Public Good will be represented as Madness, or as a Cloak for Envy, Disappointment and Malice; while the most flagitious Crimes, the most extravagant Vices and Follies, if they are fashionable at Court, will be disguised and dressed up in the Habit of the most amiable Virtues. This has formerly been the Case:—— In King *Charles* IId's Days the Play-house was under a Licence. What was the Consequence?—— The Play-house retaled nothing but the Politics, the Vices, and the Follies of the Court: Not to expose them; no —— but to recommend them; tho' it must be granted their Politics were often as bad as their Vices, and much more pernicious than their other Follies. 'Tis true, the Court had, at that Time, a great deal of Wit; it was then indeed full of Men of true Wit and great Humour; but it was the more dangerous; for the Courtiers did then, as thorough-paced Courtiers always will do, they sacrificed their Honour, by making their Wit and their Humour subservient to the Court only; and what made it still more dangerous, no Man could appear upon the Stage against them. We know that *Dryden*, the Poet Laureat of that Reign, always represents the Cavaliers as honest, brave, merry Fellows, and fine Gentlemen: Indeed his fine Gentleman, as he generally draws him, is an atheistical, lewd, abandoned Fellow, which was at that Time, it seems, the fashionable Character at Court. On the other Hand, he always represents the Dissenters as hypocritical, dissembling Rogues, or stupid senseless Boobies. —— When the Court had a mind to fall out with the *Dutch*, he wrote his *Amboyna*, in which he represents the *Dutch* as a Pack of avaritious, cruel, ungrateful Rascals. —— And when the Exclusion Bill was moved in Parliament, he wrote his *Duke of Guise*, in which those who were preserving and securing the Religion of their Country, were exposed under the Character of the Duke of *Guise* and his Party, who leagued together, for excluding *Henry* IV. of *France* from the Throne, on account of his Religion. —— The City of *London*, too, was made to feel the partial and mercenary Licentiousness of the

Stage at that Time; for the Citizens having at that Time, as well as now, a great deal of Property, they had a mind to preserve that Property, and therefore they opposed some of the arbitrary Measures which were then begun, but pursued more openly in the following Reign; for which Reason they were then always represented upon the Stage, as a Parcel of designing Knaves, dissembling Hypocrites, griping Usurers, and —— Cuckolds into the Bargain.

My Lords, the proper Business of the Stage, and that for which only it is useful, is to expose those Vices and Follies, which the Laws cannot lay hold of, and to recommend those Beauties and Virtues, which Ministers and Courtiers seldom either imitate or reward; but by laying it under a Licence, and under an arbitrary Court-licence too, you will, in my Opinion, intirely pervert its Use; for tho' I have the greatest Esteem for that noble Duke, in whose Hands this Power is at present designed to fall, tho' I have an intire Confidence in his Judgment and Impartiality; yet I may suppose that a leaning towards the Fashions of a Court is sometimes hard to be avoided. —— It may be very difficult to make one who is every Day at Court believe that to be a Vice or Folly, which he sees daily practised by those he loves and esteems. —— By Custom even Deformity itself becomes familiar, and at last agreeable. —— To such a Person, let his natural Impartiality be never so great, that may appear a Libel against the Court, which is only a most just and a most necessary Satyr upon the fashionable Vices and Follies of the Court. Courtiers, my Lords, are too polite to reprove one another; the only Place where they can meet with any just Reproof, is a free, tho' not a licentious Stage; and as every Sort of Vice and Folly, generally in all Countries, begins at Court, and from thence spreads thro' the Country, by laying the Stage under an arbitrary Court-licence, instead of leaving it what it is, and always ought to be, a gentle Scourge for the Vices of Great Men and Courtiers, you will make it a Canal for propagating and conveying their Vices and Follies thro' the whole Kingdom.

From hence, my Lords, I think it must appear, that the Bill now before us cannot so properly be called a Bill for restraining the Licentiousness, as it may be called a Bill for restraining the Liberty of the Stage, and for restraining it too in that Branch which in all Countries has been the most useful; therefore I must look upon the Bill as a most dangerous Encroachment upon Liberty in general. Nay farther, my Lords, it is not only an Encroachment upon Liberty, but it is likewise an Enroachment on Property. Wit, my Lords, is a Sort of Property: It is the Property of those that have it, and too often the only Property they have to depend on. It is, indeed, but a precarious Dependance. Thank God! We —— my Lords, have a Dependance of another Kind; we have a much less precarious Support, and therefore cannot feel the Inconveniences of the Bill now before us; but it is our Duty to encourage and protect Wit, whosoever's Property it may be. Those gentlemen who have any such Property, are all, I hope, our Friends: Do not let us subject them to any unnecessary or arbitrary Restraint. I must own, I cannot easily agree to the laying of any tax upon Wit; but by this Bill it is to be heavily taxed, —— it is to be excised; —— for if this Bill passes, it cannot be retaled in a proper Way without a Permit; and the Lord Chamberlain is to have the Honour of being chief Gauger, Supervisor, Commissioner, Judge and Jury: But what is still more hard, tho' the poor Author, the Proprietor I should say, cannot perhaps dine till he has found out and agreed with a Purchaser; yet before he can propose to seek for a Purchaser, he must patiently submit to have his Goods rummaged at this new Excise-office, where they may be detained for fourteen Days, and even then he may find them returned as prohibited Goods, by which his chief and best Market will be for ever shut against him; and that without any Cause, without the least Shadow of Reason, either from the Laws of his Country, or the Laws of the Stage.

These Hardships, this Hazard, which every Gentleman will be exposed to who writes any thing for the Stage, must certainly prevent every Man of a generous and free Spirit from attempting any thing in that way; and as the Stage has always been the proper Chanel for Wit and Humour, therefore, my Lords, when I speak against this Bill, I must think I plead the Cause of Wit, I plead the Cause of Humour, I plead the Cause of the *British* Stage, and of every Gentleman of Taste in the Kingdom: But it is not, my Lords, for the Sake of Wit only; even for the Sake of his Majesty's Lord Chamberlain, I must be against this Bill. The noble Duke who has now the Honour to execute that Office, has, I am sure, as little Inclination to disoblige as any Man; but if this Bill passes, he must disoblige, he may disoblige some of his most intimate Friends. It is impossible to write a Play, but some of the Characters, or some of the Satyr, may be interpreted so as to point at some Person or other, perhaps at some Person in an eminent Station: When it comes to be acted, the People will make the Application, and the Person against whom the Application is made, will think himself injured, and will, at least privately, resent it: At present this Resentment can be directed only against the Author; but when an Author's Play appears with my Lord Chamberlain's Passport, every such Resentment will be turned from the Author, and pointed directly against the Lord Chamberlain, who by his Stamp made the Piece current. What an unthankful Office are we therefore by this Bill to put upon his Majesty's Lord Chamberlain! an Office which can no way contribute to his Honour or Profit, and yet such a one as must necessarily gain him a great deal of ill will, and create him a number of Enemies.

The last Reason I shall trouble your Lordships with for my being against the Bill, is, that in my Opinion, it will no way answer the End proposed: I mean the End openly proposed, and, I am sure, the only End which your Lordships propose. To prevent the acting of a Play which has any Tendency to Blasphemy, Immorality, Sedition, or private Scandal, can signify nothing, unless you can likewise prevent its being printed and published. On the contrary, if you prevent its being acted, and admit of its being printed and published, you will propagate the Mischief: Your Prohibition will prove a Bellows which will blow up the Fire you intend to extinguish. This Bill can therefore be of no Use for preventing either the publick or the private Injury intended by such a Play; and consequently can be of no manner of Use, unless it be designed as a Precedent, as a leading Step towards another, for subjecting the Press likewise to a Licenser. For such a wicked Purpose it may, indeed, be of great Use; and in that Light, it may most properly be called a Step towards arbitrary Power.

Let us consider, my Lords, that arbitrary power has seldom or never been introduced into any country at once. It must be introduced by slow degrees, and as it were step by step, lest the people should perceive its approach. The barriers and fences of the people's liberty must be plucked up one by one, and some plausible pretences must be found for removing or hood-winking, one after another, those sentries who are posted by the constitution of every free country, for warning the people of their danger. When these preparatory Steps are once made, the People may then, indeed, with Regret see Slavery and arbitrary Power making long Strides over their Land, but it will then be too late to think of preventing or avoiding the impending Ruin. The Stage, my Lords, and the Press, are two of our Out-sentries; if we remove them, —— if we hood-wink them, —— if we throw them in Fetters, —— the Enemy may surprize us. Therefore I must look upon the Bill now before us as a Step, and a most necessary Step too, for introducing arbitrary Power into this Kingdom: It is a Step so necessary, that, if ever any future ambitious King, or guilty Minister, should form to himself so wicked a Design, he will have Reason to thank us for having done so much of the Work to his Hand; but such Thanks, or Thanks from such a Man, I am convinced every one of your Lordships would blush to receive, —— and scorn to deserve.

Appendix 2

Independent Television Authority–Code on Violence*

The context of violence

1 Conflict, the clash of purposes and personalities, is a major element in drama, and not least in great drama. Physical violence is conflict at the point when blows are exchanged or weapons are used. Persecution, bullying, intimidation, humiliation and cruelty are forms of mental violence, and it is well to remember that the suffering thus caused may exceed that caused by physical violence, though not a hand has been raised to strike.

2 The first rule in the control of both forms of violence must always be to examine the dramatic context in which they occur, and the ends to which they are a means. For, if need be, physical force may be used to protect the law as well as break it, to defend the guiltless or helpless as well as oppress them, to impose a just settlement as well as an unjust one, and anger may take the form of a just moral indignation against the infliction of cruelty, as well as of a vicious outburst of temper or a mercilessly sustained vendetta.

3 Therefore, in dramatic programmes likely to be seen by children, the initial question to be asked is whether they are pervaded with a clear sense of right and wrong. All may turn on the answer. For children acquire their moral sentiments from the society around them, including its aspect in television, and particularly from those they admire both in real life and in literature and drama. They tend to model their own conduct on the conduct of those they admire, and shun the conduct of those they feel to be bad. It follows that the ends for which characters presented to them as admirable resort to physical force should always be socially defensible.

Violence for its own sake not permissible

4 The second rule, which follows from the first, is that violence, whether physical or mental, should never be allowed 'for its own sake' – that is to say, simply because it attracts or secures the attention of audiences, or certain types of audience. If the nature of it, or the sheer quantity of it, go beyond its dramatic function, it should be cut. Individual brutality or the aimless violence of mobs can be shown; but there comes a point at which they have exhausted their dramatic role – and at that point they should stop. Purely quantitative control is important.

* Taken from *ITA Notes*, No. 20 (September 1970).

Intensity of violence

5 The third rule concerns the quality or intensity of violence. This may be a question of distance or closeness in space and time. A long shot of an ambush or cavalry charge is one thing, a close-up of facial agony, though part of that whole, is another. Distance in time, the remoteness of the setting from our world, may also lessen the emotional impact of violence. The senses are less vividly impressed. It may also be lessened when the story is simply not regarded as real – the fairy story, the conventional adventure story or the re-created world of the routine Western, with its stock characters, or the puppet, marionette, and mime. But not too much importance should be attached to this form of 'distance'. Reality can shrink distance, and thrust through any convention. Horror in costume is still horror.

The protection of children

6 Within this broad frame of reference, great care should always be taken in the presentation of the following:

a *Scenes likely to frighten children*
There are degrees of fear, from the mild and half-pleasurable fear of climbing a tree or a mountain to absolute unmixed terror, and children vary greatly in their susceptibility to fear. Horror deliberately presented as an entertainment should be prohibited.

b *Scenes likely to unnerve and unsettle children*
Care must be taken to guard children against the impression that they are entering a world in which they can count on nothing as settled, reliable and kind, and in which they must make their way at the expense of others, resorting to physical or mental violence whenever it will pay them.

c *Scenes likely to cause pain to children*
Pain witnessed, except by a brute, is pain felt. When witnessed, the pain of others stirs sympathy, and the desire arises to relieve suffering, and protect the weak or helpless against it. This is a stage of moral growth. But there are degrees of suffering altogether too painful for children to watch. The more helpless the victim, such as the aged, the infirm, or an animal, the greater the pain induced in a good-hearted child.

d *Scenes in which pleasure is taken in the infliction of pain or humiliation upon others*
Children should know that bullies are a fact of life, but great care must be taken to see that they despise them and do not secretly admire them. When such scenes reach the level of deliberate torture, they should be either momentary or banned entirely.

e *Scenes in which the infliction or acceptance of pain or humiliation is associated with sexual pleasure*
These should be eliminated.

f *Scenes which children might copy with injury to themselves or others*
Children are imitative and curious. The technique of hanging, or experiments with fire, or tying and locking up, or submerging in water, can easily be tried by a child.

g *Scenes in which easily acquired and dangerous weapons are used*
It is a simple fact that guns and swords are not easily come by, while knives, bottles, bars and bricks are. It is not good that children with a tendency to violence should see them in frequent use.

h *Scenes in which the less usual methods of inflicting injury are employed*
This includes rabbit punches, suffocation, the sabotage of vehicles, and dangerous booby traps.

7 In cases of doubt, cut. The risk is not one that can decently be taken.

Appendix 3

The British Code of Advertising Practice*

PART A
Preamble

All advertising should be legal, decent, honest and truthful.

No advertisement should bring advertising into contempt or reduce confidence in advertising as a service to industry and to the public.

The Code is to be applied in the spirit as well as the letter.

It covers all advertising of products and services. The advertising of medicines, treatments and appliances is subject to the additional provisions set out in part B.

A list of statutes affecting advertising is set out in Appendix 1. Particular attention is drawn to the Trade Descriptions Act 1968.

Interpretation

1·1 The word 'advertisement' throughout this Code applies to advertising wherever it may appear including advertising in leaflets, circulars and price lists and on packages, labels and point of sale material.

1·2 Any illustration included in an advertisement is subject to the same rules.

1·3 For the purpose of this Code a service is a product and is subject to the same rules.

Descriptions, claims and comparisons

2·1 All descriptions, claims and comparisons should be capable of substantiation, and advertisers and advertising agencies are required to provide such substantiation without delay when called upon to do so.

2·2 Advertisements should not contain any description, claim or comparison which is directly or by implication misleading about the product advertised, or about any other product.

2·3 Advertisements should not contain any indication that the product advertised, or any ingredient, has some special quality or property which cannot be substantiated.

---

* The two appendices to the code are omitted. One lists legislation affecting advertising, the other medical illnesses or conditions in respect of which it is prohibited to advertise any medicine, product, appliance or advice in terms likely to lead to its use for the treatment of such illnesses or conditions.

Denigration
3   Advertisements should not unfairly attack or discredit other products or advertisements directly or by implication.

Imitation
4·1 Advertisements should not imitate the devices, copy, slogans or general layout of advertisements for competing products in a way that is likely to mislead or confuse.

4·2 In the packaging and labelling of goods particular care should be taken to avoid causing confusion with competing products.

Scientific terms and statistics
5·1 Advertisements should not misuse scientific terms, statistics or quotations.

5·2 Scientific jargon and irrelevancies should not be used to make claims appear to have a scientific basis they do not possess.

5·3 Statistics with a limited validity should not be presented in such a way as to imply that their validity is greater than it really is.

Appeals to fear
6   Advertisements should not without justifiable reason play on fear.

Superstition
7   Advertisements should not exploit the superstitious.

Safety
8   Advertisements should not without justifiable reason depict or describe situations which show dangerous practices or a disregard for safety. Special care should be taken in advertisements directed towards or depicting children.

Advertisements addressed to children
9   Advertisements addressed to children should not contain anything, whether in illustration or otherwise, which might result in harming them, physically, mentally or morally, or which exploits their credulity.

Testimonials
10·1 A testimonial used in an advertisement should be genuine, not more than three years old, and related to the experience of the person giving it.

10·2 Testimonials should not contain any statement or implication contravening the provisions of this Code.

Advertisements in editorial style
11   An advertisement should be clearly distinguishable from the editorial content of the publication in which it appears. It should therefore be so designed, produced and printed that it is immediately recognizable by the ordinary reader as an advertisement.

For further guidance see CAP Bulletin No. 6, Item 40

'Free'

12   Goods or samples may be described as 'free' if they are supplied at no cost or no extra cost (other than actual postage or carriage) to the recipient. A trial may be described as 'free' although the customer is expected to pay the cost of returning the goods, provided that the advertisement makes clear the customer's obligation to do so.

Guarantees

13   Advertisements may contain the word 'guarantee', 'guaranteed', 'warranty' or 'warranted' or words having the same meaning only if the full terms of the guarantee are clearly set out in the advertisement or are made available to the purchaser in writing at the point of sale or supplied with the goods. The terms should include details of the remedial action open to a purchaser. No advertisement should contain a direct or implied reference to a guarantee which takes away or diminishes the statutory or common law rights of a purchaser, unless the manufacturer assumes a contractual responsibility to the purchaser in extent at least equivalent to such rights.

Mail order

14·1 Advertisements for goods offered by mail should not be accepted unless:

    a the name of the advertiser is prominently displayed at the address given in the advertisement

    b adequate arrangements exist at that address for enquiries to be handled by a responsible person available on the premises during normal business hours

    c samples of the goods advertised are made available there for public inspection and

    d an undertaking has been obtained from the advertiser that money will be refunded in full to buyers who can show justifiable cause for dissatisfaction with their purchases or with delay in delivery.

14·2 Advertisers who offer goods by mail order should be prepared to meet any reasonable demand created by their advertising, and should be prepared to demonstrate or where practicable supply samples of the goods advertised to the media owners to whom their advertisements are submitted.

Direct sale advertising

15   Direct sale advertisements are not acceptable without adequate assurances from the advertiser and his advertising agency

    a that the products advertised will be supplied at the price stated in the advertisement within a reasonable time from stocks sufficient to meet potential demand, and

b that sales representatives when calling upon persons responding to the advertisement will demonstrate and make available for sale the products advertised. It will be taken as prima facie evidence of misleading and unacceptable 'bait' advertising for the purpose of 'switch selling' if an advertiser's salesmen seriously disparage or belittle the cheaper article advertised or indicate unreasonable delays in obtaining delivery or otherwise put difficulties in the way of its purchase.

Direct sale advertising is that placed by the advertiser with the intention that the products or services advertised, or some other products or services, shall be sold or provided at the home of any person responding to the advertisement.

Home visits by advertiser's representatives
16 Where it is the intention of an advertiser to send a representative to call on respondents to his advertisement

a such fact must be apparent from the advertisement or from any particulars subsequently supplied and

b the respondent must be given an adequate opportunity of refusing any such call.

Homework schemes
17 Advertisements for homework schemes should not be offered to media unless accompanied with full details of the work involved and of the conditions imposed on the homeworker.

'Homework scheme' means a scheme in which a person is invited to make articles or perform services at home for remuneration.

Intertia selling
18 Advertisements should not be accepted from advertisers who supply goods without express authority.

Instructional courses
19·1 Advertisements offering courses of instruction should not promise or imply that persons completing such courses will obtain any particular employment or level of remuneration; nor offer unrecognised 'degrees' or qualifications.

19·2 Advertisements for correspondence courses in chiropody or any of the other auxiliary services covered by the Professions Supplementary to Medicine Act 1960 (i.e. dieticians, medical laboratory technicians, occupational therapists, physiotherapists, radiographers and remedial gymnasts) should not be accepted.

Franchise schemes
20 Advertisements by franchisors seeking franchisees should not be accepted until the franchisor has provided all the information required by media.

'Franchise scheme' means a scheme where a company, firm or individual (known as a franchisor) gives to a person (known as a franchisee) the right, often exclusive, to sell specified products or other specified services in a defined geographical area, or premises, in return for an initial payment and/or percentage of profits (or royalty).

For further guidance see CAP Bulletin No. 5, Item 38.

PART B Medicines, treatments and appliances
These paragraphs apply in addition to those in part A.

This part of the Code applies to the advertising to the public of medicines, treatments and appliances for the prevention or alleviation of any ailment, illness or disease. It does not apply to advertisements published by or under the authority of a Government Ministry or Department, not to advertisements for medicines, treatments and appliances addressed directly to registered medical or dental practitioners, pharmacists, registered medical auxiliaries or nurses, sent direct or published in their respective professional or technical journals.

Illnesses requiring medical attention
21   Advertisements should not offer any medicine or treatment for serious diseases, conditions or complaints which need the attention of a registered medical practitioner.

   (See in particular the list in Appendix II)

Diagnosis or treatment by correspondence
22   Advertisements should not contain any offer to diagnose or to treat any ailment, illness or disease, or symptoms of ill-health by correspondence; nor invite information in order to advise on or prescribe treatment by correspondence.

College, hospital, clinic, institute, laboratory
23   Advertisements should not contain any reference to a 'College', 'Hospital', 'Clinic', 'Institute', 'Laboratory' or similar establishment unless there exists a bona fide establishment corresponding to the description used.

Medical statements, trials and tests
24·1 Advertisements should not contain any medical statement or reference to clinical or other trials or tests which cannot be substantiated by authoritative evidence.

24·2 No product with a name containing the term 'Doctor' or 'Dr' is acceptable unless the product was marketed under that name prior to 1st January, 1944.

Cure
25   Advertisements should not contain any claim (directly or by implication) to extirpate any ailment, illness, disease or symptom of ill-health.

Appeals to fear
26 Advertisements should not contain any statement or illustration likely to induce fear on the part of the reader or viewer that he is suffering, or may without treatment suffer, or suffer more severely, from an ailment, illness or disease.

Money-back offers
27 Advertisements should not contain any offer to refund money to dissatisfied users. This paragraph does not apply to mail order advertising of medical appliances or therapeutic wearing apparel.
See Part A, para. 14.

Testimonials
28 Advertisements should not contain any testimonial given by a doctor who is not a registered British medical practitioner unless the advertisement makes it clear that the writer is not so registered.

Exaggerated copy
29 Advertisements should not contain copy which is exaggerated by reason of the use of words, phrases or methods of presentation such as the use of the words 'magic', 'magical', 'miracle', 'miraculous'.

'Natural' remedies
30 Advertisements should not contain any false claim, direct or indirect, that a product is 'natural', 'nature's remedy' or the like.

Competitions
31 Advertisements for medicines, treatments and appliances should not contain any reference to a prize competition or similar scheme.

Slimming, weight reduction, limitation or control
32 Advertisements should not contain any offer of any product or treatment for slimming (i.e. weight reduction, limitation or control) which:
a is in itself likely to lead to harmful effects
b is not directly associated with the following of a properly designed diet.

Bust developers
33 Advertisements for preparations and devices purporting to promote enlargement of the bust are not permissible.

Products offered particularly to women
34 Advertisements should not suggest or imply that any products, medicines or treatments offered therein will induce miscarriage.

Sexual weakness, premature ageing, loss of virility
35   Advertisements should not suggest or imply that any product, medicine or treatment offered therein will promote sexual virility or be effective in treating sexual weakness, or habits, associated with sexual excess or indulgence, or any ailment, illness or disease associated with such habits.

Hypnosis and hypno-therapy
36   Advertisements should not contain any offer to diagnose or treat any defect disability or condition of physical or mental illhealth by hypnosis or hypno-therapy.

Hair and scalp
37·1   Advertisements for hair and scalp products should not contain any offer of diagnosis, or any claim direct or indirect, that the product will do more than arrest loss of hair.

37·2   Advertisements for establishments providing treatment for the hair and scalp should, apart from any illustration, be restricted to the name, address and telephone number and should not refer directly or indirectly to any specific condition for which treatment is provided, although reference may be made to the type of treatment available, e.g. ultra-violet ray massage.

37·3   Advertisements for products or establishments should not contain any illustration which is misleading or which purports to show or may be taken as showing the result of the efficacy of the product or treatment.

Haemorrhoids
38   Advertisements should not contain any offer of products for the treatment of haemorrhoids unless the directions for use on the container itself or its labels include advice to the effect that persons who suffer from haemorrhoids are advised to consult a doctor.

Backache and rheumatic pains
39   Advertisements should not contain any claims for the relief of backache and rheumatic pains based upon the urinary antiseptic properties of the products advertised.

Vitamin products
40   Advertisements should not contain any unqualified claims that vitamins will give adequate protection against or treatment for virus infections, or unqualified statements that the medical profession supports such claims.

Appendix 4

Extracts from the European Convention on Human Rights and Fundamental Freedoms

Article 8

1 Everyone has the right to respect for his private and family life, his home and his correspondence.

2 There shall be no interference by a public authority with the exercise of this right except such as is in accordance with the law and is necessary in a democratic society in the interests of national security, public safety or the economic well-being of the country, for the prevention of disorder or crime, for the protection of health or morals, or for the protection of the rights and freedoms of others.

Article 9

1 Everyone has the right to freedom of thought, conscience and religion; this right includes freedom to change his religion or belief and freedom, either alone or in community with others and in public or private, to manifest his religion or belief, in worship, teaching, practice and observance.

2 Freedom to manifest one's religion or beliefs shall be subject only to such limitations as are prescribed by law and are necessary in a democratic society in the interests of public safety, for the protection of public order, health or morals, or for the protection of the rights and freedoms of others.

Article 10

1 Everyone has the right to freedom of expression. This right shall include freedom to hold opinions and to receive and impart information and ideas without interference by public authority and regardless of frontiers. This Article shall not prevent States from requiring the licensing of broadcasting, television or cinema enterprises.

2 The exercise of these freedoms, since it carries with it duties and responsibilities, may be subject to such formalities, conditions, restrictions or penalties as are prescribed by law and are necessary in a democratic society, in the interests of national security, territorial integrity or public safety, for the prevention of disorder or crime, for the protection of health or morals, for the protection of the reputation or rights of others, for preventing the disclosure of information received in confidence, or for maintaining the authority and impartiality of the judiciary.

Article 11

1 Everyone has the right to freedom of peaceful assembly and to freedom of association with others, including the right to form and to join trade unions for the protection of his interests.

2 No restrictions shall be placed on the exercise of these rights other than such as are prescribed by law and are necessary in a democratic society in the interests of national security or public safety, for the prevention of disorder or crime, for the protection of health or morals or for the protection of the rights and freedoms of others. This Article shall not prevent the imposition of lawful restrictions on the exercise of these rights by members of the armed forces, of the police or of the administration of the State.

Article 13

Everyone whose rights and freedoms as set forth in this Convention are violated shall have an effective remedy before a national authority notwithstanding that the violation has been committed by persons acting in an official capacity.

Appendix 5

Extracts from the Constitution of the Press Council

Article 2 Objects

The Objects of the Council are:

i To preserve the established freedom of the British Press.

ii To maintain the character of the British Press in accordance with the highest professional and commercial standards.

iii To consider complaints about the conduct of the Press or the conduct of persons and organizations towards the Press; to deal with these complaints in whatever manner might seem practical and appropriate and record resultant action.

iv To keep under review developments likely to restrict the supply of information of public interest and importance.

v To report publicly on developments that may tend towards greater concentration or monopoly in the Press (including changes in ownership, control and growth of Press undertakings) and to publish statistical information relating thereto.

vi To make representations on appropriate occasions to the Government organs of the United Nations and to Press organizations abroad.

vii To publish periodical reports recording the Council's work and to review, from time to time, developments in the Press and the factors affecting them.

Appendix 6

Programme Policy Governing Violence–
A Code of Practice for the BBC Television Service
A Note by the Controller of Programmes, Television*

Note: A further 'note of guidance' has now been issued, in March 1972, by Mr David Attenborough, director of programmes, television, expanding the provisions of the 1960 Code. For a summary, see *The Times*, 30 March 1972.

Introduction

It is recognized that it is difficult and undesirable to be dogmatic about a subject which has a great many and diverse aspects; the type of programme, the time of its showing and the likely composition of the audience for whom it is intended are three of the major considerations which will condition the decisions taken by producers, output heads and others responsible for what appears on the screen. To attempt to lay down laws too precisely to meet all situations would be to invite inconsistency. Nevertheless, there are certain lines of thought, certain current practices, and an accumulation of experience, which in effect constitute a policy. But it is a policy which is carried out empirically, perhaps even instinctively, and that is hazardous.

There is no reason why the main principles on which decisions are based should not be the same, and be applied in the same way, whether the programme is a studio drama or a hired telefilm, a magazine item or a documentary, part of children's television or part of that area of adult time when children are known to be viewing in substantial numbers. To talk of good taste, commonsense and the avoidance of extremes is not enough. An attempt to lay down a general code of practice may be of positive value in ensuring that, in avoiding harm on the one hand, we do not impoverish or emasculate our material on the other.

Children's programmes

(The following points are of importance also to all those concerned with programmes up to 9 p.m.):

1 The worlds which children and grown-ups occupy, though they overlap, are different. Subjects with unpleasant associations for the one will often be taken for granted by the other. Guns and fisticuffs may have sinister implications for adults; seldom for children. Family insecurity and marital infidelity may be commonplace to adults; to children they can be deeply disturbing.

* Submitted to the Pilkington Committee and taken from Report of the Committee on Broadcasting, 1960 (Cmnd. 1753, 1962), pp. 48–50.

2 A black-list is therefore impracticable. Torture is normally inadmissible, yet in 'Jesus of Nazareth' the Crucifixion was dramatized. In a particular context, many subjects which would at first sight seem wrong for children's viewing can be justified. But danger-points can be stressed, especially for those engaged in drama and in the selection of films.

3 These are the main danger-points:

a Situations which upset a child's emotional security, arising out of adoption, desertion, cruelty in the home, unwanted children, friction between parents, especially in contemporary settings. H.C.P. Tel. well says of these: 'Perhaps not violence, but violation, which is worse.'

b Portrayal of injury, illness or disablements, especially when used to sharpen a dramatic crisis (e.g. nightmares); and of embarrassing personal disabilities (e.g. stuttering).

c Dangerous examples of 'villainous' action which invite imitation, e.g. the use of intriguing weapons, traps and pit falls, from sabotaged bicycles to trip-wires.

d Bad habits in 'good' characters; e.g. chain-smoking, hitting below the belt.

e Brutality: the most difficult category. Brutality is not the same thing as violence. Violence is not the same thing as combat. Yet because combat, which is healthy, and brutality, which is not, both contain violence, they tend to become identified. Overemphasis in picture and sound is one key. Long-shot renders many affrays and battles inoffensive; closeup make the same incidents inadmissible.

f Weapons: the choice is important. Coshes, knives, whips and bottles are more suspect than revolvers, rifles or swords, because they are more easily available or improvised.

g Atmosphere: This can be more upsetting than violence because here what is essentially a subjective subject becomes most personal. To chill the spine is a legitimate part of story-telling. To create an eerie and fearful atmosphere, especially with the aid of background music, or sudden optical shock, can be more than momentarily disturbing. The supernatural, especially in modern dress, is perilous ground.

4 Commonsense, though it may not be enough, nevertheless demands that stories must have conflict, that if there are to be heroes, there must be villains also, that escapism is an inadequate basis for planning, and that risks must sometimes be run if the wholesome appetite of children for excitement and for getting to grips with life is to be satisfied.

Adult programmes

These may be divided into two categories, first, documentary and magazine programmes containing film sequences of actual happenings, and, second, dramatic programmes, whether in the studio or on film, where the scenes have been deliberately contrived.

1 Producers with library material to draw upon must always satisfy themselves first of all that the illustrations they choose which depict scenes of violence, brutality or horror are valid and essential to their theme, that the meaning of the programme is, indeed, heightened by the inclusion of such sequences. They must then ask themselves if the effect of including those scenes is not, in the case of a large number of normal viewers, going to cause such distress or resentment as to invalidate the programme altogether for those people. If we expose viewers to shock, or indeed to fear, we must be absolutely certain in advance that our reasons are good and proper ones. They may well be, but justification by hindsight is not acceptable.

2 Scenes of physical violence are an almost invariable ingredient of all American importations other than comedy or musical shows. They often occur, though customarily in less extended or extreme form, in our own plays and serials. While it is axiomatic that we do not permit, either on telecine or in the studio, the gratuitous exploitation of violence as a source of unwholesome entertainment, there are certain principles which should be common to all concerned and which may be usefully restated.

   a A sequence involving violence should arise naturally from the story, and be therefore dramatically necessary and defensible. If it is inserted extraneously for depraved effect, it should be rejected outright. This happens with many of the 'private eye' and police series which come from the United States. The 'western', on the other hand, has a formal and stylized tradition, of which shooting and slogging it out are an essential part. The latest film-makers, however, are apt to interject a sudden piece of optical or acoustic self-indulgence into an otherwise admissible fight between law and outlaw. This requires vigilance from us.

   b Any such 'natural' sequence should not be unduly prolonged.

   c No sequence should include shots which dwell upon the more gruesome and bloody physical aspects of a combat.

   d As with children's programmes, the use of dangerous implements, other than firearms, has to be watched, to avoid both revulsion and imitation in viewers.

   e Sound effects and sound track should not distort or magnify the impact of violence, e.g. the breaking of bones, the cracking of skull or jaw.

f In a fist fight, neither contestant should engage in tactics of a vicious or bestial nature.

g Violence inflicted on a woman or animal must require special scrutiny.

If there is any suspicion that a scene has been written, or filmed, deliberately to scare the imaginative and/or nervous viewer, then it should automatically be excised.

Equally important, consideration should be given to the concept of the film or play, to the purpose and intentions of the producer or author and the means they have employed to carry those out. We must not carelessly dismiss their integrity.

Finally, the most important rule for all staff is to refer for further examination anything about which they are doubtful. The effect of such reference in the long run is much more likely to be positive than negative. Responsibility shared means progress, not regression.

7th March, 1960. Kenneth Adam

Appendix 7

Principles for Television Advertising*

Preamble

1 The general principle which will govern all television advertising is that it should be legal, clean, honest and truthful. It is recognized that this principle is not peculiar to the television medium, but is one which applies to all reputable advertising in other media in this country. Nevertheless, television, because of its greater intimacy within the home, gives rise to problems which do not necessarily occur in other media and it is essential to maintain a consistently high quality of television advertising.

2 The detailed principles set out below are intended to be applied in the spirit as well as the letter and should be taken as laying down the minimum standards to be observed. They should be read in conjunction with the rules about specific classes of advertisements and methods of advertising which are set out in Appendix 1. The programme contractors, and the Authority, may in certain circumstances impose stricter standards than those here laid down and these principles do not override or supersede the standards of practice laid down by individual organizations as incumbent upon their own members and applying to their own particular trade or industry.

Definition

3 The word 'advertisement' has the meaning implicit in the Television Act, i.e., any item of publicity inserted in the programmes broadcast by the Authority in consideration of payment to a programme contractor or to the Authority.

Legal requirements

4 Advertisements must comply in every respect with the law, common or statute. In the case of some Acts, notably the Merchandise Marks Acts, rules applicable to other forms of advertising may not, on a strict interpretation of the Acts, cover television advertising. Advertisements must, however, comply in all respects with the spirit of those Acts.

* Taken from the fourth edition, published by the I.T.A., August 1961, as reproduced in the Report of the Committee on Broadcasting, 1960 (Cmnd. 1753, 1962), pp. 85–7.

False or misleading advertisements

5 No advertisement, taken as a whole or in part, shall contain any spoken or visual presentation of the product or service advertised, or statement of its price, which directly or by implication misleads.

In particular:

a *Special claims*

No advertisement shall contain any reference which is likely to lead the public to assume that the product advertised, or an ingredient, has some special property or quality which is in fact unknown, unrecognized or incapable of being established.

b *Scientific and technical terms*
Statistics, scientific terms, quotations from technical literature and the like must be used with a proper sense of responsibility to the ordinary viewer. The irrelevant use of data and jargon must never be resorted to to make claims appear more scientific than they really are. Statistics of limited validity should not be presented in such a way as to make it appear that they are universally true.

c *Imitation*
Any imitation likely to mislead viewers, even though it is not of such a kind as to give rise to a legal action for infringement of copyright or for 'passing off', must be avoided.

Disparaging references

6 No advertisement shall contain any statement intended to promote sales by unfair comparison with or reference to competitive products or services.

Testimonials

7 Documentary evidence of testimonials may be required as a condition of the acceptance of advertisements. The irresponsible use of testimonials must be avoided.

Guarantee

8 The word 'guarantee' should be used with caution and sparingly and only in relation to some specific description or quality and the detailed terms of any such guarantee must be available for inspection by programme contractors. Where the guarantee is associated with an offer to return the purchase price, it must be made quite clear to what it applies and in what way it protects the purchaser.

Competitions

9 Advertisements inviting the public to take part in competitions where allowable under Section 3(3) of the Television Act, 1954, and the Betting & Lotteries Act, 1934 (which requires the presence of an element of skill), should state clearly how prospective entrants may obtain the printed conditions including the arrangements for the announcement of results and for the distribution of prizes.

Advertising in Children's Programmes

10 No product or service may be advertised and no method of advertising may be used, in association with a programme intended for children or which large numbers of children are likely to see, which might result in harm to them physically, mentally or morally, and no method of advertising may be employed which takes advantage of the natural credulity and sense of loyalty of children.

In particular:

a No advertisement which encourages children to enter strange places or to converse with strangers in an effort to collect coupons, wrappers, labels, etc. is allowed. The programme contractor must investigate the details of any collecting scheme and satisfy himself that it contains no element of danger to children.

b No advertisement for a commercial product or service is allowed if it contains any appeal to children which suggests in any way that unless the children themselves buy or encourage other people to buy the product or service they will be failing in some duty or lacking in loyalty towards some person or organization whether that person or organization is the one making the appeal or not.

c No advertisement is allowed which leads children to believe that, if they do not own the product advertised, they will be inferior in some way to other children or that they are liable to be held in contempt or ridicule for not owning it.

d No advertisement dealing with the activities of a club is allowed without the specific permission of the programme contractor who must satisfy himself that the club is carefully supervised in the matter of the behaviour of the children and the company they keep and that there is no suggestion of the club being a secret society.

e While it is recognized that children are not the direct purchasers of many products over which they are naturally allowed to exercise preference, care should be taken that they are not encouraged to make themselves a nuisance to other people in the interests of any particular product or service.

Appendix 8

Freedom of Publication (Protection) Bill 1969

Contempt of Court

Restriction on proceedings **1** Proceedings for contempt of court in respect of the publication of any matter in a newspaper or in a broadcast by wireless telegraphy as part of any programme or service provided by means of a broadcasting station within the United Kingdom shall not be instituted except by or with the consent of the Attorney General.

Repetition of defamatory matter **2** Publication in a newspaper or in a broadcast by wireless telegraphy as part of any programme or service provided by means of a broadcasting station within the United Kingdom of –

a any matter the same as or similar to matter which is the subject of libel or slander proceedings whether against the publisher or against any other person, or

b any comment upon matter which is the subject of such proceedings

shall not, by reason only of the fact that the proceedings are pending, constitute contempt of court.

Defamation

Justification *1952 c.66* **3·1** For section **5** of the Defamation Act 1952 there shall be substituted the following section –

'**5** In an action for libel in respect of words in a publication containing two or more distinct charges against the plaintiff, a defence of justification may seek to justify all or any of the charges contained in the publication, whether or not they are contained in the words complained of in the action, and the defence of justification shall not fail by reason only that the truth of all or any of the charges contained in the words complained of is not proved, if the charges not proved to be true do not materially injure the plaintiff's reputation having regard to the truth of all or any of the remaining charges.'

3·2 In an action for libel in respect of words containing a charge of the commission of a criminal offence, a defence of justification of the charge shall succeed if it be proved that at the time of the publication of the words the plaintiff had been convicted of the offence and the conviction had not been set aside.

Qualified privilege in newspapers

4 Part I of the Schedule to the Defamation Act 1952 (which lists the categories of reports published in newspapers or broadcasts which are protected by qualified privilege under section **7·1** of the Act) shall be amended by adding the following paragraphs immediately after paragraph **7**:–

'**7a** A fair and accurate report of any proceedings before a court exercising jurisdiction in any territory outside Her Majesty's dominions.
7b A fair and accurate report of any proceedings in public of a central or local legislature in any territory outside Her Majesty's dominions.'

Judge's ruling on defamatory meaning

In an action for libel tried by judge and jury –
a any submission made on behalf of the defendant that the words are not capable of any or any particular defamatory meaning shall be made in the absence of the jury;
b whether or not any such submission is made on behalf of the defendant, the judge shall not before verdict communicate to the jury any ruling that the words are capable of any or any particular defamatory meaning.

Malice

6 Where in an action for libel tried by judge and jury the plaintiff in reply to a plea by the defendant of fair comment or qualified privilege alleges express malice, the issue of express malice and all questions relating thereto shall be decided by the judge and not by the jury.

Appeals on damages

7 Where on an appeal against a judgment or order in an action for libel tried by judge and jury the appellant appeals against the amount of damages awarded, any appellate court shall have the same power to vary the amount of the award as if the trial had been by judge alone.

Official secrets

Acts not
prejudicial
to public
interest
1911 c.28
1920 c.75

8·1 A person shall not be guilty of an offence under section **2·2** of the Official Secrets Act 1911 as amended by section **10** of the Official Secrets Act 1920 (which renders the receipt of certain specified official secrets a misdemeanour) if he establishes that the act of which he is accused was not prejudicial to the public interest.

8·2 No accused person shall be entitled to rely upon the defence afforded under this section unless not less than seven clear days before the commencement of his trial he notifies the prosecution in writing of his intention so to do.

8·3 When an accused person relies upon the defence afforded by this section the issue of whether the defence is established shall be decided by the judge and not by the jury, and the judge shall take into account together with any other relevant matters any certificate under the hand of a Minister of the Crown that the act in question was prejudicial to the public interest, and the reasons advanced in the certificate; and for the purposes of this section a document purporting to be such a certificate shall be admissible in evidence.

8·4 This section shall apply to Northern Ireland.

Supplementary

Interpretation

9 In this Act the following expressions have the meanings hereby respectively assigned to them, that is to say –

'Broadcasting by means of wireless telegraphy' means publication for general reception by means of wireless telegraphy within the meaning of the Wireless Telegraphy Act 1949 and 'broadcast by means of wireless telegraphy' shall be construed accordingly; and where words broadcast by means of wireless telegraphy are simultaneously transmitted by telegraph as defined

1863 c. 112

by the Telegraph Act 1863, in accordance with a licence granted by the Postmaster General the provisions of this Act shall apply as if the transmission were broadcasting by means of wireless telegraphy;

'Broadcasting station' means any station in respect of which a licence granted by the Postmaster General under the enactments relating to wireless telegraphy is in force, being a licence which (by whatever form of words) authorises the use of the station for the purpose of providing broadcasting services for general reception;

'Newspaper' means any paper containing public news or observations thereon, or consisting wholly or mainly of advertisements, which is printed for sale and is published in the United Kingdom either periodically or in parts or numbers at intervals not exceeding thirty-six days.

Proceedings affected and saving **10·1** This Act applies for the purposes of any proceedings begun after the commencement of this Act, whenever the cause of action arose, but does not affect any proceedings begun before the commencement of this Act.
10·2 Nothing in this Act shall affect the law relating to criminal libel.

Short title, commencement, and extent **11·1** This Act may be cited as the Freedom of Publication (Protection) Act 1969, and shall come into operation at the expiration of one month beginning with the date of its passing.
11·2 This Act shall apply to Scotland but (except section 3) shall not extend to Northern Ireland.

Appendix 9

Rules laid down by British Transport Advertising for the Acceptance of
Advertisements (January 1969)*

Advertisements will not be accepted for, or retained on, display on
British Transport Advertising sites if they:

1 depict murder, scenes of terror, horror or acts of violence.

2 are calculated to demoralize, extenuate crime, break the law or
incite anyone to do so.

3 depict or refer to indecency, obscenity, nudity or strip-tease.

4 are likely, through wording, design or possible defacement, to
offend the general travelling public.

5 advertise films which have been refused a permit for public
exhibition.

6 might wound racial susceptibilities or those of coloured or foreign
peoples.

7 refer to religious or sacred subjects in a manner which might
give offence, or seek to use our sites as a medium for religious
controversy.

8 attack a member or the policies of any Government.

9 are of a political nature, whether produced by a political party or
not, other than those which simply announce social activities or
meetings together with the names of the speakers and the subject
to be discussed. The wording used in announcing the subject
must not be politically controversial or call for support for a
particular viewpoint, policy or action.

10 might foment social unrest.

11 advertise contraceptives.

12 conflict with the British Code of Advertising Practice which
incorporates the British Code of Standards in relation to the
advertising of medicines and treatments.

13 contain illustrations or copy which are distorted or exaggerated
in such a way as to convey false impressions; are calculated to
deceive the public, or contain statements of a 'knocking' or
extravagant nature.

* Notes to these rules have been omitted but attention should be drawn to note
(vi) which provides: 'British Transport Advertising Limited reserves the right
to refuse to exhibit any advertisement without giving reasons,

14 might adversely affect in any way the organization, or organizations on whose sites a display is required (e.g. by advertising competitive services; by the use of designs or texts which might lead to confusion; or by offers of employment in competition with the requirements of the organization(s) concerned).

Notes to Chapters

Some indication is given below of where authority may be found for some of the statements and quotations in the main text. Where a book is listed in the Select Bibliography it will be referred to in the Notes only by its author's name, except where more than one book by the same author is listed in the Bibliography, when a shortened version of the book's title will be used to identify the particular book being referred to. Collective agreements quoted may all be found in the collection of labour law materials deposited in the Squire Law Library, Cambridge.

Notes

Title-page The quotation is taken from Curran's speech on 10 July 1790 on the right of election of Lord Mayor of the City of Dublin, delivered before the Lord Lieutenant and Privy Council of Ireland, in the collection of his speeches edited by Thomas Davis (London, 1845), pp. 94–5.
Curran had frequent occasion to speak in cases involving the liberty of the press and freedom of speech.

1 Introductory

p. 11 Quotation from Shaw comes from *The Rejected Statement*, included in the Preface to *The Shewing up of Blanco Posnet, Dramatic Works of Bernard Shaw*, No. XVIII (London, 1925), p. 325. Weldon quotation is from Hulke, p. 32. Radcliffe: *Censors*, p. 10.
Laswell quotation from E. R. A. Seligman (ed.), *Encyclopaedia of the Social Sciences* (London, 1930), Vol. 3, p. 290.

p. 13 Cockburn quotation: *The Times*, 27 November 1970. Muggeridge episode: *Encounter*, July 1961.

p. 14 Quotation: Seagle, pp. 20–1.

2 Legal Censorship

p. 15 Seagle, *Cato*, p. 10.

p. 16 *Korematsu* v. *U.S.*, 323 U.S. 214 (1944). P. O'Higgins, 'Unlawful Seizure and Irregular Extradition', *British Yearbook of International Law*, Vol. 36 (1960) at pp. 287–8.

p. 17 D.P.P. v. *Shaw* [1962] A.C. 220. *R.* v. *Caunt* (1947) reprinted in J. W. C. Turner and A.Ll. Armitage, *Cases in Criminal Law* (3rd edn, Cambridge, 1964), p. 624. Fenton Bresler quoted from B. Abel-Smith and R. Stevens, *Lawyers and the Courts* (London, 1967), p. 299.

p. 18 A. V. Dicey, *Law of the Constitution* (9th edn, London, 1952), p. 244. Binding over: *Lansbury* v. *Riley* [1914] 3 K.B. 663.

p. 19 *Defamation.* See H. Street, *Law of Torts* (4th edn, London, 1968), Part V. C. H. King, 'Laws that Favour Fools and Rogues', *Focus*, December 1969, pp. 12–14. Sikorski pilot: *The Times*, 31 July 1970 (*Prchal* v. *Albery*).

p. 20 Clive Irving, *Scandal '63* (London, 1963), p. 125. Wayland Young, *The Profumo Affair* (Harmondsworth, 1963), p. 14. Joseph Dean, *Hatred, Ridicule or Contempt* (Harmondsworth, 1964), p. 23. *Blasphemy.* Nokes and H. P. Bonner. J. C. Smith and B. Hogan, *Criminal Law* (London, 1965), Chapter 16(4). *Bowman* v. *Secular Society* [1917] A.C. 406. Jennings, *Law and the Constitution* (5th edn, London, 1959), p. 268. *R.* v. *Gott* (1922) 16 C.A.R. 87.

p. 21 Clive Bell, *British Freedom*, pp. 14–16.

p. 22 Home Office evidence, *Joint Committee on Censorship of Theatre: Report*, p. 103. Woodhall: Alec Craig, *Liberties*, pp. 22–23; *Daily Telegraph*, 10 January 1940, and *The Times*, 24 January 1940. Tottenham Hotspur: *Daily Telegraph*, 20 May 1963; *The Times*, 21 May 1963. J. S. Mill: Home Office Papers in Public Record Office (H.O./O.S. 3537).

p. 23 *Council of Love: The Times*, 26 August 1970. *Bubonic Plague Show: Daily Telegraph*, 19 August 1963. 'Light of the World': *Guardian*, 17 February 1967. Osborne: *Listener*, 3 November 1960; *The Times*, 7 November 1960.

p. 24 Indecent behaviour: *Abrahams* v. *Cavey, The Times*, 8 July 1967; [1967] 3 All E.R. 167.

p. 25 *Oz* case: *R.* v. *Anderson*, [1971] 3 W.L.R. 939. Havers: *Obscenity Laws*, p. 14. *Last Exit* case: *R.* v. *Calder and Boyars* [1968] 3 All E.R. 644.

p. 26 *Obscenity Laws*, p. 28. *John Calder (Publications)* v. *Powell* [1965] 1 Q.B. 509. *D.P.P.* v. *A. & B.C. Chewing Gum Ltd.* [1968] 1 Q.B. 159. G. Zellick, 'Violence as Pornography' [1970] Crim. L.R. 188–200.

p. 27 Lady Birk: *The Times*, 12 May 1970; see also *House of Lords Debates*, Vol. CCCX, cols 469–73. Newcastle: *The Times*, 21 March, 1972.

p. 28 *R.* v. *Branson*, *The Times*, 9 and 23 May 1970; *Observer*, 10 May 1970; *New Statesman*, 14 November 1969. Topless dress: *The Times*, 22 August 1964; see also *Guardian*, 1 October 1964.

p. 29 *R.* v. *Stanley* [1965] 1 All E.R. 1035. Lord Sands: *M'Gowan* v. *Langmuir* [1931] S.C.(J.) 10, at p. 13. *R.* v. *Stamford*, *The Times*, 29 February, 1972.

p. 30 *Joint Committee on the Censorship of the Theatre: Report*, p. 55. Fraser: M. Amaya, 'Cop Art', *Sunday Times*, 5 February 1967; *The Times*, 18 October 1966, and *Morning Star*, 29 November 1966. Paraksos: *Irish Times*, 21 December 1966. Beardsley: *The Times*, 10 and 11 August 1966; M. Amaya, op. cit.; *Scottish Daily Express*, 5 May 1967.

p. 31 London Art Gallery: *The Times*, 28 April 1970. Conspiracy to corrupt public morals: *D.P.P.* v. *Shaw* [1962] A.C. 220. See also I. Brownlie and D. G. T. Williams, 'Judicial Legislation in Criminal Law', *Canadian Bar Review*, Vol. 42 (1964), pp. 562–604.

p. 33 *Oz* trial: Tony Palmer, *The Trials of Oz* (London, 1971). For recent important discussions of conspiracy to corrupt public morals, see *D.P.P.* v. *Bhagwan* [1970] 3 W.L.R. 501, and *R.* v. *Keene*, *The Times*, 17 July 1971. *IT* trial: *The Times*, 10 November 1970.

p. 34 Seditious libel: *R.* v. *Tutchin* (1704), 14 Howell's *State Trials*, col. 1095; *R.* v. *Cobbet* (1804), 29 Howell's *State Trials*, col. 1. A. V. Dicey, *The Law of the Constitution* (9th edn, London, 1952), p. 244.

p. 35 *Boucher* v. *R.* [1951] S.C.R. 265; *R.* v. *Caunt* (1947) to be found reported in *An Editor on Trial* (Morcambe Press Ltd, 1947); also in J. W. C. Turner and A.Ll. Armitage, *Cases on Criminal Law* (Cambridge, 1964), pp. 624–6. Communist trial: see contemporary pamphlet, *The Communist Party on Trial* (London, 1925), pp. 20–1. Race Relations Act 1965: A. Dickey, *Prosecutions under the Race Relations Act 1965, s. 6 during the Period 1965–70* (Canterbury, 1971).

p. 36 Official Secrets: see generally, D. Williams, *Not in the Public Interest*.

p. 36   *Chandler* v. *D.P.P.* [1964] A.C. 763. Hewart: *House of Commons Debates*, Vol. 136, col. 946 (16 December 1920). See also D. Thompson, 'The Committee of 100 and the Official Secrets Act, 1911', [1963] *Public Law*, pp. 201–26.

p. 38   Aitken: J. Aitken, *Officially Secret* (London, 1971). This book not only deals with Aitken's own trial but also gives much evidence of abuse of the Official Secrets Acts generally.
D. Williams, op. cit., p. 38.

p. 39   Abuse of Official Secrets Acts: see P. Field, 'When Nelson's Letters were declared Secret', *Tribune*, 3 May 1963; and Williams, *Not in the Public Interest, passim*.
Isis case: *The Times*, 22 May 1958. Speech by Lord Tangley is quoted from a valuable article by D. G. T. Williams, 'Official Secrecy in England', *Federal Law Review*, Vol. 3 (1968), pp. 20–50.

p. 40   'Spies for Peace': *The Times*, 19 April 1963.
Contempt of Court: *R.* v. *Thomson Newspapers Ltd.* [1968] 1 All E.R. 268; *R.* v. *Editor of the 'New Statesman'* (1928) 44 T.L.R. 301. See also M. Box, *The Trial of Marie Stopes* (London, 1967).

p. 41   Lord Atkin: in *Ambard* v. *Attorney-General for Trinidad and Tobago* [1936] A.C. 323, at p. 335. *Guardian* case: *Guardian*, 9 and 10 November 1967.
'Trial by television': *R.* v. *Savundranayagan and Walker* [1968] 3 All E.R. 439. See also correspondence in *The Times*, 20 July 1968.

p. 43   Contempt of Parliament: G. Wilson, *Cases and Materials on Constitutional and Administrative Law* (Cambridge, 1966), pp. 290–7. *Report from the Select Committee on Parliamentary Privilege*, H.C. 34, 1968.

p. 44   Lloyd, p. 45.
Local legislation: quotation from J. C. Brown, 'The Advertising Control System', *The Monthly Review*, April 1968.

p. 45   *Arrowsmith* v. *Jenkins* [1963] 2 Q.B. 562. Cf. *Nagy* v. *Weston* [1965] 1 All E.R. 78.

p. 47   Wallington: *NCCL* Bulletin, December 1970. *Edinburgh Evening News*, 6 January 1971, and letter from Peter Wallington to author, dated 12 January 1971.
ACAB case: *Cambridge Evening News*, 25 May 1970.

p. 48   RAF case: *The Times*, 23 February 1963; *Observer*, 3 March 1963.
Dicey, op. cit., pp. 244–46.